THE WOMAN FROM THE WAVES

ROSLYN SINCLAIR

To Carrie: the light of my life, the love of my days, and the most human angel I know.

PRONUNCIATION GUIDE

Hæra: HIGH-rah

Each-uisge: ech-OOSH-gah

Beathag: BAY-ahk

Ætlaquoy: EYE-tla-kwhy

GLOSSARY

Ætlaquoy

Ætla is Old Norse for "fated," and "quoy" is Old Norse for a farm livestock enclosure. Due to Orkney's location and history, its place names are more likely to have Old Norse linguistic roots than Scottish Gaelic ones.

Each-uisge

Many cultures have legends about dangerous water spirits that take on different forms. Most famous from Scottish lore are *kelpies*, water spirits that can take either horse or human form and live in freshwater rivers or lochs.

In contrast, the lesser-known *Each-uisge* are ocean dwellers and known to be more vicious. In legend, they usually take on the form of a handsome man or beautiful woman to lure humans to their deaths. Often they appear as ordinary horses, enticing a human to ride them —which never ends well for their prey.

I have taken considerable liberties with the legends of the *Each-uisge*, developing culture, history, and even biology for them well beyond their traditional folklore. It was my hope to preserve their aura of mystery and danger, as well as the predatory ruthlessness that drives them.

Jorsay

From Old Norse, loosely "Horse Island." The Isle of Jorsay is my own invention and not a real Orcadian island.

Trow

A mischievous creature from Orkney and Shetland lore, dwelling underground in ancient mounds. They have a human-like appearance but are far smaller, and they usually appear old and wizened, with gray skin. If trows' mounds are disturbed by humans, they are known to take revenge. They are also known for entering unlocked houses at night and even stealing the occasional baby from its cradle. Keep your bolts fastened!

Witches

In the late eighteenth century, Orkney was home to some of the most infamous witch trials in European history. Before that, for centuries, magic was considered a reasonable explanation for many phenomena of daily life. Some folktales maintain that a witch's curse is responsible for the Swilkie, a dangerous whirlpool in the Pentland Firth. In fact, another name for the Swilkie is the Sea Witch's Wheel…

PROLOGUE

THE SEA

THIS WOULD BE A HUNGRY STORM. It would eat up the coasts, swallow the sand, and probably chew up a boat or two.

So Hæra had heard from some of her fellow *Each-uisge,* ones who'd actually ventured beyond the surface of the ocean to places she was forbidden to go. Here, down in the depths, she could only watch the storms begin. Still, the sight never failed to thrill her.

As Hæra observed from a distance, the herd's Sire led his eleven Stormhorses toward the North Sea's surface. Calder's front legs were muscular, his hooves lined with shell edges. At his back half beat his mighty marine tail, which would change to a horse's hindquarters when he ascended from the water. His fearsome horse's head pointed skyward. Between his shoulders, ocean currents began to swirl, resolving into a shape.

The shape of wings.

Before Hæra's eager eyes, Calder's wings grew into a wider span than his fellows', marking him as the Sire of the herd. The wings were a magnificent sight. Though they began as water, when he and the other Stormhorses took to the skies, they would harden into muscle, feather, and bone. The feathers, Hæra had heard, were as sharp as hoof-shells. In spite of this, her father had always said the process wasn't painful.

Not that it would matter. Hæra would take the pain a thousand times over if it resulted in a pair of wings lifting her into the sky, carrying her over the roiling sea until she and the other Stormhorses unleashed thunder, lightning, and wind over all that lay below. Those wings would keep her steady in gale-force winds that whipped the waves to madness. When Hæra finally became a Stormhorse, her wings would be the most powerful of all.

Fierce longing surged through her. Today, she'd do more than watch from below.

Carefully, darting in and out of kelp and rock formations, Hæra followed the Stormhorses as they made their way toward the surface. The Great Mare willing, they wouldn't look behind them and see a female about to trespass above the waves, seeking the forbidden air. Her father had taken her up once as a secret treat, and in spite of his injunctions otherwise, she'd sought it several times since then.

The last Stormhorse disappeared above the water. Hæra waited as long as she could bear it, pumped her tail, and propelled herself to the surface. Her head broke through the water just in time to see the final three Stormhorses transforming their marine tails into hind legs and hooves. Their mighty wings, fully formed, beat the air; around and above them, clouds began to swirl, menacing and dark.

Calder reached the clouds first and disappeared into them with one final flap of his wings. The moment he did, lightning flickered from within the cloud.

Hæra held back an eager groan. What must it be like up there? Her father, Alban, had said clouds were damp and cold. Did they also feel soft against your hide? And what was it like to feel the wind, to balance yourself on air currents?

What did freedom feel like?

Within moments, the Stormhorses disappeared completely into the clouds, heading toward the islands to the south. More lightning flashed and leapt from cloud to cloud: the Stormhorses speaking to one another without words in the language and fellowship only they knew.

Hæra could learn that language. She knew she could.

In the meantime, she'd seen what she'd come to see, and she'd better return before she was caught at the surface. The consequences for that would be…significant.

She sank below the surface and swam back the way she'd come. Silver fish scattered before her, tempting and plump, but she wasn't hungry. As she went deeper, standing rocks rose to meet her; anemones and barnacles dotted their familiar surfaces. At the bottom, a stingray slowly swam just above the seabed, its flaps stirring up the sand.

Home again. Back to the dark waters where nothing exciting happened other than orca hunts or the occasional pursuit of a selkie foolish enough to venture out alone.

"Where were you?"

Hæra whirled, and bubbles swooshed around her. Her brother lurked by a great stone behind her, his red eyes gleaming. Her front hooves instinctively pawed forward as if to strike him.

Seeing this, Asgall only laughed.

Had he seen her surface? If he had, he wouldn't hesitate to report it. Nothing would please him more than his own sister's disgrace.

"I saw a promising school of fish," she said. "But it wasn't worth telling the herd about."

"Especially now that the Stormhorses are gone," Asgall agreed. "They'd want to partake of a feast, wouldn't they?"

When it came to Asgall, going on the defensive was a bad idea. Over the turns, Hæra had learned to attack instead. "You know all about what Stormhorses want and don't want," she said. "That's funny, isn't it, since you're not one?"

Ah, yes. *There* were his teeth: sharp and pearl pale, bared at her.

"You're one to talk." Asgall's tail propelled him forward. His skin and scales were so dark that, even with Hæra's sharp vision, it was difficult to see him. Her own skin and scales, a very pale blue, made her a more visible target.

"*My* dream was within reach," Asgall growled. "It still might be. Yours? No." He tossed his head contemptuously, as if Hæra's ambitions deserved to be shaken away. "There's never been a female Stormhorse and never will be."

Hæra ignored that. He hadn't observed her trespass, although he clearly suspected it. If he knew for sure, he'd rub her nose in it before tattling. She said, "What do you mean, your dream 'still might be' within reach? You failed your trial, so-called hope of our family, and you'll never be a Stormhorse. There are no second chances. Be glad our father wasn't alive to see it."

Any defeat for her vicious brother was a victory for Hæra. Their mother, Beathag, had taken no such pleasure in it, and her disappointment had torn at Hæra. Literally. She'd worn the scars from her mother's hooves for many tides.

"And who's our hope now? You, *Hiiiira?*"

Hæra had no idea why it should be so irritating when her brother elongated her name. Probably because nearly everything he did was as irritating as an oyster's sandy insides. "I don't see why I shouldn't be. Am I not as swift as you? As cunning?" She swished her tail threateningly. "Am I not the braver hunter? The Sire's rewarded me often enou—"

Asgall snapped out with his teeth, but Hæra was prepared for that. She darted out of the way and swiped at him with her tail, catching him at his ribs. He grunted. As a foal, she'd assumed these battles were only play; the first time he'd broken her skin, she'd learned better. Now she took it seriously. Her brother would earn none of her blood.

He retreated with a snarl. "You're not as good as you think. Not nearly as good. And what makes you so proud of yourself is what shames our mother the most."

The words struck home. Asgall was right: Beathag had never forgiven Hæra for being better at hunting, fighting, everything Asgall was supposed to excel in. Sometimes it seemed she loathed Hæra for it even more than Asgall did. Her two offspring were her two greatest disappointments, but at least Asgall wasn't a *showy* one.

Now that Hæra was grown, it was easy to avoid her mother, and she did so at every opportunity. It was also better to ignore Asgall now that he no longer wished to attack her, and generally the right thing to do after he grew tiresome.

He was wrong, anyway. Hæra didn't give a damn about being the hope of her family. The depths knew her mother and brother wouldn't appreciate it.

Hæra would be her own hope. With her father's death, she had lost her only protector, and now she protected herself. And why not? Wasn't she gifted? Couldn't she swim as fast as any male, catch as many fish, maneuver as nimbly around the reefs of the North Sea? Hadn't she been the one to deliver a fatal attack during an orca hunt, feeding the herd on blubber and muscle for days? The Sire had allowed her to eat one of the orca's eyes: a great honor.

It wasn't enough.

Asgall swam away with a disgusted snort. Hæra barely noticed him. Her ambitions were more interesting than his petulance. Nearly anything was.

How ironic that through his failure, Asgall had achieved what Hæra could only gain with unprecedented success. By herd law, only Stormhorses could sire offspring. Because Asgall hadn't passed his test, he was forbidden to mate or reproduce.

Hæra wasn't nearly so lucky. Once she reached her hundredth turn around the sun—nearly 150,000 tides—she'd reach the maximum age before she had to become a brood mare. Then her life would become an endless cycle of mating with the first Stormhorse to claim her in heat, being pregnant, and giving birth...unless she was killed in the mating frenzy, of course.

Out of respect for her father who should have been Sire, and Hæra's skill as a hunter and warrior, Calder had granted her request to delay that horror well past the time she'd become fertile. She had eight turns left to go.

It seemed like a lot, but they'd swim by in a flash. Hæra had grown and was approaching her full strength. She needed to act soon.

She *would* be a Stormhorse, swift and powerful. She would be respected; even Asgall would show deference. She'd see the ocean, her home, from the distance of the clouds.

She just had to eat the right person first.

PART I
THE SURFACE

CHAPTER ONE

"It's no Stonehenge."

Sister Madeleine frowned at the girl who'd made the remark. The students of Sacred Heart should not cavalierly dismiss the wonders of the ancient world, even if some were less wonderful than others. They were lucky to be on this trip and not at home, staring at their phones all day.

At Madeleine's frown, Emma ducked her shoulders. "I don't mean to be rude, Sister. It's just less impressive, you've got to admit."

Madeleine tugged her coat around herself as the wind kicked up. Scotland's Orkney Islands had few trees or high hills, and the ocean was never far. It was a surefire recipe for wind that stung your face and cut through your layers, even in June. "Define 'impressive,'" she said. "This stone circle isn't as big or well preserved as some others—"

"Or as circular," Emma muttered.

"*But* it's the oldest in Europe, and the settlement ruins are even older. Isn't that impressive enough?"

It was true that Jorsay wasn't the grandest of the Orkney Islands. At fourteen square miles, you could walk the length of it in an hour at a brisk pace—the kind of pace Madeleine preferred. There were fewer than 250 permanent residents. The population rose in summer, but other islands in Orkney had greater claims to fame: bigger cliffs, older churches, longer shores, and visitor centers.

If the island was known for anything, it was its shape, which was remarkably like a horse's head. In fact, the name "Jorsay" came from the Old Norse word for steed: *jór*. Centuries later, it now roughly translated to "Horse Island," so named by the Norsemen who'd swept into the islands in the eighth century, conquering the populace. They had, for a time, brought horses with them. The few souvenirs for sale in the island shops tended to be horse themed.

Currently, Madeleine stood in the easternmost part of the island, where Orkney's most ancient artifacts sat. Wind flattened the green grass and clover beneath her shoes. Just beyond a hillock rose the cliffs: rough faces of ruddy sandstone and marl that stood firm against the pounding surf. Nature's dramatic variety was always a wonder and a gift.

To the north, there lay a path that led down to a strip of pale sand. Madeleine cast her gaze down to that little beach, closed her eyes, and smiled at the wind in her face. It might be chilly and gray, but it was God's day nevertheless. She was lucky to be standing here in a place so different from her home, taking it all in.

It was too bad the students didn't feel the same way, but they were still young. Hopefully, the time would come when they'd know to embrace each moment. Part of Madeleine's job was to teach them that, but only experience would drive it home.

When she turned, the Sacred Heart girls stood in a cluster, looking askance at the grass dotted with standing stones. Supposedly there had been ten stones originally erected during the Bronze Age. Now only four remained, worn down by time.

Unlike the famous Ring of Brodgar on Mainland, Orkney's largest island, this stone circle lacked a name. It held Madeleine's interest anyway. Maybe it was the crumbling prehistoric settlement nearby, the dwellings of people who would have reverenced this spot just as Madeleine worshipped in Sacred Heart's chapel, attached to the convent where she lived and prayed.

Orkney was just one stop on Sacred Heart's summer tour. The

international tour was eagerly anticipated every year by students, and this time they'd gone to Scotland. The Northern Isles were unlike the cities and highland landscapes they'd already seen. The main attraction had been the Italian Chapel, built by Catholic prisoners of war during World War II, but the neolithic history was hard to beat.

"It's cold," said Ava, another student.

Madeleine looked at the few other tourists and archaeological students examining the ruins. None of these other people seemed to be prioritizing the weather over priceless history. She swallowed down the uncharitable thought and unwound her gray scarf from her neck, which immediately developed goose bumps in the chilly air. "Take this."

"Oh, Sister, I didn't mean—"

"I know." Madeleine looped the scarf around Ava's neck, and when Ava gave her a grateful look, Madeleine smiled back at her. "I'll want it returned, mind you."

"Yes, Sister Madeleine. Thank you."

"Make sure to layer up tomorrow. Girls, go out there and take your notes. You'll probably find it's less windy if you go toward the settlement walls or the stones themselves."

"I'm not touching them," a third student, Hannah, protested. "What if they're, you know...something?"

"What if they take you back in time, like *Outlander*?" Emma scoffed. Then she gave Madeleine a guilty glance. "Not that I've seen *Outlander*."

"I certainly hope not," a cool voice said, and they all turned as one to see the approach of Sister Agnes, assistant principal of Sacred Heart and the trip's other chaperone. At fifty-four, she was nearly twenty years older than Madeleine and far less forgiving. "No Sacred Heart girl should know anything about that sinful trash."

Sister Madeleine had read the book version of *Outlander* in college, before she'd had her calling. Best to keep her mouth shut about that.

"These stones are merely artifacts," Agnes continued. "Appreciate them as part of human history before the coming of Christ. There's nothing to fear from them."

"Yes, Sister Agnes," Hannah replied, not looking totally convinced.

Maybe something else would convince her. Madeleine said dryly, "Remember how much your parents paid to send you here."

That did it. The girls scattered, some heading for the stones and others for the settlement in the packs of three or four that teenaged girls seemed to fall into instinctively. Only Emma and Ava headed off as a pair. Sister Agnes watched them leave, a frown line climbing nearly the whole length of her forehead from her eyebrows to the edge of her veil.

Their veils were coming in handy today, keeping their hair safe from the wind. Madeleine's order, the Daughters of Grace, had long since discarded the old-fashioned nuns' habits you'd find in *The Sound of Music*. Her modern habit was still undeniably modest, with a long-sleeved white blouse, a black sweater vest, a skirt that went past her knees, dark hose, and comfortable black sneakers. A black veil covered her short dark hair and fell to her shoulders, and her rosary rested at her waist. Over all of it, Madeleine wore a black puffer jacket that did a decent job of shielding her from the Orcadian weather, even without her scarf.

No high school student would call it fashionable, but at least she was warm.

"We should keep an eye on them," Agnes said, still watching Emma and Ava. "They spend a lot of time together. A…special friendship."

"They've always been good friends." Hopefully she didn't sound like she was challenging her senior sister.

"Yes, but this sort of behavior is more noticeable in a smaller group. I suppose it didn't occur to me until now that they could be— well, we all miss things sometimes. Even me." Agnes squinted. "Is Ava wearing your scarf?"

Madeleine knew where this was going. "She was cold, Sister."

"Then she should have brought a sweater. They need to learn responsibility."

Ah yes, just as Christ had said of his faithful followers: *For I was cold, and you told me I should have brought a sweater.* It might be judgmental to think poorly of Agnes, but she missed the mark on some basic things. It was fine to give a shivering child a warm piece of clothing.

And there was nothing wrong with intense female friendships in your youth. That was when you talked at all hours, shared everything, and spent every possible moment together. It was natural. And then, as God willed it, you grew up and turned that emotional energy toward a man in holy matrimony.

Or to Christ and his saints, as Madeleine had done. The Sisterhood had called to her instead, letting her know where her divinely ordained duty lay. It wasn't with a husband and children.

Which was also completely natural.

"Am I talking to myself?"

Madeleine snapped back to attention. Sister Agnes had raised her eyebrows and was employing her usual trick of looking down her nose, even though she was several inches shorter than Madeleine.

"No, Sister. I was just reflecting on your words. Very wise. I can see why you're next in line to become our convent's Superior." It wasn't the most comforting thought.

"Don't flatter me," Agnes replied, though the gleam in her eyes suggested flattery wasn't off the table. "I don't sit around daydreaming of such an honor…although one *likes* to imagine the Superior General putting her trust in one."

One? Agnes had always had a touch of Queen Victoria about her. Madeleine held back a smile. Mother Gertrude, Superior General of their order, had no such pretension. It was one reason she and Madeleine had always gotten along so well. "Of course, Sister."

"And Sister Madeleine, perhaps you too one day—in the future. How old are you now?"

"Thirty-five, Sister."

Agnes's eyes grew shrewd. "And you've chaired our history department for three years, in addition to teaching. Designing the curriculum, no less."

"It's my honor to shape our students' studies."

"A little too broadly, in my opinion. I heard you let Maria Fernandez do her senior project on the Sisters of the Immaculate

Heart of Mary." Agnes's eyes narrowed. "And she didn't condemn them."

In 1960s Los Angeles, the Sisters of the Immaculate Heart of Mary had asked to wear normal clothes instead of habits and abandon a rigid schedule of prayer and silence. The Vatican forbade it, along with other proposed reforms. In the end, most of the sisters left the order to found their own secular community.

Their disobedience was wrong. But seen in a certain light, that kind of courage was…well, admirable.

"It was international news," Madeleine said. "There's no reason our students shouldn't know about it. Maria's project was excellent. Sister Catherine agreed."

Agnes snorted. "It's incredible how permissive so many orders have become. I know *we* can't avoid popular culture when we're around teenagers all day"—Agnes's tone indicated this was a shame—"but you hear about nuns who have cell phones and get on social media!"

"Our order has a Facebook account," Madeleine pointed out.

Agnes glowered at her. "Of which I heartily disapprove."

"We have to live in the world, Sister. I believe we can do it faithfully." She knew she sounded stubborn. Sister Agnes might be her senior, but Madeleine had earned the right to speak her mind—if she could manage it respectfully.

That hadn't always come easily to her.

Sister Agnes rolled her eyes. "This is a conversation I'm tired of having. I'm not surprised to hear you've got these opinions. Maybe in these decadent times, they'll get you to a higher leadership position someday."

Currently, Madeleine's responsibilities were teaching, chairing a department, and helping Sister Catherine balance the budget—in addition to her duties as a nun. That was plenty to keep her busy. What would "higher leadership" entail?

Well—it wasn't as if Madeleine had never thought about it. She *would* be good at it, should it please God. And yet…

You're not worthy, whispered a voice that sounded all too familiar. *That's not for you. That's not right for you.*

Be quiet, she ordered it, as always.

"I don't have any such ambitions, Sister," she murmured. "That would be immodest."

"Heaven forbid," Agnes said dryly. "I do have one more question for you." She crossed her arms; the authoritative gesture immediately made Madeleine's skin prickle. This "question" was more likely to be an interrogation.

"Unlike most of us, when you joined the order you didn't change your name to honor a saint or the Blessed Virgin Mary. You were Madeleine Laurent before, and you're Sister Madeleine now. I've always wondered why."

Sister Agnes could make an inquiry about how you liked your coffee into an accusation. "My name means 'woman from Magdala,' Sister. Like Saint Mary Magdalene, one of Christ's most loving followers. I was grateful to my parents for setting me that example, and I kept my name with my Superior's blessing."

There was another reason, one Agnes would never know. Madeleine had wanted to honor her parents' memory by keeping the name they'd given her.

After all these years, the thought of their loss could still bring a cold sensation to her chest. Or maybe that was just the wind again.

Sister Agnes *hmph*ed. "Some would argue that decision means you haven't fully left the world behind. That you're reluctant to cut your final tie to the secular life. If you wish to be a leader in our order, then consider that possibility. Examine your own soul."

Madeleine looked Agnes dead in the eye. "I already have, Sister, with the help of the Church." *Not you.* "But thanks for your advice."

Advice. Or rather, interference. If Sister Agnes's words created a pit in Madeleine's stomach, it was from her presumption. Madeleine had joined the Daughters of Grace when she was twenty-two, and she'd stuck it out this long, hadn't she? Of course, she had doubts and regrets occasionally.

It was strange: Agnes's officiousness disturbed her more than it usually would have. There was something about this island Madeleine couldn't put her finger on, but it set her off balance. Something that seemed to whisper a warning on the wind…

This isn't right for you.

"Brr." Agnes stomped her feet. "It *is* cold. Must be even worse for a New Orleans transplant like you."

Praise God for a change of subject. "I can handle the cold. Worth it for a chance to see the ruins."

"Mm. Not that I'd say this in front of them, but the students are right. The ones on the Mainland are better."

Madeleine held back a sigh and found herself gazing at Emma and Ava. They stood by one of the standing stones in conversation, heads bent together and shoulders touching. Madeleine's scarf tossed around Ava's neck in the wind.

The little voice whispered again. *Beware, beware.*

Madeleine bit her lower lip and looked up at the clouds. It looked as if there was about to be a break in them.

Heaven grant that the sun shine down on them all today.

CHAPTER TWO

THE SURFACE MIGHT BE FORBIDDEN to most *Each-uisge*, but rules proved their worth by how easy they were to break. Besides, there was no other practical way to find a human to drown and eat, even if they were fishing on a boat in the middle of the water. The ones underwater always wore rubbery coverings and traveled in groups. Hæra had only dared to swim near the land a few times, close enough to overhear humans' voices, and she had yet to see a suitable candidate there.

She couldn't just kill any old sack of flesh wandering about the place. Hæra needed someone deserving. Someone strong, clever, and brave. Only the consumption of such a human would give her the power that would make her worthy to become a Stormhorse.

She'd been looking for so many turns and countless tides, but her movements were hampered. The herd lingered around the islands of the North Sea, where there were fewer people relative to other human settlements—or so Hæra had heard. Her father, Alban, had told her about flying over larger groups of humans, what he had called "cities," raining fury from his wings.

"There can be much to admire when it comes to the best of them," he'd told Hæra and Asgall once. "My human was a sea captain who guided his ship through our waters fearlessly. His ship survived one of our greatest storms, and the Sire returned and said he'd found me a suitable challenge."

"What happened?" Asgall asked. "How did you take him?"

"Because he was intelligent, he was curious. It didn't take much to lure him into the water late one night. He lowered himself into one of their little boats and rowed out toward the sound of my voice—and he brought a knife with him. When I overturned his boat…ah, that was a fight to remember. I still have the scar on my chest."

Hæra had often wondered how her father came by the scar. "Were you afraid?"

"In that moment, I feared nothing. I felt I was finally becoming *myself* as we struggled—I knew it was my destiny. You can never simply reach out and seize them, you know," he'd added to Asgall in a lecturing tone. "You have to lure them. They must desire to come to you, and then the battle begins. Remember, eat everything but the liver."

"Why not the liver?" Hæra said.

"Tradition. Something of the struggle must remain behind. It floats to the surface afterward."

"Did you take a human form to lure him?" Asgall asked eagerly.

Alban shook his head, his splendid black mane drifting in the water. "That's one way to deceive them, but I consider it the basest. Besides, they keep developing weapons and devices that make it more difficult. Such weapons make our victories more glorious—but it grows increasingly likely that we would expose our existence to them, and thus it's not worth the risk."

That made sense. Her father had told them that *Each-uisge,* selkies, and other unseen creatures were known to humans through legends and stories of their past exploits. But stories and proof were different things. Humans could hunt the herd easily now, and they would be doubly likely to if they saw a horselike creature shapeshift.

Alban continued, "Unfortunately, like all unseen creatures, our race is tied to the humans we're near to. We can speak their language. We can take their forms—but none other. And nothing but a human, my son, can make you a Stormhorse. Why this should have pleased the Great Mare and Stallion, I don't know. But I can't deny that the best ones put up a fight worth winning."

Hæra and Asgall bobbed their heads in understanding.

After a curiously long pause, Alban added: "I find much to admire in some humans, truthfully. There are times I don't wonder if we're too judgmental of them and their ways."

She and Asgall hadn't known how to respond, so they'd said nothing. You weren't supposed to voice that sort of thing, ever. At least not out loud.

"But the penalty for anyone but a Stormhorse going to the surface is a beating at best, and banishment from the herd at worst," Alban said briskly. "And the closer you venture to the shore, the more severe the penalty. Don't forget."

He'd looked at Hæra pointedly. In spite of his words, because of his fondness for her curiosity, he'd taken her on one secret trip to the surface—one of her most treasured memories. She'd heard this warning before.

"Yes, Father," she'd said obediently.

That had been long ago. Now, Alban was gone, and so were the wooden ships his captain had sailed. More and more people had left the islands. Hæra had fewer options, especially because she had to be so cautious about going to the surface: to avoid not just humans' eyes but those of her herd as well. Thanks to her caution, time was running out. It would be easy to despair.

No. The Great Mare of the Depths would heed Hæra's call, even if the Great Stallion ignored it. She must hear the justice of it.

In the meantime, Hæra was stuck with these islands and their pitifully small population. Calder was reluctant to lead the herd into new territory, saying they knew the rhythms of this place: when prey was most plentiful, where currents were fiercest. Besides, the more humans there were, the likelier the *Each-uisge* were to be sighted and hunted down.

But if Hæra risked nothing, she'd gain nothing. She just had to be clever. All Stormhorses should be. She wouldn't put the herd in danger.

Today, she swam just beneath the surface at the foot of Jorsay's great rocks and cliffs. Her tail was strong enough to keep her from being dashed against them.

Humans rarely swam in this part of the water. It was too rough by the rocks, and there were few places for them to find easy purchase if they got in trouble. Their weak little hands would slip and slide. Hæra took a risk and poked the top of her head above the surface so that only her ears and eyes would be visible, and she laid her ears flat.

Nobody in sight. Just cliffs and stones. But around the corner, the cliffs flattened out into a sandy beach that led up to the ruins of a human dwelling that dated back to the early tides of the herd itself. Farther up, she'd been told, were a bunch of tall rocks that humans seemed to find important.

She moved with the current: it was harder to be spotted that way. Besides, if she'd learned one thing, it was that many creatures—regardless of species—refused to see that which they believed to be impossible. If anyone spotted Hæra, they'd assume a land horse had wandered into the sea to drown, and she'd be gone before they could discover otherwise.

Of course, she could transform her tail into hind legs, and then she could walk about on land like one of the dumb, mindless beasts. But she didn't look enough like them. Land horses were smaller, their coats were different colors, and their eyes weren't bright yellow.

And they didn't have sharp teeth, shell-lined hooves, or mouths that slavered at the hint of fresh meat.

One option remained. Hæra could do what her father had scorned and take on human form. It might be base trickery, it might be risky, but it was technically allowed.

It would also be a last resort for several reasons. Not just those of honor, but because Hæra would wander out of the ocean without a single human garment to cover herself and with precious little knowl-edge of their customs. She'd have to be truly desperate.

She was getting desperate.

Hæra swam around the edge of the cliff and paused. Two people stood on the sandy shore, all too close to her. She kept her head low.

They were both human females. One was considerably taller than the other, who appeared to be a juvenile.

Hæra snorted in disgust, water bubbling around her nostrils. Another wasted trip. No Stormhorse had ever taken a female. They weren't strong or clever enough.

Then again…no Stormhorse had ever been a female either, and didn't the supposed reasons for that use the same sharkshite excuses? That fillies and mares weren't strong, clever, or brave enough?

Asgall was male, strong, and swift: all things that should have guaranteed his success. Nobody had thought for a moment that her brother would fail at catching a human, and yet he had. To this day, he refused to speak of it—Hæra had no idea who his human had been or what had happened. But his sex hadn't ensured his victory. Perhaps it was foolish to fall into that same error concerning her prey. Hæra might have ignored promising potential victims. She snorted again, but her disgust was only for herself.

Hewing close to the rocks, she swam closer. The females were near to this part of the shore. She wouldn't have to swim in too far and risk exposing herself.

She could hear them. The waves were loud, but sound carried to an *Each-uisge* wherever water might be found, if they were close enough. It made them dreaded hunters.

The younger female was speaking. She had yellow hair that was pulled back from her face. The elder's hair was hidden beneath a black piece of cloth.

"…something you wanted to speak to me about, Ava?" the taller one asked.

"Yes, Sister," Ava said. "I saw you speaking with Sister Agnes, and it just reminded me how much I've wanted to ask you about something that's been weighing on my mind."

As Hæra watched, the woman in black lifted her chin. "Oh yes?"

"Yes. Um, this is weird to say out loud, but I've been wondering if I have a calling."

A calling? What was calling to the young one? Hæra heard nothing other than the waves and the females' voices.

"I see," the taller one said.

"I wanted to talk to you because it was a more recent decision for you, you know? No disrespect to Sister Agnes, it's just that she's a lot...older."

The taller woman laughed. It was a low, husky sound, not displeasing. "I can't deny that, and neither would Sister Agnes. Most of the sisters are much older than I am."

Hæra's tail swished in confusion, momentarily pulling her against the current. So these two females were sisters, and they spoke of having more sisters? They must be part of a large herd.

"That's something else to think about," the taller one continued. She and Ava began to walk again, moving toward the rocks that barely concealed Hæra. "Few women want to be nuns today. Our average age worldwide is almost eighty years old, did you know that?"

"I might have guessed," Ava said. Unlike her companion, she wore brightly colored clothing, along with a long piece of gray cloth wrapped around her neck. She'd be easier to seize in the water, if it came to that. If she was worthy.

She didn't look very strong, though. Neither of them did. This was probably another failed expedition.

"The consecrated life demands sacrifices few are prepared to make. That's cause for prayer and reflection, which is why the process has so many steps. You spend time as a postulant, then a novice. Then you take temporary vows for a few years before fully swearing yourself to the order, as Sister Agnes and I have done."

"But you're happy you did it, aren't you, Sister Madeleine?"

Sister Madeleine. Hæra knew little of human nomenclature, but the words had a pleasing cadence.

"Happy?" Sister Madeleine said, after a pause. "Well...of course I'm happy. This is my life, and I can't imagine another one. It's just not for everyone, that's all. There are a lot of constraints that can inhibit a person's—" She stopped, right when it was about to get interesting, and shook her head. "Anyway, tell me: what's your experience of the call?"

"Oh…well…"

There followed a conversation Hæra couldn't understand, save that *the call* appeared not to be a literal noise but rather a summons to live in a certain way. It must be the way Sister Madeleine lived. Ava did most of the talking while Sister Madeleine listened closely and Hæra grew more bored by the second. The juvenile was definitely less interesting than her elder.

When Ava finally finished, Sister Madeleine said, "Well, how wonderful that you're considering this. We'd welcome more young women, and when the time comes, I know we'd be happy to take you as a postulant—although we'd prefer you to get a college degree. Just as long as you understand that our way of life demands many sacrifices."

She turned her head to look out toward the sea. At that moment, the wind whipped the black cloth back from her face.

It was a striking face. Hæra had never been this close to humans but could easily tell the difference between these two. The younger one seemed more hapless and unformed. Sister Madeleine looked resolute with her high cheekbones, straight nose, and full mouth, which she held in a serene line. The sun and wind had pinked her cheeks.

Hæra's heart raced as if she were trying to win one of the herd's tests of speed. There was something here, more than she'd ever sensed before. If she stayed undiscovered, she could figure it out.

Sister Madeleine lifted her head in a proud tilt as she continued gazing over the sea, looking as if she owned the entire ocean. "The life demands a certain strength of character," she said at length.

Strength of character? What sort of strength was that? Would it be enough to mark this woman as a worthy challenge? Hæra managed not to swish her tail impatiently.

"We rise before dawn every morning and spend an hour in silent prayer," Sister Madeleine continued. "Even on weekends. At seven, morning mass is celebrated, followed by breakfast. Then school begins, and those of us who teach are busy for the rest of the day, although we break for lunch and recreation. The sisters who don't teach spend the morning and afternoon working around the convent. After our school duties are done, we teachers join them again to read and pray. At five, there's the evening prayer office, supper and recreation at six, the nightly prayer office, more reading, and lights out at nine-thirty."

"That doesn't sound so bad," Ava said, while Hæra shuddered at exactly how bad it sounded. Thanks to her father and rotting books she'd seen in shipwrecks, she knew what reading was, but she didn't know how to do it. And while she reverenced the Great Mare and Stallion, prayer was as dull as a dead crab. Ava went on: "Not a lot of time to get bored or, like…overthink things. Um, what do you do for recreation?"

"We don't watch a lot of TV or movies," Sister Madeleine said dryly. "There's little leisure time. That's the point: our thoughts are turned toward duty and devotion."

Sister Madeleine probably wouldn't be impressed by how Hæra spent her own days. Except for hunts, she avoided her fellow *Each-uisge* as much as possible, straying as far as she dared to explore the ocean, and sometimes just lazing around. It was a bit lonely, but when she got her wings and the herd's respect, that would change.

"We're also involved in the community—and you might have noticed our presence at school dances." Sister Madeleine smiled. "Especially when we tell you not to dance too closely to the boys."

Dance. Hæra knew something about that. *Each-uisge* performed mating dances before the combat and frenzy began. Humans did as well? But how did they do it without getting too close to one another? It sounded as if Sister Madeleine wasn't mating with anyone, either.

Not that this mattered one way or the other, but that knowledge felt…good.

"Uh, yeah." Ava shifted back and forth on her feet. "I don't mind when you tell us that."

This caused Sister Madeleine to look at Ava for a long, silent moment. Had the juvenile said something significant, for once? If so,

Sister Madeleine didn't comment on it, and Ava added: "Do you ever see your family? Or any friends you made before you joined the order?"

There was another pause before Sister Madeleine said, "All Sisters are allowed to do that."

Her voice sounded different for a moment, in a way Hæra couldn't quite identify. Ava, however, didn't seem to notice, and it didn't last; when Sister Madeleine spoke again, she sounded as brisk as she had before. "But not often. As I said, we give up a lot. You usually do when you join an organization that requires absolute devotion."

"Kind of like the army?"

"Kind of," Sister Madeleine said dryly. "As I said, it demands strength of character. Although we must never rely on our strength alone. Our best help is in God."

That was even more confusing. What was this place called "God" in which humans found help? Best to ignore that. It didn't matter where Sister Madeleine got her strength, so long as she had it.

"Yes, of course," Ava said. "So living a normal life—I mean, not that your life isn't *normal*, but—it's easier?"

"No. Life isn't easy for anyone. Some face greater challenges than others, that's true." For a moment, Sister Madeleine's face changed. Hæra recognized the look as one of sorrow. "And we often can't know what others are struggling with. But a big life change always demands strength and courage from us, if we're to take that risk."

Warmth coursed through Hæra's blood, like the currents from the southern seas she'd heard described. Sister Madeleine was right. Change *did* require strength. Didn't Hæra know that all too well? Becoming the first female Stormhorse, changing her life and the herd's traditions so completely, would require more strength than she'd ever needed before. That must be what "strength of character" was.

It seemed, from this conversation, that Sister Madeleine led a life different from most of her kind. That also needed strength and courage.

"What you want to make sure of," Sister Madeleine said, "is that you're not looking to the order as a place to escape anything. It's a place to engage with the world, not run away from it. Is this something you're struggling with?"

Ava seemed, somehow, to shrink into herself a little. "What do you mean, Sister?"

"Only that you seem troubled. Is everything all right?"

"Everything's fine, Sister. Everything's, um, great. I'm not running from…anything."

Hæra didn't have to be human to smell the falsehood.

"I'm glad to hear it," said Sister Madeleine. Couldn't she tell the girl was lying? "But if you ever need to talk, sometimes an adult can lend a different perspective than someone your own age, even a good friend." She paused. "Like Emma."

Ava went as red as an anemone and wrung her hands—a sign of agitation. Even though Sister Madeleine's words and tone were kind, they seemed to upset the girl. There were so many human codes and quirks Hæra would never understand.

"Yes, Sister," Ava whispered. "Are you…" Her voice dropped so low that Hæra couldn't hear the end of the sentence.

Sister Madeleine shook her head. "I don't think Sister Agnes needs to know about this conversation unless you want to tell her. Do you?"

"No! That is, no, Sister, I don't want to. Um. Thanks for listening to me. You've given me a lot to think about."

"Just put your trust in God, and all will be well." Sister Madeleine patted Ava's shoulder. "Now let's get back to the others. This sea breeze isn't exactly keeping us warm, even with the sun coming out."

Oh no. They were leaving? Hæra should have foreseen it. Of course they wouldn't stay on the beach until nightfall, when it would be easier to lure someone into the water without being seen.

Not that Hæra knew for sure if she wanted to lure anyone. Not that she had decided—

Sister Madeleine looked out again toward the sea. At that moment, the wind changed and carried her scent in Hæra's direction. Hæra couldn't help herself: she lifted her nose out of the water just enough to sniff.

Then she nearly poked out her entire head. She must be imagining things. Nothing could smell that good, that pure, that...intoxicating, as if Hæra had just chewed on a stalk of the special seaweed reserved for the Sire's grotto.

Did all humans smell like this? No, they couldn't. Otherwise, they'd be the regular prey of the *Each-uisge,* for who could resist such a mouthwatering scent? As it was, within the last two generations, the herd had been forbidden from eating humans except for the Stormhorse trial. They'd been too careless before, and besides, there was much tastier food out there.

But at the moment, Hæra couldn't imagine any more toothsome fare than this.

"Build your soul's foundation on rock, like Scripture tells us to." Sister Madeleine looked down at the beach. "If you build it on sand, all will be washed away. Rock endures forever, like the standing stones we've just been looking at."

That wasn't true. The sea wore down stone over time. Sister Madeleine should look to the ocean to serve as a foundation for... whatever a "soul" was. It sounded interesting. She spoke with such conviction, such assuredness—two qualities Hæra prized in herself.

What a pity you couldn't actually talk to a human before you ate her. Hæra hadn't wanted to talk to anyone this much since her father had died. Or...perhaps she could? Perhaps if she took a human shape after all—found some clothes, somehow, tracked down Sister Madeleine, she could have a meaningful conversation and *then* drag her into the ocean...

She looked at Sister Madeleine's face with desperate hunger. The more she saw, listened, and smelled, the more certain she was. This was the one whose flesh she desired, whose blood she longed to mingle with her own. The one she'd consume and carry all the way into the sky every time she took flight.

Without replying to what Sister Madeleine had said about rock, Ava walked away, her head bent low as she trudged over the sand up toward the grassy hill. At first, Sister Madeleine kept pace with her.

Then, a few steps in, she stopped and turned around, looking at the ocean once more. Ava didn't stop.

Hæra's heart, however, did. Just for a second. Then, her common sense kicked in like a hoof to the head. She had a chance, might never get another—she *must* take it, must risk it.

This woman was worth the risk.

"Sister Madeleine!" she called from the water. *"Help me!"*

Her voice didn't sound like a proper human voice. It was too deep, rumbling with the rhythms of the sea. However, it certainly got Sister Madeleine's attention. Her head whipped round, the black fabric flapping in the breeze, as she sought out the source of the voice. She took a step forward.

Hæra stayed hidden behind her rock, her head nearly submerged. *Closer...come closer, into the waves...*

Nearly at the end of the sand, Ava turned around to see Sister Madeleine frozen on the beach. She called, "Sister?"

Sister Madeleine called back, "Did you hear that?"

Ava shook her head.

Sister Madeleine looked around again. "Hello?"

Hæra opened her mouth to repeat her cry, but at that moment, a wave crashed brutally, pushing her against the rock even against the strength of her tail. She went under. When she resurfaced, Ava was trotting back to Sister Madeleine's side. It would be too risky to call out again.

Together, the females looked over the water, paying much more attention to their surroundings than they had before. Hæra had to duck below the surface. By the time she raised her head above the water again, they'd turned their backs and were walking away from the ocean.

Maybe they were going back to that ancient settlement with all the rocks. Perhaps they resided there? Or elsewhere nearby. Her father had said Jorsay had human dwellings not too far away, lining the shore and going inland as well, to a small village where visitors stayed and others lived year-round.

Ava's and Sister Madeleine's voices weren't like the natives'. They had different accents. They were probably visitors, meaning they wouldn't stay for long.

Hæra must not despair. The Great Mare had sent this human woman to her. This wasn't the end. She had to have faith.

Sister Madeleine would clearly agree.

They were heading toward the ancient settlement, which lay to the east. Without a thought, Hæra began swimming in that direction, her tail pushing her against the current. Occasionally, she dared to crest a wave so she could look up and see if they were walking along the cliff. She had no luck until, when she had swum nearly to the island's easternmost point, she surfaced and saw Ava and someone else at the cliff's edge.

It wasn't Sister Madeleine, though. It was another juvenile female in colorful clothes. Hæra growled in frustration. Was her luck cursed?

The females were facing each other and holding hands. Then, just as Hæra was about to submerge in exasperation, she saw them lean toward each other until their faces touched and their mouths pressed together. Ava let go of the other one's hands to cup her face.

Were they eating each other? Hæra hadn't known humans did that. But neither of them were struggling. In fact, they wrapped their arms around each other as though this were enjoyable.

After a moment, Ava pulled away and rested her head on the other one's shoulder. Just then, the wind struck them and tore the long, gray piece of cloth from Ava's neck, whipping it up into the air.

Ava flailed after it, but it was too late—the fabric had gone over the cliff. That happened sometimes: human flotsam collecting in the water before drifting down to the seafloor. Ava didn't seem to know it was normal, judging by her distress.

The other female put her arms around Ava again, clearly reassuring her. Then they released each other and walked, together, away from the cliff's edge.

Well, that had been confusing. That was another way humans must pass the time together, but it didn't mean much to an *Each-uisge*. Hæra couldn't imagine mashing her mouth to one of her fellows'.

Would it be different if she did take on human form? Maybe she could do that to Sister Madeleine, once she found her again. Hæra could take her in her arms and press their mouths together in a gesture of fellowship. Oddly, the notion wasn't…offensive.

Hæra wouldn't know how to do it, though. If there were rituals or customs attached to the gesture, she'd give herself away. Sister Madeleine would certainly know all about it. She'd probably put her mouth against many other humans'. They would have tasted her lips.

The thought turned Hæra's blood into fire—her natural enemy. The image of the woman in black in a human's arms…leaning into the embrace, giving herself to another…

No. Never again. That wouldn't happen ever again. Sister Madeleine had officially touched mouths with her last human. Hæra would see to it.

From this moment on, nobody would devour Sister Madeleine but her.

CHAPTER THREE

A FEW STREETLAMPS lit the sidewalks that lined Thornhill Village's seawall. Madeleine had brought her travel flashlight anyway. You never knew when you'd need extra help to pierce the darkness.

A scarf would have come in handy too, but apparently Madeleine's was floating somewhere in the North Sea. When Ava had confessed its loss, Sister Agnes hadn't said *I told you so*, but it was clearly implied.

It was past ten-thirty at night. The sun had recently set, and clouds drifted back and forth over the moon and stars. It was colder too. It wasn't the nicest situation for a stroll, but Madeleine needed to clear her head of the words that kept tumbling around inside it.

Sister Madeleine, help me.

That voice couldn't have been real. She hadn't recognized it, and when she and Ava had returned to the group, nobody was missing. Who else could have called her by name? She must have hallucinated it.

So it was a complete mystery why she was sneaking out to that same spot in the dead of night.

No. She wasn't sneaking out. What a silly idea. She was a grown woman, and her duties were done. She'd left a note in her room, and she had her no-frills cell phone. All the girls were safely ensconced in the Merryweather Hotel, a tiny establishment that was notably less expensive than hotels and inns on Orkney's other islands, which was why she'd chosen it.

Once they'd arrived on Jorsay, Madeleine had realized why accommodations were both sparse and cheap. It was the least appealing of all the islands, at least visually. The landscapes were scrubbier, the ruins smaller, and the cliff faces less dramatic.

Then again, the other islands probably didn't have beaches that talked to you.

Madeleine swallowed hard. She had to be sensible about this. Every place had legends and wild stories, including here. Before the trip, she'd read a book on Orcadian folklore. There were stories about little troll-like creatures called "trows" that lived under earthen mounds and could either bring blessings or work mischief, depending on if you pleased them. She'd read about sea serpents big enough to shatter continents and about giants that bestrode the islands.

Worst of all was a witch who'd created a deadly local whirlpool by swinging around two dead bodies at the bottom of the ocean. One of the bodies was that of a man who had spurned her love. The other was the woman he'd preferred instead.

Even though it was only a folktale, it made Madeleine shudder. Thank heavens such a wicked creature couldn't truly exist. None of it was real. She just had to prove that to herself.

Nevertheless, Madeleine shivered in her coat as she continued down the sidewalk toward the shore. The island was small, and if you were willing to take a long-ish walk, you could reach the stone circle and settlement—and the beach.

"This is ridiculous," she muttered. It seemed like an understatement. What was she going to do if something called to her again? Walk straight into the ocean?

She shouldn't be doing this. Madeleine was a woman of both faith and reason. Neither dictated that some demonic presence waited on the beach to do her evil. Nevertheless, this was the definition of borrowing trouble. Forget ghostly voices; as a woman walking on her own in a strange place, she was much more likely to be in danger from her fellow man than a supernatural force.

Before she'd left the hotel, she'd paused by the unattended front desk, where she'd seen a pair of scissors and stuffed them in her jacket pocket. Madeleine felt the weight of her thievery now. They wouldn't be much of a defense weapon, and they didn't speak well of her commitment to turning the other cheek, but she'd return them later. Nobody had to know.

She wouldn't turn back. She couldn't, until she reassured herself that this was nothing.

This was absolutely nothing at all.

———

This couldn't be coincidence. It couldn't just be luck. The Great Mare must have heard Hæra's prayers.

In disbelief and wonder, Hæra watched Sister Madeleine walk along the seawall over the shore, flashing a beam of light in front of her from a stick.

She hadn't expected this when she'd returned to the surface, knowing she'd be safer after dark. The fishing boats had docked and the beachcombers had gone home. This was the best hour to approach the village so closely.

There was no plan. She'd only known that this might be the only chance she got. She'd go ashore in the darkness and keep to the shadows. If she were spotted, she'd run. She was faster than any land horse that had ever lived. It was worth the risk.

She'd thought also of coming ashore and taking human shape, but that still posed the problem of having no clothes. Hæra's human form wasn't strictly *human*, per se—she was just as invulnerable to the cold as she was in her real form and didn't need coverings to keep warm. But actual humans did, and she'd attract attention if she walked around without insulation.

Besides, although she knew how to transform in theory, she hadn't done it yet. As Hæra understood it, it was an instinctive process, powered by will. It couldn't be that difficult, but it would take practice to walk gracefully on two legs.

Or it would have done, if Sister Madeleine weren't heading right toward her. It seemed Hæra wouldn't have to come ashore or transform. She just had to call out again.

Although…that was much riskier here, so close to the dwellings. Night it might be, but humans were often roaming around. Sometimes they had animal companions who were more perceptive than they. The last thing Hæra needed was a noisy dog drawing attention to her. It would be better to wait for Sister Madeleine to go somewhere quieter and more solitary, like that beach.

That was, if Sister Madeleine was going to the beach. She could change direction, and if she did, Hæra might never see her again, and the Great Mare would never bestow another favor on one who so foolishly threw away a gift.

Near to where Sister Madeleine walked, a set of stone steps led down from the seawall to a small, old wooden dock. Currently, the dock's only occupant was a shabby, tiny boat. It would be simplicity itself to swim beneath the dock, hide there, and call again to Sister Madeleine. Then, Sister Madeleine would investigate. She couldn't *not*. She'd been curious on the beach.

Hæra snorted in amusement as she ducked below the surface and swam for the dock. Sister Madeleine had spoken of a "calling" that had guided her to her current life. It seemed appropriate that a second calling would remove her from it. Considering how she'd described her days, Hæra would be doing her a favor.

Come to me. She swam, curling around the current as easily as an eel. *Come to me. I'll devour you, you'll become part of me, and we'll fly for centuries. Together.*

She swam beneath the dock. The pilings were slimy and sharp with barnacles. The waves slapped against the wood. They were low but still strong enough to lift her up and down when she surfaced, bumping the top of her head against the dock's wooden slats.

She was perfectly hidden. There would never be a better time.

"*Sister Madeleine,*" she called again. "*Help me.*"

———

Madeleine was imagining things. Hallucinating. If she told anyone, they'd put her away.

Nevertheless, she couldn't move as she looked out over the dark water, where the voice had come to her. What a voice it had been! Deep, rumbling, like a wave crashing on the rocks. Vaguely feminine, if she had to specify, but…

Not quite human.

That was the thing. It hadn't sounded *human*. Madeleine had never heard a voice like that in her life.

Maybe Hannah hadn't been too far off the mark with her worries about magical forces. Madeleine should walk away right now. She wasn't one to worry excessively about the devil, but she worried just the right amount, and this seemed like his work. What else could it be?

What else, indeed?

She closed her eyes and crossed herself. "Hail Mary," she whispered, "full of grace, pray for me now. Protect me and intercede for me as I…" She took a deep breath. "As I do something absurd. But if *you're* the one who's calling to give me an answer—"

(An answer? What was her question?)

"Then let me receive the lesson with grace. Amen."

She crossed herself again and then swept the flashlight's beam down toward the sea. She saw nothing unusual: just a small wooden dock with a lone dinghy bobbing next to it.

"Hello?" Madeleine called. "Are you there?"

That wasn't what she'd meant to say. She'd meant to say, *Is anyone there?* Not to address this other presence as if it were an acquaintance!

She waited. No reply. Madeleine must have imagined it after all.

That was a relief. It was *not* a disappointment. Her life left little room for adventure, and that was just fine. She was only tired from shepherding a bunch of teenage girls all over Scotland, the remarkable scenery punctuated by arguments, complaints, and panic over lost objects. She turned to go.

As she did, she heard another cry. Not like the last one at all. It was short and sharp, sounded pained, and had no actual words. In fact, it had sounded like nothing so much as…

A neigh?

————

This couldn't be happening. Not here, not now.

Hæra tugged her head again, sharply, and got an even sharper pain in return, although this time she managed not to cry out. That was difficult, because it hurt. A lot.

It hurt a lot when your mane got tangled in the slats of a dock because the waves pushed you up in just the wrong place, and now you couldn't move because you were stuck in the most humiliating position possible right as your greatest dream was on the cusp of achievement. Nothing could make this worse.

Except another *Each-uisge* spotting her here. Maybe Asgall, who might kill her. An orca probably wouldn't come this close. The greatest likelihood was that she'd be stuck here until morning, when the humans would see her, and the *Each-uisge*'s existence would be known. Her carelessness could mean the end of her species.

Then discovery must not happen. She'd pull until her mane ripped off and her scalp bled. No matter how much it hurt, she couldn't put the herd at risk. She braced herself, her sharp teeth grinding together, prepared to pull—

Footsteps on the dock.

Hæra froze. Her ears pricked up until the wood bent their soft tips down again. Those were human feet wearing their hard coverings— shoes—moving in beats of two, not of four as beasts did. She caught a scent on the ocean breeze. A scent she already knew by heart.

"Hello?"

Sister Madeleine's voice sounded much less apprehensive than it had before. Now it sounded confused.

Hæra held perfectly still. She mustn't, couldn't move until Sister Madeleine left. Any hope of tricking her was gone, but the possibility of death by humiliation remained. If anything could be worse than discovery by humans in general, it'd be discovery by *this* human in particular. Hæra's human, or the one who should have been hers.

"Hello?" Sister Madeleine repeated on top of the dock, and then she gave a soft groan. "You dummy, is a horse going to talk back?"

If only she knew.

"Moreover," Sister Madeleine continued, sounding irritated even though she was only talking to herself, "you'd see a horse, wouldn't you?"

Then came the flash.

A sudden, sharp beam of light shone from the top of the dock and glided over the dark waves in a circular shape. After a second, Hæra realized it was harmless and had come from Sister Madeleine's little stick, but that was a second too late. She'd already startled, splashed about, and made a noise.

"Oh!" Sister Madeleine said.

Curse it to the depths and back. Maybe Hæra hadn't been blessed by the Great Mare after all. This could be punishment for daring to go against the natural order of things. What was worse: getting caught here, or Asgall being right?

The wood creaked as it bowed when weight was put on it—just slightly, but it was enough to put pressure on Hæra's head and make her tail thrash in protest.

There came another flash of light. Intolerably bright. Right in her face. Blinded, Hæra reared her head back. The tug on her mane hurt, but at least she hadn't bared her sharp teeth.

"Goodness," Sister Madeleine gasped. The flash disappeared, but it took Hæra's eyes, designed for the darkness of the deep, a moment to adjust again. "You poor thing! How in the world did you get under there?"

Hæra's vision resolved. She blinked rapidly. Sister Madeleine's face was before her, only a fin-stroke away, and it was upside-down. She'd bent over the side of the dock. The long cloth atop her head dangled down too, brushing the surface of the water. Her eyes were very wide.

They were also very green. Hæra blinked again. Sister Madeleine's eyes were as green as the grass on Jorsay's shore. Did all humans have eyes that were such a remarkable color?

"Well, never mind that," Sister Madeleine said briskly. "It's more important to get you out. I'm sure somebody's looking for you."

Not yet, but they would be. Eventually, her absence would be noticed, and someone would be sent to look. When her crime was discovered, the Sire might call for her to be torn to pieces by her fellows. Asgall would be first to volunteer.

The light shone in Hæra's face again. This time, she closed her eyes before she was blinded.

"Looks like your mane's caught," Sister Madeleine continued, sounding a bit amused by the worst thing that had ever happened to Hæra. "Maybe you should keep it short like we do."

Behind her closed eyelids, Hæra could still see the light roaming over her face. Thank the depths it wasn't penetrating far enough into the water to show her tail. As far as Sister Madeleine still knew, Hæra was a beast of the land.

"I should call someone, but…"

Hæra bucked her head in protest and neighed.

"Good grief, calm down."

Sister Madeleine's face disappeared. The dock creaked as she redistributed her weight on it, right above Hæra.

"You're just caught, that's all," Sister Madeleine said. If she thought Hæra was a land horse, why was she still talking to her, as if a dumb beast could answer back? It must be another human eccentricity. Then she laughed softly. "I wonder if this is why I found these scissors? Maybe I'm meant to rescue you. The Lord works in mysterious ways."

The who? The what? What were "scissors"? Hæra mustn't panic. There had to be a way out of this. *Think, think, think…*

Then came a sharp sound, followed by another tug at the knot of Hæra's mane wedged between the planks. It hurt—she thrashed—

"Be still!" Sister Madeleine called from above. "I'm just trying to help you!" In a lower voice, she muttered, "You silly thing."

Before Hæra could find some way to die of mortification, there came more tugs and more sharp sounds. With each tug, the pressure on her scalp lessened, and when a hunk of her mane dropped into the water, Hæra realized she was being cut free. *Each-uisge* lore told of human weapons that could slice through hide. Did Sister Madeleine have one of those?

The pressure on Hæra's scalp suddenly released. With a splash, she fell below the surface as Sister Madeleine, somehow, freed her from the trap.

Oh, thank the Great Mare for her mercy! Hæra's tail beat in relief, pushing her forward as she plunged deeper underwater. Time to go. This had officially been her last visit to the surface.

This mortifying episode was over for good, and nobody would ever have to know about it.

———

Oh, saints. Madeleine had killed the horse.

Somehow. She must have. The moment she'd cut its mane, she'd heard it go under the water without another sound, instead of splashing around as she would have expected. She'd thought that if the horse had swum under the dock, then it'd be able to swim out again. Horses could swim, couldn't they? She'd seen them in movies and on TV, fording rivers and such.

But obviously this one couldn't. Maybe it had been too tired. And she'd drowned the poor creature she'd only been trying to help. Why hadn't she sought assistance instead of trying to solve the problem on her own? When would she ever learn?

There was nobody here to help now. She was all alone. Just her and her damnable pride.

"Hello? Horse?" The words escaped her before their own absurdity could stop them. Madeleine lunged for the opposite edge of the dock where the dinghy bobbed. Maybe if she got in the little boat and looked into the water she'd see the horse, although what she was supposed to *do* if she did, she had no idea. Throw it a rope? Pray for it? There was no time to go for help.

As it happened, she didn't see anything, because a number of factors converged at once.

For one thing, she was using one hand to grapple for the flashlight. For another, the edge of the dock, which she grabbed with her other hand so she could peer down again, was slippery. For a third, she flung herself forward much too quickly and with her full body weight.

All of these factors combined into one hellish moment in which Madeleine tripped, fell, dropped the flashlight, smacked her head on the dinghy's edge, and plummeted right into the water as everything went black.

———

The water bobbed around Hæra as a sudden burst of weight displaced it. Something had fallen in. She turned.

And she watched in disbelief as Sister Madeleine's black-clad form fell beneath the surface.

Sister Madeleine's body was still, not striking out to save herself as most humans would. Couldn't she swim? Or had she actually jumped in to find Hæra after calling to her?

It only took a moment to realize neither possibility was true. Sister Madeleine was sinking, not moving. Soon, she would drown.

She saved me.

Hæra tore toward Sister Madeleine, her tail propelling her in two powerful strokes. She took hold of Sister Madeleine's coat with her teeth. The material pressed against her, along with something harder —a band of beads around Sister Madeleine's waist.

She had to act quickly. It didn't take humans long to drown. Sister Madeleine's body drifted and rolled as Hæra pulled her to shore, to leave her there and try to forget this had ever happened. A brood mare she would be after all. The Great Mare willed it so.

Then, a scent filled her nostrils. Rich. Potent. Even more intoxicating than what she'd smelled earlier on the wind.

Sister Madeleine's forehead was bleeding.

Hæra had a mouthful of cloth, but her lips pulled back to expose her teeth as she began to salivate. Her hide prickled as if a thousand air bubbles had just popped in its hairs. The scent of Sister Madeleine's blood called to her more seductively than any siren, and Hæra would know, since she'd heard the sirens.

Sister Madeleine's head lolled gently in the water. Her body twitched. Her blood smelled incredible. She was the most delectable, *edible* creature in all the seas.

And she had saved Hæra's life.

With a growl, Hæra swam for the shore, just a few more lengths away. She'd have to drag her woman onto it, and for that, she'd need to grow a pair of hind legs. She'd done it before, but only underwater and out of curiosity. Time to test the legs on land.

By the Great Mare, she wasn't just breaking the surface. She was actually going *on land*.

For a moment, she hesitated. This seemed a literal step too far. But then Sister Madeleine's body bumped against hers again, reminding Hæra what a life debt was.

On land she would go.

Her front hooves brushed against the rocks, and she began to transform her tail. It split painlessly in two, its muscles assuming new shapes, its fins becoming sharp rear hooves. Together, her four hooves touched the seafloor and then propelled her onto the shadowed beach as she dragged Sister Madeleine's body ashore.

It was...heavier up here. Everything was. Without the water buoying her, Hæra's own body seemed to weigh her down, to say nothing of Sister Madeleine's limp form. Hæra was more than equal to the challenge—the bodies of the *Each-uisge* could withstand the pressures of the deep—but already the world of things with legs was different from anything she'd ever known.

So this was land.

Sister Madeleine groaned as Hæra dragged her over the small rocks and pebbles. This wasn't like the sandy beach she'd visited earlier. Everything was hard and bumpy. The rocks were slippery and unpleasant beneath Hæra's hooves. They must feel worse against Sister Madeleine's softer form.

How soft was it? What would it be like to touch human skin—or to wear it?

Now well out of the water, Hæra opened her mouth and dropped her burden to the ground. Sister Madeleine moaned again. More blood trickled from the cut on her forehead. By the depths, to drink it! But if Hæra bent her head to sample what she craved, she'd be lost. They both would be. What began as a taste would end as a feast.

Sister Madeleine's eyelids fluttered. She coughed, and water came out of her mouth.

In a moment, she'd wake up and see a horse looming over her, bigger than any horse on land. And this time, she might notice that the horse had glowing yellow eyes and sharp teeth. Hæra needed to leave without a word, without a taste.

Unless…

Unless.

———

Madeleine's head hurt. Everything hurt, especially her chest. She was cold and soaking wet. She coughed, and that was wet too, although her chest felt better as her air passages cleared. Her mouth was salty. Where was she? What had just happened?

There had been a dock—a horse—

A woman's face loomed over her. Very close.

And with a sudden movement, the woman lay on top of Madeleine, not quite squashing her into the hard rocks beneath her back but definitely pinning her down.

In the darkness, and with Madeleine's swimming vision, it was impossible to make out the woman's features. But long hair fell over her shoulders in a wet curtain around Madeleine's head. The woman's eyes seemed to…to glow, almost, in a color Madeleine couldn't make sense of.

A hand touched the top of her head. The woman bent down, and Madeleine whimpered at a sudden, sharp sting. She must have a cut on her forehead? It burned, and the woman had just *licked* it.

The woman made a low, soft noise. Like a moan.

Madeleine moaned too, mostly because she couldn't figure out how to form words.

The woman took her hand from Madeleine's forehead. She cupped her face and lowered her head. Her lips pressed against Madeleine's own.

She tasted of salt, smelled of the sea. Her body was solid and warm and—*naked*. A naked woman was lying on top of Madeleine, between her spread thighs, her breasts pressed to Madeleine's own as she kissed her with a hot mouth.

For a moment, the pain and cold vanished. Only the heat of the kiss was real. It spread through Madeleine's limbs, warming her like coffee on a cold morning. It called her hips upward, until they rubbed against the weight atop her. She raised her knees, cradling the naked woman between her thighs—unthinking, instinctual, something she'd been waiting to do all her life.

Madeleine's deepest, most secret dreams had suddenly come true, here on a stony beach. This time, her moan wasn't one of confusion. There was nothing confusing about how good this felt.

Before she knew what she was doing, she was lifting her heavy arms in their soaked sleeves to embrace the stranger. She felt wet skin, surprisingly warm, taut with muscle. Was this what it was like to touch a naked woman? Softness and strength all at once? Blessed—no, *divine*—

The woman seized Madeleine's hands and pressed them to the ground. Kept kissing her. Her teeth curved over Madeleine's lips and chin as if she were about to bite down, and she moaned again. She was so strong that Madeleine couldn't have struggled even if she'd wanted to.

Madeleine couldn't imagine struggling. She didn't want to do anything except lie here beneath this—this—

She remembered now. She'd fallen. Hit her head. She must have gone into the water. Nobody else had been there. She would have drowned, if not for this unnaturally strong, long, shadowy…

"Angel?" Madeleine croaked.

There was a pause. The woman's—the angel's?—breath blew hot against her mouth. Her lips moved against Madeleine's as if she were about to say something.

Then, Madeleine heard a voice in the distance, a man's voice. "Hello there!" it called. "What's going on, then?"

The angel hissed. She squeezed Madeleine's wrists, and then one of her hands let go to tug at Madeleine's waist. The rosary beads there loosened, and Madeleine felt them slide from around her.

She tried to speak and only managed to whisper, "Wh…"

A warm mouth brushed against her ear and whispered three words that would haunt Madeleine for the rest of her life.

Then she was gone, and Madeleine could hear only the crash of waves upon the shore.

Rocks poked her in the back. She looked dizzily up at the stars as clouds passed over them, her mouth tingling, her forehead burning.

"Bloody hell!"

Another person knelt next to her: a man, this time. Madeleine couldn't see his face clearly either.

"You're one of those Sisters, aren't you?" he said. "I've seen you lot about. What were you doing in the—sweet Jesus, aren't you bleeding, then. Damn, what do I do when…" He leaned in. "Can you hear me?"

She could certainly smell him. There was alcohol on his breath. Madeleine wrinkled her nose and groaned. Now that the angel was gone, the pain was coming back, along with the unpleasant taste of salt. Her mouth was dry, her tongue thick.

"Right, anything broken? Can you sit up? Come on, now." The man slid one hand beneath her back and hauled her to a sitting position. She yelped at the ache in her head and her back.

"That's a girl. Stay awake, all right? My name's Jonathan." His voice was slurred. "Sit here and I'll fetch Sue Kilbright. She's a nurse."

"Yes…thanks…" Finally, she could manage proper words. She looked around, blinking, and coughed again. She could see better now, but it was still dark save for the streetlamps, which seemed a hundred miles away. Where was her flashlight? Probably still on the dock with the scissors. She should get the scissors. They weren't hers. It wasn't right to steal.

"Wasn't somebody with you?" Jonathan grunted as he propped her up straighter. She guessed that he was significantly older than she—in his sixties, maybe. "I'd have sworn blind I saw two of you, but maybe I was seeing double. I'm a bit worse for wear. I'm not usually," he added quickly.

"An angel," Madeleine muttered, turning her head to look back at the waves. "There was this horse…" She pointed to the dock, to the dinghy. "A horse in the water, and then a woman…she saved me, and she said…"

"A horse in the water?" An odd note entered Jonathan's voice. His grip on her tightened. "And then a woman, you said?"

"Yes, and she—" Madeleine touched her forehead. It stung, and her fingertips came away dark with blood. "She said—"

"Never mind what she said," Jonathan growled. "Fuck, we've got to get off this beach. Come on!"

He put his arm around Madeleine's shoulders and stood up with a grunt. He seemed none too steady on his feet, and for a moment they seemed about to fall back down, but then he caught himself. "Ah, hell. Let's go. Quickly now."

Madeleine couldn't approve of his language, but she did appreciate the sentiment. As they made their way to the steps, although her head continued to ache, it also became clear. And with the slow agony of clarification came the fear.

What in heaven's name had just happened to her? If that had been an angel—an angel in a woman's body, a woman's *naked* body that had lain atop Madeleine and awakened her most secret, shameful desires —well, what kind of angel would do that?

"Why were you alone on the beach this late?" Jonathan asked as they reached the bottom stair. "You must've had a reason. Did you see something? Hear something?"

Madeleine had no good answer to that. "Just out for a walk," she mumbled. What else could she say? She couldn't tell him about the otherworldly voice. Bad enough that she'd already babbled about the angel. She had to think about that further before she told anyone. Like the Virgin Mary did in Luke's gospel, she'd ponder mysterious things in her heart.

She'd especially ponder the three words her rescuer had breathed into her ear, captivating her, tethering her soul and her wonder to this place forever.

Return to me.

CHAPTER FOUR

THIS TIME, Hæra wouldn't get stuck under the dock.

She waited several lengths away from it. Only her eyes appeared above the surface as she watched for Sister Madeleine's return.

She'd been here all day. There was no way to tell how long Sister Madeleine would need to follow her instruction to come back, especially since she'd been injured. It had taken a lot of care to stay out of sight of the fishing boats as they'd departed that morning and returned later in the day, as well as the beachcombers. She'd only swum away long enough to hunt out two brown crabs for a snack, their shells popping between her incisors before she picked out the savory meat beneath. Then she'd returned to the surface as soon as possible, but nobody was there.

Now, hours later, she was starting to worry she'd missed Sister Madeleine in those few precious moments. It had been over a full day's cycle since their encounter, and the moon had risen high while the tide rose likewise to meet it. Hæra was exhausted, and the longer she stayed here, the greater the risk that someone in the herd would notice her absence.

She must have faith. What else had last night been about but that? Now the life debt between herself and Sister Madeleine had been paid, and they could start fresh with Hæra's original intention. She'd consume Sister Madeleine (and must remember to leave the liver), go to the Sire, and say what she'd done.

Nobody could fail to see how much Sister Madeleine would surely strengthen her, as the other Stormhorses were strengthened by their humans. Hæra must at least be allowed to prove her worth, even if the herd required more trials of her than they did of the males. She'd get her wings before Asgall's and Beathag's disbelieving eyes.

And Sister Madeleine would be with her, inside her, the entire time.

Keeping her eyes on the seawall, dock, and shore, Hæra remembered their mouths touching. She remembered all of it.

Sister Madeleine had tried to embrace her. It had been too much, and Hæra had had to hold her down. If Sister Madeleine had touched her, something would have happened. Hæra didn't know what, but it would have made it much harder to change back out of that human form.

Now, in her true form, Hæra could remember it with bemusement. At the time, her human body had been consumed by Sister Madeleine, much as she now wanted the reverse. Her blood had tasted divine, but Hæra could never have dreamed that her mouth would taste even better. And why had all that soggy cloth been bunched up between them? She knew humans wore clothes, but surely it would have felt more natural for Sister Madeleine to have been equally bare beneath Hæra's own body.

But again, that might have brought complications. Might have made Hæra feel…reluctant to change back.

This was a little worrisome. Hæra's job was not to touch Sister Madeleine with her mouth—or at least not to stop there. But how strangely disturbing it was to know that after Hæra ate her, Sister Madeleine would be no more: she'd walk along no more beaches, never again speak with that husky voice. And never again would her perfect scent carry along the wind.

They'd never get a chance to *talk*.

Hæra shook her head irritably, snorting up bubbles. What useless thoughts. She didn't need a conversation with Sister Madeleine. She already had something of her: the string of wooden beads that ended with the cross-shaped thing. Even Hæra recognized that cross. It had been part of human culture around here for so long that the herd had all sorts of theories about what it meant.

The beads now lay in the ancient chest she kept secreted away at the base of one of the cliffs.

She and Asgall had found the chest when he was a colt and she still a foal. He'd made so much fun of the object that she'd realized he wanted it. Even at that age she'd known to be wary when Asgall wanted things. He usually found a way to hurt her with them.

That night, she'd slipped away and returned to the chest, pulling it by one of its handles. Her mouth had been sore afterward, tasting of the handle's metal. She'd hidden the chest by the cliff.

The next day, Asgall had been in a terrible mood. He never admitted why, but she knew he'd returned to the chest he'd supposedly disdained, only to find it missing. He couldn't accuse Hæra of stealing it, for that would have meant he'd gone back to it. He'd lashed out at her, biting her neck and drawing blood before their mother Beathag separated them, sending Hæra away in the care of another mare while she fussed over her son.

The chest was full of things humans seemed to find valuable but which meant nothing to Hæra. There were loads of gold coins, so old their markings had faded, plus other items in gold and silver: cups and bowls, ornaments that humans put on their bodies, a jeweled dagger with a rusted blade. All items that had been around long enough that *Each-uisge* knew what they were and what functions they served. Her father had told her that cups and bowls were vessels humans used to feed themselves, since they didn't eat live prey. That had been interesting, if revolting.

Now the chest held a *real* treasure. Hæra had placed Sister Madeleine's string of beads on top of all the junk. There, the beads would serve as a permanent reminder of what it had been like for Hæra to lie atop her smaller body, something to keep after this business was done.

That is, assuming the business would ever be done. Where was her woman?

Maybe Sister Madeleine would have returned sooner if Hæra had told her that she'd bring a gift, something to replace what she'd stolen. Beneath her tongue sat one of the gold coins from the chest. Humans liked these so much; surely Sister Madeleine would come within reach to get one.

After the half moon passed its midpoint, her patience was finally rewarded. Hæra barely managed not to stick her whole head above the water as a human form appeared on the seawall in silhouette, lurching toward the little dock and dinghy. Then the human got close enough for her to see properly, and Hæra's heart fell.

Curse it to the depths and back! That was a man, not Sister Madeleine. He was no good to her.

Or was he?

It was the man from last night. The one who'd noticed them on the beach and helped Sister Madeleine away afterward. He'd taken her from Hæra's side, but perhaps he had helped care for the wound on her head.

Hæra's tail swished beneath the water in sudden agitation. The wound hadn't seemed deep, and Sister Madeleine had regained consciousness, but what did Hæra know about human health? Sister Madeleine might have been hurt worse than it seemed. Maybe that was why she hadn't come back.

Great Mare, Hæra prayed as she swam closer to the dock, *let her be well. Let the blood stop flowing. When the Last Current takes her, it shouldn't be like this.*

The man didn't walk out on the dock. Instead, he went to the rocky stretch of shore where Hæra had dragged Sister Madeleine. He didn't seem steady on his feet. Perplexed, Hæra watched as he stood at the edge of the water, looking over the sea. Then he called out, his voice reaching her through the rumble of the waves. "Show yourself, you bastard beast!" he yelled.

Hæra was so startled she nearly *did* show herself, sticking her head halfway out of the water before she pulled back down.

"She told me you were here. A bloody horse, she said! I knew you'd be back. Well, you fucked it last time, and you will this time too. You won't get her. You didn't get me."

Impossible. It couldn't be.

Hæra's head whirled. The man was older, as humans went. Forty turns ago, Asgall had failed with his chosen human. This man would have been a young adult then. Could *he* be Asgall's human? The idea beggared belief.

But she couldn't imagine who else this could be. The man seemed to know who—or at least what—Hæra was. The man had referred to a past failure. In hundreds of turns, Asgall was the only one who'd failed the Stormhorse trial. The timing matched up.

By the depths, it must be true. This pitiful, shambling creature was Asgall's human! That had to be why her brother had failed. Their chosen human prey was supposed to be noble, strong, and brave. Talk about an unworthy choice. Asgall must have been truly desperate.

It wasn't the time to feel a pang of sympathy. Her brother didn't deserve it.

"That nun thought you were an angel," the man rambled. "Seemed likelier to her than what you are. And now I find you can change into a woman as well as a man? It bloody figures."

That settled it. This was definitely Asgall's human.

"Show yourself!" The man was screaming now. Good thing nobody was out this late and that human hearing was so poor. "I'm not afraid of you!"

He was alone. He was weak. And he knew—he must know—where Sister Madeleine was.

Yes, it was an enormous risk. But Hæra was being handed another opportunity, as precious to her as gold was to humans. If she appeared to the man alone, his fellows would never believe him, and she could show him that she wasn't Asgall. That she meant no harm. That it would be perfectly safe for Sister Madeleine to come back, since she was clearly alive and talking.

Hæra's marine tail pushed her forward. Compared to the sea, the world had so little land, but the tiny stretch of rocky shore suddenly seemed as formidable as the greatest underwater crevasses.

She approached, splitting her tail when she was close enough to emerge on four legs. Gleaming strands of kelp hung handsomely from her mane. She'd polished the shells on her front hooves by rubbing them against some rocks. Altogether, it was an elegant effect. Hæra had come in her best to meet Sister Madeleine.

This sea louse of a human probably wouldn't appreciate it, but what could you do?

He was looking the wrong way. If Hæra were here to eat him, he'd be done for already. She stamped and snorted in contempt.

The man whirled on his feet, stumbled, and promptly fell on his behind. Then he sat on the ground, staring at Hæra with his mouth open. This close, she could see his grizzled beard in patches of brown and white. His face was weather-worn. His clothes were too baggy to show his shape, but he seemed neither malnourished nor covered with a large layer of insulating fat. More than that she couldn't tell.

A wet patch was also rapidly spreading over the cloth between his legs as he stared at her. He'd urinated on himself. Pathetic.

"You're different," he choked.

An understatement. Hæra and Asgall looked nothing alike, thank the Great Mare. She considered what he'd said before—what he'd called Sister Madeleine—and voiced the first question that came to her mind, although it sounded a little muddled with the coin under her tongue.

"What is a nun?" she asked, staying several lengths from him.

The human stared at her some more before gasping, "You're not him. Oh fuck. There are more of you?"

So Asgall hadn't betrayed the existence of the herd. *"Him,'"* Hæra said. *"I assume you mean my brother. Asgall is his name."*

"God. Right enough. Asgall is his name." The man seemed as shocked as if he'd just swum through an entire sea full of electric eels. "Your brother. He's got a sister. Christ."

"My name is not Christ. I'm Hæra. What are you called?"

"Jonathan," the man whispered. "Jonathan Rendall."

"Well met, Jonathan Rendall."

"Erm...just Jonathan, I..." Jonathan suddenly appeared to realize he was still sitting down. He looked between his legs at the wet patch and groaned, "You knob."

Luckily, he seemed to be talking to himself. Hæra would not be insulted or called names. *"I mean you no harm. If I did, you'd already be finished."*

"I reckon I would be, yeah." Jonathan lumbered to his feet with another groan. He bent and placed his hands on his knees, breathing heavily. "Christ, last night did my back in."

"I told you, my name isn't Christ," Hæra said irritably.

"No, Christ is—ah, never mind. That woman could tell you, and probably would for a long time."

Hæra's land tail flicked, sending drops of water flying through the air. Finally, something about Sister Madeleine. *"Why would she do that? Is it important?"*

"It is to her."

Then it was important to Hæra too, at least until this business was done. *"I'll have to ask her about it when next we meet. I saved her life, you know."*

Jonathan ground his jaw—a human gesture of agitation, she believed. "That's what she told me."

"So you see? I'm not like my brother at all." A dreadful thought suddenly occurred to Hæra. *"Did you tell Sister Madeleine about him? About what he did to you?"*

The last thing she needed was this dirty human pissing in the riptide, driving Sister Madeleine away because of Asgall's incompetence. How fitting it would be if her brother ruined Hæra's dream without even knowing it.

"Did I tell a nun I was nearly drowned by an ocean horse that had a fish tail and talked? I haven't told anyone. Bad enough to be the town drunk without folk saying I'm off my trolley too."

"I'm glad. I don't want her to think of me as a monster like Asgall."

"A monster, aye. He told me a lot of things about himself, but fuck knows it was probably all lies."

"Probably," Hæra agreed. *"Now, Sister Mad—"*

"He said he…well, I reckon both of you have some special tie to humans. You can take our shape but no other."

Asgall had betrayed so much? That was far worse than Hæra standing on the shore having a little chat. The Sire would tear him to pieces if he knew. *"He told you many things."*

"How much of it was bollocks?" Jonathan's voice was rough, pleading. His face seemed to soften, to grow open. "Not a day goes by I don't think about how mental the whole thing was. Even after all this time. Now here you are, chasing after that woman."

She must be careful now. Hæra said calmly, *"I chase no one. Did I drown her, or did I save her? That creates a bond between us, and I have no wish to break it. That's why I want to see her again."*

All true, as far as it went. She'd learned from Beathag and Asgall that the most convincing lies came from the same sea as the truth.

"Hard luck, then. She's gone."

Hæra blinked, sure she'd misheard.

"Yeah. Gone," he repeated.

She must bite back the scream of frustration. She must not lose control. Information was absolutely necessary. *"Gone where? And when will she return?"*

"Off the islands. Her group wasn't in a hurry to hang about after she cracked her head and nearly drowned. I don't think they fell in love with Orkney anyway." Jonathan tilted his head to the side, looking far too canny for a man who'd urinated on himself a few minutes ago. Hæra could smell it from here, and it wasn't pleasant. "They're from the other side of the pond—the Atlantic bloody Ocean. I doubt they're coming back at all."

No.

That couldn't be true.

"Not sure even you could swim that far," Jonathan added, a gloating note in his voice, as if he didn't stand before a creature who could rend him into pieces. "Or that fast."

"Are you mocking me?"

The words came out too coldly, as if they'd risen from the darkest depths inside her. *Be calm.* Hæra must keep her head, and she couldn't castigate herself for not eating Sister Madeleine when she'd had the chance. That wouldn't have been a fair contest, it would never have earned Hæra her wings, and it wouldn't have been right to repay a life debt by devouring her rescuer. Hæra had done the right thing. She had to remember that.

The Great Mare had willed all of this to happen—that seemed plain enough. If that were true, then Hæra and Sister Madeleine weren't finished. She'd told Sister Madeleine to return to her, and she must have faith it would happen.

"Mocking *you?* Do I want to die?" Jonathan looked down at the wet patch on his trousers. "If I did, you think the sight of you would make me piss myself? Mind you, that could be the drink…"

"I don't care what it was." Oh, depths, she had to modulate her tone. Jonathan's role had just officially changed. He was Hæra's only link to Sister Madeleine, wherever she had gone, and she couldn't afford to drive him away. If she managed this properly, he'd become her ally and never suspect a thing.

Perhaps some sort of gesture was appropriate.

"I mean the human race no harm," she said gently. *"I abhor what Asgall did. Let me prove it."*

This would be a gamble. But to gain the sky, she had to brave the winds.

Hæra opened her mouth and bent her head. The gold coin beneath her tongue hit the pebbles with a clink.

"What's that?" Jonathan asked.

"A gift I'd meant to offer her. Now I offer it to you—with my own hands."

"You haven't got hands."

"Not like this. Observe."

She closed her eyes, concentrated, and it happened again.

Her body shrank. Its muscles compacted, its bones realigned. So did her eyes, and her lateral vision disappeared so she could only look straight ahead. Her hind legs slimmed, her front legs shortened, and her hooves changed to strange, soft things with wiggling fingers and toes.

Her hide grew softer too, losing its coat of short, coarse hair. The black hair on her head made up for that, falling down in a wet slap to the small of her back and still attractively accented with kelp.

She hadn't had a real chance to examine her human body last night. Everything had happened too quickly. Now, Hæra looked down at herself.

Her shoulders seemed broad, her arms long, and her waist narrow. Her legs were long too, for a human. More dark hair lay between her thighs, covering her human genitals. She had breasts as well, although they didn't look very big. Perhaps that was because of her musculature, which seemed well developed. Pleased, she sensed instinctively that this body was well suited to swimming. That was fitting.

She raised her head to see that Jonathan was staring at her with his mouth open again.

"Bloody fuck," he said. "My head's mince."

There seemed no answer to that other than, "It's all right."

Her human voice was so strange! Softer, quieter, and without an echo. It lacked the crash of the water on the rocks. It was thus less impressive, but at the sound of it, Jonathan visibly relaxed.

She could see that easily. Her vision seemed to have lost none of its sharpness, even if it only pointed forward. Her hearing remained excellent too, as did her sense of smell—which might be unfortunate, given what the human had done to himself.

Hæra bent down—odd to do it from the waist, not the shoulders— and reached for the dropped coin. Her fingers seemed to know what to do: they closed around the coin and cupped it securely in her palm.

Then she walked slowly to Jonathan. The distance between them presented much more of a challenge than the short dash she'd made from Sister Madeleine back to the sea. Her arms wanted to move when her legs did, and she had to fight to keep them at her sides as she'd seen humans do. Her weight distribution was all wrong, and she still felt heavy out of the water. Her legs might've been strong in human terms, but they were nothing to her true form. The pebbles and rocks didn't help, creating an uneven surface beneath her soft feet.

Given all this, it was no surprise she stumbled and fell. Her gasp became a cry when she hit the rocks. This skin was so much more fragile—had it torn? It must be abraded at least. No wonder humans wore protective coverings. It was a miracle the species had survived at all.

"Oh—er—hold on a bit—"

Jonathan hurried toward her, looking none too steady on his own feet. As he moved, he took off one of his coverings, pulling it down over his arms. That seemed like an impressive maneuver, compared to what Hæra was able to manage. She hadn't even been able to keep hold of the coin. "Take my jacket," he said, holding it out to her.

Hæra looked at it dubiously. The garment would provide no protection or comfort for her lower half, which seemed to be the chancy part. And no other humans were here to see her, so she didn't have to blend in. "I don't feel the cold. I don't need that."

"Yes, you do. The cold's not why." He looked away with a grimace.

He wanted her to follow human custom, even knowing she wasn't human? Well, needs must. Hæra sighed, picked the coin back up, and rose gingerly to her feet.

It took her a moment to figure the "jacket" out. When she had it on, the weight felt unnatural and the fabric rubbed unpleasantly against her skin. Nevertheless, it covered most of her front, although she wasn't going to bother with the silly fastener that looked like a line of metal teeth. "All right."

Jonathan looked back at her. Up at her. Then he stepped back and gave a soft whistle. "Jesus. You're six feet if you're an inch. Or more."

"I only have two feet."

"No, that's—it's a unit of measurement. Dunno if you have those. I'm just saying you're tall, especially for a woman."

Hæra liked the sound of that, but she didn't have a human's standards. Maybe her height wouldn't appeal to Sister Madeleine. "Is that good?"

"Dunno," he repeated. "Depends who you ask. It just is what it is."

How helpful. "Are you more comfortable with me now that I've taken on this form?"

He laughed roughly. "Comfortable's not how I'd put it. He could look human too."

Asgall, too, had attempted the trick their father disdained. So much for being nobler than Hæra was.

"A kelpie, I thought he was," Jonathan said. "Naturally."

Hæra recoiled. Kelpies were also unseen water creatures who looked like horses and could take human shape, but as far as she was concerned, there the similarities ended. Denizens of freshwater rivers and lochs, they were smaller, weaker, less intelligent, and less circumspect in preying on people—which was probably why humans knew more about them than they did about *Each-uisge*. They dwelled alone, not in herds, and so had little protection. There were almost none left.

"Asgall's no prize, but he's no kelpie either," she snapped. "No more am I."

"So he said. Looked as disgusted as you, and I knew that was true, even if nothing else turned out to be."

Silence. She was at something of a loss after that.

"I thought it was over," Jonathan whispered. He was looking at Hæra, but at the same time, he still seemed to be looking at something else. His face had lost color. "And now it's not."

"It is," Hæra said firmly. "Asgall will never come for you again."

Jonathan blinked. Then he looked down at his shoes, so Hæra did too. They were worn and scratched. Sand crusted their edges.

After a moment, Jonathan said, "Oh." The word sounded thick, as if an anemone had just unfurled in his throat.

"You can believe me," Hæra reassured him. "I know my brother. He won't revisit a failure."

"Failure. Aye, I suppose it was." Jonathan rubbed his hand over the back of his neck. When he looked back up at Hæra, his face had some color back, and he was looking at her, not at some phantom of the past. Something else had changed, too.

"Your eyes are wet," Hæra said in alarm.

"What?" Jonathan dashed the back of his hand across his face, rubbing at his eyes. He sniffed. That sounded wet too. "Sorry. I'm a silly sod, is all."

She hadn't known human eyes could leak. Jonathan wasn't treating it as a serious condition, though. He only seemed embarrassed.

"Silly, useless," Jonathan muttered. "Failure. And here I am, forty years later with piss on my trousers and naught else. Wasted time. Wasted life."

He certainly seemed determined to waste Hæra's time. She fought not to stamp her foot, not least because it would hurt. Her side still ached from her stumble. "Then let it be different this time. Help me."

The words seemed to jolt Jonathan back into the moment. He blinked, droplets still on his eyelashes. "How's that?"

"I don't want from Sister Madeleine what Asgall wanted from you." Also the truth. Asgall saw everything and everyone as a means to an end. He wouldn't have thought twice about *honoring* this man. "Aren't my actions proof enough of that?"

"I reckon they must be." Jonathan took in a deep breath. It sounded unsteady. "And you don't sound like him. He always…laughed. Came off as if nothing mattered much."

Sister Madeleine's green eyes. Sister Madeleine's soft mouth. Sister Madeleine's response to Hæra's call. "This matters to me. It matters very much."

"Yes. I can tell. That's…different."

"Help me correct his mistake," Hæra whispered. The full force of her longing was in her voice, but that didn't have to be a bad thing, if it convinced Jonathan she was telling the truth. "Help me do what he couldn't."

"I still can't believe it happened. I can't believe he's real. The things he told me—" For the first time, sorrow and fear left Jonathan's eyes, and curiosity took their place; she could imagine the young man he must have been forty turns…"years"…ago. Maybe he'd been worthy prey for Asgall after all. "I asked him how he could talk to me. I mean —in all the stories, I know magical creatures can talk to human folk, but I asked anyway. He said he's tied to the people of this place, these islands, and sure as I could understand him, he could understand me. Same for you?"

"Same for me, yes. But speaking isn't the same thing as understanding."

"No shite." Jonathan laughed a little. Something about it reminded Hæra of the rust on the chest's ancient dagger, eating away at what had once been sharp enough to cut. "Can you read, too?"

Hæra thought again of the ruined books she'd seen in shipwrecks. "No. Can you?"

He looked insulted. "I might not be much, but yeah, I can *read*."

If Jonathan could read, then no doubt Sister Madeleine could too. He made it sound like a basic skill humans were expected to have. And it was one of their primary means of communication. She heard herself say, "I want to learn."

Jonathan's look changed to one of astonishment. "You do? Why?"

Why, indeed? The words had come to her impulsively. Why should Hæra want to acquire a silly human skill she'd never need after her goal was accomplished?

Because it wasn't accomplished. Because it would be something to share with Sister Madeleine, to…talk about.

"Because Sister Madeleine will come back," she said. "If she knows how, I want to know too. Besides, it's not that hard, is it?"

"I've got no clue how hard it'd be for you. Maybe you're a bloody genius of an ocean horse." Jonathan glanced toward the sea. Hæra was forced to turn her head to follow his gaze, which was aimed at the little dock that had started this whole farce. "She said she cut you free from there."

Hæra's face suddenly felt warmer than the rest of her. Her head and shoulders seemed heavier, as if they wanted to slump down and make her appear smaller. Perhaps she shouldn't mock this man after all—he'd probably never done anything as embarrassing as getting caught in a dock.

She lifted her chin and stood up straighter. "Yes, she did. So you see, there's a bond between us. I mean her no harm."

It would be a great honor for Sister Madeleine to be devoured, to become part of a Stormhorse that would unleash the lightning and the wind. The first female Stormhorse, no less. Sister Madeleine would become legendary, spoken of with reverence. She'd become part of the herd's lore for thousands of turns. Hæra would ensure it.

That wasn't *harming* anybody. The opposite, in fact.

"Why are you so certain she'll come back?" Jonathan asked. "She lives far off. She was just here on a tour. She's got no friends or family here."

Hæra looked him dead in the eye so he would feel the force of her sincerity. He had to. If she said it with enough faith, it'd come true.

"She has me," she said.

After a moment, Jonathan said softly, "Ah."

"Yes. And she *will* return to me. What lies between us is unfinished. Now…" Hæra held out her human hand and opened her palm to reveal the gold coin. "This is for you."

Jonathan took the coin and squinted at it with a frown. Then he lifted his chin with a sharp gasp.

That seemed promising. "I believe this is precious to your kind. Would you have a use for it?"

"Yeah, it is." Jonathan's eyes were extremely wide. "And yeah, I would."

"I have many more. They come from a shipwreck. I can bring them to you, if…"

Jonathan turned his wide-eyed gaze from the coin to Hæra. "If what?"

If you teach me to read. If you give me more clothes. If you show me your ways.

If you make me ready for her.

She pulled herself up to her full height and, for the first time, stretched her human mouth into a smile.

"I'm glad to have met you, Jonathan," she said. "Let's make a bargain. But first, you never answered my question: what *is* a nun?"

CHAPTER FIVE

WHAT A DIFFERENCE A YEAR MAKES.

Sister Madeleine dismissed the thought as she looked down at the page before her. She hadn't really been reading. Not that it mattered; she'd read this book so many times that she could recite it in her sleep.

Especially the *Catechism of the Catholic Church*'s section on angels.

The *Catechism* said it loud and clear: angels existed. Pope John Paul II had authorized it, so it was official. Each believer had an angel and protector that would lead him or her to eternal life. The creature on the beach had protected Madeleine from dying—especially from dying without one final absolution of her sins from a priest. That matched the description.

But angels must also be, as the *Catechism* put it, more perfect than all earthly creatures, full of splendor and glory. Madeleine's other-worldly rescuer hadn't seemed like that. Madeleine hadn't even seen her face. She hadn't glowed, except for the moonlight that had temporarily silhouetted her while Madeleine lay dazed and dazzled on the beach.

She'd never heard of angels that kissed you, either. At least not like that, hungry and hard, in a way that had caused her several sleepless nights while she wrestled with urges she'd thought were gone.

So…it might have been something other than an angel. That idea had kept her up at night too. Her faith had room for apparitions, the dead who came from heaven to counsel the living away from sin—but that was a *good* thing. Opinion was generally divided on ghosts. In any case, neither apparitions nor ghosts were supposed to feel so…physical, and they definitely weren't supposed to make out with you. Holy Scripture accounted for demons, but they usually possessed humans before Jesus or his saints had cast them out. It was hard to imagine why a demon would possess a human's body, kiss Madeleine, and then disappear, taking the human body with it.

No. As incredible and impossible as it seemed, an angel was the most likely answer.

Tomorrow would mark the first anniversary of Madeleine's supernatural encounter. As it approached, she'd grown nervous and jumpy, as if she were bracing for something to happen. But here in Philadelphia, far from that Orcadian beach, what could it be?

For some reason, she thought of Ava, who'd been with her that day. Both she and Emma had graduated and were now at the same university. Months ago, Ava had written to say she'd decided the sisterhood wasn't for her.

Thank heavens she'd realized it before it was too late. Imagine refusing to give the idea enough reflection, committing yourself, and losing decades to a life that wasn't right for you. It was enough to make Madeleine's blood turn to ice.

Someone cleared her throat.

Madeleine started. More than a decade spent as a high school teacher helped her detect even the sneakiest footsteps, but she'd been so absorbed in her thoughts that she hadn't heard a thing.

Before her stood Sacred Heart's only other nun under fifty: Sister Bridget, a young woman who worked diligently and was so pretty that Madeleine had spent the last year trying not to notice her delicate hands.

"What is it?" She'd sounded too sharp. "I'm sorry. What is it, Sister?"

"Sister Catherine wants to see you," Bridget said, her voice meek with deference to a senior sister.

Madeleine rose to her feet at once. "Is she in the garden?" That seemed likely. It was the hour for recreation, a rare moment when nuns had time to do what they wanted—hence Madeleine reading about angels where nobody would bother her. The garden was Sister Catherine's favorite place to rest. Madeleine loved it too, a place where things of both use and beauty grew.

To her surprise, Bridget said, "Sister Catherine's in her office." She lowered her voice. "There's someone else there too. I'm sworn not to say who."

Madeleine stared at her.

"I probably wasn't supposed to mention it at all," Bridget said sheepishly. "But I wanted to give you some warning."

"Warning?" That sounded ominous, to say the least.

"Oh, just that she's, um, not alone? I'm sure it's nothing bad? It's probably—"

"*Thank* you, Sister." Madeleine brushed her skirt down. "I'll be on my way."

She took deep, steadying breaths as she proceeded alone to Sister Catherine's office. Even at thirty-six, it was hard not to be apprehensive about going to see the principal. Especially given where Madeleine's head had been recently: all those doubts, those worries, those…unholy thoughts. Sister Bridget had long, slender hands.

Soon, she was knocking on the imposing wooden door with a brass placard that read: "SUPERIOR."

"Come in," Sister Catherine called from the other side.

Madeleine entered the familiar space, a bit fancier than most of Sacred Heart, with beautiful wood paneling, an impressive carved wooden desk with a matching chair, and a stained glass window depicting the Virgin and Child. As usual, Sister Catherine sat behind the desk with her hands folded in front of her and a calm look on her face.

More unusually, another nun stood by the window with her back turned, gazing at the brightly colored panes.

Madeleine closed the door. The other nun turned, and Madeleine gasped to see who it was. She lowered her head immediately.

Footsteps approached her. A hand appeared before her face. Madeleine took it and kissed its ring of office: a garnet set in a band of silver.

"Sister Madeleine," said Mother Gertrude warmly, and she took Madeleine's hand in both of her own.

Madeleine looked at the Superior General of the Daughters of Grace. Mother Gertrude was in her mid-sixties and, years ago, had overseen Madeleine's own novitiate. Those had not been easy years, but Gertrude was a kind and steady leader. When Madeleine had taken her temporary vows and left the convent to serve elsewhere, Gertrude had told her she "showed great promise" and invited her to keep in touch. Madeleine had.

Mother Gertrude released Madeleine's hand. "When was the last time we met in person? Five years at least. It's wonderful to see you."

Madeleine smiled. "And you too, Reverend Mother. I had no idea you were coming."

Which was strange, now that she thought about it. A visit from the Superior General should be an occasion, not a secret Sister Bridget had to keep.

Mother Gertrude and Sister Catherine glanced at each other. Gertrude said, "We'll announce my presence later. You'll have the chance to roll out the red carpet then."

"It's got holes in it," Sister Catherine said dryly. "Here's hoping our next Superior will be more successful at squeezing money from you than I was."

Gertrude clearly took no offense. "She can try. I'll open up the order's purse and let her see the dust inside."

"She'll have to be gutsy enough to push back, then."

Madeleine bit her lip at the easy rapport between two senior members of the order, so hard-working and devoted that they'd earned their places. Madeleine couldn't imagine either of them spending hours thinking about dark angels or temptations of the flesh. They focused on education, on good works, on…

Right now, they seemed especially focused on Madeleine. Looking straight at her, in fact.

Her body stiffened in alarm. Had she missed something? She'd definitely felt off her game in the last year, but she'd worked twice as hard to cover it up. This was hardly the time to space out.

Mother Gertrude gestured at the two chairs in front of Sister Catherine's desk, usually reserved for visiting parents or misbehaving students. "Sit down, Sister Madeleine."

Madeleine did, her knees a little shaky for no clear reason. Gertrude took the second chair, angling it so she could look easily between Madeleine and Catherine.

"Sister Catherine, would you like to begin?" Gertrude asked. Madeleine had always admired how the Superior General made room for others to speak first. If she herself ever reached such a position of authority, she'd want to follow that example.

Not right, her inner voice whispered maddeningly. *Not for you. Unworthy.*

"I might as well," Catherine sighed. She did look worn out, her once-sharp eyes now dull with fatigue. "It's no secret that I've been talking about stepping down. For too long, it's just been talk, but I've recently had some medical news that'll hurry things along. Nothing terminal," she added when Madeleine leaned forward in alarm. "But my rheumatoid arthritis isn't responding to the injections, and the doctor says it's time to start discussing surgery."

Madeleine looked at the swollen joints and prominent veins on Sister Catherine's hands. "I'm so sorry, Sister."

Catherine shrugged. "We're none of us without trials. The fact is, this was the sign I needed. I can't be wrangling everything while dealing with this. The pain is…" She winced.

Mother Gertrude reached across the desk and gently took one of Catherine's hands.

Madeleine's heart ached. It wasn't a surprise that Catherine was ready to step down, but what an awful reason to do it. "How can I help you, Sister?"

Mother Gertrude and Sister Catherine looked at each other. Then they looked back at Madeleine. "There is something you can do, actually," Gertrude said. "I'm considering you for the position of Superior of Sacred Heart."

Superiors General weren't known for joking around. Madeleine waited for the punchline anyway.

Gertrude smiled. "You're surprised."

"You're kidding." *That* had come out wrong. "Uh, Reverend Mother."

Gertrude chuckled as she let go of Catherine's hand. "I figured you'd say that. Sister Catherine and I have discussed this at length. I'm serious."

Madeleine couldn't speak, only stare, while Gertrude and Catherine looked back expectantly. Finally, she found her voice. "But how could I be worthy of such a responsibility when other sisters are more...um..."

Catherine asked wryly, "More eager?"

"I didn't say that."

"No, you didn't. Well done." Mother Gertrude folded her hands in her lap. "I know you're relatively young. You nevertheless have a good head on your shoulders—except for when you bonked it last year and fell in the ocean."

She and Sister Catherine both chuckled while Madeleine's face burned. She fought not to touch her forehead. It still bore a scar, about half as long as her pinkie finger, from when she'd hit her head on the dinghy. The doctor had said it would likely never fade completely.

More seriously, Gertrude said, "You've ably filled every position of responsibility we've given you. Teaching, chairing a department, helping Sister Catherine balance the budget—these are no small things to ask of someone. Now, instead of being grateful, we're asking for more."

"Don't let it go to your head," Catherine interjected. "My only reservation is about your besetting sin of pridefulness, which we've discussed—that, and your stubborn streak."

"Yes, Sister, but I really don't think I'm the best fit for the job."

"I rest my case."

"May I share my concerns, Reverend Mother?" Madeleine asked desperately, hoping that these concerns would come in a coherent form while she spoke of them. Right now, they were just a jumble of *no* and *wrong* and *can't they see?*

What was there to see, though? Mother Gertrude and Sister Catherine were wise and discerning. If they saw potential in Madeleine, it had to be there. Why did this proposal make Madeleine want to flee?

"You may," Mother Gertrude replied.

"It's not just that I'm young, but about how my other sisters would respond to that. Some of them have been here for decades. Shouldn't someone more senior take the position?" She thought about any possibility other than Agnes. "What about Sister Judith? She just oversaw our gym renovation, and—"

"Sister Judith's gifts lie elsewhere," Gertrude interrupted. "As, I believe, do her interests. Trust me, I share some of your concerns. I've given this a lot of thought, and Sister Catherine and I have been in conversation for several weeks now."

Becoming the Superior. That also meant becoming the principal. Madeleine wasn't eager to step out of the classroom—few joys rivaled those of encouraging young minds to broaden. She also took shameful pride in being kinder than her own teachers had been in Catholic school decades ago. Unlike the nuns of her youth, she'd never once thrown an eraser, slapped a student's palm with a ruler, or made anybody stand in a trash can for asking a silly question.

On the other hand, it was no secret that Sacred Heart was ready for a few changes. Madeleine had ideas, visions that could now become plans. And it would keep both the school and convent out of Agnes's hands. The list of the convent's banned books wouldn't expand, and students wouldn't need to worry about detention if their uniform skirts were a centimeter too short.

"She's thinking about it, Catherine," Mother Gertrude said cheerfully.

"So I see, Reverend Mother."

Might as well put it on the table. "Does Sister Agnes know about this?"

Both Gertrude and Catherine shook their heads. Catherine asked, "Are you afraid of her?"

Madeleine sat up straight, her eyes widening. The idea! "Not even a little, but I don't want to cause dissent in a community I—"

Don't belong in. The words popped into her mind so suddenly that she nearly gasped.

"L-love," she stammered.

"Of course you don't," Gertrude said. "This isn't a popularity contest, but a question of what we want the future of our order to look like. And your generation is the future. In this respect, your youth is an asset."

Madeleine bowed her head in acknowledgment, even as her heart continued to race like a horse straining at the bit.

"And it's not only about loving the community," Catherine added. "Remember why we signed up for this life in the first place." She pointed at the nearest crucifix. "Our love for him, so great we could never devote ourselves to anything or anyone else. Let your love for him guide all your decisions, and you can never go wrong."

Madeleine started as a new light glowed in Catherine's eyes—not something she was used to seeing from her serious Superior. Catherine's voice was full of sincerity that might as well have been a punch to Madeleine's gut.

During her novitiate, of course, there had been a lot of talk about feeling an all-consuming love for God: supposedly, it was necessary for the consecrated life. They even called it becoming a "Bride of Christ." Madeleine had never felt that passion with the fervor of some of her fellow novices, but she'd figured it manifested in her actions rather than her emotions, and that over time she'd come to feel it more. She'd been drawn to the convent life, and that had seemed like the same thing: a calling.

She'd assumed most other nuns were the same. Sister Catherine, for example, was relentlessly practical in all things. Not the kind of person to swoon with love for anyone, especially at her age.

Or so Madeleine had thought. Until right now.

"Catherine, you always hit the nail on the head. Of course it's about that," Mother Gertrude said, deepening the cold pit in Madeleine's stomach. She rose to her feet; Madeleine and Catherine followed suit, though Madeleine could have wished for steadier knees. "Sister Madeleine, spend tonight in seclusion. Consider the matter more deeply. My presence will be announced at breakfast tomorrow, the better to allow you solitude without people putting two and two together. I'll lie low until then and will speak with you in the chapel at first light."

Madeleine's answer would be expected then. "Yes, Reverend Mother."

"Thank you, Sister. You're dismissed."

Madeleine dipped her head and left the office in silence. As she closed the door behind her, she heard Catherine's and Gertrude's voices murmuring again. It was quite the effort not to commit the sin of eavesdropping.

Maybe, if she eavesdropped, she'd overhear them saying something that would reassure her and chase away the cold in the pit of her stomach. The one that said: *You cannot do this. You cannot possibly do this.*

You don't love him enough for that.

She hugged herself as she walked. Nobody was watching, thank goodness. Nobody would see Sister Madeleine, pillar of her community, sensible and respected, wondering if the last fifteen years of her life had been a horrible mistake. Reflection. She needed prayer and reflection.

There was just one problem with reflection.

Sometimes you saw what you didn't want to see looking right back at you.

CHAPTER SIX

"HAVE you got to spit all over the place?"

"I can't help it." Hæra turned away from Jonathan's kitchen sink with a grimace. "All this time, and fresh water still tastes disgusting."

"Then why do you keep trying to drink it? Run the tap, if you please."

Hæra turned on the creaky tap to rinse the sink. "Because drinking water is the most basic human function after breathing air, and I can do the first. Why not the second?"

"You're not human, though, are you?"

By now, after a year of giving Hæra lessons on human life, Jonathan could speak of it more casually. Still, there was curiosity in his voice when he continued. "You don't feel the cold, you can't abide fresh water, and there's the way you…whenever you come inland… you know."

She could do without the reminder of what happened when she came inland, which was about once every four nights. Hæra frowned as she approached the rickety kitchen table, which seemed nearly as old as the rickety cottage it graced.

Jonathan didn't live in the village, where rents were higher, but on the edge of town, looking out onto a stretch of land Hæra found desolate. Its biggest advantage was that you couldn't see the sea from any point. As long as Hæra was careful, once she was across the beach coming here and going back, she wouldn't be spotted by the *Each-uisge.*

If she were, that would be bad. These days, she thought more and more of the punishments Alban had told her about: a beating, shunning, even banishment. This trespass was severe enough that she might be exiled from the herd for good, and she likely wouldn't last long in the hostile ocean alone.

So she was cautious, reaching Jonathan's home as swiftly as she could and departing the same way. His house was a one-bedroom stone cottage with small windows and a sooty fireplace that was more reliable than the heater—and the fire was always going, including on a cool summer night like tonight. Hæra, who hated fire, had asked him to put it out, but he said that was bad luck and he got cold besides.

She adjusted her trousers as she sat. When she'd started coming ashore for her education, Jonathan had brought her women's clothing: a loose, ugly dress that was "the only thing tall enough for you." She had told him to find nicer things that would allow for more freedom of movement. After all, she was paying for it.

Now, she wore long trousers that were traditionally men's garments, and shirts with buttons that had taken a while to learn; she liked to roll the sleeves up to her elbows so the cloth stayed out of her way. She preferred boots to regular shoes, since they kept the mud off. And she kept her long, black hair pulled back in what he called a "ponytail"—a demeaning term, but it was more practical. Jonathan said it altogether made her look "bonnie, but not in the usual way."

"Here you are." Jonathan set before her a cup of cold tea. Hæra liked tea, especially when it was strongly flavored. She accepted the cup and sprinkled salt into it while Jonathan added a splash of cream to his own.

She remembered what to say. "Cheers."

He smiled and lifted his cup. Like most humans, he preferred hot tea, and steam rose from the liquid. "Cheers, lassie."

They sipped in silence for a moment, beginning their usual ritual.

They would share a cup of tea and then work. Although these lessons had begun as a means to an end, they were more interesting than Hæra had expected. Her kind had customs, but the number of rituals humans went through staggered her. At first, it had all seemed over-whelming—how was she supposed to learn enough to forge a bond with Sister Madeleine? But Jonathan had encouraged her to take it "one day at a time," and so she had.

The most basic etiquette came first. There were so many rules. On her second visit, she'd tried to be a good guest by bringing Jonathan a seal carcass, freshly killed and fragrant with blood. It turned out that wasn't polite after all.

That wasn't even the strangest thing she'd learned. Humans couldn't just take off all their clothes if they didn't feel like wearing them anymore—Jonathan had been most alarmed when she'd tried that, even though they'd been indoors. They used little utensils to eat, not just their hands. And they didn't void themselves wherever they felt the need, but went to specific places. That last part seemed espe-cially important.

Humans had done more things than even Alban had spoken of, even more than lore that had been passed down for generations. There were inventions she could never have imagined: telephones that let you talk to someone on the other side of the world, screens that gave you information about nearly anything you wanted to know, art that was made purely for its own sake.

And weapons. *Each-uisge* were violent creatures, but human brutality far exceeded anything Hæra's kind had ever managed. They had wars and prisons and whatnot. When she'd asked Jonathan why such things happened, he'd shrugged helplessly and said there was no good explanation for why people hurt each other. It was just how things were.

All of it was fascinating in its own way, and there was more besides. Hæra had heard the songs of the sirens, but they were so much less compelling than human music. She'd never have dreamed that random objects could produce such pleasing sounds when touched the right way. Jonathan had a collection of records he said would be part of her education. When Sister Madeleine returned, Hæra could talk to her about Madonna, Freddie Mercury, and ABBA.

She set down her cup and looked at Jonathan expectantly. "Shall we begin? I want to see how many words with five letters I can write from memory."

Her progress with Jonathan's alphabet hadn't been as swift as she'd expected. It was tedious, but she'd persevered and could now read basic sentences, although writing was more challenging. She'd asked Jonathan if her learning pace was fast or slow, and he'd said hell if he knew how long it was supposed to take a water horse to become literate. At first, she'd been infuriated by his insolence—and then had realized it was actually affection. Jonathan had come to like her.

How strange. And how much stranger that she'd come to like Jonathan too, as useless as he'd seemed at the start. Now, though, he was looking at her instead of answering her question.

"What's wrong?" Hæra asked.

"It's been a year to the day," he said. "One of your 'turns' since you first came ashore. Did you know that?"

Hæra blinked. Her skin prickled to realize he was right. Her kind didn't attach the same meaning to time as Jonathan's did; a "week" was useless to her, a "month" only remarkable for the phases of the moon. But a full turn of the world since she'd met Sister Madeleine felt significant. "I hadn't realized," she said.

"I just wondered if it'd matter to you."

Yes, it mattered. A turn of the world in which her woman hadn't returned. She'd never imagined it would take this long. Would there be more such turns? There couldn't be many, could there? She couldn't afford too many, not if she was to avoid becoming a brood mare.

Faith. She had to have faith. It would work out in the end.

She quoted one of Jonathan's sayings back to him. "It is what it is. Does it matter to you?"

Jonathan looked at his tea. He turned the cup so that the liquid swirled like a weak brown whirlpool. "It does, yeah."

A note in his voice grabbed her attention. After a turn, a year, she'd come to know something of Jonathan—when he was trying to be funny, when he was sad, when he had something important to say. This was the latter.

Of course, they had different definitions of "important," but Hæra would indulge him. "Why?"

"It's changed everything." Jonathan looked up at her, his brown eyes wide and earnest. "I feel like a new man. When I first went to Edinburgh with your treasure chest, I thought, this can't be happening to me. Now I'm the richest man on Jorsay—not that that's saying much, but still, nobody knows about it yet. I worried at first. Would I spend it all on drink? But I haven't, and now…" He glanced over at a desk by the window, where a computer sat next to a stack of notebooks. "I know those numbers mean nothing to you, but I'm nearly ready to make an offer on the land."

Jonathan's lifelong dream was, apparently, to buy the same desolate stretch of land Hæra could see from the cottage windows. He thought it was beautiful. It had been part of a dairy where he'd worked off and on for twenty years. The last owner had died without issue two years ago, leaving the estate to a niece in Aberdeen who clearly wasn't interested in maintenance.

Now, Jonathan wanted to raise livestock on it. At sixty-two years old, he'd given up hope it could happen. While many of Orkney's islands had thriving farms and tourism, Jorsay's only industry was fishing. The island's few young men had mostly left to work the oil terminals off the island of Flotta. The presence of a viable farm would be good for something called "the local economy."

In spite of his age, Jonathan wanted to start this enterprise. Then, he said, he'd finally have something to show for his life.

When he'd said that, Hæra had imagined a pair of wings growing from her back as she took flight.

"I'm glad it's happening," she said now. "You've held up your end of the bargain so far."

Jonathan snorted. "I haven't heard that in a while. Drunks aren't known for it. Ask anyone on Jorsay how far they'd trust me with anything important."

"Then why do you stay here?" For that matter, why was Jonathan building something that would tie him even *more* to the islands?

"Well, I...I've wondered that." Jonathan's brow creased, as it did when he was trying to remember something, or when something didn't make sense to him. "I used to try to leave, after everything happened with your brother. Why shouldn't I start over? But every time I tried, something held me back. There wouldn't be a job, or something would fall through, or I'd drink away the chance, but in the end..."

"What?"

"I just couldn't leave," Jonathan said slowly. "That's what it all comes down to. I think about leaving Orkney, and I can't. That's all."

Hæra leaned forward and placed her chin on her hand. Jonathan had never elaborated on what had passed between him and Asgall. Perhaps that was because Hæra had never asked. As curious as she was about her brother's failure, her time with Jonathan must be used efficiently. Better to focus on gaining necessary skills than revisiting a painful past.

Now that they were approaching the first year, the past was apparently calling.

"Will you tell me what happened between you and Asgall?" she asked.

Jonathan raised his eyebrows. His cheeks reddened a bit. "He never told you?"

This could be tricky. She couldn't tell him what Asgall had really wanted to do, lest he suspect Hæra's own plan. She hadn't even told him about the existence of the herd. So far as Jonathan knew, Hæra and Asgall were the only ones of their kind.

"He knew better than to tell me," she said. "I told you, I abhor what he did."

"Oh. Well." Jonathan took in a deep, shaking breath. When he exhaled, it blew away the steam over his teacup. "I was a young man, barely twenty-one. Climbing over the rocks by the cliff like a proper idiot, and all of a sudden I see a horse in the water. I think it's lost, though I can't imagine how it swam all the way out there, but then it lifts its head, and it…he…starts talking to me. A horse talking to me! I thought I'd lost my mind. But he said he knew me, he'd been watching me, figured I was a hale and hearty fellow. And I was, you know…then."

Hæra tilted her head in acknowledgment. Once, she wouldn't have believed the staggering drunk she'd met on the shore could have been an impressive specimen of humanity. Now that she'd gotten to know Jonathan better, she could imagine it.

"I was a young fool, and I thought, who the hell knows what's going on, but why *not* talk back to him? He told me I was special….chosen. Like the heroes in stories or some bollocks. And we talked. It was dark by the time we finished talking, and I'd missed my work shift. He told me to come back next evening, and I did. And the evening after that, and after that, and so on."

"How many evenings?" Hæra asked, half dreading the answer, because however many it was, Asgall had already surpassed her total with Sister Madeleine. Would it take so long to forge a lasting bond between them? How would she manage it?

To her dismay, he said, "All summer. I'd come to the rocks every night—my mates thought I had a girl hidden away. They didn't know I had a friend." Jonathan's mouth twisted. "Or so I thought."

"Asgall is nobody's friend," Hæra said. "But he can pretend."

"Aye, he pretended all right. He pretended right until the day he… changed. Just like you did." Jonathan looked off into the distance, as if into the past. "He said he wanted to prove he was telling the truth, and right before my eyes, he changed into a man and climbed up on the rocks."

"What did he look like?" Hæra asked, curious in spite of herself.

"Young, like me. Like I was, then." Jonathan still didn't look at her. What was he seeing over her shoulder, through the window? "Tall and slim. Black hair like yours, but his eyes were…I never saw anything like them before. They were almost red."

Asgall's scarlet eyes had flashed maliciously at Hæra many a time. "I expect that showed you something was wrong."

Jonathan snorted. "You'd think so, wouldn't you? It didn't. He seemed to shine in the sun. He was…"

His voice trailed off. Hæra was about to interrupt when Jonathan said, "He was beautiful."

Hæra barely held back her snort of disbelief. Her monster of a brother, beautiful? She'd believe it when she saw it.

"We talked even more, then," Jonathan continued. "We talked until the sun was setting, about things I'd never told another soul. Then he held out his hand to me. Suggested I get in the water so he could transform and take me for a ride. Said he'd show me things no human had ever seen before. I…I wanted to go, but there was a little voice in my head. And it said, *run.*"

Hæra raised her eyebrows, impressed. Jonathan was definitely more perceptive than her first impression had suggested.

"I listened to it. I didn't want to, but something inside me *made* me move, yeah? I got up and tried to leave, but he was too close, and he grabbed my hand. He was so bloody strong. I didn't have a chance, and next thing I knew, I was in the water. Then…" Jonathan ran a shaking hand over the back of his head. "He's not grabbing my arm anymore. I feel *teeth* on my leg, sharp as knives. And he's dragging me under, and that's when I really see him—not just his beauty but his horror too, there was this big-arsed *fish* tail…"

He trailed off, clenching his jaw again.

"But you escaped," Hæra murmured. That was even more impressive. Once an *Each-uisge* dragged down prey, it was hard to break free.

"You're damned right I did. I kicked him in the face—I think I got his eye—and I punched him in the nose. I remember thinking, 'You're meant to do that to sharks.' He let go, and I kicked up to the surface. Thought I was done for, but there was a fishing boat, and I waved and screamed and they spotted me. Started heading my way. I reckon that scared him off."

Scared off by the presence of a boat! Hæra's lip curled. If Asgall had stayed underwater and dragged Jonathan back down, the humans wouldn't have seen him. All that effort, and he'd given up right at the cusp of victory. Hæra had never exchanged a real word with Sister

Madeleine, and she still couldn't imagine what could separate them after they'd gotten that close.

Nevertheless…Asgall had had the chance to speak to his human at some length. Could Hæra manage something similar when Sister Madeleine returned?

"I sound like a fool for talking to him in the first place, but…life is lonely, right?" Jonathan hung his head. "It's a bugger. We come in alone, and we go out the same."

Sister Madeleine wouldn't. Once Hæra ate her, her spirit would be part of Hæra forever. And when the Last Current took Hæra, she wouldn't go by herself. No more loneliness for either of them. Hæra thought often of how Sister Madeleine had looked on the sandy beach that afternoon: strong, but solitary. That woman knew what loneliness was.

"After all, it's just you and *him*," Jonathan said. "And you don't like him much. Course you'd know what it is to look for what you can't find, to…" He glanced at the window, toward the darkness outside. When Hæra first started visiting him, the windows had been so clouded with salt and dirt you could barely see through them. Now he'd washed them.

"To what?" she snapped. "I'm only looking for Sister Madeleine. I'll find her. That is, she'll come back."

She had to, because the depths knew Hæra couldn't get to her. Once she'd gained his trust, Jonathan had obliged her by going to the hotel where Sister Madeleine's group had stayed. He'd reported back that they'd come from somewhere called "Philadelphia," a city that didn't border the ocean and was full of a million humans besides. Hæra couldn't help thinking of them all sweeping in and out of the place like krill into the baleen of a whale.

"You must think about her a lot." Jonathan had that look in his eyes, the one he wore when he was about to seek information from Hæra. "Even though you only knew her for a day."

Hæra would not shift about in the chair. She'd learned that was a gesture of restlessness that gave away more than she intended. "So?"

"I don't mean to pry," said Jonathan, prying. "Just wondering if it works differently for you—love, that is. Most humans can't fall that fast, but is that the same for you and him?"

Fall in love? Hæra looked at him, dumbstruck.

She knew, conceptually, what he meant. Humans formed emotional bonds with each other before they mated. It was part of the species' preservation. They could get very passionate about sexual coupling.

Each-uisge knew no such passion except during mating season, when mares went into heat. Their real delight was in the frenzy of the hunt, riding the currents, or tearing into a rival.

Her current body was different, though. For all that it wasn't truly human, it had responded...strongly...to Sister Madeleine lying beneath it. When she'd touched Sister Madeleine's mouth with her own—a "kiss," she knew now—she'd felt a hungry pulse between her thighs. Was that what Jonathan meant?

He said, "I just don't know what to make of the look in your eyes when we talk of her. As if there's nothing else in the world."

Hæra's face grew as hot as the unwelcome fire.

"I don't judge," Jonathan said quickly. "I, er, might if you didn't take on this body right here. But you're learning to read and act like us. God knows I'm no romantic, but I can't work out what else it means, and..."

Hæra stood so quickly that her chair toppled backward, and Jonathan cut himself off, looking startled.

She glared down at him, teeth bared at his effrontery. Implying that she would ever...

Just imagine what her father would say to that. It would serve this human right for Hæra to tear him to pieces here and now. How dare he speak such lies, presuming something that couldn't possibly be right?

Instead of looking properly terrified, Jonathan narrowed his eyes. "What's all this, then?"

"You don't know what you're talking about," she snarled. "Do you think I'd stoop to *that* sort of connection with your kind?"

"What are you doing, then?" Jonathan asked, sounding as if he didn't believe her. "You saved her life, and now you want to see her again. And truth to tell, I don't think she's the only reason you come here of nights."

Blood roared in her human ears. "Are you joking? Why else would I come?"

"Because you're lonely." Jonathan stood up. Shorter than Hæra, and weaker too. "Because you want a friend."

Hæra stared at him, and then stared some more, at this man who'd taken her gold in exchange for clothing and an alphabet. He'd pissed himself the night they met, and now he presumed such things of her? He didn't know what she really wanted. If someone didn't know what you wanted, then they didn't know you.

"My brother and I don't love," she said, her voice as cold as an ice floe. "We could never love humans in the way you say. Never."

Something in Jonathan's eyes flickered. A line appeared between his eyebrows.

"I don't have any friends," she said. "I don't need them."

"But—"

"And if I did, I wouldn't seek them on shore." Why did her human heart pound as if she were fighting her way through a riptide? Perhaps because it was so small, while her fear felt as big as ever. "You're the lonely one who hides out here because you lack the resolve to leave a place where nobody wants you."

Jonathan recoiled.

Hæra turned on her heel and stomped toward the back door. Talk about an unpleasant way to mark the turn since she'd met Sister Madeleine.

"Then what *do* you want?" Jonathan's voice was raw, as if Hæra had somehow hurt him by speaking the truth. "I know what *he* wanted, but I don't know about you!"

I want the storm. I want the thunder. I want...

Two sea-green eyes flashed in her memory like lightning.

Without a word, Hæra left, the door banging shut behind her. Jonathan didn't follow.

She headed for the shore. As she did, she inhaled deeply of the sea air and sighed in relief as her strength began to return in full.

Jonathan had referred to what happened when she came inland. The farther she got from the ocean, the more her physical strength diminished. She hadn't known that would happen until she first came to visit him.

She called this body her "human form," but it wasn't truly. It was more like her real body twisted into human shape, with an indifference to cold and wind, and a preference for salt water and raw meat. And strength and speed no human could match.

At least, to a point. Carrying the treasure chest to Jonathan's house, to say nothing of the dead seal, had been harder than she'd expected. She was still stronger and faster than any human—at least, Jonathan said so. But Hæra hated her weakness, and Jonathan was obviously wrong about many things.

And yet, with every stronger step to the sea, Hæra felt worse about how she'd left him. He was harmless. He'd kept to the terms of their bargain. He was a surprisingly effective teacher. And he was…kind, in a way her species never was.

Maybe she could have been patient. She'd kept more company with him in the last turn than she had with any other creature. She could have been kinder too.

In her imagination, Sister Madeleine regarded her seriously, reminding her that there was strength in caring for others.

Curse it. Next time Hæra came ashore, she'd have to apologize to Jonathan. She couldn't face it yet. With a groan, she continued to the beach, her steps strangely heavy even though her strength was returning.

He was still wrong, though.

Love. What an idea.

Love and hunger were not the same.

CHAPTER SEVEN

THAT NIGHT, alone in the chapel, Madeleine had waited for a voice. Maybe one that said unambiguously, *Tell Mother Gertrude yes.* That would be helpful.

No such voice had spoken to her. Now, she lay awake in one of the bedrooms reserved for visitors instead of the room she shared with another sister, so she could remain in solitude as Mother Gertrude had ordered.

If she were Superior, she'd get her own cell—along with some privacy—for the first time since she'd begun her postulancy. That'd be nice.

Just say yes.

That wasn't the voice of God. That was her own, pleading with her to make things simple and do what she was told instead of arguing.

Talk about what didn't come naturally. Besides, if she became Superior, she'd have to make executive decisions. She'd owe obedience to Mother Gertrude, but she'd have to assert herself too. That wouldn't be too difficult, even if Agnes made herself a thorn in Madeleine's side. Madeleine could pull this off.

No, you can't.

That voice came from deep inside, much deeper than the one that urged her to walk the straight and narrow path. She had a horrible feeling the second voice was the honest one, urging her to look at what she'd avoided for too long. A voice that said, *Are you* sure *you're not seeking a family to replace the one you lost? Are you* sure *you're not running away?*

Especially from yourself?

She'd heard it before, off and on, for years, and had always silenced it. She'd managed not to listen because things continued on a steady pace from day to day, and with no big changes on the horizon. Why look at what didn't bear seeing?

Now, a big change was staring her in the face, and she had to stare back. Her steady course had diverted, courtesy of a force she couldn't ignore, and it had brought her to the edge of an abyss.

Sister Catherine's words about loving God might as well have been a plague of locusts, devouring Madeleine's peace and leaving barrenness behind. Passion had lit Catherine's eyes even in the midst of her pain—a passion Madeleine had never known for her own vocation. She'd forgotten it was missing. It was easy to forget until someone rubbed your face in it, whether they meant to or not.

She could wallow in that problem all night, and maybe she deserved to. That didn't change the question, though, which was: *Now what?*

She could refuse Mother Gertrude. Then, nothing would change. She'd remain Sister Madeleine, locked and bound into a life with restrictions and rules she could never alter, a purpose she lacked, and yearnings she dared not examine.

Except it was already too late for that. Gertrude's request had opened Madeleine's eyes when she'd fought to keep them shut. To close them again would be cowardice.

Whatever else she might be, Madeleine prayed she was no coward.

In her solitary bed, she trembled in a way she hadn't since she was twenty-one and her brother had died, leaving her all alone in the world. *You're not alone,* she tried to tell herself, *you have your community.* But did she?

Saint John of the Cross had called this the dark night of the soul.

An apt phrase. In the dead of night, it was impossible to escape her thoughts. Including ones that had nothing to do, at least on the surface, with her decision.

Sister Bridget's very pretty, isn't she?

Madeleine rolled over onto her stomach and pressed her face in the pillow to muffle a groan. Oh no. These thoughts? *Now*, of all times?

Or maybe it was exactly the right time. If Madeleine were to consider this seriously, she had to confront her weaknesses. Lacking passion for her heavenly husband was one. Thinking unholy thoughts about other women was entirely another.

It wasn't unholy to reflect that another woman was pretty. Madeleine could cut herself some slack on that score. She couldn't imagine herself...doing anything...with Sister Bridget, unlike other women she'd wickedly fantasized about in the past.

Like her angel on the beach.

A shiver ran through her, along with a hot pulse between her legs that *definitely* wasn't appropriate. The pulse faded in an immediate rush of shame. It was wrong, terribly wrong, to think of her rescuer in such a way, especially if that rescuer was heaven-sent.

But would heaven have sent her a woman who'd lain atop Madeleine, her naked body as warm as if she'd emerged from a sauna instead of the North Sea? So warm that Madeleine's hips had rocked up to meet that weight, seeking something she'd craved for so long...

Return to me.

Madeleine bit her lip and shook her head silently in denial.

Sister Madeleine, help me.

The two voices had been so similar. One had come from a woman's—an angel's?—mouth, while the other had echoed like the ocean, but there was a familiar note in both. A note that seemed to come from a different world.

Otherwise, she couldn't recall exactly what the voices sounded like. Everything had been so confusing, and that was before you factored in the head injury. It was all fuzzy. She probably wouldn't even recognize the voices if she heard them again. She could only remember how they'd made her feel.

If only she could see her rescuer again and get some answers—or at least figure out what the right questions were. She'd spent a year longing for that with every fiber of her being, more than she longed for grace and peace.

More, perhaps, than she longed for God.

Beneath the covers, she shivered as if caught in the grip of a mighty wind.

The truth wouldn't be denied anymore. Madeleine did not long for God more than she longed for anything else in the world. She'd vowed that she did, and she had lied. She'd lied in a sacred place, about a sacred thing. She was no exemplar of moral behavior for her students. She was a fraud.

The shivering got worse. She pressed her lips hard together to stop a whimper. This couldn't be happening. It couldn't be *real*. But it was happening. It was real. And something else was real too.

She didn't belong here, with her sisters who trusted her without knowing her. She'd never be able to hold their hands in the simplicity of faith, like Mother Gertrude had held Sister Catherine's hand. Nor could she earn their unquestioning obedience, not when she didn't even want what she was selling.

She wanted answers. After years of living a lie, she wanted the truth. And heaven help her, she wouldn't find either of those inside convent walls.

But it would be difficult to seek them outside as well. When she'd taken her permanent vows, she'd surrendered her material possessions to the Church. She received a small salary as a teacher, but that went right back into Sacred Heart's coffers. She could get a job at a public school easily enough, but it would take time to get on her feet and set aside money to travel, especially because she had limited relationships outside the Church.

And she had no family to help her, either. No mother or father or brother. They were all gone.

She'd be so alone. She'd sacrifice everything for answers that might never come. Was she ridiculous for even thinking about this? Now that she knew how sinful she really was, if she just repented and *tried* to love God as much as she should—might that not be enough?

Madeleine closed her eyes. Tears slipped from their corners and rolled down her cheeks. The wet weight in her chest reminded her of waking up on the beach, coughing up seawater…one year ago to the day.

The timing couldn't be a coincidence. Holy Writ taught that you weren't supposed to ask heaven for signs. But that didn't mean heaven wouldn't send them to you unrequested.

She pressed a hand over her mouth to muffle a sob. Crying wouldn't stop any of this. Tonight's misery was a bell rung by a guiding Hand, awakening her from a lazy and undeserved sleep. She'd used the order as a false refuge for decades: hiding from pain, from grief, and from her own nature. Now, for punishment…for penance… came this revelation.

The word "revelation" came from the Latin *revelare*: to expose and make known. Literally, it meant "to unveil."

That seemed fitting, didn't it?

———

When Madeleine met with Mother Gertrude the next morning, she felt strangely calm. Or perhaps she was just in shock.

She and her Superior General faced each other alone in the chapel, sitting on the pew in the front row before the altar.

"Well, Sister Madeleine?" Gertrude asked. She'd said Madeleine's generation was the future of the order. Hope shone in her eyes that Madeleine would help her realize that future. "Did the still, small voice of God speak to you?"

"I don't know about that, Reverend Mother. The voice sounded loud to me. And I'm not sure it came from God—although I certainly hope it did."

Mother Gertrude frowned. "What?"

It was time. Madeleine sat up straight and folded her hands in her lap, over the rosary that had replaced the one she'd lost exactly one year ago. The smooth beads beneath her palms had to give her strength today.

She said, "I must turn away from the opportunity you offered me. I'm not fit for the position—more than you can possibly know. And last night's reflections revealed to me that I've got to turn away from more than that, too."

Now Mother Gertrude looked alarmed. "Sister, what are you talking about?"

Madeleine took a deep breath and looked away from the woman who had such faith in her, toward the altar. From there, the suffering Christ looked back. Her heavenly husband, whom she'd been trying to fool for decades.

At least now she could do right by him.

"I'm declining the position of Sacred Heart's Superior." Her voice was low but resolute. "And I'm leaving the Daughters of Grace. God forgive me."

CHAPTER EIGHT

Hæra brooded until she finally reached the rocks, but then practical concerns took over. What was she to do with her clothes? Jonathan usually handled that, bringing them when they met onshore and taking them away when she left. After their argument, he might not return for their usual appointment, and she wanted to apologize before then anyway. Tomorrow, in fact.

A large rock stood far back enough that the high tide wouldn't reach it. She looked around to make sure she was alone. Then she undressed and tucked her clothes and boots in a crevice beneath the big rock.

Naked, she transformed into her four-legged horse form and walked into the water.

The waves lapped welcomingly at her fetlocks and then rose steadily over her legs. Sand and pebbles scraped against her, borne landward by the water to blend sea and shore.

The current urged her forward, and she lunged in with relief as it buoyed her, taking the burden of her body weight. She bobbed up and down, concentrating as her hind legs fused together into her marine tail.

There. She was herself again. Her true self that needed nobody else: not a friend, and definitely not someone to *love*. Just because she'd grown used to wearing a human-shaped body once in a while, just because she'd been learning new things, didn't mean she was changed.

She crested to the point where the waves rose highest. Once she got past it, the water would calm again. Normally, she plunged beneath the surface and cut through the waves, the better to conceal herself and hurry back home. Tonight, though, the air called to her: *stay just another moment.* And so she crested the surface of the wave instead, letting it carry her higher up.

Freedom. The word flashed across her mind. Hæra, nearing the top of the wave, looked longingly up toward the sky, where freedom beckoned. Then she reached the wave's peak, looked down at the water that awaited her, and saw the end of freedom altogether.

Three pairs of *Each-uisge* eyes glowed up at her.

She'd been caught.

There was no time to feel anything but shock. The wave swept her swiftly and unforgivingly down, smacking her into the surface and then shoving her below it.

The *Each-uisge* parted before she could crash on top of them. Below the surface, she looked around wildly to see that she'd been met by Asgall, Beathag her mother, and Calder, the Sire of the herd. Calder's tail, mottled with blue and black, barely moved as he held steady in the water. By contrast, Beathag's dark green tail whipped back and forth in agitation.

Shite. Shite, shite, shite.

They all dove down and surrounded her. Asgall's eyes were bright with malice, Beathag's with rage. Calder's were only cold with purpose.

How much had they seen? Had they just witnessed her human transformation? They must have. How had they known to wait for her here, and how had they found out? She'd been so careful.

They would question her and then undoubtedly condemn her. Banishment could be her fate, and then where would she go? Maybe she should just tell the truth. She wanted to be a Stormhorse. Her rule-breaking was in aid of that, and she hadn't betrayed the herd's existence. It might be best to say that—right away, in fact? She opened her mouth to speak.

Her mother struck first.

Without a word, Beathag head-butted Hæra in the chest, driving her backward. Then she did it again. Before Hæra could get her bearings, Asgall's tail slammed against her fins; together, he and their mother sent her tumbling head over tail. Her front legs flailed as she tried to right herself, but then Beathag's teeth sank into her shoulder.

This was no reproving maternal nip, nor even the more serious bites her mother had given her in times of anger. Her mother tore into her hide, drawing blood while Hæra cried out.

Asgall laughed and slammed his own head into her back, this time pitching her forward so she was forced to look the Sire in the eye.

Hæra tried to say, *Wait,* but only "whuh" came out before Beathag's shell-edged hooves cut into the side of her neck, a hot slice of pain. Her wounds were already stinging from the salt.

The Sire did nothing. He watched impassively.

Hæra muffled her pained cries. A beating was preferable to exile, where she'd be vulnerable to predators and famine. This might be Calder's mercy, perhaps in deference to the memory of her father. If she endured it stoically, then it'd be over.

Along with her dreams. Calder would decree Hæra join the ranks of broodmares posthaste.

"Sire!" she cried pitifully. "Let me explain why—"

"Silence," Calder said, even as Beathag lunged again. Together, Hæra's mother and brother kicked and slapped and bit her, again and again until her body no longer felt like a body but a breathless sack of pain. She burned white-hot with agony from muzzle to fin. Her flesh seemed tender enough to be eaten without chewing.

When would it end? When would they be satisfied? She had broken herd law, yes. Her family was not fond of her, yes. But *this*—

It was only by chance that she rolled upward when Asgall's tail passed beneath her in a vicious swish, fast and hard enough that it would have snapped her spine if he'd connected.

It was then she realized the beating wouldn't be over. They wouldn't be satisfied until they'd torn her to pieces. This wasn't a reprimand. It was an execution. Her own mother and brother were going to *kill* her.

"Stop!" she cried. "Mother! I didn't betray us. Nobody knows about the herd. I just wanted to—"

Calder spoke, cutting her off. "Your brother has told me you do not wish to breed. I see now you'd rather take a hideous form than follow the course of nature. Banishment's too good for you. Your mother and brother will erase the shame you brought upon them."

An *honor killing?* Oh, by the depths, no one ever turned back from those. "No, wait! I—"

Calder nodded at Beathag, who bobbed next to Hæra. "I'll trust you to do your duty. Finish her."

Beathag's eyes held no hint of reluctance or remorse. "We both will. My son and I will atone for her."

"Sire," Hæra croaked. Her ribs ached. "Please, I did it for a noble reason. I was trying to—"

Before she could finish, Beathag's fin cracked across her face again. Hæra tumbled, and when she opened her eyes again, the Sire had swum away.

He was gone, and if Hæra's family showed mercy to her, then he wouldn't have to know. She could leave and never return, taking her chances in the open ocean. At least banishment was better than *death.* Maybe the unthinkable would happen, and Beathag would spare her daughter's life after all.

"I've had many disappointments," her mother said. "You, the worst of all."

Hope collapsed in Hæra's chest like one of Jonathan's structures made from playing cards. Beathag looked even more merciless now, if that was possible.

Asgall—as if sensing he was the second-worst disappointment— took this as his cue to strike Hæra again. He used less force than before, and he laughed. Now that the Sire was gone, it seemed he felt free to take his time about hurting her.

Hæra wheezed, "I only wanted to help our family...after my father..."

"Don't *dare* speak of your father." Beathag bared her teeth. "And you do nothing for our 'family.' You think only of yourself."

She tore into Hæra's shoulder again. Hæra yowled in agony. She'd never been on fire, but this pain reminded her of the awful flames in Jonathan's fireplace. This must be what it was like to burn.

She was a fighter, a hunter, wasn't she? She couldn't be so wholly passive, so complicit in her own death. She could strike back at Beathag, and she'd better do it fast. Beathag was smaller than she was, and not nearly as strong. Hæra could draw her mother's blood in one final gesture of defiance.

She looked into Beathag's eyes and saw only loathing, relentless and cold. "Always, you shame me," Beathag said. "You've never been who you're supposed to be. And now you're nothing at all."

The strength drained from Hæra at once, as if Beathag had sliced a hoof across her jugular. She floated uselessly in the water, blood drifting slowly from her salt-stung wounds.

"My son," Beathag said. "She tried to take what you should have had."

Behind Hæra, Asgall snarled. She'd nearly forgotten about him.

"You failed me too," Beathag said. "With that selfsame human, was it not?"

"He tricked me," Asgall rasped. "I wasn't like her. I didn't go ashore or betray our kind!"

You transformed and got on a rock, Hæra thought, but didn't say— Beathag cut her off.

"And you never will. No more of my family will I lose to those stinking creatures. You both are *mine*. You're for the ocean, my son." Beathag glanced at Hæra, who floated and ached. "Your sister's bones will be too. That is all the kindness I can offer."

Jonathan's kindness was different. That was a strange thought to have just now. It had to come from blood loss. To think...the sea held her death, but on land was a human who'd made her tea and taught her to read...

"End this now," Beathag told Asgall.

End it. Yes. As she began to sink toward the ocean floor, her tail limp, Hæra thought an ending wouldn't be so bad. Her body might feel like one big bruise, one long snapping bone, but her mind was mercifully numb.

She looked up at the surface and closed her eyes. Her last sight shouldn't be the family that hated her. Until now, she had not realized they did. *I am nothing at all.*

Asgall's teeth snapped at her neck. "You dared approach him," he whispered. "You *dared.*"

Jonathan, again. Of course Asgall would punish Hæra for taking something he didn't even want, something he'd surrendered. Typical. What was the point in responding? All was lost, wasn't it?

Then, behind her eyelids, appeared a woman in a nun's habit, her eyes closed and her face pale with sorrow. Her hands were clasped at her breast. Sister Madeleine. Tall and graceful, and…

And beautiful, the most beautiful thing Hæra had ever seen…

"Angel," Sister Madeleine whispered, *"I'm so afraid."*

Afraid? Afraid of what? What could threaten her when she stood alone, praying?

"If you're there, if you're good, please guide me now. Protect me."

Sister Madeleine needed protecting? Hæra curled more deeply into herself as Asgall dealt her a particularly vicious blow. She could protect nobody like this, least of all herself. What good would she be to Sister Madeleine? *Nothing…I am nothing…*

Asgall swam backward, beating his tail, building up force to turn on her. Hæra closed her eyes again, listening desperately.

"I'll do what you said, as soon as I can. It might take a while, but—"

Asgall laughed. The current shifted. He was closing in.

Sister Madeleine pressed her clasped hands to her lips. She murmured, *"I'll return to you. I swear it."*

Hæra opened her eyes. Asgall was right there. His mouth was open, his teeth razor sharp.

She struck him in the mouth with her hooves. When he reared back, blood flowed from his muzzle.

And then she fled.

Each-uisge did not flee, but they also didn't do a lot of the things she'd done already, and she knew exactly where she was going. There would be no more pleas for mercy, no more curling up and waiting to die.

Her woman had called to her, for her, and Hæra was *not nothing*.

She wasn't as strong as Asgall, but she was faster than he was, and for sure she was both stronger and faster than their mother. She was injured, but not yet broken, and although she couldn't fight, she could try to escape.

Rage could drive her. Betrayal could fuel her. But nothing, *nothing* could propel her forward so powerfully as hope.

For it had been no hallucination—Sister Madeleine had called to her. Hæra didn't know how, but Jonathan had said something similar when they'd met: that he still heard Asgall calling to him sometimes. Perhaps that had been more than idle human dreaming. When the bond formed between an *Each-uisge* and its chosen human prey, if it didn't consummate in a feast, then what could resolve it?

Of course Sister Madeleine was crying out to her, promising to return to her. Hæra couldn't just give up and die. That wasn't their destiny.

Return to me, she would have called to Sister Madeleine if she could. *I'll live for you. I'll survive this, for you.*

She could hear her mother and brother pursuing her. Her destination seemed an age away, but it was getting closer with every stroke of her tail, and then, suddenly, the swirling waters were in sight.

Behind her, Asgall shouted, "You're mad!"

She said nothing to that, just plunged on, and by the time she'd reached the edge of the whirlpool, they'd stopped chasing her. They'd have to be the mad ones to follow her this far. Everyone knew the Witch's Whirlpool was a deathtrap.

Nothing ventured, nothing gained. This was still a better alternative to being killed. Hæra threw herself into the current and wondered if she'd snap in two when it took hold of her, dragging her downward to a pit where no creature was meant to go. She curled into the inside edge of the current, extending her neck as much as she dared through the wall of water into the eye of the vortex, and then looked down.

The witch looked back up at her.

Her eyes were black as the pit. At the bottom of the seemingly endless pool, she too whirled around and around, whipping a human corpse through the water with each hand.

By all accounts, one was a human man who'd spurned the witch, and the other was the human woman he'd chosen instead. In return, the witch had chosen revenge, and for this crime she was bound eternally to her victims. Centuries later, neither would let her go. The spinning of the corpses caused the vortex that no one from leagues around would approach. Asgall and Beathag would think Hæra was dead for certain.

If she didn't pull this off, she would be.

"Ancient One—" She struggled to keep her head out of the water wall, leaning down toward the eye of the whirlpool surrounding the witch. "Help me!"

The witch said nothing. She continued to spin in place, whipping the dead bodies around.

"Do you see my wounds? My kind punishes me for pursuing a human—for following my heart, as you followed yours—"

The witch spun faster. For a second, Hæra was sucked back into the whirling water, pulled downward, before she struggled free again.

"You know what it's like!" she gasped. The closer she was pulled to the bottom, the crueler the current was. Her body was designed to withstand brutal pressures, but not this, and there was dark magic at work besides. "You know how they don't let go of you!"

The witch—for a moment—slowed. Not stopped but slowed.

Hæra thought fast. Brute strength was useless, but flattery might work. "Some called you jealous, but I call you brave. You risked everything for him." She nodded at the male corpse that clung to the witch's right hand, perfectly preserved after centuries, clothes and all. "And he was foolish to prefer *her*." She nodded at the female, whose red hair fanned out around her face. "I came here to ask your blessing, that I might have even a little of your courage!"

It was a lie, of course, but the witch didn't know that. She said nothing in reply but kept spinning the two bodies. Hæra wondered what the witch would do. Nobody knew what happened to creatures who got too close to her. She couldn't use her hands, but her teeth were sharper than any shark's.

"Help me!" Hæra screamed again, just as she'd called to Sister Madeleine a turn ago.

The witch looked up at her, her eyes darker and colder than the depths. Hæra stared back down, even as her bleeding tail beat uselessly against the currents that were now starting to pulverize her. Her ribs had never hurt so badly as they did now.

The witch said, "You will fail."

Fail? May the depths save Hæra if this creature could see the future. There were all kinds of rumors about her abilities—but if she could do that, wouldn't she have foreseen her own doom? She couldn't be right, not when Sister Madeleine herself had appeared in what must have been a vision.

"I won't, Ancient One," she pleaded. "She calls to me. She needs me!"

The witch stared at Hæra, spinning in time with her. Hæra looked back into those black eyes, as voracious as the whirlpool she'd created. She was a creature of hunger and need, like Hæra herself. She might understand, she might show mercy, and...

"Try, then." The witch's voice sounded as if it had been dragged across a seabed full of broken shells. How long since she had last spoken? "Try, fail, and despair."

"No. I'll succeed, and—"

"Fail. Despair. Come back."

Hæra stared at her. With every passing second, as the water battered her and she lost more blood, it became more difficult to focus, much less make sense of those words. "Come back?"

The witch's eyes, for a moment, held more than darkness. They held fire, hotter than anything in Jonathan's home, hot enough to turn the sea to smoke if she didn't bank it.

"Bring me your despair," she said.

Hæra's head spun like the whirlpool. That wasn't a prophecy—and something about the way the witch said it didn't even sound like a command.

It sounded like a bargain.

She didn't know what the witch was bargaining for. Perhaps she only wanted to see someone else fail as she'd done and thus share in her suffering. It didn't matter. Hæra would take any terms.

"I will," she gasped. "If I fail, I'll come back. With my despair." Whatever that meant. Despair wasn't something you could carry in a treasure chest. Not that it mattered, because she sure as sunlight was never coming back here. The vision of Sister Madeleine had given her all the hope she'd ever need. "I promise!"

As soon as she'd said the words, the dead man's mouth opened. So did the dead woman's. Together, they began to scream. Their long-silenced voices were louder than the howl of any tempest. Hæra's head tossed backward and she was lost in the water again, buffeted by its uncaring power. It was still less terrifying than the sound of the murdered lovers.

The witch's voice cut through the screams as if it were slicing through a wave to the other side. "Agreed," she said.

Hæra's head made it back through the water wall, just in time to see the witch throw one hand upward: the one gripped by the man she'd loved. The whirlpool's wild current shifted. It caught Hæra, lifting her higher even as it whipped her around, away from the stronger force at the base of the vortex and up toward the surface.

And then—suddenly—it let her go. It flung her from its embrace until she drifted limply in a slower current.

Blearily, she looked around to find herself on the whirlpool's other side, far from where Beathag and Asgall had pursued her. A startled school of pollack swam away the instant her marine tail twitched.

Now she was alone, but her wounds still bled. Predators would catch the scent, and the last thing she needed was to become an orca feast. How far was she from shore? Hopefully not far. She was at the last of her strength. Her wounds would begin to heal soon, but it might not be soon enough.

Moving as carefully as she dared, she fought her way to the surface. Thank the Great Mare, the shore was in sight—but it was another side of the island. In fact, it was the stretch of beach where Hæra had first seen Sister Madeleine.

Had the witch known? Was this a seal on their pact?

Right now, she didn't care. Hæra held back a groan—it would take too much energy—and swam for the shore. At this hour of night, it was empty. It seemed like an age before her front hooves grazed the seafloor, and then she had to fight against the waters that wanted to drag her back home.

This time, she didn't bother with four legs. Her bleeding tail dragged against the rocks and sand as she lugged herself out of the water and, shaking with fatigue, concentrated one more time.

On the shore, beneath the moon, she lost consciousness as her human body collapsed. It, too, bled.

———

When she woke up, a harsh light shone down onto her face. It was like no sunshine Hæra had ever seen. The sky was gone; in its place was a white, flat surface from which the light glared.

She lay on something soft. Her left arm hurt; when she turned her head, painfully, she saw something sharp had been stuck in it, attached to a bag full of clear liquid. She was still naked, and a long piece of cloth covered her from her chest to her feet. Her entire body ached.

A ceiling above her. Walls around her. She was indoors, away from the sea, and weak. This was entirely the human world, and she'd swum right into its arms with no guarantee of welcome.

And she wasn't alone. Jonathan sat in a chair next to her bedside, regarding her solemnly. Next to him stood a woman in a blue shirt and blue pants. "Welcome back," Jonathan said. "This is Nurse

Kilbright. You're in her practice. Jorsay only gets a doctor twice a week."

Was that supposed to mean something? Hæra tried to speak and couldn't. Her chest weighed as much as a dead whale, and her throat hurt.

"I've cleaned you off and stitched you up," Nurse Kilbright said. "You're healing awfully fast, though." Her eyes narrowed.

"Why, there's some luck," Jonathan said quickly. "Sue, can we have the room for a tick?"

Nurse—Sue?—Kilbright nodded and left. Jonathan watched her go, and when the door closed, he turned back to Hæra. "You've been out for nearly twenty-four hours," he said. "Word went round the island of a tall, naked woman who washed up on the shore, beat to shite and back, unconscious and with nobody to claim her. I came as soon as I could."

He'd come? After the cruel things she'd said to him? She hadn't even had a chance to apologize. She had a dozen questions, starting with where she was, but she felt fuzzy-headed. Nothing around her seemed real. Instead of anything pertinent, only one word made it out of her dry mouth.

She whispered, "Sorry."

"I reckon you are. Probably for all sorts of things." Jonathan sighed and rubbed the back of his neck. "Anyway, I'm here."

Hæra found another word. It was even harder to say. "Why?"

Jonathan smiled. It was a little soft, a little sad. "Well then, lass," he said. "What else are friends for?"

PART II
THE SHORE

CHAPTER NINE

LANCASTER, PENNSYLVANIA, FIVE YEARS LATER.

"Phone charger?"

"Check."

"Toiletries?"

"Check."

"Rain boots?"

"I'll wear them on the plane so I don't have to pack them."

Madeleine eyed her scruffy suitcase, which already appeared full-to-bursting even though she'd pared everything down as much as she could. Who'd have thought a former nun could accumulate so many possessions?

She glanced over at her roommate, who sat on Madeleine's bed as she read the packing list. Becca's forehead creased in concentration, as if she were the one flying to Scotland on a hare-brained mission.

"Did I put anything on the list about bringing my sanity?" Madeleine asked.

Becca gave Madeleine a wry smile. She'd been supportive of this adventure ever since it had been put in motion—the moment

Madeleine had paid back the loan she'd taken from the Daughters of Grace to start her new life. As soon as she'd signed the final check, she'd started putting her meager savings toward a trip to Orkney.

To find answers, if not her angel.

She'd miss the apartment, even if she'd only be gone for a month—plenty of time between her return and the start of school in mid-August. It had become a haven. After all this time, Madeleine had managed to make her room reasonably homey, although it had taken a while to shake off her sense of austerity and put up a decoration or two. Now there was a poster of her favorite bookstore in the French Quarter and an illustrated quotation from Emily Dickinson.

On the bureau sat an older photo of her with her parents and brother, taken when she was sixteen, only a couple of months before the car accident. It was angled so that she couldn't see it easily, but… well, it was there. Meanwhile, a crucifix hung on the opposite wall so that she saw it as soon as she woke up.

Becca propped her elbows on her knees. She was a widow in her early fifties, and five years ago she too had needed a fresh start—plus a cheap place to live while dealing with her late husband's debts. Madeleine had left Philadelphia both to save money and escape painful memories, but she hadn't known anyone in Lancaster. She and Becca had met on a site dedicated to finding roommates. Together they'd grieved the end of their marriages: Becca's to Mark and Madeleine's to Christ. At first, Madeleine had been sure they'd never be able to relate to each other, but she should have known that kinship could form in unlikely places. Becca had become a kind of sister when Madeleine needed one most, and she'd done her best to return the favor.

Too bad Becca couldn't come along to Orkney and make sure Madeleine didn't fall into the clutches of a supernatural force, but somebody had to stay home and feed the cat.

"How're you feeling, hon?" Becca asked.

Madeleine gave a rueful laugh. "Scared senseless. But excited. And kind of in shock."

Becca nodded solemnly. "There's only one place that can hold all of those feelings at once."

"Oh no," Madeleine said immediately. "I'm saving every penny."

"Relax, it's on me. You can't go off to the land of haggis without one last taste of great American cuisine."

Twenty minutes later, they sat in their booth at Applebee's, ordering their usual drinks. They'd started coming here as a joke—a tacky chain restaurant was so incongruous with Becca's grief and the minimalist life Madeleine had fled. The joke had turned serious, and now Applebee's was their Friday night routine.

Life on the outside, so to speak, had been strange at first. When Madeleine had left the convent, she hadn't drunk alcohol in years outside of the rare feast day. Nor had she worn secular clothing, gone grocery shopping alone, or slept in her own room. Strangest of all had been the excess of time, when once her hours had been full of fellow-ship. At first, she'd cried so often from loneliness that she'd wondered if she'd made the worst mistake of her life.

Becca had helped with that too. After they'd had a couple of weeks to get used to each other, she'd proposed some "retail therapy," and they'd gone to Goodwill. It had been surreal to don a form-fitting sweater, to say nothing of a pair of jeans. She'd spent decades basically pretending not to have a body and hadn't realized how it would feel to see it again. Madeleine, with only two skirts and three blouses to her name, had looked at herself in the mirror and seen a woman with shapely limbs, pleasing curves, and a head of short, dark, wavy hair. For the first time, she'd thought, *Maybe this can work.*

Now her hair was long enough to fall just past her shoulders, and she'd expanded her sweater collection considerably, along with other items. She even had a couple of necklaces that weren't crucifixes.

The server dropped off their beverages, and Madeleine raised her pink margarita glass into the air. "I'll miss you."

"Just me? Not a word for Booster?"

"Don't let him throw up hairballs in my room while I'm gone."

Becca grinned and raised her sangria. "I'll miss you too. To your adventure. May the next month be life-changing, but in a nice way."

Madeleine's heart gave a little thump at the thought. She'd wondered so often if returning to Orkney would change her life, if anything would actually happen—or if it had already happened.

Maybe the...visitation she'd experienced had just been meant to show her that she wasn't living the right life. It had been so painful to leave the Daughters of Grace, but years later, that pain had lessened. Her new life had its satisfactions, she still went faithfully to mass, and she wasn't living a lie anymore. Maybe that was the whole ball of wax.

No, that couldn't be right. Madeleine had realized she wasn't meant to be a nun, but it couldn't stop there. Not when she'd actually been ordered to go back. *Return to me.*

They clinked their glasses and drank, but then Becca's expression turned solemn. "You'll be careful, right?"

"Of course I will. I've been planning this for ages. I didn't come this far just to get myself in a pickle at the last minute."

Becca looked worried. Or maybe that was just the yellowish lighting from the lamp that hung dangerously low over the table. "I know, but that's the reason you're going, right? The 'pickle' from last time, whatever it was."

Madeleine had never told anyone the entire truth about her angel. The closest she'd come was with Becca, who was also a faithful Catholic, if more prone to left-wing sentiments than anyone Madeleine had known in her previous life. It was a year before she'd told her roommate that she'd had an "extraordinary experience" in Orkney that "hadn't quite seemed of this world" and had taken it as a sign "for a new beginning." Becca had been fascinated, but as the date for Madeleine's return to Orkney approached, that fascination had morphed into apprehension.

"I'll be as careful as I can be, but we weren't given a spirit of fear," Madeleine reminded her.

"No, but we *were* given common sense. You've got plenty except when it comes to this, so I thought a last-minute reminder wouldn't hurt. Especially if you really are messing with supernatural stuff." Becca narrowed her eyes. "And you can't poke a ghost in the eye with a needle."

Madeleine smiled. With an abundance of time after leaving Sacred Heart, she'd needed a hobby. Embroidery had been her choice. She'd told herself she was stitching her life back together with every threaded flower petal and Bible verse. "I'll keep that in mind."

"You better. Want to order the mozzarella sticks?"

Madeleine hid a grimace. She'd rather arrive at the Philadelphia airport with a peacefully settled stomach. "Pass."

Silence fell for a moment while she and Becca looked at each other. For the first time in a while, words seemed hard to come by. Becca ran a hand through her curly salt-and-pepper hair and laughed awkwardly. "So…if there was ever a moment for you to tell me about what exactly happened there last time…"

"I can't." Madeleine's hand clenched on her margarita glass. "I told you, you'd think I was crazy."

"I doubt it. I think you're dealing with something that really happened. And I'm your friend."

Becca reached across the table and took Madeleine's hand. Suddenly, Madeleine was back in Sacred Heart, watching Mother Gertrude take Sister Catherine's hand in just the same way. In comfort, an appeal to sisterhood.

She wasn't going to tear up. That'd just be pitiful. "I know you are. One of the best friends I've ever had."

"Is that why it's hard to tell me?"

That was the problem with good friends: they could see through you. Madeleine sighed, "Maybe."

"Hon, you've spent the last five years of your life trying to undo the previous fifteen. And you still don't quite know yourself yet." Becca squeezed her hand and let go. "That's okay, but I sometimes think you're waiting for this trip to tell you."

Ouch. Did anything hit as hard as the truth? But on the other hand, if a divine visitation…or whatever that had been…couldn't tell you who you were meant to be, then what could?

Therapy, Becca would say for the hundredth time, and for the hundredth time, Madeleine would reply, *Maybe later*. The days were gone when they could lock you up for babbling about angels, but that didn't mean a therapist wouldn't try to talk her out of believing it.

"There might be some truth to that," she said slowly. "Maybe that's the question."

"The question?"

How was she to put this into words, when it was so hard to articulate even to herself? "I'm going to Jorsay to find answers. But if you asked me what the question is, I don't know that I could tell you." She propped her elbow on the table and frowned at the pink dregs of her drink. "I wasn't meant for this philosophical stuff."

"Sometimes the philosophical stuff finds us."

"I like to take action. I've had to twiddle my thumbs over this for years. Now I can finally go, and…" Madeleine looked at Becca, silently pleading for her friend to have some answers. "And I wonder if I even know what to look for. If it'll come in a form I recognize. What if I miss it?"

Or what if it's not there at all?

No. She wouldn't go there. Something was calling her back to Jorsay. It had literally said, "Return to me." How unambiguous could you get?

"You won't miss it." Becca spoke so sincerely that it was easy to believe her. "I think you'll find what you're looking for, even if it's not what you were expecting. And then you'll come home and tell me all about it. Or while it's happening," she added. "You got that international phone plan, right?"

"Yes. I'll keep you updated," Madeleine promised. "And I'll send pictures. It's beautiful even when it's overcast. Which seems to be most of the time."

"But it's June! Won't it be nice and sunny?"

Madeleine only shook her head and laughed.

Becca sighed. "Maybe your next trip will take you somewhere sunny. When you get back, let's talk about a Caribbean cruise next year, okay? There are some good deals." Becca rested her chin in her hand and gave Madeleine a knowing look. "Unless you change your mind about dating when you get back and have something else to do.

No, no, don't give me that look—just, if this trip is about examining your priorities, then maybe you'll examine all of them."

Madeleine wasn't going to squirm. "I don't know how many times I have to say that not everyone is meant to be partnered. I'm fine. Don't aim at the speck in my eye until you've pulled out the log in your own."

Becca shrugged. "I date. It's not my fault the pickings are slim, especially at my age."

"Then what makes you think it'll be different for me? I'm forty-one years old. Not exactly a spring chicken."

"There's a difference between forty-one and fifty-three. If you don't know that now, then you will. Besides…" Becca appeared to hesitate. "You and I might be looking for different things. And nothing's wrong with that."

Madeleine's stomach went cold. She'd never told Becca about her feelings for women. Becca might have guessed, though. Madeleine had refused to date since leaving the order but declined to say why. And Becca would never judge—she'd once made a point of saying gay people deserved to be as happy as anybody else. Madeleine, her face burning, had changed the subject as soon as possible.

There were Catholic believers and theologians who didn't condemn homosexuality. In fact, when she was a trembling teen, Madeleine had said as much to her father, but he had replied, firmly, that there were no "cafeteria Catholics" in their family: so-called believers who picked and chose the doctrines they wanted to follow. It was all true, or none of it was.

Now her father was dead, along with the rest of her family, and that conversation was over forever, along with every other conversation. Her parents sat eternally in their disappointment, because now they knew everything. Her brother, David, would never grow up, give her a hug, and say he loved her no matter what. It never stopped hurting.

"Well, that's all I've got to say about that," Becca said, jolting Madeleine out of her abrupt melancholy. "Did you check in for your flight?"

The cold in Madeleine's stomach warmed a little. She should look to the future, not dwell in the past. "Yes. A few hours ago."

Becca grinned. "That's my girl."

It was a sweet phrase, but for some reason, Madeleine got a shiver up and down her spine. She imagined a low-pitched, feminine voice whispering in her ear, *You're not her girl. You're mine.*

As usual, heat leaped to her face, and in a couple of other places too. Was that better than icy misery? Lord have mercy. She really would have to work to keep from making a fool out of herself on this trip.

"And the hotel's all lined up?" Becca continued. "Everything's ready to go?"

"Totally ready," Madeleine said. She'd be staying at the same barebones hotel the Sacred Heart group had stayed in. Six years on, and it was still the only hotel on Jorsay.

"Sounds like you're all set. We're leaving for the airport at…" Becca winced. "Six-thirty, you said?"

It took well over an hour to drive from Lancaster to the Philadelphia airport, and there was no way Madeleine was missing her flight. "Yes. God bless you. I appreciate it."

"Happy to do it, sweetie. That's what friends are for, right? Helping each other."

"Yes." Madeleine glanced through the window at the headlights of passing cars, at the lit-up shopping center across the street. Ordinary people living ordinary lives. The life she'd come back to in a month, hopefully with her head sorted out at last. "That's what friends are for."

———

Philadelphia International Airport was nobody's idea of heaven, but at least it was familiar. Right now, standing at the curb while she said goodbye, Madeleine thought it would take all her courage to leave her friend and step into the unknown.

"You got everything?" Becca asked anxiously. "Passport?" Becca had no children, but she seemed to have a maternal instinct to lavish on Madeleine.

Madeleine patted her purse. "Passport's at the ready."

"Great. If you got that, your boarding pass, and your credit card, then you can figure out everything else as you go." She clapped Madeleine on the shoulder. "Text me when you land. Every time."

That would be several texts, considering there were no direct flights to Orkney from Philadelphia, or pretty much anywhere else. "Sure, I'll…"

A car behind them honked, anxious to pull up to the curb in their spot, and Becca called to it, "All right, already!" She turned back to Madeleine with a smile. "Be careful, hon. But also have some fun, okay? This is a once-in-a-lifetime trip, and you deserve to enjoy yourself."

That didn't sound easy. "I'll do my best."

"And try not to sleep on the plane. The time difference—"

Another honk, longer than the first one.

"I hate Philly," Becca groaned. "Okay, come here."

She and Madeleine threw their arms around each other. For just a second, Madeleine permitted herself to squeeze her friend, to take all the comfort in the embrace that she could, before the voice that had haunted her for a lifetime whispered: *Stop it. It's wrong.*

"Give Booster extra pets for me," she whispered.

"You got it." Becca held her tighter.

Madeleine let go, her heart racing. She wasn't the least bit attracted to Becca, but that voice—old, cold—was nearly impossible to silence. "Right. Goodbye."

"Bye, hon. I'll say a prayer for you. Text me!"

After yet another promise that she would, Madeleine dragged her suitcase to the glass doors while Becca drove away. The doors parted before her, but she stood still, her heart hammering. The same old voice murmured, *It's not too late to turn back.*

Turn back.

For once, she managed to silence it. However cruelly persuasive it could be, its power dwindled to nothing compared to the voice from the sea.

Return to me.

Madeleine set her shoulders back and lifted her chin. "All right," she whispered. "Whoever you are, I'm coming."

And with one deep inhalation for courage, she stepped through the door on her way to the sky.

CHAPTER TEN

THE DOGS no longer feared her. It had taken a while. Herding dogs were intelligent animals and could scent predators even when they came in unusual forms. When Hæra and Jonathan had looked for their first dog, many had snapped at her. More than one breeder had asked her, "You're not a dog person?"

"I wouldn't know," she'd replied, having never tasted dog meat.

They got on better now. Perhaps it was all the time she'd spent inland around humans. Hæra smelled less like the ocean and more like grass. She spent more time on grass than she could ever have imagined. Being outdoors was better than being cooped up indoors, and the wind and rain never troubled her.

The farm's first dog, a collie cross named Brodie, followed close behind as Hæra guided the four-wheeled Gator down the farm's "road." Said road was only the tracks created by the farm's vehicles, the grooves worn down after hundreds of drives.

Up ahead, her target came into view. Hæra sighed. Brodie barked. "I see it," she called to him. "Let's not forget whose eyesight is still better."

The cast ewe lay ahead, flat on her back and bleating in distress.

Hæra pulled up closer, turned off the Gator, and hopped down. The mud squelched around her boots, wet soil covering the dried dirt that already crusted them. A surprise storm had rolled in last night. As always, she'd stayed indoors while Jonathan and the farmhands secured everything. She couldn't risk being seen by the Stormhorses. Calder would recognize her human form.

The Sire must have been in a temper. Jonathan had said the storm was "a bad'un."

She reached the ewe, which bleated more pitifully as she approached. Once, she would have taken advantage of its foolishness in falling and being unable to right itself, as any predator would with vulnerable prey. But she'd been in need of rescue too. When this sheep fed somebody, it'd be a human who bought it at market, not her.

Jonathan had originally intended to raise cattle, which were the most popular livestock on Orkney. Hæra had convinced him to raise sheep instead. He hadn't been difficult to persuade, especially since her treasure had given him the initial funding.

Sister Madeleine's Bible talked a lot about sheep and shepherds. That meant Sister Madeleine must like sheep. It was another way Hæra would prove they were a worthy match.

Hæra crouched at the ewe's side, slid her hands under it, and easily hauled it to its feet. Then Brodie took over, chasing it back to the flock, which had eyed the whole business cautiously from a distance. With her hands on her hips, Hæra watched the ewe return to its fellow sheep and lambs. Then she returned to the Gator and began to drive again, inspecting the area carefully.

The cattle, gathered separately, seemed well also. The farm had thirty-five head of Limousin cattle to balance the grazing yearlong. They could also safely consume worms that would make the sheep sick. Hæra made sure to get a count as she drove. Thirty-five cows, present and accounted for.

Everything looked fine. Hæra put on the brakes and mashed the transmitter button on her walkie-talkie. "Jonathan?"

After a moment, his voice sounded through the static. *"What's the damage?"*

"Muddy ground and one cast ewe."

"That's the lot?"

"Seems like."

"Well, I'm not complaining. Come on back then. Or have you had your breakfast?"

"Yes. The lamb neck." As usual, she'd saved time by not bothering to cook it first. "I'll stay a little longer."

"Sure, and why not? It's such a beautiful morning." Jonathan's sarcasm had no bite in it. *"No damage. Fuck me, we're blessed."* The connection ended.

"We're something, all right," Hæra murmured. The Gator rumbled back into motion as she headed for her destination: a small hill over an unremarkable Iron Age tomb. It was more properly called a mound. When she reached it, she looked around again. Nobody in sight.

She rummaged through the leather bag at the foot of the passenger seat. From it, she withdrew a paper sack and hopped out of the Gator, squelching through the mud until she saw the small opening in the mound. It was impossible to find unless you knew what you were looking for. Unless you knew how to see.

As she did each morning, Hæra left the paper sack by the entrance. It contained a meat-filled pastry and a bottle of beer. Then she retreated several paces and waited.

After a moment, the trow poked his little head out. His face was sharp and suspicious, his eyes dark, his skin gray.

Hæra nodded in greeting. "For you, friend. Thanks for your protection from the storm. May the farm continue to enjoy your favor instead of your mischief."

The trow smirked. Without a word, he snatched the bottle and bag and returned into the mound, quick as a wink.

Five years of daily offerings, and Hæra had yet to learn his name. She would certainly never see his underground home, which—if he was like most trows—would be full of treasure. And empty beer bottles, presumably. The little mischief-makers had dwelled in Orkney and Shetland for thousands of years, myths to men, facts to other unseen creatures. And if you got on their good side, they'd bless the land where they dwelled.

Hæra and the trow had a satisfactory bargain. She brought him food and drink and paid him respect. Moreover, she didn't tear him to pieces, even though rumor said he'd be delicious. Hard to tell which he appreciated more. In return, the farm enjoyed unnatural immunity to poor weather, animal disease, and even the overabundance of geese that plagued Orkney during the winters.

Jonathan had named the farm "Ætlaquoy." He'd said they had to call it something, said it translated to "Fated Farm," and what with Hæra's insistence on her and Sister Madeleine's destiny, and how he, Jonathan, had always wanted his own farm—well, it sounded nice, didn't it? A bit posh, even if folk fussed about the spelling.

The trow had never fussed. As far as he must be concerned, this land had never had a name and never would.

Hæra brushed her palms together and returned to the Gator. Brodie remained with the flock. Were there any stragglers? Best to drive round and make certain.

The ground bumped and threw up mud on her jeans and rain jacket. She hated mud. In the ocean, there was no need to wash things or do a lot of other nonsense. Humans had to *work* so much, all the time.

At first, Hæra had despaired. Her life in the ocean hadn't prepared her to go outside at a certain time of day, throw herself into hard labor, and then rest, only to get up and do it all over again. Even inland, her human form hadn't tired easily, but her mind had, along with what Sister Madeleine would have called her soul. She'd lost everything familiar to her. Now she was trapped in a strange world she had to navigate while hiding who she was.

On the third night, she'd sat on the edge of Jonathan's couch, where she'd stayed in those days. Her eyes suddenly stung with salty water. Mucus lined her throat and nose, while heat gathered in her chest. She'd thought of the sea, and how she dared not approach it, and strange noises had begun to come out of her. That night, she'd learned what it was to weep.

Since then, she'd never cried. Too unpleasant. Instead, she'd thrown herself into her human studies and joined Jonathan in starting the sheep farm. Why not? She had nothing else to do, and besides, she'd given him the money for it.

Brodie barked up ahead as he chased a couple of stray sheep back into the fold. Hæra looked at the flock as she drove. The lambs were fattening up well. Ætlaquoy would have another good year. According to Jonathan, it was doing much better than most farms did in their first few years. Its livestock was hardy, its grass good. The Texel and Cheviot sheep, already known for the quality of their meat, sold well.

Hæra had told Jonathan about placating the trow so it would bless the farm. He was more willing to believe it than most humans would be. By now, he knew about Hæra's whole herd too—it had been impossible to keep it from him after what had happened—but humans didn't need every secret of the unseen creatures.

For example, Jonathan knew what Stormhorses were, but not how an *Each-uisge* became one. He'd just take that the wrong way. It might even change how he saw Hæra, and as it stood, they had nobody but each other. The thought of disappointing him, or worse, was... unpleasant.

She braked and looked around. Everything looked all right. She turned off the motor, ready to enjoy some time to herself. Now that he wasn't worried about the storm's aftermath, Jonathan would be making his usual fry-up. Once the ground was drier, she'd join him and a couple of other farmhands in cutting the grass to make the silage that would feed the sheep during winter. Hæra liked doing that too. You got to drive even bigger vehicles, which had beautiful sharp blades.

That was an hour or so off, though. She had time to sit by herself on a chilly morning and read. She was nearly done with a book about the history of sheep.

At first, to help her learn reading, Jonathan had given her books for children. But all too often, the books featured things that didn't exist in the world around her. It was hard enough to learn about how life *really* worked on land; if she had to read made-up stories, she didn't want them to pretend they were about *modern* life.

That was why she liked the Bible so much: it was old. At Jonathan's suggestion, she'd started reading it for insight into what Sister Madeleine believed. Now, after she'd been slowly making her way through it for years, she had a list of questions to discuss when Sister Madeleine finally arrived.

Question One: in Genesis, water existed before everything else. Didn't that suggest something about the superiority of the ocean over the land? Question Two: when Noah's great flood receded, many ocean creatures must have died—why was that fair? Question Three: why hadn't Jonah simply asked the whale to spit him out? Whales were generally polite and accommodating.

She had many such questions. Jonathan said they didn't have proper answers, but he wasn't an expert. Sister Madeleine must know, even if she actually believed the stories were true. As far as Hæra was concerned, they couldn't possibly be, but that didn't matter.

Sister Madeleine didn't know that the Great Mare had birthed the ocean and the Great Stallion had shat out the land. She might not take to the idea, but that didn't mean they couldn't *talk* about it.

What might happen next was still unclear. Was Sister Madeleine still Hæra's chosen prey? If Hæra returned to her true form and devoured her—gaining her strength—would she be able to return to the herd in triumph? Even the Sire wouldn't be able to deny that she'd played what Jonathan called "the long game" to do something remarkable.

Her dream didn't have to be out of reach forever. The stormy sky could still be hers. Perhaps.

She'd decide when Sister Madeleine finally returned. Once she saw those grass-green eyes again, she'd know what to do.

In the meantime, there was a task at hand. With her tongue pressed between her lips, Hæra made her way through a maths exercise. These were word problems, meaning she had to read as well as work with numbers. A challenging combination.

She worked until the sky was lighter and then packed her things away. She looked about and sighed. It would likely be a day like any other, wearing at her like the oceans wore at the cliffs over time. Hæra took another look round. The sheep seemed steady on their feet. Brodie sat watchfully. All was well, and it was time to go back.

———

The Gator rumbled and bumped. The morning mists were clearing, and the farm came into view through them.

The tallest structure was a barn that contained two tractors, a trailer, and room for silage bales. Next to it stood a long shed that served for lambing, shearing, and dosing the sheep, depending on the time of year.

She and Jonathan had begun the farm nearly six months after Hæra had washed up on shore. By then, they'd settled into a life together, and her physical strength and endurance could make up for his lack of the same. Jonathan handled the business; Hæra watched instructional YouTube videos (remarkable things) and got to work mucking out land and mending fences. They'd hired men to repair the barn and convert the cow shed. Two of the hires, Jim and Connor, had stayed on as farmhands; others returned seasonally when extra help was needed.

Hæra parked the Gator by the office building. It was actually a house, and the front room served as the office. Jonathan and Hæra lived in the back, where there were two bedrooms, one bath, a sitting room, and a small kitchen. Jonathan's old cottage lay on the edge of the land; he let it to Jim, one of the year-round farmhands.

Time to go in. At the back door, she knocked the mud off her boots and headed into the kitchen. Jonathan was washing dishes. He didn't look up from the sink as he said, "Morning, lass. How'd you rest after that storm?"

He never asked her how she *slept*, since Hæra didn't sleep. She slowed her metabolic system—so she had learned it was called—while remaining alert to danger. Back home, the herd took turns resting and keeping watch over one another. Here, she simply got into bed. No need to close her eyes if she didn't want to.

She could rest standing up too, but Jonathan found that unnerving, so she lay down instead.

"Well enough," Hæra replied. "Yourself?"

"I couldn't, thanks to worrying. Your lot made a dog's dinner all over the islands. Saw it on Facebook. People are going to wonder how we've escaped again and again."

Hæra shrugged and washed her hands when Jonathan stepped away from the sink. "Let them wonder. They won't guess the truth."

"You mean about your…little friend." As always when discussing the unseen world, Jonathan sounded hesitant.

"Little friend, big magic. Hang on, you've got a bit of…" A baked bean was stuck to his shirt, left over from breakfast. She picked it off with a paper towel. "All sorted."

He smiled. His life had not accustomed him to small kindnesses, she knew, any more than her own had. It was…not unpleasant to perform such things. From time to time. "Ah, thanks. Bit of a mess, am I? Anyway, I still can't believe we buy him off with a bit of pastry."

That, and I could eat him, Hæra thought. She also hadn't told Jonathan about giving the trow beer, thanks to his desire to stay away from alcohol. She tossed the towel into the bin. "A little respect goes a long way. Don't trouble yourself."

"I can't help it. I lay awake last night listening to the thunder, and kept thinking."

He shuffled past Hæra toward the sitting room, where an over-stuffed armchair and his tatty sofa faced a television he refused to replace. Jonathan had adapted to computers as necessary, but said his telly had done for him for years and there was no need to change it.

Fine with Hæra, who disliked television anyway. Too confusing. Better to watch real things happen instead of complain about the BBC, shout at footballers, or fall asleep, as Jonathan did.

"Thinking about what?" she asked.

"Among other things, letting the cottage. Jim's moving out since he's getting married." Jonathan rubbed the back of his neck. "I don't like it sitting empty."

"I'm sure you'll find somebody. Perhaps a tourist, at least for the season. Isn't there a housing shortage?"

"Tourists!" Jonathan gave an exaggerated shudder. "What tourist would want to set up near sheep dag instead of the ocean? Even if they did..." He paused. "I'd rather a Jorsayian. Someone who won't ask questions."

Indeed. For several months after her arrival, Hæra had assumed all humans were as incurious as Jorsay's residents, who didn't seem interested in looking too closely at her situation. Then, outsiders from a bank had come to look into the farm sale; they asked her about her "role in the business" and were visibly bemused when she said she'd brought some treasure. They'd asked more questions. Jonathan had called them nosy parkers and gone to talk to a different bank.

It had been a valuable lesson. You couldn't take discretion for granted, and no matter how much the islanders might talk about others behind closed doors, they didn't poke about into their affairs.

Jonathan looked out of the window toward the pastures that stretched beyond, rolling gently over the few hills that Orkney landscapes tended to boast. Hills that it was hell to herd sheep over. "I didn't tell you about running into Harry Duggan at the Cliffside Store a few days ago."

Hæra winced. Harry Duggan was the exception to Jorsay's discretion rule. He was gossipy enough to make up for the rest of the island.

Jonathan continued, "He said give you his greetings, and then asked, 'Now how old is she again? I'd swear the lass is blessed with eternal youth.'"

"What did you tell him?"

"What could I, except do the maths? We told everyone you were twenty-six when you got here. So now you're thirty-one, and not a change on your face." Jonathan crossed his arms. "We can get away with it for now, but not forever. Bad enough when you washed ashore and Sue Kilbright said you healed fast. Eventually, folk won't be able to ignore you're different, and then what do we do?"

Was Hæra supposed to have an answer to that? She put her hands on her hips and glared at him. "Why are you worried about this today?"

"Why aren't you worried about it ever? You'll have to face it at some point. We need a plan, and I've got no ideas." A helpless expression crossed his face, a sort of crumple between his bushy eyebrows. They were white now, as was his beard. Age had touched Jonathan, but not the creature who shared his dwelling place. He had a point.

Jonathan added, "I got you that birth certificate, thanks to Eileen."

He meant Eileen McKay, Jorsay's registrar. She lived just outside the village, ran the office out of her cottage, and had been sweet on him in their youth. He'd said Hæra was his daughter, the by-blow of a one-night stand years ago with a woman who then disappeared and had raised Hæra "off the grid." It would never have flown in London, he'd said, but who'd care out here?

Now Jonathan continued, "That's better than naught, it lets you exist in the eyes of the law, but it doesn't solve the problem. It doesn't make you *human*. You're not like anyone else."

Hæra tossed her head. Her ponytail bounced between her shoulder blades. "I'm pleased you noticed."

"It's not funny. You're near a century old," he said. "Stop thinking like a child and look to the future beyond the return of your Sister Madeleine."

Hæra's shoulders stiffened. Of all subjects, Jonathan knew not to make light of this one. If he had doubts, he was meant to keep them to himself. He'd been good at that so far, trusting to Hæra's belief in her destiny.

Even if she hadn't fully told him what that destiny was.

"I thought it'd be easier when the farm was a going concern." Now the furrow between Jonathan's brows could have been plowed by a tractor. "Thought money would help me see things clearer. All it's done is draw more attention. I don't know how long I can protect you."

In her true form, Hæra could easily bite someone's arm in two. She could run faster than any car, outswim any fishing boat. And her true form wasn't lost to her. "I don't need protection from humans. I repeat—why ask about this now, today? Has something happened?"

"Anniversary's coming up, isn't it? Of course I'm thinking about it, and I wish you would too. Or is it that you can't? Your kind don't look ahead that way?"

"Correct," Hæra snapped. Her *kind* was chiefly concerned with survival from one tide to the next. That didn't lend itself to planning years out. Humans made everything too complicated. Jonathan had just said they could keep doing this for a while, so why worry about it?

"Look ahead as you please," she said. "I'm going back out. The sheep won't tag themselves." Nor would the silage be cut and stored on its own, nor the pens mucked out. Nor could a cast sheep right itself again.

"Lass…"

"I'll think about it when I'm working, all right?" It wasn't a lie. She'd brood over this silly conversation. "We'll get it sorted. And don't —" She raised a hand to point at Jonathan even as he opened his mouth to object. "*Don't* doubt Sister Madeleine. I never have, and I never will."

No matter how long it took. Sister Madeleine had that strength of character she'd mentioned, the one that let her live so differently from most humans. If she could commit to such a restrictive life and endure those privations, then of course she had the strength Hæra craved. And Hæra would never lose faith in that, not in a thousand years.

How was that for thinking ahead?

For a moment, Jonathan looked as if he'd press the issue, and Hæra held her breath. What would she do or say if he did? They argued from time to time, but not about this, the thing most sacred to her heart.

"I'll be in the office," Jonathan sighed. "Farmbench needs checking."

Hæra couldn't care less about the computer program Jonathan used to track everything, but if it kept him distracted, it'd do. "Fine. I'll have my walkie-talkie."

She stomped back through the kitchen, stopping only to retrieve her muddy boots from the back door. Then it was back out to the farm, beneath the gray sky she hadn't flown into, the clouds she hadn't pierced.

Yet.

———

Sheep were stupid, but not so stupid that they couldn't sense an angry predator when it was right on top of them. Even if said predator wasn't out for their blood.

"Christ, Hæra," Jim said as she tried to tag a four-month-old lamb. The little creature struggled and cried in her grip while Brodie snapped at its mother's ankles to keep her away. The field's mud slipped beneath her boots. "Let me do it."

"I've got it," Hæra said between her teeth. She squeezed the tagger on the lamb's ear, below the vein that ran down the center, and squeezed. The lamb squealed and then bounded away the moment she released it. She sat back on her haunches. "You're moving out of the cottage?"

"Yeah, in a couple of weeks. Moving into Isla's place before the wedding. Jon's not a bugger about the late notice." He looked over his shoulder. "Speak of the devil."

Hæra turned to see Jonathan's car, an aging Vauxhall Corsa, bumping down the drive toward the road. He must be going into Thornhill for the shopping. "What time is it?"

Jim looked at his watch. "Going on three. Let's have a rest."

They sat side-by-side in the Gator while he ate a sandwich. Hæra glanced over the flock, which stood a mistrustful distance away. The newly tagged lamb remained at its mother's side.

"I'm glad lambing's over," Jim said between bites. "Come the end of April, I'm checking ewe teats in my dreams."

Dreams sounded awful. To close your eyes, be wholly unprotected, *and* experience things that weren't even true? Thank the Great Mare Hæra would never have to deal with that. "Me too," she said.

"Better than fishing, though. I used to do that."

"Do you miss the ocean?" She didn't look at Jim when she asked. In her peripheral vision, though, she knew he looked at her. It wasn't as good as in her horse form, when she could see from all directions.

"Can't miss what's everywhere, can you?" he said. "You can't *miss* the ocean on an island."

Hæra could. She didn't dare approach the beach anymore. You never knew who might be watching. She could smell the sea on windy days, she could hear it from certain distances, and that was the closest she got to her former home. What would it be like to walk by the water, or to swim in it, and feel her strength return to the fullest?

"You don't go near the water much," he said. "Not even the ferry."

Look out. That was the beginning of a deeper inquiry—the sort islanders rarely made but that Jonathan so feared. She snapped, "Can you blame me? I nearly drowned."

"Right," Jim said quickly. "Lucky you escaped that. Sounded almost like a miracle, in fact."

For a moment, his eyes were shrewd. Hæra's stomach tightened. What else had Jonathan just been saying but that folk would ask questions about her, that they talked behind closed doors?

"I was lucky," she said shortly.

"Of course. Brr, it's airish, isn't it? Have a sip of something hot." He offered his thermos.

"No thanks. I'm not cold." She never was, and hot liquid felt awful in her mouth.

He hummed and then was silent: the sort of silence that fell when a human was thinking. Was that all right, or was he speculating about things he oughtn't?

Thankfully, down the hill, she saw movement. "Here comes Connor."

"Does he?" Jim craned his head forward and squinted. "I don't see…no, I'll be damned. You've got eyes like a cat's."

Hæra liked cats. They had a healthy sense of self-worth. "Thanks. He'll take over for me when he gets here." Clearly, she wasn't in a proper mood to tag the sheep. "I'm going to hose down the shed."

"Does it need washing? The flock's been out here."

"I'm sure it does." Or at least Hæra needed to aim powerful jets of water at something and not make conversation with anyone. She hopped off the Gator. "I'll walk back."

When she reached her destination, she hosed down the shed, well used to its smell by now, and checked the equipment. The big water buckets needed refilling, along with a fresh dose of dietary supplement. There was always something. Farming never stopped. At least it kept her busy. Less time to think about what she'd lost.

One hour passed. Two. Jonathan did not return. He didn't need this much time to do the weekly shopping. It was going on five o'clock. Had something happened?

No. She would *not* worry. Jonathan had acquaintances in the village, and the farm did business with many folk. He avoided the pub nowadays, but he might be sitting down for a cup of tea with somebody. Hæra wasn't his entire world, just most of it.

I don't know how long I can protect you, he'd said, as if he weren't an aging man who relied on the unnatural strength of her arms. How long until Hæra couldn't protect him, either? Not from the herd, not from the storm, but from the brute force of human time that would grind him down faster than Hæra could keep up.

She hadn't planned to stay long enough to see that. She wasn't ready for it.

Finally, there came a welcome sound: the rumble of Jonathan's car in the drive. Hæra looked up from the straw she was shoveling. The car was rumbling much faster than usual. And when it stopped, the tires screeched, as if the driver had slammed on the brakes.

Jonathan never drove that fast. Something was wrong.

Hæra was through the pens' door in a trice, tossing the shovel to the ground. Her heart, once the size of a human head, was now the size of a human fist, and it punched her chest accordingly.

When she got to the car, Jonathan was scrambling out of it. He didn't seem sick or injured, but his eyes were wild, his face was flushed, and his mouth was stretched in the biggest smile Hæra had seen since he'd signed the deed to the farm.

She began, "What—"

"Open the boot and help me put the food away," he gasped. "We've got to make the place neat. And then you've got to scrub up while I start cooking. We've not got much time."

"Make the place neat? Time for what?"

"Not what. Who." Jonathan grabbed Hæra by her forearms. There was sweat on his forehead. He shook her, and then he laughed. "Your Sister Madeleine. She's here. I saw her at Annie's Crafts, ran right into her, no warning. She was just *there*."

Hæra's human ears rang with the force of a kirk's bell.

"She's here," Jonathan repeated, his eyes bright as the sun off the water. "Do you understand what I'm saying? Sister Madeleine is back."

Return to me. Sister Madeleine. The green eyes. The dark veil. The husky voice, the proud face, the strength of character.

The blood. The mouth. The sea, the sea, the sea.

Return to me.

"If you're joking," Hæra whispered, "I will eat your heart."

Jonathan seemed unfazed. He was still smiling. "I expect you would. No joke. I swear by God it's true. And guess what?"

"What? *What?*"

"She's not just on Jorsay. She's coming here. She's coming to dinner tonight."

Hæra forgot every polite human habit Jonathan had ever taught her. A cry escaped her with the force of an ocean that slammed against a cliff, fighting to change its shape. She bent at the waist and braced her hands on her knees. Her eyes stung with salt for the first time in years. Her face burned, her chest ached, and she cried out again.

Jonathan's hand gripped her shoulder. "Oh, lass. My lass. Shush now. All's well. It's everything you hoped for, isn't it?"

Not yet it wasn't. Sister Madeleine was somewhere on this island. And if Jonathan was to be believed, soon she'd be within reach. Close enough to touch, to smell, to seize. To taste once more.

No. Hæra must not. She *must not*. Humans weren't like that, Sister Madeleine wouldn't like that, she wouldn't understand. Hæra just had to wait a little longer. The first step was to have Sister Madeleine in sight again.

She'd waited this long for her woman. She could wait longer to get what she wanted from her.

As soon as she figured out exactly what that was.

CHAPTER ELEVEN

TWO HOURS EARLIER.

"YOU MADE IT!"

The relief in Becca's voice was palpable. Madeleine smiled at the phone display as she sat down on the hotel bed. "I think I did. I've been traveling so long, it's hard to be sure."

"You spent last night in John O'Groats, right? On the mainland?"

Madeleine chuckled. "The word 'mainland' is a bit confusing out here. The largest island is named Mainland too—and locals call it *the* Mainland."

"What? Why would you call an island Mainland?"

"The UK is an island," Madeleine pointed out. "And I stayed in last night. There was an awful storm." She shuddered. "I hate thunderstorms."

"Yeah, I remember the first time we had one and you said we couldn't sit near any windows. Booster was calmer than you were."

"Anyway," Madeleine growled, "I spent the night on the *other* mainland, and then took the first ferry to South Ronaldsay. Then I island-hopped. It took four hours to get here."

"Four hours? I looked on Google Maps. Those islands are tiny."

"Tiny on a map, but plenty to wrangle when you've got to time it with ferries and buses." The Orkney Islands featured a tiny airplane that hopped between many of the islands, but just the sight of it had made Madeleine claustrophobic. Years ago, the school group had been too large to take it, and she wasn't anxious to try it this time, so she'd stuck with alternative methods. Besides, the plane didn't go directly to Jorsay, so why bother?

That said, her stomach hadn't been thrilled with the choppy waters beneath the ferry either.

"So if you spent that long in transit I guess nothing's, you know, happened yet?"

Madeleine sighed. "Not yet."

She'd expected to feel something when she set foot on Jorsay: some shock of recognition, a sense that she was in the right place. No dice. It was ground like any other ground. But she wouldn't let herself be disappointed. Not yet. She'd just gotten here, and she had a month left to go.

"So now what?" Becca asked.

"I'm starving. I'll go out, forage, and explore the place a little more. It seems more developed than the last time I was here."

"Are you going to look for that guy right away? What's his name. Jonathan?"

Madeleine took a deep breath. "Yes. Jonathan."

The man who'd found her on the shore. The man who'd taken her story seriously, to a degree she'd found alarming at the time. He'd been drunk and unsteady, but he was also the only person she could think of who might have some answers for her.

She hadn't gotten his last name—she'd been too discombobulated to ask. By the time she'd thought of it, she was already on her way home. "Jonathan" wasn't much to go on, but this was a tiny island, and he'd given the impression of a lifelong resident. Surely, with a name and a description, someone here would know him.

If he was even still here. Anything could have happened in the meantime. She'd told herself this often, but hope was the hardest thing in the world to kill.

"All right," Becca said. "Be safe. Do regular check-ins, okay?"

"I will," Madeleine promised. "I didn't come this far to get myself into pointless trouble." *Just trouble with a point.*

"If you say so." The doubt in Becca's voice could have rivaled that of Saint Thomas as he questioned the wounds of the risen Christ. "Get something to eat and enjoy your look around."

Madeleine bade her farewell and disconnected before looking around the room. The Merryweather Hotel hadn't changed. Even the slightly musty smell was the same. Her suitcase rested on the luggage rack by an old chest of drawers and beneath a mirror that was barely big enough to show all of her face and shoulders. Next to the window sat a shabby armchair accompanied by a table with an electric kettle, mug, and two teabags.

The last time she'd been in a room like this, she'd worn a nun's habit, with no idea what was about to hit her. Now she was a woman who still struggled to recognize herself in the mirror. She'd given up so much, almost everything, to be where she was right now. Would it, *could* it possibly be worth it?

Madeleine crossed herself and bowed her head in prayer. She murmured, "Thank you, Heavenly Father, for my safe arrival, and for opening my eyes five years ago to what I had to do. Please bless my endeavors here, guide my feet, and protect me from evil. Amen."

She crossed herself again and waited hopefully for the sense of peace that had once filled her after prayer. As happened more often now, it didn't come. In fact, the closer she'd gotten to this trip, the less serenity she felt with every *amen.*

Well, God wasn't a teddy bear you hugged for comfort. He didn't promise you an easy time; her life was proof of that. If Madeleine felt unsettled right now, then she ought to.

She went to the window. Condensation fogged the glass, but she could still see the rolling green landscape beneath a gray sky. No ocean view from here. The hotel was far enough from the shore that she wouldn't be able to hear seductive voices calling to her from the waves.

Which was, Madeleine told herself, a good thing.

She took a deep breath against her squirming stomach. No point in further delay. She'd finally made it to Jorsay, and she wasn't about to hide away in a hotel room. It was time to begin her investigations.

And to pray, with all her heart, that she'd be equal to whatever she finally found.

———

She stopped by the front desk on her way out. Almost immediately, she wished she hadn't. The young woman who'd checked her in was gone. In her place stood Harry Duggan, the hotel's proprietor and manager. A busybody, as she recalled. The last time she was here, he'd asked her and Sister Agnes—in great detail—what "nun life" was like. And he had not been deterred by Agnes's glare.

Hopefully, he wouldn't recognize Madeleine. It was amazing what a nun's habit covered, and not just physically: people saw it as a part of your identity. Out of it, you were a stranger. She'd felt that way herself.

Duggan, who looked to be in his mid-sixties, stood behind the desk where she'd checked in just a few minutes ago. When he saw her coming, he beamed. By the time she reached the desk, he already had a folded piece of paper waiting for her.

"Take a map," he said as she approached. A half-finished pastry sat on a plate next to him, and his gray beard had crumbs in it. "Stepping out on your own? Or have you got friends here?" Before Madeleine could reply, he continued, "Nobody's mentioned having visitors, especially American ones. Let me see, who's got American friends or family round here? Isla, I reckon, at the pub. She went to New York once. I saw her at the chippy yesterday, and she didn't say anything about you, though. And I suppose you'd be staying with friends if that's why you were here?"

Madeleine wanted to say she wasn't here to visit anyone, but that wasn't precisely true. "I have no friends or family here, Mr. Duggan." *I have no family anywhere.* "Just visiting."

"Call me Harry. How long are you with us?"

"The next month, actually." She'd have preferred to rent a cottage for so long a stay, but Jorsay had fewer rental cottages than the other islands, and they'd all been booked. At least the Merryweather wouldn't break the bank.

His eyes widened. "Ah, you're Madeleine, then! I know *your* name —we don't have many who stay for that long. Welcome, welcome. Visiting, you said?"

Madeleine could be vague. Clearly, Harry Duggan wasn't the person to ask about Jonathan. Better to keep her eyes open as she explored, and if she didn't happen to spot him, to inquire with someone less nosy. "Um, well..."

"You'll love it. Can't say we get much sunshine, and watch out for the wind. You missed a bugger of a storm last night. I spent all morning cleaning up. Still, there's nowhere better on Earth. And you've picked a grand time to stay on Jorsay. We've got new things coming up, but it's not overrun with tourists like the Mainland. Not that anything's wrong with tourists," he added quickly. "I can tell you're the right sort, not here to run folk over with a bicycle or complain that the food's different to home."

"I'm not," Madeleine agreed. "New things on the island?"

"Right! Well, we've got some lads who work at the oil terminal, but that's not enough to make us rich, is it? And fishing's worse. Then, a few years ago, a local fella started a sheep farm that's done better'n anyone would've thought, and it's bringing in money. Money's good, right?"

Madeleine nodded. It'd be a waste of breath to speak.

"Keeps more people here working in the spring," Duggan continued. "He deals with local businesses—Annie's Crafts only uses Rendall wool now, and there isn't a restaurant in the islands where you won't find his sheep in a shepherd's pie. Fine, healthy animals. Fetch a high price at market too. Have you ever seen a sheep farm?"

"No, I..."

"Right, course you haven't. Good soul he is. Was a sot for a long time, but he's turned himself right around—well, you can change, can't you? Of course, it all happened after that lass showed up. Funny how it worked." He leaned across the desk and then glanced to the left and right, as if checking for eavesdroppers. "I shouldn't be telling you this."

That was undoubtedly true. Madeleine said quickly, "I don't need to—"

"Then again, it's not a secret, is it? His daughter arrived on his doorstep in need of a home—covered in bruises and cuts no less! Might have been running from a cruel fella, but it's not for *me* to say. I expect that'd make you clean yourself up, wouldn't it, if your lost bairn just appeared in need of help?"

Harry Duggan was surely proof that gossip kept small towns alive. "I guess, but…"

"Mind you, there's something *off* about her. We all say so." Harry's eyes glittered for a moment, lighting up with more perception than Madeleine was comfortable with. "Not to his face, of course. But thanks to him, Jorsay's got more than the chippy and the pub. Got a proper bakery and everything. A fancy clothes shop, even, if you'd like to buy something nice."

Madeleine managed not to glance down at her jacket, sweater, and jeans, which admittedly didn't look very nice.

"And there's a café too. Run by a couple of lads. They're a bit…that is, they don't *fit in*, but they're nice enough, and we all stay out of each other's business here."

Do you really? Madeleine thought. "That sounds perfect. I'm looking for some lunch."

"Why, we do a lunch here! My wife, Margaret, serves it herself. Why not tuck in before you go?"

I'd rather fall off that dock again. "Thanks, but I want to stretch my legs. Where's the café?"

He looked unoffended, probably because at *some* point she was bound to get lunch at the hotel. "Take a left from the front door and pass the civic center. It's across the street from there. Called the Sunrise Café."

She looked down at the map he'd given her. It was the same map the hotel had offered six years ago. No Sunrise Café on it. "Sounds perfect. I'll just…"

"Hang on."

A sudden, sharp note in Harry's voice caught her attention. Madeleine glanced up from the map to see that he'd narrowed his eyes at her. Her stomach flipped over.

"I know you," he said. "Don't I? But where from? I can't be imagining it. You don't forget eyes like yours."

So much for not being recognized. He'd figure it out in a moment, and now she had to deal with his questions when she hadn't even adjusted to his time zone. Or she didn't. She could tell him to mind his own business. She could even do so politely, as you should when you were stuck with somebody for a whole month. "Mr. Dug—Harry…"

"You're the nun!" He snapped his fingers as his mouth widened in a grin. "The one who hit her head and fell off the dock! You've got the scar and everything, haven't you?"

Madeleine managed, with all her willpower, not to touch the scar. As if she wasn't self-conscious enough about it.

He continued, "Of course I remember you. You were here with a whole pack of schoolgirls. Can't believe I didn't recognize you straightaway. Why didn't you say something? Special deal for repeat guests. We don't have many."

She had to play it cool. Madeleine managed a chuckle. "I guess I didn't know how to bring it up. It's nice to be back. I remember the hotel, um, fondly."

"I'd hope so. What are you doing back here? It looks as if you're, er…" He glanced down at her clothes again, and this time his brow creased. "I mean, are you still a…"

"I'm not." He wasn't owed an explanation. She'd given enough of those over the years. "But I am hungry, so I'll just head out. I'm sure we'll be able to catch up later," she added, able to find a thread of generosity for a man who might be pushy but meant no harm.

"Right, yes. I can't wait to tell Margaret. She'll never believe it. Have you got dinner plans? We'd stand you a meal. Must be quite a story!"

Blessedly, at that moment, a man and a woman came down the stairs, both of them in fleece pullovers and jeans. "Hello," the man said in a German accent. "We want to ask about bike rentals."

Harry said, "Oh, you'll want the Cliffside Store for that! They've only got five, though, so they might be out. Martin Heriot, that's the owner, he's had a devil of a time with…"

Madeleine never heard the rest. She'd already escaped.

The Sunrise Café was just where Harry had said, across the street from the civic center. The civic center itself had seen better days, its doorposts in need of a fresh coat of paint and its bricked steps crumbling. The café, however, was clearly well kept, with a trendy logo painted over the front window. A sign beneath promised free Wi-Fi.

Madeleine crossed the street. Halfway across, she thanked heaven that there were no cars, because she'd looked the wrong way again. That would take getting used to.

The bell jangled as she opened it, and the aroma of fresh coffee tugged her inside as if it had taken her by the hand. She inhaled deeply through her nose and sighed in pleasure. The café had few tables, and most of them were full: three women sharing coffee and conversation, a man in work clothes reading a newspaper, and two people who looked like tourists frowning at their phones.

Behind the register stood a slim young man with brown skin and black hair, who smiled when she came in. "Welcome," he called in an English accent.

Harry had said the owners of the shop were two lads who didn't "fit in." This must be one of them. Madeleine smiled at him. "Thanks."

"What can I get for you?"

She reached the counter and squinted up at the menu. Just a few years ago, those letters would have been easier to read. "Just coffee and one hot filled roll with sausage, please."

"Coming right up. Oi, Jeremy!" the young man called to the back.

"One sausage roll. Will that be all? Comes to £4.95, VAT included. That means you don't pay tax. And you don't tip."

Madeleine grinned at his explanation as she offered her credit card. "See a lot of Americans?"

"Mostly in the summer. Where are you from?"

The inquiry contained genuine interest but none of Harry Duggan's nosiness. That made it easy to answer. "Pennsylvania. Do you know it?"

"Is that where they make the chocolate?"

She laughed. "You mean Hershey! Yes, that's in Pennsylvania. But I grew up in New Orleans."

"New Orleans?" His smile widened. "I always wanted to see Mardi Gras. I expect everyone tells you that."

She couldn't deny it. Nor would she say, yet again, that there was more to her hometown than the French Quarter and plastic beads. It was a losing battle. "Looks like you settled somewhere pretty different. You're not local, are you?"

"What gave it away?" He handed back her card. "I'm from London originally. Name's Arjun. My husband and I came up from Edinburgh about two years ago. Wanted to take advantage of the culture shift *and* get away from it all. We sure did, didn't we?"

My husband and I. Madeleine's fingertips went cold as she took her card. Her spine stiffened.

No, she ordered herself, *don't be rude, don't be ridiculous, don't let him see...*

But he did see. Her face had frozen, and it must be obvious, because Arjun's own expression closed.

"Sit anywhere you like," he said.

What was she supposed to say? *I'm sorry,* when she hadn't actually said anything, and an apology would only hang an ugly wreath on a door that should have stayed shut?

Instead, she whispered her thanks, and when the other owner—a white man, the husband named Jeremy—brought her coffee and hot roll to her table, she whispered it again. He said, calmly, "You're welcome. We close in fifteen."

She'd been hungry, close to starving. Now, even though the sausage roll was delicious and the coffee hot and fragrant, she could barely get it down. Could she have handled that worse? Maybe if she'd actually jumped back and screamed.

You don't understand, she wanted to tell them. *I didn't expect to find it here. I wasn't ready.*

She couldn't say that. Madeleine managed to get down her food and flee the coffee shop within five minutes.

This trip was off to an inauspicious start.

————

Her first thought was to run back to the Merryweather and dodge Harry Duggan's questions as best she could. She could lie down, take a nap, and wake up to find the whole humiliating incident was a dream.

Instead, Madeleine hung a right out of the café. The cool air soothed her burning cheeks somewhat.

You'll have to deal with this, her inner voice whispered. It wasn't talking about the café. *You've put it off all your life, and now it's here. Here, you'll face yourself.*

That seemed a little melodramatic, Madeleine thought desperately. Sure, she'd struggled for decades with urges the Church told her were unholy. Yes, Jorsay was the place she'd come to find answers to a mystery. But not that one.

Unless she found herself lying beneath her angel again, kissed until she was taken into a realm of joy where everything felt right.

Nonsense. She couldn't expect that! Madeleine shoved her hands into the pockets of her jacket, walking so briskly that her legs felt the strain. Few people were out and about, unlike the enthusiastic summer crowds she'd seen on the Mainland. Jorsay might have "new things," as Harry had put it, but it hardly bustled.

Thornhill Village was tiny. She'd probably see Arjun and Jeremy again. She'd have to think of *something* to say to heal the wound she'd inflicted. One of many just like it that they'd received over the years, she could imagine.

She'd received wounds of her own. Decades of her family, her Church, her home, telling her that her desires were sinful and unnatural. Then, she'd kissed an angel and emerged into a world where there were other ideas, and now she didn't know what to think or how to feel, and when she prayed, she wasn't getting answers.

If only teleportation were possible. She could pop back into her apartment with Becca for a pep talk before returning to her quest. As it was, she was stuck here in the wind, alone under a gray sky.

With a jolt, she wondered: when was the last time she'd been *alone?* She'd lived in community with the Daughters of Grace for so long, and then she'd moved in with Becca. While it had been lonely at first, she hadn't truly been on her own. Now it was just her, standing on her own against a mystery.

"Grow up," she muttered. "You've got to do this. There's nobody else to do it for you."

She'd said the same thing decades ago, after her brother had—

"Oof!"

She hadn't seen the man coming before she collided with him on the sidewalk. The breath rushed out of them both, and she staggered backward, an apology already in her mouth. Maybe she'd save time by traveling through the whole village and apologizing to everybody in advance. She looked up and began, "I'm so—"

And found herself looking into the wide brown eyes of the man who'd found her on the beach.

Jonathan.

Judging by how his mouth hung open, he recognized her too. He stared at her. Unable to speak, she stared right back.

He looked better than he had six years ago. He stood up straighter, his white beard and hair were neatly trimmed, and no glaze of alcohol covered his eyes. And there was no drunken thickness in his speech when he whispered exactly what she was thinking:

"I don't fucking believe it."

CHAPTER TWELVE

Hæra could rip out Jonathan's throat. He hadn't gotten *anything* useful from Sister Madeleine. As they cleaned the house, he said he'd been too shocked to ask any relevant questions, so overwhelmed was he by seeing her again.

"I was in Annie's Crafts," he'd said, looking around the living room as if he'd never seen it before. "Checking in on the wool order, not that wool's worth anything these days, and having a natter with old Annie. We're having tea in the back while Ellie's at the front—not Jean, she's working at the kirk today—"

"Jonathan," Hæra said hoarsely. She was supposed to be hoovering, but the vacuum handle sat uselessly in her hand.

"Right, sorry! So we're just talking. And all of a sudden, as if it's naught, Annie tells me Harry Duggan rang her not half an hour ago to say the nun's back. The one who fell in the sea. I thought I was dreaming, as if I fell asleep after you and I talked about her just this morning. Couldn't be real, could it? But Annie was serious. Asked me, 'Weren't you the one who found her?' And I just left my tea and ran out. She'll let me have it for that one. Never forgets that shite."

Jonathan enjoyed telling long stories. Hæra usually enjoyed hearing them. "*Jonathan.*"

He looked remorseful. "Ah yes. I ran out, thinking…not thinking, really. Just that I'd find her, see if it was true. And then I ran straight into her."

Had Hæra collided with something too? Not Sister Madeleine, but something even bigger and less visible? That would explain her breathlessness. "Tell me!"

Jonathan took the vacuum from her hands and turned it on. He didn't have to raise his voice for her to hear him. "Starting where? We didn't know what to say! I said I was looking for her, and she said she was looking for me too, and we had to talk. She wanted to talk to me right away. But I couldn't. Not…"

"Why not?" Hæra nearly screamed it. How could Jonathan not get all the information he could manage?

Jonathan glared at her while he pushed the vacuum about. "Not without you."

Oh. Her indignation receded like the tide.

"So I told her, come for dinner, and we'd talk all she liked. Then I went to the provisions shop. I dunno what she likes to eat, but it's not what you do. Can you do with cooked meat tonight?"

Hæra could do with anything, even vegetables, if it meant Sister Madeleine sat at their table. "Yes. Does she know I'll be here? Does she…" She swallowed hard. "Know who I really am?"

"Am I daft? Of course she doesn't. I said my daughter would be here. That's all."

All right. That might be all right. Hæra took a deep breath. "How will she get here?"

"I offered to pick her up, but she said she'd rather bike and 'see more of the island.' She might change her mind for the ride back."

"Perhaps I can fetch her," Hæra mused, only half joking. She was more than capable, and not just in a car. What would it be like to assume her horse form and carry Sister Madeleine on her back to the farm?

Or elsewhere. Hæra could carry her to the sea and devour her. Her father told her that once a human rode an *Each-uisge* within sight of the ocean, the human could not dismount. Sister Madeleine would surely belong to Hæra then.

How strange that hadn't been her first instinct.

She looked away from Jonathan, who wouldn't understand such an instinct at all. He still thought Hæra was *in love* with Sister Madeleine. It was easier not to disabuse him.

Jonathan turned off the vacuum so he could ask, gently, "All right?"

"Of course I am. I'm always all right."

"That's good. Listen, go and collect yourself. Let me finish up here and get started on dinner. Shepherd's pie, I think—our meat's good, and we've got to show her what we've done, yeah?" Jonathan spoke in his most encouraging tone. "Won't she be impressed?"

Would she? She ought to be. How often had Hæra imagined showing Sister Madeleine everything she and Jonathan had made? There hadn't been a farm before. Now there was. Everyone said it was a good farm. You couldn't do that without strength, could you? Without that *strength of character* Sister Madeleine had, the strength that had proven her worthy prey. Now she'd see that Hæra was worthy too.

"Oh, one more thing," Jonathan said. "She looked different."

Hæra, who had been turning toward her bedroom, stopped in place without turning around. "How different?"

"She was in ordinary clothes. I dunno if that means anything. I think there's nuns who don't wear habits anymore, so maybe her convent just changed."

Hæra's body prickled from the crown of her head to the tips of her toes as she absorbed the implications of this. "You saw her?" she asked quietly.

A pause. Jonathan knew that tone in her voice. The one that rose from the deep with its teeth bared. Hæra couldn't help it. Jonathan had seen what had been concealed…seen it before Hæra had. Sister Madeleine's hair, her throat and ears, the shape of her body.

He said, "I don't know what you're thinking, but stop thinking it. And you can't sound like that when she's here. It marks you straightaway. Put your human voice on and hope she doesn't recognize you before you're ready, although…"

The world seemed to turn in the ensuing silence.

"Are you going to tell her what you are?" Jonathan asked.

I don't know what that is.

Hæra had never thought those words before. She hoped never to again; how strange and disturbing that they'd come to her now, of all times! She shook them off with a snorting sound that—she had to admit—didn't sound very human either.

"Just follow my lead," she said. Without waiting for his reply, she continued on to her room, where he'd told her to *collect herself*. As if bits of her were scattered all over the place. She imagined a seabed pitted with pearls, shell fragments, bleached bones. Would she gather them more efficiently with sharp horse's teeth or soft human hands?

At the moment, she had only the latter. Hæra closed her bedroom door and looked around the space, spare and familiar: a twin-sized bed, a bureau, and a closet. There was little decoration, save for a photo of her and Jonathan from the day he'd purchased the farm. He held up the deed for the camera, smiling broadly. Hæra stood at his side, her own smile smaller, but her satisfaction real.

That was all, and it was still more than she required, since she didn't need the bed. The one window looked out over the farm, where sheep grazed in the distance.

She strode to her bureau, opened the top drawer, and fished around in the clothing there until she found what she sought at the bottom.

With a shaking breath, she withdrew Sister Madeleine's rosary.

When Hæra had first brought the treasure chest to Jonathan, she'd explained to him that the rosary was the one thing he must not sell. She hadn't wanted to give it to him, but on land, the wooden beads wouldn't rot like they would in the sea. He'd kept it for her in the cottage, and she'd looked at it during many of her visits as a reminder of her mission. Once she'd moved in with Jonathan full time, she had taken the rosary for her own again.

Properly speaking, it belonged to Sister Madeleine. If need be…if Hæra had to prove who she was…she could return it to her.

She ought to take a shower and put on fresh clothes. Instead, with a groan, she fell down on her back on the bed. The rosary's wooden beads clacked together. It was happening. The Great Mare had finally taken pity on Hæra and willed Sister Madeleine to come to her. Now all Hæra had to do was hold up her end of the bargain and take what she'd been given.

She would. She closed her eyes as the breath shuddered out of her. She clutched the wooden beads and thought of Sister Madeleine's sea-green eyes and soft, full mouth.

Hæra would take, and take, and take.

———

Madeleine's rented bike wobbled back and forth on the road as she made her way to Ætlaquoy, her teeth chattering in spite of her sweater and jacket. The Orcadian wind turned biking into a miserable exercise. *Summer, my foot.*

She should have taken Jonathan up on his offer to pick her up. Instead, she'd had the foolish idea that biking would get out her nervous energy, as well as giving her ample time to think. So much for that. She could only think about how cold she was. Her bare hands ached on the bike handles.

At least the place was easy to find. She was already at the turn from the main road down the gravel path to the farm. A handsome painted sign marked the turn, reading, "Ætlaquoy." She'd already forgotten how Jonathan had pronounced that.

Madeleine made the turn. The farm's buildings were easily visible. Thank the saints, she was almost there, although she had to admit that parts of the ride hadn't been totally unpleasant. A bit of sunlight had emerged, and in a few hours there might be an actual sunset. It was a spirit-lifting sight.

She needed that lift. It didn't seem real that she was here, about to have a conversation with Jonathan about what had happened on that beach six years ago. Possibly Jonathan would have no answers for her. This dinner might be no more than an exercise in mutual bafflement.

The gravel driveway led past green pastures dotted with white sheep. In the distance stood some cattle. Madeleine knew nothing about sheep farming, so she supposed this number of animals must be impressive. Harry Duggan had said Jonathan's farm was successful.

Then again, Harry Duggan had said a lot of things. If only she'd realized he'd been talking about Jonathan, she'd have paid closer attention. As it was, she at least remembered Harry mentioning a "bairn" who lived with Jonathan—his illegitimate child. Someone who'd been beaten when she'd arrived and undoubtedly had a difficult background. It was hard to imagine Jonathan, even with a neat beard and clear eyes, taking care of a surprise daughter's trauma—but what did Madeleine know about him?

By the time she reached the cluster of buildings at the end of the drive, her thighs burned and her lungs ached. She'd thought she was in better shape than this. Where had Jonathan said to go? Oh, right, the office building, which also served as his home.

"It's not much," he'd said, sounding self-conscious. "But we've got room for one more for dinner."

Madeleine had thought of her tiny shared room in the convent, and the little apartment she now shared with Becca. "That's extremely kind of you."

The office sat next to the gravel drive, while the barn and a couple of other buildings lay not a far distance off. It was a brick structure that did indeed look like a residence. Another building sat on the other side of the nearest field—a little stone cottage that looked older than everything else. It seemed homey from this distance, just the sort of thing you imagined when you thought of Scottish cottages. In the United States, a plaque probably would have designated it as a historic building.

The gravel crunched beneath her tires as she braked. *Be calm. Deep breath, deep breath.* That was hard when she was already breathing heavily from the ride. Her hands stung from the wind. She should have brought gloves, but who thought of that in June?

Madeleine walked the bicycle to the steps that led up to the front door. Just as she reached them, the door opened, and Jonathan emerged onto the porch. Was she imagining things, or did his smile seem nervous?

"Welcome, welcome," he said. "Happy you found us. You look as if you've been blown about a bit!"

Madeleine touched her tousled hair. She must be a mess. "Just a bit."

He chuckled. "If you like, I'll drive you back. Come in, come in."

She followed him inside. A couple of desks filled the front room, both covered with papers and binders. One desk also had a computer. Jonathan had made some effort at neatness, but he was clearly not a natural organizer. Madeleine was already itching to put everything in good order.

Jonathan led her through a corridor to the living quarters: specifically, a living room with a small sofa, some armchairs, and a TV. It was a homely, homey space, perfect for a man whose business and life were so entwined that he needed to keep them in the same building. Madeleine thought of the convent. She could relate to that too.

An appetizing smell floated through the air. Her stomach growled, and she shot Jonathan an embarrassed look. She'd only had that sausage roll for lunch, hours ago.

He grinned. "Shepherd's pie all right, then?" Suddenly he looked anxious. "Or are you vegetarians? I should have thought of that, shouldn't I?"

Vegetarians, plural? Were there suddenly two of her? Madeleine looked at him in confusion.

"Nuns, I mean," he clarified. "Do you eat meat, Sister?"

Madeleine's mouth opened slowly; she closed it again. She looked down at her secular clothes, and then back up at Jonathan, wordlessly begging him to put it together on his own. Nothing seemed harder, in this moment, than saying, *I'm not a nun anymore.*

She didn't have to. Jonathan's eyes widened in comprehension. "Ah. I did wonder. It didn't seem the time to ask."

Thank goodness she didn't have to say the unsayable. Madeleine smiled again. "You were right. You have a lovely home."

"Thanks. It's not much, but we like it. What shall we call you then, if not Sister?"

"Madeleine will do just fine. Madeleine Laurent." Guided by an impulse, she chuckled and held out her hand. "Nice to meet you again."

Jonathan grinned and shook her hand. His own hand was warm and callused: a reassuring grip that let go without holding her too long. "Likewise. We've got the pie and some veg. Tea, of course." He cleared his throat. "No alcohol. We don't keep it about. Hæra doesn't drink either."

Hæra—that must be his daughter. It was a lovely name. In fact, something about it sent a pleasant shiver up and down Madeleine's spine. Moreover, it seemed Jonathan really had changed his ways. It was comforting to know you could do that no matter how old you were. She said, "Tea sounds wonderful."

Jonathan seemed relieved. Then he looked around. No doubt seeking the other part of the *we* he'd just mentioned. "Where is that lass?" he muttered.

As soon as he said it, the floor creaked in another room with the sound of a footstep.

Madeleine's heart did something strange. At the creak of the floorboard, it suddenly pushed hard, almost painfully at the inside of her chest. She managed not to clutch at her shirt, but couldn't quite muffle a gasp.

Jonathan looked at her in swift concern. "What's the matter?"

"Nothing," she managed. "I just…it must be…" She didn't have time to imagine what it must be, because then a woman entered the room.

Madeleine had spent fifteen years of her life surrounded almost exclusively by women. Those women had come in all shapes, sizes, and aspects. She'd thought, somehow, she'd seen every kind of woman there was.

She had never seen a woman like this.

Jonathan's daughter was tall, long, and lean, and appeared to be in her mid-twenties. She wore a white buttoned shirt with its sleeves rolled up, men's pants, and boots. Straight black hair fell down past her proudly set shoulders. Her face was long, her cheekbones high, her mouth wide. Her skin was so pale it was almost blue, as if she'd come here straight from freezing waters.

Her eyes made up for it. Madeleine looked into the hottest eyes she had ever beheld. They were an unusual color. She supposed "amber" was the closest word to it, but she'd never known amber to catch fire before. They were almost…yellow, in a certain light.

The woman stepped closer, openly looking Madeleine up and down. It should have been presumptuous, even rude. Fire should not have swept over Madeleine as those eyes assessed every inch of her. Then the woman looked into her eyes again, seeking something. Madeleine had no idea what it could be, but what if she didn't have it?

She couldn't breathe. Couldn't speak. Was her mouth hanging open? Were her eyes bugging out?

She'd been tormented by women for so long—women with pretty faces, enticing figures, and delicate hands. Feminine women. Women she'd managed to resist. Now Madeleine looked at this entirely new kind of woman and thought: *I didn't know about you.*

"Sister Madeleine," the woman said softly, and her voice rolled through Madeleine's blood like the tide. It was deep, almost throaty. For a moment it seemed familiar, although it couldn't be. "It's so good to see you."

———

Good to see you. That wasn't the half of it.

Hæra hoped she had control over her eyes. When she wasn't careful, she could wear a devouring look, or so Jonathan had warned her.

Sister Madeleine was even more worth devouring than she remembered.

There was *more* to see now. Sister Madeleine's wavy hair was dark brown, nearly black, and fell just past her shoulders, looking wind-blown. She wasn't wearing that dowdy habit anymore. Instead, she had on a blue jacket and jeans. Hæra couldn't make out much of her top half thanks to the jacket, but the jeans showed the curve of her hips followed by long legs—not as long as Hæra's, but few women's were. Sister Madeleine's cheeks were flushed, undoubtedly from the cool air that never troubled Hæra. She was... beautiful.

That is, as humans went. She met their standards of beauty. That was an objective fact. It didn't mean anything in particular for Hæra to notice it.

Something else had changed from last time. Sister Madeleine had a scar on her forehead just over her right eyebrow. Hæra remembered that spot with all the clarity of pure water. She remembered tasting it, too. Their encounter had marked Sister Madeleine as permanently as it had Hæra.

How *wonderful.*

Hæra's hand was already rising into the air. This wasn't the first time her human body had acted without her permission concerning Sister Madeleine, but it had been so long. She realized, with a jolt, that she was about to reach out and cup Sister Madeleine's face, touch that soft, blushing skin. Slide her fingers back into the dark hair. And then press her lips to the scar, tasting the memory of blood.

Hæra's hand froze in midair. Luckily, that was the perfect position for Sister Madeleine to reach out so she could shake it in greeting.

For the first time in six years, Hæra's bare skin touched Sister Madeleine's. Time stood as still as if the moon had stopped in its course, holding the tides captive.

It was just like last time. Sister Madeleine's flesh was cool from the elements—the ocean then, the brisk air now. It still didn't banish the heat that flared inside Hæra immediately. Maybe because, this time, Sister Madeleine was the one who'd reached out. The one who had sought the touch of Hæra's human hand. And their hands fit together perfectly now, two currents curling together to form a whirlpool.

Unbidden, Hæra thought of the whirlpool witch. *Bring me your despair,* the witch had told her. She'd be waiting a long time. This was the most triumphant moment of Hæra's life.

Then Sister Madeleine brought it all crashing down around her ears. "Actually," she said, "I'm not Sister Madeleine anymore."

Hæra stared at her, certain she had misheard, waiting for a correction that didn't come.

"What?" she said.

CHAPTER THIRTEEN

As promised, dinner was shepherd's pie, roast vegetables, and strong black tea. Madeleine hadn't realized how hungry she was until she began to eat. Apparently rumors of the quality of Jonathan's flock hadn't been exaggerated. The lamb was savory and delicious, and he'd perfectly crisped the potato topping. He was an engaging host, encouraging Madeleine to talk about her journey over.

That was more than Madeleine could say for his daughter. Harry Duggan had said she was "a bit off," but he'd understated it.

Ever since their introduction, Hæra had been withdrawn, as if she'd been floored to learn what Madeleine *wasn't* instead of who she was. She'd all but clammed up completely. Now she was picking at her food, ignoring her tea, and staring moodily at the saltshaker.

It didn't help that every once in a while, Madeleine glanced her way to see Hæra staring silently back at her. The heat had fled those amber eyes, and now ice had taken its place. But why? How could Madeleine have offended her?

One possibility had her blood freezing in her veins. Had Hæra noticed Madeleine's immediate attraction to her? If so, that was unfair. It wasn't as if Madeleine had seen it coming. If she had, she'd have been able to cover it. She'd been doing that sort of thing her whole life. Besides, did Hæra think Madeleine was going to pounce on her? As if she could! Hæra could easily pin Madeleine to the ground beneath that long, wiry frame.

Madeleine bit her lip and tuned back in to what Jonathan was saying.

"I expect you're wondering about Hæra," he said, giving her a nasty jolt. Could he read minds or something?

Whether he could or not, he didn't seem to notice the deadly glare Hæra had just shot him. Instead, his smile was cheerful enough, if a bit anxious, as he looked back and forth between Hæra and Madeleine.

"Wondering about her?" Madeleine asked. There, that had sounded innocent enough.

Jonathan glanced at Hæra. "She didn't live here then, but she knows what happened. And she's safe as houses. Won't speak a word of what we say here, will you?"

Hæra snorted. An inelegant sound for an inelegant woman. That was her only reply.

Jonathan looked nonplussed at this. "We just want you to know that, is all. Seeing as we're here to talk about something a bit odd."

A bit odd? That wasn't the half of it. He was right—if they were to be honest about this "odd" thing, then it didn't hurt to be honest about themselves. Then, they could talk more freely about what had happened six years ago.

"Something that changed us," Jonathan continued. "At least, it changed me…and seems it changed you too."

Madeleine smiled wryly. "Even more than it looks. Much more than a change of dress."

At that, Hæra raised her head and gave Madeleine a sharp look, although she still said nothing.

"It's why I left the Daughters of Grace," Madeleine continued. At least her voice wasn't trembling as she talked about the most painful decision of her life to two strangers. "My experience here opened my eyes to many things I'd been trying not to see. I've been dying to come back here and investigate what happened, but after I left, it took me years to get back on my feet and save the money. I gave up my worldly goods when I joined the order, you see."

Jonathan sat back in his chair and folded his arms with a sigh. "Church was happy enough to take it all from you and not give it back, then?"

"I gave it up willingly," Madeleine corrected. Even with all her doubts, it was hard to hear outsiders criticize an institution she'd given so much of her life to. "I never expected to see my money again" —what little she'd had left over after her brother's death, anyway— "and the order gave me a generous loan when I left. I don't bear them any ill will. That's important for *you* to understand about *me*."

Jonathan nodded. "Fair enough."

"I loved my sisters. I loved my home." Oh no, her eyes were smarting! She wouldn't cry, not here of all places. "I just…couldn't be there."

"Because it was too hard?"

Hæra's voice was sharp, and when Madeleine looked at her in surprise, her amber eyes were sharper.

"Excuse me?" she said.

Hæra looked her dead in the eye. Her pale cheeks took on a reddened cast. "Living such a life requires great *strength of character*," she said, laying an unnatural emphasis on the last three words. "I admired—that is, I would have admired you for that—but you left. You quit."

Madeleine's muscles all seemed to lock up at once at the naked contempt in her voice.

Jonathan began, "Hæra, what—"

"And why was that?" Hæra continued. "Because you weren't what people thought you were?"

Madeleine should say, *You don't know anything about it, so be quiet.* But all of a sudden, she found herself back at Sacred Heart, in that lonely room on the night she'd faced the truth of herself. She'd stared into the shadows and admitted that the order didn't really know who…or what…she was. And she'd known she had to leave. The charade was over.

The openness had vanished from Jonathan's face. He scowled at his daughter. "What's the matter with you?"

"The matter with *me*?" Hæra pointed at Madeleine as if in accusation. "*She's* just admitted to giving up on what made her who she was, on what proved her strength. She's not what she pretended to be!"

"Are any of us?" Jonathan's face reddened. "Are *you*?"

So much for a nice meal. Madeleine pushed back in her seat. The legs scraped against the floor. "I should leave. I—"

Hæra beat her to it. Without a word, she shot to her feet, and her own chair fell backward to the floor. It was still clattering when she bolted through the back door, slamming it behind her until the frame clattered too.

Madeleine sat frozen, barely able to breathe. She'd been part of many unpleasant conversations and witnessed more than a few shouting matches, but none of them had left her paralyzed. There didn't seem to be a single thing in the world to say except *Goodbye*, followed by another chilly bike ride. She and Jonathan would have to meet another time, *without* the maddeningly attractive woman who'd inexplicably stormed out of here.

Jonathan cursed softly and then gave Madeleine an apologetic wince. "Sorry, Sist…Madeleine. I don't know what's got into her. She can have a temper, but—"

"It's fine." Madeleine tried to smile. This wasn't his fault.

Jonathan would not be interrupted. "She's a good lass. She just has some…er, issues."

Obviously. Madeleine remembered, suddenly, that Harry Duggan had said Hæra was injured when she'd arrived on Jorsay. Maybe she'd had a lot of traumatic experiences that made her volatile.

"Will you stay here, please? I'll talk to her." Jonathan looked at Madeleine pleadingly. "Let's not leave it like this, all right?"

Madeleine remembered his brown eyes from the night they'd met: glazed with drink and anger. Now they were bright and clear, and there wasn't a spot of alcohol on the table. Whatever had happened on the beach that night had changed them both.

"I'll wait," she said. "But I can't guarantee I'll want to speak to her again."

"Hell if I'd blame you. I'll be back in two shakes."

Even under the circumstances, Madeleine couldn't resist. "Of a lamb's tail?"

Jonathan blinked at her. Then a grin widened his mouth. "Just so. Sit tight, lass. I'm off to have a word with a horse's arse."

———

Hæra leaned against the fence. The wind blew hard in her face, as if reprimanding her for her foolishness.

The foolishness of faith. The foolishness of hope. The foolishness of the last five years.

The clouds had cleared enough to reveal the sun. Full dark wouldn't fall until half past ten, and it wasn't quite eight o'clock yet. There was a little more time to enjoy the daylight.

Hæra could still remember the first time she'd seen the sun. She'd been a young filly. Her father had taken her to the surface, a secret from Beathag and Asgall. Hæra's eyes had adjusted quickly from darkness to the light. Nobody on Jorsay took a sunny day for granted, but she appreciated it even more than most.

Not tonight, though. No sunlight could reach her now. She was dark as the deep trenches, where no light existed save phosphorescence, and whose pressures even an *Each-uisge* could not survive.

"Oi!"

Hæra groaned and rubbed her forehead. Of course he couldn't leave well enough alone. "Bugger off," she said when Jonathan's footsteps were close enough for him to hear her.

"You first." He reached the fence and leaned against it with her, breathing heavily. Had he been moving too fast? The doctor at the clinic had warned him about his heart, and Hæra always told him to be careful. "The hell was that?"

"What do you think it was?" Hæra snapped. She turned to look at him. Jonathan's face was creased with worry—and more than that, with open confusion. How could he possibly not see what was the matter? "She's not a nun anymore!"

"Yeah, I noticed that upset you a bit." Jonathan's voice was as packed as full of sarcasm as if he meant to take it round the world. "So what?"

Hæra looked at Jonathan in disbelief. "So *what?*"

"It makes sense, now I think about it. D'you think she could have come all the way out here by herself if she was still a bloody nun? If she was in that order of hers, she'd still be back in America, and you'd never have seen her again."

Hæra turned back to the pasture, gazing at the sheep that appeared as white dots in the distance. Evidence of everything she and Jonathan had worked for, and to what end now? "Maybe that would have been better. At least then I wouldn't have known…"

Her voice cracked. It sounded horrible. Weak.

Jonathan sighed gustily. "It's not her fault you built her up in your head. And I still don't understand why that's what you're stuck on. You've wanted to know about her religion and that, but you never talked about her *having* to be a nun."

"Because it never occurred to me to question it," Hæra snapped. Her throat was thick. It was too much like her first night on land, when salt water had gathered in her eyes, snot in her nose, and saliva in her mouth. When she'd wept. "It was just part of who she was."

"Was, not is. She changed. People change. So do your kind, you'd know that better than anybody!"

I haven't changed. How she longed to say that. Hæra couldn't tell him why Sister…why *Madeleine's* transformation hurt so much. How was she supposed to explain it? *I was going to eat her, and then her strength of character would help me return to my kind and transform into a Stormhorse?*

Jonathan wouldn't like that much.

"All right," he said after a moment. "Do as you like. I'm going back and having a proper conversation with our guest. I'd say you can join us when you feel like apologizing."

"Would you say that?" Disappointment sharpened her edges. "Then

I'd say it's my house too, and I'll join you or not, as I please. Don't forget how you came by all this. Now leave me alone."

"Ugh," Jonathan said, and stomped away.

Hæra returned to looking at the sky. Apparently, it was a sky she'd never know for herself. Her one goal, her one dream, lost. Her one hope of returning to her own kind to find welcome among them at last.

And the end of loneliness, once she and Sister Madeleine belonged to one another for all time. That was lost too.

Unwillingly, Hæra thought of the witch of the whirlpool, looking up at her with mad, dark eyes.

You will fail, the witch had said. *Fail. Despair. Come back. Bring me your despair.*

A bargain was a bargain. The witch had spared Hæra's life in exchange for her promise—a promise Hæra had believed she'd never have to fulfill. She should have known better. Witches didn't grant requests for free.

What now? Walk into the water, transform into her true shape, and return to the whirlpool to meet her fate? Hæra had no idea what such a fate could be or what the witch could want from her. Maybe just to eat her. It seemed fitting. Better that than trapped on this island in a false human skin, aging too slowly and drawing everyone's attention. It was better to meet an honest end in her own shape. And then, when the Last Current took her, Hæra would bravely face the Great Mare and apologize for her failure.

Well. That was that. At least the last five years hadn't been all bad. At least Hæra had made...a friend.

Damn. She'd have to apologize to Jonathan again before she left. Whatever happened with the witch, she didn't want things to end between them like this.

Maybe she really had changed.

Time passed. The sun went lower. Hæra stayed at the fence post, looking at the sheep. Then, after some while or another, more footsteps sounded behind her. Softer, lighter, and slower this time.

Hæra's ears pricked up and her nostrils flared. The wind carried a scent to her—the smell of Sister Madeleine's body, which had been pressed so perfectly to Hæra's own. And curse her for a fool, even now her heart leapt at it.

Pure instinct, that was all. She set her jaw against her own weakness and turned around.

Madeleine, no longer Sister, was approaching her. Hæra might have expected hesitation in her step, but there was none. Rather, Madeleine moved with graceful dignity.

The sunlight danced over her dark hair. Her shoulders were proudly set, and when she stopped several feet away from Hæra, she folded her hands in front of herself and lifted her chin. She looked at Hæra without fear—or, apparently, resentment.

Beautiful, Hæra thought, irrelevantly.

"Jonathan told me the truth about you," Madeleine said.

Hæra's blood went cold as an ice floe. Jonathan had what? Had she angered him so much that he'd spoken the unspeakable without Hæra's permission? "What did he say?" she managed.

"That he never knew he had a daughter until a few years ago," Madeleine said.

Hæra couldn't prevent a little exhale of relief.

Madeleine continued, "That you've gone through hardships you've worked to overcome. And that you've taught each other a lot about… how did he put it?"

"How *did* he put it?" Hæra said.

"About how to be alive," Madeleine replied quietly.

The words gave Hæra an unpleasant jolt. Had she or hadn't she just been thinking about giving her life to the sea witch? "What?"

"He didn't elaborate, but I think I know what he means. I think you do too."

Now Madeleine's gaze was shrewd and penetrating, cutting past Hæra's surfaces, putting her somewhat on the back foot, as Jonathan sometimes said. She'd looked at Madeleine when she'd first arrived at the farm, looked her up and down, voraciously. This was different. Madeleine wasn't looking, but seeing.

There was a great deal that Hæra wasn't ready for Madeleine to see.

"There are many ways to be alive," Madeleine said. "One of them is by being in relationship with other people. In leaving the Daughters of Grace, I gave up the only family I had so I could strike out on my own and discover the truth. Yes, living as a nun is difficult and requires resolve. So does changing your life and starting all over." She tilted her head to the side, still watching Hæra closely. "You understand what that's like too, don't you?"

Apparently she'd recovered from dinner, when Hæra had flustered her. Now she showed no anger or resentment. In those well-remembered eyes, Hæra saw only compassion. She'd never seen such an expression on any *Each-uisge*, or another human, for that matter. It differed from Jonathan's kindness; it was more self-possessed and assured.

Was Madeleine right? She thought Hæra's presence here was a sign of strength. She didn't know that Hæra had been running away, choosing exile and a demeaning transformation over death. Few would call that courageous, even if it was the hardest thing Hæra had ever done.

It was her turn to see something. She focused her gaze squarely on Madeleine's face. "Can you truly say you weren't running away from anything?"

Madeleine pursed her lips and turned away. Ha! In human body language, Hæra had learned, that signaled either fear or guilt.

"I'd prefer to think of it as running toward something," Madeleine said eventually. She kept her gaze focused on the pasture beyond. "I just don't know what yet."

Me.

The thought struck Hæra with the force of a tidal wave. At Madeleine's words, she was tossed back into the horrible night Calder, Beathag, and Asgall had attempted to kill her. She'd curled up into a ball, awaiting her fate, when across the miles, Sister Madeleine had called out to her.

"Guide me now," Sister Madeleine had pleaded. *"Protect me. I'll return to you, I swear it."*

In that moment, Hæra had vowed to live—for Madeleine's sake. Running toward Madeleine had saved her life. And now her woman was saying the same thing?

Stricken, Hæra looked at Madeleine, feeling as tossed about as she had in the witch's whirlpool. Everything she'd just been thinking was incorrect. Madeleine was no coward who'd fled a hard life. She'd had to do that—to get here. To reach Hæra after all those years.

Me, Hæra thought again. *You were running toward me. You left your life, your family, for me.*

And you don't even know it.

The witch would have to wait. In a moment, Hæra's despair had vanished, replaced by confusion and wonder.

"What about you?" Madeleine asked, dragging her back into the present. "Were you running away, or toward? It only seems fair to ask."

"I didn't run," Hæra heard herself say. "I swam." Oh, that had sounded so silly she could kick herself. With a horse's hoof, no less.

Madeleine raised her eyebrows. In amusement? This was almost as bad as when she'd found Hæra trapped under the dock. "Jonathan said you nearly drowned on the night you came to him. Said you had some silly idea about swimming in the North Sea for good luck."

That was the same story Jonathan had told everyone after Hæra's arrival. Of course it made her sound like a nitwit.

"Ah…er…yes." Hæra looked at the beautiful woman with green eyes and delicious blood who had forsaken everything to chase what Hæra had shown her. However, Madeleine was mistaken in what that was. She was chasing life, not death, and she wouldn't understand that Hæra offered both.

Madeleine waited, as if for Hæra to elaborate. When no such elaboration was forthcoming, she exhaled through her nose. "Anyway, I wanted to set things straight. It's my greatest weakness—my pride. I won't have it said by anyone that I'm a coward or a weakling. Even if Christ's teachings tell me not to care about that."

Hæra frowned. She'd read all of Madeleine's Bible and she didn't remember that Jesus fellow saying such a thing specifically. Well, Madeleine would know better than she did. In the meantime, some truth was called for. "I see you are neither thing."

"Thanks," Madeleine said dryly. "Now, am I wasting my time if I ask for an apology?"

"Did Christ say you should?" It was an honest question. Hæra couldn't remember anything about that either.

Honest or not, it seemed to strike Madeleine as funny, since she laughed and shook her head. "I guess he didn't. So much for that, then. Goodbye." She turned to go.

"Will you return?" Hæra blurted.

Madeleine glanced back, seeming surprised by the question too. "Jonathan's invited me back tomorrow. He said he'll give me a tour of the farm."

"And—and you'll come?"

"I think so. I want to talk to him more about what happened when he's not making excuses for your rudeness."

Hæra could manage only a sputtering sound.

"There won't be any need for our paths to cross again, I think," Madeleine continued. "That'll be for the best. For various reasons."

Various reasons? The only one she'd named was Hæra's rudeness which, admittedly, was justified. "What are the other reasons?" Hæra demanded. If Madeleine thought she could so easily walk away after all this time, she was mistaken.

Madeleine looked taken aback. She turned pink. "Um...well... none. Never mind that."

"I won't be rude again," Hæra assured her. "And if Christ tells you to ask for an apology, I'll give you one."

Madeleine opened her mouth. Closed it again. She looked what Jonathan called "gobsmacked," though Hæra had no idea why that should be. Of course it was only right to offer an apology after she'd been so wrong in her assumptions.

Since Madeleine seemed to have nothing to say, Hæra added, "I assume that settles things. I'll see you tomorrow. You'll arrive in the morning?"

"I…uh…" Madeleine still looked thrown, for some reason. "I don't know? I'd like to go on a walk on the beach first. Where it happened. Just to see—"

Yet again, Hæra's human body acted beyond her control.

Her hands went around Madeleine's biceps. They tugged Madeleine close to her body, almost as close as they'd been on the shore that night, except Hæra was wearing clothes this time. Her heart raced, and her lips curled back, baring her teeth.

Madeleine gasped, "What—"

"The shore is dangerous," Hæra snarled. "The waters are treacherous. There are things in there you can't imagine." Asgall, Beathag, teeth and tails… "Stay away!"

"Good *Lord*!" Madeleine's hands were curled against Hæra's chest, but she wasn't pushing away. Her face was much pinker now. "What's the matter with you? Of course I wouldn't go swimming. It's not dangerous just to walk on the beach!"

"No?" Hæra pulled her in even more. "What happened the last time you did?"

Madeleine stared up at her, apparently unable to think of a response to that. Her face was extremely close to Hæra's. So close that Hæra could feel her breath, unsteady and warm, against her own mouth.

Her lips had been soft that night. They'd opened for Hæra, who'd found a warm place inside. They were opening now, in much the same way, as if…as if…

Madeleine turned her head away with a gasp. Had she realized what Hæra was thinking? Was she remembering—?

"I-I understand why you must feel that way." Madeleine's voice shook. "After what happened to you. But I won't swim. I'll be careful. Now I need to go. Oh goodness, let me go—"

If she wanted to be let go, why wasn't she pushing Hæra away? Was that a human thing too? Hæra wasn't experienced in holding people. She took a deep breath and forced her grip to loosen, making her human limbs obey her again. How strange, that Madeleine's presence should wrench Hæra's own body from her control so easily.

It was even stranger that their separation should cause a sense of loss that made Hæra feel as cold, as if the sun had never come out after all.

Just in case it was called for: "I'd apologize for that, too," Hæra said, "if you asked."

Madeleine stepped back, wrapping her arms around herself, not looking at Hæra. "Just don't grab me again. Don't go around grabbing people in general. It's absolutely unacceptable."

Jonathan had never taught Hæra that. He probably hadn't realized he'd need to. "Oh. Then I won't."

Without a word, Madeleine turned and walked away. Hæra judged it best to wait behind, since she couldn't trust herself to say sensible things, and the Great Mare forbid she slip in front of Jonathan. Besides, standing here gave her a chance to watch Madeleine walk— she hadn't realized what a pleasing sight that would be.

It would be even more pleasing to watch her approach tomorrow. Hæra had learned from her experience tonight. She'd be ready to have a proper conversation, the sort she'd spent years studying for, ready to stand within reach of Madeleine once more.

Not *reach*, though. Not again. She'd just promised not to do that anymore.

As she watched Madeleine return to the house, with steps less measured than they'd been during her approach, Hæra hoped that was a promise she could keep.

CHAPTER FOURTEEN

Home safe.

As soon as Madeleine sent the text to Becca, she thought: *everything about that is wrong.* She wasn't home, but sitting on a bed in a hotel where she'd had to dodge the nosy proprietor. And she was anything but safe.

Moments later, a green bubble appeared on the screen.

Good!!! So you talked to him?

Not as much as she'd planned to. After Jonathan had returned from speaking to Hæra, they'd touched on what had happened that night on the shore, but he seemed reluctant to go into much detail. Madeleine wondered how much he remembered; he'd been pretty drunk. He might be embarrassed to admit it. Mostly, he'd wanted to apologize for Hæra's behavior.

And when he'd driven her back to the hotel, Madeleine hadn't been up to saying much of anything. Hopefully their meeting tomorrow would be more productive.

Yes. He's very nice.

Did you figure anything out?

Madeleine hadn't figured anything out except one thing she hadn't wanted to. And she wasn't ready to tell Becca, "Yes. I am incontrovertibly, incurably homosexual."

For her whole life, she'd avoided thinking that word, applying it to herself. If she didn't say it, she didn't have to live with it. She could call it something else: a condition, an affliction, a cross to bear. It was all those things. It was also more.

After Hæra had held her so closely, Madeleine couldn't use any other word. *Homosexual.* Sexual. So sexual that, even through the hostility and confusion, Madeleine's body had responded wholeheartedly to Hæra's long, wiry frame. And, God help her, to those strong hands that had gripped her as if Hæra never intended to let go.

It hadn't felt unnatural at all. It had felt like the most natural thing in the world, something Madeleine was meant to do, to…have.

That wasn't right. It couldn't be.

Not yet. I'm going back tomorrow. He's got a sheep farm.

Lol. Get a wool sweater for me

Will do.

Be safe, hon. Call me if you need me. We miss you

There followed a picture of the cat, Booster, sitting on the end of Madeleine's bed with an unimpressed look on his face. In spite of herself, Madeleine chuckled.

I miss you too. Going to bed now. It's been a long day.

I bet. Night night 🩶

Madeleine sent a heart back. Then she slumped forward, her chest pulling her down with the weight of the stone inside it. She propped her elbows on her knees and closed her eyes. Her bottom lip trembled, and she set her jaw to stop it. That didn't stop one tear from rolling down her cheek at the slightest flutter of her eyelashes. It didn't stop the second one either.

Homosexual. The word summoned her parents' stern teachings. Her priests' solemn sermons. The nuns' policies against special friendships. Everything she'd been taught and had dedicated her life to following.

It also summoned Arjun and Jeremy's faces, closing before her like twin doors on iron hinges. Shutting her out of a place she shouldn't *want* to go—and yet, something in her raced forward, crying for entrance.

Or just crying. That too.

Madeleine, who hadn't allowed herself the release of tears in a long time, lowered her face into her hands and let them come. Her chest heaved and ached as she sobbed. *I don't want this. I don't want this. I don't want this. Lord, take this bitter cup away from me.*

Christ had said that before his crucifixion, begging God to spare him from an excruciating death. God had declined to do so. Nobody was immune to suffering. Certainly not Madeleine, who was already acquainted with it and—apparently—about to become more so.

She'd lost her parents and brother...she'd left her Sisters...and now this new, awful truth—something was wrong, horribly wrong, with her. Something that had been eating away at her soul, maggot-like, for decades. How much did you have to endure before God decided it was enough? And what on earth was she supposed to *do*, now that she couldn't look away anymore?

Keep looking.

Madeleine shuddered at the return of the unwelcome voice. It did love to say things she wasn't ready to hear. But every time, it was what she needed to hear. Was it the voice of God? Her own conscience? Something else? Would she ever know?

She sat up and wiped her tears away. Her breath was painful in her chest. Blowing her nose helped to relieve the pressure in her sinuses. Crying might be a release, but the aftermath was messy and inconvenient, like all the rest of this.

Okay, she told herself as she tossed the tissue toward the trash can. It bounced off the edge and landed on the worn carpet. *Okay. You're homosexual. Now you know.*

(She had always known.)

Now you know, and you can deal with it. You can live with it. You can live through it like you've lived through everything else. It's just another cross to bear. Pick it up and carry it.

Practically speaking, nothing had to change. Madeleine had never acted on her urges with women, and she wasn't going to start. She'd just keep living her life as she always had. She could begin by getting ready for bed as she always did. At the very least, she'd start life as a homosexual woman with clean teeth.

The thought chased a hiccupping laugh out of her, which was something, at least. She could still laugh at silly things. She could still hate flossing and make herself do it anyway.

She could still pray.

Madeleine prepared for bed. The end of this endless day was so close, but she couldn't skip the last step. She crossed herself, bowed her head, and said the same words she always did.

"My God," she whispered, "I adore you, and I thank you for the many favors you bestowed upon me this day—I—"

The words crowded and clogged in her throat. This time, the urge to laugh was bitter. Oh yes, how could Madeleine not be *grateful* for all the "favors" she'd received today? It was almost as bad as the night she'd lain awake at Sacred Heart before admitting she had to leave.

God could fill in the blanks for once.

"Amen," she muttered, and crawled into bed. Her limbs seemed to weigh a thousand pounds apiece, and the bed creaked beneath her. These springs must have been working hard for twenty years. The pillow was thin too. If you changed a few significant details, she might be back in her convent bedroom.

No. No more thinking about Sacred Heart or anything else. Her brain was about to give up the ghost, and she should let it before things got even worse. Madeleine closed her eyes and sought her rest.

Things got even worse.

Behind her eyelids, Hæra lounged against a metal fence and gave her the same soft, mysterious smile she'd worn when they met.

A gasp escaped Madeleine. Her eyes flew open, and Hæra disappeared, although she left some evidence behind. Chiefly, Madeleine's hammering heart and dry mouth. Somehow, this was even worse than the homosexuality thing. Maybe because it had kick-started the homosexuality thing.

Worse, and absurd to boot. Hæra was rude. She was brusque. She was much younger than Madeleine—by fifteen years, probably. An age gap was hardly the worst part of this, but it didn't help. Moreover, she was *odd*. That whole thing about Christ telling Madeleine to ask for an apology? At first, she'd been sure that Hæra was being sarcastic —and disrespectful. But sincerity had glowed in her strange eyes.

So had something else. Madeleine couldn't identify it, but whatever it was, it sent a wave of heat up and down her body.

Ridiculous. Yes, Hæra was objectively attractive, even if it was in a way Madeleine had never encountered before. That shouldn't stack up against her behavior. Especially not the way she'd seized Madeleine, hard and fast. As if she had a right to it, as if Madeleine... belonged to her.

What had she said? Something about the beach being dangerous. Madeleine had been too overwhelmed to take in everything. Hæra's body had been so warm against her own, and that was odd too. The weather was cold and windy, and Hæra hadn't even been wearing a sweater. She seemed to make her own heat: heat she'd been ready to share.

Including her own breath, which had puffed hot and unsteady against Madeleine's mouth. As if she'd been about to kiss her.

Oh God. No. Absolutely not. Madeleine gritted her teeth. Hæra might be odd, but that didn't mean she'd been aiming for a kiss! Madeleine was the one who wanted…

Odd. Rude. Too young. Get some sleep before confusion kills you.

Madeleine rolled to her side, tugging the duvet up to her chin. She closed her eyes with determination. Sleep would come. She'd wake in the morning refreshed and better able to face these demons. At least said demons were figurative, not literal. And if she was lucky, God would grant her the peaceful rest she sorely needed.

Please, she thought, before the world blessedly disappeared.

———

When the world reappeared, Madeleine was in the wrong place.

She'd just closed her eyes in her hotel room, and now she stood alone and naked in the middle of a grassy field. The full moon and stars shone overhead.

Naked, but not cold. She looked around in confusion. Considering how cool the day had been, she should be even colder out in the middle of the night without a stitch on.

How had she gotten herself into such a situation? She had to make it back to the Merryweather. Hopefully everyone would be in bed, and the whole village wouldn't see her walking down the street stark naked. Just the thought made her cross her arms over her breasts and cringe. They'd all see her…they'd all know…

"Only I see you."

Madeleine whirled on her heel with a gasp.

Hæra stood about ten feet away, fully clothed, her arms hanging loosely at her sides. Her long hair lay draped over one shoulder. She seemed even taller here than she had earlier. Or maybe it was the way she stood, straight and proud in the middle of the field, not surrounded by the trappings of civilization. Except her clothes, of course.

Madeleine said, "You shouldn't be wearing any clothes."

Hæra lifted her eyebrows. "You want to see me naked?"

"Ye…no!" Madeleine wrapped her arms more tightly around

herself. "Not like that, I just meant, it isn't fair. If I'm naked, you should be too."

Hæra said nothing, just shook her head. Then she began to walk toward Madeleine in slow, easy strides. Her chin was lifted, her lips curved in a soft, sure smile. The moonlight caught on her pale skin, and she seemed to glow.

"Please," Madeleine whispered.

"It's not time yet." Hæra flicked her hair back over her shoulder.

"When will it be?"

"When you're ready."

"I'm ready now!" Madeleine dropped her arms so they didn't cover her anymore. She stepped forward. The grass was soft beneath her bare feet. Yes, oh yes, she was ready.

Ready for what? That part was less clear.

"Are you?" Hæra extended her hands palms up, her long fingers splayed open in invitation. "Are you ready for me?"

"Yes," Madeleine gasped. She held out her own hands.

She couldn't tell who moved first, Hæra or her, but the end result was the same. Their hands met first, curled around each other, and then Hæra yanked Madeleine's naked body to her clothed one.

She'd kiss Madeleine now. She'd finish what she'd started earlier tonight by the pasture, when she'd grabbed Madeleine just like this, and it had seemed so clear that their lips would press together in the sort of kiss Madeleine had yearned for her entire life.

Hæra bent to Madeleine's throat and sank in her teeth, gently.

Madeleine's knees turned to water softer than the sea. Only Hæra's grip kept her from collapse. No, she couldn't ever be cold, not when Hæra's mouth held all the heat in the world.

That mouth drifted over Madeleine's throat, pausing to lick and suck while Madeleine grabbed Hæra's elbows. Every stroke of Hæra's tongue made her knees even weaker. She tried to beg for more, but no words would come. Just *ah, ah, ah.*

That seemed to be good enough. Hæra growled against her wet skin. "You've never done this before."

"Never." Madeleine writhed forward. Why was Hæra still dressed?

Didn't she want this too, didn't she need this, skin-to-skin? "I've been waiting so long."

"For what?"

"For—for—" *For you.* No, that wasn't right, that couldn't be right. "I don't know. For it to be all right, for…"

"It is all right." Hæra's hands cupped Madeleine's hips. "Better than all right."

Oh mercy! Hæra was touching her bare skin, and not for a handshake. She was touching Madeleine where nobody ever had, making Madeleine's hips rock forward for more.

She'd waited for *so long.*

"More," Madeleine said. She grabbed Hæra's shoulders. "Do it like that again."

"Like what?" Though Hæra's eyes said she knew.

Madeleine closed her eyes and pressed her forehead to Hæra's shoulder. It was broad, firm.

"Rough," she choked.

This time, Hæra bent to the other side of her throat, sucked hard enough to leave a mark. Madeleine would get a matching set, high up enough to be visible. Everyone would see what she'd done.

Only a few moments ago, that had been a terrifying thought. No longer. Everyone could see that Madeleine Laurent finally, *finally* had what she needed.

"Yes," she gasped. "Let them see. Let them know."

Hæra bared her teeth against Madeleine's skin. "They'll know you're mine."

Without meaning to, Madeleine thrust her naked hips against Hæra's clothed ones. Something…new…was happening between her legs. It was almost like pain, but it felt good, too. She wasn't just warm or interested. She *ached*—heavy, full. Soaked. "Yours," she groaned.

Hæra bent lower. Her mouth traveled downward. She had to crouch a little to reach her next destination.

Madeleine's breasts.

At the first hot lick on her nipples, Madeleine cried out. It was heaven, or hell, or some third unearthly place where she wanted to live forever. A place of heat and light.

Hæra switched back and forth between her breasts while Madeleine ran her fingers through all that hair and then clutched her shoulders. She held Hæra close as she sobbed with need. Her breasts ached as badly as she did between her thighs, until she was nothing but one long throb, and she couldn't stop rocking back and forth. Hæra sucked her hard enough that it ought to hurt, it *did* hurt, and she only needed more. "Please," she moaned.

"You need this," Hæra growled. "Say it."

Madeleine dug her fingers into Hæra's scalp. "I need it!"

I need it, I need it, I need it. What else could she say, or do? She was made of lack and necessity, ripe for the taking.

Hæra tugged her head back and straightened up. Her eyes flashed as she loomed over Madeleine. "Are you ready now?" She touched the top button of her shirt.

How strange to want something so much that you couldn't speak. For answer, Madeleine reached out toward Hæra's buttons herself. Her hands shook as if she was afraid—or as if she were in withdrawal. They shook so much she couldn't open the top button. It didn't want to slide through its hole. Madeleine tugged at it hard, then harder, and let loose a little cry. "I can't get it!"

Hæra laid her hand over Madeleine's. "It's not for you to do." Those blazing eyes burned their way through Madeleine. "You're not in control of this. I am."

Shouldn't that be terrifying? It was safer to be in control, to decide when to start and stop, and to dictate how things happened. How strange that her knees went weak, that her mouth softened, and her every nerve begged her to let go. Let Hæra do whatever she wanted. Madeleine would want it too.

"Thank God," she whispered.

Hæra unfastened her first button. She repeated, "Are you ready?"

"Please." Madeleine clutched her hands into fists at her sides. Otherwise, she'd reach out and do what Hæra said she couldn't. And then, would this end? No, it couldn't end—Madeleine would do anything, anything—

The second button slid through its hole. Then the third. Hæra's pale skin came into view. She didn't seem to be wearing a bra, but Madeleine couldn't see enough to know for sure. She leaned forward eagerly. What would Hæra's breasts look like?

Hæra stopped unbuttoning. "This is all you get."

Madeleine looked up into her eyes in dismay. "No! You get to see all of me. It's not fair."

"Good things come to those who wait." Hæra took hold of Madeleine's bare shoulders. Her shirt was unbuttoned just far enough to show the line of her cleavage. There wasn't much. Her breasts must be smaller, perhaps like an athlete's, part of a strong and lean body.

"I've waited long enough," Madeleine groaned. "Show yourself to me. Please!"

"I'll be the judge of what's enough. But…" Hæra traced a fingertip down Madeleine's throat.

Madeleine promptly got goose bumps and gasped. Hæra's touch left a streak of heat behind.

"But I'll learn something from you," Hæra continued, her voice a husky murmur. "Something I should have learned a long time ago."

Nothing existed beyond the skin Hæra was touching on Madeleine's throat. Until now, it had only been a patch of skin like any other skin, neither special nor blessed. Now it held Madeleine's whole consciousness. "W-what is that?"

Before her eyes, Hæra slowly sank down to her knees in the grass. Her eyes never broke contact with Madeleine's.

"How to pray," Hæra whispered.

Her strong, warm hands cupped Madeleine's hips. She leaned forward until her nose pressed into the dark curls between Madeleine's legs and inhaled deeply.

And then—her tongue—

Hot. Wet. Waking up everything it touched, welcoming Madeleine's flesh into a brilliant new world, a country discovered at last. Madeleine cried out in shock. She'd heard of this act, but she hadn't known it could turn your brain into static. Was she about to faint?

No. She wouldn't be allowed to. Hæra would make her take it. Madeleine had no choice.

"God, yes," she sobbed. She grabbed Hæra's hair, all that black hair, and pulled her in closer. "Don't stop."

"I can't stop," Hæra mumbled. She licked over Madeleine's flesh, which was getting more slippery by the moment as Madeleine writhed on her mouth. "I want you too much."

Yes. Yes. They *both* wanted it—Madeleine wasn't alone, finally not alone—

She pushed her hips forward pleadingly. "Please want me!"

"This is how I pray." Hæra's tongue went faster, pressed more firmly against the sensitive nub Madeleine had avoided touching for decades—a hot, wet, rhythmic stroke that licked her into the stratosphere, finally sending her from Earth to heaven.

Madeleine sobbed as she watched that sleek, slick mouth working between her thighs. Her hips rocked in a wild rhythm to match.

Too fast. Too fast. She cried out as she rode Hæra's face. Something was happening too quickly—she had to slow herself down—

God and all His saints, though, it felt *so* good, after so long—

Hæra's hands cupped her bare bottom. Nobody had ever done that to her before. Nobody had ever done any of this to her before. Madeleine's hips rocked faster, though she didn't mean for them to. Hæra had somehow found a perfect rhythm that lifted her up on her toes. It drew cries from her mouth too, loud ones.

"Yes, now," Hæra growled. "Do it now."

"D-do what," Madeleine gasped, but she knew what. Oh God. Oh yes. It had been so long. When was the last time? When she'd touched herself in college one drunken evening, thinking about her beautiful French professor. She'd dropped the class the next day. She hadn't been ready to feel—but now she was, and—

She dug her fingers even more tightly into Hæra's hair and looked down into her eyes as Hæra licked her. Between her thighs, the ache grew and the warmth became fire, the same fire that had burned in

Hæra's eyes tonight when she'd grabbed Madeleine as if she had a right to, and…

A soft beeping sounded from somewhere in the distance.

"What's that?" Madeleine asked, even as her thighs shook.

To her horror, Hæra stopped licking her and sat back on her heels. "It's time for you to go."

The beeping grew louder. Madeleine looked at Hæra in dismay. "No! I need to—"

Beeeeep.

As her phone's alarm grew louder, Madeleine opened her eyes. She blinked blearily.

She wasn't with anybody in a field under the stars. Nor was she naked. She was in a prosaic hotel room wearing her pajamas. The flesh between her thighs was heavy and slick.

And it was the middle of the night. Completely dark out. Why was her alarm going off?

Madeleine fumbled for her phone on the nightstand and stopped the alarm. Yes—it was three in the morning. She'd meant to set her alarm for six. She'd been so…distracted…that she must have made a mistake.

The German tourists were next door. Hopefully they hadn't been disturbed by the alarm, or any noises she might have made just a few seconds ago during that outrageous dream, when she hadn't even climaxed.

Madeleine stared at her phone's display without seeing it. Instead, she saw Hæra's seductive smile right before it disappeared between her legs so Hæra could do something that Madeleine had never even dared dream of before. With a healthy dose of blasphemy, no less.

She flung herself back on her creaky bed with a groan. Was this what happened when you…came out to yourself, or whatever? The dam broke and let the flood in all at once?

It wasn't fair. You should be able to get used to this kind of thing gradually. There should be a grace period.

Full of grace, Hæra whispered in her mind.

Madeleine groaned, rolled over, and felt again the slickness between her thighs. *Grace* didn't seem likely. Yet she'd been so happy in the dream, all that dirty shame nowhere in sight. She hadn't hated herself. Madeleine had simply wanted to let Hæra give her what she needed. It had felt like freedom, not the chaste cage her life was supposed to be.

Maybe—maybe it was possible that something that could make her feel like *that* didn't have to be a curse? Or not *just* a curse? Maybe…

Down that path lay mortal danger to her soul. She wouldn't think about it. She'd stop thinking about it right now. After all, she'd spent her whole life deliberately not thinking about this. It was second nature. She could do it in her sleep.

Madeleine groaned and rubbed both hands over her face.

No, actually. She couldn't.

CHAPTER FIFTEEN

The next morning, Madeleine promised herself not to make it weird.

She was back at the farmhouse with Jonathan, and he was making breakfast. They were going to talk. Never mind her dream. Madeleine was going to focus on what mattered today, and she was going to be normal.

The breakfast itself, however, wasn't normal for her. Even after leaving the Daughters of Grace, Madeleine kept her breakfast light: cereal or yogurt, maybe some fruit. She wasn't ready for what Jonathan called his "fry-up."

"There you are," he said triumphantly, placing before her a heaping plate of food. "A proper Scottish breakfast. These are my best tattie scones, made from potatoes. Baked beans, fried tomatoes, and black pudding."

Madeleine tried not to sound apprehensive as she looked at the round, dark slices of meat. "Black pudding?"

"Oh yes. It's made of…" Jonathan seemed to hesitate. "It's a type of sausage. This'll give you energy for the day and no mistake."

"Thanks," Madeleine said weakly, hoping it wouldn't also give her a stomachache.

He poured her a full cup of coffee and sat down, snapping his napkin out before dropping it in his lap. "Tuck in."

Not yet. Madeleine crossed herself and bent her head in prayer. Jonathan didn't seem like the religious type, so she kept her voice soft as she said grace. Then, without looking up, she began to cut into the tattie scone. "Thank you so much for breakfast."

After a pause, Jonathan said, "Ah, it's no trouble."

They gave each other awkward smiles and then looked down at their plates. Madeleine concentrated on her food and the clattering of utensils that suddenly seemed too loud.

She took a bite of the tattie scone and said in a low voice, "This is delicious. Where's Hæra this morning?"

Hopefully far away. Far enough that Madeleine wouldn't see her today and think about that dream she wasn't thinking about already.

"Out in the fields. She, er, doesn't care for a fry-up. And she likes an early start. She'll be back soon."

Madeleine's stomach flipped over, and it wasn't entirely to do with the bite of black pudding she'd just taken. Said pudding was thick and chewy, and she gulped it down as soon as she could, knowing it'd sit like a brick in her stomach. It had been generous of Jonathan to cook for her, though. "This must have taken a lot of work."

"Work? Nah. Running a farm, that's work. Sue, I mean Nurse Kilbright, says I've got to watch my diet. Thanks for the excuse to have some proper food."

Before Madeleine could reply, the back door opened, and the woman who'd haunted her dreams last night strode into the kitchen.

Hæra's long, black hair was pulled back in a messy ponytail. Her face was flushed from the air, and today she wore a windbreaker. Jeans —men's jeans, Madeleine could tell—covered her long legs, ending in muddy work boots. She couldn't have looked less like Madeleine's ladylike French professor with her pencil skirts and silk blouses.

Her eyes immediately speared Madeleine as if she, not the food on the plates, was breakfast. Madeleine's mouth went dry.

"Finally," Hæra said.

"What?" Madeleine managed.

"I was wondering when you'd get here." She leaned on her elbow against the doorframe, an insouciant pose that made Madeleine's heart literally skip a beat. "When will you be ready to go?"

"Good morning, lass," Jonathan said pointedly. "It's nice to see a guest, isn't it?"

"So it is," Hæra replied, never taking her eyes from Madeleine.

Madeleine couldn't help returning the favor. "Um. Hello."

"It looks as if you're just starting." Hæra's gaze flitted over the breakfast. "How much time will you need?"

"As much as she needs," Jonathan said in exasperation. "She came here to talk. Let her have breakfast. There's no hurry, is there?"

Hæra took hold of the third chair, pulled it out with a scraping noise, and sat next to Madeleine. She lounged against the back of the chair and spread her legs. Their knees bumped. Madeleine almost choked on her sip of coffee.

"Did you sleep well?" Hæra asked.

Madeleine would not blush. Hæra couldn't possibly know about her dream, and it was going to stay that way. "I'm still adjusting to the time change. But I slept well enough. Thanks. You?"

She could have kicked herself for the question. What next? Asking, *Did you dream about having sex with me, too?*

"I rested," Hæra said. She darted a quick glance at Jonathan, and when she spoke to Madeleine again, her words sounded a little rehearsed: "Thank you for asking. And you, Jonathan? Did you sleep well?"

Jonathan rubbed a hand over his forehead and chuckled ruefully. "Aye. We're a rested group. Well done."

"Yes." Hæra gave Madeleine a pleased smile. "You see? I've learned etiquette. No need to fear my rudeness again."

At least someone could laugh about it now. The return of Hæra's rudeness would almost be welcome, as long as it slowed the racing of Madeleine's heart. "Um, yes. Your father's a good cook. Do you cook too?"

A pause. Hæra and Jonathan looked at each other, and something seemed to pass between them.

"I was raised by another," Hæra said eventually. "He was my real father. I think of Jonathan as my friend."

That sounded like part of a much bigger story. Hæra must have quite a tale to tell—if that was why Madeleine was here, which it obviously wasn't. "Ah. That makes sense."

"Yes indeed," Jonathan agreed. "You could say our biological connection's irrelevant."

He'd said they should all be honest with each other. There were things Madeleine couldn't say—not yet—but if they were putting cards on the table, why not ask this? "Hæra, to tell the truth, Harry Duggan at the Merryweather told me you were Jonathan's daughter before I even met you."

Jonathan groaned but did not interrupt.

"He said you made Jonathan turn his life around. But I can't help wondering if that night on the beach didn't do it as well." She turned to Jonathan, who was rubbing his forehead again. "It certainly changed me."

The question was: had it been for the better?

"There's no question but it did," Jonathan said. "You could say if not for that night, I wouldn't have taken the lass in at all."

Hæra nodded, looking unsurprised. They must have talked about this many times.

"Why did it affect you so much?" Madeleine pressed. "Don't get me wrong, I'm glad it did. It looks like you've done something amazing with your life. But from where I'm standing, that night, you just helped me off the beach while I babbled after hitting my head. You didn't see what I did—and you'd be perfectly within your rights not to believe I saw anything at all."

Jonathan exhaled heavily and nodded. "I would be."

"I didn't know what to expect when I found you again…*if* I found you again. I wasn't sure you'd remember me."

"Wouldn't remember a half-drowned nun I found on the beach? I wasn't that drunk," Jonathan objected.

Madeleine sighed. "Sorry. I just didn't think what happened would affect you like it did me." Definitely not to the point where he'd sober up and take in a lost daughter. Madeleine would not look at Hæra again. Not when that long body lounged so alluringly in the chair. "*Did* you see something? I don't remember all the events of that night."

At that, Hæra's gaze snapped onto Madeleine like teeth. "You don't?"

"I had a head injury," Madeleine reminded her. Why had Hæra made it sound like an accusation? "A lot is fuzzy."

"How much do you remember?" Hæra asked, her voice surprisingly sharp.

A perfect, naked woman's body pressed against my own. A kiss like fire.

"It's surprisingly vague," Madeleine mumbled, her cheeks hot. "I woke up on the shore and thought a woman was with me. Then she was gone, and Jonathan showed up."

"That's it?" Hæra sounded disbelieving. "That's all you remember?"

Why was Hæra looking at her like that?

———

Surprisingly vague? No joke. Madeleine only remembered waking up on the shore with a woman who'd then left her behind? Nothing else? That couldn't be all. Why would Madeleine have come all this way for a memory so incomplete?

"What did the woman look like?" Hæra demanded, then wished she hadn't. Talk about a risky question. If Madeleine said, *Come to think of it, she looked like you,* they could head into territory they weren't yet ready for.

"I didn't get a good look at her," Madeleine said. "It was dark, and my head hurt. She looked more like a silhouette than anything."

She sounded a little defensive. Hæra was better than she'd been before at reading those cues, just as she was better at reading books. Best to back down for now. "I see. That makes sense."

"Does it?" Madeleine looked down at her breakfast and pushed around the black pudding patty with her fork. "I don't feel like any of this makes sense. Jonathan, back to my original question…"

Jonathan shifted in his seat, looking uncomfortable. "Why'd it affect me so much, ah, yes." He glanced at Hæra, as if seeking something, but she had no idea what it was. "I don't know what to tell you."

He meant it literally, Hæra realized. Jonathan didn't know what, or how much, to say. He wouldn't give up her secret, *their* secret, until Hæra gave him the go-ahead.

She wasn't ready to do that yet, and she gave him a minute shake of her head.

"You're the only link I've got to that night," Madeleine said. "I don't know where to get answers, other than from you and that beach." She gave Hæra a cool glance. "Which I am going to explore, thank you."

Hæra's hackles rose just as surely as if she were Brodie scenting a predator. "I warned you—"

"I know what you warned me. Of course I have to go back there, and I'll go in broad daylight. I'll be completely safe. I'm sure there will be other people around."

"What do you hope to find there?" Jonathan asked. "Your angel?"

Madeleine blushed. A blush meant the blood was getting closer to your skin. Hæra remembered licking the cut on her forehead, now marked by a scar.

"Yeah," Jonathan said. "I remember what you said, all right."

"Please don't laugh at me," Madeleine said softly.

"I wouldn't. You'd just smacked your head and weren't thinking straight."

Madeleine lifted her head. Hæra watched the proud tilt of her chin with fascination. *Beautiful.*

"I still believe it," she said. "Or at least, I'm willing to believe it. I didn't just say that because of a head injury. That might seem silly to you, but angels are part of my faith."

"No, lassie," Jonathan said quickly. "I don't dismiss you. I'm, ah, willing to believe it could be something supernatural. I don't know about angels *specifically*, but who am I to say?"

He glanced at Hæra, who said, "Who indeed. Sist...that is, Madeleine, what do you believe an angel is?"

Knowing full well that Madeleine had thought Hæra was one, Hæra had combed through the Bible to read about them, but there had been less than she'd thought there would be. If Madeleine had thought Hæra was an angel, what did that mean to her? Surely Hæra hadn't reminded her of those silly pictures of people with wings, haloes, and white robes.

As if reciting from an invisible book, Madeleine said, "Catholic doctrine dictates that angels are servants and messengers of God. They're creatures of pure spirit, not human beings."

Hæra frowned. "Then why do they always look like humans in the pictures?" And did Madeleine believe Hæra had been a *servant of God* while she was lying on top of her, kissing her?

Madeleine chuckled. "Because people relate more to things that are familiar. Scripture actually describes angels as frightening beings of fierce aspect."

"So the woman who found you had a...fierce aspect?" That was *much* better. So much better, in fact, that Hæra settled more back in her chair and grinned at the thought.

Madeleine's cheeks turned red again for some reason. For a moment, she looked Hæra up and down. It had the oddest effect. Madeleine wasn't touching her, but somehow, her eyes on Hæra felt like hands. And not in a displeasing way. Would Madeleine feel the same if Hæra looked at her like that? Would they both feel as if they were touching one another?

Hæra's throat felt thick at the thought. She had to swallow hard as she let her eyes travel over Madeleine in turn, taking in her dark hair, her high cheekbones, and those incredible eyes. The slender throat, the shoulders, the—

"Well then!" Jonathan stood up, and the abrupt movement snapped Hæra out of the haze that had taken her. He brushed his hands together and looked down at the table. "Hæra, why don't you give our guest a proper tour of the farm?"

"What?" Madeleine looked as dazed as Hæra felt.

"Sorry to cut this conversation short, but damned if I didn't just remember I've got to call the abattoir." When Madeleine opened her mouth, as if to protest, Jonathan added, "We can, er, finish later."

Now Madeleine looked lost. "But…"

"We'll talk more. Cross my heart." Jonathan's expression softened. "I dunno if I've got anything to say that'll give you the answers you want, though. I never saw an angel, fierce or otherwise. God's truth."

Madeleine dipped her head. Her shoulders slumped. Hæra had done this herself when she was very tired or sad, and the gesture made her human heart ache. Somehow, years ago, Sister Madeleine had called to Hæra through the fathoms, pleading for her protection. Hæra was fully prepared to shield her from any physical threat. But how could you protect a human from sadness?

Her body acted without her permission again. It acted, once again, to seize Madeleine. But not as it had before. This time, Hæra watched her own hand reach across the table to take hold of Madeleine's where it sat next to her plate. Madeleine's hand was smaller than her own, warm, and softer than any human skin Hæra had ever touched.

Now Hæra's face was getting hot. Heat was, in fact, spreading through her whole body. How strange.

Madeleine stared at her, eyes wide.

"There's no need for sorrow." The words were whispers. Hæra's voice inexplicably wanted to be as gentle as if she were coaxing a newborn lamb to its feet. "We'll find the answers you seek. I swear it."

Madeleine looked down toward their joined hands as if she'd never seen anything like them.

"Come with me," Hæra urged. Since she couldn't show Madeleine the sea—at least, not yet—the land would have to do. "The sun's coming out for once. It'll be a beautiful day."

"Yes." Madeleine's voice sounded as thick as Hæra's had a few moments ago. Her hand, for a moment, trembled beneath Hæra's. "Looks like it will be."

CHAPTER SIXTEEN

JUST THINK, Madeleine had been disappointed only a few minutes ago.

More than disappointed. Closer to crushed. With only a few words, Jonathan had knocked down her hopes that he could provide the answers she needed. She'd been telling herself for years to prepare for that possibility. After all, what could he have seen from such a distance, in the dark? She'd *known* that. She'd even told herself there were no guarantees that he'd be here at all when she returned.

Hope had kept her in a stranglehold, though. He was the only human link she had to that night, and he'd had plenty of his own questions at the time. Part of her had always hoped he'd seek answers too and would have them ready for her when she arrived.

But Jonathan had no answers, only sympathy. That was one avenue closed to Madeleine. The others were all in shadow and seemed strewn with rocks. For a second, after he'd told her he couldn't help, her chest had caved in.

Then, Hæra's hand.

Now, Madeleine sat in the passenger seat of a two-seater, four-wheeled utility vehicle called a "Gator" that rumbled and bumped over uneven ground. She bounced in the seat while Hæra drove across the fields with cheerful abandon. Hæra's dark ponytail flew behind her in the wind, and her cheeks were reddened in the fresh air.

At least the fields in daytime didn't look anything like the darksome plain of Madeleine's dream. The sun was indeed coming out today. Beneath its light, patches of grass flashed in different colors: neatly segmented squares of green and yellow.

She asked Hæra, raising her voice over the motor, "Why are some of those grass squares green and some yellow?"

"From moving the sheep from field to field during the summer months," Hæra called back. "So we can cut silage."

"What's silage?"

"Grass for the winter. We ferment and store it. It doesn't smell nice, but it's worse when we spread the slurry. We don't hang the washing outside then."

"Slurry?" Madeleine asked, with a feeling she already knew.

"It's mostly shite," Hæra confirmed. Then she glanced at Madeleine with a frown. "That's how the farmhands speak. Would you prefer I spoke otherwise?"

"Uh—" The Gator bounced into a large dip in the ground. "I'd prefer if you kept your eyes on the road!"

"There's nothing to hit," Hæra said reassuringly, although she looked forward again. "See? The sheep are farther up ahead. And we're not really on a road."

"That's what I mean." Madeleine set her jaw against another bump. "You could knock the axle clean off if you're not careful. Or fall out." The Gator didn't have seat belts, just metal hip restraints that didn't feel very protective right now.

Hæra's mouth pursed, and she looked thoughtful. "Are you concerned for my safety?"

That was an odd question from a woman obsessed with the dangers of a beach. "Of course I don't want you to fall. Especially with me in the passenger seat."

Hæra's eyes widened. Then she took her foot off the accelerator, and the Gator slowed down. Before Madeleine could exhale in relief, Hæra said, "I wouldn't let you come to harm. We'll slow down."

Madeleine's right hand—the one Hæra had taken in her own minutes ago—tingled. So did the rest of her skin. She managed, "Thanks."

"Of course. What do you think of the farm?"

Madeleine looked around at the rolling fields, dotted with sheep and, separately, cattle. It resembled the other farms she'd seen while island-hopping. Indeed, most of Orkney seemed, to her untrained eyes, to be pasture. Jorsay had definitely been the odd island out in that regard the last time she was here. "It's beautiful, especially on a sunny day. Jonathan started it five years ago?"

"Jonathan *and* I started it," Hæra corrected.

Madeleine winced. "Oh, of course. Sorry. I just meant..."

Hæra's lips twitched into a little smile, although she kept her eyes straight ahead. "That Jonathan masterminded this whole enterprise and his bastard's just along for the ride?"

Her hands clutched the hip restraint even harder. The metal dug into her palms, as if grounding her from the embarrassment. "I'd never have said that!"

"No. But would you have meant it?" Now Hæra cast her a shrewd glance.

Oh...darn it. Madeleine sighed. "I guess that's what I was thinking, in less colorful language."

"'Colorful'? Oh, I see what you mean." Hæra guided the Gator into two well-worn tire tracks in the grass. "You'd be wrong. I gave Jonathan the money for the farm."

That was certainly unexpected. Madeleine would have to revise, yet again, her opinion of Hæra. "Because he...took you in?"

There was a pause. Hæra looked ahead, as if mapping out her answer, which meant it wouldn't be straightforward. Madeleine had taught enough high schoolers to recognize someone searching for an explanation. She didn't think Hæra was lying about funding the farm. That said, it obviously wasn't so simple.

"Yes and no," Hæra said. "I gave Jonathan the money before I moved here. It was part of an arrangement between us. A year later, I came to him, and he bought the land. We started the farm together."

There was more to the story. So much more. To her astonishment, Madeleine found herself ravenous for it. Why? When Harry Duggan had tried to gossip yesterday, she hadn't been able to escape fast enough. The carrot Hæra dangled in front of her, however, was impossible not to grasp at. She could ask, couldn't she? They were talking about it, weren't they? Hæra could tell her if she didn't want to talk about it. She seemed blunt enough for that.

"You mentioned other family," Madeleine said. "Where do you come from originally, if not Orkney?"

Again, Hæra hesitated. Then she said, "My family were nomadic. I'm not really 'from' anywhere."

"Nomadic? Are you Romani?" The Roma encountered plenty of prejudice, which might explain Hæra's reluctance to go into more detail. It also might explain her accent, which was subtly different from Jonathan's and other native islanders'. Hæra's accent was lower, *sharper*. It sounded like the rhythms of the sea.

"No," Hæra said, putting paid to that theory.

When no more information seemed forthcoming, Madeleine said, "It must have been a challenge to settle down here."

"You have no idea," Hæra said dryly. "I grew up roaming with my h...family, and now I rarely leave the farm." Before Madeleine could ask about that, she added, "And you? Did you grow up in your convent?"

"Goodness, no." Outsiders had such strange ideas about nuns. "I was born in New Orleans. I didn't join the Daughters of Grace until after I graduated college. Most orders require postulants to be at least eighteen, preferably a little older."

"New Orleans," Hæra said slowly, as if testing the words. "A city in the United States."

A famous one, yes. Madeleine had never met anyone who hadn't heard of it. Hæra sounded uncertain, though. What had her education been like? If her family had been nomadic, as she'd said, maybe she'd bounced from school to school. Or maybe she'd been homeschooled. Or not schooled at all. It might also explain why she was so...shaky when it came to the social graces.

Under those circumstances, where on earth had she found the money to start a farm? Probably nothing Hæra would want to tell or Madeleine ought to know. She seemed to be living a respectable life now. Everyone deserved a second chance.

"New Orleans is pretty famous—or infamous—for being a party town," she said. "The motto is 'Let the good times roll.'"

"A party?" Madeleine could have sworn Hæra's ears pricked up. "That sounds like fun."

"It depends on your idea of fun. For me—"

"Ah! Look!"

Without further warning, Hæra swerved the Gator off the path. Madeleine yelped and grabbed the hip restraint tighter.

"Just a moment." Hæra drove a little way over the grass before putting on the brakes. Then she pointed at a small mound in the grass. "See that?"

Madeleine, still catching her breath, squinted at the mound. There didn't seem to be anything special about it. "What is it?"

"Some say a trow lives there."

Madeleine vaguely remembered that word from researching the island before the school trip. "Trow...that's some kind of little monster, right?"

Hæra frowned. "The word 'monster' isn't called for, is it?"

She seemed genuinely offended. Madeleine could think of nothing to say other than, "Oh. Sorry."

"Many legends surround trows. They're quite mysterious. Do you believe in mysterious things?"

Madeleine immediately thought of the mysteries of the rosary: the birth of Jesus, his resurrection, and so on. It wasn't what Hæra meant, but it was still about believing in what you didn't understand. When you got down to it, was a mythical creature all that different from...

What was she thinking? Was an imaginary trow the same thing as the life of Christ? Madeleine touched the crucifix on her breast, another kind of apology. "I do. Mysteries are part of my faith."

"Your faith?" Hæra turned off the motor. In the absence of its rumble, the wind whispered through the grass and seabirds cried in the distance. "Let's talk about that."

She leaned forward eagerly, closer into Madeleine's space. Now it was easier to see the color of her eyes. In the morning light, there was no trace of the yellow tint Madeleine had seen the night before. Today, Hæra's eyes were a bright amber with gold flecks near the pupils. And they were no less intense than they'd ever been.

"Talk about my faith?" Madeleine croaked, heart racing in a way that had nothing to do with Hæra's awful driving.

"Yes. I've read your Bible, and I have a lot of questions. Since you're a…well, you *used* to be a nun, I thought you could answer them." Interest lit Hæra's eyes. "That's what you believe in, isn't it?"

Would every conversation with this woman end in Madeleine's head spinning like a top? "Yes, of course, although it's much more complicated—"

"Excellent!" Hæra slapped her thighs with her palms. They looked like firm, strong thighs. "Let's start with Genesis."

"Most things do," Madeleine said weakly.

"How was there light on the first day of creation, but God made the sun and stars later? And why are there two different passages of him creating animals? And if the first man and woman were the only people on Earth, then how did their children have children of their own? Did they only mate with each other?" Hæra quirked up an eyebrow. "That leads to weak offspring, you know."

At least these were questions Madeleine had encountered many times before, especially while teaching high school students. "Some people take every word of Scripture literally, but I never advocated for that—nor did my order. Scripture is inerrant in spiritual truth, not scientific fact. We should see it as inspired by God, but written by men."

Hæra blinked. "No women?"

"Nope," Madeleine said dryly. "Although there are female saints and scholars. Honestly, Catholics don't spend as much time on the Bible as you'd think."

Hæra frowned. "You don't?"

"No. We've got the *Catechism,* the lives of the saints, Augustine's *Confessions,* and so much—"

"But the Bible's all I've read!" Hæra flung herself back in the seat, looking as incredulous as Madeleine felt. "You're telling me there's *more?*"

It was so absurd, so out of left field, that Madeleine laughed. "Yes, a lot more. It can answer some of those questions you're asking."

Hæra scowled. "I don't want other books to answer my questions. I want to ask you. It took me years to read that stupid thing."

Now that was *really* rude. Madeleine lifted her chin and kept her voice cool. "Tell you what. I won't call a trow a 'monster' if you don't insult something sacred to me."

Hæra pursed her lips and looked away. The wind whipped at her ponytail, teasing loose, dark tendrils of hair around her pale face and sharp cheekbones. "Very well. I'm sorry."

Madeleine stared at her. Madeleine shouldn't stare at her. Was she really sitting here talking about her faith when she couldn't resist thoughts that ran so counter to it? What right did she have to get on her high horse when last night, she'd dreamed about Hæra taking her in her arms and...

"It's okay," she whispered. "I do have doubts from time to time."

———

The low, shaky note in Madeleine's voice brought Hæra out of the sulk she'd just fallen into. To think she'd spent years making her way through that horribly long, strange book, only to learn it didn't even matter that much!

But it was hard to sulk when Madeleine was biting her bottom lip. Ordinarily, that would have occupied Hæra's full attention, if not for the distress that accompanied the gesture. It was time to say something kind and understanding.

"Of course you have doubts," she said. "Those stories don't make any sense."

"No, not about that," Madeleine said, her voice still low. She wasn't making eye contact with Hæra anymore. "I told you, they're not all to be taken literally. Never mind. Let's keep looking at the farm."

They had all day to look at the farm, and it was harder to talk while driving. It would be even harder while surrounded by animals and other farmhands. Hæra said, "Soon. Tell me about your doubts."

Madeleine's brow creased. "Why do you want to know about my doubts?"

Because I want to know everything about you. "What we don't believe matters as much as what we do. But it's in the middle where things get interesting." She'd known that all her life. She'd always been one to question the traditions of the herd, and later, many things about human existence too. "If we don't doubt or question what we've been told, we don't learn. Haven't you found that's true?"

Madeleine looked stunned at Hæra's words, for some reason. "The *Catechism* teaches the difference between voluntary and involuntary doubt. One is a sin, and the other—"

"I didn't ask what the *Cat*...thing teaches," Hæra said impatiently. "I asked what you think." A dreadful thought occurred to her. "Or don't you question it? Do you just believe whatever it says?"

"I was taught its precepts when I was a little girl, and I dedicated my entire life to following them for fifteen years," Madeleine said between her teeth.

"But then you left." A question occurred to Hæra. "Why did you join the Daughters of Grace in the first place?"

She'd never wondered that before. Years ago, when she'd overheard Sister Madeleine talking to the girl Ava on the beach, Madeleine had spoken of her "calling" to the order as if it was a fact of her existence. But now she'd left that same order, so that couldn't be the case.

"That's a personal question." Madeleine had her hands clasped tightly in her lap. "Especially given how, last night, you judged me for leaving it."

"I said I'd apologize for that if you wanted me to," Hæra reminded her. "Do you?"

After a moment, Madeleine said, "That'd be nice, actually. Yes."

"I'm sorry," Hæra said promptly. "I shouldn't have done that. Now please tell me why you joined the Daughters of Grace."

Madeleine looked at her without saying anything. Then, suddenly, she shook her head and laughed. Her smile flashed like whitecaps on a rough ocean. She propped her elbow on the back of the seat and rested her head against it, her dark hair mussed from the wind. "You're something else," she said, grinning.

Sweat broke out in Hæra's palms and lower back. *Something else.* Could Madeleine see Hæra wasn't what she pretended to be? "What do you mean?"

"You don't even know me, and you're asking me the most intimate questions about my life."

That could have been a lot worse. Hæra rejoined, "That's how I'll *get* to know you. How can I know you if we don't talk about anything…intimate?"

Madeleine's cheeks turned pink again. Maybe it was because of the wind. Her grin faded into a smaller, more quizzical smile. "Why do you want to get to know me? I guess you don't meet a lot of new people out here. Is it because I'm different? From somewhere far away?"

It wasn't clear how to respond to that. Hæra probably shouldn't say, *I want to know you because you pulled me out of the ocean and turned me into someone else, and somehow you've got to be the answer to everything, and when you belong to me, my life will make sense again.*

"Would that be a bad reason?" she asked cautiously.

"Not really. You just come on a little strong, that's all. What happened to asking someone about their favorite color?"

That seemed much less interesting, but if that was the path Madeleine wanted to walk, they'd walk it. Maybe it would lead to wider roads. "What's your favorite color?"

"Green," Madeleine said promptly. She looked around at the green fields and grass. "It's the color of things waking up when winter's over. It's the color of life."

Strange. For Hæra, red was the color of life: the blood a creature lost when giving birth, or what prey spilled before it nourished the predator. However, it made sense that Madeleine would have a different perspective. "Green's the color of your eyes, too," Hæra said, then wished she hadn't, because she hadn't meant to, and Madeleine knew the color of her own eyes. A useless observation.

Indeed, Madeleine didn't seem to know how to respond to it. In fact, she looked away, taking the color of her eyes with her.

Hæra cursed herself. "Was that inappropriate?" she asked.

"What? No, of course not." Madeleine cleared her throat. "What's *your* favorite color?"

Hæra had seen every color in the sea. Anemones clothed in red and purple; iridescent fish; the stark black-and-white of orcas; the mottled hides of seals and selkies. She couldn't choose, although she had to say something to Madeleine.

Suddenly, she remembered the seventh day she'd spent on land after her exile. It was sinking in that she wasn't leaving any time soon, she had no idea when Sister Madeleine would return, and she had to adjust to a foreign way of life. Despair had set in, and she'd left Jonathan's cottage with no objective in mind.

Then she'd seen the rainbow.

Her father had told her about rainbows, but she'd never seen one in any of her trips to the surface. Hadn't known that something so lovely could arch between heavy gray clouds. Other than Sister Madeleine, it had been the most beautiful thing she'd ever seen.

"I love all the colors," she said softly. "But especially when they're together. Rainbows are best."

For some reason, Madeleine looked delighted. "Now there's a great Bible story! Noah and the rainbow. God's promise of renewal."

"That was a sad story," Hæra objected.

"Well, yes, it's been argued that it was cruel to destroy most of humanity, but remember—don't take it literally."

That wasn't the part Hæra found sad. It had seemed a shame to get rid of all that lovely water that had covered the world. "I don't."

Madeleine shifted in her seat, appearing uncomfortable. That made sense—the padding wasn't the best. "Since we're asking…intimate questions, are you a Christian? What with reading the whole Bible and everything."

"No," Hæra said flatly. "I read it because I had to." Or so she'd thought. She evidently should have been reading Madeleine's—what did she call it? That *Catechism* instead.

"Oh." Madeleine winced. "Your family made you? When you were growing up?"

Hæra nearly laughed as she imagined Beathag's reaction to the Bible. That was a telling question, though. Maybe Madeleine's family had made *her* read it. "I think we've talked about my family enough for now. I'm glad to be rid of them, and that's that. What about yours?"

A shadow passed over Madeleine's bright eyes, and it had nothing to do with the fluffy white clouds overhead. "That's a sad story too. They're gone."

Hæra was about to ask, *Gone where?* when she remembered that sometimes humans used that as a euphemism. Maybe Madeleine was doing that.

"Do you mean they're dead?" she asked, to clarify.

Madeleine laughed shortly, although Hæra hadn't been joking. "You're blunt, too. That's okay. Yes, they're dead. My parents died in a car accident when I was sixteen, and my brother was fourteen. He… didn't cope well. Overdosed when I was twenty-one."

Overdosed. That meant drugs. It showed up in the *Orcadian* occasionally, and Jonathan always said it was a pity. Hæra wondered why Madeleine had joined the Daughters of Grace after the tragedy, instead of making another family with a mate and a child.

It seemed to be another way Madeleine and Hæra were similar, at least. "I'm sorry. That sounds hard."

"It was. Is. I don't talk about it often. They're in a better place now, and we'll see each other again someday."

That wasn't what Hæra's species believed. Hæra had been taught that when the Last Current took her, she'd feed other creatures in the ocean just as they'd fed her. That had always been enough. While it would be nice to see her father again, she had no desire to reunite with Beathag and Asgall after she'd finally gotten rid of them for good.

Plainly, Madeleine would take no comfort from that observation. She held her lips in a thin line, as if she was trying to smile but couldn't manage it. She was sad again. Hæra had made her sad. Just as in the kitchen, it was unbearable. Hæra's body leaned forward, pulled, helpless. This time, she rested her hand on Madeleine's forearm, atop her jacket sleeve.

Madeleine inhaled, softly.

Hæra wouldn't say something she didn't believe like, *Yes, you'll see them again.* There were enough lies between them already. This time, she could say something true.

"Life is very hard," she said. "But there are pleasures too. We've got rainbows, haven't we?"

Madeleine's full mouth opened, but nothing came out. Then she managed, "Rainbows, yes. Those are…great."

The sadness had left her face. Therefore, Hæra should let go of her. She tried to. But her human hand didn't want to relax. In fact, it wanted to grip Madeleine harder. Pull her closer. "I suppose we got pretty intimate," she said hoarsely.

Madeleine looked into Hæra's eyes. Her own eyes were wide. Her voice was barely audible when she replied, "We did."

Her arm was rigid, stiff, in Hæra's grip. Like last night, she didn't try to pull free, but she'd also told Hæra not to seize her. And here Hæra was, doing it again.

Curse it. Could she not learn? Hæra let go. "I apologize for grabbing you again."

"Um." Madeleine shook her head, looking as if she'd just woken up from sleep. She touched her forearm where Hæra's hand had just been. "That's okay. It was different. I know you were just trying to…" Her voice trailed off.

At least one of them knew what Hæra had been trying to do. It was time to restart the tour before she did something even more inexplicable.

Her eyes lit on the trow mound. Hopefully he had no idea what was happening just outside his home. He'd laugh his little head off, and then Hæra would have to rip it from his shoulders and the farm would lose his blessing.

"Let's go," she said, and turned the key. The motor rumbled to life. "There's plenty left to see."

CHAPTER SEVENTEEN

Madeleine was a city girl: born and raised in New Orleans, completing her novitiate in New York, and settling down at Sacred Heart in Philadelphia. She'd worked in community gardens and so on, but that was the extent of her experience with agriculture.

She'd had no idea how much work went into running a farm. If you'd asked her, she'd have said that of course it must be a hard life, but seeing it up close was different. Morning to night, there was always something to do.

The work changed from season to season. From Hæra she learned that the summer was for fattening up the lambs for sale. In autumn, rams would be put out to breed with ewes. The ewes were gravid throughout winter, and March to April was lambing season. Shearing began in May, and then summer arrived and the cycle started again.

It sounded exhausting, but in some respects it was similar to the life Madeleine had left: a routine that kept people busy all day. A chance to put in hard work and then see the fruits of it. And a community of people to share it with.

At the barn, Hæra introduced her to the full-time farmhands. Jim was a lanky man who looked to be in his early thirties. Connor seemed older than Madeleine, stocky and at ease in his environment.

The men were clearly curious about her, but Connor only said that it was nice to have a visitor, and Jim said he hoped she had a good time on the islands. No questions—the opposite of Harry Duggan.

Perversely, this made Madeleine more forthcoming. Was there anything more likely to draw you out of yourself than someone who wasn't nosy? "Thank you," she said. "I'll be on Jorsay for a month."

Connor and Jim glanced at each other, raising their eyebrows. But Connor only said, "Ah, lovely."

Maybe Hæra's presence prevented them from inquiring further. She stood with crossed arms and feet planted wide. She was taller than all three of them, and she seemed to loom. Madeleine had the impression she didn't want the conversation to go on too long.

"Well," she said, fighting against her own awkwardness, "I don't know a lot about farms, but this looks like an impressive operation."

That drew the first real smiles from both of them. "Aye, we're proud of it," Connor said. "It's backbreaking and that, but worth it."

"Have you always farmed?"

"All my life. Da was a crofter on Stronsay but gave it up when my brothers went to work at the oil terminal. Better money there, but it's not for me. Word went out that this new farm needed some hands, and I came out here. It's done better than any new farm's got a right to."

"I can see the work that goes into it," Madeleine said. "And the pride, too."

His smile broadened. He was handsome, with warm brown eyes and a strong jaw. The sort of man Madeleine had tried to find attractive, long ago. However devastating her recent revelation was, it was a relief not to have to try.

"Jim's getting married," Hæra said abruptly.

They all turned to her, but she was only looking at Madeleine, her eyes narrowed and arms still crossed.

At a loss, Madeleine said to Jim, "Congratulations. When's the day?"

"Next month," Jim said, evidently more willing to talk about himself than inquire into Madeleine's business. Madeleine didn't know much about men, but this did seem typical of them. He looked over his shoulder and pointed. "I'm moving out of there in a couple of weeks. It'll be nice to have more room."

Connor chuckled and clapped his shoulder. "Just so long as you don't expect to have any of your own things, only hers."

"At least I'll live somewhere civilized..."

Madeleine tuned out their ribbing as she looked where Jim had pointed. It was the small stone cottage at the edge of the pasture, the one she'd noticed last night.

"Jonathan used to live there."

Madeleine nearly jumped at how close Hæra's voice was to her ear. She turned away from the cottage to see that Hæra had stepped forward until her long body was nearly touching Madeleine's.

Madeleine's mouth went dry. She'd just gotten her composure back after that...intimate...conversation, for heaven's sake. Could Hæra not grant her a single moment's peace?

But did Madeleine even want peace anymore, when her dream last night had felt like freedom instead?

"He lived there when I arrived," Hæra continued, her voice strangely intense for factual conversation. "Then we dwelled there together until the farm was a going concern. It was the first place I lived here."

Connor and Jim were still joking with each other, not listening, and it gave Madeleine the courage to say, "You must have mixed memories of it." When Hæra frowned, she clarified, "Because it wasn't easy for you to settle here. A challenge, as we said."

"It's a good cottage," Hæra said. "You'd be comfortable there."

"Huh? Why would—"

"Ah, sorry," Connor said, still chuckling, yanking both Madeleine and Hæra out of the moment. "Didn't mean to be rude. I just like to remind this one he doesn't know what he's getting into."

Madeleine summoned a smile. "You're a married man yourself?"

"Aye. I'm just blowing smoke up his arse. It'll be grand." He patted Jim's shoulder again.

"It's good to have a bond with the most important person to you," Hæra said. "Something that lasts all your lives."

Now both Connor and Jim looked surprised. Clearly, Hæra had never said such a thing to them before. After a moment, Connor said, "Ah, right."

"Madeleine's Catholic," Hæra continued. "Jonathan told me once that when Catholics start being married, they never stop."

Madeleine's eyes widened. That was one way to put it.

"Ah, so they don't." Jim rubbed his hands over his denim-covered thighs. "Well, that's lovely. Now I've got a peedie lamb that needs a supplement. Pleased to meet you, Madeleine."

"Likewise," said Connor. "Enjoy the island."

Jim began, "Hæra, are you going to—"

"Madeleine and I will finish the tour," Hæra said. "After that, we'll have lunch and settle on something for the afternoon."

They would? Hæra was commandeering her entire day without asking Madeleine about it, as if she had a right to Madeleine's hours. For someone so much Madeleine's junior, she was certainly…authoritative.

They'd see about that. Madeleine said crisply, "I wouldn't keep you from your work, Hæra. I'll have that beach walk this afternoon. Connor, Jim, it was nice to meet you."

She turned and marched back to the Gator, which Hæra had parked next to a tractor. Madeleine had never been close to a real tractor before. She'd had no idea how big they were. She'd had no idea about lots of things.

Hæra's footsteps sounded behind her. Madeleine didn't turn around to look at her. Better to take a moment to collect herself. Hæra was arrogant. Presumptuous. Young. Horrifyingly insightful.

If we don't doubt things or question what we've been told, we don't learn.

Doubt was an essential part of faith. It was also the worst part, and right now it was sucking around Madeleine's ankles like quicksand. She'd come here to escape it, not be pulled deeper. But Hæra had spoken of it as if she'd seen right to the heart of Madeleine's struggle, when they didn't even know each other. Hæra wanted to get to know her, though. It was—it must be—out of pure curiosity. It shouldn't make Madeleine ache deep inside, warming the cold place where her doubts sat.

She sat down in the passenger seat with a huff. Hopefully this tour would be over soon. Then she could take her walk on the beach, *alone*, away from maddening women with long legs.

The Gator dipped as Hæra got back in the driver's seat. Instead of turning the key, she turned to look at Madeleine. "Did I offend you?"

There were polite ways to brush that off that still meant *yes*. But it was clear, after the last hour or so, that Hæra preferred things to be more direct. "I don't like how you decreed what I'll be doing for the rest of the day instead of asking me what I'd like to do."

"But…" Hæra ran a hand over her head, smoothing down the black strands. The breeze ruffled them again instantly. "You're enjoying the tour, aren't you? I assumed you'd like to keep doing it."

"You know what they say about assumptions," Madeleine said, a little snappishly, because she'd noticed that Hæra had long fingers. When Hæra looked confused, she added, "They make an ass out of you and me."

Hæra's eyes widened. "I am *not* an ass. They have no dignity! Although…" She frowned and looked thoughtful. "They're relatively intelligent and have good memories. I could do worse."

Before Madeleine could splutter out a response, Hæra's frown softened into a little smile. Her eyes gleamed with mischief as she said, "Thanks for the compliment."

Madeleine's heart began pounding again. "I might not know much about you, but I know you're impossible."

"You wouldn't be the first to think so." Hæra turned the key in the ignition. "But I'm more than possible. I'm here. And you don't know much about me *yet*." She turned her gaze on Madeleine, and it sharpened again. "How much will you learn, I wonder?"

How dry could a mouth get? "You're pretty full of yourself if you think I'm dying to learn about you. I came here to learn about something else entirely, and it's got nothing to do with you."

There was no need to mention that Madeleine had already learned a little something about herself, thanks to Hæra. She hadn't come here to uncover her sexuality, but life was full of surprises.

"It seems to me you don't know what you're here to learn," Hæra said. How could such an odd person be able to slice through to the heart of things? "It's a mystery, like we were talking about before. I think you should be open to every possibility. How else can you find whatever you're looking for?"

Before Madeleine could reply, Hæra pulled away from the barn, driving back toward the fields. "There's a nice view from the top of that hill. You can see most of the island, and you'll never find a better day for it."

"Is that the last part of the tour?" Madeleine asked desperately, holding on to the hip restraint again.

"Yes. I wanted to save this for last. It's the best part." Hæra gave a sudden little gasp. "Oh! Do you know the song 'Save the Best for Last' by Vanessa Williams? Jonathan played that for me sometime after I arrived. It's very good."

"Um, yes, I—"

"What's your favorite song? That's a good question, isn't it? Not too intimate."

One thing was for sure: this morning wasn't turning out like Madeleine had expected.

———

Hæra was relieved to find the question was, in fact, not too intimate. In fact, she learned that Madeleine divided songs into two groups: hymns and secular songs. Madeleine didn't want to pick a secular song because she liked too many, but she did admit she loved "Landslide" by Fleetwood Mac—one of Jonathan's favorites too. "Agnus Dei" was her top hymn.

As for Hæra, she liked all kinds of music, even the bad kind. Like when Jonathan played the fiddle while Hæra sang tunes she'd learned from him; he said they both sounded bloody awful, but she didn't see why it mattered when they had such a fine time.

"What does 'Agnus Dei' mean?" Hæra asked as she pulled the parking brake. They'd reached the top of the hill.

"It's Latin. It means 'lamb of God.'" Madeleine climbed out of the Gator "as if her arse was on fire," as Jonathan might have put it. Maybe Hæra had been driving too fast again.

"Lamb of God," Hæra mused, casting her gaze down to the grazing sheep, none of whom had wandered to the top of the hill yet. "There's a lot in your Bible about shepherds taking care of sheep. Do you like sheep?" Hæra hoped so. She'd been working on that assumption for five years. According to Madeleine, assumptions were bad.

It had given her a chance to tease Madeleine, though. Hæra didn't tease people often, not even Jonathan. It had felt…nice. A bit like stroking a fluffy cat.

"I've never been around them," Madeleine said, dashing yet another hope. "Not real sheep, I mean. The Bible's talking about people, not animals."

"Well, you can't farm people," Hæra growled as she hopped out of the Gator.

"Scripture draws the distinction between sheep and goats." Madeleine kept her back to Hæra as she looked around. "Sheep are obedient to the will of God. Goats are defiant."

This felt like uncertain ground. "Goats are smarter, too. Or are you still talking about people?"

"I don't know. I'm starting to wonder if I ever knew what I was talking about." Madeleine hugged herself and began to walk toward the far edge of the hill. The grass, longer up here without grazing sheep, brushed against her ankles. "Never mind that."

Hæra strode after her. "It sounds important."

"It is." Madeleine's voice was rough, a breaker against sandstone. "Too important to talk about now. Don't you ever want to think about things before you start talking about them?"

Hæra had been thinking for five years about what she'd say to Madeleine, how much she would reveal, and she still wasn't sure. "Sometimes." Now, of all times, the urge to tease Madeleine returned. "On special occasions."

Madeleine gave her a quick, startled-looking glance. Hæra couldn't help grinning at her. How could she? The sun was out, lighting the edges of Madeleine's dark hair. It changed the color of her eyes too, from the shallows of the sea to the paler grass all around them. You had to smile at something so beautiful.

"Um." Madeleine began to play with her jacket's zip, which she'd drawn all the way up to her chin. "This is...you were right. It's a great view."

Hæra raised her eyebrows. "Are you sure?"

"Huh?"

"You're not looking at it."

Madeleine's breath caught, and she turned away at once. This time, Hæra didn't mind. The sun seemed to have lit in her own chest. Right now, nothing could be finer than standing in this light, at the top of this hill, with this woman.

No, that wasn't true. It would be even finer if Hæra could touch her—slide her arm around Madeleine's shoulders as she'd seen Jim do with Isla. Could she? Madeleine hadn't objected earlier when Hæra had touched her hand, and later her forearm.

Then, Madeleine stepped away again, and the question was moot. "You really can see everything."

True. Because Hæra couldn't put her hands on Madeleine, she put them on her own hips and looked around. From the top of this hill, the green land of Jorsay rolled, stretching out toward the cliffs and shore.

The sea surrounded them on all sides. Whitecaps glistened in the distance, and milky foam sluiced over the sand and rocks of the shore. This far inland, on a sunny day with no storms, no *Each-uisge* would see Hæra. From here, she could look upon her former home. Would it ever be her home again? Would she return to prove herself, earn her wings, and take a place of honor in the herd? If she did, the Sire would pardon her, and Beathag and Asgall would never hurt her again. She wouldn't have to mate, and she'd have her full strength back. It was what she'd always wanted.

Once she returned to the sea, she'd never stand on this hill again with the wind in her hair. She'd never have another cup of cold, salty tea while Jonathan played his fiddle. And if she acted too soon, she might not learn why Madeleine had left the Daughters of Grace. Yes, by eating her, she'd make Madeleine a part of her forever. But it wouldn't be like this.

Hæra set her jaw. What was the point of thinking about that? She couldn't stay in human form forever, as Jonathan was always reminding her. This was her only way off Jorsay and away from human questions that would, eventually, be the end of her.

She didn't have to worry about it for a month. That was how long Madeleine planned to stay. Maybe she could even be persuaded to stay longer. That should be plenty of time to work out...whatever Hæra had to work out.

"There's my beach."

Madeleine pointed north, in the direction of Thornhill Village. Hæra held her breath as she followed Madeleine's gaze. Madeleine probably couldn't make out the actual stretch of beach from here, but it had been just outside the village. As for Hæra, she could see the rocks, lapped by the slowly rising tide. Rocks where her human feet had first touched the land after she'd dragged Sister Madeleine's limp body ashore.

Madeleine must be remembering the same thing, with no idea that she stood right next to the creature who had saved her.

"I know the one you mean," Hæra said. "Er, Jonathan told me. Can you see it from here?"

"I can't, but I know where it is. I can *feel* where it is." Madeleine hugged herself again, as if a human body was something that could escape its owner. "Like there's something pulling me there. Does that sound impossible?"

Not impossible, but alarming. The last thing Hæra needed was for Madeleine to be "pulled" to the beach where both their lives had changed.

It was daytime, though. A sunny day, no less. *Each-uisge* were least likely to approach the surface under these conditions. Maybe Hæra could go to the beach for the first time in years and feel her strength return with every step. She didn't have to be afraid of...

Finish her, Calder said in her memory. Her mother's teeth had torn into her hide, and Asgall taunted her as he closed in.

"It's not exactly sane," Hæra said brusquely. "I can't imagine approaching that piece of land after what happened to you."

"Good thing you're not the one approaching it," Madeleine snapped. "You might think it's a bad idea, but I'm going anyway."

"What? Alone?" Of all possibilities, Hæra had never imagined that one—Madeleine walking the beach, *their* beach, without her.

"Am I supposed to go with a tour group?" Madeleine waved a hand in the air. "'And here, folks, is the most mysterious beach in Orkney. If you ever want to see an angel, this is the place!'"

"I doubt a tour guide would say that."

"That's my *point.* I can't do this with anybody else looking at me and wondering what on earth I'm doing. Even Jonathan doesn't know what happened."

Hæra bit her lip. Her public relationship with Jonathan was built on lies. Now, thanks to her, he'd told another one. He didn't like it, she knew, but what else was there to do?

"You shouldn't go alone," she said. "If there really is something supernatural at work, then you'd just be tempting fate. It's dangerous."

"Oh? I had no idea."

"You don't have to be sarcastic. I'm concerned for your safety. Just as you were concerned for mine before." And how that had warmed Hæra, like the sun after she'd surfaced from the depths.

For some reason, Madeleine looked astonished yet again. No reason for it, though. Didn't it make sense that such feelings should be reciprocated? "Why?" Madeleine said.

"What?"

"Why are you concerned for my safety? Why's it such a big deal to you that I want to go walking on a beach in the middle of a sunny day when there are people around? You don't know me." Madeleine added sharply, "No matter how many *intimate* questions you've asked."

"Er..." Madeleine had made a point about speaking bluntly. Now that the shells were on the other hoof, Hæra found herself at a loss. Yet again, she couldn't tell the truth.

She could tell something like it, though. "As I understand it, people are meant to care for one another. Not to be alone in the world. Wouldn't you want to keep someone from harm even if you didn't know them?"

Madeleine's breath caught. She looked down at the ground. Then she said, in a low voice, "You're right. We're put here to love our neighbors. It's easy to forget that." She sighed. "Thanks for reminding me."

"You're welcome," Hæra said, since that was the appropriate response to thanks. "Must you see the beach today? You're here for an entire month."

"That's true." Madeleine looked toward the ocean again. Hæra followed her gaze. She really was pinpointing the exact location, beyond what a human should be able to see. Could it be true that the beach was calling to her? "I guess I don't have to go charging all over the island in search of answers right this second."

"Yes," Hæra said in relief.

"The truth tends to find you when you're not looking for it," Madeleine continued. "Maybe I could use a little time to…uh, absorb what I've already learned."

Hæra frowned. As far as she could tell, Madeleine was frustrated by not having learned anything yet. "What's that?"

"Something about myself. They say travel's got a way of doing that. I'm sure you'd know, if you were raised…nomadically? Is that a word?"

As far as Hæra was concerned, it could be. "Sure."

"Right! So the more we see of the world, the more we learn." Madeleine's smile was bright now, but it didn't entirely reach her eyes. Hæra hadn't known until now that human smiles could or couldn't do that. "What's the most interesting thing *you* learned in all your travels?"

I learned that you existed. I learned that I could become more than I ever thought was possible. I learned what grass and sand feel like beneath my feet.

"I don't travel anymore," Hæra said. "I almost never leave Jorsay." But her stationary time on land had taught her something too. She could tell that Madeleine was trying to distract her, turning the conversation away from herself.

"Doesn't that get boring?" Madeleine tilted her head to the side, looking as inquisitive as a barn cat.

"I keep busy."

"Best remedy for boredom." Madeleine glanced at Hæra's wrist, where an old Casio digital watch sat. "What time is it?"

Before Hæra could tell her, Madeleine reached out and took hold of her wrist, raising it so she could look at the watch. She didn't ask Hæra's permission. She just did it, and her fingertips brushed the skin of Hæra's wrist.

That skin caught fire. It was the first fire Hæra hadn't hated. Dumbly, she looked at Madeleine's slender fingers on her skin.

So did Madeleine. She kept her dark head bowed over their hands for a second as she looked at the watch. Then, with a gasp, she let go of Hæra as suddenly as she'd touched her. Hæra's wrist prickled in her wake.

"Sorry," Madeleine said. "Now I'm the rude one. So it's, uh, the time it is. Time for me to go."

"What?" Hæra asked in dismay. "But what about lunch and the afternoon? You're not walking on the beach, so…"

Madeleine wasn't looking at her. "I'll go to the Mainland. I found a Catholic church there. I checked, and they have an afternoon mass today."

"Mass today?" Did that mean the church was heavier than usual? Hæra wasn't thinking clearly, not after Madeleine's touch.

"Yes. I haven't been in over a week." Madeleine headed toward the Gator without looking at Hæra. "Would you mind driving me back to the farm? I've got to hurry if I want to make the ferry."

"I can drive you to the ferry," Hæra offered, following Madeleine. She didn't have a driving license, but nobody cared about that here.

"I wouldn't want to inconvenience you. Besides, I biked here again."

"No inconvenience." Hæra hopped into the driver's seat and started the ignition. "The bike'll fit in the Gator bed."

"You'd…uh…drive this on the road? The actual road?"

Hæra flashed her a grin. "Trust me. It goes faster than you'd think."

For some reason, Madeleine didn't look reassured.

———

"Bless me, Father, for I have sinned."

The familiar words came easily to Madeleine as she knelt in the confessional of Our Lady and Saint Joseph's Church. The priest sat on the other side of the screen, the thin latticework obscuring his face as he awaited her soul's unburdening.

"How long has it been since your last confession?" the priest prompted.

Oh good grief, how had she forgotten the second line? The one drilled into her since birth? So much for the familiar words. Flushing, Madeleine said, "It's been…" She couldn't remember. Not the exact number of days. She could always remember that, but now she couldn't. "Over a week," she managed.

"And what is the nature of your sin, my child?" His voice was deep, reassuring, the voice of Madeleine's own history.

"I—I've—"

I've realized I'm homosexual, she ought to say. *I'm so drawn to another woman that I touched her without realizing what I was doing. I'm in search of an angel I might not even want to find, when that's all I should* want.

"I've been impatient," she said. "I've been short-tempered and ungracious. And I've been…afraid."

"Afraid of what?"

"I don't know. Everything. Of not doing what I should do—or being who I should be—" Her voice cracked.

Hæra's fierce amber eyes flashed in her memory. Her smile had been carefree as she'd driven the Gator toward the ferry terminal at speeds the vehicle surely hadn't been meant for. Her wrist had been sturdy beneath Madeleine's hand. Sturdy and strong.

Madeleine hadn't even intended to touch her. It had just happened, the way both Eve and gravity had happened to the apple. Whether according to the Bible or Isaac Newton, the result was the same: a fall.

"I'm not who I'm supposed to be," Madeleine said brokenly. She looked at the wall of the confessional, where someone had helpfully tacked up a copy of the Act of Contrition, which you were supposed to recite when you were done confessing. She'd memorized a version of it as a child. She never needed to read it.

"None of us are," the priest reminded her. "But what sins have you specifically..."

"That's all I remember," Madeleine whispered. What now? What did she say now? "For these and all my sins I'm truly—truly—"

Truly sorry. Say you're truly sorry. Then let him give you penance so you'll know what to do to wipe away your sin and get rid of who you are, and say the Act of Contrition. You've done it all your wasted life—

"I can't," she gasped. She scrambled to her knees so fast she nearly hit her head on the low ceiling of the confessional. "I'm so sorry. I can't right now. I'll come back later."

"My child—?"

Madeleine crossed herself and bolted from the booth. She kept her eyes on the floor so as not to look at other parishioners who were waiting to confess. The church door seemed miles away, but she reached it eventually and emerged onto the streets of Kirkwall. Unconfessed, unabsolved, still drowned in mortal sin. Drowned worse than Hæra feared Madeleine would be in the sea.

Madeleine hurried down the streets, past the shops and restaurants, wondering how, even on land, waters could close over your head.

CHAPTER EIGHTEEN

Hours ago, Hæra's left wrist had not seemed significant. Tonight, long after Madeleine had departed for her "mass," Hæra looked at it while sitting on the edge of her bed.

It had always looked ordinary, as human wrists went. Slenderer than a man's, but not as delicate as Madeleine's. This could be no ordinary wrist, however. Not after Madeleine had touched it.

Touched it of her own free will, no less. Hæra hadn't reached for her first. This time, Madeleine had touched Hæra unprompted, and she hadn't needed to. She'd just asked Hæra what time it was. Hæra had been about to tell her. There had been no reason for them to touch.

How wonderful, then, that they had.

Hæra stroked her fingers over where Madeleine's own fingertips had circled her so briefly. She couldn't have guessed how it would feel. Was this how Madeleine had felt every time Hæra had touched her, "grabbing" her?

Now I'm the rude one, she'd said, clearly meaning it was the same thing. So she must have felt the same. Every follicle of hair on her body must have stood to attention.

Madeleine must...want her.

Hæra set her jaw. Her human teeth ground together, their blunt surfaces reminding her of all she had lost, and all she stood to gain. In her *Each-uisge* form, her teeth were like knives. They could only tear Madeleine's flesh, not caress it.

Wanting.

What was that? When Hæra thought of Madeleine, and wanting her, and Madeleine wanting her back, she no longer knew what that meant. It had been clear once. Want had been the same as hunger. This seemed like hunger too, but Hæra felt no desire to rend Madeleine's soft skin.

It would be nice to figure out what she desired instead.

It felt, as Jonathan sometimes said, on the tip of her brain. She was on the verge of realizing the truth, but the harder she tried to work it out on her own, the more elusive it became. Over the last few years, she'd learned that in times like this, you had to *stop* thinking and let the answer come to you on its own.

Hæra flopped back on her bed. At ten o'clock, it was still light outside, but today had been tiring. She'd drawn her heavy drapes that blocked out the sun, and now she picked up her mobile to play the ambient "ocean noises" sounds she liked to have at night. It wasn't the same as being in the sea, but it was a surprisingly good imitation. Humans had many skills, including being able to record the rumble of underwater currents and the call of whales. Now, Hæra could hear the sea in her bedroom.

She hit "play" and set the phone on the nightstand. She'd changed into comfortable sweatpants and a T-shirt. Needing little insulation, she used no duvet. It was time to slow her metabolism down and sink into the half-conscious state of rest that would prepare her for the next day.

On her mobile, as part of the recording, a humpback whale sang out for a mate.

The sound made Hæra's heart beat faster rather than slowing it down. Mating calls were so personal. In her former life, the herd had used them to track down whales and find the smaller fish that tended to surround them. Now, in this life, alone in this room, the song sounded different.

"*Come here,*" the whale sang to a female, "*join with me.*"

Hæra squirmed in bed.

"*Let challengers perish,*" the whale continued. "*Let us be one.*"

She squeezed her thighs together. The resultant pressure brought a warm, firm pulse between her legs that felt quite good.

She'd experienced this pulse before, but not often. She knew what it was, too. After she'd moved in, once she was getting on with reading, Jonathan had brought her a book written for adolescents about sex. He'd been embarrassed when she'd had questions but had answered some of them. For others, he'd begged her to go to the Internet. She had, which had only raised more questions, as well as making her think that the males of the human species were nearly as brutal as her own kind.

When she'd shown Jonathan the evidence of this, he'd turned purple, told her to "stay the hell away from filthy videos," and then fussed at her for giving the computer a virus. He got her another book after that, one for human adults that had more information about pleasure and less about reproduction. It had included information about men with women, men with men, and women with women.

None of it had stirred her. Hæra had no attraction to humans in pictures or videos, and she was exposed to few in person. She'd felt a similar pulse between her legs in the presence of a beautiful woman tourist she'd seen on a brief trip to the village, but it had passed quickly enough. She'd decided it was just her human form's way of consoling itself in a new environment.

Lying in bed, listening to seductive songs while thinking about Madeleine, was different.

Hæra bit her lower lip. Her incisors pushed against the soft, full flesh. All of a sudden, she imagined that she was biting Madeleine's lower lip instead.

She gasped. She hadn't meant to; the thought had drawn it out of her. It drew something else out of her too: another pulse, stronger and hotter.

Without her will, her hand went between her legs to press against the pulse, as if trying to contain it. It didn't work. If anything, the pressure of her hand made everything worse—or better. Her hips pushed forward, as if of their own volition, and Hæra's eyes fell shut.

Her imagination swam ahead on its own. In her mind's eye, she loosened her teeth on Madeleine's lip; her bite had drawn from Madeleine a groan, the kind she'd given on the beach that night. Now, Hæra's mouth softened. Both her lips pressed to Madeleine's, and Madeleine's lips opened for her in return. They exchanged the same kiss as on the beach that night all those years ago. Sister Madeleine's lips had been cold, but her mouth was warm. And she'd opened it so readily for Hæra, as if she'd been waiting for her.

Hæra's hand moved again, not just once. This time, it began to rub back and forth as she touched herself through her sweatpants. The rhythm, the changing pressure, made her hips rise and fall, chasing the sensation.

She didn't mean to do any of this, any more than she'd meant to take Madeleine's hand, or touch her arm, or pull her into a fierce embrace. What was happening to her? Madeleine had some strange effect on her—made Hæra act without thinking, pulled her *out* of herself, somehow—

It felt so good. She trembled at her own touch. There was nothing like this in her true form. Her kind had no sexual response save going into heat; she had never experienced that, and it had always sounded awful. This was pure, self-indulgent pleasure that seemed to have no purpose other than shivering through her blood.

What would it be like if she touched her flesh more directly, instead of through fabric? Would it feel even more enjoyable? Only one way to find out.

Hæra made sure her bedroom door was fully closed—both Jonathan and the books had emphasized that human sexuality was a private matter. Then, she shimmied out of her sweatpants and underwear, lay back down on the bed, and looked at the triangle of dark hair between her pale thighs. It was rather striking, in a way she'd never considered before. Did Madeleine look like this too?

At that thought, Hæra didn't feel a pulse so much as an *ache*. She bit her lip again, this time to stifle a gasp. It would have been a loud gasp.

Thinking of Madeleine's thighs, she pressed her fingers between her spread legs, against the bare flesh there. Good thing she was biting her lip, still. Without her clothes in the way, her fingers called forth a hotter, sharper response. The noise she wanted to make was in her throat.

This was remarkable—not like touching her arms or legs or any other part of herself. When she did that, her body didn't change. The rest of her body didn't grow hot and heavy, it didn't start to ache and plead for more.

Let it have more, then. Hæra let her fingers roam. When she pressed at her lips, she felt a delightful throb. When she rubbed her fingertips against her entrance, it seemed to flutter, as if it had a mind of its own. And the more she explored, the more sensitive she grew.

Sensitive, and…wet. The books had said that was normal too. It was her body's way of preparing for penetration. Hæra had never been penetrated, at least not in this way. How would it feel?

Only one way to find out about that, too.

Holding her breath, Hæra slid her right index finger inside herself. The sensation was strange. Intrusive. She wasn't sure she liked it, although when she crooked her finger a bit, it felt better. She crooked her finger more, and then faster, like the rhythm she'd tried over her pants, and her hips lifted for more of it, calling another gasp out of her. One she couldn't muffle.

It was wonderful! Were real human bodies like this too? If Hæra slipped her finger inside Madeleine like this, would it be just the same? Would Madeleine be wet, warm, and soft around her? Would she like it if Hæra went at her this way?

Hæra's finger stilled. So did her mind, as she realized: she was thinking about having sex with Madeleine. About doing to Madeleine what felt so good when Hæra did it to herself.

She was thinking, in detail, about having sex with a human

woman, with *Madeleine*, which went far beyond an idle stir of interest at the sight of a stranger.

Hæra's mouth sagged open, slack with disbelief. She stared at the ceiling as if she'd never seen it before, her finger still wedged inside herself.

By the depths, was that what it was about? Had she acclimated so wholly to this human shell of hers that she'd acquired a whole new kind of hunger? She'd never seen it coming.

Now, though, she saw something else. When she closed her eyes, she could only see one thing. She saw Madeleine lying before her on a bed, her legs spread, while Hæra knelt over her and slid a finger inside her. The same one she had inside herself right now.

Madeleine was wet too. She was naked from the waist down because…because she hadn't wanted to wait, she was too desperate for Hæra to have her. She was breathing quickly too, her breasts rising and falling beneath the sweater she'd worn last night at dinner. Hæra had no idea what Madeleine's body looked like beneath her clothes, but it was obvious that Madeleine's breasts were bigger than her own, her hips curvier.

Her body would be as beautiful as her face. There was no doubt of that. And if it had responded so thoroughly to Hæra on the beach, when it had been covered in wet clothes, then it would respond even more without them. Hæra had been naked. If Madeleine were naked too…beneath her…

If Hæra were kissing her again, only this time they were both naked, and if Hæra were also moving her fingers inside her…

She was doing it to herself again. Frantic, hard, while her thighs shook and she gasped. *Madeleine.* If she did this to Madeleine. Madeleine's face would flush, just like it had before. Her pulse would go faster at the base of her throat, and Hæra could lick it, suck it, even bite it.

"Oh," she gasped, "oh, oh." She hadn't been able to muffle it. Maybe she could make Madeleine do that too. Make her feel so good that she couldn't stay quiet. Madeleine's voice was soft, low, rich. Hæra imagined it saying *oh, oh, oh.*

Madeleine would look at Hæra the whole time while her full lips opened around her moans. Her hips would rise and fall like Hæra's were doing, chasing the sensation.

As she moved inside herself, the edge of Hæra's hand brushed something above her entrance. It was a sensitive spot, a little flap of flesh that responded with a brighter flare of pleasure. She gasped again.

Then, carefully, she spread her legs wider, tilted her right hand, and touched the spot with her left one. This time, she had to bite her lip so hard it hurt to keep from making a noise. Touching this spot felt even better. It was a little dry, though. Inspired, Hæra withdrew her fingers from herself, sighing a little at the loss. Then she stroked them, wet as they were, over the spot.

She closed her eyes and let her head fall back. It felt *incredible*. She experimented, trying different angles and pressures until she had a rhythm going that made her whimper through her nose. Faster, she should try going faster. Her thighs were shaking again.

How would she do this to Madeleine? She could lie next to her. She could lie pressed next to Madeleine with her fingers between Madeleine's thighs, stroking her just like this…after being inside her, getting her slick so that it felt good…while Madeleine writhed under Hæra's hand, pleading for more…

Then she'd turn her head. She'd open her mouth, pleading for the first thing they'd ever done together. Hæra would give it to her. They would kiss, deeply, the closest to devouring that Hæra could get while still keeping Madeleine's soft skin safe. She'd kiss Madeleine's mouth, and stroke her between her legs, and make her moan, and—and—

Hæra's muscles stiffened, and the rising ache inside her crested. She throbbed, clenched inside, exquisite spasms that scattered her thoughts into nothingness. All she could think about was Madeleine's mouth while her legs shook and a cry escaped her throat. It seemed to go on and on as she stroked herself, coaxing out more and more pleasure with her own hands.

This was what it must feel like to soar among the clouds, borne up by a great pair of wings.

Then it was too much. The wave crashed down on a rock, and Hæra's skin was suddenly too sensitive for it to feel good anymore. She pulled her fingers away, panting, reeling with shock. Between her legs she was hot now, swollen and heavy. Her entrance felt stretched, though not sore.

Still wet too. Dizzy and disbelieving, Hæra looked at her fingers. The index one was coated with fluid, evidence of what she'd done to herself.

Orgasm. That's what she'd just had. The adult books about sex had talked about it. They called it different things, although one of the most common terms had been "to come." At first, that had confused Hæra. Come where?

To a place of deep bliss, apparently. She'd never imagined having an orgasm herself, that being an experience reserved for male *Each-uisge*. They enjoyed the mating act, while females hoped to survive it. Half of her species had clearly been robbed.

Hæra sighed. Coming was incredible. Her body was relaxing now, melting into the mattress in a way it never had before. Her heart rate was slowing, and the lips between her legs were still warm. Her vulva —that was the name for it. What was the sensitive spot called? She'd forgotten. She'd have to look it up again.

Madeleine must do this to herself too. Who wouldn't? Who could deny themselves such pleasure when it was literally an arm's length away? Hæra certainly planned to do it again. Often. What a pity it had taken her so long to discover the sensation.

And what a pity she couldn't tell Madeleine about it yet, human sexual activity being private and all. They'd have to be more comfortable with each other first. More intimate.

Hæra licked her wet fingertip. It tasted salty. That was fitting. Would Madeleine taste like this too? Or was it another thing that was different for humans, like reduced physical strength and the need for fresh water?

She needed to look at those books again. One of them had mentioned something about "oral sex," which had intrigued Hæra at the time, close as it was to eating somebody. If it would please Madeleine…if Hæra's hunger had turned from blood to sex…

She wiped her finger on the sheet and blinked at the ceiling. From blood to sex. She was back where she'd started: wondering when she'd turned into someone who wanted to mate with a human.

The answer seemed obvious. She'd wanted it almost the moment Madeleine had returned to her. The question was where that desire slotted in alongside everything else: her need to return to the sea, her quest to become a Stormhorse, and what it would take to make that happen.

Strangely, she couldn't summon interest in that just now. How odd that such pleasure should make it hard to think or care about serious matters. She only wanted to wear a foolish smile and bask in the aftermath as if she were lying on the grass beneath the sun.

It had been a long and confusing day. Hæra might as well reward herself with this. She let the lazy smile cross her face and slowed her heartbeat, her metabolic system, drifting into her rest state. Everything would keep for now. Somehow, she would find a way to see Madeleine tomorrow. Jonathan would understand if she didn't work on the farm.

The sun might come out again. That would be nice.

"I have found you," the whale sang. *"Let us begin."*

She should leave.

The notion seemed inconceivable. Madeleine couldn't believe she was entertaining it after being on Jorsay for two days when she'd planned for a month.

But now she sat in the tatty armchair of her hotel room nearly at midnight, staring at the airline app on her phone. Changing her ticket would be expensive, but it might be worth it to escape.

Or she could text Becca. Call her, even. There was something about hearing a human voice, especially when it belonged to someone who loved you. Becca would love Madeleine even if she knew the truth. Heck, Becca probably already knew, based on remarks she'd been dropping for years. Remarks like *Everyone deserves to be happy* and *There's nothing wrong with wanting something different.*

It would be the next best thing to a priest's absolution. After all, hadn't Madeleine thought often that there were differing interpretations of homosexuality in Catholic doctrine? That some progressive Catholics approved of it?

In her memory, her father lifted a scornful eyebrow. *That's convenient, isn't it?* he seemed to ask. *Looking for excuses when it's about* you. Her mother nodded in agreement while David shrugged indifferently.

"It's not just about me," Madeleine muttered, and her eyes widened as she heard herself say it. She hadn't meant to.

But she wasn't wrong, was she? It wasn't just about her. It was about Arjun and Jeremy too, whom she'd snubbed yesterday in the café. (Had it only been yesterday?) It was about other people she'd met throughout the course of her life. Like her former student Ava, who'd spoken earnestly to Madeleine about wanting to become a nun. Now she was in graduate school and happy with a girlfriend.

Ava had been more honest with herself than Madeleine had been decades earlier, and now she was happy. It was the funniest thing: Madeleine had never condemned her or even feared for her soul. For all her knowledge of doctrine, she simply could not imagine a world in which God punished sweet, earnest Ava for finding a little happiness.

Why couldn't Madeleine find that same happiness for herself? Why *shouldn't* she? She'd fled from the convent, then she'd fled from the confessional. The only walls around her now were metaphorical, and she could take them down if she wanted. Couldn't she?

The phone display looked blurry. Madeleine blinked, the tears streamed down her cheeks, and it became clear again.

She'll set you free.

Madeleine gasped aloud. The thought had struck her out of the blue, and she couldn't tell where it had come from. Surely not herself. Maybe in addition to being gay and a burgeoning heretic, she was hearing voices again. Great.

That settled it. Madeleine needed to get out of here. She'd return to the safe familiarity of home and count this a wasted trip. She navigated the app, looking for the option to change her flight. Why did they make this so difficult? Didn't they want her to give them an outrageous amount of money?

It's really too annoying, the voice murmured again. *And too expensive.*

Madeleine winced as she finally found the "flight change option." Too expensive was right. She'd spent so much money already, depleting her savings for this trip that she intended now to abandon.

You should stay.

Her fingertip stilled over her phone display.

Stay here, and become free.

Free. The second time she'd thought the word. Or someone else had thought it for her. Maybe it didn't matter who'd thought it.

What would it be like to be free—set loose from the bonds that held her so tightly they cut? Tradition, doctrine, all of it. What would that be like?

It was one of the most terrifying questions she'd ever asked. How could it also be one of the most thrilling?

If she left Jorsay, she'd just be running back to her cage. And for what? To surrender to her own cowardice instead of exploring what she'd been shown?

Madeleine had done as her angel had ordered her years ago. She'd returned, and it would be the worst folly to turn tail and run before she had some answers. She was ashamed of herself. This was the thought of a coward, a defeatist—everything she'd told Hæra she wasn't.

Hæra, again.

Hæra who was strange, who was rude, who was *really* intense, who was the most inexplicably attractive person Madeleine had ever met. And who had an uncanny knack for looking right at things Madeleine would rather keep hidden.

Right. Madeleine was past being able to make sense of this. She closed the airline app and tossed her phone onto the bed, where tonight she'd have more dreams. Would Hæra, her beautiful mouth, and her wicked hands feature in them?

Madeleine blushed. Her lusts seemed to have trapped her even more than religious doctrine.

Confession hadn't helped her today, but maybe something else would. She bowed her head and crossed herself to pray the Act of Hope. "O my God," she whispered, "relying on your infinite goodness and promises, I hope for pardon of my sins, the help of your grace and life everlasting, because you have promised it through the merits of Jesus Christ, my lord and redeemer."

She paused. That was the end of the prayer, but she felt no lighter or warmer, no more beloved. One more thing seemed to be called for.

"Please," she mumbled. "I'm begging you. Amen."

CHAPTER NINETEEN

"So what the hell's going on?"

Jonathan stood in the doorway to Hæra's bedroom with his arms folded and brow creased.

Hæra frowned at him from the edge of the bed as she put proper shoes on. Muddy boots wouldn't do for this morning's excursion. "Why take that tone? I'm going to the hotel to meet Madeleine."

"Does she know that?"

"She should," Hæra hedged. True, she hadn't actually told Madeleine she'd be showing up at her doorstep first thing, but it probably wouldn't come as a surprise.

"Last night, you told me that yesterday you talked all morning, but then she ran off and not a word since. And there was her wanting to walk on the beach. What if she does that today? You wouldn't go too, would you?"

Hæra's stomach twisted at the thought. She said what she'd told herself yesterday: "It's daytime. I doubt my herd is poking their heads above the water. It's forbidden to nearly all of us."

"Loads of things are forbidden. Seems to me that certain of your lot do what they please anyway. You've gone on for years about how it's risky for me even to ferry between the islands, and now you can just go for a stroll on the beach?"

Was Jonathan concerned for her, or just annoyed that she'd nagged him for so long? Could be both. "Only the Sire, my mother, and my brother even know what I…that is, what my human form looks like."

She looked Jonathan in the eye as she rose from the bed where, last night, she'd had such an enjoyable time. That was one experience she'd be keeping to herself.

As usual, at any mention of Asgall, Jonathan's eyes clouded. He said, "I think that'd be enough. Especially your brother. He's…" Jonathan set his jaw and looked away, toward the window and the land beyond. "You know what he is, and so do I."

Hæra pursed her lips. Even after all this time, Asgall had a hold over Jonathan that she both resented and envied. Asgall had not appreciated Jonathan, had not *cared* for him, as Hæra did for Madeleine. And yet his human still felt his pull.

What a priceless gift it would be for Madeleine to be drawn to Hæra in such a way. Asgall had had an entire season to fascinate Jonathan, and Hæra was scrambling to keep Madeleine here beyond a single month. It just wasn't fair. Why should Asgall have such power over Jonathan when he didn't even want him?

"I doubt it'll be a problem," she said. "Madeleine said yesterday that she's not in a hurry to see the beach. She wants to think about what she's learned already, or something like that."

"She does? You didn't say anything about that last night."

Hæra shrugged irritably. "I didn't think of it."

Jonathan's gaze called her the liar she was. "I suppose you're entitled to keep yourself to yourself. I'm only worried for you, lass. I know this means a lot to you, but I don't know *what* it means to you."

What was there to say? Jonathan wanted a human answer, all to do with love, nothing to do with appetite. If he knew Hæra had been planning to eat Madeleine for years, he'd never understand, just as Hæra didn't understand why her plan suddenly wanted to change.

"I can't explain," she said, which was true enough. "I'm going now."

Jonathan sighed. "I hope it goes well. Bring your mobile. You're taking my car?"

"If that's all right." The Corsa would be a more comfortable mode of transportation if they needed it. Madeleine hadn't complained about the Gator ride to the ferry, but she'd looked frazzled by the end of it.

"I've got no business elsewhere today. Just don't hit anything. And wear the seat belt," he added sharply.

"I'll be careful," Hæra promised. "Especially if she's with me."

Jonathan raised his eyebrows at that, though Hæra couldn't see why. "That's good," he said eventually, with a little smile. "Have a care with her, and it'll turn out all right."

What an odd thing to say. Hæra could do nothing else. It was like telling her to remember to breathe.

———

The water pressure at the Merryweather Hotel was better than at Sacred Heart, but that wasn't saying much. Madeleine had to rinse the shampoo from her thick hair for about twice as long as she'd gotten used to in her apartment.

It still felt good. She'd woken up sweaty after dreams she couldn't remember clearly. At least they hadn't involved Hæra doing forbidden things to Madeleine's body. The Act of Hope must have worked.

Yes. Hopeful indeed.

Madeleine groaned to herself, finished her shower, and continued her morning routine. She'd slept in. It was nearly eight o'clock. Not that she had a packed itinerary or anything—or an itinerary at all, come to that.

How disconcerting. She'd come thousands of miles to have no plan for how she'd spend her days. But what was she supposed to do? Pre-book a tour for her existential crisis, or buy a ticket that would take her exactly where she needed to be? Spend every spare minute on Jonathan and Hæra's farm, ogling a woman instead of looking for answers?

She couldn't do that, but she could do *something*. On Sacred Heart's trip, the ancient human settlement of Skara Brae on the Mainland had been closed for upkeep. It hadn't ruined the trip—the settlement on Jorsay was even older, and less touristy to boot. Still, missing such a landmark had been disappointing. Why shouldn't Madeleine return to the Mainland today and take in an actual sight instead of wandering aimlessly around Jorsay? She'd be around more people, and it might unstick something in her head.

And she'd avoid a certain long and lean distraction.

Madeleine finished getting ready, grabbed her purse, and hurried downstairs, trying not to catch her foot on the threadbare stair rug. She could get breakfast at the little coffee stand at the ferry terminal. It was too soon to face the Sunrise Café again.

Then, as she reached the lobby, she heard a voice that derailed her plans for breakfast, along with possibly the entire day.

"…only asking if she's up yet."

Madeleine froze on the stairs, just hidden by the corner that led into the lobby. Hæra was here? With no warning, just like that?

"Couldn't say," Harry Duggan replied. "I've only just opened the desk. If she left early, I'd have missed her."

"Left earlier than this? But I waited until a decent hour, and I still worried I'd disturb her."

Hæra sounded dismayed. It made something in Madeleine's heart clench.

Nobody had seen her yet. She could sneak back upstairs. Soon, Hæra would leave, and Madeleine could get her day started with as little confusion…and desire…as possible.

"You could wait a while," Harry suggested.

Madeleine muffled a groan.

"We could have a bit of a natter," Harry continued. "Can't remember the last time I laid eyes on you. You're looking well. Where's Jonny? I don't think I've ever seen you out and about without him."

"Jonathan's working on the farm."

Hæra's tone didn't invite further conversation. Madeleine, who'd known her all of two days, could already imagine the shutters that had closed over her sharp eyes.

"Ah yes, the farm. Knocked me arse over kettle when he started it at his age. Let me think…I seem to remember you were with him then, but I'm not sure…"

Madeleine rolled her eyes. If Harry Duggan didn't have a photographic memory for gossip, then she was a ballet dancer.

"Yes," Hæra said tightly. "We did it together. You're sure you haven't seen Madeleine?"

"Positive, but it's likely she's here! Nothing's open, and she's bound to be still on American time. Shall I just call for a cup of tea? How do you like it?"

Now it seemed Madeleine had to choose between saving herself and saving Hæra, who didn't seem eager to talk about her personal life. That was no choice. Of course she had to do the right and generous thing.

And if it meant seeing Hæra again…well, that wasn't *Madeleine's* fault.

She hefted her purse strap, straightened her shoulders, and descended the steps. She'd already had some progress in fobbing off Harry Duggan's nosiness; she could handle this with grace and dignity.

That plan, too, went by the wayside as the toe of her sneaker caught on the carpet on the last stair, and she tripped into the lobby with a yelp, crashing to the floor while both Hæra and Harry looked on from the front desk.

That didn't happen, Madeleine lied to herself as soon as she could form a real thought. She'd landed on her right side. At least it wasn't flat on her face. Maybe she could bolt for the door and leave Jorsay forever after all. Face burning, she stared at the floor and made to sit up. Then, before she could, someone's arm slid behind her back, and another beneath her knees, and next thing she knew, she was being lifted up in the air.

It wasn't by Harry Duggan, who was gaping at the scene from behind the desk.

In shock, Madeleine looked into Hæra's eyes. They were level with her own as Hæra adjusted her into a bridal carry.

Madeleine slung her arm around Hæra's shoulders. Instinctively. For balance.

"Are you all right?" Hæra asked.

For a second, Madeleine forgot how to talk. Her side ached. Hæra's grip was unfathomably strong. She showed no sign of effort. Madeleine might as well have been a feather pillow. After a moment, she managed, "Um."

Hæra scowled and cast her sharp glare around the lobby. "I'll set you on the sofa. Duggan, call for that nurse, that Sue Kilbright."

"Er—right—" Looking stunned, Harry reached for the phone before he frowned. "Hang on, she just took a little tumble. Miss, can you stand at all?"

Could anyone stand when their knees were made of jelly? "Uh, probably."

Hæra made no move to put her down. She was strong and taut and warm. Madeleine swallowed, or tried to, her mouth as dry as if she'd swallowed all the salt in the ocean. "Let me try to stand," she whispered.

Hæra ground her jaw. Without a word, she lowered her right arm from beneath Madeleine's knees until Madeleine's feet were touching the floor. Her left arm she kept around Madeleine's shoulders, tightly. Perhaps the jaws of life could not pry her away. She was still looking into Madeleine's eyes.

"Well?"

Madeleine and Hæra turned as one to see Harry with his arms crossed, raising his eyebrows. Madeleine's face filled with heat again. Harry's eyes were those of a lifelong gossip, after all, and here he was, seeing whatever there was to see.

She was supposed to be doing something.

Oh, right. Standing. Madeleine put her weight first on one foot, then the other. "Everything's fine. Like you said, only a tumble." She managed a laugh. "I just bruised my pride."

"I thought as much," Harry said lightly. "You're the tumbling sort, looks like. At least you didn't fall into the ocean again!"

Madeleine grimaced. "That's tr—"

"Madeleine is graceful," Hæra said coldly. She still had her arm around Madeleine's shoulders and showed no inclination to let go. "And an elegant person. You don't know anything about it."

Hæra's defense was vigorous, her grip firm. Madeleine's face heated even more.

Harry lifted his chin. "It's a rude lass, isn't it? Calling me 'Duggan,' manhandling ladies, and that." His mouth twitched into a curious, unfriendly smile. "There's always been something odd about you, hasn't there? Is that why old Jonny keeps you tucked away?"

The air around Hæra seemed to change. There was no other way to describe it: it shivered, and so did Madeleine as Hæra's lips pulled back over her teeth. Her incisors looked oddly pointed. Her amber eyes flashed, and...

...it had to be the light, that was why they looked *yellow*...

Madeleine stepped away. Hæra's arm fell from around her shoulders, and she looked at Madeleine, blinking as if she'd just woken up.

"Let's go," Madeleine said, since staying here was a terrible idea.

"Yes," Hæra agreed, although Madeleine had named no destination.

Madeleine picked up her purse from where it had hit the floor. Her knees still felt shaky, and her heart was racing—from the fall, the rescue, and the hostility in the air. Only that.

"Good morning, Harry," she managed, but she couldn't manage to look at him as she headed for the front door. Hæra's tread sounded behind her. Harry said nothing.

They emerged into the cool morning air. Madeleine managed not to trip down a second step of stairs, and then they were on the sidewalk together, facing a day she'd intended to spend alone.

Now she looked at Hæra's fierce face, thinking: *I'm not spending this day alone. I won't.*

"That was dramatic," she said.

"Harry Duggan is a gossip," Hæra growled. "He speaks all sorts of nonsense."

"I'm pretty good at figuring out what's nonsense and what isn't. Comes from teaching high school." She took a deep breath. "And I meant you picking me up."

Hæra frowned. "You fell. And you cried out."

"I was just startled, not hurt."

"I couldn't know that." Hæra's gaze sharpened, though not like it had in the lobby, when Madeleine had been afraid she'd say something unforgivable to Harry. "Do you wish I hadn't done it?"

Why had Hæra asked that? *You shall not lie to one another* was one of the Ten Commandments. Madeleine worried her lip and went for something both true and acceptable. "I appreciate the thought. I know you wanted to help."

"Maybe I shouldn't have." Hæra pursed her lips. "It's not always best to move people if they might have broken something. I wasn't thinking."

Fair enough. From the moment Hæra's arms went around her, Madeleine hadn't been thinking either. "Well, nothing's broken, or even sprained. You're...um..."

"I'm what?"

"Strong," Madeleine mumbled. "Must come from lifting hay bales or whatever."

Hæra didn't look pleased, as she might have expected. Instead, she gazed away into the distance. "We're closer to the ocean here than on the farm. I can hear the waves if I listen closely enough."

What did that have to do with anything? "I can't seem to."

"I have excellent hearing. Now, where do you want to go? Have you eaten?"

"Not yet. I was going to have something at the ferry."

"The ferry?" Hæra looked alarmed. "You're leaving the island again?"

"Yes. I'm going to see something I missed out on six years ago."

"What is it?"

Madeleine tilted her chin up, looked into those eyes, and felt the memory of strong arms around her. Another memory—her father's voice—admonished her, warned her against the feelings that swallowed her like the sea.

Today, even if just for today, Madeleine would drown the voice instead.

"Come with me," she told Hæra, "and find out."

CHAPTER TWENTY

The tour bus to Skara Brae slowed as the road narrowed and led into a parking lot. Pedestrians crossed to and fro, not seeming to take much notice of the enormous vehicle bearing down on them. On the other side of the parking lot sat a visitor center where people, some of them clearly in tour groups, swarmed around the doors.

Skara Brae was Orkney's most famous prehistoric human settlement—not as old as the settlement on Jorsay, but more complete. It consisted of ten flagstone houses, some of which still had their original stone-built furniture. There was even a primitive sewer system. Even with her head and heart in a whirl, Madeleine was excited to see it.

Once off the bus, Madeleine led the way into the center and purchased two tickets. "Do you want the dual admission?" she asked Hæra at the window. "The one that also lets us into Skaill House?" She nodded at a picture of the seventeenth-century mansion that sat on the Skara Brae site and required a separate ticket.

Hæra looked at the stately house that loomed judgmentally over the flat, green land. "I've never been in a house that large."

"Then let's go. My treat." Madeleine gave her credit card to the cashier. "Is it a long tour?"

"Self-guided," the cashier said brightly. "Take as long as you like."

Madeleine gave Hæra a wry look. She didn't seem the type who'd want to spend hours looking at antiques. "I warn you, I'm a history teacher. I take my time in places like this."

Hæra shrugged and picked up a brochure. "I don't mind. Time passes faster when it's with you."

Madeleine's face caught fire. Hæra just glanced over the brochure as if she hadn't said something that was almost—almost *romantic*. Something that made Madeleine's heart race again.

"Aww," murmured the young woman at the counter, wearing a little smile as she gave Madeleine her card and receipt.

She'd assumed the wrong thing. Madeleine should correct her. Except nobody had actually *said* anything that needed correcting, nobody had *said* that Madeleine and Hæra were...together, or something like that, so what was there to correct?

Madeleine, her face hot, shoved her wallet back into her purse. "Right, let's move."

"The exhibit starts there." Hæra pointed at a corridor that led toward the back of the building.

Madeleine eyed the door that led directly outside to the settlement. You had to go through the gift shop to enter and exit, of course. "Uh, maybe we should just get straight to it."

It was warm. The crowd, probably. Fresh air was just the thing.

"But the exhibit tells you all about the things we're going to see, doesn't it?" Hæra sounded confused, but Madeleine wasn't about to look at her face. She could visualize it perfectly: a slight crease between Hæra's dark eyebrows. "And they've got things from the settlement you can see up close. You said you were looking forward to that."

"Well, I..."

"Come on." Hæra patted Madeleine's back. "We've got all day. It's this way."

She kept her hand on Madeleine's back, between her shoulder blades, as they made their way toward the corridor.

Torture ensued.

When they sat down on a bench for a brief movie about the settlement's history, their thighs and knees pressed together. Hæra seemed fascinated by the large screen, propping her elbows on her knees as she leaned forward and watched the grainy, black-and-white footage of the site's excavation.

The narrator's voice seemed low and far away, although maybe that was just the blood roaring in Madeleine's ears. Hæra smelled like the outdoors, all wind and earth. Her thigh felt firm, even through the layers of their jeans. It'd be even firmer without the jeans, probably. If their legs were bare, then Hæra's muscles would—

Without warning, Hæra turned and leaned in until her mouth was almost brushing Madeleine's ear.

Madeleine's heart stopped. What on earth? Was Hæra about to kiss Madeleine's cheek? Or—if Madeleine just turned her head a little bit, their mouths would—

"I didn't know it was uncovered by a storm!" Hæra whispered.

Madeleine looked dumbly at the screen. It showed black-and-white photos of the site's excavation, images of both men and women standing in the newly uncovered pits. The narrator's voice was saying something about how female archaeologists had been there too. "What?" she said. "I didn't catch that part."

"How'd you miss it? They said nobody knew the site was even here until a great storm stripped off the earth in 1850. I've never heard that before."

At least one of them had been paying attention. In fact, even in the low light, Hæra's eyes sparkled with excitement.

"It's pretty amazing," Madeleine managed.

"Let's go. You don't want to finish the movie, do you? You don't seem interested in it." Hæra rose and turned to stand in front of Madeleine. Her tall form blocked the light of the screen, sending her into silhouette, her face no longer visible.

For a moment, Madeleine's head spun for a different reason. Hæra above her...in silhouette, her face invisible...why did it seem so familiar?

Hæra held out her hand.

Maybe Madeleine was dreaming. Maybe that was why she took Hæra's hand and let herself be pulled up instead of rising on her own. Maybe that was why she let Hæra keep her hand, tugging her toward the rest of the exhibit that would eventually lead them outside.

The strange feeling of déjà vu faded. Their hands fit so well together. As if they were meant to curl in one warm grip wherever Madeleine and Hæra should go.

Madeleine had been looking forward to seeing the display: ancient tools, pottery behind glass, preserved articles of clothing. Now, instead of admiring human ingenuity, her entire consciousness was in her palm.

After an eternity that wasn't long enough, they emerged from the exhibit into the open air that would lead to the actual site. But first, there was a replica to explore: some anthropologist's best guess as to what one of the huts might have looked like.

Hæra let go of Madeleine's hand. That wasn't the loss it might have been, because a narrow stone tunnel required her to stand close, her warm front pressed to Madeleine's back. Close enough that Madeleine could feel the rise of her breasts.

In Madeleine's dream, Hæra had declined to unbutton her shirt, as if even Madeleine's subconscious couldn't figure out what her breasts looked like. They wouldn't be big. Maybe they were proportional to her frame, which was lean and muscular instead of curvy. They'd be as pale as the rest of Hæra's skin, although now Madeleine knew that skin could flush too, turn pink and—presumably—warm.

There wasn't enough air in this tunnel. Her lungs ached from trying to breathe. Everything ached. She hadn't been this close to a woman since…since…

Return to me.

Madeleine bit her bottom lip and trembled. Since her angel had lain atop her, kissed her, and turned her life upside-down. Now she was practically plastered to a mortal woman who seemed determined to upend everything yet again.

They emerged from the tunnel back into the fresh air. Thank heavens for the breeze. It cooled her burning face.

"There it is! The real thing." Hæra grabbed Madeleine's hand again and tugged her toward the path that led to the settlement. "Hurry."

Even through the magic of Hæra's touch, Madeleine could think clearly enough to ask, "What's the big rush?"

Hæra kept her eyes firmly forward. "Why shouldn't we hurry? Don't you want to see what's ahead?"

Part of Madeleine would give anything to see what was ahead right now—the future and whatever it held. That wasn't given to people, though. Goodness knew what rash or foolish decisions they'd make if they knew what was coming.

She held Hæra's hand tighter.

———

It seemed her human shell had unexpected benefits. Even if Hæra were a Stormhorse, looking down at Skara Brae from the sky, she might never have known its history.

She definitely wouldn't be here now, beholding her father's work up close.

The storm had happened in 1850, when Alban was a young Stormhorse. His wings would have been part of the gale that blew the sand away and uncovered the settlement she was looking at. How could she ever have imagined she'd have the chance to see something like this?

Yet again, her human eyes stung with saltwater. She blinked, but that only made more of it. Her throat grew thick too.

Father, she thought, *if only I could speak to you one more time. You'd have wisdom for me. You always did.*

She still didn't know how he'd died. The former Sire had said only that his body had been found torn to pieces, as if *how* it happened didn't matter, and now that Sire was dead too.

Hæra would never know the truth, but something of her father had returned to her. Here on land, of all places.

He'd been able to do this because he'd eaten that sea captain, the one he'd spoken of so fondly. Alban had said that, in battling and consuming his chosen human, he'd truly become himself. In fact, he'd spoken far more generously of humans than the rest of their kind did; Hæra had overheard her mother chastising him for that. Beathag had warned him not to "fall under a human's spell," as if such a thing was possible, as if—

"Remarkable, right?"

The soft voice startled Hæra out of her memories. Madeleine, standing next to her, gazed into one of the pits. There were eight in total, called the "houses." Flagstones supported and surrounded them. Side recesses showed more stones from ancient, collapsed roofs; evidence suggested the buildings had been rather sophisticated for the time. Around them all, the tourists looked down from rolling knolls of grass.

"We've come a long way," Madeleine said.

Their jacketed arms touched. Hæra's heart thumped. This was the first time Madeleine had stood so close to her of her own accord.

"Think about it," Madeleine continued. "They sat around stone fire pits and burned seaweed for fuel. Now, ask me how central heating works, and I couldn't tell you."

Everyone Hæra knew used radiators, but to be fair, she didn't know how those worked either. "I don't think people are so different now."

The ancient house had beds, a gathering place, containers, a privy. It wasn't wholly unlike the stone cottage she'd first lived in with Jonathan, or even the more modern quarters they shared now.

"Not in some ways," Madeleine acknowledged. "But our fight's always been to improve on what we've got. Thousands of years after these people lived, I have a hand-held device that can tell me nearly everything I want to know." She held up her mobile. "It's not always a good thing, but we don't like to remain stagnant."

Clouds passed overhead, rendering the color of Madeleine's eyes as changeable as the sea. The sea never remained stagnant either.

The *Each-uisge* were different, though. In all its history, had the herd ever changed its customs? For how long had mares been forced to subject themselves to a violent mating cycle and the interminably long pregnancies that followed? For how long had males been forbidden to take partners if they failed the Stormhorse trial? Hæra had been told that these were facts of existence itself, unchanging and unchangeable.

But humans changed. They had changed enough that while once they'd been easy prey for the *Each-uisge*, now they had to be avoided because they'd become so dangerous. They'd devised aeroplanes that could fly in defiance of nature, they'd created weapons that could kill from far away, and they'd built stronger houses that could resist most storms.

What had her father said about humans, all those years ago? The same father whose presence Hæra could sense now? *I find much to admire in them.*

The sea was so near. It was the source of Hæra's strength and the place to which she sought to return. And for the first time in six years, she thought: *Why?*

She'd spent as much time as she could in isolation from the rest of the herd, and the rest of the time trying to prove herself. Her only dream had been one that would let her break with generations' worth of precedence.

Suppose she was allowed to return without being executed. If she couldn't become a Stormhorse, her fate would be a cycle of mating with one so he could breed her for centuries. Each pregnancy lasted roughly ten years, and only one foal was born at a time, which was why her kind's numbers were so few in spite of their long lifespan. Why in the Great Mare's name would she risk that for the slim chance at a dream?

"Are you okay?"

Madeleine was looking up at Hæra with wide eyes; she wore an expression of concern, of caring. Because Madeleine cared about Hæra. As did Jonathan. People here on land cared about Hæra, while her own family had attempted to kill her. Why go back?

Because you have no choice, she told herself. *Because you aren't human, no matter what you look like. The only land creature who understands you is an underground trow.*

"Hæra?" Madeleine prompted. "What's wrong? You look like you're a thousand miles away."

A thousand leagues underwater, perhaps. Hæra should say nothing was wrong: a human custom that had been easy to pick up.

"This place reminds me of my father," she heard herself say instead.

Madeleine blinked, and then her face softened. "You don't mean Jonathan, right? You mean the man who raised you."

"The one who raised me, yes." Hæra looked restlessly over the pits and the swarm of tourists. "I can imagine him here."

"He liked this kind of thing? Archaeology, history?"

"Yes." As Hæra said it, she realized it was true. Her father had taught her much of the history of the sea, the herd, and humans too. Beathag had approved of the first two, but not the last.

She should stop now, before Madeleine began to ask questions she couldn't answer. Especially because, for the first time, Hæra wanted to answer those questions. That was a bad idea. If anything could make Madeleine stop caring about her, it'd be the truth.

She began, "Shall we—"

Madeleine put a hand on her forearm, and Hæra ran out of breath to speak.

"It's strange what makes us remember, isn't it?" Madeleine asked. Her gentle voice wound around Hæra's heart like a leafy vine. "I miss my family too, although some of the things they taught me..." She seemed to hesitate. "Well, never mind that. I lost them a long time ago, but even now something will remind me of them when I'm least expecting it. It hurts, even though I'm glad to remember."

A sudden breeze ruffled her hair, and she let out an "ooh!" It must be a cold breeze. Hæra wasn't the best judge of temperatures that bothered humans. Because she couldn't yet speak, she angled her body so that she stood between Madeleine and the wind.

"Better?" she asked.

Madeleine's hand still rested on her arm. How strange, that the touch could anchor Hæra to earth at the same time it made her feel light enough to fly without wings.

"Yes." Madeleine sounded breathless. "Very chivalrous of you."

Hæra didn't know the word *chivalrous*, but she could guess from the context. It was clearly a compliment. "If you're cold, we should go inside that big house you got the tickets for."

"You're done looking at the ruins?"

"I think I've got the idea." Hæra tilted her head to the side. "I'm ready to see something newer, if you are."

"I…" Madeleine took a deep breath. "I'm ready to move on, yes."

"Then let's go." Madeleine might take her hand off Hæra any moment now. Best to prevent that if she could. Hæra placed her own hand over Madeleine's and tucked it so that it rested in the crook of her elbow. "Your hands are cold."

Madeleine's face had reddened. "I should have brought gloves. I keep forgetting."

Hæra squeezed her fingers. They were cool indeed—and long, so maybe their circulation wasn't good. Maybe Madeleine's blood traveled too slowly in her veins to keep her warm, and it needed coaxing.

"You don't need gloves." She rubbed Madeleine's fingers gently. "You've got me. Let's go somewhere warmer."

Madeleine said nothing, but she didn't take her arm from Hæra's either. Together, they walked toward Skaill House, turning their backs on the ancient past.

CHAPTER TWENTY-ONE

WHAT A LONG, strange day it's been.

The words danced through Madeleine's mind as she looked at Hæra across the table in the little restaurant near the Kirkwall ferry terminal.

Hæra's reaction to their mini-tour of the Mainland had let Madeleine know she was telling the truth: she didn't leave Jorsay much, and she'd seen precious little of the rest of Orkney. In fact, you'd think she'd never seen a city in her life. Even Kirkwall—which Madeleine struggled to think of as a "city" per se—seemed to astonish Hæra. She kept her eyes wide open, looking in shop windows with fascination and pointing out people who struck her as remarkable in one way or another. A husband and wife speaking Russian ("I've never heard that language before!"), a man so tall he loomed over everyone else ("I suppose he feels self-conscious a lot."), and another couple shepherding their five children through the streets ("They must really enjoy having sex.").

Madeleine hadn't been able to summon even a choked reprimand at the last one. Hæra's tone hadn't been suggestive or mischievous at all—she might have been making any ordinary observation. Not that anything about Hæra was ordinary.

That was as evident now as ever. They'd been served ten minutes ago, and Hæra had still spent more time looking around the restaurant than eating. "How's your dinner?" Madeleine asked.

Hæra started—she had been looking at the bar—and glanced down at her plate of fish and chips. "It's very…cooked," she said.

"You mean overdone?" Their haddock filets seemed perfectly golden and crispy.

"I suppose. Yes." Hæra looked back at the bar. "Do you enjoy alcoholic drinks?"

No way was she telling Hæra about the Applebee's cocktails. "On occasion. You?"

"Jonathan doesn't keep alcohol in the house, and my family didn't drink. I've never tried it."

Madeleine's eyes widened. "Really?"

"On my honor." Hæra turned her sharp eyes back on Madeleine. "Should I try it tonight?"

"You've honestly never had a drink until now." Yes, she sounded skeptical, but so what? At least that was honest. "You never snuck a beer with your friends or tried it on your own?"

Hæra didn't seem offended by Madeleine's naked disbelief. "I didn't really have friends. Alcohol wasn't part of our culture. And I've heard it's sad to drink alone."

More puzzle pieces to put together. Madeleine could barely keep up with them all. Hæra had grown up moving from place to place with a spotty education and few social skills. She'd also indicated that she might have been forced to read the Bible growing up. Now Madeleine learned alcohol wasn't "part of the culture." Had Hæra been raised among religious extremists? Maybe even in a cult?

Maybe you shouldn't judge people whose lives were shaped by dogmatic religious practice, she thought ruefully, *especially when they get away from it.*

"If you want to try your first drink tonight, don't let me stop you," she said. "Just don't go overboard."

"You mean drink so much I'll fall off the ferry? I doubt it." Hæra flagged down their waitress. "Here she comes. What should we get?"

"Uh…you can't go wrong with a nice glass of wine. And white wine goes best with fish."

The waitress arrived. Hæra said, "We'll have two glasses of white wine, please."

"Right." The waitress smiled. "Do you know which white you'd like?"

Hæra frowned, then cast a sidelong glance at Madeleine. "Do *you* know?"

Madeleine hid a smile and leaned forward toward the waitress. "I don't," she said. "Can we see the list?"

———

"The wine-dark sea," Madeleine murmured.

Hæra wasn't sure what she meant by that. She was sure, however, that Madeleine's body was quite close to hers as they strolled along the dock outside the Jorsay ferry terminal. Their arms were touching, even though they had their hands in their pockets.

Wine was interesting, it turned out. She hadn't minded the Pinot Grigio after the first couple of sips. It wasn't salty like she usually preferred her beverages, but neither was it sweet. A bit sour, perhaps: not unpleasant.

Having finished two glasses, she felt calmer. The restaurant had been a disturbing experience at first—far more than Skara Brae. It was one thing to be surrounded by a load of humans when you were outside and moving around. It was another to sit still and be packed in like a sardine swarm within an enclosed space, unable to smell the sea.

But the wine had had a relaxing effect, and now she walked with Madeleine in a merry mood as the sun dipped lower over the horizon. It had stayed out all day today, and there was still over an hour left before dark fell completely. How rare to have felt sunlight on her face for so long.

That said, the amount of light made Madeleine's statement even more puzzling. "The sea's not dark," Hæra said. "Nor was the wine."

"I know. It's a quote from the *Odyssey*."

The title was familiar. "Isn't that a story about somebody going on a long journey?"

"Yes! Odysseus." Madeleine sounded impressed by Hæra's knowledge; Hæra couldn't help puffing out her chest a bit. "He's trying to go home, but it takes him so long that when he finally gets back, everything is different." She giggled. "Reminds me of…well, me."

Madeleine had also ordered two glasses of wine, though she hadn't finished the second. She looked more relaxed as well. In fact, she'd been wearing a little smile ever since they got off the ferry, where the wine hadn't agreed with her as much.

"Are you different?" Hæra asked. "Or are you more your true self than you've ever been?"

"Wow. You're deep when you've had a drink or two."

Then Madeleine slid her right arm into the crook of Hæra's left one. That put them even closer together.

Hæra managed not to stop in her tracks. This was even more intimate than when they'd held hands in the Skara Brae museum. She'd done that so the crowd wouldn't separate them—a thin excuse, but at least it was one. There was no excuse now for Madeleine to link their arms together. Hæra wasn't about to protest. A few days in, and there was already nothing like Madeleine's touch.

"I've been pretty deep, yes," she said, thinking of the marine abysses into which she'd plunged until her body couldn't withstand the pressures. The witch's whirlpool had been deep too. By now, Hæra understood enough of humans to know Madeleine meant metaphorically deep, but the two experiences felt similar.

"I'm sure you have been. Given what you've told me about your upbringing, I bet you've been to some pretty deep places. Maybe some dark ones."

Dark. Yes. Hæra hadn't seen the sun for years after she was born. The witch had looked up with no light in her hollow eyes as two corpses whipped around her. And Calder, Asgall, and Beathag had tried to kill her in the dead of night.

Hæra turned her face from the sea. "Let's get farther inland, toward the village. You must be chilly in the wind."

"I think I'm getting used to it. And the wine helps. And you."

Hæra looked down at Madeleine to see her looking back. The lowering sun turned her eyes the color of spring grass again.

"You're warm," Madeleine continued. "On the night we met, you were standing outside without even wearing a jacket."

Oh dear. That had been a careless slip on Hæra's part. "I was cold, I just didn't show it. In fact, I'd like to get out of the wind myself." She tugged gently and turned them away from the dock toward Thornhill. The closer they got to evening, the more dangerous it was for her to be within sight of the sea. She'd already indulged herself too much today.

Madeleine went without protest and kept her arm linked with Hæra's. Together, they climbed an uphill paved path that led to a wide alley between two brick buildings. The alley would lead up to the main street, and from there it was only a few blocks to Madeleine's hotel.

The inhabitants on either side of the alley had gone to some effort to beautify the place. Boxes and barrels of flowering plants lined the path. Greenery climbed the stone walls, dotted with the occasional rose or speedwell. Humans did this sort of thing: adding decoration to places for no practical reason. It didn't conceal them from predators or attract mates. Yet it stirred…something…in Hæra to see the bright colors against the drab stone. A bit like her rainbow.

"How lovely," Madeleine said as they walked down the alley. "Look at the flowers. In fact, hold on a second."

Hæra waited for Madeleine to start snapping pictures with her mobile. Humans were fond of doing that in moments like this. But instead, Madeleine bent to sniff a pink, fluffy rose. The movement pushed out her bottom. Her jeans fit her well. Hæra swallowed.

"Wonderful." Madeleine straightened up. "There's a reason they tell you to stop and smell the roses. Come on, you do it too."

At least she hadn't caught Hæra ogling her arse. "If it'd please you."

Madeleine looked in her eyes. "It would."

Hæra's heart hammered as she bent to inhale the scent of the rose.

It was sweet, almost overpoweringly so, but pleasant. She was used to how land plants smelled by now, and this was nicer than most.

"Tropical plants grow well in New Orleans," Madeleine said. "It's hot there. You might melt."

Hæra turned to face her. Madeleine was standing closer now, her face upturned as she gave Hæra an earnest look. She was very beautiful.

And far more relaxed than Hæra had ever seen her. There could be a reason for that. "Did you drink too much?"

Madeleine laughed. "One-and-a-half glasses isn't enough to knock me over. Just enough to make me think that some things I was worried about aren't that terrible, you know? And it's such a beautiful night, and these are such beautiful flowers, and you're..." She trailed off and kept looking into Hæra's eyes.

Hæra's heart was whale song: a thundering, irresistible call. She whispered, "What am I?"

Before Madeleine could answer, Hæra's hand did what it had wanted to do that first night in the kitchen. It reached up to touch Madeleine's face. Her skin was soft as the rose petals.

Madeleine's exhalation was barely audible. Perhaps human ears could not have heard it. But the dilation of her pupils was obvious, as was the soft parting of her lips.

At that moment, Hæra knew what she was. *I'm hers.*

And after six years, drawn to Madeleine's heat like sea fog to the land, Hæra kissed her.

CHAPTER TWENTY-TWO

WARM.

At first, that was all Madeleine could think. Hæra's mouth was so warm, a point of heat and delight that drew the wind's chill from Madeleine's bones.

Gentle, too. Such gentleness, from the woman who'd scooped up Madeleine in her arms—had it only been that morning?—with astonishing strength. Soft lips, followed by a puff of breath against Madeleine's own mouth. A tender hand on the side of her face.

Then the hand moved.

Swift as a riptide, it moved from Madeleine's cheek to the back of her neck, curling possessively around her. Madeleine's warmth flamed to the heat of an inferno as Hæra wrapped her other arm around her waist, dragging her even closer. Then Hæra's mouth opened and the kiss changed into something else entirely.

She wasn't kissing Madeleine. She was devouring her.

There was no other word for it. Hæra kissed her like she was starving, and Madeleine was a feast she'd seen through a window and broken in to take. And she wouldn't finish taking until she was sated, no matter what anyone had to say about it.

So why Madeleine was throwing her arms around Hæra's neck

was a mystery. Not one to be solved—a mystery like they'd spoken of before, a divine one, integral to who she was. Here, in Hæra's unrelenting embrace, Madeleine stumbled over all her questions and, finally, into herself.

She kissed Hæra back wildly. It was what her mouth had been made to do. Not to mouth prayers or stammer excuses, but to kiss this woman. Her breasts pressed just beneath Hæra's own, their bodies fit together perfectly, they aligned without a molecule of air to interfere between them.

And the ache from her dream returned in full force, as if it had only been lying in wait. In a breath's space, she became an empty vessel, hollowed out and absent her purpose until she was filled. She cried out softly.

Hæra opened her mouth, and the kiss grew deeper, and deeper. Madeleine dug her fingers into Hæra's strong shoulders, feeling as wobbly as when she'd fallen to the floor this morning. She couldn't fall. Not if falling would end this, the moment in which she was finally coming to life.

She didn't have to worry. Hæra wouldn't let her fall. Hæra was pushing her back toward the alley wall, between two planters, until Madeleine's back was pressed against leaves. No roses here, no thorns, only the soft rustle of ivy. And yet the scent of flowers filled the air, along with Hæra's own scent—salt and sea.

"Yes," Hæra breathed, "yes."

"Yes—" It broke from Madeleine in a moan.

Hæra growled. She cupped Madeleine's rear end, just like in her dream, only Madeleine wasn't naked this time. Layers of clothing separated them, and Madeleine whined in the back of her throat at the deprivation. Skin on skin—oh God, what a delight that would be, what a *necessary* thing, and she didn't have it—

But Hæra's hands were warm through the thick fabric of her jeans. And her thigh pressed between Madeleine's own, urging her forward, making her rock.

Pressure. Divine pressure in her most sensitive place. Madeleine cried out softly against Hæra's mouth, her hands scrabbling over

Hæra's shoulders as she rose up on her toes, seeking more, and then more.

She got more. Hæra gave it to her, rubbing Madeleine back and forth on her thigh with that inexorable strength, making Madeleine sob with need. It couldn't be possible. How was she this turned on, this quickly—?

Not quickly. It was the work of decades, and Madeleine was starving too. She ground on Hæra's leg in search of more while they kissed and kissed, moaning against that ferocious mouth. Back and forth, faster, harder.

"More," Hæra gasped, as if she'd read Madeleine's mind.

Faster. Harder. "Yuh-yes—"

"More!"

Her thigh withdrew, taking the glorious pressure with it. Madeleine bucked her hips forward, a gasp of protest escaping her, but then—then something else was there—

Hæra's hand—

Madeleine's knees buckled. It wasn't enough. She didn't know anything could feel like this much, and she still didn't have *enough*.

Hæra cupped her through her jeans, finding the same perfect rhythm. Her other hand still grabbed Madeleine's rear, holding her firmly in place to be fondled, stroked and rocked and cradled. She created the pace, dictated the speed of Madeleine's pleasure, as if it didn't occur to her to do otherwise.

It got Madeleine wetter than anything ever had in her life.

She cried out again, muffled by kisses. Between her legs she was heavy, swelling. The seam of her jeans was a torment, but she rutted against it anyway because it was stimulation, it was *something* after decades of nothing, and even discomfort was better than lack. She'd had so much of lack. Now she might have—

"I can make you do it." The words curled in a hot promise from Hæra's mouth into Madeleine's. "I can make you come."

"Oh!" Madeleine's hips rocked faster, chasing that promise. More, she still needed more. She was so wet—was it enough to soak into her jeans? Could Hæra *feel* how wet she was?

"You're so beautiful!" Hæra tore her mouth from Madeleine's, and suddenly that mouth was at Madeleine's neck, nuzzling at the skin above her jacket collar. "I'll do it to you. I can do it, I know how."

"Do it to me," Madeleine whimpered, unable to stop herself. "Oh God, my God, do it—"

For a terrible moment, Hæra's hand went still. Her mouth moved against Madeleine's skin. "I," she whispered, "am not your God."

Then her teeth sank into Madeleine's neck.

It should have hurt, probably. It should have been terrifying, certainly. Instead, the pressure of Hæra's teeth made spots dance in front of Madeleine's eyes. Seeing stars while the sun was out. Pain at her neck, pleasure between her legs, two halves that made a thing complete. She couldn't have one without the other, she needed Hæra's teeth as much as she needed her hand, she needed *all* of it, and this was why she'd come to Jorsay. It was here, the answer was right here, she hadn't known, she'd had no idea—

Oh dear Jesus, she was about to—

"Oi! Keep it to yourselves!"

The words rained down from above like a bucket of cold water. Hæra's head reared back, and Madeleine pulled her own head away so quickly she bumped it against the wall. Together, they looked up to see a window slamming, the voice's owner unseen.

The shutting of the window shut something inside Madeleine too. There was no air in her lungs, and that was no longer because of Hæra's kiss. Her arousal drained away instantly.

You did it. You did it, and someone saw *you.*

Her body curled in on itself. She tugged her arms from Hæra's neck to hold them in front of herself, her hands shaking until she clenched them into fists as she looked away from Hæra toward the ground, at the cobblestones' uneven height. She couldn't move. She could barely breathe.

"I'll kill them."

Hæra's voice was rock-rough. It dragged Madeleine right back into the moment. She gaped at Hæra, who was looking up at the closed window with her teeth bared.

"What?" Madeleine choked.

"I said, I'll..." Hæra looked back down at Madeleine, who pressed back farther against the wall at that look. Her amber eyes had turned all to golden fire, like nothing Madeleine had ever seen in her life. Such eyes didn't belong to an ordinary person—they couldn't possibly—

Madeleine's eyes widened as several images collided in her mind, knocking shame into the background. Hæra looming over Madeleine now in the alley, eyes aflame. Hæra towering over her in the movie room at Skara Brae, all in silhouette—a moment that had taken Madeleine out of herself because it was so familiar, because—

Because it had been a woman's shape looming over her with a shadowed face, with burning eyes, while Madeleine lay helpless and overwhelmed on the beach...

"That is, of course I won't. I only meant..." Hæra's shoulders rose and fell with her rapid breath. Her pulse raced at the base of her throat. She curled her hands around Madeleine's arms again. "We don't have to stop. Let's go somewhere else. The farm...no, your hotel is closer, isn't it? Let's go, *please*—"

No, Madeleine could have said, or *I can't do this, it's wrong,* but none of that came out of her mouth. Something else did instead.

She whispered, "Are you my angel?"

Angel. Madeleine had defined that for Hæra not so long ago. She'd said her Scriptures described them as beings of terrible aspect, more frightening than comforting.

Right now, that seemed fitting. When they'd been interrupted, Hæra's instinct had been to tear the interloper apart with her teeth. *I'll kill them,* she'd said, with no idea who "they" were, only knowing that they must be destroyed for interfering with destiny. *Her* destiny—to kiss and touch Madeleine forever, or at least until they'd both reached that shattering climax she'd only experienced with herself so far.

She couldn't say that. She could only look down into Madeleine's face, flushed and beautiful, looking back at Hæra as if she'd never seen anything like her before. Her eyes begged for an answer while her body strained in obvious panic against Hæra's embrace.

"I'm not an angel," Hæra said, which was completely true.

"Then what are…"

Hæra's heart stopped. Her breath did too, frozen in her chest. Madeleine was about to ask, *What are you?* Only moments ago, the question had had a different tone. Now, either the truth or a lie would destroy Hæra.

"Madeleine," she blurted, but no other words followed. What words even mattered, next to that name?

Madeleine stared at Hæra, but the flush was fading from her cheeks, and the wildness from her eyes. Hæra's gaze dropped to the mouth she'd just kissed. She'd kissed it once before: that night on the beach. How could it be even better now? Even more all consuming?

Madeleine closed her eyes and groaned. "Oh, my goodness. You must think I'm insane. I can't believe I just said that."

Relief weakened Hæra's knees. "I'll take it as a compliment."

"I can't believe I just *did* that, either." Madeleine was shaking, minutely, in Hæra's arms. "I'm…I'm sorry. So sorry. It must have been the wine."

Oh no. If Hæra couldn't excuse her way out of this mess, Madeleine couldn't either. "You told me it wasn't affecting you that much."

Madeleine still didn't look at her. "Maybe I was wrong. I must have been. I don't do things like that, I don't…I don't kiss women, that's not right, it's…"

"You kissed me," Hæra said. "And it was very right."

Madeleine went still against her.

"Is this about everything you've read?" Hæra pressed. "Is it those *doubts* you told me about? Your questions?" She let go of Madeleine's arms to take her hands instead, pressing them to her own chest. "Were they about this? About me?"

"No! That is—" Madeleine tugged her wrists backward. "Yes and no? Please, I can't think. Let me go!"

"If I do, will you run?" If she did, how fast? Madeleine couldn't be as swift as Hæra, certainly not in Hæra's horse form, when she could tear up a field's soil with the sharpest hooves that had ever seen land.

"No, I won't *run*. Let go, I said."

Hæra saw that Madeleine wouldn't run, and she let go. Madeleine probably couldn't, considering that her knees wobbled the instant Hæra set her free.

Madeleine looked up at the closed window. "Who saw us?"

"I don't know." *Which is for the best.* Hæra couldn't help a snarl. "It doesn't matter. You don't know them. Why should you care?"

"I know I shouldn't." Madeleine pushed a stray lock of hair from her face. Her hand had stopped shaking, but she seemed to be having trouble meeting Hæra's eyes again. "I know I shouldn't put stock in earthly opinions, and I know I didn't hurt whoever that was, I know..."

Hæra's lips pulled back farther over her teeth. "You don't know much at all. That's why you're here."

Madeleine looked at her again, eyes wide.

"Here I am!" Hæra spread her arms. "You said you came here looking for answers. I'm one of them, even if we don't know the question. Can't you see that?"

Madeleine might not know Hæra for what she truly was, but they were bound together by a greater force. Whatever name it bore—God, the Great Mare, or something else—didn't matter.

"Impossible," Madeleine said. "I *can't* be here just to meet you, find you attractive, and realize I'm gay!"

At the last word, she went pale, then clutched her jacket over her heart. Her eyes looked up at Hæra as if she couldn't believe what she was looking at—or what she'd just said.

"Gay?" Hæra said, when it became clear Madeleine had no follow-up. "You mean homosexual, right?"

"Oh my Lord." Madeleine pushed past Hæra toward the mouth of the alley that led to Thornhill's main thoroughfare. Hæra couldn't help it: her hand extended after Madeleine to seize her, pull her back. Madeleine tugged away and kept going.

"You said you wouldn't run!" Hæra shouted.

Madeleine froze in place. Then she turned, the look in her eyes so bleak that anything Hæra might have said died between her teeth like a fish.

"I need time, okay?" Madeleine whispered. "I didn't expect any of this. I have to think."

"What's there to think about?" Hæra took one step forward. If that interfering bastard opened the window again, she wouldn't be responsible for her actions. "I want you, and you want me. Can't we figure it out together? Let me go wherever you're going, I don't care—"

"Hæra—"

"Don't leave me behind!"

Oh shite. She'd barely managed to choke down one more word: "again." *Don't leave me behind again.*

Return to me.

Madeleine wrapped her arms around herself like she had that night she'd come to dinner, when she and Hæra had spoken by the pasture with no idea this lay ahead. She repeated, "I need time to think."

"How much time?" Maybe Hæra should slow down—Jonathan said she tended to "charge like a bull"—but nothing seemed less possible right now. If she slowed down, Madeleine might speed up.

"I don't know. A couple of days."

"*Days?*"

"Or more. It's up to me," Madeleine snapped. She seemed to see something in Hæra's face—desperation, maybe—and for a moment, her own expression softened. "We'll talk again. I promise. But I have to go. Don't follow me, just go home."

Without another word, she bolted out of the alley, turned the corner, and was gone. Hæra stood alone, surrounded by flowers whose purpose she didn't understand, body still aching for what had left her.

Just go home, Madeleine had said, meaning the farm. If she'd stayed another moment, Hæra could have explained something important.

She'd found her home at last, and it was in Madeleine Laurent's arms.

———

Madeleine couldn't go back to the hotel. The front desk was officially closed by now, but Harry Duggan was the type to linger and chat up anyone who came through the door. After what had happened earlier that day—her tumble down the stairs, Hæra sweeping her up as if she were a fainting maiden—it would be better to jump off a cliff than face him.

Where was there *to* go? The shops were closed, and the chippy didn't have tables, just a counter where you ordered food. The Sunrise Café stood across the street, dark and silent.

Madeleine shivered as she walked past it. The sun touched the horizon now, and the night's chill was drawing in. She couldn't just pace Thornhill's streets, waiting for some sign that she wasn't delusional or damned.

One place was still open, and it'd stay open later than everywhere else on the island. Neither Hæra nor Jonathan were likely to show up. Madeleine turned her steps toward the Kestrel, Jorsay's only pub. One-and-a-half glasses of wine had been enough to get her in trouble. She'd just buy a drink for courtesy's sake, no matter how tempting it was to lose herself in an alcoholic haze.

Then again, she'd had a hard time resisting temptation lately.

CHAPTER TWENTY-THREE

"You can't work out why she's ashamed? Really?"

Jonathan's eyebrows came together in a scowl that made no sense. He should be on Hæra's side here. He had been so far, hadn't he?

"She was a nun," Jonathan continued. "You read the Bible, even if you didn't know the other books she told you about. Don't you remember what that bloody thing says about men who shag men, and women with women, and so on?"

Hæra winced. "Oh. A bit." There had been a few passages about how humans weren't supposed to mate with other humans of their own gender. It hadn't seemed relevant at the time, since Hæra hadn't known she'd want to have sex with Madeleine, much less that Madeleine would want to have it with her.

Dammit. This was going to be a problem. Hæra offered, "She cares about other books more, she said. About saints and whatnot. Maybe those are different."

"I seriously doubt it."

"You don't know, though. You're not like her, you don't even believe in God. Maybe you're wrong."

"I'm more like her than you are, aren't I?" Jonathan asked.

The words cleaved between the two of them with the sharpness only truth could carry. Jonathan had his arms crossed and a hard look in his eyes. "You don't understand her. You're not even trying."

Unbelievable. It wasn't even one of Jonathan's bad jokes. He looked much too serious.

"How can you say that? I've done everything to understand her!" Hæra began to count on her fingers. Her *human* fingers. "I learned your customs. I learned to eat and drink the disgusting things you do. I learned to read. All so I could talk to her and ask her the right questions."

"Did you learn how to listen to her answers?" Jonathan stalked over to his computer, looking much too upset about this. After all, it was Hæra's crisis, not his.

"She didn't give me any answers. Not proper ones. She just ran away after I...after *we*..."

"Kissed. You said." Jonathan threw himself into his desk chair and stared at the monitor, which Hæra couldn't see from the other side of the desk. In the window behind him, the day's sun sank toward the horizon. Not much time left.

"I didn't know your lot did that," he said after another moment. "You've told me how different my body really is from yours...and his."

She groaned. Jonathan ought to know that now wasn't the time to talk about Asgall, of all things. *Never* was the time to talk about Asgall. They had to solve Hæra's problem, once they worked out what it actually was.

"You've been queer since she got here," he continued. His knobby fingers rubbed over the white hair at his chin. "And now you've got a look in your eyes that reminds me of him."

Hæra stiffened.

"I thought he cared about me," Jonathan said to the monitor. Whatever he saw there appeared to fascinate him. "And then he tried to drown me."

Hæra stepped forward, heart pounding. She hadn't seen such a distance in Jonathan's eyes since the night they met. "I am not Asgall," she said, with all the force the words could hold.

"No? You want to hold her, same as he did me. And I don't mean for a sweet little kiss."

Nothing had been sweet or little about that kiss. It had eaten up Hæra as surely as a storm ate up the shore. As surely as she'd intended to eat up Madeleine at the beginning, which Jonathan didn't and mustn't know.

"We talked about this at the start," she said evenly. "I saved Madeleine's life. I care deeply for her. It's not the same as Asgall and you. Did my brother ever kiss you?" She said the last in a lighter tone, thinking the situation could use some levity.

"What do you think?" No levity in Jonathan's voice. Instead, there was something deep and dark, like pain.

That must mean *no*. Of course it did—the idea of Jonathan and Asgall *kissing* would be laughable, if anything about this was funny. "There you are, then. It's not the same thing at all."

"It better not be."

Hæra started. Jonathan had never sounded like that before: his voice low, heavy, almost cold. It sent a chill through her blood. "Where's this coming from?" she managed. "You've always supported me."

"I don't know. Like I said, you got that look in your eyes when you were telling me about what happened. And I remembered you're not like me. You'd think it'd be hard to forget, wouldn't you? What with how you eat raw meat and don't sleep. But it's *that look* that makes me see you as you are."

"As I—" Finally, Hæra could move. She rushed around the desk to kneel next to Jonathan's chair, where she looked imploringly up into his weathered face. That face had smiled at her for years. It wasn't smiling now.

"I dreamed of him, you know," Jonathan said. "All the time."

Hæra started.

"It felt like more than just dreams. I *saw* him, I heard his voice clear as day, and he was always calling me back to the rocks. For so long, I wondered if he was coming for me...if he wanted to find me."

"I—I didn't know that," Hæra stammered. "Why didn't you tell me?"

"The hell's the point? It hasn't happened. Nothing's ever happened in decades." He pursed his lips, and the white bristles of his mustache rose. "Except for you. Thought that meant something."

Something? Surely it meant more than *something*. Was it time to tell him the truth after all? They were friends—he was the only friend Hæra had ever had. Perhaps after all their time together, he wouldn't hate her if she explained the situation.

Hæra took one of his hands. It was cold, although the house wasn't. His circulation was bad, the doctor had said. "It does mean something," she said. "It's true I'm not human. I can't help that. But listen…"

"I know you can't help being what you are." Jonathan didn't pull his hand away. He didn't curl it around Hæra's either, though. "That's what worries me now."

"What do you mean?"

He looked at her, finally. His eyes were hooded, unreadable. "If I thought I'd been wrong about you this whole time…if I thought you meant her harm…"

Her entire body froze. She clutched his hand harder, but he didn't wince or tug away. Just kept looking at her. So much for telling him the truth.

"I don't want to hurt her," she said hoarsely. "Jonathan, I swear it."

That, at least, was true. Whatever must happen between them in the end, Hæra didn't *want* to hurt Madeleine. Not the woman she'd kissed, who'd spoken to her about things that mattered.

Jonathan kept looking into her eyes. All of a sudden, Hæra was back in the whirlpool, staring into the black eyes of the witch who sought her innermost self. Her heart stopped. She'd thought, only hours ago, that the trow was the only one who understood her. Had she been wrong? Jonathan seemed to be looking into the heart of her.

What would he find? Would he see the truth, whatever that was…?

Then he closed his eyes and sighed. When he opened them again, they looked as they always did, and a rueful smile tugged at his mouth. "Sorry, lass. I ought to know better."

Relief made Hæra's head dip down. Her heart began beating again. Jonathan did not hate her.

"This mad situation's carried me back, is all," he continued. "Last night, I had a dream he was calling me again. I woke up half ready to walk into the ocean. Scared the hell out of me. Then you came home tonight and…" He shook his head. "Never mind that now."

Hæra felt another chill. Years ago, when her family had tried to kill her, she'd had a vision of Sister Madeleine promising to return to Hæra. Nothing like that had happened since. Hæra had certainly not been able to call Madeleine to her side. She'd never heard of any *Each-uisge* doing that with their prey. Then again, no *Each-uisge* had failed with their prey in living memory, nor spent the sort of time that Jonathan and Asgall had together.

"You didn't tell me about that either," she said.

Jonathan shrugged. "It was only a dream. I just said I've had it off and on for decades. It makes sense, doesn't it, after all that's happened?"

She wouldn't know. *Each-uisge* didn't dream. Jonathan did, though. He'd know what was normal and what wasn't. Other problems loomed larger now.

Hæra didn't want to hurt Madeleine. She didn't want to hurt Jonathan. She didn't want to be found out as inhuman. She didn't want to return to the ocean and be torn to pieces by her kin, or give herself up to a witch.

She stood, feeling heavier than she had the first time she'd stepped on land, dragging Sister Madeleine's unconscious body with her. "I'm going out to the barn. Perhaps we can talk more later."

Jonathan nodded, and Hæra glanced toward the computer monitor he'd been staring at for so long.

The power wasn't on. She could see nothing but the two of them, their shapes reflected and distorted in the darkened screen.

———

There would be no whale mating songs for her tonight. Nor self-pleasure or any other rewarding thing.

It was after midnight. Jonathan was long abed, but Hæra couldn't rest. Not after the events of today. She leaned against her bedroom windowsill. Her breath fogged the glass as she glared at the dark pasture outside. The farm: her gift to Jonathan.

So far, her only legacy.

She could imagine what her family would say to that—even her father Alban, who'd been so intrigued by humans. Hæra's legacy shouldn't be making a human man happy for a time.

That, and kissing a former nun into a state of confusion until she ran away.

Hæra smacked her palm against the window, welcoming the sting and the coolness of the glass. It wasn't supposed to be like this. It was supposed to be some other way. Sister Madeleine was supposed to return to Jorsay as the nun she'd been before. She and Hæra were meant to meet, have some sort of instant understanding, and talk. Then, Hæra would eat her, return to the sea, and become a Stormhorse. Simplicity itself.

Becoming a human was much less simple than being an *Each-uisge*. Hæra couldn't figure out how…

Hæra wasn't *becoming a human*.

She recoiled from the window as the obscene idea crawled over her mind like a roach. Becoming human? Where had that come from? Ridiculous. She wore a human form around herself like a rough oyster shell hiding a pearl. Hadn't Jonathan just pointed out how inhuman she was? He'd know better than anyone.

Human! Why? Because she'd drunk wine and learned to read books? Because of her flimsy trappings, was she thinking of herself as one of *them*, weak and pathetic as they were? What was next? Starting a collection of useless objects, or whinging about Parliament, or the other pointless ways they spent their short time in the world?

This was going too far, too fast. Within the span of a few days, since Madeleine's reappearance, Hæra's life had spun more out of control than ever. And that was saying something. If thoughts like these were occurring to her, that had to be a sign. Of what, she didn't know, but it couldn't be good.

Hæra stormed to her bureau. She yanked open the top drawer and dragged out the wooden rosary she'd pulled from Madeleine's drenched body on the beach.

For years, Hæra had treasured it as a reminder of what they had together. Now, it was just another symbol of something that separated them: something Hæra couldn't understand but that was so important to Madeleine that it made her run from an all-consuming kiss.

Maybe she should march over to Madeleine's hotel right now, wake her, and confess everything. That would show exactly how inhuman she was. Then she'd do what she had to do, return to the sea, and never have to face Jonathan's disappointment and anger.

She could persuade Madeleine to leave the hotel. Go for a walk out of sight. Transform into her true shape. She hadn't done that since she'd come to live on land. That must be part of the problem. She'd forgotten what it was like to be herself.

She would transform and watch Madeleine's eyes widen with horror as she beheld the monster she would believe Hæra to be.

Then, this would all be over. Hæra would eat Madeleine, and Madeleine would be a part of her forever. She'd return to the sea in triumph, gain her wings, and take to the sky. No more confusion or desire, no more deluded reflections about wanting to stay on land. No more worries about a human man's opinion of her.

And definitely no thoughts about *becoming human* herself.

She'd remember who she was. *Each-uisge*, predator of the seas, destined for the skies. Not a woman with a cold current in the pit of her stomach and skin that prickled with panic.

She'd take care of this once and for all.

Hæra threw the rosary back in the drawer—neither she nor Madeleine would need it, after all—and stormed through the house. Time to leave and never come back.

She paused briefly by Jonathan's closed bedroom door. He was snoring on the other side.

She'd never see him again. He'd wake up to find her gone. Eventually, he'd hear that Madeleine had disappeared, he'd put two and two together, and he'd know that Hæra was what he feared. As bad as Asgall.

Well then. He would be correct. But he'd be all right, wouldn't he? She'd made him prosperous. The community respected him now. He'd found a purpose in running the farm. Once Hæra left, he'd no longer share his home with a creature who was everything he despised.

Jonathan would be better off without her.

Hæra swallowed down a groan and fled what had become her home for a brief and brilliant time.

CHAPTER TWENTY-FOUR

"Closing time, love."

Madeleine looked up from her drink, blinking more slowly than she usually did. Iona Darrow stood over her table, drying a beer glass with a towel.

Iona and her husband, Elliot, were co-owners of the Kestrel. They'd met when they were teenagers and had lived here their whole lives. They had one son who worked at the oil terminals. Plus a dog. Elliot was allergic to walnuts.

Madeleine had learned all of this during their multiple visits to her table, because she'd been here for a while. Now it was after midnight and she was the only one left in the pub.

"I'm sorry," she said. The words didn't sound right, maybe because her tongue felt thick in her mouth.

"No need to apologize."

There was, but Madeleine couldn't remember to whom, or why.

"We've got to close up. Why don't you just finish that one?" Iona raised an eyebrow. "Or not, maybe."

There was still a swallow or two left in Madeleine's second whisky. She didn't love whisky but had needed to order something, and gin or vodka hadn't felt right. The Kestrel didn't do fruity little cocktails. She didn't like beer, and wine was right out.

Turned out whisky wasn't too bad, especially once you'd finished the first one. After that, a second seemed like a great idea. Madeleine picked up her glass and knocked back a swallow. Her throat stung and her eyes smarted. The ice cubes clinked against her teeth.

"You know how to find the Merryweather?" Iona looked worried. "I can ring Harry, he'd come and fetch you. Or Elliot could walk you there."

Madeleine might be drunk, but not so drunk she'd welcome anyone else's company right now. "I can find the hotel. I leave, hang a right, and walk two blocks."

"Three. You're sure you—"

"I'll just be on my way. Thank you." There, that sounded polite. She'd enunciated every word perfectly. You'd never know she was intoxicated.

She paid for her drinks and stood up. Everything spun around her. The Kestrel was a welcoming place with old wooden tables and a bar that seemed to have been hewn from the Stone Age, like Skara Brae. It was also a little out of focus.

Nevertheless, Madeleine held her head high as she left. Was she walking in a straight line? It didn't matter; she wasn't driving. She just had to hang a right, walk two blocks—or three or ten or whatever— find the Werrymeather, and go to bed.

Just hang a right.

Madeleine's feet turned to the left and started walking, with her bemused permission, toward the sound of the ocean.

At this hour, even the main thoroughfare was deserted. She had the street to herself. In fact, it seemed like she might be the only person in the world. What a lonely thought. Madeleine shoved her hands in her jacket pockets. The sea grew louder as she walked toward it. At least she wasn't cold. That might be the whisky too. Was there anything it couldn't do? Dull her senses, warm her up...make her brave.

Brave enough to find her beach.

She'd put it off long enough. She should have gone to the beach the same day she'd arrived on Jorsay. Why hadn't she? It didn't make any sense. She'd stayed away from it just because Hæra had asked her to for no reason.

Hæra.

Madeleine laughed roughly into the wind.

Hæra had asked an awful lot of her in the space of a short time. To stay away from the beach, to talk about damningly personal things, and—just recently—to go to the hotel together. To finish what they'd started. Hæra had sounded so desperate, as much as Madeleine herself had felt.

That couldn't have been possible, though. Madeleine had been desperate enough to ask if Hæra was an *angel*—a sure sign of a woman losing her mind.

The street weaved crookedly in front of her. That was okay. Just put one foot in front of the other. The beach was getting closer. No matter how drunk she was, she was heading in the right direction. She could find that beach with her eyes closed right now. It seemed to call to her.

There was a noise behind her.

Madeleine held still and listened. For the first time, a prick of worry made its way through her haze. It wasn't the best idea for a woman to walk, drunk and alone, in a strange place in the middle of the night. What if she was being followed?

She turned unsteadily, but behind her was only the empty street, dark but for where the lamps cast ellipses of light onto the pavement.

Must have imagined it.

Maybe she'd imagined all kinds of things. Maybe this trip—maybe the last six years of her life—was just one big hallucination, a fever dream, and she'd wake up in Sacred Heart to find none of it had happened.

But on the off chance that wasn't true, she kept walking toward her beach.

Eventually, she stood at the same seawall she'd walked years ago with a tiny flashlight she'd lost and a pair of scissors in her pocket.

She might have changed in the meantime, but the beach looked the same. It must *be* the same. Those must be the same rocks that had sat there six years ago.

There, several yards away from the rocks, stood the same dock she'd fallen from.

Madeleine didn't have a flashlight this time. She had a phone, though. Its flashlight function, combined with the streetlamps behind her, provided just enough illumination for Madeleine to make her way down the steps that led from the seawall to the shore. As she went, the wind carried the scent of the sea to her: thick and a little rotten, as if it was about to roll ashore and leave something behind to decay.

Even with the flashlight, the darkness was oppressive. The rocks were slippery. She was probably going to twist an ankle, or maybe her neck. Madeleine laughed giddily as she made her way to the dock. This was ridiculous, and so was she. If her students could see her now, sensible Ms. Laurent—Sister Madeleine no more—they'd be astonished.

The wind slapped her face, as if encouraging her to sober up. Her hair followed suit. Madeleine pulled it back, and in so doing, dropped her phone. It hit the rocks with a clatter.

"Dammit!" she gasped. Then she laughed again. It felt great to curse. How long had it been since she'd done that? She picked up her phone, saw that its case had protected it, and turned toward the sea.

"*God damn it!*" she screamed. The words tumbled away into the wind. Her throat hurt. She'd yelled with all her might. Maybe somehow, across the sea, someone would hear the sound of her frustration.

She took another step toward the dock. She'd found a horse under there, of all things. Then she'd drowned it by trying to save it. What did it say about a night when *that* wasn't the strangest thing that had happened?

Her vision was even blurrier now as her eyes watered. Must be the wind. It was so loud. She couldn't hear anything over it. She dashed a hand across her eyes. Took another step toward the dock and the dark water beyond it.

At that moment, the wind ceased.

With it, so did the noise. For the first time since she'd gotten out of bed this morning, Madeleine was surrounded by absolute silence. Now she could hear only the sound of her heartbeat.

And something else.

Another noise behind her. Clattering. Slow, measured, deliberate. Something…someone…was walking over the rocks.

Walking in her direction. The footsteps were getting closer.

Sudden fear did more to sober you up than wind or water. Was it someone taking advantage of a drunk woman on her own? Her phone didn't get a good signal out here, but maybe she could still call 911— wait, the UK used a different emergency number, what was it—

Madeleine turned on her heel, barely managing not to fall, her heart in her mouth. Would she see an assailant? No.

She saw a horse.

It stood on the rocks perhaps fifteen feet away, silhouetted by the streetlights above the seawall. It held perfectly still as it stared Madeleine down. It made no sound.

Madeleine was no expert on horses. She'd drowned the only one she'd ever come into close contact with. But she was pretty sure they weren't supposed to be this big. The horse in front of her looked large enough to carry three full-grown adults. It couldn't be real, could it? Was the whisky making her hallucinate this?

She was drunk enough to wobble when she walked, but she wasn't drunk enough to hallucinate.

Madeleine raised her phone with its flashlight. Her hand shook so much that the beam darted all over the place. The horse seemed unbothered by this. It began to walk toward her again, its hooves sure and steady against the rocks. Its pace was slow and measured. Its eyes never looked away from her face.

Madeleine could think of nothing so much as being stalked, but that was ridiculous. Horses didn't stalk people. They weren't predators. They also weren't this enormous, and they didn't randomly appear on beaches in the middle of the night.

Making an effort to steady her hand, Madeleine managed to get the light onto the horse's face, flashing the beam over its eyes. The horse stopped in place, closed its eyes, and shook its head.

It also bared its teeth.

Its long, *pointed* teeth.

Madeleine's hand began shaking again, so badly that she nearly dropped the phone a second time, and the flashlight beam dipped away from the horse. She'd seen enough, though. She'd seen that its flesh was a pale blue color, that its eyes were bright yellow, and that it had sharp teeth. This was not a normal horse. And in this place, at this time, only one possibility suggested itself.

"You were the horse under the dock," she said raggedly. "The one I drowned."

The horse's long, black tail flickered. It looked an awful lot like confirmation.

"Oh God." Madeleine clutched the collar of her jacket. "You're a ghost or something."

But that couldn't be, could it? Horses couldn't become ghosts, because animals didn't have souls. Doctrine was clear on that.

Doctrine seemed to have little bearing on what stood before her now.

The horse took a step forward. Madeleine took a corresponding step backward. She was past the rocks now, and onto the sand at the water's edge.

"Are you angry?" she managed. "I'm so sorry. I didn't mean to. I just wanted to help."

The horse kept coming forward. Madeleine kept moving backward. But there was nothing behind her save for the sea. There was nowhere to go.

"I didn't know you'd drown. I thought you could swim. How else could you have gotten under the dock?"

The horse made a soft, low sound. It wasn't a neigh or any other noise she knew horses could make.

It was a growl.

Her blood ran colder than the North Sea. Madeleine gasped, "Oh

Lord, Blessed Virgin, protect me. Listen, you—you stay right there, you—"

She stepped back. The heel of her shoe hit the water, which lapped around her foot, soaking frigidly into her sneaker.

Should have worn those rain boots, she thought nonsensically. *Becca's going to fuss at me about that.*

No, Becca wouldn't. Madeleine was never going to see Becca again because she was going to die on this beach, *her* beach, murdered by a *horse ghost.* She had to be dreaming. This was the worst nightmare she'd ever had.

"I was trying to save you!" she cried.

The horse stopped in place.

"You were caught up, remember? In that dock?" She tried to raise the phone again to use the flashlight. Her arm wouldn't move. "I only wanted to set you free."

The horse turned its huge head. It made no sound as it cast its gaze over the darkness of the sea. Its tail twitched, and it stomped one hoof against the stones, as if agitated.

It seemed distracted. Could Madeleine make a run for it? Could anyone outrun a horse the size of a delivery van, whether it was a ghost or not? Especially when the path was strewn with slippery rocks?

She'd damned well better try, considering the alternative.

Madeleine lurched toward the right, eyeing the seawall stairs, which seemed to be a thousand miles away. Everything remained fuzzy from the whisky she'd guzzled. Her legs wouldn't move as fast as she told them to. Even if they would, they wouldn't be faster than the horse. It darted in front of her, baring its sharp teeth once more.

Madeleine staggered backward again. Her feet slid into the wet sand and water. "Stop!"

The horse didn't seem inclined to comply. It just kept walking while staring Madeleine down with that unnerving glare of intelligence.

She looked around wildly. The dock was just a few feet away, much like when she'd woken up on the rocky shore beneath... beneath...

Madeleine's breath caught. This was the spot. This was the same spot her angel must have dragged her ashore. She looked back at the horse.

"You should leave me alone," she said, her voice ringing like a bell. "Something here protected me last time. It will again. I know it."

The horse took a sudden step back, as if startled. So it did understand her. That much was obvious. Somehow, this monster understood English.

Then it looked over her shoulder at the sea and flicked its tail again.

What was it looking at, or for? Before she could think better of it—must have been the alcohol—Madeleine turned as well.

Bad idea. The sudden shift in perspective disoriented her. She was drunk, the ground was slippery, and for the third time, Madeleine Laurent fell down on Jorsay at the worst possible moment.

Her feet went out from under her. Her phone flew out of her hand. She landed on her bottom with a cry, right in the sand. She put a hand back to steady herself and the icy water rushed over it. Was the tide rising? She couldn't tell, didn't know, and it didn't matter because in the space of a breath, the gigantic horse was looming over her, blocking out any source of light.

Her angel was nowhere in sight. Madeleine was all alone.

No small stones lay within reach. Neither did her phone. She had nothing to throw at the beast or blind it with. She had nothing but her hands, soft and useless. Helplessly, Madeleine stared up at the terrifying creature that was about to kill her.

The horse lowered its massive head. Madeleine closed her eyes, unable to breathe as that muzzle descended toward her. Its breath blew hot against her forehead, stirring the loose hairs there. Here they came, the razor teeth, ready to tear her to shreds.

Then, the horse inhaled, deeply, as if smelling her. A low, soft noise rumbled out of its throat.

Madeleine's heart stopped.

The horse lifted its head. It made another low noise. Instead of tearing into Madeleine with its teeth, it paced around her, toward the sea.

Madeleine sat frozen. The sea behind her splashed and sloshed as the horse walked into the water. What was happening? Had it heeded her pleas and warnings, was it returning to the sea where it had died?

Suddenly, something hit Madeleine between her shoulder blades, hard enough to drive the breath out of her. Then it happened again.

The horse was nudging her with its head.

She tilted forward, gasping, as the horse bumped her with its head once more. Then it whinnied impatiently.

Madeleine scrambled to her feet and staggered toward her phone. It took her a couple of attempts to pick it up, precious moments in which the monster could easily kill her, but no such thing happened. Instead, the horse remained behind her.

Certain she was dreaming, Madeleine slipped her phone into her pocket. She didn't seem to need it right now, if it was even working at this point. It didn't seem like the moment to stop and check.

The horse nudged her shoulder with its nose again, pushing her away from the water, in the direction of the seawall.

Madeleine stumbled forward. A few steps in, she stepped on a rock that tilted beneath her foot, and nearly fell again.

The horse caught the back of her jacket with its teeth and dragged Madeleine back to her feet. It made another impatient sound, as if telling Madeleine to be more careful.

In this impossible way, Madeleine made her way back to the seawall. The horse walked behind her. Halfway up the steps, the wind kicked back in, cutting through her jacket as the whisky's warm protection officially wore off. Her feet and bottom were soaked from landing in the water, and her toes felt like blocks of ice.

Knees trembling, she reached the beginning of the central thoroughfare. As she did, the horse bumped her shoulder again and made a sound of warning. Unable to help herself, Madeleine turned and looked up. Closer to the streetlamps, she could see that the horse's eyes were indeed a flashing yellow—although when they rolled a certain way, they looked almost red.

This close up, away from the sea and all its terror, she noticed something else too. The horse...smelled nice.

Which shouldn't be possible. Shouldn't it smell however monsters smelled? Like fire and brimstone or something? Instead, the horse smelled like the sea. Not the rotting smell of earlier, but like the first time you caught the scent as you approached from shore. Refreshing, exciting, the hours ahead full of possibility.

The horse tossed its head and growled again. Then it turned its nose toward a side street in an unmistakable gesture. It wanted to go that way instead of walking down the main thoroughfare.

Maybe it preferred to kill its victims in alleys like any murderer would. Madeleine shook her head. "If you want to kill me, you can do it where people might see you. And I'll scream. They can hear me now."

The horse growled again.

Madeleine lifted her chin. "You should go back to the ocean, or wherever you came from. I guess you know now that I didn't mean you any harm? Although..."

She hesitated. Well. Even if the horse was about to kill her, she ought to do the right thing.

"I am sorry about what happened," she repeated softly. "I tried to set it right, but I couldn't. If you are a ghost, then I hope you find peace now and go to...horse heaven. Or wherever you'd go."

The horse snorted. The sound was bizarrely familiar.

"Look." She ran a hand over her mussed hair. "You're not supposed to go anywhere. Animals aren't supposed to have souls. But here you are, and I can't think what else you can *be*, so that must mean you've got one, and—and—" She laughed suddenly, painfully. "And Hæra was right."

The horse tilted its head to the side, appearing inquisitive now.

"This wasn't anything I was ever taught. Maybe other things are wrong too? Maybe everything's wrong." Madeleine wrapped her arms around herself as the wind cut through her again. "You started it all, you know. Everything that's happened."

She looked into the horse's yellow eyes, which pierced her in return, like a pin pressing a butterfly into a glass case.

"You already ate me up," she said thickly. "There's only bones left. Spiritually speaking."

The horse looked down at her. As she might have expected, it was silent.

Madeleine whispered, "Of course, you can't say anyth—"

The horse moved again. Not to bite her. Instead, it walked past her, toward the main thoroughfare of Thornhill Village, out in the open.

Then, as Madeleine gaped at it, it turned its head and jerked its head toward the street. Clearly saying: *Well? Come along, then.*

This really had to be a dream. The horse, the village, this entire trip—all of it.

In that case, there was no reason for Madeleine not to go to the horse, which waited for her. And together, they walked down the pavement on the left side of the street.

The horse walked closest to the wall, farther from the streetlamps. It kept its pace slow and stately next to Madeleine, who felt no less rubber-kneed than she had on the beach. The windows along the street were dark. She and the horse were alone and, it seemed, unseen. The lamplight threw their shadows heedlessly around as they walked. The horse's shadow looked even larger than its owner when it stretched out into the darkened street or along a wall.

Away from the sea, the only sound was the clop of the horse's pointed hooves and the steady susurration of its breath. It was the strangest and most silent stroll of Madeleine's life.

Eventually, they reached the steps of the Merryweather Hotel. Madeleine looked up at the door. Then she turned to regard the horse. "Uh, am I going to run into you again?" She devoutly hoped not, no matter how good the creature smelled.

The horse flicked its tail.

"Is that a yes or a no?"

The horse just flicked its tail again.

"Right," Madeleine muttered. What else was there to say? *Thanks for not killing me?* That seemed like a great way to revisit the possibility. She settled for, "Good night."

She turned around. Climbed the first step.

Hard pressure at her shoulder.

Madeleine wheezed in shock as the horse sank its teeth into her jacket and tugged. Instead of tearing into her skin, it ripped off a patch of fabric.

Then, before she could scream, the horse stepped back, turned, and galloped down the sidewalk.

Madeleine stared after it in disbelief. Its massive body moved with unbelievable speed as it raced away and turned down the first side street in view. Then it was gone.

She looked at her shoulder, at the rip. The jacket's fabric was tough. That was the whole point of it. That creature's teeth must be razor-sharp. Its mouth and jaw must be able to exert tremendous pressure.

Did that just happen? No. No. This is a dream.

Yes. That must be it. She was dreaming, so she'd better go to bed. That made sense.

Madeleine stumbled into the hotel and made her way to her room. She knew she should brush her teeth, say her prayers, and sleep.

Wobbling a little, she eyed the spot at the foot of the bed where she knelt to pray.

"Not tonight," she mumbled, and then collapsed on the bed fully dressed, shoes and all, as everything went black.

CHAPTER TWENTY-FIVE

I couldn't do it.

Hæra sat on the back steps of the house, staring at Ætlaquoy's fields. The sun was rising, but it was only a patch of light through the clouds. Today would be gray.

Fitting. She felt gray inside too. She felt as heavy as she had the first time she'd walked onto land, when the water had stopped carrying her.

I couldn't do it.

It should have been perfect. In human form, her head on fire, Hæra had gone into the village and sought out the hotel. From a distance, on the street, she'd seen Madeleine—clearly drunk—heading toward the sea. Toward their beach.

The Great Mare had arranged it, Hæra had been sure. It was a sign that it was time for this to come to an end and for Hæra to embrace her destiny at last. What else could it be, when Hæra had finally found her resolve, only to see Madeleine heading for the beach of her own accord?

Hæra had transformed for the first time in years. For a moment, as she'd stretched and grown and shifted her shape, she'd thought: *I forgot.* She'd forgotten what it was like to wear the body she'd had for nearly a century. Well—that would change, she'd decided, once she did what she'd come to do.

And she hadn't been able to do it.

Madeleine had stood before her under the moon and stars, the wind making a mess of her hair. Her mouth, the same mouth Hæra had kissed, hung open. Her sea-green eyes bugged out. She'd been shocked, and then terrified.

And beautiful.

And edible.

Hæra hadn't been around Madeleine in her true form since the night they'd met. She'd forgotten what that was like too. Madeleine's scent was delicious when Hæra wore a human shape. It made her want strange, complicated things.

When Hæra was in *Each-uisge* form, it made her want something simpler: to devour. To feast.

I couldn't do it.

How was it possible? To stand in front of what she wanted most in the world and be unable to take it?

Unclear. In the moment, all Hæra had known was that she couldn't rend the same face she'd kissed only hours ago with more desire than the sea could hold.

She could have spoken. Explained herself. But faced with Madeleine's horror, the words wouldn't come. Hæra hadn't been able to identify herself as the woman who'd vowed to protect Madeleine, kissed her, and was now about to eat her.

"I only wanted to set you free," Madeleine had cried, her voice raw with fear Hæra had never wanted her to feel. Set Hæra free? It was funny how human intentions often led to the opposite effect. Madeleine had slammed a prison door in Hæra's face and turned the key.

Hæra hadn't been able to hurt a hair on Madeleine's head, and she never would be.

So it was over. There would be no wings for her. No sky. For her whole life, she'd wondered what it was like to be borne aloft by the wind. She'd longed to know what clouds felt like. Now she never would, and her chest ached so much she wanted to weep, to release the cold agony of lost hope.

She wouldn't. She wouldn't ever weep again. She'd promised herself, and this would at least be one promise she could keep.

Now what? She'd always pushed Jonathan aside when he'd told her to think about the future. She should have listened. Last night's plan—leaving the farm to return to the sea—was clearly a nonstarter. She was back at the farm because she had nowhere else to go, until she couldn't stay here anymore either.

No flying. No storms. Hæra was much more likely to meet her end at the hands of the whirlpool witch after all. Or at the teeth of her own kin.

Her kin must've been on her mind lately. Last night, she thought she'd seen one of them. On the beach, just for a moment, Hæra had been sure she'd seen a horse's head popping above the water. But when she'd looked more closely, there had been nothing. Only the dark waves. She'd been paranoid.

Nevertheless, she'd urged Madeleine off the beach and back to her creaky hotel with its talkative proprietor. Even if no rogue member of the herd had been lurking, Madeleine might have run into other dangers, drunk as she'd been. If Hæra couldn't kill her, nothing else was going to either.

At least there was one consolation. Hæra had clearly made as big an impression on Madeleine six years ago as Madeleine had made on her.

You already ate me up, she'd said. *There's only bones left.*

Hæra snorted. Metaphors only got you so far. Now the literal truth had her sitting on the back steps while she contemplated her inevitable demise.

But she'd given herself one gift. She'd known Madeleine might try, this morning, to tell herself it had all been a drunken hallucination. Humans were fond of mental tricks like that.

Hard luck. A shred of blue fabric lay crumpled in Hæra's palm.

She wouldn't let Madeleine pretend everything was ordinary. She couldn't hurt Madeleine's body, but her clothes were fair game. Let there be proof that something had happened, something that mattered.

Hæra would remember too, for however long she was able, however long her life kept a shape she recognized.

Possibly not for long, then.

———

Madeleine's day was not off to an optimal start.

Her alarm kicked it off with its insistent buzzing at seven-thirty. It only got worse from there. Someone had stuffed cotton in her mouth overnight and put weights on all her limbs. They'd also shoved a hot poker into her brain. Nothing else accounted for how much her head hurt.

Madeleine pried her eyes open. The room spun for a moment. Was she still drunk? She'd knocked back enough whisky that she could believe it. How could she have been so careless?

Never again. Madeleine wasn't touching so much as a bottle of cough syrup from now on. No more alcohol. Except, she supposed, Communion wine.

Her stomach revolted at the thought, and she clapped a hand over her mouth. Nothing came up, though.

Nothing except the sudden memory of last night.

Her eyes opened wide, which hurt too. The beach. The rocks. The night. The *horse*.

"Dream," she croaked around a thick tongue. "Just a dream."

She sat up. Her bottom ached. Lord in heaven, she hadn't even taken off her shoes last night. She still wore her jacket, which…

Which had a rip in the right shoulder. A patch of fabric had been torn clean off. Madeleine stared at it.

Teeth had torn it off. Enormous, sharp teeth.

And her shoes were damp because she'd walked backward into the ocean. Her rear end hurt because she'd fallen down on it on a stony beach with a huge horse looming over her.

Some time passed in which she couldn't move, speak, or think.

Shock numbed her body. Only one word kept circling through her thoughts like a hamster on a wheel.

Real. Real. Real.

She lowered her head into her shaking hands. Okay. She could make this make sense, somehow. Spiritual sense. Many Church scholars argued for the existence of ghosts and apparitions. Beneficent souls could return from the dead to visit as part of God's ordered universe…

Animals weren't supposed to have souls…

And now that she was thinking about it, that horse had been corporeal. Ghosts were supposed to be ghostly. The horse had bumped her with its head. Its hooves had made noise as it walked next to her on the sidewalk and then taken off at a gallop.

Madeleine looked at the hole in her jacket again. Yes. It had been extremely corporeal.

A…demon? She'd never spent a lot of time thinking about those. It seemed better to focus on God's bounty. She'd been put on earth to help others, not perform exorcisms. But what else could that wicked-looking, long-toothed, flame-eyed creature have been?

Something new, a voice whispered inside her. *Open your eyes. Wake up.*

Madeleine had just woken up a few moments ago. It had been a painful experience. She wasn't ready to do it again. But she was starting to think she had no choice.

Her head throbbed. She hadn't had a hangover since college, and they were probably worse in your forties than your twenties. What was supposed to be the cure? Hot coffee and lots of greasy food? No thank you. Ibuprofen and water? That sounded better. Then, taking off her salt-crusted clothing, followed by a shower and a quiet morning to recover.

Quiet, not *peaceful.* She had the feeling that peace wasn't on her horizon anytime soon.

Not with the research she was about to do.

———

Over the next hour, Madeleine showered, changed, cringed away from Harry Duggan's attempts at conversation over breakfast ("Iona said you got a bit tipsy last night and wanted to know you'd made it here!"), and fled back to her room. Now she sat curled up in the armchair, researching on her phone.

During her last visit, she'd read up a little on Scottish folklore, including folklore specific to Orkney. She'd read about trows, and then forgotten all about them until Hæra mentioned them again. She'd read about selkies, seals that could take human form. Orkney used to have fairies too, before the arrival of Christian priests had driven them away. That one had been a little on-the-nose.

Then there were the kelpies.

Madeleine gulped as she combed through another website on Scottish lore, remembering what she'd read years ago. A kelpie was a water demon in the shape of a horse. It assumed an attractive human guise to lure people to their deaths.

Kelpies inhabited freshwater lochs and rivers. They dwelled inland. Their goal seemed to be getting humans into water, drowning them, and eating them. Why? Nobody knew. General malevolence, apparently.

The website said kelpies had black hides. Some legends said they had snakes in their manes.

Her heart flipped in her chest when she saw there was a version specific to Orkney, a shape-shifter called a "tangie." But that one was also supposed to be a merman sometimes, and lived by the lochs as well.

Madeleine's horse had met her by the ocean, not inland by a river or loch. Its hide hadn't been black, and she hadn't seen any snakes. And it definitely hadn't assumed human *or* merman form. It hadn't tried to lure her, either. It had just walked her inexorably backward toward the sea.

Good grief, what was she doing? Trying to convince herself that whatever beast she'd met last night was *normal*, not one of these terrifying creatures? Legends started somewhere. Maybe this was how the legend of the kelpie had begun.

Madeleine dropped the phone in her lap, bent over, and hid her face in her hands with a groan.

How did this square with anything? She'd thought the massive horse was a vengeful ghost. The coincidence of it standing there on the same beach from six years ago seemed too great to ignore. If it was a kelpie, why had it been trapped under a dock in the ocean instead of lurking in a loch? And why would it seem to hold a grudge against Madeleine for setting it free? Clearly, if it was a kelpie, it couldn't have drowned, so it had nothing to accuse her of on that score.

But she'd encountered something supernatural, that was for sure.

A dark road lay ahead of her. If she walked it, she'd start thinking things like: *You gave up your entire life, your community and calling, because a demon tricked you. This was all for nothing. Worse than nothing.*

She wouldn't walk it, then. Even if her time on Jorsay had wrecked her life, it had made her confront what needed confronting. She hadn't belonged with the Daughters of Grace, and she'd known that for longer than she'd wanted to admit. Certainly before she'd visited Jorsay the first time. She just couldn't face it until something extraordinary happened.

"The Lord works in mysterious ways" was a saying for a reason. Who was to say Madeleine wasn't getting a divine lesson in unexpected form? The horse had listened to her and spared her life. That wouldn't have happened if she wasn't supposed to learn something from it and change herself for the better.

Whatever "better" looked like.

In her memory flashed Hæra's face with its bright eyes and mysterious smile. Of course.

Maybe there was a reason for that too. Hæra had told her about a trow living under a mound in Ætlaquoy's pastures. She hadn't talked about it like it was nonsense. She knew the local folklore. And she was odd enough herself not to think Madeleine was crazy. Bizarrely, if Madeleine could talk to anyone about this, it would be the beautiful woman who haunted her dreams and dragged out feelings she'd repressed for decades.

You said you came here looking for answers, Hæra had told her yesterday. *I'm one of them, even if we don't know the question. Can't you see that?*

Madeleine was starting to see that, yes. For better or worse. Moreover, it seemed she wasn't the only confused party here.

Hæra had said, "*We* don't know the question."

What a strange—and telling—way to put it. In the moment, Madeleine hadn't exactly been focusing on pronouns. Now, Hæra's words reverberated in her memory with astonishing clarity.

She drummed her fingernails against the front of her teeth in an unsteady, clicking rhythm. She'd told Hæra that she'd need time to think about what had happened between them. It had been less than twenty-four hours, and it already seemed like that time was up. They needed to speak, and soon. This wasn't going to be easy.

What else was new?

CHAPTER TWENTY-SIX

"I don't suppose you talk, friend?"

The trow blinked up at her.

Small surprise. In all the years Hæra had been dropping off his breakfast, she'd never attempted to engage him in conversation. Unseen creatures weren't known for being chatty, least of all outside their own species. The trow and Hæra might both be unknown to humans, but that didn't mean they had much in common otherwise.

In fact, given her species' proclivity to eat anything meaty that moved, the trow's current suspicious expression was justified.

"Sorry." Hæra ran a hand through her hair. "I just wanted to thank you for protecting the farm. I'm not sure how much longer I'm going to be here."

The trow raised his eyebrows.

"I thought I'd tell Jonathan about where to leave your food. That's my human friend. You can trust him." Hæra hesitated. "I won't tell him about the beer, though, so you might start getting juice instead."

The trow glared.

"It's the best I can do." Hæra's shoulders slumped. "I ask for your generosity. I've put a lot of work into the farm. So has he. I don't like to think of him losing your blessing when I'm gone."

Now the trow cocked his head to one side.

"I don't know when. Perhaps not for a while, but it could happen quickly." If a human asked the wrong question. If one of her kin saw her. "And I might not be able to say goodbye. I haven't…" A lump filled her throat, and she swallowed around it. "I haven't got a place like you have. I've only got the sea."

The trow said nothing. He clearly didn't intend to. Perhaps he couldn't talk at all.

"You'll get your usual tribute until I'm gone," Hæra said roughly. "When Jonathan shows up instead, you'll know it's happened."

She turned on her heel and marched toward the Gator. When she was about halfway there, she turned, unable to help herself. The trow was gone, returned to his home with the meal she'd left him.

So much for shared understanding and allegiance. She should have known better. They weren't the same.

Hæra threw herself back into the Gator. Several meters away, Brodie watched mistrustfully. The smartest of the dogs, he was the only one who accompanied Hæra on her morning rounds because he knew to leave the trow alone. When she gunned the motor and drove away, he ran alongside the vehicle.

She'd gotten a late start today. She needed to return to the farm and work with Connor and Jim. They undoubtedly wondered why she'd been less present the last few days.

Or perhaps they'd put it together after meeting Madeleine. Maybe they'd realized Hæra's life had changed, even if they couldn't know how. It didn't matter. She had a job to do until she couldn't do it anymore. She'd just have to trust she'd recognize that time when it came, assuming she had a choice in the matter.

As she approached the farm, Connor came forward, waving. She stopped next to him. "What's wrong?"

"Nothing, I hope. Jon just said you should see him before you start work. He's in the office."

"I already started," Hæra snapped. "What does he want?"

Connor raised his eyebrows. "He didn't say. Did you two have a row?"

"No. I expect I'll be out soon." She pursed her lips. "I know I haven't worked as much lately."

"Lady who helped buy the farm can take a day off. It's not as busy as lambing season. Jim and I will see you when we see you." At that, he turned and ambled back toward the barn.

Hæra headed to the house and banged open the rear door. She wasn't in the mood to be subtle or chat business with Jonathan. Her body needed to move, whether in the fields or the barn, until the anger and doubt that had plagued her for hours sloughed off in sweat. She growled, "Connor said—"

Madeleine and Jonathan looked at her from the kitchen table.

Hæra stopped dead in her tracks. Her heart seemed to stop too.

"Good morning, lass," Jonathan said. "Look who's dropped in."

———

Jonathan had offered to leave Madeleine and Hæra in the kitchen for privacy, but even with the cold, Madeleine had needed to be in the open air. Now she and Hæra walked away from the house, and she gathered her courage.

"I wasn't sure you'd want to talk to me." Madeleine zipped her jacket all the way up to her chin. "And I'm sorry for how I behaved yesterday."

"Is that why you're here?" Hæra asked.

It would be easy to say yes. Now that Madeleine was actually here, surrounded by the everyday business of a farm, it seemed impossible to talk about magical creatures as if they were real.

But then, she'd built her life around believing in things many said were impossible. Maybe some of those specific things had been wrong, but she stood by the general principle.

"Not just for that," she said. They were walking across the yard toward the field, to the same fence where they'd talked on the night Madeleine first came to dinner. "I wanted to talk to you about something that happened to me last night. After we..." *Kissed until I lost myself.* "Uh, parted ways."

Hæra gave her a quick look, appearing startled. "About something that…happened to you? Afterward?"

This was going to be tough. There was no way for it to sound believable. Madeleine would sound either like she'd imagined the whole thing or was lying.

"Yes," she said. "I'll warn you—it sounds beyond strange. You might think I'm making it up or that I hallucinated. All I can say is, I swear it happened."

They reached the fence. She leaned forward and rested her elbows on a rail. Easier to look at the white sheep in the distance than at her companion.

"All right." Hæra sounded wary. "Tell me."

Given the go-ahead, Madeleine suddenly had no idea how to proceed. She'd been rehearsing this during the bike ride. Now her carefully planned retelling fled her mind. How was she supposed to begin, again?

She could only do her best. "Like I said, it sounds impossible, and I…I don't know if I'm ready to tell you *all* the details yet. But remember how you told me about that creature that lives under the mound? In your field?"

Hæra said nothing, so Madeleine turned to look at her. Hæra's expression was completely neutral, but her eyes pierced Madeleine like a lance. "The trow."

"Um, yes, the trow. So I figure, you must know about…um, legends and creatures, and…"

She definitely had no idea how to begin this, much less end it. *Can you tell me whether kelpies are real? Have you ever seen one? Would you like to refer me to a good therapist?*

"I saw one," she blurted. "Last night. On the beach. Not a trow, a…I think it was a kelpie."

Hæra's eyes widened.

"That's what they're called, right? The water horses?" Madeleine waved her hands helplessly, as if they could describe the creature. "It was all by itself on the beach, and I don't know if Jonathan told you this part, but on the night I fell in the water, I was trying to rescue—"

"A *kelpie.*"

Madeleine's words stumbled to a stop, maybe because Hæra's lip was curling. She looked completely disgusted.

So much for finding a sympathetic ear. Madeleine's cheeks scalded at her own foolishness. Telling Hæra had seemed like a halfway decent idea while her hangover was still wearing off. Clearly, hangover ideas weren't much better than drunk ideas.

Fine, let Hæra think she was nuts. It didn't change the truth. "I know it sounds unbelievable, but…"

"Kelpies live in fresh water. They're afraid of the ocean. And there aren't many left." Hæra bared her teeth. "Mainly because they're *stupid.*"

Madeleine blinked.

Hæra turned her glare toward the pasture. "Whatever you saw wasn't a kelpie. Trust me."

"Then what was it?" Madeleine demanded. "Because it wasn't a regular horse. It was huge, and it had—it had these *teeth*, and it acted like it was trying to push me into the ocean."

"But it didn't. Clearly."

"Don't tell me I'm imagining things!" Madeleine curled her hands into fists. "I admit it—I was drunk. I went to the Kestrel after I left you because…"

"Drunk," Hæra interjected. "There, you see—"

"No! I'm not making this up, and I didn't imagine it. I went to the beach where everything happened the first time. *That* beach."

"I told you to stay away from there." Hæra's voice dropped into a growl. "I told you it was dangerous."

"You did, yes, and…" The lightbulb went on. "Do you know something about that beach? Is that why you warned me away?"

Hæra inhaled deeply. Her nostrils flared.

Madeleine's heart, already beating quickly, tripped into overdrive. She stepped forward, her face getting hot. "Well? Is it? Is there some local legend that everyone just decided not to tell me about?"

Maybe so. There were hundreds of stories about places that held supernatural secrets protected by locals. Madeleine might have stumbled onto a Jorsayian secret not meant for outsiders to know. That might be why Jonathan said he also didn't know what had happened.

"Would you believe me?" Hæra snapped. "What about your Bible and your saints and all the rest? How would such a legend square with who you are?"

"The Bible and my saints have even stranger stories to tell, and I don't *know* who I am." The words felt rough and hot in her chest. Her eyes pricked. "That's why I'm here. I think you've figured out that much, and I know it's got something to do with that beach and whatever's there, I know—I know—"

"Madeleine…"

"I know I have to face it!" Madeleine cried.

Hæra's mouth snapped shut.

It was just as well, because now that the words had started, they didn't want to stop. "My life's totally different, don't you understand? I *chose* that. I'm not going to look away now, even if it scares the daylights out of me."

Hæra said nothing. Her face was still again, as impossible to read as the stone cliffs looming over the sea.

"You said, last night, that you were one of my answers," Madeleine whispered. "You have questions too. I know you do."

After a pause, Hæra said, "Yes. I do."

"Can you help me?" Madeleine stepped forward and looked up into Hæra's eyes. "I'm not saying I deserve it, or that you owe me something, but…"

"Owe you something," Hæra said softly.

"I just *said* you don't," Madeleine growled. Couldn't Hæra let her get through this? "I'm asking anyway. Just talk to me about this. And after that, you don't ever—"

Her breath caught on the next words, but she had to say those too.

"You don't ever have to talk to me again, if you don't want to," she said thickly. "I wouldn't blame you, honestly."

How could she? Nobody could blame Hæra for not wanting to talk to a woman more than a decade her senior who'd pushed her away after a few kisses and was now talking about a supernatural horse.

Hæra said nothing. She looked into Madeleine's eyes, seeking something that Madeleine must let her find, no matter how frightening the thought.

"You have great strength," Hæra said, after an endless pause.

"No, I don't. If I did, this would have happened before." Madeleine swallowed hard. "But it's happening now."

"Because now you're ready."

"I am *not* ready. That's not the point." Madeleine shoved her hands into her jacket pockets. Her right shoulder was chilly from where the horse had torn the fabric off. "But I'm doing it anyway. Will you help me? Can you?"

Hæra turned to look at the pasture for a long, silent moment. Then she returned her gaze to Madeleine. She pursed her lips. Inhaled through her nose. Closed her eyes. "Wait here," she said. "I'll be right back."

"What? Where are you going?"

"To get something."

Without further explanation, Hæra returned to the house, her shoulders slumped and her hands in her pockets.

Madeleine stared after her. What could Hæra need to "get" in the middle of this conversation? Maybe she was going to tell Jonathan that Madeleine needed to be taken into professional care right away. Let her, then. Madeleine knew her truth, or was beginning to. She set her jaw, crossed her arms, and leaned back against the fence post, keeping her eyes fixed firmly on the closed door. Whatever came through it, she was ready for it.

As it happened, only Hæra came through it a few minutes later, still with her hands in her pockets. This time, she held her head higher, and she strode more quickly. In fact, she made for Madeleine like a ship cutting through water, her eyes hard with purpose.

When she got closer, Madeleine said, "So what did you—"

"I brought you this." Hæra pulled her left hand from her pocket and held it out. Wrapped around her palm was a string of wooden beads ending in a cross. A rosary.

Madeleine looked at it in confusion. What was this? Was Hæra telling Madeleine that she was actually a Catholic or something? That made no sense after…

"Recognize it?"

Startled, Madeleine looked up to see Hæra's amber eyes slicing into her. A lean and hungry look.

"No?" Hæra said. "I thought you would. It was yours."

"Mine?" Madeleine looked back down at the rosary. It looked like a thousand other rosaries. Plain lacquered wood, with a…

With a chip on one of the beads from when she'd dropped it during the second year of her novitiate. Mother Gertrude had advised her to take better care of her things. Then she'd gone and lost it during her first trip to Orkney after she'd fallen off the dock and…

The rosary blurred as she looked at it. So did everything in her peripheral vision. She couldn't move.

A second thing appeared in front of her. Hæra's right hand, with something else in its palm.

A torn, blue scrap of jacket fabric.

Madeleine's fingertips went numb. Her whole body went numb. Maybe she was having a stroke. Maybe all of this was one last hallucination before she died.

She looked up, barely breathing, and ran smack into Hæra's gaze again.

That gaze was no longer sharp as a knife. Instead, its edges had rounded and softened. Hæra's hard mouth had softened too, into a smile that looked a little sad.

"I'm not an angel, but I am your answer," she said quietly. "And I always knew you would return to me."

CHAPTER TWENTY-SEVEN

MADELEINE HADN'T TURNED and run after Hæra's revelation, which was a surprise.

True, for a few moments, it seemed she couldn't move at all. She'd gaped up at Hæra, face drained of all color, body rigid. She hadn't taken either the rosary or the scrap of blue fabric from Hæra's hands. Hæra wondered if she was going to pass out and need to be caught for a fourth time.

Madeleine hadn't passed out. Instead she'd said, "I need a second," and leaned against the nearest fence post to stare off into the distance. After that second had passed, and then a few more, Hæra had suggested they go for a walk, and Madeleine said she couldn't think why not.

Now here they were: tromping over the fields Hæra had learned to call home. Madeleine stuffed her hands in her pockets. Hæra let hers swing free and easy at her sides to match her long stride.

The secret was out. Finally, Hæra had found courage to match Madeleine's. No more lies.

Madeleine looked at the green grass as she walked. "You saved me on the beach."

"Yes."

"But you're not an angel."

"Definitely not."

"Then what are you?" Madeleine stopped and looked up with an expression of frank fear. "The opposite? A demon? You can tell me. I can handle that. I just want to know."

Madeleine's pallor didn't suggest she could "handle that," so it was just as well Hæra could say, "I'm not a demon either. I'm an *Each-uisge.*"

Madeleine shook her head in incomprehension.

"Like a kelpie," Hæra clarified. "But from the ocean, and smarter." Bigger and stronger, too, and a mighty hunter with a herd, not a loner who lurked in a loch. She'd never been so insulted as when Jonathan and Madeleine had confused the two.

"Like a kelpie," Madeleine repeated, sounding numb. "So you're a… horse. Or at least you look like a horse sometimes. And sometimes you look like…"

She looked Hæra up and down and didn't finish her sentence.

"I'm not a horse," Hæra said forcefully. She mustn't grab Madeleine again, as urgent as it seemed to make her point right now. "Horses are dumb beasts of the land. My other form resembles them, yes, but we're not the same. I can…" She hesitated. "Even in that form, I can speak."

"Speak?" Madeleine narrowed her eyes. "You didn't speak to me last night."

"No," Hæra admitted.

"Why not?"

"I…didn't know what to say." It sounded foolish, but what could she have said? *Please walk back into the ocean so I can drown and eat you, and we'll see what happens next?*

Please don't hate me?

"I can think of a few things!" Madeleine hunched her shoulders and looked back toward the farm, where Connor and Jim were moving around the barn.

They didn't need an audience for this. Hæra said, "Let's keep walking."

"I'd like to stay within sight of other people, if it's all the same to you. This is bad enough without worrying if you're going to eat me. Which I thought you were last night."

"I wasn't," Hæra said quickly, with the benefit of hindsight.

"Then what were you doing? No. Wait." Madeleine held up both hands in a warding gesture. "Go back to the beginning. Tell me everything. What the hell's going on?"

Hæra raised her eyebrows. Madeleine hadn't sworn in her presence before. She was obviously agitated, and why wouldn't she be? This had to be handled carefully.

No more lies, but that didn't mean Madeleine had to know *every* insignificant detail. Like how Hæra had originally intended to eat her to become a Stormhorse. She wasn't going to do that anymore, so it wasn't relevant. She'd be able to tell Madeleine eventually and deal with whatever look came into her eyes. Just not now.

"Let me tell you first about what I am," she said. "Instead of what I'm not."

The explanation ran long. By the time Hæra had finished telling Madeleine about the *Each-uisge,* they were sitting on the side of the hill, the damp earth soaking into their trousers.

"That explains a lot." Madeleine wrapped her arms around her legs and rested her chin on her knees. The wind whipped her hair. "Everything you said about your family being nomadic, and how you don't…"

When she didn't finish her sentence, Hæra prompted, "I don't what?"

"How you don't fit in," Madeleine said slowly. "How sometimes you sort of…miss the mark when we're talking. Behaviors that are just a little bit off, basic things you don't know that most people would."

Hæra's face grew hot. Madeleine wouldn't do much better if she suddenly became an *Each-uisge.* She snapped, "I've not done badly. I help to run a farm, don't I? I even learned to read and do maths."

"That's impressive, yes." Madeleine pursed her lips and turned back to Hæra. Her beautiful eyes missed nothing now that they'd been opened. "I want to know how you did all that," she said. "But first, I want to know *why*."

She and Hæra looked into each other's eyes. For a moment, Hæra's foot seemed to dangle over the edge of a cliff—the highest one on Jorsay, maybe, with a sheer face down into the sea.

"For you," she said.

Madeleine's face went from pale to red. She flinched but didn't look away.

"That night changed me too," Hæra said, her heart thundering like a storm. "Like it did you and Jonathan, all three of us. You know who I am, don't you? Not only your rescuer, but the horse you cut free from the dock, too."

Madeleine picked at a loose thread on her jeans. "I thought I'd drowned you when I was trying to save you."

"You did save me. If I'd stayed stuck, either a human or an ocean predator would have found me. You cut me loose, and I was going to swim away, but then you fell into the water."

Madeleine grimaced.

"A life for a life," Hæra said. "I couldn't let you drown after you'd rescued me. I dragged you ashore."

After a pause, Madeleine said, "And then you became human."

"No, I didn—"

"Or you looked human, whatever! Why?" Madeleine curled her hands into fists. "Why didn't you drop me on the beach and then go back into the water? Were you staying with me until help arrived?"

"I..."

"But if it was only that, then why would you kiss me?"

The words, and the memory too, rang like a bell. Madeleine's mouth under Hæra's, soft and hot.

I kissed you because I couldn't eat you. Hæra couldn't say that.

"I didn't understand why." That was true. Even in human form, the urge to *kiss* had been alien. "I just knew I had to do it. You were there, and I needed to..."

She looked at Madeleine's mouth, which she had kissed years ago, and again only yesterday. That and more, only yesterday.

"I needed to," she whispered.

Silence. Hæra looked at Madeleine's eyes again; they were wide and dazed.

Hæra continued, "You're not the only one looking for answers, but I know you're mine."

You're mine. Would Madeleine understand the double meaning? Judging by how she gulped, she might.

Still holding her knees, Madeleine turned back to the farm. Jim was on the tractor. Connor was opening a fence. It all looked ordinary —or would, to a human.

Which Hæra was not, and would never be, no matter what thoughts occurred to her at night. "This was all so strange to me when I got here. Life on land. How humans live every day."

"It must have been. So how did you end up living with them? That is, us?" Madeleine asked in a low voice.

Hæra's laugh tasted bitter. She could try being completely forthcoming about this part and see how it went. At least it would show Madeleine her commitment to a goal.

"I returned to the beach the night after I pulled you out of the water," she said. "I hoped you'd come back, as I bade you."

Madeleine blushed again.

"You didn't, but Jonathan came instead. He, ah…well, that's a long story, and he should tell you himself. But he'd encountered my kind before, and based on what you said, he thought one of us might be involved. He was drunk and angry, and he yelled over the water, and I went to him. I knew he'd helped you and might be able to tell me about you."

She'd been so hungry then. For everything, including information. The last few years hadn't fed her enough.

Madeleine frowned. "And you became friends after that?"

"So it seems." It had been such a shock to realize what seemed normal now. "I made a deal with him. I brought him a treasure chest from the ocean, which he used to buy the farm, in exchange for him teaching me your human customs."

"Why did you want to learn those?"

"I think you already know."

They looked at each other again in silence.

"Tell me anyway," Madeleine murmured.

Well. All right. Hæra smiled wryly. "I wanted to be able to talk to you," she said. "To understand you when you returned."

Madeleine hugged her knees more tightly, as if holding herself together. "How did you know I would? Did you—did you—"

Hæra frowned. "Did I what?"

"Did you cast a spell on me?" Madeleine blurted. "Did you compel me to come back?"

What a question. Did Madeleine think Hæra was a witch at the bottom of a whirlpool, full of magic and still unable to save herself? "If I could've done that, you'd never have left in the first place."

That didn't seem to reassure Madeleine. "So…you would have compelled me if you could."

"Didn't I just say that?" Hæra turned toward Madeleine so she faced her rather than sitting parallel to her. "I would have then. It's different now. I don't want to trap you here."

"No?"

"No. I've learned about being somewhere because you're forced to." Hæra looked back down the hill toward the farm. Her life's work. "You can find good things about it, but it's still not your choice. Why would I want you to feel that way about me?"

Madeleine was silent. Hæra kept looking at the farm, waiting.

"You're forced to be here?" Madeleine asked eventually.

"Yes." It was hard to look at Madeleine for this part. How strange. "My family caught me transforming and coming ashore. I'm not sure how. I think it was Asgall who saw." He was much more likely to have been lurking around the surface than Beathag or Calder.

"Asgall?"

Hæra pursed her lips. "My brother."

Madeleine looked horrified. "Your own brother turned you in?"

"Asgall hates me. He always has. He's a creature of bitterness and spite." Hæra heard plenty of bitterness in her own voice. "My mother—Beathag—isn't fond of me either. When I returned from Jonathan's one night, she and Asgall were waiting for me, along with the Sire of the herd. They tried to kill me. I escaped, although they believe I'm dead."

So she hoped. Yet again she thought uneasily of the horse's head she thought she'd seen in the water last night. All those precautions she'd taken for all these years couldn't be for nothing, could they?

But she'd seen nothing else. Out of everyone in the herd, only Calder, Asgall, and Beathag knew her human form. If they'd seen her alive, they'd have come ashore to destroy her for good. The presence of one lone human wouldn't have deterred them. In fact, Madeleine would have been a bonus prize.

The thought led Hæra to grab Madeleine's hand. Madeleine hadn't been eaten by anybody last night, including Hæra, she was alive and well, but touching her still felt necessary. Just to make sure.

Madeleine didn't pull away. "Your family tried to kill you," she said softly. "That's horrible. I'm so, so sorry."

Hæra blinked. The horror was still in Madeleine's eyes. It was easy to forget what a different view some humans could take of matters like this. What to Madeleine was an atrocity was simply a fact of life to Hæra. In the moment, of course, she'd known rage and pain, she'd felt such betrayal, but...

But...

You've never been what you're supposed to be, Beathag had snarled, her disgust wounding Hæra as surely as her bite had done.

"Never mind," Hæra said gruffly. "It brought me here."

Madeleine bit her lip. "And you've been here ever since?"

"Yes. Jonathan used the treasure I gave him to buy the farm, and we run it together. I didn't intend to be here, but...but..." She leaned forward, holding Madeleine's hand more tightly. "Do you remember what I said about rainbows?"

For a moment, Madeleine looked uncomprehending. Then her brow cleared. She even smiled a little. "Life is hard, but there are rainbows."

That smile, tiny as it was, was the emergence of the sun from the clouds. Hæra exhaled deeply to see it. "Yes. That's the farm. That's Jonathan. That's…"

You. She didn't say it, but they both heard it.

"You know," Madeleine said after a pause, "I'd be well within my rights not to believe any of this, even if you do have my rosary and a piece of my jacket."

"Unless I demonstrate? I can, although perhaps not here." She'd prefer not to change shape while Connor, Jim, and the dogs were all in plain sight. It might raise a few questions.

"Not here," Madeleine agreed. "And not now."

"Tonight, then?" It would be much safer to transform under the cover of darkness.

"I don't know." Madeleine looked at their joined hands. "If I see you do it, then…it's real."

Hæra frowned. "Of course it's real. That's the point. I'll prove it."

"I'm sure you would. I'm not ready for that." Madeleine raised her green gaze to Hæra once more. "I know I said I could handle it. But none of this is anything I was brought up to believe. I need time to get used to it."

"Maybe not. You said you'd need more time to think about our kiss, but here you are."

It sounded like airtight logic to Hæra. It didn't seem to strike Madeleine the same way, since she chuckled ruefully.

"When I do something, I go all the way, don't I?" she asked. "It wasn't enough just to stumble over a magical creature. I had to go and kiss it."

Hæra didn't like the sound of that at all. "I'm not an *it*. I'm a…"

How did she finish that sentence? She couldn't say *person*, and *Each-uisge* wouldn't make anything better.

Neither term felt right, either.

All she could think of was, "I'm myself. Just as you are."

"Whatever I am." Madeleine tugged her hand free of Hæra's and looked back over the fields. "Turns out I came here to discover that and got more than I bargained for."

"These beliefs you speak of," Hæra said carefully. Here was something else that needed delicate handling. "Isn't it good to know more about the world, even if it means you were wrong about some things? I've learned that too."

"I didn't say I was wrong about anything," Madeleine snapped. She glared at Hæra. "I told you I believed in mysteries. You're definitely one, even if you're no angel. And just because you exist doesn't mean I have to throw out every single thing I was taught!"

The fear was back in her eyes. That meant she might not believe what she was saying. However, that didn't mean it wasn't true.

Hæra agreed, "That's right. You have to think about it. I did. And I've had much longer to do that than you have."

"No kidding." Madeleine propped her chin on her knees and hugged herself again. If she hugged herself tightly enough, Hæra wondered, would she be able to contain whatever surged in her now? "And I've got less than a month to do it."

Was that a joke? Hæra leaned forward. "What are you talking about? You can stay longer. You can stay as long as you like."

"I can't. I have a life." Madeleine bent her forehead until it touched her knees and Hæra couldn't see her face anymore. "I've got a job that starts in August and a place I pay rent on. And I have a plane ticket it'll cost me a fortune to change. I don't have any treasure chests to tap into."

Hæra said impatiently, "August is longer than a month away, and we can help with your plane ticket. Even if we couldn't, would that be more important than what's happening here?"

Madeleine didn't reply or look up.

"It wouldn't. You know that, don't you?" Hæra placed her hand, lightly, between Madeleine's shoulder blades, atop the torn jacket. Madeleine trembled at her touch. Fear, or something else? If only Madeleine would look at her.

She said, "Jim's moving out of the cottage soon, and you can stay there. I already said so, do you remember?"

Madeleine's voice was muffled. "I remember."

"You returned to me." Hæra swallowed hard. "Now stay with me. At least a little longer."

A shiver ran through Madeleine's body, more pronounced than the tremble.

Hæra mustn't panic. Not even if the moment—if Madeleine—felt like sand falling through her fingers, something that couldn't be held or made to stay.

"You don't have to decide right now," she said, with some difficulty. How awful it would be not to have Madeleine's answer immediately. But it'd be much worse to get a negative one when, if she waited, that might change.

Maybe she was learning to think ahead. Jonathan would be pleased.

Madeleine finally raised her head. She turned her face to the cloudy sky, her expression unreadable. "I might leave, I might not," she said. That was better than *I'll definitely leave*, at least. "What about you?"

"Me?"

Madeleine's gaze was sharp. "I understand why you stayed here. But did you never at least dream of leaving? Seeing the rest of the world instead of this one, tiny island near the family that tried to kill you?"

Put like that, it sounded only logical. "I don't dream. But you're speaking in metaphors—yes?" When Madeleine smiled a little and nodded, Hæra continued, "My kind remains around the islands of the North Sea. And I can't leave the ocean no matter what form I wear. My strength deserts me the farther I get from it. I couldn't survive inland."

For the first time, Madeleine's expression softened. "Forced to be here…as you said. That's unfair. I'm sorry."

If Madeleine had seemed sorry *for* Hæra, that would have been infuriating. Madeleine seemed sorry about something else, and it brought compassion to her eyes. That alone gave Hæra the courage to say, "But you can choose. When you're ready."

At the word *ready*, Madeleine's eyes hardened again. She didn't look angry, though—at least not at Hæra. Instead, she turned that sharp, resolved look up to the cloudy sky. And Hæra knew Madeleine wasn't going to wait to make her decision.

She held her breath.

———

When you're ready, Hæra had said, as if Madeleine could ever be.

Foolishly, when setting out for Orkney, she'd vowed to be ready for anything. In hindsight, she'd only prepared herself for a limited set of options. She would meet her angel, or not; she would find answers to questions she didn't know how to ask, or not.

She'd found other things instead. Chief among them, the existence of something that didn't exactly mesh with her belief system— although it wasn't entirely incompatible. God had made all kinds of creatures, and science couldn't account for everything. Madeleine believed in things both seen and unseen, and what else was a miracle but an impossible thing made possible?

Hæra ought to be impossible. And yet, when Madeleine had realized the truth, she'd thought: *Of course.*

Of course she's magical.

To the descriptors "odd," "rude," and "wildly attractive," Madeleine now had to append "magical." It seemed of a piece with the rest. Madeleine had taken one look into Hæra's eyes, and a part of herself she'd buried long ago had leapt instantly to life.

Resurrected, you might say.

Hæra wanted something from Madeleine too, that much was clear. For one thing, sex, which wasn't on the table. It was definitely *not* on the table. For a lot of excellent reasons. But Hæra wanted more than that. When you just wanted to have sex with someone, you didn't pepper them incessantly with personal questions—or spend years of your life learning to live as a different species.

Madeleine's fingers trembled, and not just because of the cold air.

She squeezed her knees more tightly and kept her eyes on the sky instead of on Hæra, since looking at Hæra would only throw her into confusion again.

Hæra was trapped here, but Madeleine wasn't. Choosing to leave would definitely be the smarter option. She could return home and start figuring herself out in the absence of any supernatural elements. She'd find a way to reconcile the beliefs she'd cherished all her life with what she'd learned about the world, and about herself. The ground would steady under her feet again. She just had to go home.

No, whispered a voice inside her. The same voice she'd heard in her hotel room when she'd been ready to change her flight. *You'll regret it. When else will you ever have an opportunity like this?*

She'll set you free.

Freedom. Answers. In their own ways, Hæra and Madeleine sought the same things. They weren't going to find them separately.

Madeleine took in a shaky breath, exhaled it, and turned back to Hæra, whose expression was grave—bordering on worried. Hæra, of the apparently limitless confidence, worried? If the situation weren't so serious, it would have been adorable.

"I don't want to leave," Madeleine said.

Hæra's eyes lit up again.

"In fact," Madeleine continued, "whenever I've thought about leaving, I've felt the strongest pull against it. Like a little voice telling me I need to stay here until I figure this out. I don't *think* it's a bad voice. Not that I'm saying I'm hearing voices, it's not like that, it's just…" She trailed off.

Hæra said nothing, which seemed like its own kind of miracle. She waited.

"Look, whatever's going on, I'm not ready for—for what we did in that alley." Madeleine's face burned. "It isn't just that you're not…like me. Although it is that. It's a lot of things. It's—I mean, for one thing, you're a lot younger than me, aren't you?"

"No," Hæra said. "I'm nearly one hundred years old."

For a second, Madeleine grew dizzy. She put her hand to her forehead. "Oh."

Hæra frowned. "Why would our ages be important?"

Okay. Madeleine could deal with this too. She could deal, somehow, with all of this. "I, um...I guess in the bigger scheme of things they're not. Listen, I can't imagine I'm the only one who should think about this. If you're not like me, then I'm not like you. Doesn't that give you pause?"

Hæra pursed her lips. Then she nodded, looking as if she didn't want to.

A strange feeling squirmed in Madeleine's stomach. It felt like an improbable mixture of relief and disappointment. "There you are. We both have a lot to figure out. But..." She took in a breath so deep that it was painful to exhale it. "I think we should figure it out together."

Hæra's face changed again. Its long, sharp planes softened. Her eyes glowed. In relief, possibly. How could Madeleine learn to interpret her?

Unless she stuck around?

"However it happened, we were brought together for a reason," she said in a low voice. "I don't know what to believe anymore, but I believe that. And I want to see what it means."

"So do I," Hæra said. "I thought I knew what it meant once. Now, I'm not sure."

"What did you think it meant?"

Hæra hesitated. "Nothing. Never mind. It wouldn't make sense to you."

Did any of this? Madeleine stuffed her hands in her jacket pockets again. "I'm not saying I'll stay all summer. But my plans just got more flexible."

She'd have to tell Becca, who might be supportive of her extended stay. Or Becca might think she'd lost her mind, and she wouldn't be shy about saying so. And that was without putting the whole "supernatural creature" element into the equation.

"I'm glad." Hæra scooted toward her on the ground. They didn't touch, but it was close enough that Hæra was sharing her warmth. "In spite of everything, I'm glad all of this has come to pass. It's shown me so much about the world. I hope it will to you, too."

Madeleine wasn't sure what to hope for, other than for everything to make sense again, which didn't seem likely to happen anytime soon. Only one thing was certain now.

Whatever path lay before them now, she and Hæra were destined to walk it together.

PART III
THE STORM

CHAPTER TWENTY-EIGHT

"Decorating your dwelling place is such a human thing to do."

Hæra's words rang from behind Madeleine, throughout the stone cottage's modest living room. At the sound of them, Madeleine pivoted on her heel to stare at her. An entire month had passed since Hæra's earth-shattering revelation, and Madeleine still wasn't used to statements like that.

You'd think she would be. Over the last month, Hæra had been more-or-less forthcoming about her species. Madeleine had learned about the average *Each-uisge* lifespan (centuries), diet (carnivorous), mating rituals (brutal), and role in the natural world (unseen, impossible, magical). And yet, when Hæra referred to something ordinary as "human"—as if it were strange or absurd to her—Madeleine found herself taken aback once more.

Hæra didn't seem to notice she'd said anything amiss. She set Madeleine's suitcase by the front door. She'd insisted on carrying it both from the Merryweather's curb to the car, and then from the car to the cottage.

"It's etiquette," she'd said as she lifted the suitcase in one fluid movement while Madeleine fought not to stare at her muscular arms.

Now Hæra looked around the cottage with her hands on her hips and one eyebrow raised. Her black ponytail lay draped over one broad shoulder.

She certainly *looked* human, if more…compelling than any human of Madeleine's acquaintance.

Madeleine gulped. Not the time to think about that. They'd agreed.

"I'm not going to do much decorating. But it's one thing to be in a hotel room for a month"—maybe the longest month of her life, what with Harry Duggan's gossip—"and another to be in a cottage for… however long…without anything to look at."

"There's furniture," Hæra objected.

True. The stone cottage Jim had just vacated, following his wedding, came furnished—with furniture Jim had owned as a bachelor, and which his bride refused to allow into their home. There was a faded yellow sofa whose cushion springs had seen better days. A brown Naugahyde armchair cracked on the left arm. A card table and folding chairs in place of a real kitchen set.

"There is furniture, technically," Madeleine agreed.

Hæra dropped onto the armchair and leaned back, spreading her legs wide. "It's comfortable."

Madeleine's mouth still went dry. She would not stare at the seam of Hæra's jeans between her legs. She'd keep her eyes squarely on Hæra's face, with its sparkling eyes and mischievous grin.

Maybe Hæra's face wasn't such a safe place to look either.

"You'll be comfortable too," Hæra said. "It's not so bad, is it? Jim left a few things on the walls. What about that picture over the fireplace?"

With difficulty, Madeleine looked away from Hæra's eyes to the picture in question. "Dogs playing poker. It certainly is a picture. I'd rather look into a nice fire, personally."

Now wouldn't be a bad time. She shivered. The stone cottage wasn't as well insulated as her room at the Merryweather had been, and the radiator was working twice as hard to be half as good.

"I don't like fire," Hæra said.

They faced each other across the length of the living room, such as it was. Just a few feet. It still felt like too short a distance for Madeleine's pounding heart.

It felt too long as well.

"Because it's your opposite element?" she asked.

Hæra smiled. She always did whenever Madeleine showed any insight into her…state of being. "Yes. I'd never seen it before I came to this cottage for the first time. Then I hated it at once."

"Is it the heat?" That was a shot in the dark, but Hæra seemed impervious to cold. She'd even told Madeleine that she didn't take hot showers. After that revelation, Madeleine had needed a few minutes to stop picturing Hæra in the shower, hot or otherwise.

"That, and the way it…" Hæra seemed to hesitate. "The way it eats everything up when it gets out of control. And how quickly that happens."

Madeleine bit her bottom lip. She could think of something that had a similar effect on her. How funny that Hæra should fear fire's power when she, a creature of the cold ocean, still threatened to burn Madeleine alive.

Hæra slapped the arms of the chair and rose to her feet. "Never mind that. I'm going to check the back door."

"Why?"

"The bolt looked a little rickety last I checked. Not that we've got to worry about burglars out here, but I'd have you be secure."

Madeleine's face heated as Hæra strode toward the back of the cottage, followed by the thump of the back door opening and closing.

Hæra often spoke of wanting Madeleine's safety. Over the last month, she'd made Madeleine feel safer than anyone ever had—and less safe too. She was confident in her abilities to the point of arrogance, and she had a way of making everything seem under control. She was also no less alluring than she'd been when they met. Her lean figure was an increasing torment that never failed to make Madeleine's heart pound. Each day, Madeleine's self-control strained against an increasingly gossamer-like leash.

Her phone pinged with a text, and a hot, relieved breath rushed from her chest. A distraction. She looked at the screen.

Move-in day! Good luck!!

Becca's text brought a welcome smile to Madeleine's face. It wasn't as good as seeing her friend's face or hearing her voice, but the timing was perfect.

Thanks. What are you doing up so early?

Boostie needs the new shot every 5 hours for the next 2 days. It's so much fun

There followed a picture of an enraged Booster, his golden eyes narrowed as he plotted revenge.

Poor baby. How is he?

Getting better. How are YOU?

Madeleine worried her lip and debated sending a picture of the living room. Maybe later. Becca would be horrified by the furniture.

Doing fine ☺

Don't ☺ me, what about H? Is she so excited you're staying??

Madeleine had told Becca a little about what was going on. Emphasis on *a little*. She had omitted the tiny fact of Hæra's supernatural origins. She'd said she was staying in Orkney longer to get more answers, with the help of "a friend" she'd made here—a woman.

After that, Becca hadn't been able to rest until Madeleine's "friend" had a name, and said it would be amazing for Madeleine to have a "friend," and Becca wouldn't be opposed to hearing if there were any further developments concerning this "friend."

In other words, Becca had been extremely supportive. Maybe excessively so. She wouldn't object to Madeleine having a relationship with a woman, that was clear, and Madeleine still didn't know how she felt about that. Appreciative? Afraid? She'd go with confused.

That was partly because Madeleine couldn't tell Becca the whole truth and see what kind of 180-degree turn her support would take. Either Becca wouldn't believe her and would think she'd lost her mind—or, worse, Becca *would* believe her, and think she'd lost her mind even more.

Just then, the back door banged open again, signaling Hæra's imminent return. Madeleine hastily typed a farewell text to Becca, saying yes, "H" was very excited, but now Madeleine had to go. She urged Becca to please get some sleep and ended with two heart emojis to make it nice.

She put her phone back in her pocket right before Hæra strode back into the room. "How's the bolt?"

"Needs fixing. I'll take care of it this week for you. I don't often get to work with metal."

Her eyes were alight with pleasure at a new task. It was one of her most appealing characteristics. She'd told Madeleine about how overwhelmed she'd been when she'd come to live on land. Every challenge had seemed insurmountable, and there was so much to learn. "But I've always been good at doing things," she'd said casually, "and I like to do them better than anybody else, so I worked it all out."

Madeleine had thought of how Hæra had felt her up in that alley, which was clearly the first time she'd ever done that. Yes, Hæra could work things out beautifully. The throb of recollection had taken over Madeleine, as it did now, and it was only getting worse...

Or better, that heavy ache, that...

She had to think about something else immediately. Hæra had mentioned working with metal. A memory of Madeleine's mythological studies surfaced in her mind. She glanced at the front door, which presumably had the same bolts and locks as the back one. The metal was black and thick, rough in places, and rubbed shiny in the spots where people had touched it over the years. "The bolts are iron, aren't they?" she asked.

"Yes. Well done," Hæra said, in a way that would have been sarcastic coming from most people. Hæra, however, sounded genuinely pleased that Madeleine could identify a basic material substance. Probably because it had been yet another thing she'd had to learn, herself.

It was kind of adorable, and Madeleine's chest warmed. She smiled in spite of herself. "I read that iron is dangerous to magical creatures. It hurts you if you touch it. That's why people used to put horseshoes above their doors, to keep wicked fairies away."

Hæra frowned at her right palm. Then she sniffed it. "Hmm. Come here."

Madeleine came here, as if Hæra were a magnet and Madeleine herself an iron filing. Hæra held out her hand, palm forward, in front of Madeleine's mouth. "Smell that."

The meaty part of her palm did have a little scrape on it, along with a brown smudge. Madeleine bent her head. The tip of her nose brushed the flesh of Hæra's palm, warm and roughened with work. It smelled sharp, metallic. A little dirty, but in the honest way of the earth, not of filth.

If she moved her head just a little more, Madeleine could nuzzle that palm with her lips, her whole face. She pressed her lips together against the urge—and the ache that spread through her body—and raised her head. "Smells like iron, all right," she mumbled.

"I like the smell. Iron's no danger to me. I'm not a fairy, anyway. They all died. It's a pity—the lore of my kind says they were delicious." Hæra sniffed her palm again. "Ah well, I'm off to wash my hands."

And she walked off, full of swagger and jaw-dropping observations, seemingly unaware of both.

Madeleine's mouth hung open, and she snapped it shut. Okay. Hæra's palm was warm, her skin smelled incredible even when it had iron smudges on it, she walked as if she owned the ground beneath her feet, and she made Madeleine's body hot and unfamiliar to herself, but that was…fine. Madeleine would deal with it. She'd had a month's practice by now.

She's remarkable, Madeleine's damnable inner voice whispered, *she's extraordinary.* And heaven help her, that wasn't wrong.

Within moments, Hæra returned to the living room and seemed not to notice that Madeleine hadn't moved an inch. "You're doing some shopping in the village today? For these decorations you want?"

The village. Oh, right. There was a world beyond this cottage, a future beyond this moment. Madeleine had forgotten. "Uh, yes," she said. "I'm sure you have to work, but you're…"

Hæra's amber eyes looked softly into her own.

"Welcome to come," Madeleine whispered.

By now, she didn't need to say it. Hæra was always welcome. Madeleine never tired of her company: her questions, her observations, her candor. You could say she was a breath of fresh air—if the air was a sharp wind that blew in from the sea.

Together, they'd rambled all over Jorsay, although Hæra was still leery of spending time on the shore. Madeleine had accompanied Hæra during her work on the farm, learning more about sheep than she'd ever planned to. They were always in company, and Madeleine —an introvert by nature—found that when they parted at the end of each day, she was already looking forward to the next one.

Hæra's first smile of the morning had become the sunrise.

Now Madeleine looked up at Hæra, who was remarkable and extraordinary and all the rest, and she fought not to sway forward, though her body longed to. She thought: *Take me in your arms, like you did before. Hold me close so I'll forget all the rest.*

I want so much to forget it.

Lord in heaven, Madeleine was in so much danger. She prayed the Act of Hope every night, along with other prayers that seemed to be losing their efficacy by the hour.

"I'll go anywhere with you, you know that," Hæra said. "I expect we'll need the car."

Madeleine's mouth was dry. *I'll go anywhere with you.* Hæra just *said* things like that, as if it wasn't a big deal. For her, maybe it wasn't.

For Madeleine, if she wasn't careful, it could become everything.

"Yes," she said. "I'd expect so."

"You should try driving again. You've nearly got the hang of going on the left."

"Maybe I will. It's less hair-raising than when you do it."

"I'm a good driver," Hæra objected. "My reflexes are better than everyone else's."

"That doesn't mean you can go three times as fast as everyone else. Curves in the road don't un-bend for your reflexes. Maybe we should get you a book on physics next."

"Maybe you should just close your eyes." Grinning, Hæra looked around the living room again. "You can't want to get that many things. This place isn't all bad. The bed's nice at least, isn't it?"

She wandered through the open bedroom door, as if to check for herself. Her hips swayed easily as she walked.

Do not follow her into your bedroom. Or any bedroom. But especially yours.

Ignoring her completely, Madeleine's feet followed Hæra into the bedroom. She entered just in time to see Hæra sit down on the edge of the bed and bounce a little. "See?" Hæra said. "Brand new. Seems comfortable enough to me."

No doubt it was. The bed was the one item Jonathan had replaced, saying he didn't want to shame himself by making Madeleine sleep on Jim's ancient mattress, and it'd be good for future tenants too.

Madeleine, though used to sleeping on ancient mattresses, had decided a man's used one was a different thing, and she'd thanked Jonathan wholeheartedly. Now, though, she saw Hæra leaning back on a clean, firm, queen-sized mattress. Maybe it would have been a good idea to make the bed as unappealing a site as possible.

"Have you tried the bed yet?" Hæra asked. "To see if you like it?" She leaned back on her hands, her legs spread again, her eyes gleaming.

It would be an invitation from anyone else. With Hæra, Madeleine could never be sure. The…woman…before her operated by no rules Madeleine understood. Hæra sat like this all the time, lounging on surfaces and taking up all the space she wanted. It might not mean anything special.

Was Madeleine staring at her? Again? Her face flamed. "No, I haven't tried it."

Hæra patted the mattress next to her. "No time like the present."

Maybe this was a dream. Yet another dream, all too like the ones that had plagued Madeleine over the last several weeks. Hæra's lazy smile and her long body, on offer if Madeleine's desire finally overcame her resistance.

Madeleine sat next to Hæra on the bed because her knees didn't want to support her anymore. That was the only reason.

Their knees bumped. Their thighs almost touched. Madeleine could barely breathe.

"What do you think?" Hæra asked softly.

Madeleine looked at their touching knees, both covered in denim that might as well not exist, given how she seemed to feel the contact against her skin. The pressure was warm, firm, because she and Hæra were close together on a bed. "Um...think?"

"About the bed. Is it comfortable?" The mattress moved beneath Madeleine's bottom as Hæra bounced on it again. Their knees bumped some more.

"It seems fine," Madeleine said, her mouth dry. She couldn't look up.

A pause. Then Hæra said, "What's the matter?"

Oh, for heaven's sake. Madeleine had to do better than this. She looked up to see a frown on Hæra's face: a look Madeleine had long since learned to recognize as one of concern.

"Nothing," she said, her breathless tone giving the lie to that. "I guess we should get..."

"Something's wrong," Hæra said firmly. "Was it something I did? You have to tell me, or I won't know."

Those eyes missed nothing, when they cared to look. Amber-colored again, in this light. Would they be the same color in Hæra's horse form...her *real* form? Madeleine still hadn't found the courage to watch her transformation. Too much, too hard, too real.

She said slowly, "When a human invites another one into a bedroom, sits on the bed, and asks the other human to join them, that's usually…I mean, maybe not usually, but *often*…"

Hæra looked uncomprehending.

"I mean, that kind of invitation is…intimate. A lot of times it means you're asking someone to—to have sex."

Dear God. Had those words just come out of her mouth? Madeleine rose from the bed at once, even though her knees had grown no steadier in the past minute. It was better than letting them brush up against Hæra's.

Behind her, Hæra said quietly, "I didn't know that."

Madeleine's face heated as she stared at the wall. She really was ridiculous, clutching her pearls and worrying about her virtue. "Of course not. Why would you?"

"You set boundaries with me." Hæra's voice was tight. "I wouldn't ask such a thing of you, even if I…"

Madeleine couldn't turn around. She couldn't move, except for the hot throb of her heart in her chest. She croaked, "Even if you what?"

The bedsprings creaked. Hæra was standing up. Then her heat was behind Madeleine's back, their bodies nearly touching, as close as they'd been in the tunnels of Skara Brae.

"I was going to say 'even if I wanted to ask,'" Hæra said. "But I don't want to ask you for sex."

If Madeleine's face had been hot before, it was on fire now. So was all the rest of her, burning with instant humiliation. It looked like Hæra found her pearl-clutching exactly as ridiculous as it was.

Then, Hæra's mouth was at Madeleine's ear, her breath hot against Madeleine's neck. "I don't like asking," she whispered. "It's not my nature. My kind doesn't 'ask' for what lies right before us."

Her hands closed around Madeleine's shoulders. She didn't grab or squeeze. Rather, she held Madeleine with an easy grip that only served as a reminder of what she *could* do, if she chose.

At Hæra's touch, Madeleine's knees nearly buckled again. She kept her balance but could not swallow a sharp gasp that Hæra surely heard. *Take me in your arms,* she wanted to moan again, *make me forget—*

"You followed me into the bedroom," Hæra growled. "You accepted my *intimate invitation.*"

"I didn't know!" How was Madeleine finding the air to speak, even if it was barely audible to her own ears? "I wasn't sure you meant it like—like—"

"Like you would have, in my place?" For a moment, Hæra's grip tightened. "I see."

"H-Hæra…"

"Are there any more human *intimate invitations* I should be aware of?"

There were thousands of them, but at the moment, Madeleine couldn't think of a single one. She couldn't think of anything at all. "I don't know," she choked. "Nuns don't do that."

"You're no longer a nun." Now Hæra's lips brushed the shell of Madeleine's ear. She smelled, again, the sea. "So, Madeleine…"

If Hæra leaned in even a millimeter further, she'd be nuzzling Madeleine's throat. If Madeleine turned her head, their mouths would meet. There was nobody here to stop them—to save them—

Please, Madeleine thought, as her head began to turn, as her body began to melt. *Please…*

"Do not put yourself in a position," Hæra said, "when you think I might take, and hope that I won't."

She let Madeleine go.

Madeleine was left standing on shaking legs, with a desperate throb between them. Her vision swam as if she were about to lose consciousness. Would that be a bad thing? The last time she had, Hæra had awakened her on the beach with a voracious kiss.

Madeleine would never make sense of her. One moment, Hæra was a bright-eyed, inquisitive creature who seemed as if she couldn't hurt a fly. The next moment, she was all teeth and appetite, someone who'd spent nearly a century gliding through the waves toward her prey.

Her prey had probably never wanted to be caught before.

Madeleine brushed her fingertips against the little crucifix she wore. It felt heavier than usual around her neck.

Behind her, Hæra said brusquely, "Let's see Jonathan before we go to the village. He'll have his fry-up ready."

Ah. Jonathan. Yes. Someone else, someone not Hæra, yes.

Blessedly, at the mention of an old man and his fry-up, her arousal began to cool. She pulled her phone from her pocket with a shaking hand and checked the time. It was nearly nine in the morning. "This late?"

"He had a lie-in. He's been tired this last week. Says he's been having odd dreams and doesn't sleep well."

The worried note in Hæra's voice made Madeleine turn her head. Hæra's expression, whatever it had been, was concerned again. She frowned a little.

Then Hæra's eyes snapped up, locking on to Madeleine's once more like teeth closing around a throat. "I've never dreamed," she said.

Madeleine needed a moment to get her breath back. "You've told me."

"I don't sleep, dream, or feel the cold. And..." Hæra's eyes narrowed. "I don't ask."

Without thinking, Madeleine touched her crucifix again and felt her pounding heart beneath.

"Remember that," Hæra said, and stalked through the bedroom door.

———

The air was brisk, the wind sharp, and by the time she'd finished the walk from the cottage to Jonathan and Hæra's flat, Madeleine was back to herself somewhat.

Whoever *herself* was these days. At least it was someone who could smile at Jonathan when she and Hæra entered the kitchen and say, "Good morning."

Jonathan looked up from the stove. He didn't seem like a man who'd been plagued with "odd dreams." Rather, he had a big smile on his face. "Good morning," he said cheerfully as he pushed bacon around in a frying pan. The grease popped and hissed. "All moved in, Madeleine?"

"Yes, not that there was much to move. Just my suitcase."

Hæra opened the door of the fridge and bent down. "She likes the new bed."

Madeleine's face flamed, but thankfully Jonathan was looking at the pan again. He said, "Ah, good! Couldn't see forcing a lady to sleep on Jim's...well, never mind that. You're going into the village?"

For a moment, Madeleine was unsure. Hæra had said she'd go earlier, but she was clearly unhappy with Madeleine now. Did that mean the trip was cancelled? She could have slapped herself. Was she planning to curtail a trip just because Hæra might not go with her for once? That was ridiculous.

"Yes," she said, her voice a little sharper than she meant it to be. She cleared her throat. "After breakfast. Thanks for inviting me."

Jonathan grinned again. "My pleasure. Sit down, sit down."

Hæra put the cream on the table. Jonathan laid generous amounts of bacon and fried bread onto two plates.

Madeleine couldn't forbear a quick glance at Hæra, who sat down with no plate before her, just a cup of tea. "Um, have you eaten?"

She and Hæra had shared a few meals now. Enough for Madeleine to know that an *Each-uisge* didn't prefer cooked meat. It should have been disgusting, not fascinating, to watch Hæra dig into a raw sheep's neck, but, well, there you were. At least Hæra used utensils.

Hæra gave her a long look. Then her lips twitched softly in a little smile, and she relaxed in her chair, sitting back and crossing her arms. "Haggis," she said. "Only without the suet and oatmeal. Or the onions. Or the boiling."

"So you had a plate of raw sheep's liver, heart, and lungs," Jonathan said dryly.

Hæra never took her eyes from Madeleine's. "I'm a growing girl."

If she wanted to fluster Madeleine, too bad. Hæra had already set her off-balance enough for one morning. Madeleine placed her napkin in her lap. "That should hold you for a while, then."

Before Hæra could reply, she bowed her head, said a quick, silent blessing, and crossed herself. By now, after several meals at Jonathan's house, neither Hæra nor Jonathan seemed awkward around Madeleine's prayers. In fact, when Hæra reached for the salt, she said casually, "I tried blessing my breakfast today too."

Madeleine almost dropped her fork before she could start on her bacon. "You did?"

"Yes. I said the same words you do, except I thanked the Great Stallion."

Madeleine wasn't used to this either: such casual references to a supernatural creature's religion. But surprisingly, it was getting a bit easier. Hæra believed in things, and that was something they had in common.

Even if Hæra's beliefs didn't seem to dictate how she acted, which was something they didn't have in common.

"What was it like to say a blessing?" Madeleine asked.

"I didn't feel anything, but I've never thought a lot about the Stallion. *Each-uisge* don't have as much to do with him. But he's the one who made the land, and that's where my food came from, so I had to thank him." Hæra pursed her lips consideringly. "I suppose on the nights we have fish, I should thank the Great Mare. Maybe that would feel more meaningful."

"How did the Great Stallion make the land?" Madeleine asked, curious to know what kind of mythology a mythological creature lived by.

"Shat it out," Hæra said promptly. "And the Mare gave birth to the ocean."

Jonathan groaned. "Over breakfast and all?"

Hæra shrugged and sprinkled salt into her tea. "She asked me."

There was no denying that. Madeleine chuckled. "So I did."

"I didn't." Jonathan popped a piece of fatty bacon into his mouth.

"You need to eat less of that stuff," Hæra said with a little frown. "That nurse Sue Kilbright told you not as much salt, didn't she?"

"That's funny, coming from the one who puts salt in everything she drinks."

"It's not…" Hæra gave a quick glance at Madeleine. "It's not the same for me, you know that."

Rather than looking chastened, Jonathan appeared pleased. Every reminder of Hæra's true nature, spoken in front of Madeleine, seemed to delight him.

The first time they'd all sat down to a meal together, after Hæra had told Madeleine the truth, he'd beamed. His relief had seemed palpable, so intense it was almost joy. Carrying that shared secret must have been nearly as hard on him as it had been on Hæra.

It was worth it to him, though. Jonathan had spoken of his happiness that Hæra had come to him. He'd wasted so many years, he'd said, but now he had a new lease on life, and wasn't that grand? Anyone could take a page from his book.

Madeleine had known what he was really saying. *Start over. Learn what I did. It's never too late.*

They'd see about that. For now, it was all Madeleine could do not to ogle Hæra's long, lean body every chance she got. That was more than enough to contend with.

Especially after her little slip a few minutes ago.

They had vowed to be friends, and only that. They didn't talk about where they might be going. Hæra wasn't one to look to the future, as she admitted herself, and when Madeleine tried to look at the road ahead, it went out of focus.

It was much easier to live day by day, spending time with Hæra and taking moments as they came. Whatever Madeleine was supposed to learn from this would come to her when it was meant to —right?

Breakfast ended, and Madeleine insisted on helping Jonathan clean while Hæra went out to bring the Vauxhall around. "Guests don't wash up," he objected as he set the bacon pan to soak.

Madeleine began to wash their coffee cups. "Am I just a guest now?"

She glanced at him. He looked back. Through the window over the sink, the rare morning sunlight landed on his face, turning his white beard whiter. "I dunno what you are," Jonathan said. "But more than a guest, that's true. You're good for her. And I thank your God, or her Mare, or whatever, that you came."

Madeleine dipped her head. "So do I."

"It's been hard, though, hasn't it?"

His look was full of compassion. Madeleine still found herself unable to answer it beyond saying, "Yes."

"We should talk," he said. "You and me."

Jonathan and Madeleine hadn't had a heart-to-heart yet, mostly because Hæra was always present. Madeleine knew they'd both been wanting one. Who else could understand the situation they'd both found themselves in: their human lives changed forever by an *Each-uisge*?

But what would he say if he knew what she and Hæra had just gotten up to? Madeleine still wasn't clear on what he and Hæra were to each other. Not biologically related, but they were kin. They were protective of each other. How would he feel about his... friend?...having such a relationship with a human being? A woman?

The Vauxhall rumbled and then came to a stop outside, reminding Madeleine why it was hard to find time alone with Jonathan. They smiled wryly at each other.

"How are we going to manage that?" she asked.

"It'll be easier now you're living here. Come over tomorrow morning when the lass is out in the fields. And tonight..." He grinned. "Tonight we'll have a proper housewarming, the three of us, if you don't mind an old man's company."

He must have been so lonely for so long. Few would believe that Madeleine had felt the same way, since she'd spent decades in community with other women. But there were different ways of being isolated, and she could recognize a kindred spirit. "Of course I wouldn't mind. That's kind of you."

"Well, tonight's a good night. Slovakia are playing Iceland in the Euro, and I don't care about that."

Jonathan's devotion to the European Football Championship mystified Hæra, but Madeleine had grown up watching the New

Orleans Saints. She understood not wanting to miss a big game. "That's lucky. What will this housewarming involve?"

"Ah, wait and see." His eyes twinkled. "But a fiddle might feature, so prepare yourself."

The back door opened. The Vauxhall rumbled beyond it as Hæra called, "Madeleine? Are you ready?"

Will I ever be? "Ready," Madeleine replied, and she gave Jonathan a smile as she headed for the door.

Outside, Hæra held the passenger door open for Madeleine. The sun limned her dark hair and flashed off her smile.

"Ready," Madeleine whispered again, only to herself, not at all sure it was true.

CHAPTER TWENTY-NINE

The words hadn't left Hæra's head since Madeleine had first uttered them. By asking Madeleine into a bedroom, Hæra had invited intimacy. As Madeleine had put it—with surprising forthrightness—sex.

Hæra kept her eyes firmly on the road ahead and tried not to think about having sex with Madeleine, possibly in the passenger seat where she now sat.

It wasn't easy. In the past month, Hæra had learned about a new kind of torture. It wasn't the agony of waiting she'd known in the sea, hoping to take to the skies. It wasn't the incalculable pain of being attacked by her own family. It wasn't the dull misery that had beset her during her first months living on land.

There was nothing dull about this torture. It was sharp, relentless, alive.

And it didn't always feel like pain.

Sometimes it even felt good—a warm pulse between her thighs that had Hæra "seeing to herself" more often. Most nights, in fact. She'd lie in bed in the dead of night, touching herself and thinking of Madeleine.

She'd imagine that they hadn't been interrupted in the alley. Instead, they'd had perfect privacy while Hæra finished what she'd started: unzipping Madeleine's then-untorn jacket, slipping her hands under Madeleine's sweater, finding what there was to find. All the while, Madeleine would have kept grinding on Hæra's thigh, seeking release with those helpless whimpers coming from the back of her throat.

She'd have found it. Madeleine would have shuddered in Hæra's arms with the same ecstasy Hæra found from her own touch. Then she would have relaxed as Hæra always did, panting, her muscles going limp. She'd have gone loose in Hæra's arms, happy and grateful. She'd have said—

"Are we going to park somewhere else?"

Hæra blinked. They were nearly in the village. So much for focusing on her surroundings.

And she'd driven right past the four spaces set aside for public parking. Thornhill didn't have a proper car park. Not much need for one.

"I'll park at the curb in front of that café," Hæra said, as if she'd intended to do this all along. "The Sunrise. I can fit between those two vehicles." She squinted. "That van is Jimmy Howisher's. He's been late on our deliveries. Jonathan'll be cross if it's because he's been here drinking coffee."

Madeleine didn't reply. She was probably looking at her mobile or something. Hæra glanced over to find Madeleine staring at the Sunrise Café as the car approached it, her eyes wide and her face pale.

Hæra began to slow. "What's wrong?"

"Nothing." Madeleine swallowed visibly. "I'm just not sure the car will fit there. You should find a space with more room. A couple of blocks down, maybe."

A challenge. Hæra's skin already prickled with the urge to meet it. "Can't fit? You watch."

"But...we don't want to damage..."

"Have faith." Haera pulled up parallel to the van and reversed her car. "My sense of perception is excellent." She checked the mirrors as she backed into the space—which, admittedly, would be a tight fit. "Not as good as when I'm in my real form, mind you. Then I can see from all sides."

She waited for Madeleine to say a horse would have a hard time driving a car in other ways. Madeleine didn't. She was silent.

Hæra focused on backing the car expertly into the space. When she put it in park, she gave Madeleine a triumphant grin. "See? Perfect."

"Let's go." Madeleine unbuckled her seat belt with unsteady hands. She wasn't looking at Hæra. "Hurry, please."

Now Hæra's skin prickled for a different reason. Madeleine wasn't just upset. She was afraid. Hæra could smell it on her. But why? There was nothing to hurt her here. No threats were visible on the street. Hæra's lips pulled back over her teeth anyway; her fingers curled tightly on the steering wheel. Better than reaching out and grabbing the frightened woman trying to escape the car.

It was too late anyway. Madeleine was out of the car, and there was nothing for Hæra to do but follow her.

As she did, she glanced in the window of the Sunrise Café. To her surprise, she saw a man with black hair and brown skin looking through the window too, but not at Hæra. Rather, he was looking after Madeleine with two raised eyebrows. He'd clearly noticed her haste.

That wasn't remarkable. You noticed people when they seemed distressed. But something about the man's expression stopped Hæra in her tracks. He didn't just look curious—he seemed a little upset himself. He frowned.

Hæra realized that she and Madeleine had never been to the Sunrise Café during their little trips to the village, or even gone near it. That was surprising, since Thornhill was so small. But Madeleine always cut across the street or chose routes that went other directions, sometimes taking side streets even if they were less efficient. Had she been avoiding this place?

The man glanced up and saw Hæra looking at him. His frown vanished, replaced with surprise.

Knowing she ought to chase Madeleine, Hæra spent a precious few moments staring back at him. Her brows drew together, and knowledge shivered through her. This man had recognized Madeleine.

Had he frightened her? If so, there was no time for the dire retribution he deserved. Hæra would make sure he suffered it later. For now, she had to chase Madeleine down.

Dallying at the window meant she had to jog rather than walk. She caught Madeleine at the end of the block, in front of the Cliffside Store. She caught her literally, in fact, grabbing her elbow before she could cross the street in front of an oncoming car. The car honked and drove past.

"One car on the whole street and you try to get hit by it?" Hæra snapped. Her heart raced unpleasantly in her chest. That had been too close.

"I looked the wrong way. It's still a habit." Madeleine kept her eyes turned from Hæra. "Thanks for catching me."

Hæra kept Madeleine's elbow in her grip. That might not be wise, but she couldn't do anything else. It had been a while now since Madeleine had attempted to run from her. She'd forgotten how it had felt: like being marooned.

"What's the matter?" she asked. "Don't say, 'Nothing.'"

Madeleine laughed roughly. "I know better. Let's just walk for a second, okay? I'll gather my thoughts."

What an odd way to put it, as if thoughts could fall out of your pocket to be retrieved. The first time Hæra picked up something with human hands had been the night she'd offered Jonathan a gold coin. It had been solid and wet in her palm. How much had changed since then.

How little had changed, too. She couldn't tell what had upset the human at her side.

"Where are we going?" she asked as they began to walk.

To her astonishment, Madeleine said, "Back to the beach."

Hæra stopped in her tracks. "Beach? You mean *our* beach?"

"That's exactly what I mean."

They hadn't returned to that beach since the night Hæra had met

Madeleine in horse form. It seemed like a bad idea, as it always had. But Hæra had grown bolder about being near the water lately. It was daytime, when most *Each-uisge* were forbidden to come to the surface. She'd broken the rules herself, but nobody else had, that she'd ever heard of.

The same conditions applied. Only Asgall, Beathag, or Calder would recognize her like this. The odds were minuscule that any of them would come above the surface, today, in front of that particular stretch of beach. And Madeleine wanted to go.

Hæra only had one question. "Why?"

Madeleine wrapped her arms around herself, keeping her eyes focused straight ahead as she marched in the direction of the beach. "I don't know. I just need to be there. Where we were, where..." She trailed off.

When she didn't finish, Hæra said, "Where we met?"

Madeleine nodded. "Will you be safe there?"

Hæra took in a deep breath. "Yes. I think so."

They said nothing else until they'd reached the seawall and climbed the stairs down to the rocky shore. How strange to think that less than a month ago, they'd met here in the dark and their lives had changed for a second time.

Only a moon's turn since they'd reunited? Impossible. It seemed she and Madeleine had been bound to one another since the creation of the world, whoever had done that.

As they reached the shore, Hæra felt herself grow stronger. Here, she'd be able to pick up four Madeleines if she wanted to. Not that she'd get the chance. There could never be another Madeleine.

Today, others were on the beach. Not close: a man and woman standing by the water in brightly colored jackets—tourists, probably. Farther down the beach, a bearded old man walked by himself, his hands in his coat pockets. His shuffling steps reminded Hæra of how Jonathan used to be.

To the left, Jorsay's cliffs loomed in jagged layers of sandstone with moss-covered outcroppings. Slippery rocks rose from the ocean floor above the water's surface. They were like the cliffs and rocks Hæra had hidden behind when she'd eavesdropped on Madeleine talking to that juvenile, Ava, about what it was like to be a nun. The sound had carried clearly to her, Madeleine's voice enchanting her as surely as any witch's spell. It seemed so long ago.

"What happened in the Sunrise Café?" she asked.

Madeleine looked at her, wide-eyed.

"There was a man inside who watched you," Hæra clarified. "I think he recognized you. He looked upset."

Madeleine groaned and hid her hands in her face.

Hæra's breath caught. "Did he hurt you?"

"No," Madeleine mumbled into her palms. "I hurt him, I think. And I hurt myself too."

"What?"

Madeleine lowered her hands and told Hæra of the day she'd arrived, when she'd ordered food at the Sunrise Café and reacted poorly to learning that the owners were gay men. She spoke of her panic, followed quickly by humiliation and regret.

"I know what they thought of me," she said. "I haven't been able to face going back." She snorted. "Even though that sausage roll was amazing."

"What do you mean, what they thought of you?"

"That I'm a homophobe. You know that word? Someone who hates gay people. That's what they thought I was." Madeleine seized the top of her zip, which was already pulled up to her chin. "They were right."

The back of Hæra's neck prickled. The word "gay" felt heavy, significant to the moment. Madeleine hadn't used it since their passionate encounter in the alley. Hæra had figured it was just part of her desire for them not to become sexually intimate in general, but it had to be more than that, if using it made her look so miserable.

It seemed they were talking about it now. So talk about it she would.

"You don't hate anyone," she said. "You're not made that way. Besides, you told me you're gay, didn't you? So that would mean you'd hate yourself, and that's absurd."

The logic seemed foolproof to her. Madeleine would realize she wasn't a homophobe because she couldn't possibly hate herself. How could anyone hate her?

Madeleine pressed her lips together and closed her eyes. For all the world, she looked as if someone was about to strike her and she was just waiting for the blow.

I will protect you from blows, Hæra thought, *nobody shall strike you while I'm here.*

"Maybe it's absurd," Madeleine said softly. "Maybe it's prideful and un-Christian. But it's still true."

Hæra boggled. Madeleine could have said nothing more unbelievable. As such, Hæra could not believe it. "Hate yourself! For *that?*"

Maybe Madeleine just didn't have a grasp on the concept of hatred. She was too kind. If she knew how Hæra felt about Asgall, Calder, or even her mother sometimes, she'd know the difference.

"It's wrong," Madeleine said.

Hæra scowled. Loads of things were wrong, but she couldn't imagine why this was one of them. Wasn't Hæra resigned to her attraction to someone from another *species*? It couldn't be wrong when it felt so natural. "I know your books say it's bad. I just don't know why that matters so much."

Madeleine kept her eyes shut. "I couldn't expect you to."

"No," Hæra said sharply. "It's not just because I'm not human. Those men in the café must not care about your books either. Neither do a lot of other humans. If your books and saints and whatever else are more important than people..."

"They're not!" Madeleine cried, opening her eyes. They were full of anguish. "That's the point! You can't separate the Scriptures from people. They teach us how to live with each other. How to behave, how to *be.*"

Hæra turned her eyes away from what she didn't understand and toward what she did. Ahead of her, the North Sea churned, iron gray beneath the clouds. Whitecaps crested the waves that carried sediment to shore, blending sea and land.

"Hæra?"

Even the plea in Madeleine's voice couldn't get Hæra to turn her eyes from the sea. It was great, it was powerful, it was greatly and powerfully lonely.

"My kind don't live in community as humans do," she said eventually. "We only cluster for safety. We hunt and travel as a herd. Everyone knows their place. There was never a place for me."

Madeleine's hand landed gently on her upper arm. The sea sighed.

"There's no music or entertainment," Hæra continued. "The closest I came to idle conversation was my brother's taunts. I sought often to be alone—it was less lonely than being with the rest of my kind. It's different here. I'm not lonely with Jonathan. Or with you."

She turned, finally, to Madeleine, who looked up at her with wide eyes.

"I would still rather go back there," she said, "than live by your books and hate what I am."

Madeleine's hand gripped Hæra's arm, as if in a spasm. She looked as if she couldn't speak.

Just as well. Hæra was out of words herself. She couldn't continue with the truth: that she would have to return to the sea eventually and either seek to live alone as a rogue *Each-uisge* until she couldn't fend for herself anymore, or face execution by the herd. A lonely end, no matter how you looked at it.

But she would know who she was and who she'd been, and she'd have no regrets.

"I've learned so much," she told Madeleine. "I've learned that life isn't what I always thought it was. I wish you would too. Then…"

Madeleine blinked once, then twice. Her eyes were wet. As Hæra watched, a tear streaked down from one of them, down her cheek. She choked, "Then what?"

There were so many options. *Then you could share this world with me. Then we could be together, for a time. Then I could have what I want, which is…which is…*

"Then you could be happy," Hæra said, her voice quiet with the truth. "That's what I want."

Madeleine gasped. She clapped a hand over mouth, and more tears flowed from her eyes while her shoulders shook.

Madeleine's pain burned Hæra, as painfully as fire must. This time, she'd inflicted it. One month ago, on a darkened street, Madeleine had told her, *You already ate me up. There's only bones left.*

Without permission, swift as thought allowed, Hæra wrapped her arms around Madeleine's bones and flesh, pulling her close. Madeleine clung back, digging her fingertips into Hæra's back while she pressed her face into Hæra's shoulder and wept. "I don't deserve to be happy," she sobbed.

"Why not?" Hæra tightened her grip. If only she could pull Madeleine into her own body somehow and keep her safe from these awful ideas.

"I've hurt people—"

"Who?"

"And I've done wrong—"

"How?"

"Because I'm bad, I'm just bad, that's all!" Madeleine dug her fingertips into Hæra's back even harder. It hurt, but it couldn't hurt nearly as much as what seemed to torture Madeleine now. "I've never been what I'm supposed to be!"

Hæra choked back a gasp. Beathag had said nearly the same thing right before she'd tried to murder her own offspring. She'd said it about Hæra as if it were the foulest curse she knew. Now Madeleine used those words as cudgels against herself.

"That's not true," Hæra said fiercely. "You're kind. You're generous. Aren't you supposed to be those things?"

Madeleine didn't seem to hear her. "I hate what I've been taught, I *hate* it, and that's wrong too, and that's—t-that's—" She shook her forehead rapidly against Hæra. "Oh God!"

Hæra's nose rested against Madeleine's hair. This close, she could smell Madeleine better than ever. It was the most perfect scent in the world, the most tantalizing. How could Madeleine believe any part of her was bad, wrong, or anything less than perfectly beautiful? If Hæra had been wronged by her kin, Madeleine had been poorly served by her faith. No one should have dared to make her feel this way.

While Madeleine cried in her arms, she looked around. The man and woman at the water's edge were watching them, but at Hæra's glare, they quickly turned away. The old man was nearly to the end of the beach now.

"If that's what you hate," she said, "then what do you love?"

Madeleine took a deep, shaky breath, and let it go. She did it again, a couple more times, while her trembling slowed. Her face was still pressed against Hæra.

"I love springtime," she said after a moment. "When I see the first crocus or daffodil. I love my coffee in the morning. I love starting a new piece of embroidery, all the possibility of the blank fabric."

These did not seem like significant things, but plainly they were significant to Madeleine. Hæra waited for more, trying to do so patiently.

"I love singing, I don't think I've told you that." Her voice was muffled. "I love the first day of school, getting to know my students. I love the farmer's market Becca and I go to sometimes. I love Becca, I really should call her soon. I love so many people I haven't seen in so long. People who've gone, and I pray I'll see them again, I love them too."

Hæra said into Madeleine's hair, "Even if you don't see them again, you still loved them."

"Ah!" Madeleine pressed her face hard into Hæra's shoulder again, but it was only the truth. Hæra had spent years waiting for Sister Madeleine to return to her. But if she never had, then Hæra would still have had the memory of their meeting on this very beach. She understood that now.

She stroked the back of Madeleine's head. And, as she had seen Jonathan and the farmhands do with upset animals, she gently hummed. Madeleine was no animal, but she was Hæra's to hold nevertheless. "What else do you love?" she whispered into the shell of Madeleine's ear. It was cold from the wind.

Madeleine shivered and exhaled again. She stepped back a little, although not out of Hæra's arms, and wiped the tears from her face. She looked into Hæra's eyes, sniffled, and bit her bottom lip.

For a moment, Hæra's lungs—which could hold more air than a

human's—couldn't function. Her eyes couldn't either, since even her peripheral vision was gone, and Madeleine's face was all she could see.

Madeleine said hoarsely, "No, it's not like that. I've only known you for a month. I don't know how to describe it. Just that…" She placed her hand over Hæra's human-sized heart. Maybe she could feel it slamming against Hæra's human-sized ribs.

"For years, I thought you were an angel," Madeleine said. "Or I hoped you were. Church doctrine says everyone has an angel who's assigned to us, who protects us, and I thought…if you were my angel, then maybe I was all right."

"You *are* all—"

"And now I know you're not, but it's like I opened a door I couldn't close. I keep *questioning*. I keep *wanting* who I am, what I am, to be okay, because I'm so tired of fighting myself."

Why in the Great Mare's name would Madeleine want to be anything other than her generous self? Hæra said through her teeth, "I'm not an angel. I said so."

"I know! But you've been with me for years. Wherever I went. Now we're here, together, and I want you with me all the time—I don't understand it, it's like you're part of me, even though you can't possibly be when we're not even the same *species*."

Hæra wanted to cry out that it didn't matter, but she couldn't say a word. Not now, when Madeleine was saying what Hæra had dreamed of for so long. It was exactly how she felt too, and she couldn't find the words to say so.

"But that's not love," Madeleine continued. "At least not like I've ever understood it. It's something else, isn't it?"

It was hunger. Hæra had always known that, and it wasn't the same as love.

Or was it? Hunger could be sated. You could rend your prey to pieces and feed yourself to bursting, and it would be enough. It was impossible to have enough of Madeleine.

That…might be love. No, it must be. One sort of love, anyway. Hæra had learned, during her time here, that there were supposed to be different sorts of love that meant different things. It hadn't occurred to her to apply that idea to herself.

"And you? Can you love?" Madeleine sounded—and looked—desperate as she voiced the question in Hæra's mind. "That is, I know you can. But *what* do you love?"

Hæra held back the most obvious answer—the word "you" that Madeleine wouldn't believe. She felt unsteady inside as she pondered the question and sought easy answers that wouldn't frighten either Madeleine or herself. She tucked a loose strand of hair behind Madeleine's ear, and thought she would say, *Rainbows,* or *hunting,* or *the power of the storm.*

She heard herself say, "Jonathan."

Her breath caught in shock, but Madeleine didn't look shocked at all. In fact, her face softened, and some of the distress left her eyes. "Yes," she said softly, as if it were obvious.

It was the farthest thing from obvious. Hæra thought, *I didn't know that. I didn't know.*

But she loved Jonathan's patience, his persistence, and his kindness. She loved how he'd set out the salt for her tea on the second time she'd visited. She loved how he'd put a pillow and duvet on the sofa for her on the night he'd brought her home, battered and grieving. She loved his white beard. She loved how he loved her too, because he must, he must, it was the only explanation for what they were to one another. All told, that added up to loving…

"Jonathan," Hæra repeated numbly. "I love him."

"And he loves you." Madeleine's voice was full of certainty now.

Certainty must be nice. Hæra looked toward the sea again, where her kin were, where Jonathan was not. Where there was no farm, or sunlight, or rainbows, or Madeleine. Once, she had meant to drag Madeleine with her under the waves. Now that wouldn't happen either.

She squeezed her eyes shut before she could begin to cry too. Maybe Madeleine had felt like this when she'd realized she was attracted to other females. Something out of the order she'd been taught to believe in, and something that couldn't be changed.

Madeleine's hand touched her cheek, brushing over it with the back of her knuckles. "Hey. Are you okay?"

The self-recrimination was gone from her voice, replaced with soft concern. Hæra already knew how kind her eyes would be, if she looked at them.

"They never told me I could love," she choked. "Not this way. I could only take or be taken. It was sharkshite. It was all sharkshite. I didn't know until now, until Jonathan, until—until—" She looked wildly down at Madeleine, whose eyes were as compassionate as Hæra had known they'd be. "Until *you.*"

Madeleine grabbed Hæra's shoulders, as if to keep her feet. After a moment, she said, "This is what we're supposed to learn."

"What?"

"I mean, this is it. I think?" Madeleine pressed her face again to Hæra's shoulder. "No, I know it is. This is why we were brought together, to learn this."

Hæra dug her hands into Madeleine's hair again, her fingers shaking. "Learn what?" Water dripped from her eyes down her cheeks. One drop touched her lips. She tasted salt that should have been familiar but wasn't. Tears tasted different from the sea.

Maybe she was sick of salt.

Madeleine's arms slid down from Hæra's shoulders to around her waist. She looked into Hæra's eyes with an expression so earnest that it made Hæra's hands release their fierce grip on her hair.

"I think," Madeleine said slowly, "that there's so much about the world I don't know. This world and the next one. The last month's taught me that. And you told me yourself that doubt isn't a bad thing. It's how we learn." She took in a deep, shaking breath. "You're brave. You're *so* brave. I have to be too. And that means…"

She hesitated, and Hæra couldn't parse the meaning of the pause. Everything needed to be spelled out clearly for her just now. "Means what?"

"Taking a risk," Madeleine whispered. "A big one. Because if I don't…maybe I'll never be happy. Maybe I'd die without ever being happy. Or free."

"What does that mean?" Hæra pleaded. Happiness and freedom might not be the same for Madeleine as they would be for her. "What would make you free? Or happy?"

Madeleine looked into her eyes. Her chest didn't move against Hæra's; she was holding her breath. And without a word, she reached up and traced her fingertips over the edge of Hæra's jaw, back and forth.

"This," she said shakily. "Trying this."

Hæra couldn't reply. She could only lower her forehead, slowly, until it touched Madeleine's. She closed her eyes.

"Oh, Hæra," Madeleine murmured. Her other hand slid up and down Hæra's back. "We'll figure it out. We can do it together. Don't you think?"

I can do anything with you, except survive the sea. Hæra couldn't say that. It didn't seem like the right moment to explain her inevitably grisly fate.

Besides, it was still true: whatever happened in the future, they had right now. Hæra would have no regrets. Especially not about turning her back on an opportunity.

She tilted her head. Just a little. She made a soft, small sound, and there was wanting in it as she touched Madeleine's chin with her human fingertips. "I want to learn about love," she whispered.

Madeleine trembled again. Her breath was warm on Hæra's lips as she said, "Me too."

There, before witnesses—the humans, the shore, the sea—they kissed.

Madeleine had been sure that she lacked the courage to return to the Sunrise Café. She'd avoided it as much as possible, always walking on the other side of the street even if it meant going out of her way. And, today, actually running away from it as if it had been on fire.

You don't lack the courage, she told herself. *You don't lack anything you need.*

She lacked certainty, yes. But she didn't need that. Hæra's hand was in her own, and it sufficed.

The memory of Hæra's kiss was on her lips. It had been different from the other kisses they'd shared: soft and sweet. When their mouths had parted, Hæra sighed and rubbed Madeleine's nose with her own. They'd laughed, both of them sounding surprised. Joy had bubbled in Madeleine's chest: a feeling she could never have allowed herself only twenty-four hours ago, when she'd still clung to her view of how the world worked, in spite of all the new evidence that said otherwise.

She'd thought: *This is what it's supposed to be like. This is how it's supposed to feel.*

As she pushed the café door open, the bell rang. Arjun was standing behind the counter, taking another customer's order. He lifted his eyebrows when he saw her but said nothing as he rang it up.

Madeleine led Hæra to the counter, and as they reached it, the customer took his coffee and walked away. Arjun looked at them impassively. "Good morning," he said.

"Good morning," Madeleine said, before realizing she didn't have a speech prepared, or even an opening remark. Righteous determination could only power you so far before you had to say something coherent. Yet again, she stared at Arjun and tried to think of what to say.

"I'm sorry," she blurted.

Arjun tilted his head to the side. "For what?"

His eyes said he knew very well *for what*. It was no different from when Madeleine made high school students admit to their transgressions. She could do the same. She opened her mouth.

"For not reading the menu before we ordered," Hæra said. She slid her arm around Madeleine's shoulders loosely, her massive power leashed for now.

Madeleine's face heated as Arjun looked back and forth between them.

"What did you have last time, Madeleine?" Hæra continued. "The sausage roll?"

Madeleine's hand crept up to touch Hæra's where it rested on her shoulder. It covered the rip where she'd torn Madeleine's jacket with her teeth.

Hæra's fingers stiffened. She clearly anticipated rejection. She began to move her hand away.

Madeleine placed her own hand over it and held it in place.

"Yes, that's what I had," she said, looking at Arjun. "It was really good. I'd just gotten here, and it was the first thing I tried." She took a deep breath. "But I wanted to come back and try something else."

Arjun looked at Hæra's hand on Madeleine's shoulder. Then his mouth quirked up halfway. "Never too late to try something new," he said. "Especially if it's something you've been wanting to try for a while. Jeremy could tell you so."

Madeleine blushed again and smiled at someone who was like her and whom she did not have to fear, unless she chose to. He smiled back.

"We'll have whatever you suggest," Hæra told him. Her thumb rubbed against Madeleine's shoulder. Madeleine kept her own hand over Hæra's, using it to protect the tear beneath.

CHAPTER THIRTY

Madeleine, sitting on the bed, stared down at Becca's texts. There was not a single indication of surprise in them. Typical Becca.

She bit her lip, then, and her eyes stung with tears.

On the screen, green bubbles started, and then stopped, and then started again. Madeleine could picture Becca with her tongue between her lips, concentrating as she worked out the right thing to say. Finally, Becca replied:

Madeleine dipped her head. This time, a tear made its way down her cheek.

A phone call. One where Madeleine and a friend could hash out all the details of a thrilling kiss, of a new romance. The sort of experience Madeleine never had growing up but had watched other girls having, and always wondered what it was like. Her heart raced with eagerness.

Moments later, the phone rang, its bright tone lighting up the room with promise. Smiling, crying a bit, Madeleine finally answered.

———

Hæra had said Jonathan was "a shite fiddler," which had seemed harsh. Tonight, before the cottage fireplace, Madeleine had to concede she'd been correct. Jonathan's bow was less than precise, the fiddle's notes high and screechy as he played traditional Scottish folk songs "to welcome an American lass properly."

It was still delightful. She, Hæra, and Jonathan all sat together in the cottage's little living room, with a fire going to keep out the evening chill. Hæra had pulled the couch back and sat farther away from the heat, but she insisted she was fine, if Madeleine and Jonathan needed the fire to stay warm.

There was a space at Hæra's side. Madeleine looked longingly at it from where she sat on the floor with her back to the fire. Maybe once she warmed up, she'd sit with Hæra for a few minutes, and next time she was in town she'd buy a blanket from Annie's Crafts. Then they could sit together.

At least looking at Hæra was its own reward. Hæra lounged on the couch in her usual posture: legs spread, arms draped over the back of the couch, casual and confident. She'd let her hair out of its ponytail. Now it fell, long and straight, around her face and over her shoulders. Her eyes were sharp, her mouth tilted in a thoughtful little smile as she watched Jonathan.

Madeleine smiled too. Hæra had said she loved him as if it was the greatest shock she'd ever known. Meanwhile, Madeleine had had something of a shock herself. The scales had fallen from their eyes today, as they had from Saint Paul's.

Paul had harsh things to say about homosexuals—things that had tormented her for her whole life. He had also said, *If I have not love, I gain nothing.* Catholics weren't overly fond of Pauline theology, but you couldn't just discount that kind of declaration from an apostle of Christ.

She didn't have to throw it away entirely, nor the other teachings that had sustained her through good times and bad. She did, however, have to think about them in new ways. And if that made her a cafeteria Catholic after all, picking and choosing what seemed right to her, then maybe it wasn't the worst fate in the world.

Becca had agreed. They'd spent most of their conversation talking about Hæra and the kiss—with a few key details left out, obviously. But Becca had agreed it was high time for Madeleine to embrace a new way of thinking.

It couldn't be this simple. One conversation on the beach, followed by one chat with a friend, wouldn't erase a lifetime's worth of doubts and fears. But for the first time in decades, she felt something like peace. There was nothing wrong with holding on to it as long as it lasted.

And to think, she owed it all to a supernatural creature. She looked at Hæra again. Maybe tonight, she could ask Hæra to transform into her *Each-uisge* form. She might be ready to see it now.

Jonathan's song drew to a close. Madeleine and Hæra applauded politely. "It was shite," Jonathan confessed as he set the fiddle in his lap.

"Usually is," Hæra agreed. "Can I sing with the next one?"

Jonathan laughed. Madeleine sat up straight and said, "You sing?"

"Worse than I play," Jonathan said on Hæra's behalf. "How about 'The Rowan Tree'?"

At Hæra's enthusiastic nod, his fiddle launched into a folk melody Madeleine didn't recognize. The original composer, whoever it was, likely wouldn't recognize it either. Hæra's singing didn't help. However attractive she was, she had a singing voice like…well, like a horse's. Madeleine grimaced.

Nevertheless, when they were done, she clapped. Thankfully, Jonathan said, "That's it, my wrists and fingers are giving up. Madeleine, would you honor us?"

Hæra leaned forward on the couch. "You told me you like singing."

It was another piece of Madeleine she seemed eager to consume. In spite of the day's revelations and her newfound peace, the greed in Hæra's eyes made Madeleine's stomach flip over in a not-unpleasant way.

"I do," Madeleine said. A lightbulb went on over her head. "Some folk songs, even. French ones my mother taught me."

As always, at the memory of her lost family, her heart clenched. Though somehow, it wasn't so bad talking about it with Hæra and Jonathan. Even with the Daughters of Grace, a wall had raised itself around her heart as she tried to tell herself Christ's love was enough. It hadn't been.

Or maybe this was just a new way of feeling it. She wasn't sure yet.

Hæra smiled. The greed had gone from her eyes, replaced with the most human expression Madeleine had seen there yet: simple under-standing. Hæra had lost her family too. She said, "Go on then."

Madeleine cleared her throat. "I'll have to do it *a capella*. This one's 'Le Petit Cheval'—'The Little Horse.'"

When they nodded, she began to sing. "Le petit cheval dans le mauvais temps, qu'il avait donc du courage! C'était un petit cheval blanc…"

She wasn't half bad, especially compared to Hæra, and heaven knew she'd gotten enough practice with hymns. Her voice was a pleasing alto that glided nimbly through the notes.

When she finished, Jonathan clapped, and Hæra frowned. "That was short. There isn't any more?"

"Hæra," Jonathan sighed.

"What? I like her voice. Madeleine, is there more?"

"I only remember the first three verses," Madeleine admitted. "It's been a while."

"What do the words mean?"

"It's about a horse who's brave in a thunderstorm." As she said it, Madeleine bit her lower lip. She'd chosen the song deliberately, but now that she said it aloud, maybe it seemed heavy-handed.

Hæra sat up straight. Jonathan shook his head. "Best not to speak of that."

Before Madeleine could look around in alarm, Hæra said brusquely, "Don't be superstitious. It's not as if the herd can hear or see us. Madeleine, thank you for the song. You have a beautiful voice."

"She does," Jonathan agreed. "Finer than any I've heard in church."

"You don't go to church." Hæra darted a quick glance at Madeleine, as if making sure this topic wasn't off-limits.

What could Madeleine do but shrug? Jonathan could talk as he pleased, and it was good for her to be with people whose lives didn't revolve around worship. She herself hadn't been inside a church since her disastrous attempt at confession. After today's events, she felt no rush to return.

"There's other ways to find what's holy," Jonathan said. He crossed his legs at the ankles and settled his weathered hands on his stomach. "Singing's one. I sang a lot when I was a young man. Village kids would follow me about asking me to." He glanced at Hæra. "He said that's how he first noticed me, you know. Heard me singing. The song went out of me after him."

Hæra stared at Jonathan. "You never told me that."

"Must I tell you everything? Anyway, it's true."

Madeleine's mother had taught her not to ask intrusive questions, even if people were speaking in front of her about something she didn't know. It sure was a temptation now. Yet she held her tongue. If Jonathan wanted to elaborate, he would.

As if he'd read her mind, he smiled wryly at her. "Sorry. I'll tell you more later."

He must be referring to their talk tomorrow. Curiouser and curiouser. Madeleine nodded, already alight with interest.

"You should sing again," Hæra told him, voice taut. "Don't let him take away your pleasure anymore. I want to hear your song." She leaned forward toward where Jonathan sat in the hideous Naugahyde chair, eyes narrowed.

I love Jonathan, she'd said. *They never told me I could love.*

But Hæra could love. At the thought, Madeleine's blood ran hot in her veins, in a way it didn't even when she burned with desire. The fire at her back was nothing in comparison. Hæra wanted to learn more about love, and maybe someday, together, she and Madeleine could both learn…

Too bad she wasn't facing the fire. Then she'd have an excuse for her reddened cheeks.

Jonathan shifted in the chair. "My voice isn't what it used to be."

"None of us are," Madeleine heard herself say.

They both glanced at her. Jonathan's lips twitched. "That's true."

"Will you sing?" Hæra asked softly. "For us."

She held Jonathan's gaze with an expression Madeleine recognized now. It focused on you until you wanted to do nothing more than whatever Hæra desired. It was half order, half plea, both halves equally hard to resist.

Jonathan cleared his throat. "I can't promise I won't sound like a sheep."

"We're used to sheep," Hæra said. "And it can't be worse than your fiddle."

"Fair enough," he chuckled. "What to sing, then. Let me think…ah. I know the one."

He closed his eyes and seemed to settle into himself, going away somewhere. Madeleine had the feeling she was watching someone returning to the past. When Jonathan began to sing, Madeleine realized quickly it was meant to be a dialogue between two lovers.

Oh lad of mine, where do ye go?
To the high hills, my own one, to the high hills I go.
Why go to the hills, and not come to my arms?
I'm afraid your embraces will do me some harm.

He was a tenor. His voice was scratchy and unpolished after decades of neglect, but it would have been marvelous when he was younger. As he sang, he seemed to *become* younger, his lined face relaxing into the memory of a lost, happy time. He must have been good-looking, too. Like this, Madeleine could see it in him. A beautiful young man with a beautiful voice. Then he'd lost it to alcohol. Her throat grew thick at the lost potential.

Hæra leaned forward again, putting her elbows on her knees. For some reason, her mouth was pinched as she listened, her knuckles white as her hands gripped each other. Why? There didn't seem to be anything unusual about the song. It just sounded like folk music.

The song continued:

Why should my embraces then work ye such woe?
You are my true love, but sorrow will show.
How shall ye get to the hills high above?
Farewell, I'll take flight on the wings of the dove.

Jonathan drew out the final note, making the word "dove" soar like the bird itself. At the last moment, his voice shook, and he stopped at once. His eyes opened, and when he saw Madeleine and Hæra staring at him, he blushed.

This time, Madeleine's applause was entirely sincere. "That was wonderful!"

Jonathan blushed more deeply. "Eh, you must not be used to much if that was 'wonderful' to you."

"I've heard enough lousy singing to be a good judge," Madeleine said dryly. "Back me up, Hæra."

"It was good," Hæra said. "I wish you had sung to me before."

At the wistful note in her voice, Jonathan rubbed the back of his neck. "Ah, well. Now I have, haven't I? Anyway, it's gone past nine, and I'd best leave you. Maybe I'll catch a bit of that football match after all. Hæra, you coming with?"

Hæra shot Madeleine a glance.

It had been a long, emotional day. Madeleine had much to think about, and that was best done alone. It would be best for Hæra to say goodnight. Madeleine should tell her so.

"You're welcome to stay," she said. "Unless you want to watch football."

"Then I'll stay," Hæra replied at once. "Jonathan's club hasn't won in ages."

"My club isn't even…never mind." Jonathan stomped toward the door. "Come home when you're ready to appreciate sport."

"Chance'd be a fine thing," Hæra called after him, and he laughed as he shut the door.

That left Madeleine and Hæra facing each other: Hæra sprawled on the couch, and Madeleine's heart went into overdrive again.

"Quite the day it was," Hæra remarked.

Only yesterday, Madeleine would have broken eye contact and tried to collect herself. Now, that didn't seem possible. Hæra's eyes hooked her like a lure. "You can say that again," she replied. Then she added, "Not literally."

Hæra's lips quirked. "Thanks for the clarification. I don't always know."

Madeleine laughed shakily. Were her palms sweating? How absurd. After the emotional roller coaster of the day, sitting in front of a fire couldn't undo her.

Again, Hæra leaned forward, looking as intently at Madeleine as she'd looked at Jonathan while he sang. As if she was trying to figure something out: what to see, do, or say. "I don't know a lot of things," she said after a moment. "I'm not like you. Remember?"

How on earth could Madeleine forget? "It's crossed my mind once or twice. Why do you ask?"

"Jonathan's song." Hæra looked over Madeleine's shoulder into the fire. Its glow turned her eyes into that yellow shade that Madeleine remembered so clearly from her horse form. "I know why he chose that one. He wants to tell you the story himself, and I'll let him, but it's got me thinking about what I am. Or what I was."

What I was. Jonathan's story. The song went out of me after him.

She said slowly, "You told me at the beginning that Jonathan had met another *Each-uisge* before you."

A muscle spasmed at the side of Hæra's mouth.

"Is that what he was singing about?" Madeleine pressed.

"I can't tell you what happened. That's his story." Hæra ran a hand through her hair, mussing it in a way that called to be fixed by Madeleine's fingers. "But he told me it ruined him. Drove him to drink. And he sang? Now I learn he lost that because of…"

Her eyes filled with anguish as she stared at Madeleine. "What if I don't know when to stop?"

Whatever that meant, it certainly stopped Madeleine's heart. Stole her breath, too, making a reply impossible.

"We weren't taught how to love," Hæra whispered. "Only take. I would take everything from you if I could. I can't help it."

The words should have been a warning. A sensible woman would take them for one. A sensible woman's body wouldn't go soft and weak with wanting. It wouldn't throb between the thighs.

Hæra must have seen it on Madeleine's face, because her nostrils flared.

"You said you want to know how to love," Madeleine said hoarsely. She curled her hands into fists. That way, she couldn't hold out her arms in a moment that had gone from calm to wild in the blink of an eye. "You can. Anyone can, no matter what or who you are."

"And what does that mean?"

Before Madeleine could answer, Hæra rose from the sofa. All six lanky feet of her unfolded into the air. She came forward—one step, two, three. Her legs were long and that was all it took. She loomed over Madeleine on the floor. Her fists were clenched. Her teeth bared.

Madeleine remembered her jacket ripping beneath those teeth. She remembered one of those hands covering the rip, too. Which would win now? The teeth or the hands?

Which one did Madeleine want to win?

Hæra slowly lowered herself to her knees before Madeleine. Quite close to the hearth, to the fire. "What does that mean?" Hæra repeated. "For me to love you? It's not the same as it is with Jonathan. I don't know what this is. It's not—what I used to think—"

Her hands curled around Madeleine's upper arms, taking all the air out of the room while they were at it.

"It's not love," Madeleine managed to croak. Hæra's touch was as firm, as possessive as ever. "I told you…too soon…"

"I have had *six years* to want you."

What burned brighter, the flames or Hæra's eyes? "You wanted your idea of me. Sister Madeleine the nun, you said so." At the memory of Hæra's disappointment and anger, her chest ached. "But that's not who I—"

"I knew what was real," Hæra hissed. "I knew then, and I know now. I know what you felt like under me."

Madeleine lost her breath again. She knew what that felt like too, even if the memory was fuzzy from a head injury. She'd lain weak and helpless, the cold chased away by the searing heat of the woman who held her now.

"*That* was real," Hæra said. "And so was your strength. I thought I didn't need anything else, but now…" Her eyes grew impossibly hotter. "What would be enough of you? Can you tell me?"

Madeleine rocked forward, rising up on her own knees so she and Hæra were almost of a height. Her heart beat so hard that she swayed to its rhythm. "L-love isn't possession."

She'd never said anything less convincing in her life.

"Then what is it?" Hæra moved forward until their knees bumped. "Something that gets me near this fireplace?"

Hæra hated the heat. "Will that hurt you?"

"It confuses me. Like you." Hæra leaned in. Their noses were almost brushing. Again, Madeleine could feel Hæra's breath on her mouth. "So. Love?"

Yet again, nothing came to mind but Saint Paul's most famous words. No matter how Madeleine felt about her faith, they seemed appropriate now. "Love is patient," she whispered. "Love is kind."

Hæra snorted and looked unimpressed.

Her voice shaking, Madeleine continued, "Love does not envy. It doesn't boast. It isn't proud. It…"

"That's enough." Hæra curled one hand around the back of Madeleine's neck. "It seems clear that I don't love you."

The words created a cold pit in Madeleine's chest, even though Hæra was only agreeing with what Madeleine herself had said. Of course they couldn't love each other yet. At least not more than people were supposed to love one another in general.

"I'm not kind," Hæra whispered. "I've been known to boast. And I'm a proud creature, Jonathan's told me."

So am I. A lifetime ago, Sister Catherine had said pridefulness was Madeleine's besetting sin.

"I'm patient, though, you must agree." Hæra's face was changing in a way Madeleine couldn't explain. Not like someone about to change their shape into a magical being. More like someone changing from a person into…into… "I've waited a long time. So have you."

"What about envy?" Madeleine croaked.

"Oh yes." Hæra rubbed her nose against Madeleine's—a gesture that might have been sweet, even silly in another context. Here, it just felt like another step toward the edge of a cliff.

What a thrill it would be to fall at last.

"I envied everyone who spent that time with you," Hæra said. "Now I want all the time with you I can get."

Was it Madeleine who was moving her right hand to rest on Hæra's shoulder, and her left to touch Hæra's cheek, just beneath the sharp cheekbone? Was that Madeleine's thumb brushing over Hæra's bottom lip? It must be.

Hæra inhaled shakily. She opened her mouth. She must be about to say something else, and Madeleine held her breath for it.

Hæra didn't speak. Instead, she closed her incisors gently around Madeleine's thumb. The tip of her tongue flicked against Madeleine's flesh. As she tasted it, Hæra's eyes fell shut, as if in bliss.

This wasn't like the kiss they'd shared on the beach: cathartic, sweet, almost innocent. Nothing was innocent about Hæra's mouth savoring Madeleine's skin. It couldn't be, not when Madeleine's whole body lit up hotter than the fire at her back.

Too fast, she tried to tell herself, *this is too much, too soon.* She was still wrestling with so many things.

Hæra's eyes opened again. The firelight reflected in them. She released Madeleine's thumb from her mouth with a soft, wet noise, and in that moment, Madeleine Laurent's walls collapsed into rubble. It wasn't too soon.

It was much too late, in fact.

Madeleine opened her arms. As Hæra's own arms wrapped around her, as Hæra bent to take her mouth, her soul whispered: *Better late than never.*

CHAPTER THIRTY-ONE

THE SEX BOOKS hadn't prepared Hæra for this.

Not the basic books that explained the mechanics, nor the longer ones that focused on pleasure and technique. Even with illustrations, they'd all been so abstract.

Madeleine wasn't abstract. Her body in Hæra's arms was soft, real, and warm.

Quite warm. They were on the rug right in front of the hearth, closer to fire than Hæra had ever dared approach. Now its heat crept over her skin, more primal than if it came from a radiator or stove, unconfined by device or design.

As Hæra kissed Madeleine, the heat swept through her from within and without, and she welcomed it as she never had before.

It was different from the beach, different even from the alley. Tonight, Madeleine's mouth opened eagerly, and her body surged forward. Her generous breasts pressed beneath Hæra's smaller ones, their bodies coming together in a perfect fit.

They were both upright on their knees as they clung to each other. Hæra's legs threatened not to support her. Her body melted before the flame, before Madeleine. Would it be better to lie down? To be on the cooler floor, where their bodies could be together from head to toe?

But Madeleine might not be ready. She hadn't issued an *intimate invitation*.

Hæra's hands shook where they clasped Madeleine's back. She'd warned Madeleine about her nature so many times, but that didn't mean she couldn't fight it. She hadn't been able to hurt Madeleine on the beach. She could not hurt her now.

I won't hurt her, Hæra thought deliriously, as she tore her mouth from Madeleine's and placed it on the soft curve of Madeleine's neck.

I won't. She bared her teeth against the skin.

I won't. She began to suck.

"Lord!" Madeleine's hands spasmed on Hæra's shoulders. "Hæra!"

Hæra released her skin with a gasp. Had that been pain? What had she done? "I..."

Before she could finish, Madeleine's hands swept up into her hair, carding through it. Nobody had ever stroked Hæra's hair before. It tugged against her scalp, making it tingle, as if Madeleine were caressing the rest of her body too.

Then Madeleine tightened her grip in Hæra's hair, and she pressed Hæra's face more firmly to her neck. Holding her there. Madeleine's body trembled, and she barely seemed to be breathing.

She wanted it.

Hæra panted against her wet skin. Opened her mouth. Bared her teeth. "On your back," she said.

A little sob came from Madeleine's mouth, but she was moving, doing as she was told. Hæra kept one arm around her shoulders, lowering her to the floor. The stone had to have been cold beneath the rug, but Madeleine didn't protest. She kept her fingers in Hæra's hair and opened her mouth as Hæra settled on top of her.

Like she'd done that first night, on the beach.

They seemed to realize it at the same time. Hæra and Madeleine stared into each other's eyes when Hæra came to rest, her long body covering Madeleine's completely, although she put her weight on her elbows in one last gasp of consideration.

"Oh my God." Madeleine's voice was barely audible. "It really was you."

A growl rose from Hæra's throat. "Did you ever doubt me?"

"No, no, it's just—you feel—" Madeleine's fingers trembled in Hæra's hair. "You feel like everything." Her body trembled too. "You changed everything."

Hæra looked at Madeleine's mouth, full and parted, and licked her lips.

"Do it again," Madeleine whispered. "Change me."

Hæra didn't need asking twice. She bent and took Madeleine's mouth again, deep and hungry.

Kissing was even better than eating. How could she ever have known that? Madeleine's mouth was a meal all on its own, soft and warm as she kissed Hæra back. It was easy, it was *natural*, that she should feast on her woman's mouth until little noises came out of the back of Madeleine's throat.

It was better than Hæra's nighttime fantasies when she touched herself. Better to have Madeleine with her, responding to her, making Hæra's body do what it had only done alone until now. She ached painfully, sweetly, between her legs. She was swelling, softening, growing wet.

Was Madeleine as well? Hæra moaned at the thought. She pushed her hips forward, seeking pressure from the body beneath hers. The seam of her jeans rubbed between her lips, pulling a little cry from her. So much—not enough—

Madeleine made a tiny, helpless sound. And then she spread her legs.

An intimate invitation.

Hæra was swept into the sea with blood in the water, hunting down her prey by scent and taste. Madeleine's scent, just here, as Hæra rubbed her nose into that thick, dark hair. Madeleine's taste, as Hæra licked her throat.

"Hæra," Madeleine whimpered. She began to move. Her hips rocked up and down like waves. She was hunting something too. "What's happening? What are you doing to me?"

"You're doing it to me too." The words came from Hæra in a snarl. "You want me." She rolled her hips down again, rubbing against Madeleine and calling a cry from her. "I can smell it, taste it on you."

Madeleine's head fell back. She panted, "I don't know what to do."

Humans *thought* so much about things. How could Madeleine think now, when Hæra's mind was narrowing into a blade of pure instinct?

"You know what to do," she growled. "Do what you want. Take what you need."

Madeleine looked into Hæra's eyes. She opened her mouth as if she was about to say something, but instead she grabbed Hæra's hand. Her own hand was shaking.

And when she placed Hæra's hand on her breast, a low cry came from her.

There were too many layers. Madeleine had on a sweater, and then a shirt, and presumably a bra underneath that too. How much could she feel? Maybe her breasts really were that sensitive. Maybe, even with the slightest pressure, they thrilled to Hæra's touch.

Not enough.

Hæra shoved her hand beneath Madeleine's sweater. Her breast was warmer here, and the jersey cotton was less of a barrier. Hæra's thumb brushed over the edge of her bra beneath. Madeleine made a low noise and grabbed Hæra's hand through the wool of her sweater.

Hæra paused. Was *not enough* for her *too much* for Madeleine? Would they have to stop?

I can stop, she told herself frantically, *I can, I can.*

"Like that," Madeleine whispered. "Just hold me, please."

Oh, thank the depths. Hæra's resolve would not be so sorely tested. "Am I hurting you?"

Madeleine laughed shakily. "Definitely not."

Her cheeks were red, her eyes bright, her mouth full. Hæra couldn't help herself. She leaned down for another kiss. Madeleine returned it, still clutching Hæra's hand against her breast. Then she murmured, "Nobody's touched me like this before."

Hæra looked down at her in astonishment. That couldn't be right. Madeleine was so beautiful that someone from another *species* desired her—she must have known another human's touch, surely? "Why not?" she demanded. "You weren't always a nun."

"No, but I was always…like I am." Madeleine briefly closed her eyes. "I avoided boys. When I did date, I told them I didn't want to go too far before marriage. As in, not far at all." Her lips quirked up. "You know, in some respects, religion was convenient."

It wasn't convenient right now. Hæra fought not to pant like one of the farm's dogs. Madeleine had often spoken of needing to take things slowly. They could do that.

For another minute or so.

Hæra closed her eyes and took a deep breath, about to ask the Great Mare for patience, because maybe Madeleine was right about the power of prayer. Anything was worth a try.

Then, suddenly, her right hand—the one on Madeleine's breast—stung. Madeleine had just curled her nails into it. Hard. Hæra looked down again to see that Madeleine's facial expression had changed completely in the last couple of seconds. Her eyes were wider, her flush had gone pale, and she bared her teeth. Hæra began, "What—"

"And you?" Madeleine asked. "Have you ever done this with someone else?"

It turned out that your heart could beat, not just in your chest, but in your temples, your throat, and between your legs. The look in Madeleine's eyes—hot, wild—scattered Hæra's heartbeats everywhere, from her head to her toes.

Instead of *I could never,* Hæra said, "What if I have?"

Now Madeleine grabbed Hæra by both shoulders. Her fingers dug in harder. Hæra hissed in a sharp breath. It hurt.

It felt so, so good.

"Tell me!" Madeleine squeezed Hæra's shoulders even more tightly. "Am I the only one? Please just tell me—" She pressed her face into the curve of Hæra's throat. Her voice was barely audible. "Tell me there was nobody else."

Hæra's eyelashes fluttered as pure bliss spread through her, more potent than the wine they'd shared weeks ago. Her mouth pulled wide. Fire warmed her teeth and gums.

And with her thigh, she bore down between Madeleine's legs, as she'd done in the alley.

Madeleine scrabbled her nails over Hæra's back. Her hips rolled up into the pressure. "Hæra!"

"You understand." Triumph dizzied her, and she wrapped both arms around Madeleine once more. "You understand what it's like, how I feel."

"This can't be how you feel!" Madeleine shook her head back and forth against Hæra's shoulder. "It's not right. I shouldn't care if you've been with anyone else."

Hæra pulled back. She cupped Madeleine's face in her hand and looked into her eyes. She waited.

"But I do," Madeleine said brokenly. "I just thought about it, and suddenly I wanted to kill anybody who might have…"

"They haven't." Hæra rubbed her thumb along the exquisite edge of Madeleine's jaw. At the base of Madeleine's throat fluttered her pulse, beating with blood from her heart. "I want only you. I'll have only you."

Madeleine tugged, and their mouths collided, a joining that was almost brutal. The room spun around them. There wasn't enough air in it. There wasn't enough of anything, most especially of Madeleine. There could never be enough Madeleine.

"And," Hæra breathed against her mouth, "I'll have *all* of you."

―――――

All of you. It should be a terrifying thought. This whole scenario should scare Madeleine out of her wits—it was too much, too soon.

Maybe tomorrow it would feel that way. Tonight, Madeleine was done with everything she *should* do and be.

Tonight, Hæra would have all of her, and Madeleine would return the favor.

She'd never done anything like this. It didn't matter. For the last month, her body had been beyond her control, moved only by its own genius. It had frightened her at first—what right did her skin have to tingle, her breasts to ache, her sex to pulse?

Now she could only bless her body's wisdom. She lay on her back while Hæra crouched over her, eagerly rubbing her nose beneath Hæra's ear as she inhaled her scent. A scent she recognized with a shock.

It was the scent of the creature that had met her on the beach and walked her safely back into town, a scent both animal and elemental that had won her over even in the face of danger. This scent was meant for Madeleine, and Madeleine alone.

Mate.

The word flitted through her mind, there and gone, before her mouth opened in a groan. The groan led to her teeth brushing over Hæra's flesh. And then her tongue. She tasted salt and skin, warm and delicious.

She needed more of it. Closing her eyes, Madeleine began to suck Hæra's skin. Maybe she could drink it right down if she went hard enough.

A gasp. Then Hæra's fingers grabbed her hair, tugging her head back. Had Madeleine sucked too hard, hurt her? There was already a reddening patch on her neck.

Hæra's eyes were wildfire. She bent her head, and now her mouth latched onto Madeleine's neck once more. Teeth came with it. Their edges sank into Madeleine's skin at the same moment Hæra's hand cupped Madeleine between her legs.

Pain and pleasure, equally fierce. How could she ever want one without the other? Madeleine cried out in joy and arched up into Hæra's hand and mouth.

"More," she pleaded. "All of me."

Hæra reared up. Even on her knees she loomed over Madeleine, body edged with firelight. Her chest rose and fell with her panting breath. What did she look like beneath her shirt? Her breasts would be smaller than Madeleine's—probably pale, probably soft, definitely perfect.

As if she'd read Madeleine's mind, Hæra began to unbutton her shirt. The breath stopped in Madeleine's lungs. That dream she'd had —when Hæra had refused to reveal herself, but now—

"Take yours off too," Hæra said hoarsely. "Unless you want me to tear it."

Madeleine's sweater was sturdy wool woven from Ætlaquoy's own sheep. She grabbed at it. "Y-you could tear this?"

Hæra's eyes flashed. "You haven't seen the limits of my strength. Would you test them?"

"Yes," Madeleine gasped before she could stop herself. "Show me."

Hæra grabbed the collar of Madeleine's sweater. The wool tore as if she were ripping a piece of notebook paper in half. The threads snapped apart, crackling with static electricity. If the shock pained Hæra, she gave no sign of it. She only stared down at Madeleine's knit shirt.

No, not at the shirt. At Madeleine's breasts beneath it.

Nobody had looked so openly at her body since she'd put on a habit. Nobody she'd wanted had ever looked at her body at all. Hæra's gaze made it unfurl like a flower reaching for a single bright ray that pierced the clouds.

Pierce me again. Madeleine arched up helplessly into that look. A soft whimper came from the back of her throat.

"I won't tear anything else," Hæra whispered. "Bare yourself for me. Show me."

She started unbuttoning her shirt again. Was it Madeleine's imagination, or were her hands shaking now? Madeleine's certainly were. She sat up, tugged off her torn sweater, and then her shirt. And then she held her breath as she removed her plain, white bra.

Hæra slid off her shirt, revealing she wore no bra at all. She could get away with it. Her torso was lean, with small breasts. They were as pale as the rest of her, tipped with light brown nipples. They were perfect. So was the rest of her.

Firelight gilded the muscles of her long arms and broad shoulders. Her torso tapered down to a narrow waist. Like this, she looked elemental, primal, strength in her every line. And yet no outsider could guess at the true power of her frame.

Madeleine opened her mouth to whisper a compliment—not that she knew where to start—when she saw that Hæra was staring fixedly at Madeleine's breasts too. Her mouth was open slightly, her eyes glazed.

There were about two seconds to figure out what was happening before Hæra pushed her back down to the floor. Madeleine lost her breath with the impact, and also lost any desire to protest, because then Hæra bent her head and took Madeleine's right breast into her mouth.

Madeleine's hips bucked up. A sob tore its way out of her throat. Hæra's mouth was hot, her tongue rough as she licked Madeleine's nipple eagerly. Then the licking became sucking, harsh and hard, enough that it ought to hurt—it *did* hurt—pain and pleasure, once again—

And once again, Madeleine moaned, "More."

There was more. So much more. Madeleine hadn't known there could be so much of anything under heaven. Hæra's mouth was everywhere: Madeleine's breasts, and then back to her neck, sucking another mark to life. Then she kissed her way down Madeleine's belly, pausing occasionally to bite and lick that too, moaning over every dip and rise of skin.

The whole time, Madeleine could do nothing but dig her hands into Hæra's strong shoulders and hold on. Was this more of Hæra's magic: the ability to paralyze her with pleasure, to destroy her mind? She should act—touch Hæra in return, demand her own rights. She should run her hands over Hæra's long body, make Hæra melt too, make Hæra's body surge against hers and—

Even as the thought made her moan again, Hæra unzipped Madeleine's jeans.

Madeleine's heart stopped. So did her breath, when Hæra slid her hand beneath her zipper, beneath…beneath her underwear…

Hæra's fingertips brushed the soft hair between Madeleine's legs, and then her lips. There wasn't much room. Hæra's hand was pressed tightly against Madeleine's aching flesh.

An ache could be powerful enough to swallow an entire sea.

Madeleine hadn't known that before. She hadn't known anything before this moment, when Hæra touched her where she'd yearned to be touched by another woman for so long.

"You're wet," Hæra said hoarsely. "So am I."

Madeleine's hips rocked against her hand. Hæra didn't have to say it so boldly...it shouldn't feel so *good* to hear something so...

"I do this to myself," Hæra said. "Almost every night. I think of you and do this to myself."

"Ah!" The cry escaped Madeleine before she could stop it. Hæra touched herself? She stroked these long, strong fingers over her own wetness—maybe she went inside, maybe she throbbed like Madeleine was doing now, so hard she lost her mind—

"I did it the first night you came back." Hæra's breath was quick, unsteady like she was about to lose hold of it. "I never did before, but then...after I saw you again..."

"Hæra," Madeleine sobbed, rubbing her hips frantically into that maddening touch. It wasn't enough. There should be more, but what more could there be?

Hæra showed her.

She yanked Madeleine's jeans down to her knees. It prevented Madeleine from spreading her legs wider, and Madeleine wanted to spread her legs as wide as they could go, wanted to make more room for Hæra to do whatever she wanted. To claim Madeleine before being claimed in her turn.

"Have you ever done that?" Hæra rasped. "Thinking about me?"

No, only about my college professor twenty years ago. Madeleine couldn't say that. Or should she? Would it bring that possessive fire back into Hæra's eyes, make her claim Madeleine at once—?

"I dreamed about you," she blurted. "That same night."

Oh Lord, she hadn't meant to say that. She'd never meant to confess that. Nobody was supposed to know about that dream, much less the person who'd starred in it. But when Hæra's eyes widened, Madeleine couldn't find the shame she ought to. She could only groan again.

"About me doing this to you?" Hæra rubbed her knuckle against the throbbing, hot little nub that had driven Madeleine out of her mind so long ago. The one she'd avoided touching ever since. "Was it about this, me touching you this way?"

"No, it—it—" She couldn't say it. She *couldn't.*

"Tell me. Tell me—"

"Your mouth!"

The words burst out of her, unstoppable as a storm and just as impossible to calm. They made Hæra stare down at her, her mouth going slack, while Madeleine stared right back. She'd really just said that.

"My mouth between your legs," Hæra said. "You want me there too."

It wasn't a question. That look was back in her eyes. Consuming. Madeleine could only whimper in response before it.

"Yes," Hæra breathed. She looked between Madeleine's legs, at the thatch of dark hair and her own pale hand. "That's right. You were made for my mouth from the start."

And she slid back, lay over Madeleine's spread legs, bent her head, and devoured.

Madeleine cried out, high-pitched and helpless. It wasn't like fingers. Hæra's mouth was warmer and softer, her tongue was wetter, and it seemed to be everywhere at once. She licked Madeleine into swelling, sparing no time for tenderness—only starvation.

Who was making those noises? It couldn't be Madeleine herself, not those abandoned cries that echoed off the cottage's stone walls. She wanted to spread her legs wider, and she couldn't, and somehow that deepened the ache even more. Her hips rolled until Hæra grabbed them. Those strong hands kept her from moving, chasing Hæra's lips and tongue. She could only take what Hæra gave her.

Take it, and take it, and take it some more. Hæra licked, sucked, and kissed her until Madeleine heard wet noises. That was her. By now she was so wet that Hæra's face was sliding against her. Her flesh was swollen, practically pulsing.

Hæra had done this in her dream too, all those weeks ago. She'd taken her time, licking leisurely, tormenting Madeleine. She'd been in full control of herself.

Not this time. Hæra licked Madeleine like someone who'd starved for eons and wasn't about to let a feast escape. She growled against Madeleine's soaked flesh, made guttural sounds of savoring.

Madeleine sobbed. Her back arched as high as it could. She couldn't help herself. Women did this to each other...all her life she'd yearned, and now...

She grabbed Hæra's head and dug her fingers into her hair. The fire had warmed that too, and it was soft and fine in Madeleine's hands as she held Hæra's face against her. Her hips rose and fell like waves, and Hæra's grip tightened even more. She found Madeleine's clitoris again.

With her tongue this time.

"Oh God," Madeleine gasped.

Hæra began to lick her there, directly, hungry and quick.

"Oh God. G-god..."

Hæra went faster. Madeleine's flesh was so sensitive. It almost hurt, *almost*, the pleasure and pain at once, she couldn't do without both, she was pulling Hæra's hair now, she was gasping—rising—oh, it was too much, she couldn't take it, surely she couldn't—

Hæra folded her lips around Madeleine's aching clitoris and began, relentlessly, to suck.

"Oh *God!*"

Madeleine's hips bucked up as climax took her for the second time in her life. The tension of decades broke inside her, a rope made of deprivation finally snapping. Answered prayer. The face of God.

She closed her eyes, the world too bright to bear while she throbbed and moaned. So long, it had been so long, and she couldn't stop moving. Hæra's tongue kept her pulsing, made her keep coming, until her throat was raw with crying out. Too much.

Never enough.

She didn't want it to end, but it had to, or she'd die. She'd just come until she died at Hæra's hands, or mouth, and suddenly there was so much to live for. Madeleine loosened her grip in Hæra's hair and pushed her head instead. "No more…no more, please…"

Hæra gasped against her. She must have been holding her breath. She could probably hold her breath for a very long time.

The room was out of focus. Only Hæra was clear. She wiped her mouth with the back of her hand, licked her lips, and closed her eyes as if savoring the flavor. She sighed. Then she surged forward, relentless and implacable, and pressed her mouth to Madeleine's again.

Madeleine tasted—that must be *herself*, what Hæra just licked from between her legs. It was the taste of pleasure. Did all women taste like this? Would Hæra?

Their naked breasts pressed together, warm and soft. The memory of ecstasy lapped between Madeleine's thighs. She was boneless, and Hæra's greedy kiss stole what little breath she had.

"I fuck myself," Hæra rasped. "That's what it's called. Now I want you to do it to me instead."

Madeleine made a soft, wheezing noise.

"I like how my fingers feel in me." Hæra grabbed Madeleine's wrist. Her hand trembled. "Yours will be different. I've thought about it so many times, do it to me *now*, please!"

Her breath was hot on Madeleine's mouth. She was all strength and salt, but for the first time, Madeleine wondered if she might not make Hæra weak and sweet instead.

Was she dreaming? Not this time. Hæra's jeans button was real beneath Madeleine's hands as she fumbled with it, and then the zipper, while Hæra rose up on her knees. Her legs shook on either side of Madeleine's.

Madeleine yanked the zipper down and tugged at Hæra's jeans. Hæra helped, pushing down the jeans to her knees, and then down to her ankles, where her boots stopped her progress. Her underwear followed. They were both half dressed on the floor, couldn't even get their pants all the way off; that wasn't how it was supposed to happen, was it? For your first time, weren't you supposed to be naked in a bed, taking your time?

She tried to imagine making slow, sweet love with Hæra in bed, and the image faded away like mist in sunlight. No, Madeleine couldn't make Hæra sweet. She could, perhaps, make her something else.

Upright on her knees, Hæra tugged Madeleine's hand between her naked, pale thighs. There was black hair there, softer and sparser than the hair on Hæra's head. It covered soft lips, and when Madeleine's fingertips brushed them, Hæra gasped. "In me!"

With Hæra's urging, she slid not one finger, but two, up into soft heat she'd never dared imagine. Soft, tight, *wet* heat.

Because of her. Hæra was wet because of Madeleine. Here was the proof, clenching on Madeleine's fingers as Hæra tossed her head back and groaned.

To the end of her days, Madeleine would never forget what it felt like to be inside another woman for the first time.

"Oh my God," she gasped, looking up at Hæra, stunned. "Oh mercy."

"No mercy." Hæra rolled her hips, her head still tilted back as she began to move on Madeleine's fingers. She thrust her hips back and forth. "Oh—your fingers are smaller—but they feel so *good*." She began to move faster.

Hæra was so wet that Madeleine's fingers made noises going in and out. She was buried inside Hæra, and white liquid was starting to drip on her knuckles. What did it taste like?

She had to know. She couldn't wait.

Gasping and greedy, Madeleine stroked Hæra with her other hand as well, swiping her thumb between those lips and seeking moisture. She found it, slick, and licked it off her thumb. Salty and sharp.

Hæra cried, "Do that again!"

Madeleine did. She moved her fingers in Hæra. She kept her gaze fixed on Hæra's own as she stroked with her thumb again, brought it to her mouth, and sucked.

And with that, Hæra came. It couldn't be anything else. She clenched inside, throbbing around Madeleine's fingers. Her hips arched forward and she cried out, never looking away from Madeleine.

"Taste me," she gasped, "*taste me,*" and then clenched again, cried out, and folded forward until she crouched over Madeleine on all fours.

Madeleine kept moving her fingers and licking her thumb, savoring a flavor so good it could only be called divine. She only stopped when Hæra finally grabbed her wrist again and groaned. When she slid her fingers out, they were coated. Now there was even more to taste.

It might have horrified her once, might have struck her as dirty, but this had happened because Madeleine had pleased Hæra. Because they'd come together to please each other. Because for the first time, Madeleine had dared to reach for happiness instead of shame.

"Yes," Hæra whispered, and like any glutton, any creature of pure appetite, Madeleine licked her fingers clean.

CHAPTER THIRTY-TWO

Hæra had never held anyone while they slept. Her kind didn't know the practice, and she'd had no reason to embrace a sleeping Jonathan, although she'd watched him once out of curiosity.

She must have been saving it for Madeleine, whose body was warm in her arms. They lay in Madeleine's new bed—the one they'd sat together on only this morning. Hæra was curled up behind Madeleine. From the sky, they must look like a nautilus shell.

They were a perfect fit. What else could they be?

She had finally claimed her mate.

Her mate had claimed her in return. Hæra hadn't expected that—not from cautious, reserved Madeleine. But the woman who'd once worn a nun's habit had teeth to match Hæra's own, and she'd devoured Hæra, body and soul.

Depths below. Hæra had thought there could be no pleasure more primal than Madeleine's fingers inside her, fucking her so eagerly. She hadn't counted on what it would be like to see Madeleine licking Hæra's juices from her fingers, as hungry as any *Each-uisge* had ever been. Seeing that—having the sure knowledge Madeleine, too, had starved—had driven Hæra to climax immediately. She'd come so hard she'd almost lost consciousness.

But she'd managed to stay awake, and instead she had lain atop Madeleine, both of them almost naked. They had kissed and kissed. Hæra hadn't known you could kiss anybody like that, when you were sated instead of just wanting more. She hadn't known kisses could be lazy, soft, and tender.

There must be all sorts of kisses, then. She and Madeleine would share them all.

Eventually, Madeleine had groaned and said the floor was hurting her back, and they'd had to get up. She'd seemed oddly shy. What would happen next, Hæra had wondered. What was the human custom after sex?

Whatever most humans did, Madeleine had invited Hæra to stay.

"I don't want you to go." She was blushing again. "We can figure out the rest tomorrow."

Hæra approved, and carried Madeleine to bed to prove it. For some reason, that made Madeleine blush again. She'd blushed more when she'd put on her pajamas as Hæra watched appreciatively.

Hæra had to wear her clothes to bed, but she didn't mind. She was more than willing to lie here, accepting Madeleine's *intimate invitation*, and curl their bodies together. Somewhat to her surprise, Madeleine had gone right to sleep. She'd relaxed against Hæra's body instantly, as if someone had flipped a switch inside her and told her she was perfectly safe.

Which, of course, she was.

Now Hæra, too, began to relax against Madeleine's warmth. It was much less threatening than the fire's. Said fire was banked now, leaving Hæra to feel much the same way. It was a fine feeling. How long since she'd known satisfaction?

She'd thought, once, that it would come from beating a pair of wings against the wind. She'd never do that now. That was clear enough. It had been folly to think she ever could. Why would the Sire and herd have taken her back just because she reappeared and said she'd killed a human? That had been her desperation talking. She'd needed to believe that her dream could not be beyond her grasp forever.

Well, it was. In exchange for centuries with wings, Hæra now had an uncertain handful of weeks with the sleeping woman at her side. Should Madeleine stay beyond the end of summer (and she'd said nothing about doing so), that didn't change the particulars. Even if they somehow managed to remain together without trouble, Madeleine would grow old and die long before Hæra would.

Not so long ago, Jonathan had told Hæra: *Stop thinking like a child and look to the future.* She'd replied confidently that Madeleine's return would solve every problem, but of course Jonathan had been right. How irritating that humans, short-lived and limited, could see the bigger picture better than she could.

They were far from perfect—their history showed as much—but humans did a lot of things better. Like grow. Like change. Madeleine had said so herself.

Perhaps now wasn't the time for deep reflection, though. This bed was so comfortable. Jonathan had done well to get Madeleine a new one. And strangely, it seemed to have a magical property. As she lay on it, Hæra grew heavier. It was like the first time she'd come on land from the buoyancy of salt water. Unlike then, her muscles also relaxed, and she was warm.

It was time to slow her metabolic system and rest. She'd had a long day, to say the least. She might close her eyes, although that wasn't necessary. Even her eyelids weighed her down tonight.

Hæra snuggled closer to Madeleine and closed her eyes, sinking into the heaviness.

The sea witch looked upon her.

Instead of resting on Madeleine's bed, now Hæra stood in the middle of the whirlpool. She was in human form. Her feet, shod in her work boots, rested upon the sandy ocean floor.

The witch stood a few feet away. Her face was hard as fossil.

She wasn't swinging the other two humans in a circle—the man she'd loved and the woman he'd preferred. Instead, the man and the woman stood behind her. Their arms hung at their sides, and they looked at her with empty eye sockets. Their faces appeared translucent as jellyfish, their skulls visible through the skin.

Hæra looked around wildly. Where was the bed and the cottage? Where was Madeleine? Or—no—it was a good thing Madeleine wasn't here. Madeleine should never come within a mile of this creature and her victims. For that matter, Hæra had no idea why she was here either.

"Bring me your despair," the witch said.

Her eyes were an abyss. Light could not penetrate there. Nevertheless, years ago, Hæra had managed to appeal to her. She'd made the selfsame bargain the witch referenced now.

"You said I had to come back when I failed," she said. "I haven't. Madeleine has come to me."

The witch said nothing.

Hæra lifted her chin and looked into the abyss. She said, "Even if I die for all this, I don't regret my choice. I won't despair. There's nothing for me to give you."

The witch's mouth sliced open into a grin. She was missing some teeth. Those she did have, bleached white as any other bone, were sharp enough to put an *Each-uisge*'s to shame.

"Not long now," she said.

Hæra recoiled. "Why do you say that? And why—" She looked down at her human form. "Why am I like this when I'm in the sea? How did I get here?"

"You are what you are."

"Of course I am! What else could I be?"

"You are this." The witch pointed one long, thin finger at Hæra. "This, no more. Begone."

"But..."

Behind the witch, the man and woman began to walk forward, toward Hæra. They said nothing. They made no sound. Last time, they had begun to scream—

Hæra opened her eyes to find herself back in the bedroom with Madeleine still asleep. She was so cold that even Madeleine's body couldn't warm her. She was shaking. She leapt from the bed with a cry, looking around to make sure the witch and the whirlpool were gone.

Madeleine woke up with a gasp. "Hæra?"

"How did it happen?" Hæra looked around again, and then down at Madeleine, who was propping herself up on her elbows and looking thoroughly discombobulated. A lock of hair fell over her eyes.

"How did what happen?" Madeleine sat up and pushed the lock behind her ear. "What's wrong?"

"I was here, and then I was in the sea. With the witch. The one I told you about, in the whirlpool." She was as spun about as if she truly were in the whirlpool. "I closed my eyes, and I was there, and I opened them, and I was back here."

Madeleine blinked, not looking nearly as alarmed as she ought to.

She probably didn't believe it. Hæra must sound out of her mind. She pleaded, "I swear it. I can't explain it, but it happened."

"You were dreaming," Madeleine said softly.

Hæra stared at her. Then she shook her head. "No. I told you, my kind can't dream. We can't even sleep."

"Not ever? You *never* sleep?"

"No, we…" Hæra's voice trailed off. She frowned. "It's not safe. We slow our metabolisms—it's easier to rouse from that if we're attacked." By a predator, or each other.

"That makes it sound like you *can* sleep." Madeleine sounded remarkably reasonable for a woman who'd been awakened under these circumstances. "It's more that you don't. You're positive you can't?"

"I…never thought about it." Hæra was still shaking. "I never have before. None of us did. It wasn't safe."

Madeleine regarded her. Then she held out one hand. "You're safe here. Maybe your body knew that, and it let you sleep. And then you dreamed."

The hand, slender and soft, was irresistible. Hæra took it. It was warm too. "That wasn't safe," she said unsteadily. "The witch. It felt real. It must have been real."

"Dreams usually feel real when we're having them." Madeleine squeezed her hand. "It's strange. But if you magically went to the whirlpool and came back, wouldn't you be wet?"

That was a good point. Hæra was perfectly dry, except for the sweat breaking out beneath her arms and in the small of her back. Strange, to sweat when you were cold.

Strange to be cold at all.

"I dreamed?" That couldn't be her voice, so small and afraid.

Madeleine squeezed Hæra's hand gently. "Do you want to tell me what it was about?"

Talking about the dream seemed like a bad idea. Hæra had told Madeleine a little of how the witch had helped her escape from her family's attempt on her life. She hadn't mentioned the witch's specific demand for her despair. Why bother explaining something so grim and impossible? Better to avoid that. She said gruffly, "I'd rather not discuss it."

"Okay. But do you want to…"

"No. Just go back to sleep. My…dream…is over."

"We call bad dreams nightmares."

"Yes, I know. *Night mare.* It's ungenerous to horses."

Madeleine laughed, sounding surprised. "I never thought about it like that. I wonder if that's where the word comes from?" She rubbed a hand over her eyes. "Maybe I'll look it up in the morning. But are you sure you're…"

"I'm fine. It wasn't real." If she said that again, then it might make it true. The witch was not here. Her thralls were not here. "It wasn't real."

"No. It wasn't." Madeleine squeezed her hand again. "But I'm sorry your first dream was so unpleasant."

That was an understatement. She placed her free hand on Madeleine's shoulder. "I'll lie back down with you."

"You're sure?" Madeleine's expression was both sleepy and hopeful.

To prove it, Hæra lay back down and pillowed her head on top of her folded arms. "Positive. Perhaps dreams aren't so bad if I wake up again to this."

Madeleine beamed, and in that moment, the witch's cruel laugh was worth it. "Really? I can't look that good. I bet my hair's a mess."

It was, but Hæra had learned you weren't supposed to agree with people when they said things like that. She considered. "Is this what Jonathan calls 'fishing for compliments'?"

"Caught." Madeleine placed her hand on Hæra's elbow. "Pride's one of my weaknesses, you know."

"So you must like compliments." That seemed easy enough to do. There was no shortage of things to compliment Madeleine on.

Madeleine blushed in the shadows. "I shouldn't, but...no, you know what?" She propped herself up on one elbow. The lock of hair fell from behind her ear again. "I *should*. People like to be complimented, and that's normal. Yes, I would like a compliment, if it's a sincere one."

"You have excellent breasts," Hæra said, sincerely.

Madeleine stared at her. Then she fell back down on her back and laughed. Hæra frowned. "I wasn't trying to be funny."

"I know." Madeleine rubbed a hand over her mouth and laughed again. "Sorry. That's sweet. Thanks. Yours are lovely too."

Hæra immediately stopped being annoyed. Madeleine was right: it was nice to be complimented. "Thank you. You also have beautiful eyes." Understatement. "Many other things about you are beautiful. I could keep going."

Madeleine's smile softened, and those beautiful eyes glowed. "Maybe you'd better not give me a big ego. Let's see, I owe you another one...you're very curious."

Hæra remembered her reading. "'Curious' has different meanings. Do you mean I'm odd?"

"No." Madeleine's fond smile suggested, however, that Hæra might be a little odd—just not in a bad way. "I mean you've got lots of curiosity about the world and how it works. That's a wonderful trait."

Hæra's bad dream was already nothing more than a dimly unpleasant memory. "I'm glad you think so."

"I—" Madeleine yawned and covered her mouth. "Sorry. I do."

"Don't apologize." Hæra had kept her from rest long enough. "Go back to sleep. Do I get another goodnight kiss, or is the custom only one?"

Madeleine's lips twitched. A look of wonder appeared in her eyes. "I think you and I might have to make our own customs."

"Then let's begin now."

Madeleine leaned in. Her kiss was softer than lambswool. If all nightmares ended like this, they might not be so bad.

But she didn't mean to chance it. She'd stay on guard against sleep from now on.

There would be no second dream.

———

She left Madeleine before dawn with a soft kiss to her cheek. "I must work."

"Okay," Madeleine mumbled, and she went promptly back to sleep. Hæra chuckled and left.

It was nearly five in the morning, when the work of the farm began. A raw sheep's liver awaited her at home, and after last night's activities, Hæra was ravenous.

Sex had fed another sort of hunger. Sex with a human! Not so long ago, she couldn't have imagined it. How ashamed her mother Beathag would be. Even her father, who had admired humans, couldn't have countenanced it. As for Asgall, he'd be insufferable.

None of that mattered, Hæra thought, as she tromped across the muddy ground toward the farmhouse. Her biological family was gone. Her chosen family was here, for however long it could last. And she had work to do. If she hurried, she could finish the morning's first tasks and return in time for breakfast with Madeleine and Jonathan.

Jonathan would be insufferable too, if he guessed what had happened between Hæra and Madeleine. Just in a different way. Oh, he'd be so pleased, with all his talk of *love*.

Hæra grinned up at the cloudy sky. He didn't have to know yet. Madeleine would probably appreciate discretion. It could be a delicious secret. Hæra was tired of secrets that weighed her down, but this one was different. It made her want to laugh in delight.

Delight. Madeleine's mouth beneath her own. Her fingers inside

Madeleine's softness, until Madeleine cried out in shocked pleasure. They'd do it again, too. That was delight, all right.

What was a nightmare compared to that? This was real.

As she approached the farmhouse, her lips pursed. A funny noise came from between them. She'd heard Jonathan and the farmhands making such a sound. A whistle. She was whistling. She never had before.

Better not. Jonathan would guess instantly, if he heard her whistling.

No lights shone from the farmhouse windows. He'd still be asleep, then. Easier to slip in. Hæra glanced at his bedroom window as she passed it. Then, by chance, she looked at the ground beneath it and stopped dead in her tracks.

There were footprints beneath Jonathan's window.

Hæra frowned down at them. The mud had hardened a little around the prints' edges. Whoever had left them must have done so hours ago.

She placed her own foot next to a print. The footprint was longer, but its outline was slimmer. Probably because she was wearing boots —there were toeprints too. Someone had been creeping about while barefoot?

Had that someone broken in?

Taking a deep breath, Hæra unlocked the back door and slipped inside. If an intruder awaited her, believing he'd face another human's strength, he was in for a surprise. If he'd hurt Jonathan, he was in for worse.

Silence and shadows. Nothing moved.

Hæra took a knife from the block and proceeded forward. No muddy footprints in here. Wouldn't an intruder have tracked dirt in? She caught no unfamiliar scent. She didn't hear anybody breathing. Her hunter's instincts felt nothing strange in the air.

Jonathan's door was shut. She pushed it open slowly, holding her breath. *Please...*

He lay beneath the duvet, his chest rising and falling regularly. A quick glance round proved him to be the only occupant of the room.

Everything looked normal.

Hæra exhaled and shut the door again. Good thing he hadn't awakened to see her in his doorway brandishing a butcher knife.

She continued her inspection, already knowing that whoever had come last night was long gone. Had someone wanted to burgle them? She'd never heard of a barefoot burglar, and nothing seemed to be missing. None of the windows were ajar or broken; the front door was also locked. The television and computer were still here, and both Jonathan's and Hæra's bedrooms looked in order. The strange intruder probably hadn't entered the house at all.

She hurried out to the barn, still carrying the knife just in case. No intruder lurked there either. No equipment was missing, and that was the most expensive stuff they had. The livestock dotted the green grass and hills. She hadn't heard any disturbance from them last night.

Then again, she'd been...distracted.

Hæra bit her lip, harder than she'd bitten Madeleine's. Nothing bad had happened, she reminded herself as she turned back to the farmhouse. Jonathan and Madeleine were both safe, as was the farm.

Disturbed, she replaced the knife and took a quick, cold shower. Then she tried to sneak back to her room, wrapped in a towel...just in time for Jonathan to shuffle through his bedroom door. He rubbed the sleep from his eyes and startled to see her.

Shite. She must stand up straight and not be embarrassed. She should be imposing, even. Hæra threw her shoulders back and then had to stop the towel from falling down.

Jonathan stared at her. His eyebrows went up. A little smile found its way to his mouth. "Morning," he said. "When'd you get in?"

"Late," she said in a clipped voice. *A secret. Our secret, Madeleine's and mine.*

"Mm. I was up till two." His smile grew. "Must've been late indeed."

Oh, curse it. He knew already. At least he seemed pleased about it, but Hæra glared at him anyway.

"Well, pay me no mind," he said gently. "I'm happy if you are, and that's all I'll say."

She softened. Just so long as he said nothing to Madeleine—but he would never. "I'm happy. Why were you up so late?"

"Couldn't sleep." He yawned.

That was odd. Once Jonathan had stopped drinking, his sleep schedule became regular as clockwork. Had he heard something?

"Someone was here last night," she said.

Jonathan smoothed down the few strands of hair over his bald spot. "What's that?"

"I saw footprints outside the house. Just one person, I think."

He stared at her. "What the hell?"

"I know." She couldn't keep having this conversation in a towel. "I checked everywhere. Nothing's missing from the barn, and nobody got in the house. But someone was walking about outside last night. You heard nothing?"

Jonathan frowned. "No, but my ears aren't what they used to be. Where did you see footprints?"

"Let me dress and I'll show you." She adjusted her towel again. "You know, the oddest thing? Whoever it was, was barefoot."

She headed toward her bedroom, which had also been undisturbed. Behind her, Jonathan was silent. Then he said, "Barefoot?"

His voice sounded strange, but that was no wonder. Someone had crept round their property. Hæra felt strange about it too. "Yes."

He made no reply. She dressed quickly, led him outside, and pointed at the footprints. "There, you see?"

"Someone was right here?" Jonathan asked faintly. He still wore his pajamas beneath a jacket, along with his work boots. "At my own window?"

"Clearly. You didn't hear anything?"

"No. I didn't." He shoved his hands in his jacket pockets and stared at the footprints. "Barefoot. Sure enough."

"Who might have done it?" Hæra asked in bewilderment. She'd lived among humans for five years but still hadn't heard of any customs that had them walking round in the mud without shoes.

Jonathan never looked away from the footprints. "Some village lad, I'd think. Sloshed and that." At Hæra's skeptical look, he added, "When

I drank, I'd get into scrapes that made no sense. Did I ever tell you I woke up near those standing stones once, by the settlement? All I remember is I was singing 'Dancing Queen' at some point. Rest is a blur."

Now wasn't the time for Jonathan's memories of darker days. They ought to figure out the timing of this. "You said you were up until two. It must have happened after that. Or were you watching television? You might not have heard anything if so."

He laughed, though it sounded forced. "I thought you hated those detective programs. Now you sound like one."

"Jonathan…"

"If nothing's missing and nobody was hurt, then I'll not fret about it."

Even for Jonathan, this was too laid-back. "What if they return?"

"Well, that's what the shotgun's for, isn't it?" he asked lightly.

Hæra stared at him. "The shotgun's for sick or injured animals."

"Christ, lass, you still haven't learned sarcasm." He patted her shoulder. "Let's get you something to eat before you work. You used up some energy last night, eh?"

Hæra pursed her lips. She wouldn't blush or stammer. She *wouldn't.* "Breakfast sounds good."

"There's still that sheep's liver in the fridge." He was smiling, but something about his expression still looked peculiar. She couldn't tell what. It was in his eyes.

"Thanks," was all she could say.

"Go on then. I'm away to bed." At her raised eyebrows, he said, "I was up late, wasn't I? I'm not half knackered. I'll be up again soon."

He gave the footprints one last look and turned back toward the front door, his head slightly bent.

"Did you have any dreams last night?" Hæra blurted.

Jonathan stopped in his tracks. He looked halfway over his shoulder, but not enough to meet her eyes. "Why do you ask?"

Because maybe you could tell me what it means to dream. "I—I don't know. Does it matter?"

"You tell me." He shrugged. "Maybe I'll dream when I go back to sleep."

Beware it, she wanted to cry, *it's awful.* Why say that? Jonathan had been dreaming his whole life. All humans did. "Then sleep well."

"I'll do my best," he said, and continued on, his boots gathering the mud with his shuffling walk. His shoulders were stooped. He looked old.

Dreams were an affliction. Hæra glanced back toward the cottage where she'd left Madeleine sleeping. Dreams were a condition of being human too. Was Madeleine dreaming now?

If so, may they be kinder dreams than the one that had attacked Hæra. May Madeleine dream about their incandescent night together. May Madeleine dream about love.

CHAPTER THIRTY-THREE

A WARM STRIPE of light crossed Madeleine's face through a crack in the curtains. She squinted as she opened her eyes.

It was sunny outside? Seriously?

A soft laugh escaped her before she rolled over to find the other side of the bed empty. Hæra was gone.

For a moment, her heart fell. Then she remembered Hæra kissing her cheek and leaving much earlier in the morning. What time was it?

One look at her phone told her it was 8:35. Not as late as she'd thought, but she and Jonathan were supposed to have breakfast together while Hæra worked in the fields. He was probably wondering where Madeleine was.

Madeleine bit her lip. Maybe she wasn't up to facing Jonathan anyway. The events of last night must be written all over her face.

A smile crossed her face. It grew bigger. Then it turned into an actual giggle.

Good grief. This wasn't a moment for giggling. She'd done it. *They'd* done it, herself and Hæra, what Madeleine had been yearning to do for so long—and what Hæra had clearly yearned for too.

I want only you, she'd said. *I'll have only you.*

Madeleine touched the side of her throat. Hæra had bitten and sucked her there. She pressed down with her fingertips and inhaled at the soreness. Hæra had wanted to mark her.

Madeleine had felt the same. At the thought of Hæra with another lover, some kind of frenzy had seized her, and nothing eased it until she knew Hæra was hers alone. And then…later…after Hæra had a nightmare, there had been comfort and teasing, as soft as the sex had been sharp.

No. This was no laughing matter.

It might, however, be occasion for joy.

Joy wasn't the same thing as happiness: happiness could be something you didn't necessarily *feel*, but was an overall state of being you hoped to attain. A low, steady fire burning in the hearth all day. Joy was a flaming torch. It inevitably went out, but while it lasted, it dazzled with heat and light.

Madeleine, greedy for light, would hold on to this torch as long as she could. Maybe Hæra didn't like fire, but she'd certainly put up with it last night. Besides, it was just a metaphor.

She looked at the other side of the bed where Hæra had lain, holding her. And had that nightmare. Hæra had always said she never slept, much less dreamed, but last night she clearly had.

A night of firsts for both of them.

They could talk more about that later. Madeleine should get moving. It would have been…nice…to wake up still snuggled in Hæra's arms. But it was nice to have time for herself too: to prepare herself for whatever this new day brought.

There was one thing she wouldn't do, however.

She wouldn't spiral. She wouldn't panic like she had after their kiss in the alley. Yes, she and Hæra had gone farther the night before than she'd intended to. Much farther. A panic attack would be an understandable reaction, especially given everything she'd been wrestling with.

Wrestling with Hæra had been much more thrilling, though. More than thrilling, it had felt right. So like their first kiss, that night on the beach years ago. That had felt sanctioned, sanctified, divine—and it was just a kiss. Last night, when Hæra had come on Madeleine's fingers, calling out her pleasure, it had felt like ascending to an even higher heaven.

The old, cold feeling of shame tugged at her with frozen fingers. Madeleine took a deep breath and pulled free of them. Not right now. Shame was for certainty, and certainty was its own kind of sin.

There would be time later for shame, if it came to that. But maybe it wouldn't. The sun was out this morning. It was occasion for joy.

———

To Madeleine's surprise, Jonathan was still in his pajamas when she arrived. He stood at the kitchen sink with a cup of coffee in his hands. His gaze was fixed upon the window.

Madeleine cleared her throat. He didn't move. She cleared it more loudly, and then he twitched and turned around, his eyes widening.

She took a hesitant step into the kitchen. This was strange. Jonathan slept later than Hæra and the farmhands, but he was always up and dressed by now. "Good morning. Am I here too early?"

"No," he said quickly. "Sorry. I lost track of the time. I knew you were coming over, didn't I?"

He wasn't usually so scattered. "Um, you said I should, yes."

"Right, right." He ran a hand over his balding head. "Coffee? I've not made my fry-up yet."

"Coffee sounds good, thanks." A greasy fry-up didn't, and besides, Jonathan looked exhausted. She didn't feel right having him wait on her. "Please don't go to any extra trouble for breakfast. Cereal's fine. In fact, I'm happy to get it myself."

"No, no, sit down. No trouble at all, let me just get my head together, I…" Jonathan glanced around the kitchen, looking restless. "Strange night. I couldn't sleep. Then Hæra told me we've had some mischief round the place."

"What?"

Madeleine listened, astonished, as Jonathan told her about muddy footprints beneath his window. He insisted he wasn't worried, that it was just some childish prank from a villager. "No matter where you are, there's always foolish lads, aren't there? I was one, once upon a time...I remember..."

She ignored his request to sit—he didn't seem to notice—and fixed herself a bowl of Weetabix while he talked. By the time she sat down with her breakfast, Jonathan had finished his story and looked a little more settled, although there were bags under his eyes.

"We all made some silly decisions when we were young," she said lightly.

A shadow crossed his eyes. "Aye, so we did."

"In fact..." How did you bring up something like this? "Um, I think you asked me here today so we could talk about what happened when you were younger. With another *Each-uisge*. Right?"

Jonathan pursed his lips and looked down at his coffee. He'd barely touched it. It must be cold by now. "Not much to tell."

He couldn't be serious. Not much to *tell* about an encounter with a supernatural creature? Especially to the one person on this island who might understand?

"I don't want to push," she lied. "But it'd be nice to compare notes, right? We could learn something from each other."

He shrugged. Just yesterday he'd said they should talk about this. What had changed? "Perhaps, perhaps not. Your situation's completely different to mine."

"Okay, but that doesn't mean—"

"Hæra's different."

The name sent a jolt through Madeleine's body. The look in Jonathan's eyes said he'd intended it to.

"I've seen how you are with each other," he said. "I'd be blind not to. And she was different when she came in this morning...from your place."

Madeleine's face heated as surely as if she were back in front of that fireplace, with Hæra on top of her.

Jonathan gave a little smile. "Just so."

"I..." She looked down into her coffee. *Remember the joy,* she told herself, *remember how right it felt,* but words only went so far. The old shame, kneaded into her soul by unkind hands, rose.

"No, no," he said quickly. His hand covered her wrist while she clutched her coffee cup. "I'm happy for you both. I hope you are too? It's not too hard, is it?"

Thin, almost translucent hairs covered Jonathan's wrist and the back of his hands. That was something to look at, instead of into his eyes. "It's all pretty unexpected."

Jonathan snorted. "I'm sure. Look up, now. Our Hæra's a good one, even if she is odd. And you're all the world to her."

At that, Madeleine did look up. Jonathan's eyes were wide and earnest. His earlier exhaustion seemed to have vanished; he was much more like himself. At least, the self he'd become after Hæra came into his life.

"I'm not all her world," Madeleine said. Hæra herself had said, on the beach, all the things she loved. "But that's good. I shouldn't be. And she's not just odd—she *is* different from me." The mug was hot against her palms as she held it even tighter. "From us."

They regarded each other in silence, for a moment.

"Aye," Jonathan said heavily. "There's no changing that."

"I don't know what's going to happen. How long I can stay. Even if I did—even if *somehow* we worked this out—"

And what would "working it out" mean? Hadn't Madeleine said, only yesterday, that it was too early for love? That meant it was *way* too early to think about…whatever this was. A long-term commitment to someone outside her own species?

She swallowed. "She won't get older. People will notice."

"I know." Jonathan bowed his head, as if in defeat. What else could he do? It was only the truth.

Maybe now Madeleine could have that panic attack. It wouldn't be useful, but at least this situation deserved it. "She can't go back to the sea, can she? Her own family tried to kill her. What's she supposed to do?"

There had to be a plan. Hæra could lie in Madeleine's bed, their naked bodies could glide together, their mouths could mate. They could roam the island hand-in-hand and talk about anything. But, even if they wanted to, they couldn't grow old together. What then?

"There's money," Jonathan said quietly. "More than she knows, I think. That bloody trow means we do all right."

Madeleine had never seen the trow. Just something else she wasn't ready for.

"I set aside some for her every month," Jonathan continued.

It took Madeleine only a moment to understand. "So she can leave."

"Aye, if I don't die in time." At Madeleine's startled look, he added, "I mean if I live long enough so folk notice she doesn't age, and then she has to run before she can inherit the lot."

"Doesn't she already own at least part of it?" After all, Hæra's treasure chest had paid for the place.

Jonathan shook his head. "We didn't have her birth certificate when I bought, and I was nervous that folk might look too close. I offered later, but she wasn't interested. Now at least I can give her enough to get started."

Another silence between them held the truth. It would only be a start. And there was something else to consider.

"She told me she can't go inland," Madeleine said in a low voice. "She loses her strength if she's too far from the ocean. That limits her options."

Jonathan leaned back with a gusty sigh and crossed his arms. His pajamas seemed too baggy on him. "I know. There's islands with few people and always have been. The Hebrides might suit for a while."

For a while, until she had to leave there too. Hæra would have to roam the world for centuries in a borrowed form, alone. There were probably worse fates, but at the moment it was hard to think of one. Unless…

"Maybe that's far enough away from her family," Madeleine ventured. But even if it was, would it be any easier for Hæra to survive the sea by herself? "Maybe there are more *Each-uisge* somewhere else, and she could find a new herd and be safe."

"Yeah. Maybe."

The look they exchanged said it all. What did "safety" mean where

Hæra was concerned? If she wasn't like humans, she wasn't like her own kind either. That was how she'd ended up here.

"Have you two talked about this?" Madeleine managed.

"I've tried, but she puts me off. She's always said that when you came back, everything'd be sorted. She never told me how." Jonathan sighed again. "Maybe you can make her see sense when I couldn't. You're a practical lass. Suited to this, I'd think."

A strange weight settled on Madeleine, then. As if Jonathan had taken a heavy mantle off his shoulders and placed it on her own. He was worried about Hæra. He was old, and probably not in the best shape from decades of drinking. Now here Madeleine was, younger and with a deep connection to Hæra. Jonathan wanted her to take over and figure out what to do with the woman he'd sometimes called his daughter.

Ah, there was the panic. It snapped and bit at Madeleine's insides. She said, haltingly, "I'll try to, but…there's only so much I can do."

Jonathan gave her a sharp look.

"Or anyone," Madeleine added. Her palms were getting damp. *I'm not ready for this,* she wanted to plead with him. *I can't take responsibility for this.* She was just re-learning how to be responsible for herself, for heaven's sake.

"No?" he said. "Let me tell you what I know."

His eyes were as piercing, now, as Hæra's had ever been. Madeleine sat up straight and faced him squarely back. "Okay," she said.

"There's ties that can't be cut. If you try, you learn they're your veins and you bleed out. And I don't believe in your God, but I know there's something outside ourselves as puts things in our keeping."

Her heart thundered in her chest like a storm, or a herd of wild horses. "And you think Hæra's been put into mine? I hope you haven't told her that. She'd hate it."

"Would she? The lass thinks you've been put in her keeping too. And so you were."

Madeleine dug her hands into the fabric of her jeans. "How can you know a thing like that?"

His eyes were hooded. "Experience."

Footsteps sounded beyond the kitchen door. Hæra was returning from the morning's first work and kicking the mud from her boots.

Jonathan lowered his voice. "Just remember: what's for you won't go by you."

"Yes, but—"

The door banged open. They both turned. Hæra stepped in, tall confidence and swagger, someone who didn't see the future coming at her like a bullet.

"Good morning." Her voice was warm, and her eyes were too, as she looked at Madeleine. "Glad to see you up and about. How did you sleep?"

How did you? Madeleine didn't ask. Best not to bring up the nightmare. "Well. Thanks."

"Good. Jonathan knows I spent the night, by the way." Hæra sounded apologetic. "I didn't tell him, but he worked it out."

At least the cold sensation in Madeleine's stomach vanished when her face heated up again. "Um, yes, I know."

"Just as well." Hæra sat down and slouched back in the chair, smiling openly now. "He told me human sexuality is meant to be private, but I am *very* happy about it, and I don't think I can hide it."

Madeleine swallowed a gasp, even as a warm wave swallowed her. Hæra's eyes were bright with pleasure now that she was here, with Madeleine, at this table.

Put in your keeping, and you in hers.

Hæra had spoken, often, of keeping Madeleine safe. Protecting her. Shielding her from the wind, catching her when she fell. It seemed to delight her. It came so naturally to her.

As if Madeleine was for her, and Hæra wouldn't let her go by. She'd always believed that.

"So am I," Madeleine said. Her voice was low, but it didn't shake. "No need to hide anything at all."

CHAPTER THIRTY-FOUR

Borrowed time.

Jonathan and other humans used this phrase occasionally. Hæra knew what it meant but hadn't *understood*. How could you borrow something insubstantial? And from whom?

Now, two weeks after she and Madeleine had started having sex (Hæra wouldn't call it *sleeping together*, since she hadn't slept again), it made more sense. Time felt like something she'd been granted temporarily when the witch had saved her life. It couldn't last forever, and now that she'd given up her mad fantasy of eating Madeleine and becoming a Stormhorse, Hæra had to face facts. This couldn't last forever.

It was so easy not to talk about it, though. It always had been, although Jonathan had tried to press her on it.

Madeleine didn't. After two weeks, she still wasn't interested in discussing the future. How odd. For once, Hæra was the one who looked ahead, and a human was the one who turned away.

Best not to push it. These were happy days. The happiest of Hæra's life, in fact: the pleasures of a century squeezed into a summer.

She'd thought nothing could be more thrilling than a successful hunt, pursuing a great creature like an orca until her teeth tore into its flesh. Someday, she'd believed, getting her wings would be even better. Wrong. Nothing could be better than taking Madeleine into her arms for kisses, caresses, and more. *Here* was the flesh she wanted most beneath her mouth, *here* were the dazzling heights she'd sought.

Madeleine seemed to feel the same. She and Hæra walked about Jorsay less and worked on the farm more. It was hard work—"Smelly, too," she said—and she was exhausted at the end of each day. Even so, she would reach for Hæra every night with eager hands.

Hæra had tried playing the whale mating songs to enhance the mood. Madeleine didn't find them alluring, but it turned out they didn't need the extra help.

"You no longer care about your church," Hæra had said exultantly on their third night together, for so it must be.

Madeleine, sated in Hæra's embrace, frowned. "I wouldn't say that."

"But why else would you have sex with me? I thought that was why not."

"It's complicated." Madeleine looked away. "I'm trying to look at life in a different way. Like we talked about. But that doesn't mean it's simple. Let's talk about it later?" She caressed Hæra's bare shoulder. "I'd rather focus on being here with you."

That suited Hæra down to the ground, and she'd pressed her lips to Madeleine's forehead, where the scar was.

She'd been content to put the matter off for another day. Two weeks later, *another day* had yet to arrive. Maybe it would have been all right if that were the only problem. It wasn't. Something felt wrong with the farm, and it was nothing she could put her finger on. No more footprints appeared. Nothing went missing or got damaged. Nothing had *happened*.

And yet.

The humans didn't seem to notice anything. But the sheep were a little more nervous than usual, ewes likelier to bolt from their lambs. The dogs raised their hackles more and wagged their tails less.

It was enough to disquiet Hæra too. In *Each-uisge* form, her ears would have been folded constantly back. And yet she couldn't tell why.

The feeling crept in everywhere. At night, Madeleine's cottage seemed chillier than it had when Hæra and Jonathan had lived there. Hæra didn't mind the fireplace so much now, and holding Madeleine close always helped. Madeleine herself didn't seem to notice, which was strange, since she was more sensitive to cold.

On two occasions, outside the cottage while Madeleine slept, Hæra could have sworn she heard whistling. The second time, she'd slipped out of bed, dressed, and gone to investigate. By the time she'd made it outside, there was nothing. No footprints either. Then again, there was less mud around the cottage and more grass, where it was harder to see indentations.

Of course Madeleine, Jonathan, and the farmhands had all told Hæra it must have been the wind. Nobody else seemed to think anything was wrong, although Jonathan had refused to look directly at her when he said the wind was responsible.

What else could it have been? Hæra knew how unnerving the wind could be. Until she'd started taking human lessons, spending more time on land, she'd never heard how it sounded away from the sea. Now she knew it could moan and hum in the night. And whistle too.

Maybe the trow was up to mischief. Trows were known for that sort of thing: it was all fun and games until they crept into your house to steal a baby from its cradle, though Ætlaquoy didn't have any babies. Perhaps the trow was bored and had forgotten what Hæra could do to him? Perhaps, when she'd told him she might be leaving soon, he'd decided she was no longer a threat. He would learn otherwise, before this got out of hand.

She needed no shotgun to deal with him. Or anything else. Her own teeth would suffice.

And so, early one morning, when Hæra brought his breakfast, she intended to give him a piece of her mind. However, when she set the food and beer bottle on the ground near his door, he did not appear.

She waited. And waited. She waited over ten minutes, until she was grinding her back teeth. She eventually called out, "I want to speak to you!"

The trow did not emerge. The pasty and beer stayed right where it was.

"Are you causing this mischief? Something's wrong. I know it is."

Silence.

"If it's you, then leave off!" Hæra snapped. Why was she shivering? It was July, and she didn't even feel the cold in January. Nevertheless, she hugged herself against a chill. "I've found a wee bit of joy, and you can leave me to it, can't you? Just for a while!"

Silence.

"Do you even know what joy is? Have you never—" The wind cut into her, and she gasped. "Never loved a thing and wanted to keep it close?"

No answer.

She could threaten the trow. Maybe that'd keep him in line if pleading wouldn't. Why should an *Each-uisge*, great hunter of the North Sea, plead with an underground trickster? She should show him his place.

"Just reconsider," she snarled. "It's a fine arrangement, this. You eat well without having to hunt voles. Don't ruin a good thing."

It was as close to a threat as she could manage, which was pathetic. She must be going soft.

It wasn't as if she was *fond* of the creature.

———

When she said so to Madeleine that evening, Madeleine only smiled. "Are you sure about that?"

Hæra tugged her in closer on the couch and began to play with her shirt collar. "Of course. Why would I be fond of him? We've never had a proper conversation."

"No, but he's…like you."

Hæra thought of the day she'd gone to the trow's mound to ask him to protect the farm when she was gone. He'd said nothing, just looked at her inscrutably. Was that kinship? "I don't think so."

Madeleine studied the base of Hæra's throat. She began to trace the dip in Hæra's clavicle with her fingertips. "Isn't he more like you than I am?"

Hæra frowned and caught Madeleine's hand in her own. "What do you mean? He's a little thing who lives under the ground all alone and doesn't want anything but food and beer. That's not like us." She squeezed Madeleine's hand. "Come with me sometime. If he comes out, I'll introduce you. You'll understand then."

Madeleine looked at her, and Hæra held her breath. *Come and look,* she pleaded silently, *see the unseen. Don't turn your face from it.*

After a pause, Madeleine said, "What about the day after tomorrow? I told Jim I'd help him tomorrow first thing, but the next day…" She took a deep breath. "You're right. I've been saying I want to learn new things, haven't I?"

Hæra's heart soared higher than if she had grown wings. "Really?"

Madeleine gave her a tiny smile. "Really."

"And after that, perhaps you'll be ready to watch me transform into my real shape?"

The tiny smile faded. "Um…"

Hæra drooped.

"I will," Madeleine said quickly. "I'm working my way up to it. I do want to understand your world, I know it's time, just…baby steps, okay?"

Hæra hadn't spent much time around human babies—and wasn't anxious to change that—but she understood the metaphor. "Of course it's okay."

Maybe her disappointment was inappropriate. Madeleine was slowly reordering her entire belief system, thanks in large part to their relationship. It was more than Hæra had a right to expect after how they'd begun. She tucked Madeleine's hair behind her ear. "Your willingness means a great deal to me. As do you."

Madeleine blushed. She drummed her fingertips against Hæra's clavicle until Hæra released her hand, and then began stroking Hæra's skin again. "You mean a lot to me too."

She didn't make eye contact when she said it. Did that mean she wasn't sincere? No, that wasn't right. Hæra "meant a lot" to Madeleine, that was obvious. So why the furtive expression?

For the first time, Hæra felt reluctant to ask. What if she upset the delicate balance they'd achieved and drove Madeleine away? It was probably nothing.

When Madeleine leaned forward and nuzzled the side of Hæra's neck, it was even easier to convince herself of this. Madeleine had grown much bolder in the last couple of weeks. No more pink cheeks and fluttering eyelashes, although Hæra had enjoyed that too. Now she reached for Hæra when she wanted something, and she took it. An urge Hæra fully understood.

She tilted her head to the side and sighed as the kisses wandered higher up her neck. Could there be anything else like the stroke of Madeleine's lips on her skin? She'd spent so long wanting to devour Madeleine. She hadn't thought how pleasant it might be to get devoured in her turn.

Madeleine nipped her earlobe. Hæra chuckled. "Trying to eat me alive?"

"I hear that's your specialty," Madeleine said lightly.

Hæra's heart stopped. Did Madeleine know somehow, had she guessed—?

Surely that wasn't possible. The longer they were together, the less Hæra could imagine telling her the truth about her original plan, calling a look of anger and disgust into those beloved eyes. Why ruin what brief time they had together? But if Madeleine had somehow realized…intuited, or…

"Sorry," Madeleine said.

"What?" Hæra asked, startled.

"You got all stiff. I guess I shouldn't joke about that." Madeleine touched Hæra's shoulder, and now she looked into Hæra's eyes, her expression penitent. "I just—sometimes I think, if I can joke about it, it's not a big deal."

"It's not a *big deal*," Hæra said, relieved. "We are who we are, and we're obviously compatible. I just…want you to understand that I…"

Madeleine blinked at her. "You what?"

"That I could never harm you," Hæra said hoarsely, remembering the night on the shore when she'd taken horse form and tried to drive Madeleine into the sea. Instead, she'd realized she could never hurt a hair on Madeleine's head.

To her dismay, instead of saying, *I know that*, Madeleine shook her head. "Of course you can. And you will."

"What? No, I…"

"That's what people do," Madeleine said gently. "If we're close to someone, then we can hurt them, and sometimes we do. No matter how much we, um, care for them. That's what it means to be human, and…" She trailed off as they looked at each other.

"Is it?" Hæra asked quietly. "To hurt each other, to care, and to dream? I've experienced all three now."

Madeleine swallowed. "Yes."

"But I'm not human." At the words, Madeleine flinched, and Hæra sighed. "I can't change that, although…"

"Although what?"

Although I don't know what I am instead. A creature inhabiting one world after being driven from another, belonging to neither. "Never mind. Right now, I'm more kin to you than to a trow. I think you were about to prove it?" Encouragingly, she rubbed her nose against Madeleine's forehead and inhaled the scent of her hair.

"I think I was," Madeleine agreed. She kissed the side of Hæra's mouth.

That was more like it. Hæra had something to prove too, and she sent her hands and mouth wandering. She discovered, again, the swell of Madeleine's breasts. Then the curve of her thighs, and—soon enough—the soaked secret that hid between them.

By then, as Hæra stroked deeply inside her, Madeleine was moaning and holding her close. Her breasts were bare, the tips of her nipples salty with sweat as Hæra tasted them. She rolled her hips desperately. "Please," Madeleine groaned. "More. Oh God, more."

"I told you, I'm not your God," Hæra said hoarsely.

Madeleine's eyes flew open. She arched her hips and gasped.

Hæra bared her teeth and looked down into Madeleine's flushed face. Tunnel vision. She could only see forward, could only see those green eyes looking back at her. "He's got no business here."

"Ah," Madeleine whimpered, rocking her hips, "ah…ah…"

"It's just me." Hæra thrust faster.

"Oh, oh—"

"Just me and you." She watched Madeleine's eyes close, watched her head tilt back. "And I…"

"Hæra—H-Hæra—"

"Am going to fuck you straight into heaven." She curled her fingers.

Madeleine's thighs went rigid. She wailed. And around Hæra's fingers, she clenched and throbbed, thrusting her hips until—a sudden, wet surge—

Hæra looked down, astonished and delighted, as Madeleine squirted all over her hand while she came.

Her reading had mentioned that, and one of those dirty videos had shown it too. It hadn't sounded all that appealing until now, when it was happening right in front of her, the clearest possible sign of Madeleine's ecstasy.

Slowly, Madeleine's trembling subsided, and she sank back down into the couch with a moan. "Oh, my G…gosh." Then she grunted, propped herself up on her elbows, and looked down the length of her body with widening eyes. "Oh my *gosh*. What…"

Hæra grinned and held up her wet fingers and hand. "Nicely done."

Madeleine put her hand over her mouth. "I'm so sorry! I didn't mean to—what *is* that?"

"A compliment." To prove it, Hæra licked her fingers. Delicious. "It's a sexual response that means you came extremely hard."

"Oh. I, uh, I've never heard of…" Madeleine pushed her hair out of her face with a shaking hand. "I made a mess."

She had. The wetness was on the couch cushions too. But cushions could be cleaned, and Hæra had no interest in stopping now for a bit of housekeeping. "Then let's move to the bedroom."

Madeleine looked dizzy. "But I…"

Hæra rose to her feet and looked down upon Madeleine's body, sprawled naked on the couch. Her pale skin was flushed red, a sheen of sweat over her breasts and belly. Beads of moisture gathered on the dark hair between her legs. Her magnificent breasts rose and fell quickly, even as she got her breath back.

Then she looked into Madeleine's eyes. She couldn't know what her own expression was, but whatever it was, it stopped Madeleine in her tracks and made her mouth softly open.

"My turn, now," Hæra said softly, and bent down.

Madeleine slid her arms around Hæra's neck and rested meekly in her arms as she was carried to bed. That was the last of her meekness, though. By the time Hæra was naked too, it was her turn to cry out as Madeleine licked between her legs, hungry and eager. She'd been hesitant about this at first but had insisted on trying, and now she couldn't seem to get enough of it, said she loved Hæra's taste and texture, loved bringing her pleasure.

Yes, it was a pleasure indeed to be devoured. Who could have known it?

Afterward, while Hæra's thighs were still shaking, Madeleine surged over her like a wave. She wiped her mouth with the back of her hand. "Was that good?" she panted.

For answer, Hæra hauled Madeleine into her arms, rolled her on her back, and kissed her wet mouth. "Better. I love when you taste me, my Madeleine."

The possessive escaped her before she could stop it. Beneath her, Madeleine's breath hitched, which meant she'd noticed it too. Hæra held her own breath.

After a second, Madeleine whispered, "Glad to hear it…my Hæra."

Hæra gasped. She propped herself up on her elbows so she could get a better look at Madeleine's face. "Yes. I *am* yours. Do you understand it?" *Finally?*

Madeleine bit her bottom lip. When it slid back out from between her teeth, it shone. After a seeming moment of deliberation, she touched Hæra's face. "Sometimes, God puts things...or people...into our keeping. We might not know what to do with them, but they're ours anyway. I'm learning that."

On the surface, it sounded like Madeleine spoke of a burdensome obligation. The look in her eyes, thoughtful and sincere, made much more of it than that.

"I agree," Hæra said. What else had she known all along, but that the Great Mare had put Madeleine into her path? "We belong to each other. It's simple."

"*Simple?*" Madeleine's lips twitched. "Never change, Hæra."

Too late for that. Hæra didn't bother saying so as she bent down for another, sweeter kiss.

CHAPTER THIRTY-FIVE

Normally, Madeleine slept well in Hæra's arms. Tonight, although Hæra held her as securely as always, she couldn't nod off. She'd lain awake for two hours. That wasn't good, since the coming day would be another long, busy one. They all seemed to be.

She loved them, although her muscles ached at the end of each one. Even on rainy, cloudy days, there was immense satisfaction in working hard for a good purpose. It wasn't like teaching, which, while rewarding and difficult, didn't involve tractors, shovels, or sheep poop.

Admittedly, she could have done without the sheep poop.

Leaning into doubt and change seemed to be good for her. She was happier than she could ever remember being. Why ruin it by wishing for the impossible? Why look to the future?

She'd spent years thinking ahead to when she'd return to Orkney and find her angel. She'd found something else, and for once she was trying to live in the moment. The moment was wonderful. The future was bleak.

She groaned and sat up. She could embroider on the sofa until she got sleepy. Hæra loved the piece she was working on now, a seascape. She couldn't fathom how Madeleine had the patience for all the tiny stitches and had been astonished when Madeleine said the little details were her favorite part.

Madeleine glanced back at Hæra, who lay breathing deeply and evenly. Her body was relaxed. You'd think she was asleep, except her eyes were open, if unseeing. She was "resting," slowing her system down for the night. Hæra had told Madeleine she hadn't slept since their first night together, when she'd had a nightmare she didn't want to discuss.

Another way they weren't alike.

They were alike in others, though.

My Hæra.

Madeleine slipped out of bed. Hæra inhaled and stirred, but she calmed and returned to rest when Madeleine said, "It's all right, I'm just getting up for a minute."

A few minutes later, Madeleine looked down at the still-damp patch on the sofa and wondered who she was kidding. Telling Jonathan she couldn't be responsible for Hæra? Then clinging to Hæra every night like she was Madeleine's only lifeline, craving her more each day? She'd had no idea she was capable of this recklessness, much less this ravenous need. So ravenous she'd made this mess.

Madeleine groaned to herself and cleaned the couch. Then, once she'd finished, she pulled out her embroidery kit.

The repetitive push and pull of the needle soothed her. The colorful thread slid in and out of the fabric, leaving it brighter and more textured than before.

We belong to each other. It's simple.

Simple? No. True? It seemed so. Jonathan had told her, effectively, that she couldn't escape her fate. She wasn't sure about that. She believed in free will; otherwise, how could you ever be held accountable for your own choices? How could you deserve the happiness you'd worked so hard for?

God sent his children opportunities. It was up to Madeleine to recognize one such, and then choose to take it or not. She'd chosen to take it. So had Hæra, even if she'd phrase it differently. The Great Mare or something.

Why did it feel like a decision lay before Madeleine, when so much of this was completely out of her hands? She should be so lucky as to get to *decide*—

"What's wrong?"

The voice was right behind her, and Madeleine stabbed her fingertip with the needle. She yelped.

Hæra swiftly rounded the sofa. Her hair was rumpled. She frowned. "All right?"

"Yes. Oh, shoot." A droplet of blood had welled up on Madeleine's fingertip. "Can you get me a Band-Aid? They're in the bathroom cabinet."

Hæra looked down at Madeleine's fingertip as the blood drop swelled. She inhaled, and a familiar expression crossed her face. The same expression she wore in bed, only sharper. Wilder.

Madeleine's breath caught.

Hæra sat down without a word and took Madeleine's hand. She looked at the welling scarlet drop and then looked into Madeleine's eyes. Asking, silently.

A memory stirred, swift and violent, of the night Hæra had saved her from drowning. Madeleine had been half conscious, but she'd felt Hæra's tongue licking the cut in her forehead. It had stung. She'd forgotten it until now.

She laughed unsteadily. "Oh boy. Sure you're not actually a vampire?"

"Please," Hæra whispered. Her eyes never left Madeleine's. "I won't hurt you."

Heat swept through Madeleine, and she ached as if she and Hæra hadn't had sex on this same sofa just hours ago, which was weird, because this was *blood*, and all she could manage to do was nod.

Hæra lowered her head. Her hot, soft mouth closed around Madeleine's fingertip, and she began to suck.

She might as well have licked between Madeleine's legs. Madeleine's head tilted back, her eyes closed, and she moaned. The faint sting melted into the warmth, until the only thing left on earth was Hæra's eager mouth.

Hæra gasped and pulled away. When she raised her head again, her face was flushed, her eyes glazed over, as if she were drunk. Her mouth was still open. She clearly wanted more, although there was no more from such a tiny wound. Her black hair curtained her face when she turned aside and let Madeleine go. She said roughly, "Sorry."

Madeleine's fingertip wasn't bleeding now, but it tingled. "Th-that's all right. Are you—um—what does that do?"

Hæra didn't look up. "Do?"

"I mean, tasting blood. Does it...do something to you?" Maybe that's why Hæra wouldn't turn to her. "A feeding frenzy, like sharks?"

"Sharks!" Hæra laughed, sounding a little scornful. Maybe that was another insulting comparison, like with the kelpie. "No. There's no frenzy. I'm still myself." She turned to Madeleine then. Her eyes weren't glazed anymore, and she wore a little smile, but the hunger was still there, written all over her in a language Madeleine ached to read. "Just want every bit of you there is, I suppose," she said.

Madeleine's face grew hot. *I want the same,* she could reply, *minus the blood part.*

"Can't sleep?" Hæra asked. Her knee bumped Madeleine's. She was warm and close, the living room was dark and cold, and embroidery could only get you so far.

Madeleine tossed the wheel and thread aside. "I'm sure I can now."

Hæra's eyes gleamed. "In my arms, you mean."

"There's no end to your ego." It was as good as an admission. Madeleine stood up. She held out the hand with the finger that had bled, but wasn't anymore.

Hæra regarded it silently. Then she took it as she rose to her feet, and kept holding it as she led Madeleine back to bed.

The next morning, Hæra left before Madeleine was awake, although Madeleine got up earlier now that she was helping out round the farm. Hæra loved how enthusiastically she'd taken to it. Yesterday, she'd learned how to drive a tractor. She embraced every opportunity to help out. Madeleine said it was only fair since Jonathan was letting her stay in the cottage for free, but Hæra knew she liked to be useful. More than that, she enjoyed working with her hands and being outdoors. Strange, she'd said, for a city girl.

It had been stranger still for an ocean creature. Hæra and Madeleine surely had more in common than Madeleine seemed to think.

But—*my Hæra*, Madeleine had said. And just a couple of hours later, she'd blessed Hæra again with the taste of her blood. Its savor had warmed her from head to toe. By the depths, there was nothing like it.

At the first taste, she'd feared she wouldn't be able to stop. How could she, when it was the taste of bliss? Madeleine had moaned, as if she'd felt the same.

Well. That wasn't going to happen again. Next time Madeleine pricked her finger, Hæra would get her a plaster as requested. And she wouldn't even look at the blood.

What a night. Madeleine had claimed her *and* let Hæra taste her. Hæra hoped the sea witch didn't really expect her to return with her despair. No despair could touch her when she had something like this, even if it was temporary.

As she approached the farmhouse from the cottage, she stopped in her tracks and frowned. Jonathan stood outside the back door in his pajamas. Standing in profile, he looked blankly toward the pastures and hills.

"Jonathan?" she asked in alarm as she hurried forward.

He didn't move. Just kept staring into the distance.

"*Jonathan!*" Hæra snapped as she reached him.

That did it. He gasped and turned around. "Lass! You near gave me a heart attack."

That better be an exaggeration. He was too pale, and doctors had warned him enough. Hæra's own heart galloped unpleasantly. "Are you all right? What are you doing out here like this?"

"I…erm…" Jonathan looked down at himself, seeming to notice his own pajamas. "I thought I heard something."

There was nothing in the pastures but sheep, cattle, and dogs. The only sound, as always, was the damned wind. Hæra said through her teeth, "Like what?"

"My name, I think." He shook his head. "I must have been only half awake. I probably thought it was you calling me."

"Well, I wasn't." Hæra looked around. Nobody else was in sight. Connor and Jim wouldn't arrive for another hour or so to start the day's work. "Were you dreaming? Perhaps you sleepwalked."

Jonathan scoffed. "I haven't done that since I sobered up. Never mind it. I'm not hurt, and all's well."

All wasn't well if Jonathan was hallucinating voices and walking about in his pajamas. Hæra's stomach lurched as she remembered what she'd learned of aging humans. How they could begin to misremember things or think they were elsewhere. They might forget their own loved ones, or even who they were. "You should see the doctor next time he's on the island," she blurted. "I could go with you."

The glare Jonathan turned on her didn't seem forgetful at all. He looked fiercer than he ever had, in fact. "I'm fit as a fiddle. Haven't we got work to do? Look to your part, now."

He was never so brusque. It startled her so much she couldn't think up a suitable retort while he stalked back into the house. The kitchen door slammed behind him.

She was shaking a little. How curious. How strange.

Was this the trow? Trows were tricksters, but they weren't known for luring folk outside to hurt or kill them. They preferred simple mischief, even if it could be destructive.

And when Hæra went to the trow's mound, yet again he did not appear.

"I don't have your food today," she growled at the earth. "I'll come back with it tonight. Perhaps your hunger will make you willing to answer my questions."

No reply.

Madeleine, she thought, *I'll ask Madeleine about Jonathan.* Madeleine had worked with sick humans when she was a nun, helping all kinds of people. She'd know.

But when Madeleine showed up for the day's work, and Hæra recounted the incident, she had no ready answer. Instead, she looked troubled. "He didn't seem to know where he was? That's not a good sign."

"I know that." Hæra dragged a huge hay bale closer to the barn wall. It was taller than she was, and it seemed to take more effort than usual. Her arms ached with the strain. "He said he wouldn't see a doctor."

"Has this happened before?"

"Not that I've seen. He's sharp since he stopped drinking."

"Then maybe it really was sleepwalking. He might have been embarrassed or confused, especially if he's never done it before." Madeleine sighed. "We'll keep an eye on him."

It sounded reasonable. There was no need to assume the worst.

That didn't stop Hæra's skin from prickling for the rest of the morning, nor her head from swiveling at every unexpected sound, nor her heart from racing at odd moments. Something was wrong.

And after lunch, when Connor said, "Forecast says a storm's building off the coast—might be coming this way," Hæra knew she was right.

"That'll be no roostan hoger," Jim grunted as he hefted a sack of feed. A light rain he meant. "Here's hoping we're lucky as usual. Funny how we never get damage like the other farms do. Jon must be touched by the angels," he added, his voice lighter. "What d'you think, Hæra?"

Hæra and Madeleine made eye contact. Madeleine pursed her lips and looked away. Before Hæra could answer, Madeleine said, "Connor, can you show me how to whistle for the dogs again?"

"Oh, aye, there's a trick to it…"

By midafternoon, the temperature was dropping, and the air smelled of rain: earthy, the atmosphere's moisture calling scent from soil. The omnipresent clouds grew darker and heavier overhead. The hairs on the back of Hæra's neck remained up.

Jonathan stayed inside, saying he had work to do on the computer in case the storm took out the electricity.

"We never lose the electricity," Hæra said, trying to sound calm. "Remember?"

"Aye, your little friend." Jonathan didn't look away from the screen. "I'd rather not completely trust to him, if it's all the same to you." His index finger clicked the mouse. "I've never seen him, after all." He clicked again. "Sometimes I wonder if he's real."

"You're joking." Hæra's mouth was dry. "Why would I invent such a thing? Do you believe it's *coincidence* we've suffered no damage from storms in the past five years?"

"How should I know what to believe?" He began to type, furiously. "Sorry. I'm in a pisser of a mood. Best to leave me to myself. Go on, now."

She had no choice but to go on. It would make things worse to push; when he was truly upset, Jonathan dug in his heels. Setting her jaw, Hæra left.

The sky had darkened since she'd gone into the house. The air had sharpened. For the first time in her life, Hæra wished she'd put on a jacket.

From a distance, thunder rolled. The storm was nearly here. But that'd be all right. They'd be all right. It was always all right.

Wasn't it?

———

After supper, the rain began.

The wind lashed it into their faces as they secured the barn and urged the dogs into the safety of the sheep pens. As usual, the sheep and cattle themselves would wait it out in the fields. It would be a colossal effort to round up hundreds of animals for one night's storm, especially since you'd have to roam over the hills and fields to collect them all. There wasn't time.

Jim shielded his face from the rain with his jacketed hand. "I'd best be getting home," he said, his voice loud over the wind. "Isla's texted four times."

"Married life!" Connor laughed. They hurried together toward their cars.

Hæra turned to Madeleine, who had her hood pulled up and was visibly shivering in the cold and wet. "You should go back to the cottage," she said.

The rain left beads of water on Madeleine's nose and cheeks. "Aren't you coming too? Don't you need to stay indoors in case Calder sees you?"

"I'll be there soon." Hæra looked at where the Gator waited by the fence post, the only piece of equipment she hadn't put into the barn. "There's just one thing I need to check. Quickly."

———

What had happened to the trow?

With the wind and rain growing all around her, Hæra stared at the ground in confusion. It was now dark enough that she'd turned on the Gator's headlights, but her vision was still good enough to see beyond the beams.

The trow's mound was gone. In its place was mud and torn grass, as if something had churned up the ground where his home had been.

Hæra looked around wildly, but she was alone. She called out, "Hello? Are you there?"

Like this morning, like yesterday morning, there was no reply.

"Answer me, you wretched thing! Are you all right?" Silence, except for the howl of the wind. "Are you hurt? If you are, I'll—" Her wet ponytail slapped her in the face. She shoved the hair out of her mouth. "I'll help you, I promise. I'll bring you any food you want. Just stop this storm!"

The wind changed direction. A new smell touched her nostrils, then. New, but dreadfully familiar.

The smell of blood, somewhere on the ground.

Not a human's blood, nor that of sheep or cow or dog. She'd never smelled this particular sort of blood before. She went icy with dread as she stumbled forward, toward the mud, in search of what must be there.

Let me be wrong. Let it be something else. A vole, a bird, a...

A little gray hand poked out from beneath a clump of mud.

Hæra gasped. She fell to her knees and wiped the water from her eyes before she pushed the mud away, seeking the rest of the arm.

It wasn't there. The hand lay alone on the ground, dark blood pooled beneath the torn flesh of its wrist.

Hæra groaned. She kept digging, her hands slipping through the slimy earth in search of more—perhaps the trow was still alive here, somehow, with only his hand cut off? Her fingertips pushed into something soft that wasn't mud. She leaned forward and saw a thin, reddened, fatty string of something.

Intestines.

Shite. Oh shite. Hæra sat back on her heels with a cry as the wind roared around her.

How? What could have done this? The trow had powerful magic. No dog or bird of prey could have caught him. It certainly wasn't the work of a sheep or a cow. Save Jonathan and Madeleine, no human knew of his existence. So what...

Lightning flashed, illuminating a patch of earth just a couple of feet away.

Hæra squinted at it, and when the light faded, lurched forward. She slid on her knees, looking for what she must not have seen, what could not be here, what must not be here.

But it was here. An indentation in the earth, followed by another, and then another. The first few were shaped like human footprints. Then they began to change shape, into prints that were larger, but heavier and rounded, with a pointed tip.

In the darkness, with her enhanced vision blurred, Hæra stared down at a hoofprint with a sharp edge. She looked at the trow's severed hand and ripped-out guts. She smelled the blood. And then she knew.

CHAPTER THIRTY-SIX

Madeleine hated storms.

She wasn't one to hide from the sound of thunder, but she did brace herself against power outages and structural damage. And, of course, she prayed for everyone's safety. Coming from New Orleans, she knew about the power of wind and rain, but there hadn't been anything in the cottage she could use to board up the windows. She had, however, filled the bathtub with water. Reflex.

Hæra had told her, weeks ago, that Ætlaquoy had nothing to fear from storms because of the little trow in his mound. She brought him food, and his magic kept the farm safe. It sounded like an unequal bargain to Madeleine: daily breakfast for the protection of an entire property? But Hæra had assured Madeleine that it was enough for the trow; he wanted the respect signified by a daily offering. His kind, Hæra said, were big on offerings. "And," she'd added, "I think he likes being seen for what he is instead of having to hide."

Now, as Madeleine sat on the cottage couch while the wind howled outside, she looked at her hands. Hæra had wanted her to meet the trow, and she'd wanted more than that. She'd wanted Madeleine to see the unseen world from which she came, even if a trow and an *Each-uisge* were very different creatures.

Tomorrow morning, Madeleine would. It was past time. Hæra had been patient with her, more than she was about pretty much anything else. If Madeleine wanted to keep leaning into doubt as a way to reshape her faith—and herself—then she'd better put her money where her mouth was. Even if the idea made her stomach squirm with apprehension.

The current state of affairs wasn't likely to calm her down. Summer days in Orkney were long, and it was just the early evening, but the storm clouds had turned the sky as black as night.

Thunder clapped outside, loudly enough that she gasped. Moments later, lightning flashed beyond the rain-hammered windows. Good Lord, it *was* starting to sound like a hurricane. Much worse than the forecast had said.

Hæra was still out there.

Madeleine's heart thumped unpleasantly. Hæra was supernaturally strong, but she wasn't proof against a lightning bolt. She hadn't said where she was going or how long it would take for her to return. She'd left on the Gator, which could easily get stuck. Or, given how Hæra drove, it could turn right over.

Madeleine pulled out her phone. She'd call. Cell reception on Jorsay wasn't the best, but she had to try.

No bars. Madeleine stared at the display. *No* reception? The storm must have taken out a tower somewhere.

"Shoot," she muttered as she hurried to the kitchen. The landline phone was mounted to the wall by the back door. She couldn't reach Hæra's cell, but she could at least call the house, where Hæra might be taking shelter instead. If not, Jonathan would pick up, and he might at least know where she'd gone.

Then, as Madeleine was only a few feet away from the phone, the power went out.

The cottage darkened. The rattling radiator quieted. The only sound came from the wind, rain, and thunder. Madeleine didn't have the fire going yet, and there was no light source.

If this was what the trow's protection brought during a storm, Madeleine hated to think how bad things would be without it. She used her phone's flashlight to make her way to the landline without stubbing her toe on anything.

It's only the dark, she told herself. *Nothing's here that wasn't here before. You just can't see it as well.*

Her parents had always warned her and David that talking on the phone during a thunderstorm could get you electrocuted. She'd take the risk, she thought, as she fumbled the receiver from the cradle and held it to her ear.

As her finger hovered over the buttons, she froze. No dial tone.

That shouldn't be. Landlines were supposed to work even during power outages. At least, they did in the US. Was it different out here? Something to do with being on an island?

Regardless, neither of her phones worked. She was stuck here alone in the dark, and she'd be an idiot to go outside in this weather just to get some company, as if she were a frightened child.

Lightning flashed. The sudden brilliance summoned her gaze to the nearest window, the one over the kitchen sink.

A gigantic horse looked back at her.

The shriek was barely out of her mouth when the lightning faded, and it was dark outside the window once more. Her heart jumped into overdrive nevertheless. She stared at the panes. Had she imagined that?

Had it been Hæra?

Madeleine's hands trembled. Now was a fine time for Hæra to show off her horse form again: without any warning, in the middle of a tempest, scaring Madeleine half to death. Then again, maybe it was safer for her in the storm, in that shape? She might be more resilient, except...what was it Hæra had said?

Storms come from Stormhorses. Each-uisge *who grow wings and unleash their power.*

She'd also said, *If my herd saw me, and it was easy to catch me, my life would be forfeit.*

Hæra would never wander around during a storm in her true form. Or her human form, for that matter, although she said only three *Each-uisge* would recognize it: the herd's Sire, her mother, and her brother. So what in the world had just looked at Madeleine through the window?

She heard a noise outside, loud enough to be heard even over the wind.

A neigh.

Not like any horse's neigh she knew, though. It was low-pitched but hideous in its volume. As if it had come from enormous lungs. She'd never thought a neigh could sound *menacing* before.

Her flashlight guided her toward the sink. Seriously, was she imagining things? Or *was* Hæra foolish enough to walk around in her true shape? If so, she'd better get in here. Madeleine could give her a piece of her mind, then kiss her, then say she was absolutely ecstatic to meet the trow. She'd do anything Hæra needed her to do, because they were in each other's keeping. Just as long as Hæra was safe.

Getting near a window was something else you weren't supposed to do during a storm, but she'd thrown out so many commonsense rules by now. What was one more?

Thunder clapped so loudly that she cringed. It sounded as if it were directly above the cottage roof. She found the edge of the sink with her hands and leaned forward toward the window. Nothing but darkness and barely visible streaks of rain on the glass.

Mere seconds after the thunderclap, lightning struck again—a bolt striking the ground itself within easy view of the kitchen window. By itself, that would have been enough to frighten Madeleine, but tonight she could only stare at the horse that did, indeed, stand on the other side of the glass.

She only saw it for a few seconds. But that was more than enough time to know it wasn't Hæra.

It was huge, bigger even than Hæra had been on the shore. It was black, where Hæra had been pale. Its eyes were—oh, she must be imagining this, she absolutely must—*red*.

The lightning faded. Spots danced before her eyes. She blinked, readjusting to the darkness even as her soul began gibbering in terror.

The neigh, again. Even darker and deeper than before.

Not Hæra. One of Hæra's kin, an *Each-uisge*. It had to be. And probably not here for a friendly reunion with a long-lost member of the herd.

She stepped back from the window. Her knees weren't steady. It was so dark in here, and she was all alone. Meanwhile, Hæra was out there somewhere—

Wasn't she? Had she already been found by the other ones, however many had come here? Was she dead?

Dead, Madeleine lunged back toward the window, *she can't be dead*, Madeleine grabbed the sink, *not dead*, Madeleine leaned forward until her breath fogged up the glass, *Hæra can't be dead, I would feel it*. She would say so, yell it loud enough to be heard on the other side. She would make that horrible horse tell her that Hæra was alive.

Lightning flashed again. Cloud-to-cloud this time. There was nothing on the other side of the window.

Madeleine clung to the counter. Outside, the wind and the rain began to lessen—the storm must be passing, and quickly. Did that mean the Stormhorses had found Hæra and taken what they'd come for?

Oh God, if only she could call the main house! Why wasn't the landline working? Had that creature out there cut the line to the box? That couldn't be. How in the world would it know what a phone line even was? Hæra had said *Each-uisge* avoided humans unless they were preying on them.

Preying on me. Her blood turned to ice.

She strained to hear anything. The wind had gone from a shriek of rage to a low moan, as if saying, *My work here is done*. When thunder rumbled again, it sounded more distant. The sky, however, remained dark.

Otherwise, everything was silent except for the percussive slam of Madeleine's own heart.

Until the creature neighed again.

Madeleine whirled on her heel. The sound had come from the left. She stared at the curtains hiding the nearest window in that direction, just as lightning flashed again.

On the other side of the pale curtains stood a giant horse's silhouette.

Madeleine could barely breathe.

The horse moved on as the lightning faded. It walked slowly, taking its time.

Madeleine, biting her lip against a groan of fear, looked at the front door. She'd left it unlocked for Hæra. Not that it mattered, right? Horses couldn't unlock doors.

But this was not a horse. This was a creature out of myth, and it could take a human shape, with human hands.

The thought was enough to unfreeze Madeleine's knees. She sprinted toward the door. Every foot seemed like a mile, and every second she expected the door to open and a human-that-wasn't to be on the other side, ready to tear her into pieces.

It didn't happen. She reached the door and turned the lock. There. Now she had to get to the back door. Both doors were made of thick, heavy wood—even an *Each-uisge* wouldn't be able to shove them open easily.

But just as Madeleine turned on her heel to race to the back door, a voice spoke.

"Come out, little sister."

She froze.

"It's been too long. Don't you want to see your family?"

The voice was deep, masculine, and unearthly. It resounded with an echo no human voice could, and it could only belong to one creature.

Asgall said, *"It's dead, you know. The trow. I ate most of it in just a few bites. No more magical protection for you, although you might have guessed that by now."*

Madeleine shuddered. Yes, on some level, she had guessed.

"Madeleine?"

She hadn't been ready to hear her own name in that voice, sinister as a cold hand in the dark. She gasped.

"If my sister's too cowardly to come out of her own accord, perhaps you

could encourage her? Perhaps you could tell her that if she comes out, I will spare you."

Oh God. Oh God. Madeleine stumbled backward a step, and then she turned and dashed to the back door.

Even as she did, she heard hooves pounding the ground outside of the cottage in the same direction. Asgall must have heard her moving inside—of course he did, *Each-uisge* had supernatural hearing, and she wasn't being quiet—he was keeping pace with her. He was so fast, would he actually beat her to the back door?

Madeleine slammed her body, shoulder first, against the door as she threw the bolt—the new, sturdy iron bolt Hæra had installed only a couple of weeks ago.

Asgall's steps came to a stop on the other side. She'd barely made it. The door seemed to be the only thing keeping her upright.

He'd answered one question. Hæra was alive, or at least he hadn't killed her. Apparently he'd do Madeleine no such courtesy.

Hail Mary, full of grace. Her lips moved silently around the familiar words even as she trembled from head to toe. *Pray for us sinners now and at the hour of our death.*

"Hello, Madeleine."

His voice might have been right in her ear. Madeleine stepped back from the door, her eyes going to the glass panels at her eye height. There were only four of them, and they were small—not enough to break and get into the cottage. They were, however, large enough to see the horse's eyes looking right at her.

"She's not in there, is she?"

Madeleine and Asgall stared at each other. Her mouth was as dry as if she'd swallowed half the ocean.

"She'd come out if she were. She cannot allow another to hurt you. I heard what she said to you on the shore."

What?

"I'm there fairly often, you know. It's not difficult to conceal myself. I saw her standing before you in her true form as well, on another night. Ready to push you into the sea, drown you, and eat you."

Madeleine shook her head mutely. Hæra would never have done that, she'd said so.

"*Ah. She's never told you about that? She must have forgotten.*" His rumbling voice growled with scorn. "*Perhaps she was too busy learning about* love."

Oh Lord. He *had* been there; he'd seen and heard everything. Were those the only times they'd been spied on?

Hæra had been reluctant to walk on the shore but had convinced herself otherwise, for Madeleine's sake. Madeleine should have paid attention to Hæra's instincts, not her own.

She kept looking into his eyes. Maybe that was wrongheaded—he might take it as a challenge—but this *thing* had tried to kill Hæra and might be set on doing it again. She wasn't about to cower before him. "What do you want from us?"

Asgall's laugh had no joy in it, but it was a nightmare breed of horse and man, both of them cruel. "*You say, 'us.' As if you share the same life. As if you understand what she wants.*"

Madeleine lifted her chin. Just because his words were confident didn't mean they were right. "I'm pretty sure I understand Hæra more than you do. It seems you weren't exactly close."

"*True. She was always a fool. Why our father indulged her, I'll never know.*" Asgall slowly backed away from the door. One step, two, three. Was he leaving? Would that be a good thing, or was he going to find Hæra?

Either way, it gave Madeleine a better look at him as the sky began to lighten in the storm's retreat. His hide seemed to shift from black to dark blue, depending on how he moved. His head was longer than Hæra's, his body larger by several…inches, or whatever you used to measure horses, she didn't remember, she couldn't remember anything.

"*Still,*" he continued, "*we had something in common. A desire to take flight and unleash the storm.*" His dark tail swished. "*Did she tell you about the Stormhorses?*"

Madeleine swallowed. "Yes. I take it that some of them just passed overhead?"

"You take it correctly." When Madeleine flinched, he snorted again. *"Calm yourself. Calder died several tides ago. None of the others save our mother know her human form."*

"You never told them?" she asked in astonishment. "Not you or your mother? And…isn't it a risk for you to come on land too, if they could see you from the sky?"

"My mother's motives are her own. As for me—some chances are worth taking, as is cloud cover. Why should I want anyone else to have what is mine? That's something else Hæra understands."

Jonathan had told Madeleine that some things were put into your keeping. He'd been right. "We both understand it." She thought of Hæra's family savaging her, how lonely Hæra had been in the herd. "Better than your kind ever could."

Asgall tilted his head. His eyes held an uncanny intelligence. No one could ever mistake him for an ordinary horse. *"So,"* he said, *"she is not 'my kind' any longer?"*

"You should go," Madeleine said, shaking. "The storm's passed. Someone might see you. You should go back to the sea and leave us alone. We're not hurting anyone!"

"Not hurting *anyone?"* His lips pulled back. His teeth were bigger than Hæra's too, and just as pointed. Made to rend flesh and scale. *"A human would think so. It's time for my sister to pay me back. Tonight, I'll finally take what I want."*

Madeleine's fists clenched. "And what is—"

"After I take what she wants, first."

He turned around and kicked the door with his hind legs, so hard the wood groaned as if he'd knocked the breath out of it. The cottage itself seemed to shake. The whole door shuddered with the first kick, and a long crack appeared with the second. The new, strong iron hinge on the door creaked and began to bend.

Madeleine fled, although there wasn't anywhere to go. She could hide in the bedroom, but that door was much flimsier, and he'd find her right away—it would gain her a few seconds, perhaps. It'd be even more useless to run outside, where he'd chase her down in moments.

There was a block of knives in the kitchen. Shaking and hot with adrenaline, she grabbed the butcher knife. Why did she have to shake? Wasn't adrenaline supposed to make you strong and sure, like those stories of women picking up cars to save a child? Madeleine had the wrong kind of adrenaline. She was about to rattle into pieces.

Asgall kicked again, and his back hooves appeared through a crack in the wood. His next blow would finish the door.

Madeleine backed away, holding out the knife with both hands, for all the good it'd do her. She'd be lucky to get within striking distance before he cut her down. Would he make it quick? Or would she suffer as he ripped her limb from limb? *Hail Mary, full of grace—*

Someone screamed outside.

It was so wild and loud that Madeleine dropped the knife. That wasn't a human scream, but an animal cry of fury, and again, she heard something galloping around the cottage.

Hæra.

"Oh God." Madeleine grabbed the knife, her hand shaking so badly she almost dropped it again. "Oh God, oh God."

Moments later, Hæra cried out again, wordlessly: a ringing bell of challenge that Asgall answered with his own bellow. Madeleine dashed to the door, in which Asgall had kicked a substantial hole. She looked through to see Hæra and Asgall facing each other on their hind legs, their front hooves kicking the air. They hadn't made contact yet. Maybe it was just posturing, Hæra warning Asgall away. Maybe he'd come to his senses and actually go.

Asgall lunged, so quickly Madeleine could barely track it. His hooves struck Hæra's chest and she staggered backward, turning enough to show he'd drawn blood. Their hooves must be sharp as razors, just like their teeth, they could hurt each other so badly, he could hurt Hæra so badly—

"Please," Madeleine moaned, to any god out there who might listen. "Please, no."

Hæra shrieked and turned around. When Asgall immediately went for her hindquarters, she kicked backward. He staggered, and Hæra whipped back around, snapping at his neck. She must have bitten him; he yowled. When she darted away before he could bite her too, her muzzle was bloody.

The siblings circled each other, snarling and panting, going up and down on their hind legs. Air steamed from their nostrils. Asgall's eyes flashed red in his dark face, and Hæra's eyes glowed golden as the sun. They were massive in their size and power as they attacked each other again, and this time, Asgall got his teeth in Hæra's mane, between her shoulders.

Then everything happened fast. Hæra shrieked again and butted him with her head, but it was too late. Asgall bowled her over, pushing her down to the ground on her side. Then he was atop her, his teeth fastened to the back of her neck while she screamed and kicked him. She drew more blood from his hide, but it wasn't enough. He was too big, too furious.

Madeleine yanked the door handle. Why wasn't it opening? Oh, right, she'd thrown the bolt, Asgall hadn't broken that, she had to unlock it, had to rush out there with her pathetic knife and do *something*.

Asgall didn't look up when she charged through the door. He was focused on Hæra. Maybe Madeleine could get in one stab or something—or at least startle him so he'd pull away—

"Stop!"

Madeleine turned. Jonathan was running toward them, his gait unsteady and effortful. Maybe that was because he was clutching a shotgun across his chest.

They used a gun to put down sheep, she remembered dizzily. Connor had told her that. She hadn't wanted to think about it.

Asgall cried out. Jonathan's arrival must have distracted him, and Hæra had bitten his neck. When he reared back, she rolled up and slammed her head into him, driving him away enough that she could stagger to her feet.

Asgall backed away, looking at her, his teeth bared. Hæra lowered her head, clearly ready to charge again.

"I said *stop!*" Jonathan yelled, as he came to a stop himself, by the corner of the cottage. His face was red, and his chest heaved. "The both of you! Stop!"

Asgall took one step backward, and then another, looking back and forth between Hæra and Jonathan.

Hæra remained still. Her legs shook, and she seemed to be keeping weight off the front left one. She bled from her back, where he must have sunk his teeth in. And he'd rolled her over, leaned on top of her with his weight—had he broken any of her ribs?

Whatever he'd done, she was hurt, that was clear. Otherwise, she'd ignore Jonathan's order not to attack. Madeleine could feel the rage coming from her, had heard it in every snarl and scream.

Asgall's rage, however, seemed to have banked. He seemed, moreover, to have forgotten Hæra existed. He looked only at Jonathan, who looked back at him, bent over and breathing heavily.

"Leave her be," Jonathan said between gasps. "Leave us all. Oh fuck, it's really you. I knew it—the lights went out, and somehow I knew—" He groaned. "Fuck off. Go."

"Why would you say that?" Asgall asked. He was panting too. *"When you've called to me for so long?"*

Madeleine's mouth fell open, because that could only mean one thing. *Asgall* was the *Each-uisge* Jonathan had known? Hæra's own brother? Why had neither of them told her that?

Jonathan shook his head. The rain came down on his jacket, on his bare head. It soaked into Madeleine's hair and clothes too. "It's you who's been calling me. Haven't you? With the dreams? The other day, I woke up standing outside—because I heard a voice, I heard your bloody voice."

Asgall pawed the mud with one hoof. *"We call to one another—you and I. It's always so when our kind bonds with yours. I expect my sister and her victim are the same."*

"Victim?" Madeleine blurted.

"She's not," Jonathan said. He hefted the shotgun and cradled it to his chest, not aiming it. It looked heavy in his arms. "Hæra's not you, and Madeleine's not me, and I won't let you hurt them. I'll shoot you first. I swear to Christ I will."

Asgall laughed. It sounded as awful as the first time. *"Madeleine isn't like you? So my sister never told you the truth. Of course she didn't."*

"Shut up," Hæra snarled. *"Get out before he kills you or you're seen. Or don't you care anymore about exposing the herd?"*

"A fine accusation for you to make. How many lies have you told them about us?" Asgall turned to Madeleine. *"Let's find out."*

"Shut up!" Hæra repeated. *"Madeleine, go back inside!"*

"I won't leave you," Madeleine said hoarsely. Something pressed against her chest, and she realized she was clutching the butcher knife there with both hands, just as Jonathan held his shotgun. "I'm not afraid of what you are. You can—you can—" She clutched the knife even tighter. "You can change in front of me, you can do anything, I don't care. Just as soon as he's gone."

"What's going to chase me away?" Now Asgall's voice was low, mocking. *"That mighty blade of yours? The truth will cut you worse."*

"Hæra's told me the truth." Even though Madeleine's courage was arriving later than she'd have liked it to—probably because someone was here with a gun—at least it had come. "I know everything."

"Madeleine," Hæra said.

"Everything," Asgall repeated. *"Like the Stormhorses."*

"Like the Stormhorses," Madeleine said between her teeth. "And I've kept it to myself, because I'd *never* betray—"

"And how I want to be one—as does she?" Asgall looked at Jonathan. *"Do you know how Stormhorses come to be?"*

Hæra tried to charge Asgall again, but she staggered and groaned. How could they treat her injuries once Asgall finally left? Because he had to leave, with Jonathan's shotgun, with the danger of discovery. But afterward, Madeleine and Jonathan couldn't exactly call a veterinarian. If Hæra changed back into her human form, what would happen to her wounds?

"Get out," Jonathan said, but he still didn't point the gun at anything. "Go back to the sea, you bastard, you're the one who tells lies—you told me nothing but lies!"

Asgall bared his sharp teeth. *"I told you lies and truths then, when you were beautiful. Now you're a pitiful old..."* He stomped his front hoof again and shook his head wildly. *"A pitiful old man, I thought I saw you on the shore not long ago—just wandering along, head bent, it wasn't you, but it* could *have been..."*

An old man on the shore? The memory struck Madeleine, of the day she and Hæra had spoken of seeking their truth, learning how to love in front of the whole ocean. An old man had been walking the beach alone, and yes, he'd reminded her of Jonathan. She said, "That's why you were there? You thought you saw him?"

Asgall stared at her, and his frame shuddered. For a moment it seemed he would charge her, and Hæra took an unsteady step toward him again, groaning.

He didn't charge, but turned his attention back to Hæra. *"I saw you, sister,"* he said, roughly, as if there were barnacles in his throat. *"Standing on the shore in your true shape. I returned again and again, to see if—to find out if he, too, would"* —he looked at Jonathan— *"but he didn't. Just you and her. And you spoke of love."*

"What do you know about love," Jonathan said raggedly.

Asgall looked at him for a long, sharp moment before speaking. *"An* Each-uisge *becomes a Stormhorse by eating a human of great worth. He was my human, or should have been. Not now, when he is...this."*

Unable to help herself, Madeleine looked at Jonathan, whose shoulders slumped, face slack with misery.

"And you are hers," Asgall told Madeleine. *"My sister's way to her wings. Or so she believes—"*

"Kill him!" Hæra cried out. *"Jonathan, kill him!"*

Jonathan stayed still. He stared at Asgall as if nothing else existed, and he made no move to aim the shotgun.

"She wants to be the first female Stormhorse, and she'll kill you to get it. She'll drag you into the sea and eat everything but your liver."

Madeleine might drop this knife if she couldn't keep her hands steady. Nothing but lies, Jonathan had just said. Asgall only told lies. Hæra would never hurt her, she'd sworn it. How many times had she acted to protect Madeleine, starting on the night they met?

Except—just last night, Hæra sucking her finger, seeking her blood—

"She saved my life." Madeleine's voice shook. "She could have drowned me instead, and she didn't. I think that proves you wrong. Hæra? Tell him."

Hæra's head swung low. Her body swayed a little too. Was she going to collapse?

"Yes, sister. Tell me," Asgall said encouragingly. He could easily attack Hæra now and make an end of her in front of Madeleine's eyes. Jonathan still wasn't doing anything with the shotgun. But Asgall stood quite still before his sister, and Madeleine knew he'd try to destroy her with his words instead.

He couldn't do that, though, could he? Not if Hæra was innocent. His accusations couldn't hurt her or any of them. Hæra only had to deny it.

"Tell us all that I'm lying," Asgall said. *"Or even mistaken. After all, you and I never spoke of this. You held your secret dear. I'm only guessing—and possibly I'm wrong. Say you never intended to devour your Madeleine so you could take to the skies. Swear to it."*

Blood dripped down Hæra's sides from the bite Asgall had given her back. Maybe that's why she wasn't instantly denying what he said. She would, though. Of course she'd say Asgall was lying. She'd wanted to connect with Madeleine, explore the bond between them, as she'd sworn so many times.

Just say it. She only had to say it.

"Kill him," Hæra said. *"Jonathan, please."*

Madeleine's heart grew cold. Colder even than when Asgall had stalked her in the cottage.

In her peripheral vision, Jonathan finally took a step forward. Then another. He looked unsteady in the mud. His face had gone from red to pale, white to the lips. "Lass?" he said, looking at Hæra. "It's not true, is it?"

Hæra lunged toward Asgall, if you could call it that. Her bite would have been more of a nip if it had landed, which it didn't. She was too far away, and Asgall only laughed, even as blood turned patches of his own hide even darker.

"And you came back for more," he said to Madeleine. *"You couldn't help*

yourself, could you? Even after so short an encounter, you were bound to her. You had to return, just as this one"—he looked at the gaping Jonathan—*"can never leave me."*

Jonathan's gaze went slowly back and forth between Hæra and Asgall like a pendulum.

Madeleine's voice finally dragged itself out of hell. She croaked, "Hæra? He's lying, isn't he?"

If Hæra said yes, Madeleine would believe her. Even now, when the depth of her soul knew Asgall spoke the truth. Denial was the most wretched, impoverished face of love.

Hæra turned to look back at Madeleine. Her yellow eyes were dull with pain and with something else, something Madeleine recognized all too well.

Confession.

Madeleine had brought the knife with her to use in Hæra's defense. Now it fell from her nerveless hands. Hæra watched it fall. Her head lowered again, and she swung it back toward Asgall, though she faced the ground. Then she bowed forward, going down on her front knees, and lowered her head until her muzzle touched the ground. *"Finish me,"* she said. *"I can't make it to the witch."*

The witch? Hæra had only ever told Madeleine about one witch, the one at the bottom of a whirlpool who'd taken pity on Hæra and flung her ashore to save her. Hæra had never said why she'd done it, just acted as if it was a random act of mercy. Then she'd dreamed of her, and Madeleine had dismissed it as a nightmare. Was that the witch she meant?

If Asgall knew, he didn't seem to care. He opened his mouth, and saliva stretched between his teeth, as if he meant to strain his sister's blood through it.

For a blighted, blistering moment, Madeleine wanted him to. In the next moment, she opened her mouth to scream in protest.

"You'll die with her, then."

Madeleine turned so quickly that her wet hair smacked her cheek. Jonathan had finally raised the shotgun and was aiming it straight at

Asgall. The barrel held steady, not shaking a bit. "Piss off before I shoot you between the eyes."

Asgall backed up and lowered his head like a bull about to charge. *"You cannot. You'll never bring yourself to do it. No more than I..."*

He trailed off, but Jonathan seemed to know what he'd meant. Now the shotgun wavered.

"I spent too much time with you," Asgall spat. *"You made me weak. It won't happen again. Lower the gun, you sad old man, and let me give her what she deserves. She deceived you worse than I ever did."*

Jonathan set his jaw and hefted the gun more firmly. "Then she'll answer to us, not you. I said go."

Asgall pawed the earth, drawing ruts in the mud. *"She said she loved you. I heard her!"* His voice had lost its superior, mocking edge. *"Do you actually believe it?"*

"You don't know what love is!" Jonathan's shout was another thunderclap, as shocking as the one that had hit just over the cottage. For a moment, his eyes flashed like lightning too. "I knew the second you dragged me into the water! And for *that*? To shit out lightning?"

"To fly," Asgall said. *"You'd have been part of that. You'd have flown with me."*

Hæra cried out softly when he said that.

"You bastard." Jonathan's chest heaved. "You ruined me. Years I've spent thinking—no, decades—" He stabbed the gun's muzzle forward. "You took decades from me, the two of you stole my whole fucking *life*, didn't you? Mine, and hers too."

He glanced at Madeleine, who could neither move nor speak. Hæra, still kneeling, groaned.

"Stole *your life? You dare say that?"* Asgall's voice rose with new fury. *"When I let you keep it? I could have—"* He went up a little on his hind legs, as if preparing to fight again.

Jonathan said nothing, but his eyes closed, and he pressed his lips into a thin line.

"I still can," Asgall rasped. *"I will, you pathetic—you wasted what I gave you."* He looked down at Hæra. *"As soon as I finish this business first. The new Sire will reward me for it. For all three of you. I'm sure of it."*

He rose up again on his hind legs, higher this time, and poised right over Hæra. When he brought his hooves down, he'd crush her head.

"No," Madeleine cried, as if that'd help anything, "no, stop—"

The gun's percussive roar split the air worse than the loudest thunderclap. Madeleine cried out, and Asgall staggered backward as dark liquid bloomed on his chest.

Smoke drifted from the double barrels of Jonathan's gun. The barrels trembled. His eyes were wild.

Asgall groaned and stepped back again. Blood dripped from where Jonathan had shot him. Was it near any vital organs? Where did *Each-uisge* keep their hearts?

"You'll need...more than that." Asgall's head dipped before he raised it again, as if with great effort.

"I've got it." Jonathan's voice was thick. "Have you?"

Asgall bared his teeth again and looked at Jonathan with flashing eyes. Would Jonathan be able to shoot him again? He seemed reluctant, as if he couldn't understand the danger they were all in.

Madeleine had grown up with the Ten Commandments, including: *You shall not kill.* But if she had the gun and knew how to fire it, she'd break that one. "He killed the trow," she heard herself say. "The trow that protected the farm."

"I noticed," Jonathan said. "Everything looks proper fucked. I expect that was your plan," he added to Asgall.

"You..." Asgall stepped backward unsteadily. *"You have no idea what I've done. The lengths I've gone to."*

"I know you've been creeping 'round the place at night in the man's skin you wore to fool me. I knew it was you, I just couldn't face it." Jonathan bared his teeth too. "Even the dogs didn't bark."

"They knew better." Asgall's breathing was labored. *"Well? End it, then."*

The gun shook in Jonathan's hands.

"Hæra and I both betrayed you," Asgall said. *"We both intended to slay those who only sought to love us. This is your moment, old man. Have your revenge."*

Jonathan looked at Madeleine then, for some reason.

Hæra sank lower to the ground, bleeding from the wound on her back.

"Not her," Madeleine choked. They couldn't kill Hæra. The thought turned Madeleine's bones to lead. She'd come all this way to find her angel, find her answer, and even if that answer was full of lies and bleeding in the mud, they couldn't kill her.

In the distance came the sound of a motor. A car. No doubt Jim or Connor, coming to check on the farm.

"Get out," Jonathan said again to Asgall. He waved the gun, his face haggard. "Now."

Asgall's head turned toward the sound of the motor. He looked again at Jonathan, at the pointed gun.

Then he turned and loped away with an uneven gait, a smudge of darkness against the green field. White sheep cried out and scattered before him in panic. Some of the sheep, Madeleine saw now, lay dead on the ground. That lightning strike, maybe.

We've never lost an animal in a storm, Connor had bragged to Madeleine once.

The motor sounded louder. It'd be at the head of the driveway now. From the driveway's angle, a driver wouldn't be able to see behind the cottage, but there was no time to waste.

Madeleine nevertheless stood frozen, looking at Hæra slumped on the ground. Blood wasn't gouting out of her, exactly, but it came in a steady stream.

Jonathan kept his eyes on Asgall until he was out of sight. Then he cursed, set down the gun, and went to Hæra. His gait looked none too steady either. His motion snapped Madeleine out of her trance, and she hurried forward too, until she could kneel in front of Hæra.

Hæra's mouth hung open as she breathed too slowly. Asgall's blood covered her muzzle and sharp teeth. Her yellow eyes were dull, and she didn't seem to see Madeleine properly.

"Lass." Jonathan knelt too, with more effort and a groan. "Change back. Hurry. They'll be here soon."

"What happens to her wounds?" Madeleine demanded. If they got worse when Hæra transformed…

"They turn into the human version. I think?" Jonathan rubbed a hand over his forehead. "That's what happened after she washed up on shore. Hæra, change, we'll take you to Sue." When Hæra said nothing, he grabbed a hank of her mane and tugged. "For God's sake! Can you hear me?"

"Change," Hæra said slowly. *"Yes."*

She rolled slowly on her side, the one without the bite. A pained whinny escaped her anyway. Madeleine held her breath and waited for the transformation to begin. What would change first? Would Hæra's long *Each-uisge* face become her inhuman human one?

If it did, then she'd become the Hæra Madeleine knew. She could explain everything. In spite of everything Asgall had said, maybe there was still some misunderstanding.

Hæra's hind legs quivered. She pressed them together. They seemed suddenly to fuse into one shape. The hooves began to lengthen.

They spread out into two fins.

Her hide changed too. As Madeleine stared, Hæra's bottom half turned from flesh to scale, her powerful hind legs becoming a fish tail.

"Oh God," Jonathan choked. "Like him…like he was…"

"Yes." Hæra lay in the mud, her tail flopping weakly, as if she'd been caught in a net and dragged onto the deck of a ship. *"This is what we are."* She turned her head with a groan and looked into Madeleine's eyes. *"This is what I am."*

Wrong, Madeleine wanted to protest, *you're the woman who kissed me on the beach, you're the woman I left my whole life for, you're the woman I—*

"No more lies." Hæra tossed her head, dragging her mane in the dirt. *"I was going to—what he said. I was going to kill you."*

No.

Madeleine stared into Hæra's pleading eyes. They weren't human eyes, not with how they rolled in distress. They weren't horse eyes either, not with their supernatural intelligence.

She said slowly, "You were going to kill me."

Hæra made a low, pained sound. *"Yes."*

Madeleine clutched her wet sweater. She had to be missing something. "But you saved me."

"Hang on," Jonathan said, his voice strained. "She should change back to human, we should talk inside—"

"No!" Madeleine leaned forward, on her hands and knees, getting mud everywhere. "You saved me on the night we met!"

"You saved me first." Hæra rubbed the side of her head into the ground. *"As you said yourself, you set me free. I was in your debt. I paid you back. And then..."*

And then the debt was paid, and Hæra had owed Madeleine nothing else. She was free to—to—

"Eat me," Madeleine managed. "You were going to *eat* me. This whole time I've been here—that was your plan?"

All their nights together, the way Hæra loved to nibble and suck at Madeleine's skin, how she whispered that she wanted to eat Madeleine alive. How she'd licked the blood from her finger. It had felt so good, and it had only been a poor substitute for something else.

For what Hæra had wanted all along.

"At first," Hæra whispered. *"At first, yes. So I could regain honor with my herd. So I could become a Stormhorse."*

Jonathan cursed again. Madeleine fell on her bottom and scooted away from the monster in the mud.

"But I couldn't." Hæra's voice rose into a plea. *"Didn't you see, that night I found you on the beach? I couldn't do it. I couldn't hurt you. I'll never hurt you...I swear it on the Great Mare, on all the tides..."*

Madeleine couldn't go back into the cottage. Not the place where she and Hæra had lain in each other's arms for so many nights now after Madeleine had thrown aside the teachings that had defined her life. She couldn't stay here either.

Madeleine rose to her feet. She had to leave.

"Wait," Hæra moaned. *"I'm not just this."*

She closed her eyes and seemed to concentrate. Her fish tail split again and took the shape, not of horse legs, but human ones. Her body shrank, her barrel chest slimmed down and grew two breasts, and her front legs became her muscular arms. Before Madeleine lay the naked form she'd enjoyed for weeks, but bleeding and bruised.

Asgall's blood still covered Hæra's mouth from nose to chin. "I'm also this." Hæra's voice was now the one Madeleine knew, even if it was rough with pain. "Please, I'm sorry, I'm—I'm also *this*, and you love me like this, don't you? You love me." Her voice rose again, cracked with desperation. "I know you love me!"

The truth will cut you worse, Asgall had said. "I—I—"

"And I love you." Hæra held out a hand to her. It trembled. "I know what that means now, I understand, I won't hurt you—"

Madeleine turned. Her feet carried her with more speed than she'd have thought possible under the circumstances. She'd grown stronger while working the farm. She ran across the wet fields while Hæra's anguished cries faded behind her.

She didn't know where she was headed. She'd just go until her legs wouldn't carry her for another step, or until she reached the cliffs, the land ended, and there was only the sea. The sea where Hæra had meant to drown Madeleine.

She had succeeded and didn't even know it. Madeleine was drowning now. There was no rescue in sight.

CHAPTER THIRTY-SEVEN

From the refuge of Madeleine's bed, Hæra dimly heard Jonathan outside the cottage ordering Jim and Connor to start inspecting the worst of the damage. Yes, he *obviously* knew about the broken cottage door, that wasn't their first concern. Hæra had been hurt in the storm and was resting inside until Sue Kilbright could get here. Naught anyone else could do. Jonathan would just tend her until help came. Madeleine? Oh. Yes. Madeleine was inside too, now he thought of it. She'd help Hæra, sure enough. Jonathan would just go inside for a few more minutes and then be along to see the wreckage.

Get on now, look to the dogs, they were in the sheep pens. Hope to Christ none were hurt, with the mad wind and that.

Never mind the gun.

His voice wove in and out of her hearing, which felt less sharp than usual. Perhaps that was because her left arm hurt so much that she couldn't pay proper attention. Asgall had injured her front left leg, and now it translated into an ache that ran from Hæra's shoulder to her wrist. Broken? Maybe.

Her heart, too.

Madeleine knew everything. And she hated Hæra for it.

The bedroom door opened and shut. Hæra blinked. When she

stopped blinking, Jonathan stood over the bed, lantern in hand. The light threw shadows into the crevasses of his face and the corners of the room. His shirt and jacket still looked damp, and his trousers were dirty from where he'd knelt in the mud. He looked exhausted and held the shotgun loosely in the other hand.

Hæra looked at it and then raised her eyes to him in silent question. She wouldn't blame him.

"Don't be daft." Jonathan propped the gun up against the wall.

"You said you would." She remembered the night Jonathan had looked at the dark computer monitor, his face blank and cold. "You said if you thought I meant Madeleine any harm, you'd..." She trailed off. Jonathan hadn't said what, specifically, he'd do.

"And do you mean her harm?"

"*No.*" She said it with a force that made her ribs hurt worse.

"Well then." Jonathan looked away, and Hæra remembered she was naked, as she'd been on the night they'd met. "I'll call Sue. Can't use my mobile, some bloody *Stormhorse* must have buggered the tower."

He took the lantern and left the room, leaving it in darkness again. Hæra looked at the wall. Her bones hurt. Beyond the bedroom, Jonathan moved around. After a moment, he called, "The landline's out. Hold on a tick."

Hæra held on a tick, and then another tick, until he came back. His face was pale as he set the lantern on the dresser. "Someone cut the wires from the phone box. No, not cut. Tore."

The implication was clear, but absurd. "How would Asgall know to do that?"

"I told him about telephones all those years ago. He was fascinated by them, how you could talk to someone on the other side of the Earth. And he's been skulking about the place for weeks. Must've figured it out." Jonathan rubbed his hands over his face. "Clever bastard. Never forgot a thing I said. Nobody ever listened to me like he did."

Hæra knew what Jonathan meant. She thought of how she'd hung on Madeleine's every word. That had to be different, though. She'd cared for Madeleine from the first moment. Soon, that caring had become more, something Hæra had never believed she could feel.

Asgall wasn't capable of that. He couldn't be.

"Years ago," she rasped, "on the night my family attacked me... before that, we were sitting out there at the kitchen table, and you asked if my kind could..."

"Wait," Jonathan said sharply. "Tell me what hurts worst."

Where to begin? Oh. He meant her body. She said, "My left arm. Mainly my wrist, I think."

Jonathan winced. "Yeah, that's a funny angle. Hold your arm up, and I'll get some ice, it should still be frozen. Then..." He pinched the bridge of his nose as if he had a headache. "We'll clean you up. Put you in some of her clothes. Get you back to the main house, and if he didn't cut that fucking landline too, I can call..."

They looked at each other, realizing at the same moment that Asgall had definitely cut that fucking landline too.

Jonathan swore and stormed out of the bedroom. When he returned, he held a plastic bag full of ice, along with a washcloth.

Hæra gingerly held the ice to her wrist. The sharp cold, which normally wouldn't trouble her, stung. It should slow the swelling, at least.

Madeleine had ibuprofen in the bathroom, but human medicine never had much of an effect on Hæra. That wasn't the only difference, though. After she'd washed up on Jorsay, Jonathan had hustled her out of the doctor's office as quickly as possible, but Sue Kilbright had noticed how fast she'd begun to heal.

While Hæra held the ice bag, Jonathan wiped Asgall's blood from her face. Then he looked at the red-black smears on the cloth without saying anything.

"That night, you asked me if I was in love with Madeleine," Hæra said. "You asked if it could happen so quickly to my kind."

Jonathan closed his eyes. His face screwed up as if he were about to weep.

"Did you..." He'd told Hæra that, on their last day together, Asgall had taken on human form. "Did you and he..."

"Don't," Jonathan choked. "Fuck's sake, don't ask, or I'll go as far as I need to for a drink."

By now, she knew Jonathan better than to take that as a yes, as it might have been for another human. He might mean yes, he and Asgall had lain together on that day. He might mean no, and the possibility now was too much for him to bear.

They sat together in silence. Hæra could think of nothing to say as Jonathan's shoulders rose and fell unevenly while he kept his eyes shut. His lips pressed together. A tear crept from the corner of his eye and ran down his weathered cheek into his beard.

"I'm sorry," she whispered. "Sorry for everything he did."

"Don't say that either. The hell do you know about it?" Jonathan dashed a hand across his face and wiped the tear away. He sniffled and coughed.

Fair question. Hæra knew little, only that Asgall had hurt Jonathan for decades—Jonathan had said he'd ruined his life—and she couldn't risk doing the same thing to Madeleine. She couldn't give Jonathan his life back, but she could spare the other person she loved from sharing his fate.

"You should have left me to him," she said. "Now he'll return and put you in danger."

"He was hurt too." Jonathan cleared his throat and looked at the gun again. "Next time, I'll—I'll be able to do it." The promise seemed to lack conviction. "And if he waits long enough, you'll be well enough to help me. Let's clean you up."

"If the power's out, the water is too." The farm drew its water supply from a well with an electric pump. "We can't use the reserves just to wash me."

"We need to clean this mud off your cuts. They'll have the lights back on soon, you'll see. We'll sit you on the toilet and I'll fetch enough water for you to wash."

He let her lean on his shoulders to the bathroom, but she didn't like how labored his breathing sounded. She said, "You should rest."

"With the farm in a shambles? Connor and Jim'll already be wondering what's taking me so long. Oi, is that water in the tub?"

It was. Together, Hæra and Jonathan looked at it in confusion.

"Madeleine must have filled it," Hæra said. "Why?"

Jonathan made a sound of comprehension. "To save water in case the power goes out. Which it did. Clever lass, except she ran off in the rain."

Hæra groaned as she stepped into the tub. Cool water sloshed against her calves. "I have to find her. I have to explain."

"Not until you've got some strength back." He set the lantern by the wall; shadows draped the corners of the room. "You look done in."

"That doesn't matter." Even as she said it, she swayed. She remembered their first real conversation, out by the fence on the night Madeleine had come to dinner. She'd been rude and had to say sorry afterward. This seemed like occasion for greater regret. "I need to apologize."

"Only to her?"

The quiet reproof, the pain in his voice, would have felled her if she hadn't already been sent sprawling.

Hæra lowered herself into the tub, groaning with the strain in her muscles and the burn in her wrist. She almost slipped, and she dropped the ice bag so she could catch herself on the lip of the tub with her right hand. It thumped wetly on the tile floor, and a few cubes shattered. She sat in the water, hissing at the sting in her cuts. Dried mud softened and flaked off her skin, while blood began to turn the water a cloudy red.

"I lied to you," she said, with difficulty. "For so long. Longer than he did. That makes me worse."

Jonathan gave her a washcloth, lowered the toilet lid, and sat on it. After a moment, he said, "What the hell did you mean to do, exactly?"

As she dragged the washcloth over her stinging cuts, Hæra spoke her plan aloud to another for the first time. She explained her yearning to grow wings, her desire to avoid the breeding cycle, her belief in her own destiny. To be the first female Stormhorse. To escape the sea and storm the skies. And how devouring a worthy human was the only way to do it.

"And Madeleine, your Sister Madeleine, was worthy?" Jonathan asked.

"The most worthy." Hæra looked at her bare knees, poking above the water and flecked with goosebumps. "I knew it from the moment I saw her. And when she returned—when I got to know her—I knew I was right." She shuddered. "Now I look back on it, and I don't know what I was thinking. I don't think I ever could have hurt her, not even at the start. Or maybe I could've, if I hadn't…"

"If you hadn't what?"

"Spent so long trying to understand her," Hæra said. "Coming to you and living here for years so when she finally came back…I saw her, and it was as if…" She pressed her right hand, her good one, over her heart. It didn't stop the ache.

Madeleine had looked at Hæra as if she hated her.

Jonathan didn't reply but stared into the distance. Maybe he saw Asgall there. She was almost done cleaning herself when he said abruptly, "I always wondered what you'd do when you didn't age. But all along your idea was to eat Madeleine and then grow those wings?"

"I suppose." Her wrist burned.

"So you could go back to your herd and not get killed, or have to breed and all the rest?"

Hæra swallowed. Her stomach felt as if it had another ice bag inside it. "It made sense at the time."

"Would it work?" Jonathan's gaze was suddenly, unusually sharp. "If you ate a worthy human, would they take you back? He just talked as if they would—a reward for killing the three of us."

"I-I don't know," Hæra stammered. "Nobody's ever tried. But I won't hurt Madeleine." She leaned forward; the water sloshed. "I swear it on whatever you need me to swear. I must—"

"Then eat me."

Now was not the time for Jonathan's jokes. Hæra had to find Madeleine before it was dark again, make sure she was safe, and apologize. She'd run in the opposite direction of Asgall, and Asgall was hurt, but that didn't mean she couldn't encounter some other danger.

"Very funny," she growled. She dropped the washcloth into the water with a plop. "Will you help me up? Madeleine's out there some-where in…"

Jonathan grabbed her right bicep and squeezed it, hard. He'd never done that before. "I'm serious. Look at me."

Hæra looked. She hadn't seen such a wild expression on his face since the night they'd met on the beach, when he'd been drunk and screaming for Asgall to come ashore and face him. "It'd save your life, would it? You'd go home and be all right?"

"What?"

"He must've thought I was worthy once. Am I still? He looked at me tonight the same way he did years ago, just before he tried to…" Jonathan shivered. He was red in the face. "I'm not much now, but…"

"*Eat* you?" After tonight's other events, she'd thought she could hold no more horror, but this offer… "Are you mad?"

"What about this isn't!" He let go of her arm so he could throw both hands in the air. "And what the hell else am I meant to do?"

Had tonight broken him? Had seeing Asgall done his brain in for good? "There are plenty of alternatives to being eaten!"

"Really? For me?" Jonathan leaned forward, eyes flashing. "Like what? Dribbling on myself in a care home until I'm buried and prayed over by people who don't know me?"

"Jonathan, what…"

"It's my bloody *destiny.*"

Hæra gaped at him. A purple vein pulsed at his temple, beneath his reddened skin.

"I've always known it," he said. "Ever since they pulled me up on that boat while I bled from my leg. Spent decades as a sot, dreaming of him, and then I met you that night, and I thought—here it is, it's time—"

"You thought…?"

"But it didn't happen like that. You were different from him."

Hæra hunched her shoulders. "I'm not, I…"

"*You were different,* and I thought, Maybe it's all done with, maybe it won't come to pass after all. And you know what that did?" His eyes were wide and wet. "It broke my fucking heart."

Her ears rang. She was faint. Maybe she was losing more blood than she thought. "You…want to be eaten?"

"I want to *do* something, and for him to… How many deaths mean anything? Not just pissing off one day and hoping your mates raise a glass. I haven't got mates. I've only got you and…"

Somehow, Hæra knew Jonathan wasn't going to say *and the farm* or *and Jim and Connor* or *and Madeleine* or and *the bloody sheep* or anything else that might have made sense. She knew who he meant.

"Meanwhile, you've got her," Jonathan said hoarsely.

Madeleine. Who had fled across the green fields to the depths knew where. "She hates me. She should. I don't *have* her."

"It doesn't matter if she hates you," Jonathan said raggedly. "You've got her anyway. But you could leave her be, you could give her life back. Take me with you, do what you've got to do, and go back to the sea. Get your damned wings."

The bathwater was too cold now, and her wrist ached worse. She put her right hand over her face. "Stop. No more of that nonsense. I can't think. I have to find her."

"But…"

"I said no! Forget it. That's final." Hæra stood up and nearly lost her footing. Jonathan caught her slippery arms and almost fell down himself.

"Oh hell." He sounded very tired. "You've got to lie down before you do aught else. She'll come back."

It was a titanic effort to lift one foot out of the tub onto the mat, never mind the second one. "How do you know that?"

"Because I know." He left her sitting on the toilet and returned with plasters, ointment, and bandages. "Your bleeding's already slowing down."

"I heal faster than you." The blood of her kind congealed quickly; a survival mechanism to keep predators from scenting it in the water.

"Good job nobody else saw. We've been lucky, lass." Jonathan patted the wound on her back dry with a towel while she held back a hiss of pain. "We didn't do too badly, did we? All told?"

Gently, he wrapped her wrist and dressed her other wounds as best he could. When he was done, Hæra knew she was unable to chase after Madeleine or anybody else. She could only make her way to the bed. Jonathan was right: her blood no longer soaked freshly into the bandages and plasters, but she was more exhausted than she'd been since the last time Asgall had attacked her along with her mother. What would Beathag say about all this?

Beathag wouldn't say anything. She'd just deliver the killing blow.

Jonathan pulled back the duvet, the top of which was muddy and bloody from when she'd lain on it a few minutes ago. The sheets beneath were clean. She was still naked. Her clothes and boots lay somewhere outside in the mud, shredded to bits from when she'd transformed.

Her eyelids sagged as she lay down.

No. She mustn't sleep. She had to put her body into a state of metabolic rest; she would not *sleep*. She just had to rest a little, only a little while, so she'd be strong enough to find…

"Madeleine," she groaned.

Jonathan covered her with the duvet. "Hush now. I'll tell one of the lads to look for her. She ran east."

It seemed vitally important that Jonathan understand something. Hæra's eyelids sagged even as she said, "I love her."

"Yes. You said." Jonathan sat down on the edge of the bed. Then he put a gentle hand on her shoulder.

"You'll be all right," he said.

How? she wanted to ask him, but it was too late. Her eyes closed. She was going to sleep. The last thing she knew was the warm weight of Jonathan's hand.

CHAPTER THIRTY-EIGHT

Madeleine was covered in mud.

It was nearly dry now, and it caked her shoes, the palms of her hands, and her jeans over her knees and bottom—everywhere she'd touched the wet earth when she'd knelt before Hæra. Now she was dirty all over, and there was nowhere to wash.

Whatever plumbing the neolithic Orcadians had managed was long gone.

She hadn't realized where she was going until she got here: the standing stones of Jorsay, near the most ancient human settlement in Europe. Six years ago, her students hadn't been impressed by the tiny size of the stones and settlement compared to more impressive sites on the Mainland.

Madeleine had found it interesting, although she hadn't felt any particular urge to revisit it since her return. It wasn't like Skara Brae or the Ring of Brodgar, which were well traveled and roped off. The ruins on Jorsay still felt wild, as if you could fall into trouble in some other world.

That'd suit her. It couldn't be worse than the trouble she'd found in this one. Even in the darkness, with the only light coming from her phone, this place held less horror than what she'd just left behind.

Hæra...

Her legs shook with exhaustion and her lungs ached. Had she run all this way, or at least most of it? She wasn't a runner. Her body, smarter than her brain, must really have wanted to get out of there.

With a whimper, Madeleine sat on the ground—what could a little more mud hurt?—and leaned back against one of the standing stones. Its rough surface tugged on her sweater's wet wool. She closed her eyes, for all that there was nothing to see in the dark. Behind her eyelids, Hæra's face stared back at her. It shifted back and forth between human and *Each-uisge,* but its eyes always glowed. Not the amber that had been almost human, but yellow, the yellow eyes of the beast that had tried to walk her backward into the ocean one night.

I was going to kill you.

No. Madeleine shook her head, even as Hæra's voice echoed in her memory.

To regain honor with my herd, so I could become a Stormhorse.

A Stormhorse, like her father had been—Hæra had told her that her father, Alban, had been part of the great force that uncovered Skara Brae. She revered his memory. Of course she'd want to follow in his footsteps. Hoofprints. Whatever. And of course she'd take extreme measures to get there. Hæra always did whatever was necessary to get what she wanted.

Including getting Madeleine in bed after turning her away from beliefs she'd held sacred her whole life. All for the purpose of killing her.

Maybe that would have been less painful than this. Again, there came the wrench of loss. Over the last few weeks, she had learned what it was like not to be lonely. It had taken so little time for Hæra to creep into Madeleine's heart like a worm boring into an apple. Madeleine had spent decades keeping herself apart from the world, even her fellow nuns, even Becca. Then she'd let someone in, and it had changed her, and she hadn't been alone, and she'd thought maybe she could question everything she'd believed *her whole life* and it'd be okay, and...

She sobbed and wrapped her arms around her knees, squeezing

them as if she could shrink into something too small for the world to notice. Too small for it to hurt. She'd given up her life and vocation for someone who'd intended to betray her in the worst possible way.

No, she reminded herself yet again. *You had to leave, the convent wasn't right for you. No matter what, you did the right thing.* At the moment, that didn't make anything feel better. It didn't change what Hæra had done, or what Hæra was.

Not human, just a creature that wore a human face when it suited her. Madeleine had feared to see that transformation all along, and now she knew why. It exposed the awful truth, and while Madeleine had spent the last few years facing a lot of new truths, she wasn't ready for this one.

The memory of Asgall's words blew through her worse than any gale.

He hadn't just said that Hæra intended to eat Madeleine. He'd said that Madeleine had had no choice but to return to Jorsay—that she and Hæra were "bound" together, and Madeleine would never be able to leave.

She remembered that night she'd tried to change her plane ticket so she could leave Orkney sooner. She hadn't been able to. Some inner voice had talked her out of it, promising *freedom* of all things— what a cruel joke. Was it Hæra's voice? Forcing her to stay through some enchantment?

She'd asked Hæra that, on the day Hæra had told her what she was. Hæra had denied it, but that could have been a lie like everything else.

If that was so, if they had a "bond," then what would be left of Madeleine at the end? Would she be like Jonathan, who'd stared at Asgall with a broken look on his face—still tied to him after years of pain and enmity? Jonathan had said Hæra and Madeleine had been given into each other's keeping. He'd been in a position to know, but he hadn't told her the truth either.

Hæra had just protested she'd never hurt Madeleine. Her eyes had been wild, her hand extended in a plea. *I love you,* she'd cried— screamed—with more desperation than Madeleine had ever heard in anyone's voice. *I know you love me.* She'd cried that too.

"It's not love," Madeleine choked, her eyes still closed. "You don't know how to love. Oh lord Jesus, forgive me. I went so far astray. Blessed Virgin, pray for me." She hunched her shoulders. "Help me, please—just some help, some guidance, *please*—"

A huge, crashing sound drowned the last word.

Madeleine's eyes flew open. That had sounded like a giant wave striking nearby—but the ruins were atop a great cliff face. No wave could reach this far up, not even pushed by the hurricanes Madeleine had known in New Orleans. It was too dark to see, but she *smelled* the water, as if a surge of seaweed and salt had landed a short distance away.

The clouds split open to reveal the bright curve of the half moon overhead. Everyone talked about the unnerving quality of full moons, but Madeleine had always found half moons to be eerier—the even split between light and dark.

The half moon granted just enough light to show another great surge of water splashing over the edge of the cliff. The water did not, however, fall to the ground. Instead it rose higher, and higher still, and began to arch forward through the air in a graceful curve tipped with foam.

Whatever this was, it wasn't natural, and she'd had enough of the supernatural to last her for eternity. She had to get up, turn tail, and run again. "Anywhere but here" seemed like a fine destination.

But there was no time to run. She only managed to brace her feet and tense her thighs before the water coalesced before her, spinning like a tornado. Her face caught salty, misty spray from its edges. As Madeleine wiped the spray from her stinging eyes, the spinning water expanded into a dreadfully familiar shape.

Another horse. One made not of flesh or blood but of the sea. It stood higher than the cliff, a surging giant. Its head alone seemed as large as her entire body.

As it floated in the air, water defined its form, rippling and reflecting the moonlight. Seacap foam curled around its front hooves. And also around the fins of its massive, fish-shaped tail.

Madeleine, frozen on the ground, gaped up at it. Maybe she'd fallen asleep at the foot of the stones and was having a terrible dream. Or a beautiful one. The creature was both. Its eyes were pits of darkness, like the bottom of an abyss.

And it was looking straight back at her.

"I AM THE GREAT MARE," said the leviathan. "AND YOU ARE VERY SMALL."

———

In sleep, Hæra dreamed. In dreams, the witch found her again.

Hæra stood before the witch as she was: naked and bruised in her human form. Asgall's blood was on her face again. Around them spun the whirlpool's waters, but now the witch was alone. No corpses of her victims. She and Hæra faced one another on the sand.

"The bargain," the witch said.

Hæra bowed her head, just as she had before Asgall, when she'd realized all was lost. "Yes, Ancient One."

"Bring me your despair."

"I will. As soon as I'm well enough to come to you."

The witch's eyes, pits of black, flashed with displeasure.

"Your whirlpool is too far away." Even in a dream, her body ached. "I cannot swim that distance while I'm hurt. And I cannot take a boat." Everyone would be inspecting the damage to the fishing vessels. Even if Hæra knew how to pilot a boat, which she didn't, she'd never be able to steal one.

The witch took one step forward, and then another. She frowned, as if in concentration; perhaps she wasn't used to walking. But she came forward, and Hæra found herself helpless to move away.

The witch cupped Hæra's face. Her hands were so cold that even Hæra flinched at her touch. Her skin was coarse as sand. She leaned forward and licked Asgall's blood from Hæra's cheeks. Her tongue slid, slimy and kelp-like, over Hæra's flesh. When it passed over her bloody lips, the witch sighed, "Hungry."

Hæra's stomach flipped over. The witch's breath was icy against her mouth. This wasn't like Madeleine's kisses, which Hæra would never taste again. "You're going to eat me?" she asked shakily. That'd be fitting, all things considered.

"I like your brother's blood," the witch said. "Bitter salt. He belongs to the sea."

Hæra knew, somehow, that the witch was not really tasting Asgall's blood but a dream's echo of it—perhaps Hæra's own memory of its taste. How strange, that you could *know* things in dreams.

"Walk to the shore," the witch told her. Her thumbs stroked Hæra's cheeks. "Walk into the water. I will bring you here."

"What? How? Aren't you trapped in your whirlpool?"

"I will bring you here," the witch repeated. "Hurry. Hurry to save a life."

That didn't make sense. "Save a life? What do you—" She turned colder than any current could ever be. "Madeleine. She's in danger. On the shore?" Madeleine hadn't been heading in the direction of the shore, but she might have changed her mind.

"Your woman is safe. Someone else is not." The witch stopped stroking Hæra's cheeks and pressed her thumbs in, hard. The edges of her nails were sharp enough to cut. "Hurry, hurry, hurry. Hurry to me. And to despair."

Hæra opened her eyes.

It was fully dark now. This time, she didn't look around for the witch; she was still in Madeleine's bed. It was only a dream. Not real. Not...

Her cheeks hurt where the witch had pressed her thumbs in.

Hæra touched one cheek with a shaking hand. She felt no cuts from those sharp nails, but the dread had her body in its grip nevertheless, and she thought: *Real.*

The witch had said: *Hurry to save a life.*

How long had she been asleep? How healed was she? There was only one way to find out. She sat up and groaned. Everything was sore, but she no longer bled. She flexed her left wrist. Painful, fragile, but not broken. It would have to do. She struggled to her feet.

Hurry to save a life. Not Madeleine's. The witch had said Madeleine was safe. There seemed no reason for her to lie about that—it could neither amuse nor benefit her. There was only one other person Hæra would care enough about to make her way to the shore.

But Jonathan wouldn't have gone there. Would he? Why…?

Head spinning, she looked at the wall where his shotgun had rested. It was gone.

It's my bloody destiny, he'd said, the sea's wildness in his eyes.

"No, you dolt," she whispered, and stumbled to the front door even as horror drenched her limbs.

She was stark naked. It didn't matter. There was no reason to put on Madeleine's clothes only to tear them up again. She couldn't make it to the shore fast enough in her human shape. Her *Each-uisge* body was swifter than the Gator, swifter even than a car when she was in top form.

This was far from top form, but it'd have to do. It was dark now, for the electricity hadn't come back, and nobody would see her so long as she avoided torches. Connor and Jim would be working round the farm to clean up whatever damage there was, and maybe Madeleine was there too. Maybe she'd come back by now. They'd be distracted.

And if Hæra was seen, she was seen. This was more important.

She poked her head through the front door to make sure. Nobody in sight. In the distance, around the sheep pens, two torches waved about. A dog barked, so at least one had survived.

Setting her jaw, Hæra closed her eyes and transformed one more time. As her body expanded, so too did the discomfort. Her left front leg wasn't broken, but it would be beyond foolish to move at a full gallop.

Hurry to save a life.

She had done more foolish things than this. With a low neigh of pain, Hæra ran as fast as her bruised body could carry her to the shore where everything had begun, and where everything seemed likely to end.

CHAPTER THIRTY-NINE

THE GREAT MARE. The creature who'd supposedly given birth to the ocean. The only thing Hæra had ever seemed to reverence. She'd never used the word *goddess*, but it seemed apt.

For a moment, Madeleine's brain dug in its heels. Supernatural creatures made of flesh and blood were one thing. But the First Commandment was extremely clear: she must worship no other gods before God himself.

However, that didn't mean she shouldn't be polite. As the creature had said, Madeleine was very small. "Good evening," she croaked.

The Great Mare made a wet noise. It wasn't horselike, as Hæra's sounds were, but an echo of the ocean depths. It sounded like a chuckle.

Madeleine's eyes darted back and forth. The moon shone off the Great Mare's liquid hide; she cast a glow all about her that caught the edges of the ancient stones. This place no longer seemed of the human world at all. "Is—is this your home? Is that why you, uh, came here?"

"MY HOME IS NOT OF THE LAND." Scorn roiled in that voice, for Madeleine in thinking something so ridiculous. "BUT THIS SPOT IS SACRED AFTER A STORM, WHEN APPROACHED BY A HUMAN CONNECTED TO

MY KIND. SUCH A HUMAN IS WORTHY. THAT DOES NOT HAPPEN OFTEN—
SUCH A CONNECTION GENERALLY MEANS YOUR DEATH."

Madeleine shuddered.

"IT IS A PLACE OF POWER, AND I CAN BE HERE FOR A LITTLE WHILE.
BESIDES, DID YOU NOT CALL FOR AID?"

Madeleine could say, *I didn't mean you,* but that seemed unwise.
Was it rude to stay on her rear? It probably was, right? She pressed her
dirty palms against the stone behind her and slowly rose to her feet.
"It's, um, an honor to meet you."

Her voice was shaking. Why couldn't she sound respectful but
calm?

Because a horse made out of the ocean was towering over her,
that's why. If only there was time for a real prayer to Mary or one of
the saints, a prayer for intercession and protection. As it was, she
didn't even dare cross herself. It might anger the creature.

It might not work.

It might not even mean anything.

"I WAS HERE NOT SO LONG AGO," the Great Mare said, "SOME FEW
TURNS OF THE WORLD AROUND THE SUN. AFTER ANOTHER STORM, I
APPEARED TO A MAN WHO CAME TO THIS PLACE, WHO WAS BOUND TO
ANOTHER OF MY CHILDREN. HE WAS DRUNK."

Jonathan. It must have been. The Great Mare had appeared before
Jonathan, and he'd never said anything about that either.

"HE SANG TO ME," the Great Mare said. "A SONG ABOUT A YOUNG
QUEEN OF SEVENTEEN TURNS WHO LOVED TO DANCE. HE DANCED FOR
ME. IT PLEASED ME." She cocked her head to the side. A spray of water
hit the ground. "FOR THIS, I OFFERED HIM A BOON. DO YOU SEEK ONE
TOO?"

Madeleine had read enough folklore to know you should be
careful about asking "boons" of supernatural creatures. They always
came with a catch. "That's generous, but no thank you."

"YOU SHOULD NOT REFUSE ME UNTIL YOU KNOW WHAT IT IS." She
sounded amused. "ONE QUESTION HE COULD ASK ME, ABOUT ANYTHING
AT ALL, AND I WOULD ANSWER TRUE."

An answer? That was the boon? No offer of infinite wealth, absolute power, or worldwide renown?

Just an answer.

In that moment, no prize—not even salvation—had ever seemed greater.

Madeleine grabbed her sweater over her heart. "What question did Jonathan ask you?"

"Nothing. He asked to forget that he had ever seen me."

Madeleine's mouth fell open.

"Now." The Great Mare floated forward, between Madeleine and the moon. The moonlight wavered and grew dim, filtered through her body, as if Madeleine were looking up at it from underwater. "What will you sing and dance for me?"

Those eyes—dark— "I...I don't dance much. And I'm not..."

"Sing, then. Sing for your answer." A wave crested down the Great Mare's back and settled again. "Sing for your life."

It would be hard to sing; her lips had just gone numb. "My...life? You mean you—you'll kill me if I don't?"

"That is not what I said. Do not sing to avoid death. Sing for your life. Sing to the sea, and hear what echoes back to you." The Great Mare flicked her tail and sent spray backward over the cliffs. "The world is full of wonder. The other human chose smallness. Will you?"

The world *was* full of wonder. Madeleine's faith was based on mysteries, and all her life she'd been told some answers would only be revealed in the afterlife. But here—now—

No one ever grew wiser, or more holy, by turning away from revelation.

Madeleine cleared her throat and began to sing. Only one song came to mind. It wasn't one she'd have wished for, but it'd have to do: "Le Petit Cheval," the French song she'd sung for Hæra and Jonathan on the night she'd moved into the cottage.

At the time, she'd thought it was fitting: the story of a little horse who went bravely out into a storm. There was never good weather where he lived, but he did his duty joyfully, pulling his cart through the wet fields as he hoped for spring's arrival.

Her voice trembled as she sang the first, familiar words. "Le petit cheval dans le mauvais temps, qu'il avait donc du courage…"

"Ah yes." The Great Mare sounded pleased indeed. "I have heard humans sing this one, over warmer waters. Continue."

Madeleine did. Thank heavens, her voice steadied. As the Great Mare watched her, she lifted her voice and sang as if she were in Mass. Maybe she wasn't worshiping the Great Mare, but something powerful whirled around her all the same. The moment deserved her best, didn't it?

I will not be small anymore.

Then, as she had that night in the cottage, she got to the end of the third verse and had to stop. "Um, yes. There you are. I'm done."

The Great Mare narrowed her eyes. "There is more to the song."

"Yes, I know. My mother sang it to me, but I…I don't remember all of it." She shifted back and forth from foot to foot. "I could try to think of another—"

"The little horse's courage is not enough. The storm kills him. He perishes without ever seeing the sun."

Whatever words Madeleine had meant to speak next died in her mouth.

"How human of you," the Great Mare said, "to turn your memory from such an ending. To be unable to face pain and death."

"No!" The word burst from Madeleine, high and fierce. Unwise too, no doubt, but the Great Mare was wrong and had no right to say such a thing. "I lost my entire family. My parents and brother were killed. Trust me, I know about pain and death, and I want to know—I want to know so much—" Her voice cracked. "Was that good enough for me to ask you a question? What more do you want from me?"

The Great Mare regarded her silently. She flicked her tail again, and this time, the end of it dissolved. "Very well. But hurry. I cannot stay much longer."

There were so many choices. So many things Madeleine wanted to know, from the pathetic (*Does Hæra really love me?*) to the terrifying (*Am I damned?*), and a dozen questions that fell in between. But in the end, only one of them seemed worthy of this moment.

"How much of it is true?" she asked hoarsely.

"How much of what?"

"Everything. Everything I was taught. God, and His saints, and heaven and hell and—and how to live—"

How to live, and who to love. A sob made its way out of her throat, and she grabbed her hair with her muddy hands. She was cold everywhere, save for the heat behind her eyes. Cold, wet, covered in dirt. Her chest ached with all the screams she wanted to release.

This might be the worst mistake she'd ever made, depending on what she learned now. It might destroy her. She groaned, "How much is true? Do you know? Will you tell me the truth?"

Madeleine had sung for her life. This was her life. Everything else came from this, and whatever she did with whatever she was about to learn would show her how small, or big, she could become. Maybe, like the little horse, her courage wouldn't be enough to save her. She could only try and hope she'd see the sun again.

"That is what matters to you?" The Great Mare sounded incredulous.

"Yes!"

The enormous head tossed, as if in resignation. "Very well. Something moves the Earth and stars, and it has no name, and it has all names. There are saints, and there are not saints. You have lived in heaven and hell already. Your rules for how to live were devised by other humans, and I cannot explain them. If everything is true, then nothing is true too. That is your answer."

It had to be a joke. *That* was the "boon"? Madeleine had never heard anything so unhelpful in her life. What a ridiculous cop-out. What kind of wishy-washy nonsense...

Unless—

Unless maybe, possibly, it wasn't, because—

"Devised by humans," she said numbly, thinking of priests in pulpits, of angry slogans on signs. Of God and the saints, she knew no more than she did before, but maybe she wasn't supposed to. That was where faith came in. As for the rest…

"THAT WAS A VERY LIMITED QUESTION," the Great Mare said. "YOU SHOULD HAVE ASKED HOW A WHALE FEELS WHEN IT FINDS ITS MATE THROUGH SONG. THAT IS THE ANSWER TO EVERYTHING. BUT AT LEAST YOU ASKED ABOUT SOMETHING OTHER THAN HOW TO FIND RICHES OR FAME." She tossed her enormous head. "OR LOVE."

Madeleine looked up into the blackness of her eyes and thought she saw stars there. Or maybe those were the stars above, shining through the water. "I think we have to find love on our own."

"AND YOU FOUND MY UNRULIEST DAUGHTER. SHE IS UNLIKE MY OTHER CHILDREN, BUT I HAVE A FONDNESS FOR HER. I PUT BEFORE HER A GREAT CHOICE. IT MIGHT NOT, HOWEVER, HAVE BEEN A KINDNESS."

The lightning, thunder, and wind. Madeleine shuddered. "You mean—the opportunity to become a Stormhorse. To eat me."

"NO," the Great Mare said, to her astonishment. "SOMETHING ELSE. SHE COULD NEVER HAVE EATEN YOU. STILL, HER LOVE IS UNLIKE YOURS, AND PERHAPS YOU CANNOT RETURN IT. YOUR LOVE IS NOT HER HUNGER."

In her mind's eye, Madeleine saw Hæra's face. It had been a study in agony as she lay in the mud, begging for pardon. In bed, it had relaxed in pleasure and relief. In conversation, it had creased in concentration whenever Madeleine spoke. Madeleine saw all of these things, and her heart ached so much it might have killed her.

"Has she changed?" she whispered. "She told me she has, but is that possible for your kind?"

"YOU EARNED ONLY ONE QUESTION," the Great Mare said. "ASK YOURSELF IF YOUR KIND CAN CHANGE INSTEAD. AND THEN ASK YOURSELF IF YOUR KIND ARE WISER THAN MINE."

Madeleine staggered a little, knees unsteady. She knew the answer to that.

"I don't know if I can forgive her," she said slowly. "But I'll talk to her. I can do that."

The Great Mare's body shimmered. Was she about to vanish? "THEN YOU MUST HURRY. SHE GOES TO THE WITCH."

"The…witch?" Hæra had referred to a witch, when she'd knelt in the mud before Asgall, in tones of deepest defeat. The thought cut through Madeleine worse than any wind. "Do you mean the one in the whirlpool? What—"

"And even if she escapes that fate, the witch is not all she has to fear. There is one other in her family."

Madeleine froze. Hæra had told her that she'd almost been killed by Asgall and… "Her mother? Beathag?"

The Great Mare's watery body was rippling, becoming transparent. "The *Each-uisge* all carry some aspect of myself in them. Hæra is like one of my heartbeats: swift and strong. Her brother is like one of my ribs, hidden and frail."

Madeleine gripped the collar of her sweater. Her own heartbeats were out of control. "And—and Beathag? What part of you is she?"

The Great Mare's body rippled again, and its shape began to dissolve. Her tail and hindquarters spun, again, into the waterspout that had first arced up into the air from the cliffs. Ocean spray struck Madeleine's face.

The mighty head was the last to melt away. But before she turned into the tide, the Great Mare had time to tell Madeleine one last thing.

"My teeth."

CHAPTER FORTY

THE BEACH WAS DESERTED. There were no fishing boats here, no houses or structures, no reason for anyone to rush here in the wake of a storm. Only one man would.

Atop the seawall, Hæra looked wildly down across the beach, seeking what she didn't want to find. It was too dark even for her. She had to get closer. Her leg aching, she picked her way down the stone steps to the shore.

She couldn't see anything but rocks that faded into sand that disappeared into dark water. The storm had cast flotsam on the shore, along with human debris like a broken old dinghy.

"Jonathan?" she called.

No reply.

Oh, how foolish of her, of course he wouldn't be able to hear her over the wind and water. She needed to be louder. She screamed, *"Jonathan!"*

His name disappeared into the wind. No sign of him.

Had he gone into the water? He wouldn't be so reckless, would he?

He wouldn't leave her?

Hurry to save a life.

Hæra had hurried. She must hurry more. If he was in the ocean, she'd find him. It couldn't be too late. Gritting her teeth against the pain in her leg, Hæra cantered toward the water.

At the water's edge, moonlight gleamed off a long, thin, metal surface. It was the barrel of Jonathan's shotgun, which lay alone on the sand.

No. Oh no.

She stopped in her tracks, panting, to sniff the gun. The barrel was cold, and she smelled no lead or discharge. If Jonathan had brought the gun for self-defense, he hadn't been able to use it. Had he dropped it so he could go into the water? Or had Asgall snatched him, dragged him down? She had to—

In her peripheral vision, something caught her eye.

To the left, a dark lump lay on the sand.

She turned, slowly, because it could not be what it was. It could not be a human body. It couldn't be—

Two human bodies?

Her legs shook like a newborn foal's as she made her way over. Like the gun, the bodies lay at the edge of the water, which lapped at them. They didn't move as she approached. They didn't breathe.

One of them was Jonathan. She knew his scent, although it was dulled by salt water. His trousers were wet up to the waist.

The other was a naked man, covered in wounds. His hands were curled into Jonathan's jacket as if he'd been trying to drag him somewhere. The man's face was half turned into the sand, his eyes closed, but she saw the family resemblance. A long nose, a full mouth. A lean, pale body with rangy muscles.

Asgall's human form.

She stared dumbly at him. That didn't make sense. None of this made sense.

Never mind it, then. Forget Asgall! He could go to the deepest depths and beyond. She needed her friend. Her best friend. Her *real* family.

Jonathan couldn't be dead. Not truly. She had to wake him up.

Hæra nudged Jonathan's body with her nose, rolling him over. *"Jonathan?"*

He didn't move. His eyes, wide and glassy, looked up at the night sky. His face was gray, his lips blue. But there were no cuts or bruises. His clothes weren't ripped. Asgall hadn't wounded him.

"Wake up," she whimpered. *"Jonathan, I'm here. Wake up."*

His chest was still. No breath lifted or lowered it.

This couldn't be right. There must be something here to explain what had happened. Something, anything. Hæra rammed Asgall's body with her head, hard enough to kill him again, to expose more of him.

His hands were too stiff to let go of Jonathan's clothes, but she saw the cuts and bites she'd given him—not as well healed as her own injuries. There was also the wound in his chest from when Jonathan had shot him. Dark blood leaked sluggishly from it.

The picture came together, horribly. Jonathan had pursued Asgall to the beach, on foot, clearly out of his mind. He had strained his heart, which doctors had been warning him about for years, thanks to all the drinking and the salty food he loved. He'd pushed himself to his limits, and then he had found Asgall.

And Asgall? He'd taken human form. No doubt to confuse Jonathan, perhaps try to lure him into the waves. Maybe it had worked. They were at the edge of the water and Asgall had grabbed Jonathan's clothes. There must have been a struggle, and it had stopped Jonathan's heart, and Asgall had been dragging his body back into the sea when his own wounds had overcome him. Now he too was dead. They were both dead. Jonathan was dead.

Jonathan, who had taken her in, who had taught her humanity, who played a bloody awful fiddle, had died. He had died. Jonathan had died, and he was no more, and he would never call her "lass" again. He would never smile when she said good morning. He would never do anything ever again.

He was gone, and she was here. She hadn't been fast enough to save his life.

Air clogged thick and suffocating in her chest. She had wanted to save his life because she loved him. She loved the dead man lying on the beach, but she'd never told him. She had never said, *Jonathan, I love you, thank you for everything.*

Now the words clawed her throat with burning talons because they were trying to get out, to follow him, but there was nowhere for them to go. A howl ripped out of her instead. Her denial shrieked its way into the wind, which carried it away. Nobody could hear her, nobody would *know* the horror of this moment. She was all alone. She stomped her leg, her injured one. She stomped it again and again, until her whole body was white hot with pain, and howled some more. It wasn't enough. It didn't hurt enough. It didn't bring him back.

Try again? Try just one more time? She bent to Jonathan and nudged him once more. She wailed, *"Please,"* and then, *"Please,"* again, and he didn't listen.

Nobody listened. Not Jonathan, and not the Great Mare, who might have been able to save him. But she didn't. The Great Mare did not wake him up again. Madeleine was wrong about prayer. It was useless.

Madeleine.

Madeleine had left too. She'd left, because she hated Hæra.

She hated Hæra. Jonathan was dead. All Hæra loved in the world was gone, and it was all her own fault. Her lies had driven Madeleine away, and she hadn't been fast enough to save Jonathan from her own brother.

And in the sea, the rest of Hæra's kin would tear her to pieces. Her own mother would be the first to do it. There was nothing left for her anywhere.

Hæra's lungs ached from her cries, and her whole body trembled. Her head weighed more than it had before. It was too heavy to hold up. She could only stare down at Jonathan's and Asgall's bodies, empty shells now. The Last Current had torn away everything that mattered. There was no love, or comfort, or peace.

There was only despair.

The witch had known all along how this would end: that Hæra's ambitions could only poison everything she touched. What began with a lie could never end happily. Maybe that had happened to the witch herself. Maybe that was why she was trapped forever with the people she'd murdered.

Hæra might find out quite soon. She had a bargain to fulfill.

That was all she had. There was nothing left for her here. She'd go to the ocean and swim for the whirlpool—the witch had said she'd bring Hæra to her, somehow. She would or wouldn't, if the *Each-uisge* happened to see Hæra first. What did it matter? What did anything matter now?

She bent to Jonathan once more and sniffed his cold forehead, inhaling his beloved scent one final time. It was mingled with Asgall's smell. Polluted. If Hæra had the strength, she'd rend her brother's human body into pieces for daring to intrude on Jonathan this way.

She had no strength. Her leg ached—it must be nearly broken. She'd use the last of her energy just to make it to the ocean, much as she had years ago when she'd washed up on shore. She'd been shattered then too.

There was no Jonathan to put her back together this time.

Head bowed low, Hæra limped toward the ocean. On her back, she carried her despair like a rider: a cold, thin thing that dug its heels into her hide. It urged her on without mercy or grace.

Good. She deserved neither. She deserved only the whirlpool. Only the witch.

———

Madeleine found Connor by the beam of his flashlight. He crouched by the fence near the sheep pen. The winds had torn out a couple of posts. Behind him, the half moon shed just enough light to reveal the corpses of two lambs.

She glanced around as she approached. The pen's metal roof was intact, but one of the doors had been blown off the hinge and hung loosely to the side. Straw lay all over the ground.

Her legs were unsteady and sore from her frenzied run to the stones. She'd walked back as quickly as she could, clutching her side against a painful stitch. The Great Mare—

—the impossible Great Mare—

—hadn't exactly made her life *easier*, but she'd certainly opened Madeleine's eyes to a few urgent things. She had to find Hæra. They could figure the rest out later. *Beathag...my teeth...*

"Connor," she called.

The beam of his flashlight blinded her. "Madeleine! What the hell happened?"

His voice was sharp with concern. She'd come to like him and Jim —they were kind and never showed the slightest curiosity about her relationship with Hæra. Around them, it was hard to feel ashamed, and easy to feel that everything was normal. That she was.

She held her hand in front of her face to block Connor's beam and turned off her phone's own flashlight. The battery was nearly drained by now. "Uh, well..."

"You're covered in fucking mud!" Usually Connor and Jim avoided profanity around her. "You look as if you were blown about in that gale, were you outside? Jonathan said you were looking after Hæra in the cottage—"

Madeleine looked over his shoulder, where the cottage lay, although she couldn't see it in the darkness. Hæra must be there. "Um —yes. I need to..."

"But Jim went to look, and nobody was in there. We can't find Jon or Hæra anywhere. Jim said the bed was covered in dirt and blood!"

He looked Madeleine up and down, clearly taking in the dirt that was on her too.

Oh no. Did he think *she*—? Madeleine grabbed her throat. "I'm looking for them too. Something happened."

"No shite it did. Neither of them's picking up on the walkie-talkie. The phones don't work either. Jim's gone to the village to fetch Isla and see if anyone there can call around." His eyes narrowed. "Doubt all of *them* had their boxes cut."

Please don't let that be an accusation. Would he believe Madeleine if she insisted she didn't know how to disable a phone box? "Where have you looked?"

"Everywhere. It took us a bit to realize they were gone—we were busy checking everything. There's dead animals, some structural damage. Not like usual."

"Um, okay, but we have to find—"

"Something's gone wrong," he said. He looked her right in the eyes, his gaze even sharper than before. But something was missing from it.

Surprise.

Connor didn't look in the least surprised or confused by this turn of events.

"It's her, isn't it? Something's gone wrong with *her*. And you know whatever it is." He took a deep breath. "You know whatever *she* is."

Madeleine lost her breath. No denial found its way to her lips. She could only gape at him.

That seemed to be confirmation enough. He ground his jaw and inhaled deeply through his nose.

Madeleine began, "Connor—"

"Do you lot think we're stupid?"

The words burst out of him in a roar, and Madeleine gasped. Connor held up his free hand, palm facing forward, to silence her. "Come on! She washes up on shore, starkers and beaten half to death, and Jonathan gives this cock-and-bull story about her being his long-lost daughter? This isn't *Coronation Street*."

"Um—well—"

"We all knew something was off straightaway. Sue Kilbright told Iona Darrow how fast the lass healed up before Jon hustled her away. And then Eileen McKay talks about how he came to her asking for a bloody birth certificate because Hæra was born 'off the grid,' and she let him have one because she didn't see the harm and she was glad he was doing better now. Christ!"

The Great Mare hadn't exactly given Madeleine a script for this. "I don't—"

"Oh, and she's strong as Superman. Harry Duggan told everyone how she scooped you up when you fell. More than that too. You think

Jim and I worked here for *years* and never once noticed how fuck-off hay bales got moved, but nobody'd been using the machines?"

Hæra had been so careful not to be seen. Apparently she'd never worried about the evidence afterward. To be fair, neither had Madeleine. She'd thought that if Hæra had gotten away with it for five years, it must be working.

It hadn't occurred to her that Hæra wasn't getting away with it.

"And storms came and we got away with nary a scratch. Until now." Connor ran an agitated hand over his hair. "I knew something had changed as soon as I got here and saw the damage. Now she and Jonathan are nowhere to be found."

Silence fell. Madeleine searched for an excuse or explanation she could give. There was none.

"And you never said anything?" she eventually asked. "You just kept working here?" That might be just as strange as Hæra's true nature. If you thought something supernatural was afoot, wouldn't you want to avoid it?

Madeleine's own case to the contrary.

"Me and Jim like her," Connor said, to her astonishment. "She works hard. Keeps herself to herself. Everyone says she turned Jon around, and he's got a heart as big as the sky. They're good folk. The farm's a good place."

The last part, Madeleine understood. She'd loved Ætlaquoy from the moment she'd set foot on it. It just *felt* good. Was that the trow's now-lost magic, or something to do with the love Hæra and Jonathan had put into the land?

"You don't ask questions of their sort," Connor added. "Whatever she is."

Madeleine had asked plenty of questions, and none of the answers had made her life easier. "That was…probably a good idea."

Connor sighed gustily. "And now you're all mixed up in it. The hell happened at the cottage? Mud's churned up at the back door. There's hoof prints all over, and not from a cow or sheep."

Asgall and Hæra, circling each other between vicious attacks.

Madeleine couldn't hide a shudder, and Connor's eyes narrowed again.

"Jim had a look round," he said. "Said one set of prints left from the back, and then another started from the front door. They both looked to be going east before the grass covered 'em."

Both prints. Asgall had left from behind the cottage. Hæra must have followed later, but why in her *Each-uisge* form, especially when she was injured? Connor had said she healed quickly, but even so, why would she take such a risk? What would make her so desperate?

Jonathan was missing too.

The beach lay to the east.

Madeleine wrapped her arms around herself. Her clothes and hair were still damp, and the night wind was cold. There was no time to go back to the cottage and grab her jacket, the one with the torn shoulder, the one she hadn't stitched up because it proved all of this was real.

"Do you know what's going on?" Connor asked. "Do you know where they are?"

Madeleine's mouth was dry. "I think so. But I have to hurry." She glanced at the silhouette of Jonathan's Vauxhall. "I need the car." She certainly wasn't jogging to the beach. Jonathan kept the car keys by the office door, and she'd had practice driving on the left side by now. "You should stay here," she added.

Connor scoffed. "No fear. I'm worried about them, but I'm not a fool."

"I am," Madeleine snapped as she hurried toward the house. The last few months had given ample proof of that. How ironic: she was finally what Christ said everyone should be.

A fool for love.

CHAPTER FORTY-ONE

THE MOMENT she'd submerged and changed her hind legs to a marine tail, a current had grabbed Hæra. It had wrapped around her like a rope and dragged her through the water, past rocks and kelp and schools of wondering fish.

The last time Hæra had taken this route, she'd been bruised in body and spirit, maimed by the betrayal of her family. The more things changed, the more they stayed the same.

At least this was faster. The witch's cold current whipped Hæra forward so quickly that she closed her eyes against the water pressure. Her tail beat fruitlessly. But why resist? This was why she'd come.

Survival was an instinct. She'd have to suppress it shortly.

With her eyes shut, she couldn't see the whirlpool, but she felt its rhythms beating the water harder as she was drawn closer. Two currents collided, creating a vortex. Humans didn't truly believe the legend that said a witch was at the bottom of it.

Just as well.

When Hæra hit the vortex's wall, the current released her. No more need of it. She was sucked into the water and slammed about. The whirlpool dragged her right down to the bottom, to the sandy pit where the witch spun with her victims. This time, Hæra didn't fight it.

Instead, when she landed on the sand, she lay sprawled there as she had in the mud behind Madeleine's cottage. Her fins twitched against the seafloor, and when she looked up, she could see the night sky.

The whirlpool slowed.

Before her, the witch stopped spinning and let her arms fall. The two corpses floated down to the sand, but neither released the witch's hands. Instead, they slumped on the ground like puppets with only one remaining string apiece.

The water rushed in to fill the void. The surface closed and the sky disappeared. The witch looked at Hæra with eyes like a sky that never saw stars.

"How did you call to me in dreams? How did you pull me here?" Hæra asked. "You can't even leave this spot yourself."

The witch looked at the dead man who clung to her. "I cannot leave. But I can summon." Her eyes sliced back into Hæra. "You owe me your life."

Hæra dipped her head low in acknowledgment. She had made the bargain; she had created the debt. "I'm here," she said. "I've brought you what you asked for. What will you do with it? With me?"

"Don't know yet." The witch walked forward, dragging the bodies behind her. Clouds of sand rose beneath them and her bare, knobby feet. "Won't know until I taste."

In Hæra's dream—a vision—the witch had licked Asgall's blood from Hæra's human face. It wasn't difficult to figure out her desire.

"His was bitter," the witch said when she reached the place where Hæra lay. "It belonged to the sea."

Between one breath and the next, she went to her knees, leaned forward, and sank her teeth into Hæra's neck.

Even though Hæra had foreseen this, instinct kicked in again. So did her front legs as she tried to knock the witch away from her. But the witch was immovable as stone, and Hæra's left front leg only hurt worse for it.

Besides, it was done. Blood floated from the wound the witch had just left in Hæra's neck, right next to one from Asgall that had healed over. Yet again, the witch's tongue passed over Hæra's flesh.

Hæra had tasted Madeleine's blood last night. It had been thrilling, tempting, intimate—nothing like this. *This* was the absence of all joy and hope.

This was despair, and Hæra had brought it to the witch as promised.

The witch did not linger. After one lick, she rose to her feet and looked down on Hæra, her expression inscrutable.

Hæra's neck ached. "Well? Finish me," she croaked.

But the witch shook her head. "You do not belong here. The sea does not own your blood."

"I don't belong anywhere," Hæra said wearily. "If the sea doesn't own my blood, what does?"

Silence while the witch regarded her. Hæra's heart pounded, sending more blood to cloud the water from her wound.

Then the witch said, "The sky."

It must be a taunt. Somehow, the witch knew Hæra's doomed desires and was mocking her with them before she killed her. If so, Hæra deserved it. She'd destroyed everything she'd touched.

"Go," the witch said.

Hæra boggled. Had the bargain been fulfilled? The witch had only wanted a bite of her?

That was no mercy. "I have nowhere to go. I have nothing else to be."

The witch said, "Wrong."

Suddenly, Hæra's vision swam. For a moment, she was in a car, a familiar one, Jonathan's Vauxhall, as it rattled down a road. Madeleine, still wet and dirty, was in the driver's seat. Her face was ashen.

It was just like the vision Hæra had had years ago, when her family attacked her. She'd been ready to give up until, across the miles, Sister Madeleine had called for her aid. Why did she look so frightened now? Was she in imminent danger?

Hæra groaned. One more chance. If she could protect Madeleine from whatever chased her...if she could do the right thing, just once, so it hadn't all been for nothing...

"Is it real?" she asked.

"Yes."

"Then please." Hæra dipped her head until her muzzle touched the sand. "I beg you…please, I'll return afterward…"

"You swear this?" the witch asked.

"I do." Hæra was shaking.

"You would return," the witch asked. "For this chance, you would return here to be imprisoned forever. Tortured forever. Why?"

Hæra looked at the dead man clinging to the witch's hand. The man she had loved and betrayed, and for which crime she was trapped eternally.

The witch looked at him too. Then she laughed, as she had years ago, like the blades of two knives sharpening each other. "You know how they don't let go of you," she said.

The words echoed in Hæra's memory. Where had she heard them before? Oh…she recalled…she had spoken them herself. When she'd first met the witch and pleaded for her life. Had the witch remembered Hæra's words so clearly for years? Of course she had. Who better than the witch to understand—to *empathize*—with being bound to the human she loved?

"Then let her hold me." Hæra yearned to stand but couldn't rise up without her hind legs, only flop uselessly on the sand. "Ancient One, I surrender…please…"

"You would do this?" the witch repeated.

"I would do anything! It can't be worse than losing her!"

At this, the witch flung up the two corpses. As she began to spin once more, the currents resurrected, and the whirlpool resumed its shape. Her robes, rotted from the sea, spun with her. Her knobby bare feet kicked up eddies of sand. She was silent, silent, and Hæra wanted to scream—

"Then do anything," the witch said.

The surface opened. The stars reappeared. Around Hæra, the water roared, creating a tunnel between sea and sky.

"Don't come back," the witch said. "You are not ours."

The current wrapped around Hæra's fins again. This time, it acted like a lasso, flinging her through the wall of the vortex with such force that she cried out. Then it released her, but it had thrown her so fast that she kept going, spinning until she couldn't tell up from down. Her tail flailed as she sought to slow down and right herself. But her tail wasn't working properly. It was growing weaker—

It was *shrinking*—

So were her front legs. So was her face, along with everything else. Without her willing it, Hæra's body was enacting a transformation it had done so many times before.

Wildly, Hæra pumped her tail toward the surface, even as she felt it begin to split in two. But not into her horse legs. Into her *human* legs. She'd never gone straight from this shape into that one, without being a four-legged creature in between.

She broke the surface of the water, gasping for air. She'd never had to do that before. Whether in water or on land, her body knew how to breathe. She'd never worn her human form underwater, though—maybe that was why?

The water was cold. Nearly freezing.

Hæra strove for air. Her teeth began to chatter, her muscles to lock up. She squinted ahead—was it darker than it had been when she'd first gone under? Everything was blurrier.

Nevertheless, she could make out the shore in the near distance, the one where she had kissed Madeleine and where Jonathan now lay. The witch had thrown her back the whole way, and she could easily make it to land.

Madeleine was out there somewhere, terrified, and Hæra had been given the opportunity to make things right. She'd figure out the rest afterward.

She struck out toward the shore and immediately knew something was wrong. Here, in the sea, she ought to be at her strongest. But her arms and legs felt weak, and when she swam—at least this body knew how to swim—she struggled as she never had before. Waves slapped her face, and she gasped around their salty taste. It made her thirsty. The salt water got in her eyes. They stung, as did the wound on the side of her neck.

Her left arm ached, but not just because it was injured. Her heart was straining at twice its normal rate while she went half her normal speed. Her lungs strained for more oxygen. Was she going to drown? That wasn't possible. *Each-uisge* didn't drown.

Humans did.

"Depths!" she gasped, and then more salt water slopped into her mouth. She spat, her tongue thick and dry. No. She wasn't. She couldn't be.

But she was.

Her body wasn't like before. It was fighting to survive in the waters she'd known all her life. Weak. Cold.

Human.

The witch. She'd said, *You do not belong here.* And instead of killing Hæra outright, she had done…this. Now Hæra hadn't just lost everyone she loved. She'd lost herself too. How was she supposed to help Madeleine like this?

She'd have to figure it out. The witch had shown Hæra Madeleine's terror and said, *Do anything,* and if this was how Hæra could save Madeleine, she'd do it.

The waves pushed her forward, closer to the shore. Closer now, she could see someone hurrying across the beach, from the seawall to the water. They carried a torch, and they were heading toward Jonathan's and Asgall's bodies.

Even freezing, probably drowning, and with salt-stung eyes, Hæra would know that human anywhere. It was Madeleine. And she looked perfectly safe, not pursued by anything.

The witch had lied. Hæra had nothing useful to do, no way to atone. She might as well stop fighting and go under the waves right now.

Madeleine reached Jonathan and Asgall. She stopped and looked around, waving the flashlight. Then she crouched next to the bodies.

She was looking at Hæra's worst failure. And that would be the last thing Hæra ever saw.

If her human lungs were strong enough, she could have cried out, *I'm sorry,* loudly enough for Madeleine to hear. The same way she'd called, *Sister Madeleine, help me,* years ago. Full circle. But these lungs weren't strong enough to yell. They were barely strong enough to breathe.

This was the end, then. It wasn't how she'd ever imagined it. Ruined…wasted…a failure, useless, *wasted…*

A rising wave, closer to the shore, caught her eye. Specifically, what was cresting atop it.

An *Each-uisge.*

One of Hæra's fellows was going to shore, where Madeleine was, alone and defenseless. Not just any *Each-uisge.* One Hæra would have known anywhere.

Her mother, Beathag.

Hæra didn't know why Beathag was here, nor did she care. It could only end one way for Madeleine. The witch had spoken true after all.

She struck forward again, wildly. Forget the cold. Forget her weakness. Forget, even, her despair. She was going to reach the shore, draw her mother's attention, and save Madeleine one more time.

Or die trying.

———

Madeleine had taken a flashlight before she'd left the farm. Now she wished she hadn't. Not if it was helping her see this.

Jonathan lay immobile on the beach, with another man clutching him.

"Oh God," she choked as she picked her way over the rocks, extra slippery in the storm's aftermath. The flashlight beam wavered with her unsteady steps. The wind felt even rougher here than usual, almost pushing her backward, as if it was trying to blow her away from this.

That might have been a mercy, but Madeleine had opened her eyes to the world, and the world could be hideous and unjust. She bent into the wind and forced her way on until she stood over the two dead bodies.

For dead bodies they were. She'd dared to hope, just a little bit, that maybe they weren't—at least Jonathan wasn't. But neither of them breathed, and their forms were unnaturally pale, rigid.

She didn't recognize the other man, until she did. He was naked and lean, his body covered in wounds. His facial features were like someone else's she knew.

"Oh God," she whispered again as she beheld Asgall's human form, clinging to Jonathan in death.

Asgall's face was a miserable rictus, his jaw set in a grimace. He looked as if he was in the middle of some great effort—or had been.

Killing Jonathan, apparently, however he'd done it. Jonathan had no visible injuries. But what else could have happened?

Jonathan lay on his back, looking at the night sky with unseeing eyes. His gray lips were slightly parted. He looked oddly at peace. As if *his* great effort, whatever it had been, was accomplished.

Madeleine pressed her lips together, but a soft sob emerged, hot in her throat. She hadn't known Jonathan well, but he'd been kind to her. He'd loved Hæra. He'd been a good man, and he deserved better than this.

She swung the flashlight's beam around. No sign of Hæra or anyone else. This beach had no infrastructure to manage in the wake of a storm. Everyone would be too busy looking after their homes and businesses, if they hadn't already gone to bed.

She was alone, and nobody could give her any answers—tell her if Hæra was safe, or what had happened between Asgall and Jonathan, or what in the world Madeleine was supposed to do now. Go to the village? Summon the police? She'd have to think of some way to explain this.

Or maybe she wouldn't. Connor said everyone suspected Hæra was different, even if they didn't know exactly how. They might not be surprised at all.

Madeleine swept the flashlight over Jonathan and Asgall again. High tide was rolling in. She had to move them or they'd be submerged. She'd never manage to carry them up the stairs to the seawall, but at least she could drag them farther up the beach before she went for help. The villagers could figure out what to do with them while Madeleine searched for Hæra.

She crouched and set the flashlight down. As she did, she saw two long, parallel furrows in the sand, next to a series of footprints. The incoming tide was washing them away.

Madeleine stared at the furrows. They led from the ocean to Jonathan's feet. Jonathan's pants were wet up to his waist, and drying sand crusted the fabric. He'd been in the water, obviously—but now he and Asgall lay on the sand, and there were furrows and footprints heading *toward* land, not away—

Jonathan's face was pale and gray. *Think of your heart,* Hæra had growled at him many times over meals while he'd waved her off.

No wounds. In the water up to the waist. Furrows in the sand. Asgall clutched him with a look of agony.

He had been dragging Jonathan ashore, not under the waves. Then he'd collapsed from his own wounds. Or something else, maybe a force more powerful than blood.

A cry escaped her, impossible to stop. She clapped her hands over her face to block out the sight of them. Had Asgall experienced a revelation here, while Madeleine was doing the same by the standing stones? Had he realized, like Hæra, that he couldn't kill his chosen human—and tried to save him, at the last? If so, it had been too late. Now, after decades of suffering, he and Jonathan were both lost.

This couldn't be how Madeleine and Hæra's story ended. She wouldn't let it. She'd learned too much. Where was Hæra? Had she been involved in this somehow? Madeleine needed answers. She needed *Hæra*. She'd come so far. It couldn't end here.

A wave crashed on the shore. It sounded the same as all the other waves, and Madeleine would never be sure why it made her look up. She turned the flashlight on it.

From the foam and dark water, an *Each-uisge* emerged.

"Hæra?" Madeleine whispered, but she already knew better.

This *Each-uisge* was smaller than both Asgall and Hæra had been, but still bigger than any horse had a right to be. Its hide looked black at first, but when the flashlight passed over it, it showed itself dark green, like seaweed washed ashore. Its mane was dark as night, as were its eyes.

Its teeth, however, looked every bit like Hæra's and Asgall's. Long and sharp, which was easy to see, since they were bared.

The *Each-uisge* slowly approached, the tide lapping around its hooves. It looked at Madeleine, and then at Asgall and Jonathan. It made a low noise.

"My son," it said.

Madeleine had known who it was. The Great Mare had said there was another member of Hæra's family to fear. Madeleine just hadn't expected to face her alone in the middle of the night.

Beathag turned her head toward Madeleine. *"I have never been on land,"* she said.

Madeleine hadn't expected conversation instead of an attack. She managed, "Oh."

"The human world holds no fascination for me, as it did for my children." Beathag stepped forward. *"As it did for my mate."* She stepped forward again.

"Your mate? Hæra's father?"

"They got it from him, this curiosity. This obsession." Beathag continued walking—prowling—and Madeleine stumbled backward. *"You've taken them all from me."*

Madeleine's stomach turned to water, as did her knees. "That's not true. Your kind prey on us. We don't take anything!"

"So it should *be. It wasn't so with them. I refused to lose my mate, but my children are gone."*

Refused to lose her mate? That implied he was still here. Hæra had said her father was dead. And moreover… "H-Hæra told me the reproductive cycle is terrible on females. She said the *Each-uisge* don't know how to love. Are you really that sad?"

Beathag tossed her head back and whinnied a laugh, otherworldly and bitter. *"I kept the thing I needed. Now I need more. Where is my daughter?"*

Okay, that was one good thing: Beathag clearly hadn't murdered Hæra. "I don't know."

"You are bound to her. Her chosen prey."

"No—it's—" It wouldn't go over well to say that Hæra had pledged her love to Madeleine and sworn never to hurt her. "I don't know where she is, I promise you!"

"I have no use for promises. Alban gave me many, and they're worth even less from you." Beathag bared her teeth. *"Help me, human. Help me find her, and I'll spare your life."*

Madeleine's heart might break through her ribs. "Oh? And what will you do when you find her?"

Beathag gave her a level look. *"I'll finish what I started, and I will get what I need."*

Madeleine had no idea what Beathag needed, but she knew all too well what Beathag had started: the murder of her own child before Hæra had escaped. She lifted her chin and sent one swift, silent prayer to whoever was listening: *Give me strength to do the right thing.*

She said, "I wouldn't help you even if I could. And if there's a hell for your kind, you can go straight there."

Beathag's tail tossed. She pawed the sand, lowered her head, and snarled. Asgall had done that when he'd prepared to charge. Madeleine was about to be torn to pieces, and it was going to hurt a lot, and—

"Mother!"

Madeleine whipped around to behold Hæra staggering out of the ocean in her human form, naked as the dawn. She'd wrapped her right arm around herself while her left arm dangled at her side. She barely seemed able to stay on her feet.

Beathag extended her head toward her daughter. The wind blew into her face, and she sniffed it. Then she recoiled, stamping a hoof.

"No," she said.

Madeleine turned the flashlight fully on Hæra. She looked different. It was hard to say how. Her body was the same, tall and lean and muscular, but she seemed smaller. Maybe it was the way she hunched over as she stumbled toward them.

"Stop," Hæra called. Her voice cracked with strain. She shivered as she clutched herself, as if she were freezing cold—but Hæra was never cold. And she was never weak, especially this close to the sea.

There was a small, dark patch on the side of her neck. As she got closer, Madeleine gasped to see it was a bleeding wound.

"What have you done?" Beathag's voice was a whipcrack.

"The witch in the whirlpool." Hæra stopped, swaying in place. "She changed me. Now I'm...I'm..."

Beathag spoke it like a curse: *"Human."*

Oh.

That was it.

Madeleine stared at Hæra. Of course. Of course that was it.

"You don't want Madeleine." Hæra took another shaky step forward. She slipped on a rock but righted herself at the last second. "She's never wronged you. Or anybody. But I have—I—" Her shoulders slumped even more. "I betrayed everyone. It's me you want. You want to finish me."

Beathag said slowly, *"You would surrender yourself to protect this... thing? Have you lost your warrior's instinct?"*

"If I could fight you," Hæra said, "I would."

She turned her haunted eyes on Madeleine. In them, Madeleine saw more longing than ever before, even when Hæra had wanted her most fiercely. But this was different too. For the first time, next to the longing, Madeleine saw grief.

If she'd needed any more proof that Hæra was now human, that was it.

Beathag turned to where Asgall and Jonathan lay on the beach, and then she looked back at her daughter. Hæra tried to lift her shoulders, perhaps in defiance, and didn't succeed.

"Please," Madeleine heard herself say, with no idea of a follow-up. Was there *anything* she could say that might save Hæra, save them both?

Hæra gave her a horrified look, which suggested not. "Madeleine. Go!"

Did Hæra think Madeleine could outrun a vengeful *Each-uisge*? Madeleine's disbelief must have shown on her face because Hæra said,

"I can slow her down. I'll stop her, I'll…" She lurched toward Beathag, holding out her good arm like a shield. Blood dripped down her neck. "Mother. Look at me!"

Beathag was already looking. She seemed unmoved by her child's injuries. *"You think to defeat me like this, when even your father fell before me?"*

Hæra stopped dead. Her mouth opened, as did Madeleine's. "What?"

"I saw his fascination with humans. Your father talked ceaselessly of them, admired them. *He called the human he took, that sea captain, his 'other half.'"* Beathag took a step toward Hæra and pawed the ground again. *"Would you say the same thing?"*

"Yes," Hæra said with no hesitation. "I would. I do."

"Alban was mine. He was my *mate, mine for life. The other Stormhorses never spoke of their humans as he did. And when I saw him infecting you and…"* Her head swung back to Asgall's body. *"I couldn't allow it. I knew I would lose him forever if I didn't act."*

"What do you—"

"And so I killed and ate him."

The only sound was the wind. That, and the ringing in Madeleine's ears. She looked on helplessly as Hæra and Beathag faced each other, one tall and proud, the other shivering and small.

"Now he is always with me," Beathag said. *"I lost him to gain him. I made that sacrifice. That is the measure of my love."*

Hæra appeared speechless. Madeleine certainly was. Beathag regarded Hæra for a moment that felt too silent and too long.

"I don't love you enough for that," she said.

Hæra staggered backward. Beathag didn't appear to notice; she merely turned and paced toward Jonathan and Asgall. When she reached them, she bent her head and took Asgall's leg in her mouth. Then she began to drag him toward the sea.

After a couple of feet, Asgall's grip finally released Jonathan, who continued to lie on the sand and look sightlessly at the stars.

Hæra said nothing. Did nothing. She just watched with a dull expression as Beathag dragged her brother's body away, farther back into the breaking waves, until the ocean swallowed both of them, and they were gone.

The moment the waters closed over Beathag's head, Madeleine's feet unlocked. She rushed to Hæra, managing not to slip or trip on the rocks.

Before Madeleine could reach her, Hæra listed to the side and collapsed.

———

Hæra had never been so glad not to be loved.

Not if love was like Beathag had said, like Hæra had once believed: possession at all costs. Beathag had killed Alban to keep him forever. What else had Hæra meant to do to Madeleine? Thank the Great Mare she'd failed.

Madeleine knelt next to her and pulled her back upright. The torch clattered to the ground. "Hæra! Are you all right? Good grief, of course you're not. What happened to your neck?"

Hæra looked numbly at the patch of beach where Jonathan lay. She touched her neck and winced. It hurt. She was so cold that her skin ached. It was better than feeling…whatever this was, all the rest of it…

Feeling human.

It must have started long ago.

Hæra looked at Madeleine's hand on her bare shoulder. It started on the night they met, on this beach, when Hæra was as naked as she was now. She'd kissed Sister Madeleine with passion she couldn't understand. Human desire. How strange, not to understand it until now.

"*Hæra.*" Madeleine's grip tightened on her shoulders. "Can you hear me?"

"Yes." She squinted at Madeleine's face. Only yesterday she'd have seen it in the dark with perfect clarity. "The witch bit my neck. She said my blood didn't belong to the sea and she made me into a human. That is, after I…"

When she trailed off, Madeleine said, "After you what?"

"After she showed me you were in danger," Hæra said slowly. "And I begged to be allowed to protect you, just one more time."

Even in the dark, she could see the tears glimmering in Madeleine's eyes, reflecting starlight and sea.

"I ruined everything," Hæra said. The wind blew; she couldn't stop shivering. "I would have died for you both. A thousand times. Instead, I *lost* you, and..." She slammed her fist against her chest. "And I'm weak, and cold, and he's gone, and you hate me, and I—"

Madeleine hauled Hæra into an embrace. She wrapped her arms around her fiercely and clutched her, as if she wanted to pull Hæra into her own body. And she pressed her nose into Hæra's wet hair when she said, "Wrong. I don't hate you. You're not weak. And if you're cold..." She squeezed tighter. "I'll warm you."

Hæra turned her face against Madeleine's neck. Madeleine's skin was cold. Her clothes were damp and covered in mud. And yet she was right. This was possibly the only warm place in the world.

"I'm sorry she was so horrible." Madeleine's voice was choked. "I didn't know how to stop her. Maybe it's wrong to feel this way, but I wish I'd had that shotgun."

"It's lying over there," Hæra mumbled. "Down the beach."

"Down th...oh my God. I didn't see it."

"It's wet. I don't think it works anymore. Jonathan didn't even fire it." She shuddered. "Asgall killed him."

And Hæra hadn't stopped it. Jonathan's corpse lay mere feet away in silent reprimand. *After all I did for you,* it seemed to say.

Madeleine said, "I don't know about that. I actually think...never mind, we can talk about that later. I've got to get you out of the cold and—and take care of him."

Hæra peered up at Madeleine. For six years, she'd hungered ceaselessly for the sight of her. Sister Madeleine had been the whole object of her desire; then, six weeks ago, Madeleine had become something else. Something more. But still, Hæra had hungered.

Not so, now. Instead, when she looked at Madeleine, she felt an ache that had nothing to do with her wounds. It wasn't the usual, primal urge to hold her. It was a sudden and desperate need to be held.

Madeleine looked into Hæra's eyes in a way that suggested she understood all of this, somehow. "We've got to get off the beach, okay? Lean on me."

She hauled Hæra to her feet. Then she hooked her left arm around Hæra, aimed the flashlight with her right, and moved toward the steps that led up to the seawall.

"We can't leave Jonathan h-here," Hæra said. Her teeth chattered.

"We can't carry him either. We'll need help. Wait here."

Hæra, useless and freezing, sat on the bottom step. Madeleine dragged Jonathan's body far enough that high tide wouldn't wash over it before "help" could get here. He was probably too heavy to be swept out to sea, but the ocean was vicious when it wished to be. Though Jonathan might not have minded, given everything he'd said in the cottage. About how Asgall was his destiny, and he'd been *heartbroken* that he hadn't been *eaten*. He might have preferred the dark waters.

Hæra hid her face in her hands. Well, too bad. Asgall couldn't have him. Jonathan would remain with her at the last. She would honor his death with human rites, whatever they were. She would show everyone what he'd meant to her, even though she'd never told him. It was the least she could do.

"What about the gun?" she asked when Madeleine returned.

"I'm not touching it. In case of…fingerprints or whatever. Is that the right thing to do? I don't know." Madeleine pushed away a frizzy lock of hair. She looked a fright. "I can't think straight. I'm so tired, but we have to keep going. Can you climb?"

Hæra had last taken these stairs on four legs. It would be easier on two. "Yes."

"Then we'll get you to the car. There's a blanket in the back seat, I think. Then I could—should I go to the police?"

Hæra didn't think much of the police. They'd never bothered her, but Jonathan had always told her to stay out of their way in case they asked the wrong questions. Now they would be likely to ask different questions. Probably the right ones.

"It doesn't matter," she said as they climbed. Gritty sand dug into her bare feet on the concrete. "It won't change anything."

"The heck it won't. I actually think we should go back to the farm."

"But Jonathan—"

"Isn't going anywhere," Madeleine said gently. "We can ask Connor and Jim for help with him. They'll know more about how the island handles this kind of thing."

"There *isn't* 'this kind of thing.' How can we explain any of this to them?"

"Um…we might not have to explain as much as you think. I'll tell you in the car. Okay, next step."

Carefully, they made their way to the top of the stairs. Madeleine had parked near the seawall. The village sat in the background, the streetlamps dark like everything else. No other people were in sight.

At the top, Madeleine went to unlock the car while Hæra leaned against the railing for support. She looked over the railing, down to where the dark sea thundered, and to the sand, where Jonathan lay without Asgall. Her brother had released his grip at last.

"Hæra?"

Madeleine sounded anxious. It tugged at Hæra's heart, but not with the wild urgency she'd known as an *Each-uisge*. She'd have done anything to save her mate from fear or harm. No, she hadn't known the witch would turn her into a human—but if she had, she'd have made the bargain gladly.

Would a human make the same bargain? She turned slowly to see Madeleine right behind her.

Madeleine put a hand on her arm. "Come on. Let's go home." Her voice was as soft as the fuzz on a new leaf.

Maybe not every human would have made that bargain. But Hæra would, again and again, in a heartbeat.

"Yes," she said. "Home."

CHAPTER FORTY-TWO

It was half-past one in the morning. Hours ago, Connor had gone to find Jonathan's body on the beach. Then he reported to the police that he'd found it, which was technically true. He didn't mention Hæra and Madeleine, however, nor the shotgun. Madeleine had no idea what he'd done with it. The police came out to recover the body for a postmortem, and it seemed there was nothing else to do for the moment.

"Heart attack, right enough," Connor had said when he'd returned to the house, his shoulders slumped. "My uncle went the same way and looked just like that. Coroner'll say for sure. Poor bugger. Still, he looked peaceful enough."

Now Madeleine, Connor, Isla, and Jim all sat in the living room of the main house; the broken back door made the cottage a non-starter. Battery-powered lanterns provided the only lighting. Madeleine had changed her filthy clothes and used just enough reserved water to wash her face and hands.

Hæra was in her bedroom, hopefully asleep. Hopefully not dreaming. Madeleine had guided her straight into her bed and she'd gone without a protest, losing consciousness the moment she lay down.

As for Madeleine, she didn't know what to feel. Or how to feel.

The adrenaline had worn off, and she was completely drained. The last few hours seemed like a dream, especially right now, in an ordinary cottage with ordinary people. Even as she was recounting the story, she thought: *Could that really have happened?*

"Bloody hell." Jim took a long pull of one of the beers he'd brought from home. "That's a story, isn't it?"

He didn't sound doubtful. Madeleine had been right. Not a single one of them had been as shocked or skeptical as Hæra had expected.

"It sure is." She rested her elbows on her knees. Good grief, she could sleep for a year. It was amazing she'd been able to talk to the three of them with any coherency. Thank God she hadn't had to speak to the police. "Some things I'm keeping to myself, but you've got the gist of it."

The gist: that Hæra had been an *Each-uisge,* that she was now human, and she'd had a brother who'd tried to kill her before dying himself. That she and Madeleine had met when Madeleine was a nun, and years later Madeleine had come back to learn more.

No need to say they'd become lovers. That seemed pretty obvious to everyone.

Connor rubbed the back of his neck. "Fuck. Poor Jon. You don't know why the other beast grabbed him?"

This Q&A session wasn't what she'd ever expected, but at least Connor, Jim, and Isla didn't need convincing of Hæra's supernatural nature. Apparently, nobody would. Still, Jonathan's relationship with Asgall...whatever it had been...wasn't Madeleine's secret to tell.

"No," she said. "Hæra tried to save him, but it was too late. By the time I got there, he and her brother were already dead, and she was..."

How did you finish that sentence? *With a witch, becoming human?* Madeleine couldn't explain something when she had no idea how it worked. She groaned. Her head felt heavy as lead. "I know it doesn't make any sense."

"That it doesn't," Jim agreed.

"But you believe me?" She glanced at Connor. "I know you said you already suspected, but even so this *has* to seem insane."

"Oh it does," Connor replied. "But I saw those hooves. And everything else I told you about. And we don't laugh off fairy-tale creatures and such."

"We always knew she was something like that," Jim added. "Didn't suspect a kelpie, or whatever they're called. Ech-thing. That's scary shite." He glanced at Hæra's bedroom door. "I thought she'd be a bonnie selkie lass."

Isla snorted. "You *would*."

Connor scoffed. "She's too hard to be a selkie. She was always going to be something that could kill you." He sighed. "At least I knew she wouldn't."

Good for Connor, but that was still a bet Madeleine wouldn't have taken in his place.

"I saw a tangie when I was a peedie girl on Shapinsay," Isla said. She was tall and fair with an Orcadian accent, a lifelong native of the islands. "That's a bit like what Hæra is. Was. Told my mum, and she said to keep my mouth shut and stay away from that place."

Isla's mother had been sensible. Madeleine asked, "Does everyone know the truth?"

"Of course not," Jim said. "Not newcomers to the place, like the lads with the café. But the old-timers, those of us who've been on the islands all our lives, we talk. You should have heard Harry Duggan bitch and moan about all the hints he dropped that Jonathan refused to pick up."

"Harry Duggan's a numpty," Isla said. "Was Jonathan supposed to tell him the truth? Christ. Some things you can't say."

"Until you have to," Madeleine said quietly. "And Hæra's human now."

Silence fell for a moment.

"So what's that mean?" Jim asked.

"I don't know."

"Is it something to do with why the farm's damaged?" Isla said. "Jim's always told me nothing ever happens to it, somehow."

"Um. Possibly," Madeleine said. "I think something happened to the trow."

After a brief silence, Connor sighed and went for his own beer.

"What happens now?" Isla asked. "Jon's dead. What does she do? What do *you* do?"

"Heck if I know," Madeleine replied. "I can stay until the middle of August. Then school begins and I have to go back to work."

That didn't seem real. Whenever she thought of her classroom or apartment, it all seemed to belong to another life, one lived by a different woman. How could she go back to it? She wouldn't even be able to tell Becca the truth.

And she'd have to leave Hæra behind when they'd been given into each other's keeping. That didn't seem real either.

She continued, "Jonathan told me once he intended to leave Hæra the farm, although he wasn't sure how that'd work given her lifespan. I guess that's not an issue anymore."

"He was always fond of her," Jim said. "And she of him, I think. She'll take it hard."

She thought of how it had been during the car ride to the farm. Hæra pale and silent, her gaze locked on the road ahead. "He was her family."

"And what are you?" Connor flopped back in the chair and took a pull of beer. "Other than an American who's swung in here for a summer fling, and who's going to bugger off in a month."

"Back off," Isla said sharply. "She's done in, can't you see? What sort of night do you think she's had?"

Isla was right, but Connor's words had sent one last surge of energy through Madeleine's blood. She narrowed her eyes. "Actually, let me ask a question. You knew Hæra wasn't human, and that we were...um..." *Whatever we were. Are.* "Were you ever going to say anything? *Warn* me?"

"Who am I, Harry Duggan?" Connor shrugged. "You'd have thought we were off our heads or lying at first. And soon enough we could see you knew. You got the same look as the two of them—the one that said you were in on it."

"You weren't in a hurry to share your business either," Jim pointed out. "We don't put our noses where they don't belong. Although if you didn't want gossip, you shouldn't have had a go at each other beneath the Frasers' windows."

Madeleine barely managed not to hide her face in her hands. Before she could think of a reply, noise came from behind Hæra's bedroom door.

All four of them looked at each other. Connor, Jim, and Isla stood. Isla said softly, "There's nothing else that can't wait until daybreak. Madeleine, will you want someone to stay?"

"That's kind, but no," Madeleine said. It was politer than yelling at them to get out so she could be alone with Hæra, especially when they'd been so helpful. "Connor, thank you so much for taking care of Jonathan. I had no idea what to do."

"Jon was a good'un," Connor said gruffly. "Least I could do."

"He doesn't deserve everyone nosing round and asking questions," Jim added. "Let him rest in peace."

Isla patted Madeleine's shoulder. "We'll come back tomorrow. Rest if you can."

"And look after her," Connor said, nodding at Hæra's door. "God knows what'll happen in a case like this."

Does he? Madeleine wondered as they left. *Does he know?*

The Great Mare had said something moved the universe and had refused to be more specific. Maybe that was good enough for now. It was too late, and she was too tired, for these existential questions. Someone else needed her more.

Madeleine squared her slumping shoulders and gently opened the door to Hæra's room.

———

Low voices came from the living room. A few hours ago, Hæra would have been able to hear them perfectly. Now she'd have to strain to listen, if she cared enough to do so.

Everything felt muffled. Her hearing and eyesight were less sharp. The lights were out and she couldn't see as well. Her body felt weak, although it remained muscular—was she still strong compared to other humans? How fast would she be able to run?

When they'd gotten out of the car, Hæra had tried to transform. Just to make sure. It hadn't worked, and it'd never work again unless she pled her case to the witch.

No. She never wanted to see those malicious eyes again. Nor risk the chance of running into the mother who'd killed her father, and who loathed Hæra so much she wouldn't do her the same courtesy.

So Hæra faced a future of growing old faster, living by human rules she still didn't understand, and...and there was no Jonathan to help her, and Madeleine…

The bedroom door opened. A beam of light struck the opposite wall—must be one of the lanterns. Madeleine whispered, "Hæra?"

Hæra, facing the wall, couldn't bring herself to roll over. Still, one more moment of solitude might drive her insane. "What?"

"I heard you moving around, or I thought I did." The door closed. The beam of light moved down as Madeleine set the lantern on the floor. Moments later, the mattress dipped as Madeleine sat. She put her hand on Hæra's shoulder, comforting through the layers of Hæra's sweatshirt.

For the first time in her life, Hæra had been truly cold.

"Did you sleep at all?" Madeleine asked.

"I don't know." She'd closed her eyes and gone somewhere else, but when she'd opened her eyes again, she couldn't remember any dreams. It hadn't been too bad. She clutched the duvet to her chest. "Is Jonathan…?"

"Connor went to the village and called the police, although it took them a while to get out here. He had to," she added when Hæra gasped in protest. "Then he called Sue Kilbright, since there's no doctor in residence tonight. She pronounced him dead and the police took him away to the Mainland for a post-mortem."

Jonathan's body was no longer here. No part of him was. That didn't seem possible. His fiddle still rested in its case by the sofa. How could there be a fiddle with no Jonathan to play it? Or a closet full of clothes with no Jonathan to wear them?

Madeleine continued, "Once the cause of death has been established, we'll get a death certificate. Then we can hold a funeral."

"There are rites," Hæra said to the wall. "Ceremonies for the human dead."

"Yes. Do you know what he would have wanted?"

"Probably to be dragged with my brother into the sea." It was a bitter truth.

"I don't know about that. Hey. Let me see you, okay?"

She set the lantern on the nightstand. Hæra winced. Even such a minor change in illumination was a new adjustment. She rolled over. Like everything else, it hurt, and she groaned.

Madeleine peered at her neck. When they'd gotten back to the cottage, she'd cleaned and disinfected Hæra's wound and put a bandage over it. "Is it still bleeding? I think I see a red spot. Let's have a look."

The underside of the bandage was red with blood. It looked awful to Hæra, but Madeleine said, "It's not as bad as before." Then she dressed the wound again, her touch gentle but sure. "We'll have the nurse here in the morning. Keep your hand on it and apply pressure, like I said before."

"I couldn't stay awake." Hæra pressed down on the bandage and winced. At least it didn't seem to hurt worse than it would have when she was an *Each-uisge*. "To answer your question, Jonathan never spoke of what he wanted after death. He just worried about what would happen to me after he was gone."

Now, in his absence, she and Madeleine looked at each other. Madeleine put her hand on her shoulder again and squeezed.

"He worried about me living for so long and people noticing," Hæra continued, her throat thick. "He worried about everything that had to do with me not being human. Now I learn that everyone already knew."

"Not everyone, but…"

"And I'm human now. I'll get old and die when…"

A thought occurred to her. A big one. For the first time, not everything was awful.

"When what?" Madeleine asked.

When you do, or close to it. Hæra couldn't say that. Madeleine was being kind now, but there was still unfinished business between them. She might not have forgiven Hæra's deception. Maybe she was only being nice until Hæra was on her feet again. Still, though. There was some comfort in knowing she wouldn't outlive those she loved by centuries.

When Hæra didn't finish her thought, Madeleine took her hand. Hæra looked at their joined hands in astonishment. She'd learned something about the nuances of human gestures in the last six years, especially in the last month and a half. Holding someone's hand was more intimate than patting their shoulder, and even after Hæra's betrayal, Madeleine was holding hers.

"I'd like to pray for him, if you'd like to join me," Madeleine said.

Hæra snorted. "Why? Jonathan didn't believe in God."

Madeleine looked beyond Hæra, toward the window. "Catholics are taught that you can pray for people's souls to ease their way to heaven after death."

"No," Hæra said at once. "He'd hate that."

"I know. Not that kind of prayer. Something that feels right for him. I'm trying to think of one—you'd think it'd be easy, I know hundreds."

Hæra lay on her back and looked up at the ceiling. After a minute, she said, "There was one he liked. He'd say it sometimes, on holidays or when he was really happy."

"Do you remember it?"

Right now, Hæra remembered Jonathan down to the last white bristle of his beard and the age spots beneath his eyes. After time passed, would she forget him? *Each-uisge* never forgot, but humans were different. Might the time come when Jonathan's memory faded, and she lost what little she had left of him?

Even if she didn't usually pray, she would say this one now, while she remembered. "Yes."

As she did at meals, Madeleine bowed her head and closed her eyes. She didn't cross herself, however.

Hæra closed her own eyes and imagined his smile. "May the road rise up to meet you. May the wind be always at your back. May the sun shine upon your face and the rains fall soft upon your fields."

She stopped. Madeleine kept her eyes closed. Oh, right, you were supposed to end prayers with *Amen*, but Jonathan hadn't.

"That's it," she said. "There's a bit about God at the end, but he always left it out."

Madeleine opened her eyes. They gleamed with unshed tears.

"He said the sun and the road were the important parts," Hæra said. "I think so too. When I die"—which would be sooner, now—"I'll nourish other things. That's enough for me."

Madeleine tilted her head. Her eyes seemed, suddenly, to hold a great truth. It was like how she'd looked at Hæra on the beach when they'd kissed and said they'd learn how to love. "I saw the Great Mare tonight," she said. "After I ran away from you."

She seemed completely serious. Just to make sure, Hæra said, "Are you joking?"

Madeleine shook her head and told an incredible story of an enormous *Each-uisge* made of seawater that had appeared to her at the standing stones. Her description matched the stories of the Great Mare Hæra had heard all her life. Madeleine spoke of the Great Mare's deep, echoing voice, and of the peculiar "boon" she'd offered if Madeleine sang a song for her. An answer for a question.

By the time she was done, Hæra's head was spinning. The neck bite didn't help; it pounded with every beat of her heart. "What question did you ask?"

Madeleine looked to the window again. "I'll tell you later. That's not the point. I'm saying I *saw* her. She was real. I...don't know exactly how I feel about that, but it's certainly in keeping with everything else that's happened to me. She said the world is full of wonder."

Right now, Great Mare or not, the world only seemed full of pain —and exhaustion. Hæra's human body was staging a rebellion against consciousness. She couldn't think about faith, gods, or grief. She lowered her head back to the pillow. Her eyelids were too heavy to keep open. "I'm so tired."

"Of course you are." Madeleine rubbed her thumb against the back of Hæra's hand. "Sleep. We'll figure things out tomorrow."

Hæra was weak. So weak. That must be the only reason she said, "Don't go."

Ever, she meant. That couldn't be. Madeleine couldn't stay on Jorsay forever, it wasn't legal, and even if it was, she wouldn't want to.

"I won't," Madeleine replied, to Hæra's shock. "Scoot over. I think there's room for both of us."

Oh. Madeleine thought Hæra meant just for tonight. Well, tonight was better than nothing at all, and even with the sweatshirt, Hæra was still so cold. She moved back, and Madeleine kicked off her shoes and eased into bed, fully clothed.

"Roll over?" she suggested.

Hæra did. Now apparently it was her turn to be the "little spoon," as Madeleine called it. Madeleine's warm body pressed against her, and Madeleine's arm slid around her waist.

"I've got you," she said quietly. "I'll keep you safe. Like you kept me."

"But..." The world was fading. "I put you in danger...Asgall, my mother ..."

"You saved me. From drowning before, and from them tonight." Madeleine kissed her hair, still stiff with ocean salt. "Sleep now."

Lacking any other choice, Hæra did. She dreamed of ocean currents carrying her from shore while her human body fought uselessly against them. She dreamed Madeleine was chasing after her in a boat, calling out for her to stay above water just long enough to be rescued.

She woke up before she could decide whether to be saved or drown. Madeleine was asleep. She still held Hæra. She was still warm.

Saved, then, for one more night. Hæra closed her eyes, returned to sleep, and didn't dream.

CHAPTER FORTY-THREE

THERE WAS a lot to take care of after a death. Madeleine knew that all too well, but it took on an extra dimension when you had to do it in another country.

Not that she *had* to do it—she'd only known Jonathan for a short time. But Hæra was in no shape to learn the logistics right now, and Madeleine was good at keeping track of details and organizing.

She had help, too, and not just from Connor, Jim, and Isla. Islanders came out of the woodwork once word got out. There was old Annie, who owned a crafts shop that bought Ætlaquoy's wool for practically nothing; Iona and Elliot, who owned the Kestrel and remembered the days when Jonathan was a regular; and Robert, who said Jonathan used to work with his father at the dairy that Ætlaquoy had once been. All of them sent cards and condolences, offered to run errands, and so on.

Hæra and Madeleine even received a surprise delivery of sausage rolls and pastries from the Sunrise Café. Neither Arjun nor Jeremy accompanied it, but the note said: *We're sorry for your loss. Come by any time. - A&J.*

Madeleine's eyes stung to see the note. How remarkable, to be forgiven. For all that her faith had been deeply shaken, she'd once built her life around a man who'd preached about forgiving those who sinned against you. That was one thing, but it was another to see it at work in the world—and to receive it. Their grace made her bow her head, humbled and grateful.

It lent her strength she badly needed. Every night, she held Hæra as close as she could, but one thing hadn't changed: when she woke up in the mornings, Hæra was gone.

Hæra got up early to tend to the farm's work, as always. She also spent more time looking out of windows and walking through the pastures by herself. On the day they got the call confirming that Jonathan had died "of natural causes," she'd disappeared for hours. Madeleine had been panicked until she came back, saying she'd wandered up to the cliffs and watched the crashing surf for a while.

Madeleine would have liked to stand on the cliffs too, if only to be sure Hæra didn't get any ideas about jumping off them. It didn't seem likely, but Hæra had already told Madeleine that twice she'd been ready to surrender to death until Madeleine had needed her. She was a tireless warrior, but she needed someone to fight for.

"If you're going to be gone for a while, just let me know," Madeleine had said, hoping she sounded reasonably calm instead of terrified. "So I don't worry."

For the first time in days, Hæra's face had softened. "Or you could come with me next time."

Madeleine did.

They were spending their nights in the cottage again after boarding up the back door. Hæra said it was too hard to be in the main house, where she expected to see Jonathan everywhere; once, Madeleine caught her sitting on the sofa, crying softly with his fiddle in her lap. At night, Madeleine held her close and woke her from bad dreams. Hæra refused to discuss them but always pressed closer to Madeleine in their wake.

The funeral happened two weeks after Jonathan's death. Madeleine had found a will in one of his desk drawers, drawn up by a law practice in Kirkwall. It clearly stated that Hæra was to inherit everything if she was still around, and if not, the property was to be sold. His only stipulation was that it couldn't be used for real estate development. Madeleine had no idea if that could be legally binding, but his wishes were clear.

As for his funeral, he had asked for no ceremony or celebration. He only asked for his ashes to be scattered at sea. There was no crematorium on Orkney; they'd had to send the body to Inverness and await its return in a different shape.

Now, on a cloudy day, Madeleine and Hæra stood on a rented boat. Hæra carried a pillow-shaped, biodegradable urn designed for disposing of ashes into water. She clutched it to her chest. "I never hugged him," she said to Madeleine when the boat's motor cut off. "I never thought of it. I wish I had."

Madeleine could say nothing to that. She could only rub Hæra's back through the warm jacket she now required.

The moment came to drop the urn overboard. Hæra stepped to the railings. She showed no sign of fear, no worries that an *Each-uisge* would rise up from the waves—a fear Madeleine had entertained a few times. Rather, she looked at the urn, and the ocean, and then the urn again.

"I told you," she said. "He wanted to go back to the ocean. I don't want that. I want him to stay on land, here with me."

Tears ran down her face, and on the last word, she sobbed.

A lump, cold and solid, sat in Madeleine's throat. It was so hard to watch your loved ones disappear for the last time. She remembered her own family's coffins being slid into above-ground graves to keep them safe from New Orleans floods. She and David had held hands while they watched their parents being sealed away. When it was David's turn, Madeleine had been alone. She'd joined the Daughters of Grace shortly thereafter and had told herself she'd never be alone again.

"We can bring him back if you want," she said, with some difficulty. "You're not legally obligated to scatter him here. But..."

"But it's what he wanted." Hæra bent her head until her chin touched the urn. "So I'll do it. I just need a moment."

Madeleine waited. So did the boat's captain, who stood a decorous distance away with his hands behind his back.

"Put your hand on me again," Hæra said hoarsely.

Madeleine could do better than that. She slid her arm around Hæra's waist as Hæra leaned over the rails and dropped the urn into the water. Together, they watched it bob on the surface before it began to sink. Once submerged, it would dissolve, and the ashes would scatter into the ocean.

She hadn't thought to, but Madeleine found herself quoting a psalm. "'For He maketh the storm to cease, so that the waves thereof are still.'"

Hæra propped her elbows on the railing and lowered her head as if it weighed a thousand pounds. "He does a shite job, then. The storms always come back, and they wreck everything."

"Then they go away again, and we rebuild." Madeleine rested her head on Hæra's shoulder. "It's not the same as it was before, though."

Hæra kept staring at the spot where she'd dropped the urn. "It's not fair."

"It rarely is," Madeleine agreed.

"It wouldn't be the same if I were still *Each-uisge*." Hæra hunched her shoulders. "You heard Beathag. We—*they*—don't love like humans. It wouldn't hurt like this. It didn't when my father died."

"That seems like another kind of suffering to me." Madeleine thought of her family and the Daughters of Grace. There were a lot of ways to lose people. "Grief is another face of love. I'd rather choose that. And are you so sure you wouldn't have mourned as an *Each-uisge?*"

Hæra pushed away from the railing so quickly that Madeleine yanked her arm from her waist. "I don't know. Let's go. I hate this place."

The words put a knot in Madeleine's stomach. Hæra had longed to return to the sea, and now she spoke of hating it? The words might come from her grief. Hopefully the feeling would pass, and Hæra wouldn't hate her own origins forever.

Madeleine knew where those feelings led, and it was nowhere good.

This wasn't the time or place to say so. She nodded at the captain, who returned to the wheel. The motor roared again, and within moments, they were cutting through the waves on their way to the land.

———

Connor, Jim, and Isla came by to pay their respects after the funeral. They took Hæra and Madeleine to the Kestrel and sat them at a table while they ordered drinks.

At first it was silent, which suited Hæra fine. She felt sick—had it been the rocking of the boat?—and the beer wasn't helping. She sipped it while Madeleine sat next to her in the booth.

It had been so hard to let him go. That made no sense. It wasn't *Jonathan*. It was a package full of something that had burned. The sea had killed him, but fire had claimed him next.

Well. Now the sea had him again. She'd never thought about Jonathan's funeral rites, but if she had, she'd have thought he'd want to be buried at the farm he'd built with Hæra.

But Connor had said that wasn't legal anyway. Perhaps that was why Jonathan had chosen Asga...the sea over her.

A couple of days ago, Madeleine had told Hæra that she didn't believe Asgall had actually killed Jonathan. That he might have been trying to save his life instead. She'd laid out some case based on furrows in the sand, until she noticed that Hæra was about to start screaming, and then she'd taken Hæra's hand and said, never mind, it didn't matter right now.

As far as Hæra was concerned, it would never matter. At least she wasn't on the boat anymore. If she never went out on open water again, it'd be too soon. The sea was no longer her home—if it had ever been.

Someone cleared their throat.

Hæra looked up from her beer to see two older women standing at the table. She recognized one of them: old Annie, who ran Annie's Crafts. Probably here to offer quick condolences, as she had the day after they'd brought Jonathan's body back.

"May I sit down?" she asked, to Hæra's surprise. Maybe it was business. Ætlaquoy sold wool to her, although it cost more to shear the sheep than they made back in sales. Gave back to the community, Jonathan always said. Was Annie here to ask Hæra to keep doing that?

"I knew Jonathan since I was a lass," Annie said. She signaled Iona Darrow for a drink and smiled at Hæra. "Was mad about him for a bit. We all were, us girls. Good-looking bastard. Did he ever tell you about the time he played the fiddle right here at Christmas? Had the whole village stomping its feet and calling for more. Must be over forty years ago."

Hæra stared at her. "No, he didn't."

"No? Ah, well then…"

As Annie told the story of a young Jonathan, another older woman appeared. Eileen McKay, the island's registrar who'd given Hæra a false birth certificate. She talked about how Jonathan had played pranks on the teacher in Jorsay's one-room schoolhouse, as it had been then, but was so good-natured that even mean Miss Magurdy couldn't stay angry for long.

Others came too, enough that eventually extra chairs had to be pulled up to the table. Villagers with whom Hæra had never exchanged a word sat down and talked their memories of a Jonathan Hæra had never known. Some of the memories were quite old.

These people hadn't forgotten him, even though they were human. Maybe she wouldn't either.

In the middle of Harry Duggan's endless anecdote about Jonathan and the time a dairy cow got loose on his watch, Madeleine put her hand on Hæra's arm again and bumped their knees together beneath the table.

Madeleine had touched her on the boat too. It had been the only thing that got Hæra through that awful trip without losing her mind.

Even after all of this—or maybe *because* of all this—there was nothing like Madeleine's touch. Whether she was human or not, Hæra seemed to be made for it. It was her only comfort.

Harry stopped talking and raised his eyebrows while he stared openly at Madeleine's hand. Then he gave a knowing little smile. "It's good to have friends in times like this, isn't it?"

"Fuck off, Duggan," Connor said affably. "Does this story end with the cow kicking your head in?"

"What? I only meant—"

"Yes." Hæra looked him dead in the eye as she put her hand over Madeleine's. "It's good. And Connor's right. You can fuck off."

Something of an awkward silence fell.

Madeleine cleared her throat. "Thanks for coming, Harry. Maybe it's time to get the check."

Afterward, Hæra waited on the sidewalk with Jim and Isla while Connor and Madeleine settled the bill. Jim sighed, shoved his hands in his pockets, and said, "How are you bearing up?"

He'd never asked her such a thing before. Nobody had. Madeleine had told her this was how people showed kindness.

She replied, "I miss Jonathan. I'm not used to being human. My body's all wrong, and I have to learn how it works. And I also have to learn about business. It's horrible."

Isla and Jim exchanged a wide-eyed look. Had Hæra been too honest? She hadn't spent enough time among people to tell. Apparently that had to change. Jonathan was no longer here to serve as both bridge and shield between herself and humanity. Hæra would have to learn to live in the world beyond Ætlaquoy.

Perhaps she should sound more positive. "But Madeleine's here. She's a great help."

What an understatement. Hæra couldn't have survived the last couple of weeks without her. Madeleine knew how to handle banks and solicitors and so on, and she explained everything to Hæra as many times as she had to. She cooked, because now Hæra couldn't subsist on raw meat. She accompanied her on walks even on rainy days.

And she held Hæra close every night, bringing her back from dreams of drowning. Yes. Thank the Great Mare that Madeleine was here.

"Aye, for sure," Jim said. "Hasn't she got to go pretty soon, though? She's a teacher. School's bound to start soon."

Hæra's whole body went rigid.

Isla seemed to notice this. She elbowed Jim, who grimaced. "But, ah, when she does go, you've got us, haven't you? Connor and me. And we know folk who'd be glad to help—Bruce Cursiter on the Mainland has a good spread and could give advice."

Hæra heard it all and understood perhaps half. Madeleine was leaving soon. She knew that. Hadn't she thought about it on the terrible night everything had happened? But then Madeleine had crawled into bed with her, held her, and for a moment, things were bearable. Hæra hadn't thought about it once since then, not even on her solitary rambles.

She hadn't let herself think about it.

To be without Madeleine—now of all times. It wasn't just now, though. Ever since the night she'd realized she couldn't kill Madeleine, the end of summer had hung over her like an axe on a fraying rope. She'd known their time together must end and had tried to focus on embracing every moment before it did. She'd never imagined it ending like this: not with her returning to the sea to die, but living a drastically shortened life on land without the man who'd been her mainstay for years.

And without the woman whose memory had sustained her, and whose reality had surpassed her wildest dreams.

The pub door closed behind her, and someone lightly touched her elbow. Madeleine, of course. "Ready to go?"

"Yes," Hæra said, her mouth dry, instead of asking the question she really wanted to.

Which was, as she looked down into Madeleine's verdant eyes: *Are you?*

———

The day had wrung Madeleine dry. She ought to stay awake and keep Hæra company, but her eyes were sagging shut. Hæra didn't seem inclined to talk anyway. She was pretending to sleep while Madeleine held her.

When Hæra had been an *Each-uisge,* she'd done the holding. Now, her softer human body lay curled in front of Madeleine's each night. Its warmth usually lulled Madeleine to sleep after a series of long, difficult days.

Yes…sleep…Madeleine needed…

"You have to leave soon," Hæra said roughly.

Madeleine's eyes opened wide.

"Jim said so. Your school starts soon. You have to go home."

She was right. It was nearly August. Lancaster public schools started in less than a month, and Madeleine had to be there a week before then. She had under two weeks to stay in Orkney.

It would be enough time to help Hæra sort out what remained of the logistics. They'd already met with the lawyer in Kirkwall; Madeleine had taken diligent notes while Hæra remained silent and subdued. She'd sent copies of the death certificate to banks and insurance companies. She'd worked with Connor, whom Jonathan had named his executor, and who'd clearly been taken by surprise by that.

That wasn't what Hæra was worried about.

Lightly, Madeleine said, "Anxious to get rid of me?"

She should've known that was the wrong tactic. Hæra's grip on human humor wasn't the best even on good days. She rolled over. Hæra might be human now, but she still had amber eyes Madeleine had never seen on a human face. Now they blazed. "I don't want you to leave."

This conversation was always going to happen. Madeleine still wasn't ready for it. It was easy to bungle sensitive subjects when you were exhausted. Especially when the answer you most wanted to give —*I won't leave*—wasn't the one you had to give.

"I know it's terrible timing," she said carefully. "You must feel like I'm leaving you when you need me the most, but Jonathan…"

Hæra's eyes grew even fiercer. "No. You can't replace him."

Madeleine opened her mouth to say, *I didn't mean that.* But she'd meant it, and Hæra knew it.

"It's not just that. I *never* wanted you to leave. For years, all I've thought of is what would happen when you returned, and it was so much more than I imagined." Hæra touched Madeleine's face, but not with her accustomed fierceness. Instead, she brushed Madeleine's cheek with trembling fingertips. "I know we should have more time before we talk of what could be."

Madeleine's heart stopped. Feelings tangled inside her, knotted like one of her uncooperative embroidery threads. Apprehension and anticipation in equal parts, impossible to separate.

Especially when Hæra was touching her skin. They hadn't made love since that terrible night. As Hæra stroked her, Madeleine's body whispered its need, too long denied.

Down, girl. Definitely not the time.

"I know what you'll say," Hæra continued. "We need time to get used to who we are. I understand what that means now. But you were the one who said we should figure it out together, weren't you?"

Used to who we are: Madeleine, a lesbian, and Hæra, a human. Pretty massive revelations to cope with before you jumped into a committed relationship. Until now, Madeleine and Hæra had been…what would you call it? "Friends with benefits"?

There wasn't really a term for what they'd been.

She swallowed. For a moment, she felt as if she was back on the boat while the deck rocked beneath her. "We don't have to figure it out tonight. We've got three weeks."

"Jonathan used to say I needed to look ahead," Hæra said bitterly. "I refused. Now I know how he felt."

Madeleine propped herself up on one elbow. Her face grew hot at the reprimand, all the worse because it might be true. "Hæra, it's late, and we're both exhausted. Now isn't the time to make any big decisions. You're having to make enough smaller ones as it is."

Hæra gave her a hooded look. "You mean with the solicitors and the banks."

"Well, yes, and figuring out who's going to run what, and…"

"You're helping me with all of that. I don't understand any of it until you explain it to me. Jonathan tried, but I didn't pay attention because I never thought I'd be around long enough for it to matter."

"I want to help." Her throat was thick and hot. "As much as I can before I..."

She didn't end the sentence. She didn't need to.

Hæra said, "Is your help meant to be a substitute for you?"

Madeleine flinched.

"Are you helping me because you feel guilty about leaving?"

"No!" At least she could say that honestly. She leaned toward Hæra, her elbow granting her extra height. "I'd help you no matter how long I was going to be here. I want to, and I'm good at this stuff." She put her hand on Hæra's hip. "You can be too. I know it seems like a lot right now, but you can."

"I won't do it alone," Hæra said. "Jim told me he and Connor would help, and he'll ask some other farmers if they'll teach me about how to be in charge. And it's not as if I don't know *anything* about what Jonathan did. I'll be all right."

Madeleine's stomach clenched. She forced a smile. Of course Hæra would be. She could do anything she put her mind to, including running a farm or becoming human. If she wanted to become the best farmer in Orkney, no doubt she'd...

Madeleine blinked.

"What is it?" Hæra asked.

Madeleine said, slowly, "Do you want to be a farmer?"

Hæra frowned.

"I mean, we've been working on the assumption that you're going to take over the farm. But you don't have to." Madeleine's heart began to hammer in her chest. Wherever she was going with this, it could lead to something big. "You could sell it and live some other way."

Hæra stared at her. Then she rolled over on her back. Madeleine's hand fell from her hip. "And do what?" she asked. "Come with you?"

The word *yes* was already halfway in Madeleine's mouth. As preposterous as it would seem to anyone else, she didn't want to imagine anyone other than Hæra sitting next to her on the flight home. Instead, what about introducing Hæra to Becca, who'd exclaimed happily over every photo Madeleine had sent? She could picture taking Hæra through a city bigger than Kirkwall, introducing her to new ways of life. Showing her Madeleine's favorite bookstore in New Orleans, or…

"Because I would," Hæra said tightly. "If you asked, if that's the only way. I would."

On the last word, anguish split her voice. Madeleine realized: even if Hæra's lifelong dream wasn't to be a farmer, she still didn't want to leave her home. The sea that had birthed her, even if it was painful. The farm she'd built with her best friend. She would do it for Madeleine—she'd said she'd do anything for Madeleine—but it would hurt her. And she'd been so hurt already.

Too much, too soon. For both of them.

"I don't think that's the answer," Madeleine said around a lump in her throat. "And I don't think you *want* to do that, do you?"

"I would. For you."

That was the problem. If or when Hæra finally left Jorsay, it should be for her own sake, to embrace a new life, not because she felt she had no other choice. "I…I don't think that's the only way. I'm sure we can think of something."

"Can we?" Hæra turned back to Madeleine, pain still in her eyes. "I want to believe so, because I'm greedy. I wondered if that would change now that I'm human, but it hasn't. I want both the farm and you."

I want that too. Madeleine almost strangled on the words. Anyone would call this crazy, but this summer had changed her. It had been painful and confusing, yes, but before Jonathan's death, it had also been the happiest time in her life. She loved Ætlaquoy, the cliffs and beaches, even the terrifying standing stones. There were mysteries on Jorsay she could spend her life trying to unravel, never succeeding. The best mysteries were like that. Hæra was like that.

"I'm sorry," Hæra said.

Startled, Madeleine asked, "Sorry for what?"

Hæra rolled back over and took one of Madeleine's hands in a firm grip. She looked at them, joined, and traced a fingertip over the back of Madeleine's hand. Following the veins. A couple of weeks ago, Madeleine had pricked her finger, and Hæra had tasted her blood. Madeleine had wanted her to. A sort of communion. Now they needed other things to share.

"Many things," Hæra said. "I'm sorry I lied to you. I'm sorry for what I was going to do to you. Although—although I don't know if I ever could have. But I thought I could."

Hæra hadn't properly apologized to her for any of that. Everything had been so overwhelming that Madeleine honestly hadn't realized. Hearing the words now made her lungs expand again. Hæra's look was haunted and intent.

"It hurt you, when you found out," Hæra said.

It hurt now, remembering it. As much as she wanted to shield Hæra tonight, now was the time for honesty. Madeleine nodded wordlessly.

Hæra held her gaze, as one determined not to turn back or be afraid. "I never wanted to hurt you. I realize how that sounds. But of course I would have."

"The Great Mare said you couldn't have," Madeleine replied. "I agree with her."

"It might be dangerous not to." Now Hæra was trying, and failing, to sound light. "Either that, or you have too much faith in me."

"Faith's sort of my thing." Even though she looked at it from a different perspective now, to say the least.

"You looked so frightened that night." Hæra tightened her grip on Madeleine's hand. "You didn't look as if you thought I wouldn't hurt you."

The mud had been slick under Madeleine's feet while rain soaked into her sweater. She'd been holding a kitchen knife as if to ward off the truth's horror. Every inch of her skin had crawled in protest. "I wasn't exactly thinking," she said. Just reacting. She shivered. That had been the last time she'd seen Jonathan alive—and Hæra as an *Each-uisge*. The first was horrible. The second...

"You did hurt me. Just not like you were planning to." She remembered something else the Great Mare had said, something about love, and how Madeleine had replied. She remembered food from the Sunrise Café. "I forgive you," she said. "You're sorry, and you tried to make amends. You offered yourself to your mother for my sake."

Hæra looked away. Her dark hair hid her face. "The least I could do. She came after you because of me."

"She came after me because she wanted to," Madeleine said firmly. "And she was more interested in you, remember? The way Beathag behaves isn't your fault."

"She killed my *father.*" Hæra flopped back down onto the mattress with a groan, although she didn't let go of Madeleine's hand. "If I actually loved anyone in my family, it was him. She did to him what I'd thought to do to you."

"Yes and no." How strange, to speak of her own planned gruesome fate this reasonably. "You wanted to grow and change. To escape what life had in store for you. She wanted to destroy your father rather than lose him."

Hæra blinked at her.

"Granted, you still shouldn't have planned to kill anyone," Madeleine conceded.

"Correct." Hæra rubbed her thumb against the back of Madeleine's hand. "I've learned that much of human morality already, haven't I? But you're eager to excuse me for something awful."

"I am *not* excusing you," Madeleine said flatly. "Forgiving you is different."

"Ah. I see." Hæra pressed her lips together. "You forgive me. That's more than I deserve. Do you love me as well?"

The question landed between them with enough weight to crack a new fissure in the seabed. Madeleine searched for words. Well, one word. A simple one.

"I told you that you did," Hæra said. "I should have asked you instead."

Madeleine's back and underarms began to sweat. Her heartbeat kicked into high gear. Even she couldn't tell if it was hitched to anticipation or terror. "I ..."

"Because I love you," Hæra said. She rolled over and rose up over Madeleine, propping herself on one elbow and looking straight into Madeleine's eyes. Her own eyes were as clear and fearless as they'd been when she was a creature of the ocean. "I don't know if it's how I'm supposed to love somebody. I don't even feel like a person sometimes. I feel like a collection of pieces that got scattered all over, in the sea and on the land, and somebody's picked them up and thrown them all back in the same place, only they don't match anymore and they don't *look* like anything..."

"Hæra..."

"But the pieces all love you. That's what they have in common, and that's me, I'm somebody who loves you with all that I am. For whatever that's worth. Maybe it's not worth anything." Hæra's nostrils flared, her eyes were wild, and for a moment she looked inhuman indeed. "But it's yours. So am I."

Madeleine could barely breathe. Her eyes stung, they were wet, and she was gasping.

"Madeleine? Have I made you cry? I didn't mean to—I—"

"My Hæra," Madeleine choked. "Oh my God." She threw her arms around Hæra's neck and dragged her down, right on top of herself, which didn't make it any easier to breathe. She didn't care. All that mattered was holding Hæra as tightly as she could.

Hæra clutched her too, rubbing her face into the curve of Madeleine's throat. "Yes. Yes, I'm your Hæra. Do you understand that, do you believe me?"

Madeleine pressed her nose into Hæra's hair. It smelled like the apple-scented shampoo she'd used in the shower this morning. She preferred hot water now. She said it felt good. She'd changed.

All of Madeleine's previous objections held true: they hadn't known each other long enough. The current circumstances weren't conducive to level-headed decisions. They both had enough baggage to fill an Airbus's cargo hold.

None of that stacked up against Hæra's beauty in the night, the passion in her voice, her desperate courage, and all that had passed between them for six years.

"I love you too," Madeleine whispered into her hair. The words shook her to the core. Before her, love's yawning chasm opened wide, ready to swallow her whole and break her for good if things went wrong. She would leap anyway. She already had. "I really do."

Hæra gasped and rolled to her side, bringing Madeleine with her. She turned her head, angled her mouth, and kissed Madeleine. She kissed her with the same mouth she used to laugh, to eat, and to say *I love you*. She could do a hundred other things with her lips and tongue, but she wanted to kiss Madeleine the most.

The kiss was a homecoming, one that spread warmth through Madeleine's limbs as surely as the fireplace on a chilly night. Hæra didn't kiss Madeleine like she wanted to eat her up, though. Rather, she invited Madeleine in, and when she surged into Madeleine's embrace, she made a soft, plaintive noise. Not her usual possessive growl. And when Madeleine pulled back for a look into her eyes, Hæra's face was slack and vulnerable with desire.

"I need it," she said hoarsely. "I need to feel good."

Madeleine realized: Hæra didn't want one of their usual rough, passionate encounters. Her eyes begged for tenderness and care. And every cell in Madeleine's body sang out that she was ready to give it.

She couldn't swear to stay on Jorsay or make any other unkeepable promise, but she could give this to the woman she loved.

When she tugged at the top button of Hæra's pajamas, Hæra whispered, "I thought you were exhausted."

"I am." Madeleine traced her fingertip down Hæra's warm throat and then back up and over the line of her jaw. Hæra was every bit as rangy and muscular as she'd always been, even if those muscles had less supernatural strength. She seemed to consider this a downgrade. Madeleine had to disagree. "I'm in no shape for vigorous shenanigans. We'll have to take it slow. Nice and gentle."

Hæra's eyelashes fluttered, and for a second, longing was naked on her face. "If—if you'd like that, I suppose we could give it a try."

Madeleine suppressed a chuckle as she leaned in for another kiss. "Wow, try not to give me an ego, okay?"

"I'll give you something else." Hæra threaded her fingers into

Madeleine's hair. Her body was taut with an eagerness Madeleine knew well by now. Straining at the bit.

But there weren't any hickeys or scratches tonight. Nobody got picked up and flipped over or held down. For the first time, Madeleine explored Hæra at her leisure.

Hæra's flesh was a treasure to be cherished and protected. Her mouth too. They kissed and came closer, undressing each other layer by layer until they were twined together, naked. The rub of Hæra's breasts against her own, Hæra's body beneath her hands, Hæra's soaked heat around her fingers.

Somehow a bold, brilliant creature had landed in the middle of Madeleine's life: Hæra the shooting star. Madeleine would catch her so carefully in the palm of her hand.

When they were done, Hæra tucked her face into the sweaty curve of Madeleine's throat. "Today was awful. I needed that. Thank you."

"I needed it too." Did Hæra understand that?

"What else do you need?" Hæra stroked the slight roundness of Madeleine's bare stomach. There was more muscle there now. "Do you know?"

It might be a loaded question, but Hæra's gentle touch, combined with the echoes of pleasure, had Madeleine melting into the mattress. Her eyelids were heavier than ever.

"I'll figure it out," she said. "Tomorrow. I promise."

———

Madeleine had promised tomorrow. She kept her promises. Hæra shouldn't have pushed. If she gave Madeleine more time, maybe Madeleine would say *Yes, I'll stay with you forever, because I love you.*

Madeleine had told Hæra she loved her. Nobody had ever done that before. It was like being thrown a shining rope in the darkness. For a moment, Hæra had seen things clearly, and they weren't all horrible. Madeleine loved her, and that was worth everything.

As fast as her mind was whirling, her body felt loose and contented for the first time in days. Madeleine had taken the lead tonight, and she'd been gentle and generous. She'd seen to Hæra's pleasure and treated her as if she were more precious than anything in a treasure chest.

Madeleine slept now. Her eyelashes fluttered; her eyes moved beneath their fragile lids. Maybe she was dreaming. Dreadful thought. Hæra's dreams were all nightmares: Asgall reaching for her beneath the waves in his human shape, the skull visible beneath his skin. Beathag returning to tear her apart, before turning away because she didn't love her enough to take her life. Jonathan dissolving into ash and drifting away on the tide while Hæra begged him to return.

Hæra gently pushed a stray lock of hair from Madeleine's brow. "I want to dream about you," she whispered.

If wishes were horses, Jonathan used to say, beggars would ride.

There must be something she could keep. Some trace of herself, the self she was both then *and* now. Her life had a "before" and "after" period, divided between the night she broke and the weeks she'd spent afterward picking up the shards. There had to be more to her than that. She wouldn't be a ruin.

Her mobile lay on the bedside table. Hæra considered it and then crept out of bed, reaching for her underwear.

Moments later, she sat in the overstuffed armchair, phone in hand, with her music app open. Her fingertip hovered over the track she wanted to play: the humpback whale songs that used to get her in the mood, or make her feel as if she were back in the sea.

As an *Each-uisge*, she'd understood whale sounds perfectly. It had assisted in hunting them when the herd had good numbers and enough strength to take on a whale. Humans couldn't hear that way; they measured whale sounds in terms of frequencies and found patterns to say that this was a mating song, that was a challenge, and so on.

The sounds weren't science. They were speech. As a human, Hæra might no longer understand them.

The thought tore the inside of her lungs. Maybe it'd be better not to know.

No. She had to know. Madeleine would be brave enough to listen. Hæra must be too.

She pressed "play." No sound at all came at first, only ambient water noise. What was taking so long? Could she no longer hear whale voices, period? If so…if she had lost what had given her such comfort…

"I'm here," a male humpback announced. *"I've been seeking you for so long."*

Hæra covered her mouth to stop the cry that crowded into her throat.

"I've waited for you," a female replied.

"Let me prove my worthiness."

Tears pricked Hæra's eyes. No reason to hold them back; nobody was here to see. Thank the depths and the Great Mare, not everything was lost to her. She still had the whales, and she still had their song.

She looked up at the ceiling and exhaled so hard it hurt, and she spent the next few minutes listening to the whales court one another. Their songs were jubilant. She hadn't heard anyone expressing joy since Jonathan's death. But joy was still out there, somewhere. Perhaps someday she'd know it again too.

She'd remember Jonathan, she'd remember how to listen to whales, and she'd hold on to everything she'd been. She'd do all this while discovering who she would be.

"You okay?"

Hæra turned. Madeleine stood behind the sofa, rubbing her eyes.

"I'm all right." It felt true for the first time in a while.

Madeleine didn't seem convinced. Her smile had a slant of worry to it. "You're crying. That doesn't have to be a bad thing, but I wanted to check."

Not a bad thing. Madeleine was right. Yes, Hæra was crying, but these tears didn't make her chest feel cold and heavy.

"Are you listening to whale sounds?" Madeleine asked. "I remember when you tried to play them in bed."

"And you didn't appreciate it one bit." Hæra lowered the volume on her phone, but she could still hear the song.

"Can I ask *why* you're listening to whale sounds?"

Hæra took a deep, shuddering breath, one she exhaled into a smile. "I wanted to know if I'd still be able to understand them. And I can."

Madeleine's eyes widened. She rounded the sofa and perched on the chair's arm. The chair rocked forward; Hæra braced her feet against the floor to keep Madeleine steady. "Really?" Madeleine said.

"Yes. They're mating." Hæra listened, grinned, and hit pause. "This part's actually a bit filthy. Let's give them some privacy."

Madeleine's smile lit up the room until there was no more space for shadow. "Is 'congratulations' the right thing to say? I wonder what else you're still able to do."

"Perhaps nothing. This is enough." Hæra placed her hand on Madeleine's thigh. "It's the only music I knew when I was growing up. I'd have hated to lose it."

"I'm so glad you didn't." Madeleine, still smiling, combed her fingers through Hæra's hair. The pleasant, gentle tug brought more tears to Hæra's eyes, and she sniffled. "When we were out with Jonathan's ashes and you said you hated the sea, I worried. I know you were unhappy in your herd, but…well, hating the entire ocean didn't seem good for you. I'm glad there's something you want to keep."

Hæra tilted her head back for more caresses. Madeleine's fingers caught on tangles here and there, but the small tugs were fine, they made this more real. "Is there anything you're keeping too? From what you were before?"

Madeleine's fingers stopped stroking. She frowned. "That's a good question."

"That's the only sort of question I ask." Hæra bumped her head against Madeleine's hand pointedly.

Madeleine chuckled. "Did you like having your mane petted before? Maybe you kept that too."

"Nobody ever petted my mane. I might have liked it. Well?"

"I don't know," Madeleine said slowly. "I'll have to think about that."

"If I should keep something, you should too." What was good for the mare was good for the stallion. Or in this case, another mare.

"You might be right." Madeleine began stroking Hæra's hair again. "Am I petting you all night while you listen to dirty music, or can we go back to bed?"

If they went to bed, they'd go to sleep, and tomorrow would come. Tomorrow, when Madeleine would make her decision about what to keep and what to throw away.

"Let's stay up," Hæra whispered. "Just a little bit longer."

CHAPTER FORTY-FOUR

When someone did you a favor, you ought to be properly appreciative. Thank-you notes were out of style, but Madeleine had been raised to send them, and the Daughters of Grace had taught their students the same. She'd sent a few on Hæra's behalf, until Hæra found out and insisted on writing them herself, in her own personal style.

Madeleine's favorite was:

Dear Mr. and Mrs. Darrow,

Thank you for the flowers you sent. Jonathan didn't like lilies but I do. They look pretty in the house. Thank you also for not acting as if I am strange because of everything that happened and for being nice to me even though he's dead.

Sincerely,
Hæra North

"North," Madeleine had belatedly learned, was the surname Jonathan and Hæra had invented when he'd cadged the birth certificate from Jorsay's registrar. She'd assumed it was Rendall, but it wouldn't make sense for Hæra to have Jonathan's last name since she'd supposedly been born without his knowledge.

When Madeleine had asked Hæra about the choice of name, she'd said, "I come from the North Sea. We weren't very imaginative."

Imaginative or not, now that the first shock had worn off, Hæra seemed determined to adapt to her new circumstances. If that included writing thank-you notes, she'd do it. She was gritting her teeth and learning how to be human as best she could, her ability to understand whale song notwithstanding.

For example, she'd asked Madeleine for a declaration of love instead of stating it as a *fait accompli*.

Madeleine sighed as she biked into the village. Last night, Hæra had asked her to figure out what she wanted. She'd promised to do it today. In the light of morning, that seemed a little hasty. Why hadn't she asked for a little more time? There were nearly two weeks left before she had to leave.

She did have to leave. She needed money to live, and obtaining a work visa didn't seem easy. Orkney had no teacher shortage. Hæra would have to get a sponsor license to hire Madeleine to work on Ætlaquoy, and that didn't feel right. Whatever the job was, Madeleine wasn't ready to move to a new country on a moment's notice after the most tumultuous season of her existence.

No matter how beautiful Hæra was in the middle of the night. No matter how incomplete Madeleine felt without her embrace. They had to be sensible, didn't they?

She groaned as she reached her destination. She'd gotten into better shape after over a month of working on a farm, but her thighs still burned from a long bike ride.

It was just past ten in the morning, and the Sunrise Café was open for business.

Madeleine hadn't been here since she and Hæra had stopped by after their pledge on the beach. She hadn't been *avoiding* the place, exactly. It wasn't a crime not to patronize a restaurant, and she'd made up for her earlier mistake, so everything was squared away.

Except it wasn't.

Sending a thank-you note for their gift would have been enough. And yet, Madeleine found herself here in person to extend her gratitude. Was this what they called "full circle"?

The bell jangled when she opened the door, and Arjun looked up from the register. She'd timed her visit to avoid a morning rush, and the café was otherwise empty. An audience would make things awkward. "Good morning," Madeleine said shyly.

He smiled. "Hello there. No need to hover in the doorway."

"Right, right." Madeleine slipped into the café, face hot.

"What can I get for you?"

Her planned words deserted her. While she struggled to find them, Madeleine glanced at a nearby corkboard, papered with notices for events all over Orkney: music performances, livestock exhibits, art classes. Hæra could go to all of those things if she wanted, after Madeleine was gone.

Madeleine cleared her throat. "Ah, actually, is"—she was going to say *Jeremy*—"your husband here too?"

At the word *husband,* so bald and bold, her spine tingled. She kept looking Arjun in the eyes. Hopefully her smile didn't look forced or weird.

"Sure," Arjun said cheerfully, so it must not have. "Oi, love! Visitor!"

Love, somehow, seemed even balder and bolder. And more beautiful. Madeleine's face must be tomato-red now.

Jeremy emerged from the back, wiping down a wet carafe. "Visitor?"

"The lady from New Orleans." Arjun raised his eyebrows at Madeleine. "Stopped by here a few weeks ago with a friend."

Jeremy's expression said he needed no reminding—that he remembered perfectly well who she was, after she'd snubbed him once and made a veiled apology later.

If Hæra were here, she'd stride confidently up to the counter and just start talking. Madeleine could take a page from her book. She threw back her shoulders and walked forward. "I wanted to thank you for the food you sent to that same friend," she said. "After Jonathan Rendall died."

Any amusement in Arjun's eyes faded into sympathy. "Poor old fellow. Never did meet him, but everyone was talking about it."

Hæra would have asked, *If you never met him, why did you send us food?* Madeleine had to put her own spin on it. "It was kind of you to send those rolls when you didn't know him. Or Hæra, really."

"Arjun said she made quite an impression," Jeremy said dryly, and added, "Oof" when Arjun elbowed him.

"She usually does." Was Madeleine blushing again? "Anyway, I just…wanted to stop by and say thank you. It meant a lot." She bit her lip. Hoped they'd hear what she was actually saying.

Arjun and Jeremy looked at each other. Somewhat to Madeleine's dismay, Jeremy leaned forward and rested his elbows on the counter-top. "So," he said, in the manner of a man with something on his mind.

"Jer," Arjun said warningly.

"No, no. I come in peace." He raised one hand, as if to prove it. "Just seems as if there's unfinished business, and I hear you're leaving soon."

Madeleine's shoulders slumped. "Does *everyone* talk about *every-thing* here?"

"Not everything," Jeremy replied. "There's certain things they're remarkably close-mouthed about. At least to us outsiders. I'm sure they're nattering nonstop to each other." He tilted his head to the side. "It takes a while to be accepted in a place like this, but you seem to have managed it much faster than we have."

"I don't think so," Madeleine hedged. "Everyone's been really nice, but I think it's different when you're just visiting."

"Dunno about that." Arjun leaned back against the coffee bar and crossed his arms. "You moved in with one of the islanders and started working his farm. Took up with his daughter, they say. Everyone talks about you as if you're one of them already. Then they stop talking if we get too close."

She almost said *I'm sorry*, but she wasn't responsible for other people's behavior, even when it involved her. "I don't know what's up with that, but it's too bad they haven't made you feel welcome."

"We're not unwelcome, exactly," Jeremy said. "Just held at arm's length. At first we wondered if it was because we're gay, but given how the villagers have taken to you two, I reckon that's not it."

Having laid down the gauntlet, he returned to drying the carafe.

Madeleine had completed her errand, and she'd be within her rights to march out of here and never come back. She could tell them to mind their own business, for good measure. She didn't owe anyone any explanations.

She'd also never had other gay people to talk to before, and she still wasn't used to thinking *other*, applying the word to herself as well.

"The first day I was here, I didn't behave well," she said carefully. "I think you remember."

Arjun nodded while Jeremy replaced the carafe.

"I was working through some issues. When Hæra and I came here, Jeremy, Arjun implied you'd done something similar."

Jeremy sent a startled look to Arjun, who shrugged and said, "You thought you were straight until you were twenty-six."

Ah, discovering yourself at the ancient age of twenty-six. They couldn't be out of their early thirties now. Madeleine said dryly, "These things are relative."

"Sounds like," Jeremy said. "Heard you used to be a nun."

Madeleine raised her eyebrows.

"Harry Duggan stopped by," he admitted. "Seems you've got a story. Things'll be quiet until the lunch rush." He tilted his head in invitation.

Apparently a conversation was happening. It should happen. She was long overdue for a conversation like this. "Can I get a cup of coffee first?"

Arjun turned to the cash register. "I was hoping you'd ask."

Minutes later, they sat at one of the little tables, both men glancing at the door in case a customer came in. Madeleine's heart remained curiously steady as she recounted her story. It was the expurgated version: she said years ago she'd had an "encounter" with a woman that showed her she needed to leave the Daughters of Grace, but not how or where. She said she'd returned to Jorsay because she'd liked it on the field trip, leaving out the part about seeking answers. And she said she'd met Hæra, and everything had changed, omitting the little fact of Hæra's supernatural origins. There was such a thing as too much detail.

Becca knew a version of this, but telling it to other gay people felt different: as if she didn't have to explain or excuse anything. By the end, they were nodding along and making sympathetic sounds.

They understood.

Halfway through her story, Arjun had taken Jeremy's hand. Madeleine fought not to stare at it. The air on her palm suddenly became lack; Hæra's hand should be there instead.

The coffee was nearly cool by now, but a sip steadied her. "Anyway, that's the story of a stranger. Thanks for listening to it."

"I like these sorts of stories," Jeremy said. "Reminds me I'm not thick for not figuring myself out during puberty like some people here."

"Love," Arjun said gently.

Love, Madeleine thought, and Hæra's smile flashed in her memory.

"We wondered if you and she would come back. I reckon she's busy taking care of loads of things."

Or walking around the farm, or diving into work, or staring off into space. How could Madeleine leave her now? She looked down at the table. "Yes. Lots to do after a death."

"You've been helping her? That's kind."

Madeleine moistened her lips. "It's what people should do for each other."

Neither replied. When she looked up, they were regarding her with identically raised eyebrows. How long did it take before spouses had the exact same mannerisms?

"Sure," Arjun said. "Takes a village and all. But you're leaving? How's that going to work?"

It isn't. It's not going to work. I have to leave her, and I can't bear it. I don't know how it can work. "What do you mean?"

"I mean are you going to try an LDR?" Arjun said. At Madeleine's blank look, he said, "Long-distance relationship. Jeremy's company moved him to Edinburgh, and it was almost six months before I could follow him, but we managed. Still, I suppose your circumstances are different..."

"And they say Harry Duggan's the nosy one," Jeremy said.

"What? At least I ask, instead of poking about for a confession like the bloody police. Madeleine? Are you all right?"

Her hands were stiff around her coffee mug. She must have the strangest look on her face, but that was fitting when an obvious solution landed in front of an oblivious person.

Hæra hadn't mentioned an "LDR" either, so at least she wasn't the only one. Unless Hæra had, in fact, thought of it, and hadn't said anything, because she didn't like the idea.

There was a lot to dislike about it. It would be incredibly difficult. But the Gospel of Matthew said, "With God all things are possible."

God might be chancier than before, but possibility seemed bigger than ever.

"I'm fine," she said. "I have a lot to think about. That's all."

CHAPTER FORTY-FIVE

"SUPPER SMELLS GOOD." Hæra kicked the mud from her boots and left them at the cottage's back door, which they'd finally replaced. "What are you cooking?"

Madeleine was just removing a tray from the oven. "Lamb chops."

"From the farm?" Hæra was only joking. Madeleine could be sentimental about the livestock. She said it was hard to eat something whose face she'd seen.

"Yep." Madeleine met Hæra's surprise with a smile. "Just got our shipment from the butcher. I bought rosemary at the provisions store. They should come out nicely."

"Who are you and what have you done with Madeleine Laurent?" Hæra asked, rehearsing a phrase she'd heard on television. It seemed appropriate.

"You know, I've been wondering that. Want to pour some wine? There's a bottle in the fridge."

They'd never had wine with dinner before. Hæra was still dodgy on the social cues of alcohol. It could mark a celebration, as if Madeleine's decision would both make them happy. But everyone had gathered in the pub after Jonathan's funeral too, so perhaps they'd both be sad.

Her stomach had been in knots all day. Madeleine had been running errands and working in the office while Hæra tended to the livestock. Hæra knew why: Madeleine needed space between them so she could think. What if she'd thought herself right off Jorsay forever?

Then—then Hæra would survive. Somehow. Jonathan would want her to, and her mother wouldn't, and she'd be just as happy to honor one and spite the other. It'd be heart-wrenchingly difficult, that was all.

They sat down to dinner. As usual, Madeleine briefly prayed. When she finished, Hæra said, "Do you pray to the Great Mare now?" When Madeleine looked startled, she clarified, "You've seen her, but you've never seen your God. I assume you pray to the one you know is real."

Madeleine huffed out a soft laugh and snapped her napkin into her lap. "That'd be logical, wouldn't it? But no. I still ask God to bless my food. I don't know if I could eat otherwise. It's too ingrained."

Hæra frowned. "That makes it sound like a bad habit, not a good one."

"I wouldn't say so. It makes me pay attention to my food and reminds me to be grateful that I have some. Even if I'm questioning a lot of things, I don't believe in throwing the baby out with the bathwater."

Hæra had never heard that phrase. The resulting mental image was so arresting she couldn't reply.

"Anyway, never mind that." Madeleine began to slice her meat. "I went to the Sunrise Café today, to thank Arjun and Jeremy for sending us that food."

"I was going to send a note," Hæra protested. "It just takes me a while to write them. I told you I wanted to do that myself."

"I know," Madeleine said quickly. "You still can. I went because—well, I wanted to talk to them. The food was just an excuse."

"Why would you need an excuse to talk to them?" Hæra asked in bewilderment. "They run a business, and they talk to people all the time."

"I meant an excuse for myself, I guess. Not for them." Madeleine sighed. "I haven't been around gay people much. Although Jonathan…" Her voice trailed off.

This conversation was getting harder and harder to follow. "What about Jonathan?"

Madeleine shook her head. "Never mind." Then she popped a piece of lamb into her mouth.

Maybe Madeleine didn't want to talk about it, but it wasn't hard to pursue her train of thought. On the night he'd died, Jonathan had shed tears when Hæra had asked him if he'd ever consummated his bond with Asgall. It hadn't occurred to her that he might prefer males in general. He'd certainly never told her.

Her throat grew thick. Thanks to Madeleine, she knew how such preferences could make humans feel lonely and ashamed. If Jonathan had felt like that for so long, and lived with it in silence, never sharing it with anyone—even her—

"I'm glad you talked to those men," she blurted. "What did they say? Did it help?" Then she shoved a piece of lamb into her own mouth and chewed. She'd make that lump in her throat go away. And it did taste nice. Cooked meat wasn't half bad when prepared correctly.

"Uh, it might have. They gave me an idea. I was hoping you'd hear me out." Madeleine sounded a little unsteady on the last few words, and she reached for her wine with a deep breath, as if bolstering herself for whatever she was about to say. She took a long drink and looked Hæra in the eye. "So. I can't stay on Jorsay, and you're not ready to leave. That's a problem, right?"

I can't stay. The words crawled down Hæra's spine, and she couldn't hold back a shudder. Hopefully Madeleine didn't notice. "You've decided to go, then?" she asked in a low voice.

Madeleine set the wineglass down and began turning it in circles, her fingertips on the flared base. It scraped against the table's wooden surface. She kept her eyes on the pale-yellow liquid within as she said, "I have no choice. I have to go back—I can't just abandon my responsibilities. Including my job."

The lump in Hæra's throat expanded to fill her lungs and stomach.

She shouldn't have taken that bite of lamb. She had to know something. "Tell me, is that an excuse to go? Is it that you don't want to stay with me, but you're saying it's about your job? I'd rather have the truth."

Madeleine's head snapped up. She said firmly, "It's the truth."

That was good, but it didn't help much. "So does that mean you care about your job more than you care about me?" That sounded needy, pathetic, but there didn't seem to be any other way to interpret Madeleine's reasoning.

"*No!*" Madeleine sounded so forceful that Hæra nearly jumped. "I care about you more than I knew I could care about anyone since I lost my family. I've learned I don't have all the answers, and maybe I never will. But I meant what I said last night. I love you."

They stared at each other. Madeleine's expression was open and earnest, as if she was willing Hæra to feel her sincerity across the plates of lamb and glasses of wine.

"I meant it too," Hæra managed. "But if you're leaving, then how—"

"We should do long distance," Madeleine said.

Hæra waited for a few more words to end that sentence. They did not. She said uncertainly, "You're going a long distance. What do you mean?"

"I mean a long-distance relationship." Madeleine leaned forward until her sweater almost touched the roasted potatoes on her plate. Her eyes were alight now, her earlier reticence gone. "I mean you and I stay together even though we can't be together physically all the time. I feel silly for not thinking of it before, like it's got to be all-or-nothing."

Hæra's head spun. "How could we be together without...being together?"

"We'd call each other. Every day if we can." Madeleine tapped her fingertips against the table's edge in an anxious, arrhythmic beat. "I'd want to talk to you every day. Hear your voice."

Talking—yes—but what about embracing? What about kissing, holding hands, and having sex? They couldn't do that if Madeleine lived in America.

Madeleine seemed to read her mind. "We'd see each other as often as we could. I'm good at saving money and finding deals. I'd come here every summer and on longer holidays, and you could visit me too."

Visit? Hæra had never considered that she could leave the farm for a little while and then just…come back. As an *Each-uisge*, she'd been bound to the sea by nature and to Orkney by habit.

Madeleine's eyes sparkled like morning dew on pastures. "Lancaster isn't exciting, but I don't live too far from Philadelphia. We could even go to New York, or take a trip somewhere else—somewhere with mountains, maybe. You've never seen mountains, right? There's so much I want to show you. And you'll love Becca."

Love wouldn't come so easily to Hæra as it did to Madeleine, even as a human. She was prepared to *like* Becca, however. This solution might not be the worst? At least it was better than Madeleine leaving for good.

She gnawed her bottom lip. "And—we'd do this for the rest of our lives?"

The words' significance didn't hit her until they were out of her mouth. She'd spoken often of wanting to be with Madeleine. She'd never said, specifically, that she wanted it to be for a lifetime. Madeleine might think it was "too soon" for that as well.

Hæra would never be human enough not to want her forever.

"No, I wasn't thinking that," Madeleine said.

The cold lump returned to Hæra's throat tenfold. She clenched her hands in her lap so they couldn't do something wrong, like reach over the table and haul Madeleine into her arms, plates and glasses be damned. Her old instincts whispered, *Make her stay. Make her your own.*

That wouldn't do anymore. Madeleine must choose, and it seemed she had. Hæra bowed her head.

"No, no." Madeleine sounded alarmed. "I mean eventually we'd be together all the time!"

Hæra raised her head again, as if a puppeteer were moving her with strings made of hope. Her eyes went wide. "We would?"

"Good grief, yes." Madeleine sounded incredulous, as if Hæra was supposed to have known this already. "I don't want to fly back and forth, and see you only every few months, for the rest of my life."

There the words were. Madeleine had released them into the wild, and there was no taking them back. The intent look on her face suggested she knew it too.

"So how long would we be distant?" Hæra asked hoarsely. "You mentioned multiple summers. Two years? Three? Or—or ten, or—?"

Madeleine shuddered. "Lord, not ten. I couldn't stand to live away from you for so long. I'm not getting any younger, and…" She trailed off and winced.

"And neither am I," Hæra finished. "There's less time."

"You probably still have more than I do. I spent so much of my life hiding from myself. Then you came along, on the beach that night, and you changed everything. You changed *me*."

Madeleine reached across the table, palm up. Hæra seized her hand without thinking twice. It was warm, firm, and slightly damp. Madeleine must have been nervous about how this would go.

"I think I made you more yourself," she said. After all, Madeleine was no more or less courageous, resolute, and stubborn than she'd been six years ago. She was just trying to be happier in her own skin. So was Hæra. "You did the same for me."

A look of wonder crossed Madeleine's face. "If that's true—oh, sweetheart, what a gift. What an amazing thing."

Hæra gasped. She and Madeleine had never used endearments before. Was that allowed now? If so, Hæra needed to choose a suitable one for Madeleine. People in romantic relationships did that. *Humans* did that. She'd lost so much, but right now the cottage was crowded with things she'd also gained, from words to wisdom.

"No more than two years," she said. Though even that seemed like an eternity. "That's long enough for us to figure out everything about ourselves, isn't it?"

A soft laugh escaped Madeleine. "It looks like some things about you will never change. That's weirdly comforting."

"*Well?*"

"Yes." Madeleine squeezed her hand. "Two years. And then we'll close the distance."

"You'll come home to me." A disconcerting thought occurred to her. "Or would I move to America?"

She couldn't imagine doing that, at least not now. But if Madeleine wanted it—if it was the only way they could be together all the time— then she'd manage. Anything was possible as long as they were together.

"I want us to want the same thing," Madeleine said gently. "We don't have to figure that out tonight."

Hæra thought about it and nodded. "Because we'll try both places and then decide. That's a good plan."

"I can't wait." Madeleine's voice cracked. Her eyes looked wet again, and a flush covered her cheekbones. "To show you everything— go places with you, see things through your eyes—everything's going to look new."

Hæra knew how she felt. She'd grown used to living on the farm, but when she'd taken Madeleine on the tour, it was as if she was seeing it again for the first time. She hadn't known time could collapse and expand that way, just because of who you were with.

It was Madeleine's turn. Whenever Hæra visited her, she'd get to do the same thing. And Hæra would be able to do things she'd never thought she'd be able to do. Leave the North Sea behind, get on a plane, and—

And—

And *fly*.

She'd watched aeroplanes so many times, including the little hopper that flew between the islands. It didn't come to Jorsay, and on the rare occasions she'd had to leave, she'd taken the ferry. That had seemed right anyway, since the closer she was to water, the stronger her human form was.

The stronger it *had been*. No longer.

Her human body knew other joys now. Judging by the flush filling her face, Madeleine was thinking about them too.

"So what do you think?" Madeleine's voice cracked again. "Will we do it? If—if you're all in, so am I, I'm—I'm *all* in, Hæra, I…"

Hæra's hands shook. Not with fear. She knew this feeling all too well. If she let her hands move, they would grab. She was barely breathing.

"I love you," Madeleine whispered. "You asked. I said yes. It's true."

Hæra's heart began to race. She didn't bother trying to slow it down; she couldn't. She could only race alongside it. "Good," she said.

Then she shot up from her chair so fast it fell over. She held Madeleine's hand as she rounded the table and dragged her to her feet too, while Madeleine looked at her with wide, wild eyes.

"You love me," Hæra said. For the second time, it wasn't a question.

Madeleine's lips parted, but no words came out. She only nodded, flushed and panting.

"You want me." A familiar feeling surged through Hæra, hot and relentless and *powerful*. Enough of her old nature remained for her to understand whale song. Enough remained for her to feel this way too.

Human or not, love or not, she had to claim what was hers.

Madeleine nodded again and grabbed the front of Hæra's shirt. Familiar shivers ran through her body. She'd trembled for Hæra ever since she'd lain half drowned on the beach, and she'd wanted it then too.

"You…" Hæra bent her head. "Need me."

"Ye—" Madeleine began, and then gave the word's last letter to the kiss.

This hadn't changed either. When Hæra plundered her mouth, looking for treasure, she found it. Madeleine's soft lips opened for her, and she pressed closer, begging for more without words. Her hips already moved restlessly against Hæra's own.

Hæra grabbed her arse. It fit perfectly into her hands. So did all of Madeleine. Judging by how she groaned, Madeleine agreed.

Where to? The bedroom, of course, where they'd lay claim to each other again. Hæra gasped, "Let's go."

"Just a second." Madeleine whimpered the words against Hæra's mouth. "Oh please, I just need a second. Give me—give me your—"

She grabbed the side of Hæra's thigh. "This. Like before, when we were—outside, do you remember, like then—"

She meant the alley, when Hæra had nearly had her beneath a window before someone had interfered. Hæra had been ready to murder whoever had pulled Madeleine from her arms.

Nobody was here to stop them now. She snarled, "I remember."

Madeleine spread her jean-clad legs, and as she'd done on that night, Hæra wedged her thigh between them. Madeleine went up on her toes and rubbed her hips back and forth, making tiny noises in the back of her throat.

"Just for a second?" Hæra whispered. "You just need this for a little while?"

"Please—" Madeleine moved faster. She pressed down harder. Hæra met her by pushing her leg forward, and Madeleine groaned. "Just some pressure, just a little bit, please…and then…"

Hæra seized Madeleine's hair, tilted her head back, and hissed in her ear, "And then you'll be ready for my fuck?"

Madeleine grabbed Hæra's shoulders. "Oh!"

"You'll be ready for me"—Hæra grabbed Madeleine's arse again with her free hand and pushed Madeleine forward—"to give it to you hard?"

"Ah!" Madeleine pressed her face against the side of Hæra's throat and clutched her harder. "S-so crude—!"

"Ready for me to hold you down on our bed." Hæra was getting tunnel vision. Soon, Madeleine would be the only thing she could see. Thank the Great Mare, some things never changed—she could love, but she could hunger too. "To take you there, fill you up?"

She could see it now. Madeleine, naked and sprawled beneath her, hair tumbled over the pillow, her skin flushed and damp. Her mouth open as she begged for what she'd get.

Now, it had to be now. Hæra turned to the bedroom.

"I can't wait," Madeleine gasped.

Her hands dove between their bodies. It took a moment for Hæra to realize Madeleine was unzipping her own jeans.

Her vision whited out. As Madeleine fumbled with the zip, Hæra shoved her sweater and shirt up, revealing her bra; she pushed the bra up too, until Madeleine's breasts bounced free.

Madeleine cried out as Hæra pushed her to the nearest wall. "Please, I—"

Hæra shoved her jeans and panties down her thighs…and stopped there. "Hold up your shirt. Hurry!"

Madeleine obeyed her, gasping.

Hæra stepped back just enough to look her up and down. The sight made her moan. Madeleine held her shirt and bra up over her breasts, which were full and flushed. Her jeans and panties stopped mid-thigh, revealing her thatch of dark hair as she exposed herself to Hæra in the middle of the kitchen.

"You shouldn't look at me like that," Madeleine gasped, which were fine words for a woman who lifted her shirt even higher. "It's shameless."

"So are you," Hæra said hoarsely. "Offering me the only parts I need."

"Oh!" Madeleine turned her head away, even as her legs parted as far as they could before her jeans stopped her. "I-I'm not like that!" Her hips rolled forward, giving the lie. "Please, I can't wait, do something to me!"

"Ah, never fear," Hæra breathed. Her mouth was wet. So was something else. "I will." She stepped forward, crouched, and feasted.

As Hæra sucked her breasts, Madeleine arched up into her mouth and cried out again. "Oh God, oh God! It's so much!"

"Too much?" Hæra nipped the tip of one tight nipple. "I should stop?"

"No. No. More, please—" Madeleine shuddered. "H-harder—"

Hæra gave it to her harder. She sucked one breast, and then the other, going back and forth while Madeleine writhed and begged for more, hips circling frantically, as if hunting again for pressure between her thighs.

"Enough," she gasped. She grabbed the back of Hæra's head, sliding her shaking fingertips into Hæra's hair. "I need—below—"

Hæra licked her nipple and growled, "Not in bed."

"No. C-can't wait. Can't—"

"Turn around." Hæra seized her hips. "And brace yourself."

"You're going to...from *behind*?" Madeleine sounded shocked.

"From behind." This had been in her reading too. They hadn't tried it. She always looked in Madeleine's eyes when they made love, and tonight should have been the perfect time for that—a tender seal on their pact—

But Hæra would never be a tender creature, and she knew Madeleine didn't want her to be.

That would explain why she was already turning around and bending forward so she could place her palms against the wall. She spread her legs as wide as she could again, just wide enough to expose the waiting space between them. Her lips were swollen, her flesh was pink as a rose in bloom.

And she was wet. Hæra could see it. She could practically smell it. And she could definitely feel it, as she plunged two fingers straight into Madeleine's dripping slit.

"*Ah!*" Madeleine shrieked at the wall. She went up on her toes and then thrust backward, hunting for more of Hæra's fingers.

She got it. Hæra braced her own feet on the ground and moaned as she began to thrust. The angle was different. She couldn't go in as deeply, but when she curled her fingers she stroked Madeleine in a new way, and it had Madeleine scrabbling at the wall with her short nails.

"Filthy!" Madeleine gasped. She thrust her hips desperately back on Hæra's hand. "You're just—oh!—taking me like—"

"Like I should have taken you at the start." Hæra's own hips were moving, as if they could find some satisfaction too, but nothing was there. No pressure to ease her own ache. There was only Madeleine's wet, *tight* heat around her fingers. "On that beach, in those nun's clothes."

She never would have, obviously. Madeleine had been half conscious with a concussion, and Hæra had barely understood the urge to kiss her, much less do more. But she'd learned much about the power of fantasy, reimagining a thing until it happened in a different way that turned you on *now* even if it wouldn't have *then*. Now, Hæra could imagine claiming Sister Madeleine that night, fucking this sweet place between her legs until she swore she belonged to Hæra alone.

"Oh, yes," Madeleine sobbed, so she must understand it too. "I'd have been yours."

"You're mine *now*." Hæra leaned over Madeleine's bent body, pressed her face into the back of Madeleine's neck, and drove her fingers in deeper, until Madeleine could do nothing but squirm on them and wail. She was clenching already, on the edge from Hæra's rough words and rougher touch.

Give it to her, Hæra thought, and throbbed so hard she moaned aloud. "You're mine no matter where you go. Mine no matter how far apart we are."

"Yours, yours, yours," Madeleine chanted. Her thighs were shaking. She was on the edge—she just needed a bit more, and then this tight little hole would convulse around Hæra's fingers—

Hæra snaked her free hand around Madeleine's body until she found her breasts. She took one nipple between her fingers, and rolled it, and pinched, at the same time she sunk her teeth into Madeleine's neck.

Madeleine's body went rigid. Then she shouted, "Oh my *God*!" as she throbbed around Hæra's fingers, coming so hard that if Hæra curled her fingers and went faster, right here, right now…

Warm liquid squirted around her hand, splashing her wrist while Madeleine screamed like a banshee and curled her own fingers hard enough to scratch the paint.

Then Madeleine collapsed forward, nearly knocking her head into the wall before Hæra caught her about the waist. She wheezed, sounding as if she were trying to talk but couldn't.

Hæra ought to ask if she was all right, but she couldn't manage to speak either. She could only place her sweating forehead between Madeleine's shoulder blades as she clung to her and slid her fingers out. They were so coated that strings of fluid trailed between them.

Madeleine whimpered and managed to turn her head. Her hands

were still pressed to the wall, although the depths knew how much work they could do to keep her upright. "Oh...oh, Hæra, my Lord... did I, again?"

For answer, Hæra showed Madeleine her coated fingers. Then she pressed them against Madeleine's mouth. "You've tasted me." Hæra's voice sounded as if it had been dredged up from the bottom of the ocean. She pulsed between her legs as desperately as if she'd been waiting to come for hours, not minutes. She needed Madeleine's touch, but first... "Now taste yourself."

Madeleine must still have been wrecked from her climax, because she opened her mouth without protest. Hæra pushed her fingers in, past another pair of soft lips, into another sort of wet heat, and sobbed when Madeleine eagerly licked her own juices.

Hæra yanked her fingers away. Her hands shook and she could barely breathe as she unzipped her own pants. Even the pressure of the zipper nearly finished her off. No, she couldn't—she had to wait—

"My turn?" Madeleine asked breathily. She still looked dazed as she turned around, as exposed as ever, but relaxed and flushed with satisfaction. "My turn to give it to you?"

"Yes," Hæra choked. She was nothing but one long, hungry throb between her legs, and she couldn't live like this a moment longer. "Hurry, give me your...your..."

Madeleine's full mouth gleamed as she licked her lips. "Pants down. Not off. Same as me."

Then, as Hæra watched, she stripped off all her clothes and went to her knees.

Hæra stared at her breasts again, fully exposed now, along with her shoulders and arms and all the rest. Madeleine smiled beatifically, looking far too serene for a naked woman who'd just gushed all over the place.

"Remember how I told you about my dream?" she said. "How you knelt in front of me?"

How could anyone forget a thing like that? Madeleine had dreamed of Hæra kneeling before her, offering her mouth just like... like...

"Now I'm going to show you what you did," Madeleine said.

She leaned in, and it was her turn to grab Hæra's bare arse as she buried her nose in Hæra's curls. She didn't start slowly. She didn't tease, as she often liked to do, with a gentle beginning. Instead she found Hæra's clitoris and rubbed the flat of her tongue against it, fast and hard and firm as any finger—

Hæra grabbed her hair and dug her nails in. She went up on her toes, threw her head back, yelled, and came.

Oh, thank the depths. Thank the Great Mare. Thank God. Thank *everything* that might have been involved in shaping this moment of all moments. Hæra wailed her release like a prayer and surrendered herself to what was too much, and not enough, to bear.

Eventually, the balance tipped toward "too much," and Hæra had to tug Madeleine away. She moaned at the loss, and Madeleine's eyes glowed up at her with pure delight. She licked her lips. "I wasn't the only one ready for it, was I?"

"Shut it," Hæra groaned. With little effort, she hauled Madeleine to her feet and into her arms. Madeleine laughed softly and held Hæra in a tight embrace. It was enough—just—to tether Hæra to earth.

Her hair was damp with sweat and smelled wonderful. Hæra inhaled it deeply and savored the press of Madeleine's naked body. She must gather these impressions, as many as she could, before Madeleine left.

She wanted to ask right away, *How long until you come back?* But Madeleine wouldn't know yet, and it'd wreck the mood. Best not to.

Madeleine intuited it, though, judging by how she ran her hands soothingly up and down Hæra's back. She kissed the underside of Hæra's jaw. "I'll always return to you," she whispered.

It turned out Hæra didn't need her former strength to carry Madeleine to bed. She yanked her pants back on and swept Madeleine up into her arms.

This seemed to put Madeleine into some kind of overjoyed swoon, but when Hæra lowered her to the bed—admittedly, with an effortful grunt—she came back to herself. "Oh gosh. We never finished dinner."

"We will. I'll have what you cooked for me." Hæra lay atop her, putting her weight on her elbows. "I won't waste a bite of what you give me."

Madeleine's eyes glazed over again, which was wonderful. In that moment, her nose was irresistible, and Hæra playfully bumped the tip of her own against it.

Madeleine laughed. "Glad to hear it, but I'll be giving you a lot. Sure you're up for all of it?"

She sounded as if she were joking. She wasn't. A little wobble at the bottom of her voice told the tale.

Hæra said, "Do you think I'm up for *less*? What's worth wanting, if not everything?" When Madeleine's forehead creased—meaning she was about to make a principled objection—Hæra touched her mouth. "The secret lies in wanting the right things. You'll see."

Madeleine's eyes grew wide and wondering. She cupped the back of Hæra's sweaty neck and rubbed her thumb there. Hæra closed her eyes in pleasure. *Made to be touched by you.*

"The *Catechism* teaches that the existence of angels is a truth of faith," Madeleine said quietly.

That got Hæra's eyes open again. She frowned. "I'm not an angel. I never was. And now I'm human."

Madeleine pulled, gently, until Hæra's forehead pressed against her own. Hæra's eyes fell shut at the sudden, solid reassurance of her. Madeleine slid her other arm around Hæra's waist and held her close once more.

"Every angel is, I think," she said.

EPILOGUE

THE SKY

ÆTLAQUOY, FIVE YEARS LATER.

"How soon can you be here?"

Over the phone, Hæra's voice was equal parts impatience and excitement. Madeleine focused on the latter and grinned. "Soon," she said. "I've got a few things to take care of before I leave, and you've got a few things to take care of before I arrive. Don't you?"

"I'm almost done. Are *you* almost done? I don't want to wait much longer, and you still have to get here."

"I'm less than ten miles away," Madeleine pointed out.

Hæra *hmph*'d. Then she said, sounding warmer, "Those words are still nice to hear."

Madeleine's grin grew wider. "They're nice to say."

Yes. Even after living on Jorsay for three years, it was nice to say that she was no farther from Hæra than ten miles rather than by thousands.

"However," Hæra continued, "you could be even less than ten miles. You could be less than ten feet."

The impatience in her voice was of a different sort now. Rather than the anticipation of an exciting event, it was the desire for

Madeleine's presence—immediately. Hæra was human, but sometimes the hunger was the same, and it came out at the most unexpected moments.

Madeleine didn't mind. She felt the same way. Nobody was getting hurt by it, and it felt wonderful, so it was just fine. Her therapist in Lancaster had helped her see that.

"I will be soon. I can't wait," she said, and grinned. "Even though you've only been gone a few hours. Listen to what a pair of lesbians we are."

"I thought we were lesbians because we're attracted to each other instead of men." Hæra sounded puzzled. "Or—oh! You mean it like one of those jokes online."

Madeleine laughed. "Yes, like those jokes."

Over time, she'd come to love the jokes. They were about U-Hauls, getting attached to one another too quickly, being emotionally needy, and somehow they were still funny. Probably because lesbians had made up the jokes about themselves. She was now in a place where she could read them, and think *Yes, Hæra and I are like that,* and feel like she was a part of something. A group she belonged to more than she'd belonged in a convent.

"Well, this is about more than just wanting to see you," Hæra said. "I don't want to lose the weather."

Madeleine looked up into the blue sky. This was the sunniest day Jorsay had seen in weeks. It was ideal weather for Madeleine to putter around in the garden, where she was now, and it was even better for what Hæra had planned. The forecast said it would stretch into tomorrow.

But Hæra had been bursting with excitement about this for weeks, and Madeleine couldn't blame her wife for wanting to take every precaution.

"Then I'm on my way," she said, smiling. "Let me just grab my things."

"Drive safely," Hæra cautioned, as she always did. "I'll be waiting."

They bid each other farewell, and Madeleine took one last look around the garden. The Honey Angel Crocosima was flourishing, but the cheesewood struggled. Next year, she'd have to pack it in with a hardier plant that could shield it from the wind. Both gardening and farming involved lots of trial and error. There was always something new to learn, as Jonathan had told her more than once.

That seemed fitting, since this was his memorial garden. Madeleine and Hæra had begun planning it three years ago, when Madeleine moved here permanently and said the back yard ought to have something nicer than gravel and grass. She'd expected Hæra to resist—say the last thing she wanted to do after wrangling sheep all day was wrangle plants.

Instead, Hæra bought bags of fertilizer the next day. Now, after some missteps and false starts, Jonathan's memory flourished, nourishing the land he'd adored. His body might belong to the sea, but both Madeleine and Hæra believed something of his spirit was here.

Madeleine hurried into the house. She neatly placed her gardening apron and gloves in their spot by the back door and continued to the bedroom to change into cleaner clothes.

The bedroom had come a long way. For years, Hæra had just used it as a place to store her clothes and few belongings. There had been no decoration or hint of personality. She'd seemed reluctant to make any changes to the home she'd shared with Jonathan.

That had begun to change when Madeleine moved permanently to Jorsay. They'd lived apart for the promised two years before the island called her back to stay. Not for any mystical reason—whatever pull Hæra had had over her as an *Each-uisge* was gone. It was the pure and simple desire not to waste another day.

They'd needed the time apart to grow into themselves. Madeleine had to come to terms with her sexuality for her own sake, and Hæra had to learn to be human without Jonathan or Madeleine constantly at her side. Now, Madeleine organized monthly events for Orkney's queer social group, and Hæra chatted confidently with Thornhill's residents when she did the shopping. The distance had been a good thing.

Intellectually, Madeleine knew this. On a deeper, almost primal level, nothing had ever been as joyful as the moment Hæra met her in the Kirkwall airport on the day Madeleine returned to Jorsay for good. Some of her ribs still remembered that embrace.

The house had become not Hæra's, but theirs. They had a bigger bed, covered by a duvet in a merry checkered pattern and a couple of extra pillows whose purpose Hæra claimed not to understand. Madeleine had put aside her embroidery and instead spent long winter evenings sewing blue curtains. Instead of stark white, the walls were now a welcoming, warm shade of peach.

They'd hung up photos that marked various occasions. There was the day Hæra and Jonathan had purchased the farm; a beaming Jonathan held the land contract and Hæra wore a small smile at his side. Next to it, in a selfie, Madeleine and Hæra laughed with Times Square in the background. Below that was a candid picture of Madeleine browsing in her favorite French Quarter bookstore. On the next wall, Hæra and Becca's cat Booster regarded each other suspiciously.

One special photo held pride of place. Over the dresser hung a large picture of Madeleine and Hæra beneath an arch of flowers at the stone cottage's front door. They held hands while Arjun stood in the doorway, reading from the ceremony script. Madeleine wore a white cocktail dress; Hæra stood tall in a suit. A cord wrapped around their joined hands.

Having an outdoor wedding in Orkney was a gamble at the best of times, but the sun had shone on that day as well. Madeleine had clung to her stubborn faith that it would. After everything they'd gone through, it shouldn't have dared to do otherwise.

It would have been a wonderful day even if there had been a downpour. That was obvious from the looks on their faces. Dozens of islanders had turned out for their wedding, but you wouldn't know it from the picture. Hæra and Madeleine gazed at each other as if they were the only people in the world.

Oh gracious. She'd zoned out looking at a photo she'd seen a hundred times. Madeleine shook her head, changed her clothes quickly, and grabbed the overnight bag she'd set by the door. At least she was already packed.

She hurried through the house, through the living room that she was *determined* to refurnish piece by piece, but she paused by the door to Jonathan's old room.

Yes, she was in a hurry, but it seemed important to do this on a day like today.

Madeleine entered the room. Jonathan's bed and his other furniture were long gone, although his fiddle retained a place of pride on a shelf. Now Madeleine and Hæra used the space for something that honored him, themselves, and the journey they'd all taken together.

On a table by the window sat...she wouldn't call it a shrine, exactly. That didn't feel right. But Madeleine had found an extraordinarily beautiful stone from the cliff where she'd met the Great Mare and got it polished. It was the size of her hand and gleamed in mesmerizing swirls of midnight blue, black, and cream. She and Hæra had set it in a glass bowl full of water from the North Sea, and together, they refreshed the water every week. They said no prayers, but it was an intentional reminder of the mysteries that moved the world and summoned their awe.

Madeleine inhaled deeply as she looked at the stone, and then she let out a slow, controlled breath. She whispered, "May it all be well." Not a prayer, but a hope. The two weren't so different.

Now she could leave. Peaceful and purposeful, Madeleine hurried out to the car.

On the way past, she waved at Connor, Jim, and Kevin, another farmhand they'd hired for the summer—really a college student who wanted to have a "rural experience." Judging by his daily shell-shocked expression, he wouldn't return next year, but Connor said he was decent help and he didn't cost much.

"You off, then?" Connor called.

"Yes! I'm going to be late!"

"Be safe," Jim said.

Kevin waved, looking a little awkward.

Madeleine gave them all a thumbs-up and hopped into the Vauxhall, throwing her duffel bag into the passenger seat. She turned the ignition and eased the car into first gear, heading down the drive.

As always, she took the opportunity to survey what she could. The farm might have lost the trow's protection, but five years on, it continued to prosper. It didn't enjoy the same immunity from storms or drought, but it remained in the black, even if the profit margins were slimmer. Madeleine sometimes wondered if the Great Mare might not have a hand (or hoof, or tail) in it. Best not to wonder too much, though. She reverenced the memory of what had happened to her but hadn't seen a supernatural creature in the last five years, and she was fine with keeping it that way.

Never mind water spirits and underground creatures and so on. It was enough to spend every day in honest labor. A *lot* of honest labor— more than she'd realized that first summer here. Farming never stopped. She and Hæra hadn't had a vacation longer than a two-night stay in Edinburgh since she'd moved in.

Well. She liked managing things. A farm was a bigger challenge than a classroom, and there were days when she wanted to throw her hands in the air and give up. But Hæra was always at her side, reminding her why they did what they did, and why it was worthwhile.

Of course, lately Hæra's mind had been less on the farm and more on her other project.

Madeleine drove through the village. Jeremy was sweeping the sidewalk outside the Sunrise Café and smiled at the brief honk of her horn. He and Arjun had to come for dinner soon—it had been too long. Maybe when Becca visited in a couple of weeks? They'd all get along like a house on fire. Perhaps Jim, Isla, and their three-year-old son could make it too. They'd all want to know about Hæra's latest venture. Everyone was asking about it.

She exited the village and kept going north. On the way, she passed the small stone kirk and kept her eyes fixed straight ahead.

After her first return to the States, she'd realized shortly that regularly attending mass no longer resonated with her. Her visits grew more infrequent; she stopped going to confession, which worried Becca but felt quite liberating. After all, Madeleine had eventually been forced to accept she'd confronted an actual god. It hadn't looked like anything she'd ever believed in. She had to redefine the sacred for herself. Now she couldn't say she *disliked* the sight of a church—something about it would always call to her—but there was pain at its doors. Instead of trusting entirely to doctrine, Madeleine had decided to place a bit of trust in herself. It was working so far.

Most of her prayers were undertaken in private these days. That was all right. She'd found other communities worth belonging to, and other ways to worship than standing shoulder-to-shoulder next to others in a sanctuary. The Blessed Virgin had pondered divine mysteries in her heart; there were worse things than following her example.

Within a few minutes, her destination came into view, along with the main attraction there. Madeleine smiled to see it even through a sudden surge of apprehension. This was going to be fine. She'd been telling herself that for days. So had Hæra, but that was different.

Madeleine reached her destination and parked. Hæra was in view, her back to Madeleine. Her shoulders were set proudly straight as she inspected her work.

Madeleine's apprehension vanished. Front or back, Hæra was so beautiful. She always would be. No matter how long their life together was—and Madeleine intended it should be as long as possible—Hæra would never be anything less than a miracle.

"Thank you," she whispered. It didn't matter if nobody was listening. The gratitude was enough.

Before Hæra, a single-engine Cessna airplane sat patiently on Jorsay's new airstrip. Its white paint gleamed in the sun, and light glanced off the edges of the propeller blades.

Looked like it was ready to go.

Madeleine inhaled deeply through her nose as she got out of the car. This was going to be fine. It would be absolutely fine.

"Please," she murmured, just in case somebody was listening after all.

———

After a period of internecine warfare, the Orkney Islands Council had voted yes on a Jorsay airstrip. Now the little island hopper took passengers to and fro, meaning swifter commute times and slightly less reliance on ferries. People were more likely to live on Jorsay, especially since it was relatively cheaper. The population had grown, if not exponentially, and the economy had too. Good news for the islanders, the village, and Ætlaquoy.

Good news for Hæra, too.

It had taken her nearly a year to obtain her LAPL: a light aircraft pilot's license. Thirty hours of flight instruction were required, plus exam study, and she didn't have loads of extra time. Or cash. The farm was profitable, and she and Madeleine lived modestly, but flying lessons weren't cheap. Nor was it easy to travel regularly to Inverness, where the flight school was. On top of it all, fair weather for training could be hard to come by.

Harry Duggan had said Madeleine was "a true saint" for indulging Hæra's "wee hobby" in the midst of running a farm. Luckily, he hadn't said this in Madeleine's hearing, or he'd still be getting an earful about it. The first time she'd seen Hæra looking wistfully at the website for Highland Aviation Training, she'd sat down and said: "Let's make it happen."

Madeleine was an expert at making things happen. Hæra had been thankful for this talent many times, but she'd expressed her gratitude that evening so thoroughly that they'd overslept the next morning.

"Hæra!"

Hæra turned on her heel to see her thoughts' object and heart's desire hurrying toward her across the grass that led to the airstrip. Madeleine carried her overnight bag and wore a smile that looked *almost* bravely enthusiastic.

She was apprehensive, but there was no need. Hæra had changed in many ways over the last five years: she liked hot tea, disliked rare meat, spent far more time talking to people (they were so *interesting*), and had grown to enjoy mystery novels. But one thing would always remain the same: she'd never allow Madeleine Laurent to come to harm.

Hæra jogged forward to greet the woman Connor had called her "bonnie bride," a term Hæra had decided to use well past the wedding day. The wind tugged her ponytail playfully. When she reached Madeleine, she bent down to kiss her cheek and took her overnight bag. She'd carry it for Madeleine; that was chivalrous. "Ready?" she asked eagerly.

"Hello to you too," Madeleine said with a dryness that didn't cover her obvious nerves. She glanced behind Hæra to look at the Cessna, which she'd once compared to a pack of gum.

"Ah yes. I forgot my etiquette again." Hæra checked to make sure the airstrip attendant wasn't looking, then gave Madeleine's rear end a quick squeeze. "How are you, petal?"

"Ooh!" Madeleine swatted her hand away, but she laughed breathlessly. "I can't believe I'm doing this."

"You're going to love it." Hæra seized Madeleine's hand and tugged her toward the plane. "Think how posh you'll feel when we land and walk past people who had to fly commercial."

"Just as long as we don't crash into posh little pieces." Madeleine slid her arm around Hæra's waist to show the complaint was without teeth.

Hæra slung her arm around Madeleine's shoulders in return. She might no longer be able to lift hundreds of pounds without breaking a sweat, but she'd lost no muscle mass working on the farm day in and day out. Her arms were plenty strong enough to hold Madeleine tight, no matter the occasion. "I'll throw myself between you and the ground. Fine cushion, that."

"Now I feel better. You've got all your stuff?"

Madeleine always said you needed so many *things* to go places. She said Hæra always forgot something, but what was the harm in sharing the occasional toothbrush? It didn't seem very different from kissing. "Oh, probably. We're only gone for one night. I know I've got my nice shirt and pants for dinner."

Madeleine gave a muffled sigh. Then she patted Hæra's arm affectionately and looked up at the Cessna. "I wish he could be here for this," she murmured.

After five years, a reference to Jonathan no longer felt like a blow to the gut. This one put a lump in Hæra's throat, though. "He'd ask me why I wanted to do something so damned silly as get in an aeroplane when there's a perfectly good ferry. And he'd refuse to climb aboard."

"I'd get the honor of your maiden passenger voyage no matter what," Madeleine said firmly. "I almost died of fright the first time you took off with your instructor, and that wasn't for nothing. But he'd be proud of you, and you know it."

This was the first time Hæra would fly without an instructor *and* with a passenger on board. She'd worked hard to get here. Jonathan had always praised her work ethic and how she'd never tried to skive off, even when it was so hard at the start. She'd worried she'd forget him, but thank the Great Mare, she knew now that wasn't true.

"Yes." She swallowed the lump. "He would be. And I'm proud of myself."

It had taken a while to stop hating herself for her mistakes and castigating herself for being a terrible human. She saw now that all humans made mistakes and weren't always good at being themselves. Even Madeleine said an unkind thing occasionally. The main thing was to learn and then to do better next time. Her first flight hadn't gone perfectly, but she'd stuck the landing.

Madeleine grabbed Hæra's arm. She beamed. "I'm so glad to hear that, sweetheart. Well? What were you saying about taking advantage of the weather?"

A few minutes later, they were situated in the familiar cockpit. The Cessna 152 was rented from the flight school. Hæra had trained in it, and by now she knew it as well as she used to know the shoals off the island. She'd already run through the pre-flight checklist twice—no sloppiness for her, when her wife was along for the ride—and she'd flown the plane here this morning herself. Everything was in order.

"Right." Madeleine's shoulder harness fastened with a *click*. Her pallor had returned somewhat. "I'm all set."

"No you're not," Hæra said at once. "We haven't had the passenger briefing."

"The what?"

"I'll begin with a flight overview," Hæra said. "Then, since you already did the seat belt, I'll skip that bit and go to the evacuation procedures, followed by the fire extinguisher location and how to secure our belongings. Today we're flying from Jorsay's airstrip to Aberdeen International Airport. We anticipate a cruising altitude of— what is it?"

Madeleine quickly put a hand over her mouth, but wasn't fast enough to hide her smile. "Nothing."

"There's a procedure to follow," Hæra said in exasperation.

"I know." Madeleine cleared her throat and appeared serious. Her eyes still sparkled, though. At least she didn't look green about the gills anymore. "I'm sorry, Captain. Proceed."

"You know," Hæra said, "for someone who gets in a flap about how dangerous these planes are, you're awfully cavalier about this."

"I'm just covering up my nerves, trust me. I'm curious about what the evacuation plan is." Madeleine prodded her window. "This, I assume."

"Only if the ejector seat doesn't work," Hæra said, straight-faced.

"Ha-ha." Madeleine's eyes widened. "Wait. Really?"

"We anticipate a cruising altitude of eight thousand feet," Hæra continued. "And a flight time of approximately an hour and a half. The fire extinguisher is mounted to the wall behind your seat. Our belongings are already stored in the baggage area, so there's nothing to say about that. Any questions?"

"One. You're joking about the ejector seat, right?"

"Let's hope you don't have to find out." Hæra pretended to reach for the ignition and laughed when Madeleine wailed and grabbed her wrist. "Yes! I'm joking."

Madeleine huffed and let her go. "Safety is no laughing matter."

"You're right." Hæra pushed a lock of hair back behind her wife's ear. "Especially yours. Not to me."

Madeleine's outraged look softened, and she held Hæra's hand to her cheek for a moment. "Glad to hear it. I'm scared stiff, but still excited. And ready for liftoff."

Hæra would explain the difference between "takeoff" and "liftoff" during the flight. Surely Madeleine would find it fascinating. "Not yet, you're not. Here."

She offered Madeleine the passenger headset. Madeleine's eyes widened. This part seemed to delight her, judging by her gleeful smile as she donned the headset. "Gosh, this feels so *official*."

"It's standard-issue gear."

"It's not standard for me." Madeleine tapped the handles of the passenger-side yoke. "I get my own steering wheel?"

"You do not," Hæra said sternly. She put on her own headset. "Don't touch anything. Sit on your hands if you've got to."

"What a grouch." Madeleine settled back in her seat and took in a deep breath. Then she exhaled heavily. "How do you turn this thing on?"

"The same way I turn you on." Hæra reached for the ignition again. "With a steady touch and fine attention to detail."

The engine roared to life. The propellers began to spin. Madeleine's voice sounded tinny over the headset when she said, "I'll hold you to that tonight."

Hæra grinned. The flight itself was the trip's main event, but she was looking forward to their evening in Aberdeen, and she knew Madeleine was too. It wasn't the most exotic locale, but they got away so rarely. The farm was a demanding, sometimes cruel mistress.

Years ago, Madeleine had asked Hæra if she'd consider giving it up. Hæra hadn't been able to imagine it at the time. But now...

It wouldn't be a huge leap to go from her LAPL to a private pilot's license. Then she'd have greater freedom over when and where she could fly. And perhaps—if *that* went well, and she kept going—

She couldn't imagine herself in the cockpit of a giant Airbus, ferrying passengers around the world. Not if it meant leaving Madeleine behind for long stretches. But there were less demanding pilot jobs that could take her above the clouds, if she chose. And while Madeleine loved the farm, it exhausted her too. She could be ready for a change. She spoke of missing the classroom; she might like to be a teacher again.

Perhaps not in Orkney. Perhaps they'd go somewhere else. Hæra loved seeing the world with Madeleine—there was so *much* of it out there.

They might not be filthy rich, but they had options. That was worth more than anything you could find in a treasure chest.

"Hey," Madeleine said.

Hæra looked up from checking the oil pressure gauge. "Hmm?"

"I'm proud of you too." Madeleine squeezed Hæra's shoulder, her grip firm through the warm layer of Hæra's jacket. "I'm so, so proud of you, sweetheart. Do you know that?"

Hæra grabbed Madeleine's hand and brought it to her lips. She kissed her wife's knuckles and felt the calluses on her palm. "The feeling is mutual," she said.

Madeleine beamed, and kissing her hand was not enough. Hæra leaned in. Madeleine tilted her head. It took some quick work to avoid the microphones, but their mouths came together in a kiss as sweet and soft as the landing would eventually be.

She finished her flight checks and signaled the attendant, Neil, who cleared her for takeoff by giving her a thumbs-up at the side of the airstrip. The Cessna taxied forward, gaining speed until the glorious moment when it gave up the earth in favor of the open air. As always, Hæra felt as if the plane had scooped her off the ground and was lifting her to where she most wanted to be.

The first time she'd been in an aeroplane was to visit Madeleine in Pennsylvania. She'd looked out over the wing, holding her breath at takeoff, unable to believe that she was finally flying. She'd known, then, that nothing would do but to try it for herself. She should have known Madeleine would encourage it, when the time was right.

Now an aeroplane was under her full control, and she navigated the crosswind confidently. Below them, the ocean shimmered under the sun. Waves broke against the mighty cliffs, leaving white curls of foam that looked deceptively small and gentle from up here. The summer fields of Orkney flashed yellow and green. If Hæra craned her head just so, she'd be able to see the farm and the white sheep dotting its pasture.

With Madeleine at her side, solar-bright joy blazed warmly in

Hæra's chest. She'd thought she needed the storms to fly. It turned out that she belonged in clear skies instead.

Madeleine clasped her hands to her breast. "Oh my God. We're doing it. We're flying." She turned to Hæra with sparkling eyes. "I mean, you're flying. I'm just along for the ride."

"No." Hæra briefly took her hand from the throttle to place it on Madeleine's knee. "You're more than that. We're both flying. You made this possible."

Things hadn't turned out like Hæra had intended when all this began. But she'd been right about one thing: she'd needed Madeleine in order to soar.

"If that's true, then I'm glad. Only God and the Great Mare know how glad I am." Madeleine cleared her throat and pointed at the throttle. "But, um, should you keep your hand on that thing? Is that how it works?"

Hæra laughed, wild and free. She squeezed Madeleine's knee. She put her hand back on the throttle.

Together, she and her wife left both land and sea behind, and sought the sky.

ACKNOWLEDGMENTS

The Woman from the Waves took me over two years to write, from start to finish, and it would not be what it is without the help of many incredible people.

Thanks to the talented professionals who put the book's best foot forward: Syd Mills as cover artist, Fay Lane as cover designer, and Kelly Cozy as copy editor.

I was fortunate to work with extraordinary beta readers. Fran Ringley, who helped me both with Scottish vernacular and Catholicism. Caroline Swift, who helped me *more* with Catholicism. Avery Friend, who asked really good questions. Jade Lovewell, who read the whole thing with a gimlet eye and provided insight into the characters and plot that I lacked.

A very special thanks must go to Fenella MacLean of the Mainland, Orkney, who reached out to tell me that the Ladysmith Sapphic Book Club had enjoyed *The X Ingredient*. Next thing I knew, I had a beta reader who could give me the inside scoop on the culture, language, and farming practices of the Orkney Islands. I will forever believe the universe did that on purpose.

I'm also grateful to Haley Cass and Monica McCallan, who helped me navigate the world of independent publishing. Their advice has been invaluable, and their friendship more so.

Orkney itself deserves a shout-out: when I went there to research the book, I was blown away by its beautiful landscapes and friendly people. It's one of the most extraordinary places I've ever been. I owe a particular debt to the books of Tom Muir, an Orcadian folklorist who enchanted me with the traditional tales of Assipattle and the

Stoor Worm, the Mother of the Sea, and the Mermaid Bride. None of these stories made it into *The Woman from the Waves*—but the wicked witch of the whirlpool found her way in.

I want to acknowledge as well the stories of real queer nuns, both those who left their convents and those who stayed. Like many sapphics, I dreamed of being a nun when I was a child. *Lesbian Nuns: Breaking Silence* by Nancy Manahan and Rosemary Keefe Curb is an extraordinary read, as is *Queer and Catholic* by Amie M. Evans and Trebor Healey.

And, finally, infinite thanks to my wife and fellow author Carrie Byrd. She was my alpha reader, developmental editor, book formatter, publicity whiz, organizer, and biggest cheerleader. Whenever I got discouraged, she refused to let me give up. When I finished, we celebrated together. We do pretty much everything together, and I'm unspeakably happy that we get to do that for the rest of our lives. Carrie: thank you, thank you, thank you. Madeleine and Hæra wouldn't be here if not for you. My love and gratitude, always.

ALSO BY ROSLYN SINCLAIR

The Lily and the Crown

The X Ingredient

Truth and Measure

Above All Things

"Ladies on the Rocks"

ABOUT THE AUTHOR

Roslyn Sinclair knew she was destined to be a writer when her second-grade teacher took one look at her "What I did on my summer vacation" essay and said, "You wrote a novel!" It was all over after that. She is married to fellow sapphic romance writer Carrie Byrd, and they live in the greater Philadelphia area.

You can keep up with Roslyn by subscribing to her newsletter. Subscribers get first access to book news, exclusive giveaways and promos, and a free steamy sapphic novella. Sign up using the QR code below!